T. Csernis & Julia Bland

NOSFERATU
NUMEN CHRONICLES VOLUME ONE

ORIGINAL EDITION

For more information on the world, this series, other books, or to contact the author, head to:
https://www.numenverse.com/

Cover designed by Tate Csernis
Cover drawn by Simon Zhong
Cover edited by Julia Bland

ISBN – Paperback: 978-1-7384052-0-6
ISBN – Hardcover: 978-1-7384052-1-3
ISBN – E-Book: 978-1-7384052-2-0

THE NUMEN CHRONICLES is a collaborative work written by

Tate Csernis (T. Csernis) and Julia Bland (Julia B.)

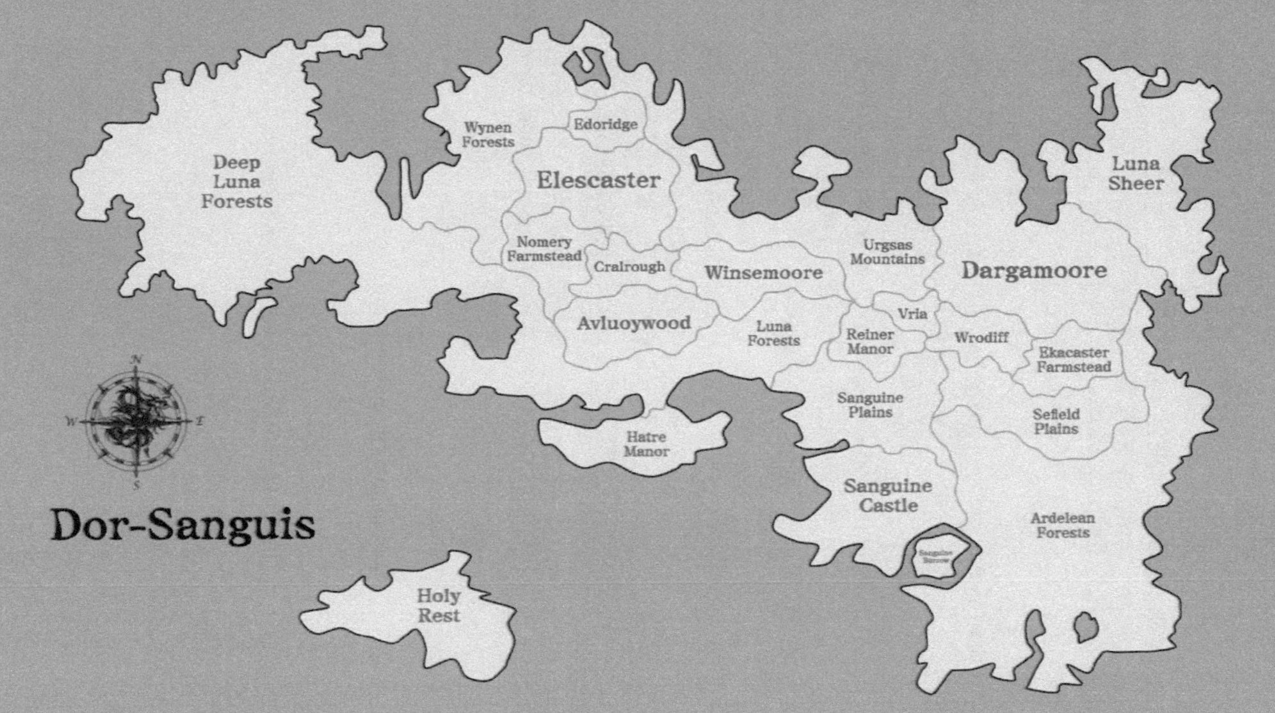

Dor-Sanguis
Deep Luna Forests
Wynen Forests
Edoridge
Elescaster
Nomery Farmstead
Crairough
Winsemoore
Urgsas Mountains
Luna Sheer
Dargamoore
Avluoywood
Luna Forests
Vria
Reiner Manor
Wrodiff
Ekacaster Farmstead
Sefield Plains
Hatre Manor
Sanguine Plains
Sanguine Castle
Ardelean Forests
Holy Rest

GLOSSARY

Ethos [ee-thos] - The energy within someone that can be used to create or manipulate other energies

✝

Aditus-Insula [adee-tus-in-soo-la] - Translates roughly to Island of Doorways *[Latin]*

✝

Dor-Sanguis [door-san-goo-wis] - Translates roughly to Pain *[Portuguese]* and blood *[Latin]*
(aka, Romania)

✝

Numen [noo-men] - God-like beings that chose to show themselves to the world rather than remain anonymous

✝

Aegis [ee-gis] - The Dragon Gods, children of Letholdus

✝

DeiganLupus [day-gan-loo-pus] - Translates roughly to 'refused to turn to the wolf' *[Icelantic, Latin]*
(aka, UK)

✝

Aegisguard [ee-gis-guard] - The world
(aka, Earth)

✝

The Void - The space between the Realms
(aka, space)

✝

Proselytus [pros-elly-tus] – A heart-like organ which creates ethos inside a body

The Months and Currency

Months

January – Primis
February – Cordus
March – Tertium
April – Aprilis
May – Quintus
June – Iunius
July – Quintilis
August – Tria
September – Novem
October – Decem
November – Undecim
December – Clausula

Currency

Copper – Equivalent of $0.01
Bronze – Equivalent of $0.20
Silver – Equivalent of $2
Gold – Equivalent of $10
Coronam – Equivalent of $100
Cidaris – Equivalent of $1 million

CONTENTS

ARC ONE || THE MISSION

ARC TWO || AN UNLIKELY ALLIANCE

ARC THREE || THE VAMPIRE LORD AND THE WARLORD

ARC FOUR || DESPAIR

ARC FIVE || FAREWELL

ARC ONE

— ✝ —

THE MISSION

Chapter One

— ⸲ ✝ ⸴ —

Vampires, Werewolves, and Demons

| Alucard |

Alucard flicked the blood from his rapier and watched the werewolf's severed head drop to the ground to join the beast's twitching body. A satisfied smirk stretched across his pale face, baring the tips of his fangs. It brought him relief knowing he was closer to his task's completion, and all he had to do now was face the Alpha.

With a vicious snarl, the white-furred wolf which stood across the field rose to its hind legs in a display of threat.

But Alucard wasn't unnerved. He extended his claws from his fingertips and awaited the beast's charge. And when it burst towards him—kicking the ground beneath its feet up in its wake—Alucard sprung forward much faster than it could comprehend. He arrived at its side before the grass where he'd been standing settled and gripped the wolf's throat, digging his claws into its skin. It yelped when he lifted it off its feet and slammed its back into the ground, and before it could attempt to defend itself, Alucard sliced the Alpha's head from its body.

It was done.

He flicked his sword, removing as much of the blood from it as he could, and then with the crimson, white fur-trimmed cape he wore over his shoulders, he cleaned his blade and sheathed it at his side. From his pocket, he pulled a folded sack large enough for the beast's head, which he picked up by its muzzle with a disgusted grunt. He unfolded the sack, eased the head inside, and glanced at each dead wolf.

They were all there, and with a jerk of his hand, he sent them up in blood-red flames. Although he'd severed their heads, he wanted to ensure none of them would become hellhounds. That was the last thing he needed. Killing werewolves for the people of the city was tiring enough; if he had to deal with their reanimated corpses, too, he'd feel as though his work was worth more than the treaty he was trying to create with the humans.

He headed into the woods and navigated the late-night gloom to where he left his black stallion. Its crimson eyes shone like a beacon, and from its nostrils oozed dark, twisting fog.

"Vank you vor vaiting," he said, his Dor-Sanguian accent thick and distinguishable.

In response, the possessed horse snorted and waited while Alucard attached the sack to its saddle.

Then, he mounted the horse and took hold of the reins. "Let's go."

The horse carried him through the murky fir forest and into the open fields lit by the kaleidoscopic light of the six moons. In the distance, the glow of Dargamoore City cut through the murk.

Alucard made the horse move faster across the farmland, following the dirt roads until he reached Dargamoore's black iron gates. That was where he dismounted and escorted the stallion to a tavern. He hitched the animal and took the bloody sack.

"Vait 'ere," he said and then headed inside.

The place reeked of beer, cigarettes, and piss. It was a building he'd only ever visit if he had no other choice, and in this case, he didn't.

Alucard approached the bar and pulled the werewolf head from the sack by its muzzle and slammed it on the counter, ensuring that the collision splashed blood in every direction. It sent two patrons running, made another retch, and the bartender dropped the glass he was cleaning in startlement.

"Zhere you go." Alucard patted the head. "I even brought you zhe 'ead so you can put up zhere vith zhe vest of zhem." He nodded at the display of taxidermy wall mounts behind the bar.

The bartender snapped out of his state of stupor. "Are you fucking serious?"

He chucked the sack at the man's face. "You vanted zhe fucking ving."

"Not literally!" he exclaimed.

Alucard took a piece of crumpled paper from his pocket. He laid it flat on the bar and pointed to the words as he read, "Vanted, dead and 'ead severed. Is zhis not to your satisvaction?"

With an irritated grunt, the man turned around and went into back room while muttering, "Fucking psycho."

Alucard waited, ignoring the crowd's murmurs—murmurs which he heard whenever he walked these streets. 'Vampire freak' and 'undead monster' were two common insults. He was used to the berating stares, too…but he wasn't familiar with the look he was getting from the man sitting in the far-right corner.

He didn't recognize the guy, but he evidently wasn't from around here. He was wearing an expensive suit, his dark hair was combed back over his head, and although his eyes were black, Alucard noticed a red shimmer when the light hit them. And his sulphur-like scent was hard to miss.

That man was a demon; Alucard could feel the creature's power like a bitter breeze in the night's air. He didn't like the smirk on his face, nor did he like the fact that his eyes were looking him up and down as though he was sizing up his next meal.

"Here," the bartender uttered.

Alucard wordlessly snatched the coin pouch from him and headed for the door.

"Hey!" the bartender called. "You're just gonna leave this here?!"

Without answering, he left the tavern and walked to his horse. His job was done, and all he wanted to do was finish his patrol of the surrounding woods and get home before daylight. He'd had enough human interaction for one night.

But just as he was about to get on his horse—

"Excuse me," came a smooth, silvery voice. "Sorry to interrupt whatever it is that you're doing, but are you Alucard?"

Alucard let go of the saddle and turned to face whoever said the name very few knew him by, and when he saw that it was the demon who smirked at him inside the tavern, he scowled. "Who's asking?" he questioned cautiously.

The demon held out his hand, which possessed claws in place of his nails. "Zalith. I assume Damien told you about me?"

That was how he knew his name. Damien told him, but despite that this demon knew Damien, Alucard wanted nothing to do with him. "No, 'e zidn't," he replied, ignoring his hand.

Zalith lowered his hand and frowned. "Well, in that case, I suppose he's expecting me to fill you in. I've come from Eltaria to meet you and discuss a relocation mission involving the vampires of my world. He mentioned that you're the Lord of the Nosferatu—the vampire society—right?"

The vampire looked him up and down. "I zon't vork vith ozzer people and I never 'ave. Zamien vouldn't suddenly change zhat." He climbed on his horse.

"Well, it would seem that he had a change of heart," Zalith said, glaring up at him. "I'm frankly a little surprised that he hasn't said anything to you yet."

"If zhis vere true, 'e *vould* 'ave said someving." He made his horse turn towards the city gates. "Good luck vith your vampire mission." Then, he headed for the exit.

The demon walked at the horse's side. "Can't you take my word for it and reach out to him to make sure?"

Alucard glanced down at him. "No." And once he was past the gates, he tapped the horse's side and took off, racing away from the city and Zalith.

"Lives are at stake!" Zalith called.

He wouldn't tell himself that he didn't care; whenever vampires were involved, he couldn't help but care. But what he *didn't* care about was that demon, and he wasn't interested in working with him. If there really *was* a mission involving vampires, then he'd do it alone, just as he'd always done things.

As he rode towards the forest, Alucard pulled one of his colts out of his coat. He ensured the barrel was loaded with silver rounds, reloading those he used fighting the werewolves. He wasn't sure whether he'd come across more tonight, but he was ready either way.

When he reached the tree line, he climbed off his horse. But as he was about to head into the murky woods, a cold shiver ran down his spine, and the scent of ash and sulphur snatched his attention.

With a quiet whoosh and crinkle of the leaves in the grass, something landed behind Alucard.

He wasn't afraid, though; he knew who had come.

"He wants to see you," came a cold, slithering voice.

Alucard turned to face the faceless spectre hiding under draping black robes. "Vhere?"

"Eltaria. Five minutes."

With a heavy sigh, Alucard nodded.

The spectre transformed into a whisp of black smoke and raced off.

"You can 'ead 'ome," he told the stallion. "Somevone vill put you in zhe stables."

The possessed beast grunted and left.

Alucard had five minutes to get to Eltaria and he'd not risk being late. So, he morphed into a vermillion smoke-like apparition and, much like the faceless wraith, he sped up and through the sky.

He moved quicker than any creature could, flying over the farmland and the dark sea, heading towards the island in the distance. When he landed on the black rock, he was greeted by the endless rainfall and rhythmic cracks of thunder.

As he made his way towards the darkness-filled archway sitting a few feet from the water's edge, he glanced at the skyfish and watched them swim around inside the storm. Considering what happened in Dargamoore, he felt it was safe to assume that he was being summoned so late because of that demon. Was he going to have to work with someone else? And not just anyone, but a *demon*? He snarled quietly and clenched his fists.

There was only one way he'd find out.

He walked through the archway and emerged on the other side, finding himself in the gloomy, eroded hall of an old castle. The damp smell was disgusting and burned the insides of his nose. Vines had twisted their way through the crumbling white brick, which was covered with leaf litter and dried dirt.

It wasn't that which made him grimace, though. A sudden ache spiralled through his head and throbbed behind his eyes. Could this pain be a result of his transition through worlds?

He took a small steel flask from his pocket. As he made his way down the hallway, he unscrewed the lid and took a sip of the blood that was inside. He hoped that it would help with this pain just as it helped with any other. And to his relief, it did.

The hallway took him to a staircase, and while he climbed it, he glanced at the silvery moon through the windows. What kind of pathetic little world possessed only one moon?

Once he reached the top of the tower, he saw that he was alone, so he wandered to the edge and stared at the world below. The empty grassland went on as far as his eyes could see, as did the forest on the other side.

Alucard's attention was snatched by approaching footsteps, but he didn't bother turning to face whoever walked onto the tower. He knew it wasn't his boss. But when he noticed that their aura wasn't human or vampire, he scowled irritably. It was the aura of a demon… and one he'd felt before.

He glanced over his shoulder and saw *him*. Zalith, the demon who approached him outside the tavern. His dark eyes shimmered crimson while he looked at Alucard, and as he approached, a pleasant smile appeared on his face.

"Hello again," Zalith said with a quiet laugh.

The vampire scowled at him. "Vhat are you doing 'ere?" he asked, but he was sure that he knew the answer.

"I'm here to meet Damien, which I'm sure isn't far off from what you're doing here yourself."

His scowl thickened, but angst accompanied his aggravation. If Damien sent Zalith to Dargamoore, then he was certain that he was about to receive an earful. But it wasn't his fault. He'd worked solo for four hundred years. Why would his boss suddenly change that without warning him?

He wouldn't have time to reply even if he wanted to. The sound of incoming wings made them both turn to face the east; a feather-winged man flew over the forest, breaking through the clouds, and it sent fear spiralling through Alucard's body.

Damien was coming.

Zalith moved closer to him, but much too close for Alucard's comfort, so as Damien soared down and landed on the tower, Alucard took a few steps away from Zalith.

With a condescending glower, Damien folded his dark, purple-tinted wings against his back. His perfectly centre-split black and white hair floated in the breeze, and his four charcoal-black, foot-tall horns shimmered in the moonlight. "You found your way here, then," he said, shifting his red and blue eyes from Alucard to Zalith.

They bowed respectfully; Damien wasn't only Alucard's boss, but also a Demon God.

Damien smiled amusedly. "I'm surprised you haven't torn each other apart— disappointed, even," he said, walking to the edge of the tower where Alucard had been standing. He leaned against the wall and glared at them.

Alucard frowned cautiously, trying his best to remain calm. "You…sent zhis zemon to vind me in Dor-Sanguis, vight? Vorgive me, but I 'ave alvays vorked alone; I zidn't vink zhat vhat 'e vas telling me vas true."

His boss held out his hand, and as he did, Alucard flinched. He expected Damien to scold him, but the man instead scoffed and pointed at him with his black claw-tipped finger.

Damien told him, "You upset one of my favourite demons."

Alucard kept his eyes on him. "I'm sorry."

Damien's sights shifted to Zalith. "Do you accept his apology?"

"Of course I do," Zalith replied.

Alucard didn't have to look at Zalith to know he was smirking. He could hear it in his voice. But he kept a vacant expression, waiting for Damien to continue.

Damien said, "I have a job for the two of you."

Zalith and Alucard glanced at one another. While Zalith looked skeptical, Alucard adorned a confused frown.

The demon took his eyes off Alucard and looked at Damien. "I assume this is related to the cause. The child?"

"Of course," Damien said with a shrug.

Alucard's look of confusion thickened. Cause? Child? "Vhat cause?"

Zalith rolled his eyes.

The vampire scowled irritably—

"Overthrowing my brother. The best way to do that is to fill his world with creatures he didn't create. It just so happens that Zalith possesses what I need, and I possess what *he* needs," Damien drawled, tapping his chin.

"Vhat…is zhat?"

"Well, *you* are the Nosferatu's leader. You are the only one with the resources to assist Zalith."

Alucard didn't want to help Zalith—he barely knew him—and in the short time they'd interacted, he was sure he was going to hate him. He wanted to ask Damien *why* he should help this demon, but he knew better than to question his wishes.

"A war has broken out in this land," Damien continued, "and it has endangered vampires. Zalith wishes to save them, and the only other realm that can harbour vampire ethos is Aegisguard. You will assist Zalith in transporting his vampires to your world since your aura will mask theirs from Letholdus' detection."

Zalith looked at Alucard. "We must begin momentarily," he said with the same supercilious tone as Damien.

The vampire scowled irritably. He *hated* that they were both talking to him like he was incapable; if the circumstances were different, he would have hit this demon by now, but he had to contain his frustration. "I vould like to know more about zhis plan bevore vushing in like a moron. Vhat are zhe visks?"

"If Letholdus finds out, I'm sure he'll kill you. But that wouldn't be such a tremendous loss, would it?" Damien answered.

Alucard tried to keep an embarrassed expression off his face, but he struggled when he saw Zalith smile amusedly.

Damien continued, "Letholdus is aware of your existence, so I'm confident that he'll think nothing of you travelling back and forth from Eltaria."

"It's a simple plan," Zalith said, glancing at Alucard.

Alucard glared at the demon. "Vhy do you care so much about vampires? You are zemon; ve are natural enemies."

"I owe it to them," Zalith answered. "They were loyal throughout the war, and their numbers are withering. Those who remain deserve to survive, and I want to find a safe place for them until I can make everything right."

Alucard had no choice but to do what Damien said, but he wasn't finished with his questions. "You never 'ave me 'elp anyvone vithout zhem giving me somevthing in veturn. Vhat vill zhat be?" he asked Damien.

"Your father is still after you," Damien grumbled. "You are only safe because *I* am keeping you hidden. Perhaps Zalith will play a part in your father's demise. Or perhaps…something else that causes your life to be in danger. That wouldn't surprise me. You often get yourself wrapped up in things I'd rather not deal with."

Alucard looked at Zalith, ignoring Damien's derogatory speech. "And you are on board vith zhis?"

"I am. But if you need more time to understand, please…it's not like we're in a rush," he uttered sarcastically.

With a vexed frown, Alucard set his sights on Damien. "'Ow vould zhis zemon kill my vather?"

Damien shrugged. "He has many skills I can put to use."

If his father was killed, then Alucard would be free of Damien. That sounded *so* relieving—*so* relieving that he required no further convincing. But having to work with someone would be frustrating, especially when that someone was a demon. However, if completing this task would give him the freedom he longed for, then he'd put up with Zalith.

"Vine," the vampire muttered, holding his hand out to Zalith. "Let's start again."

Zalith smirked and shook his hand. "I look forward to working with you."

Alucard knew that was a lie. "Likevise."

Damien sighed deeply. "Come up with a plan. I want all those vampires in Aegisguard in a year. If Letholdus catches on, you're on your own," he muttered, pointing at Alucard. He glared at Zalith. "And you…be careful. If you lay a hand on him,

I'll cut it off—permanently." Then, he aggressively flapped his wings and raced into the sky, disappearing through the clouds.

Alucard snarled. "*Dracului*… arrogant… fuck."

The vampire caught a smile of amusement leaving Zalith's face when he looked at him, but before he could tell him to stop smiling, the demon adorned a firm glare.

Zalith told him, "There are one hundred and fifteen vampires. We'll meet here before each transferal; Damien may have given us a year, but *I* need them moved as soon as possible—over the course of a month would be preferable."

Alucard frowned disapprovingly. "Ve vere given a year, and I can only take vivteen a time at most. I vill also begin no earlier zhan tomorrow; I 'ave someving to clear up bevore I start bringing vampires 'ome. Vhether zhat is okay vith you or not, I'm now leaving."

Zalith sighed tiredly. "He left us here to discuss a plan."

"Zhere is noving more to discuss."

The demon scoffed. "Logistics, meeting places, plans for if things go wrong. I'd like to know more about this Nosferatu, too. Unless, of course, you'd rather play things by ear and deal with the repercussions of fucking up."

Glaring at him, Alucard clenched his fist. "Zon't talk to me as if I zon't know vhat I'm doing. I've vorked vor Zamien *all* my life. I zon't need to stand avound discussing anyving vith you. Ve vill meet 'ere, I vill take vampires, and zhat's all. If zhere *is* anyving to discuss, ve vill do so *only* vhen I'm 'ere."

Zalith frowned condescendingly and slowly shook his head. "When Damien told me he had an answer for my problems, I didn't expect to be lumbered with such an arrogant fool."

Alucard scoffed, looking him up and down. "I could say zhe same ving." Then, he headed for the stairs. Zalith didn't say anything else, nor did he follow, and Alucard was glad. If that insufferable ass said *one* more thing, he was sure he would have broken his jaw.

He didn't understand why he had to work with a demon, but it was Damien's order, and he knew that if he didn't do as that creature asked, he'd be the one with the broken jaw… or worse.

With an irritated sigh, he made his way downstairs and towards the portal. This was the strangest assignment he'd been given, but there was no point questioning it. Damien wanted to undermine Letholdus by bringing outside ethos into Aegisguard, and he was certain that this was going to be his first of many missions involving that goal.

Chapter Two

— ⸲ ✝ ⸱ —

The Bard

| **Elvin** |

lvin flew out of the tavern's wide-open door, grasping his beloved lute against his chest. His pecan-brown hair was scattered with pieces of rotten tomato and peanut shells, and as the crowd inside hollered in revolt, he pouted sadly.

"You don't know a good story when you hear it!" he yelled, shaking his fist.

"Get lost!" the doorman shouted, pulling the door shut.

Alone on the street, Elvin scowled sullenly. He had so many other things he could say, but what was the point of wasting his breath? No one wanted to hear his stories; nobody wanted to hear the *truth* about the vampires they shared Dor-Sanguis with. *He* was the only one that could tell that story… but he'd not give another second to the hapless drunks inside that establishment.

As he shook the food from his hair, he walked down the cold, lantern-lit cobblestone street. He pulled his feather-tipped hat from his inside pocket, and once he put it on, he glanced up at the star-filled sky. He admired the array of beautiful colours spread throughout it as a result of the six brightly glowing moons. The mixture of purple, red, blue, and gold shined like sunlight through a stained-glass window, and if there was anything Elvin found beautiful in this world of darkness and misery, it was that.

He looked up and down the road, but there wasn't a single person in sight. The quietness sent a shiver down his spine, and he didn't know where he was going. He thought he'd be in the tavern much longer than he was, and for all he knew, it could be *hours* before it was time to meet Alucard.

A small school of shimmering, silver fish swam around the lantern he was approaching. What were they doing out? Skyfish didn't descend past the clouds unless it was raining. Was it going to rain *soon*? That was the last thing he needed. His hat wouldn't keep his head dry and he'd surely catch a cold.

He started thinking about the tavern again, and it made a sour scowl warp his face. "I'm better than all the other bards," he told himself as he turned left at the crossroad. "All they sing about is nonsense about some ugly lady and her stupid man friend. No one wants to hear about that. Stupid love stories. Stupid bard. Stupid tavern. They should be *pining* after my stories!" He looked over his shoulder as the wind raced past him, almost swiping the hat from his head. "I'm talented," he muttered, pouting. He *was* talented…right?

His words hadn't gone unheard.

He sharply turned his head to stare ahead as a low growl ruptured the night's ominous silence. The bard frowned and gripped his lute tightly, watching a pair of dim yellow eyes shimmer in the dark alley across the road. He tensed up and dropped his instrument as he screamed in horror, but before Elvin could flee, a blurred beast burst out of the shadows and crashed into him, pinning him against the wall. The bard let out a hysterical screech, and the wolfish monster snarled ferociously in his face.

Elvin whimpered and cried as he tried to escape the monster's grip. He knew he couldn't do anything, though. What was a measly little human going to do against a werewolf?

But the beast was suddenly torn away from him as it yelped and snarled. He stumbled forward, and when he set his eyes on Alucard, relief struck him. Alucard was the best werewolf slayer Elvin knew.

The vampire had his arms around the wolf's neck, but it looked like he was *struggling*. With several angry snarls, the wolf broke free and turned to face him. Alucard pulled his rapier from its sheath, but as he swung it towards the creature, it dodged and lunged at him—

"Aleksei!" Elvin shrieked.

Alucard slammed his fist into the side of the wolf's face, though, and sent it tumbling across the road. It hurried to its feet, but just as it was about to charge, Alucard pulled his colt from his pocket and fired.

The bullet collided with the beast's face, and once it burrowed inside its skull, the round exploded, sending blood and brain matter all over the place.

Elvin retched when a piece of bloody brain splashed onto his face, and once he was sure the beast was dead, he stomped his foot down and glared at Alucard. "You always do this to me!" he exclaimed, wiping the mess from his face and clothes. "Covering me in blood and guts and even mud that one time!"

Alucard took his hellish eyes off the beast and glared at Elvin. The light of the lanterns shone oddly on his red hair, which fell to his jaw in length and was tied loosely behind his head—much like Elvin's. A small, gold-looped earring shimmered in his right, sharply pointed ear, and an irritated look clung to his face. "Do you 'ave to complain *every* time I save your life, Elvin?" His accent was thick, and he spoke much faster than anyone else Elvin knew. He didn't hail from the same land as him, but he had been around him so long that he understood every word.

"Sorry," he said with a pout. "What the heck was that wolf doing here anyway?! They haven't been brave enough to come out of the forest in weeks."

"I zon't know," he grumbled, putting his colt away as the surrounding buildings' lights started flicking on. "But zhat ving vas a lot stronger and vaster zhan zhe verevolves I usually vace."

Elvin frowned worriedly. "What does that mean?"

The vampire sighed and turned around. "Ve should leave bevore zhese people come out and start screaming at me," he said, ignoring his question.

With a nod, Elvin swerved past the corpse and hurried to catch up to him.

Alucard glanced down at him. "Vhat are you doing out 'ere? I told you to stay in zhe tavern."

He scoffed and muttered, "They kicked me out, that's what."

Alucard smirked amusedly. "Not vans of your singing, no?"

Embarrassed, Elvin scowled at him. But he couldn't stay angry. He almost became that thing's dinner, and he couldn't help but linger on the fact that Alucard struggled to kill it immediately. "You've been killing werewolves for months like they're nothing. Why would one strong enough to break free from you show up *now*?"

"I zon't know, Elvin," he said tiredly. "I vill vind out, zhough. Zhe last ving I need vight now is vor zhem to become a pain in my ass again."

"Maybe Tobias can help." He looked up at him, waiting for him to respond, but it looked like he was thinking...very angrily. "Did you get your things done for tonight? The things you refuse to tell me about," he asked, hoping that a different subject would wipe the gloomy look off Alucard's face.

"*Da*," the vampire muttered.

"So...will you tell me about them *now*?"

He didn't reply.

"Tell me...please?" he pleaded.

"No."

Elvin frowned irritably. "You never tell me anything."

Alucard looked at him and sighed. "I killed a verewolf Alpha vor somevone, and zhen Zamien summoned me to meet 'im."

"Oh, Damien, huh?" he asked with a look of angst smothering his once eager face. Even the slightest mention of that man discomforted him. "What did you have to do? Meet someone again? Even *more* werewolf stuff? Or...Diabolus?"

"Zhe virst vone," the vampire said, glaring ahead as they followed a dirt path out of the town and towards a small forest.

The bard eyed him sceptically. "Did you...have a date, Aleksei?"

"Vhat?" he snapped, glowering at him. "I zon't care vhat zhat vas."

A nervous laugh broke free of Elvin's sigh. He might humour the idea…but thinking about Alucard dating made him feel anxious. "Yeah, true. Well, whatever it was—probably *not* a date—I want *all* the details when we get back home. I feel like this might be one for my manuscript."

"If you are vailing as a bard, vhat makes you vink somevone is going to vant to publish your manuscript?" the vampire questioned.

Elvin shrugged. "I'll make it one day; I gotta find the right angle, you know?"

"Vight," Alucard mumbled, glaring ahead again. "Vell, good luck vith zhat."

"Aww, Aleksei," Elvin said, smiling at him. "You're so supportive."

"Am I?" he grumbled, stepping aside before Elvin could place his hand on his shoulder.

Elvin frowned in discontent, but then bounced up and down. "Oh, oh, can I write down that little rescue back there? I bet you were chasing that wolf for miles, weren't you? If it weren't for me being there at that *exact* time, you would have never caught up with it, would you?"

Alucard glanced at him. "Zhat is not vhat 'appened at all."

"Yeah, but…you told me to switch things up; people don't wanna hear about a scary, rich Vampire Lord killing things, saving people, and buying fancy stuff; they wanna hear about a mere, struggling bard saving a vampire!"

"Do zhey?" he asked doubtfully.

As they came out of the other side of the forest and onto a white sand beach, Elvin nodded confidently…but then saddened. "Sometimes, I feel like you don't believe in me. I so happen to think this idea would make a great story."

"You vink everyving makes a great story."

"Well, it does if you tell it right."

The vampire rolled his eyes. "Vait 'ere vor me."

"Come on, man, you're making me wait on a beach? What if more werewolves come? Or pirates? I could be mugged!"

Alucard looked him up and down. "You vouldn't exactly make a grativying snack vor a volf, nor do you possess much at all vor a pirate to steal. You just said zhat yourselv: mere, struggling bard," he mocked, smirking.

"Wow. Crude as ever. *Please*, can't I come?" he begged, holding his hands together. "I'll keep my mouth shut; I'll stand in a little corner and observe. You won't even know I'm there."

"No," he refused again.

Elvin crossed his arms and pouted stubbornly. "Fine, but if I get eaten, *you'll* be the one digging me out of whatever creature's stomach and sending my remains to my next of kin."

Alucard frowned strangely at him. "You zon't 'ave any next of kin, Elvin. You came vrom an orphanage."

"Yeah, well…you never know. I could have *someone* out there."

"You zon't. I checked. Go and sit over zhere," he instructed, nodding at a tree. "I von't be long; I just 'ave to talk to zhem zhis time."

Sighing, Elvin dragged himself over to the tree, slumped down, and crossed his arms. "Whatever. I could have cousins…or a long-lost auntie who bakes cookies and gets drunk all the time. Those places are notorious for failing to keep records, you know!"

Alucard shook his head and dragged his hand over his face. "Vhatever you vant to tell yourselv." Then set his eyes on the open sea. In the distance, a ship was barely visible on the horizon. The vampire disappeared into vermillion smoke and sped across the water, leaving Elvin on the beach.

Elvin scrunched up and tried to focus on working out how to get more information out of Alucard, but all he could think about was his family. *Did* he have anyone out there? No, he wasn't going to let himself make up some story about fake relatives. He was alone, and Alucard was right. He was *always* right.

| **Alucard** |

Alucard reached the ship. He landed on the deck with a thump and waited impatiently as a tall, sleek man dressed in a black long coat stepped out from the cabin beneath the quarterdeck.

Attila, one of Alucard's subordinates. "Long night?" he called, his face as vacant as Alucard's.

"Vhen is ever not?" Alucard replied, glaring into the man's crimson eyes, the only thing visible under his hood.

He chuckled. "What's the news?"

"I vill be vorking vith a zemon," he mumbled irritably, taking his eyes off the man to glare at the ocean. Just *thinking* about Zalith aggravated him. "I am moving vampires vrom anozzer vorld—Eltaria. Zhey vill be staying 'ere in Dor-Sanguis," he explained, setting his eyes back on the man. "Zhere von't be enough space 'ere soon enough, so ve need to 'urry up and re-establish zhe empire I vuled bevore I disappeared. Zhe Nosveratu needs to resurface"

The man nodded. "Don't worry, I've got the Deiganish king eating out of my hands."

"Make 'im beg," Alucard mumbled. "'E vill not be our vriend; 'e vill vork vor me, not vith me."

"Of course," the man said, bowing apologetically.

"I suspect zhe volves are up to someving, too. I just vound vone 'unting zhe bard in Wrodiff. Zhis ving vas strong enough to break out of my arms and vasn't scared of me like zhe vest. I vill be 'eading to my castle tonight to tell my vampires to be cautious, so you should do zhe same."

"You are concerned greatly, My Lord. Do you suspect another war?" Attila asked worriedly.

"I veally 'ope zoesn't come to zhat. I vill get to zhe bottom of zhis," he said with a heavy sigh. That wolf was certainly something to be worried about. What if there were more? He needed to find out as soon as he could.

Attila chuckled again. "Does it make you miss the simpler times, Alucard?"

He looked at him and frowned. There was a part of him that missed the days when Damien's hold on him wasn't so tight, but he wouldn't let himself get wrapped up in old memories. It never did him any good. "No. If anyving, I am glad zhey are over, and zhat Luther is 'oled up in zhat castle vith 'is new vife."

"No, no," Attila laughed, shaking his head. "I mean before Year Zero. This treaty you have worked so hard for; you wouldn't have had to spend half your fortune building castles and forts if our kind decided to stay hidden from the world."

Alucard sighed. "Zhere are some zhat might agree, but I do not. I believe is better vor zhe vorld to know about us and learn to live vith us—less superstition and mysterious deaths zhat vay, no?"

Attila chuckled and nodded. "Of course."

"Go," he then said. "I vill see you in less zhan a month, no?"

"I'll see you then."

As Attila morphed into a bat and disappeared into the clouds, Alucard turned to face the beach in the distance. His eyes shifted to the forest, and the worry that the werewolves were scheming made him frown worriedly. With Damien's new mission, he wouldn't have time to deal with werewolf attacks. Elvin was *lucky* that he turned up when he did, or that beast might have killed him.

He needed to reach out to Tobias. If there was anyone who could get him answers, it was him.

Chapter Three

— ⸃ † ⸄ —

Damien's Cause

| **Elvin** |

Elvin scribbled in his notebook, glancing at the ship every so often while he waited for the vampire to return. But as each moment passed, he grew more and more impatient.

He slammed his notebook shut and tucked it and his quill into his pocket. What could be taking Alucard so long? Why did he have to fly over to some ship? Who was he talking to? The bard rolled his eyes and pouted, resting his chin on his knees as he wrapped his arms around his legs. It was cold, damp, and miserable. He wanted to go home; he wanted to hear about what Alucard had been up to tonight.

But he couldn't stop thinking about that werewolf. If *one* came out of the woods, would more follow? If that happened, they'd mess up the treaty Alucard was finalizing with the city. He'd worked so hard for it, and Elvin had no idea what might happen if it didn't go through. Would Alucard have to leave Dor-Sanguis? What would happen to all the vampires?

Alucard suddenly emerged on the beach with an aggravated look on his face.

Elvin pounced to his feet. "So?" he asked eagerly. "How did it go?"

The vampire glanced at him and rolled his eyes. "Vantastic."

He frowned at Alucard's answer and followed him along the beach. "Are you going to tell me about your night? What happened?"

"Stuff," he muttered, following the stone path.

Elvin pouted and followed in silence. He knew he wasn't going to get answers just yet; Alucard evidently needed time to cool down.

They approached Alucard's home. The towering black-brick manor's sharp, pointed roofs cast sinister shadows across the grass, shrouding the majority of the grounds in darkness, and the tall walls stretched a mile around the estate, cutting it off from the rest of the land.

Dargamoore sat a few miles in the distance; the city's glow emanated through the grassy hills. Huge, werewolf-infested forests surrounded the grassland, and black, nightmarish mountains graced the sky.

Elvin and Alucard reached the black steel gates which sat between the walls of his manor, and when they opened, the vampire led the way through the grounds.

Perhaps enough time had passed. Elvin looked up at Alucard and asked, "Okay, what stuff?"

Alucard rolled his eyes and snarled irritably. "I met a zemon."

Elvin held back a victorious grin. "A demon? But…demons and vampires are enemies; that's like getting you to meet a werewolf—well, one that isn't Tobias. He's cool."

"Vell, I'm supposed to be 'elping 'im move some vampires vrom 'is vorld to zhis vone."

"You're bringing vampires from some other world…to this one?"

He nodded, reaching the manor's black front door.

"Is…it really a good idea to bring more vampires here? It's only been six months since you outran the Diabolus; what if they find you again? What will you do with all these new vampires? Especially if more werewolves are gonna come out of the forest."

Alucard sighed. "Zhe Diabolus von't vind me 'ere. Zhe last place zhey vould expect to vind me is living among 'umans. As vor zhe volves, I'll deal vith zhem."

Elvin pulled out his notebook. "True…." He shuffled around excitedly. "A whole new world?!" he squealed, scribbling on the paper as he followed the vampire into his house. "What was it like? Was it like Aegisguard? Was it magical?"

"Vone moon," Alucard said with a shrug, taking off his cloak, and then he hung it on the coat rack. "Some…eroded castle, not much to see."

Nodding, Elvin went with him through the dark entrance hall and into a lounge. "And these vampires: why do you have to bring them here?"

Alucard clicked his fingers, and in response, the lanterns lined around the room lit up with small flickering flames. He then slumped onto the black leather couch and put one of the red cushions behind his head. As he rested his right leg over the arm and looked at Elvin, the bard sat in the armchair across from him.

Elvin took a moment to rest, looking around the gloomy room. All the furniture was dark and looked antique. The walls were black with oak-brown panelling lined around them, and the front wall possessed three tall, arched windows.

The vampire said, "Zamien vants to undermine 'is brover, Levoldus."

"The…god?" Elvin asked with a frown.

He nodded and looked at the fireplace. "Zhe virst step in doing so vould be to vill zhis vorld vith ethos zhat's not of 'is origin, zherevore not of 'is control. So, ve are starting vith zhese vampires. 'E 'as me 'elping some zemon zhat apparently vants to 'elp zhe vampires of 'is vorld because zhey vere loyal to 'im vhroughout a war. Now, I 'ave zhis night and 'alf of tomorrow to vind somevhere to put zhem and to try and 'urry up zhis treaty I 'ave been vorking on vith zhe city."

Elvin scribbled in his notebook as Alucard spoke. "The human-vampire cohabitation treaty?"

The vampire nodded. "*Da.*"

"I don't know if they'll hurry that up," Elvin said sadly. "But maybe you can convince them."

"Zhat's zhe plan."

"Why does Damien call Letholdus his brother?" he asked curiously. "Why do *all* the Numen call themselves brother and sister? They're not related."

"I zon't know. Must be a God ving," the vampire muttered.

"Hmm. Well, why does Damien wanna overthrow Letholdus?"

Alucard shrugged and flicked his hand, lighting the fireplace with red fire. "Zamien 'ates 'is siblings; 'e vants to be on top. Zhere's noving more to zhat, veally."

"What's he doing once he has other ethos in this world?"

As he glanced at Elvin, Alucard shrugged again. "Outside ethos vill corrupt zhe ethos 'ere. Zhe more zhere is, zhe more damage is done. I gazzer zhat Zamien vants to veaken Levoldus and zhen kill 'im."

Elvin wrote it down. "Kinda barbaric."

"Eh, not my problem. Gods vill do vhat gods vant to do," he grumbled, staring into the fire.

"So, are you gonna do it? Help the demon?"

"Vhat choice do I 'ave? Zamien asked me to do zhis; I can't exactly say no."

Scribbling, Elvin nodded and looked back at him. "What about this demon?" he asked with a smirk. "He? She? What was it like?"

The vampire scowled. "Must you know?"

"Well, yeah. I need all the details. How else am I supposed to write this book? Could this book…possibly become a story of romance?" he teased, fishing for a reaction. "A love triangle!"

Rolling his eyes, he glared back into the fire. "Insufferable, stuck-up businessman type; suit, blazer ving…I vink 'e 'ad a tie. I actually met 'im virst outside a tavern; seems like Zamien sent 'im to meet me on 'is own. I zon't know vhy he vhought zhat vould vork."

"What happened?"

"I told 'im to fuck off."

Elvin sighed, but there was amusement in his voice when he said, "Oh, Aleksei. Perfect description, though. Love that." He wrote it down.

"Seems like Zamien loves 'im," the vampire grumbled.

Elvin then stopped writing and frowned at Alucard. "From what I've heard, I really don't think that creature of a man could ever love anyone; he probably loves the fact that this demon guy does what he's told," he assumed.

"*Da*," Alucard mumbled.

"Okay, do you have a plan?"

The vampire looked at him. "Vor vhat?"

"The whole…moving vampires from there to here thing."

"Vhat is zhere to plan? Go zhere, bring zhem 'ere. Simple."

"Okay, but where will they live? You haven't got the treaty sorted yet with the humans in the city, so they can't exactly live there, can they?"

"My castle, I guess."

Writing it down, Elvin nodded. "And the treaty?"

"I'll try and sort zhat tomorrow; 'umans sleep zhe night avay like babies."

"So, you'll use tonight to prepare the castle, I assume?"

"*Da*," he confirmed.

Elvin smiled. "See, why can't you be like this all the time? You only seem to answer me when I'm asking for the book. You really *do* believe in me, don't you?" He grinned from ear to ear.

Alucard didn't answer.

The bard sighed and closed his notebook. "Well, are you okay?" he then asked with concern in his voice.

Alucard frowned, glancing over at him. "Vhy vould I not be?"

"I worry about you. You never really talk about how you feel, and you always look miserable when you get back from seeing Damien."

"Zon't you 'ave a 'ome to get to?" Alucard dismissed.

Elvin pouted. "Well…yeah, but don't you want me to help you tonight? I don't have anything else to do."

"No," Alucard denied. "Go 'ome."

The bard stood up and huffed. "Will you let me get chased by wolves? Attacked by pirates? Walk me home…please?"

Alucard glanced at him. "No, no, and no," he grumbled, scowling. "Sergiu is outside vith zhe carriage. Tell 'im I told 'im to take you 'ome."

"Mean," Elvin mumbled as he turned around, heading for the door. "Where should I find you tomorrow?" he asked, looking back over his shoulder at the vampire.

"The city, outside zhe 'Ouse of Commons," he instructed.

Elvin made his way to the door. As he left, he glanced back at Alucard, watching him as he made himself comfortable on the couch. He was worried about him; he knew how much Alucard despised Damien. But as much as he wanted to try and be there for him, he knew that Alucard didn't want his company right now. He knew him well enough to know that he wanted to be left alone for the rest of the night.

With a pout on his face, Elvin pulled the door shut behind him and started searching the courtyard for Sergiu.

| Alucard |

When the bard left, Alucard looked back into the fire. Tonight hadn't been what he expected. This was the first time Damien sent an associate to find him on their own, and the first time he'd forced Alucard to work side-by-side with someone. At least all working together involved was meeting to drop off and pick up the vampires, though.

Alucard was glad, however, that he didn't have to see Damien alone. The last thing he wanted was to be in that creature's presence by himself. But the meeting had been somewhat humiliating; this new demon—Zalith—clearly thought that Alucard was incompetent and that he couldn't do what Damien asked of him. But Alucard was going to prove them both wrong. There had never been a time where he failed at a task—not since… *then*. But he didn't want to think about that.

Then, he scowled. Zalith had mentioned 'the cause'—what was *the cause*? He hadn't been made aware of any cause. Clearly, Alucard had been left out of something once again. Did he care, though? Yes, he did. Damien made sure to always involve him in some way or another. So, why hadn't he been told what this cause was?

Not only did he have that to worry about, but it also looked like the werewolves were testing the waters. They hadn't set foot in any of Dor-Sanguis' towns or villages since he'd scared them off, so why had one been brave enough to hunt in Wrodiff tonight? He hoped it was just a stray desperate for food, but part of him knew that things could never be that simple. The wolves were up to something, and he needed to find out before someone was killed; that would ruin *everything* he'd been working so hard for.

"Don't you have a job to do?" came Damien's harrowing voice.

Startled by his appearance, Alucard sat up straight and looked over his shoulder.

"Vampires need moving," Damien said as he made his way over and slumped down in the chair Elvin had been sitting in. "And yet you sit around here like some useless fool. Not a surprise, though." He sighed, tapping his claws on the arm of the chair.

Staring at him, Alucard frowned cautiously. "I vill be starting tomorrow. I need time to prepare a place vor zhem to stay."

Nodding slowly, Damien glared at him. "You still keep that human around—why?"

"'E's…my vamiliar," Alucard answered.

"Hmm…you tell him an awful lot, don't you?"

"'E's vriting a novel."

Damien scoffed. "Pointless frivolity. To sit somewhere for hours looking at written words when you can simply speak from memory. Human minds don't have such a capacity, though. Do *you*, Aleksei?" he asked as a smirk crept across his face.

Keeping his eyes on the Daegelus, Alucard frowned slightly, unsure whether he was meant to answer or not.

But Damien then huffed. "I suppose I should tell you about my new cause since I'll be needing you for it."

Alucard tensed up. He wasn't wearing his cape, so he didn't have the dragon fur to shield his mind. Damien had evidently poked around inside his head; why else would he have suddenly mentioned *exactly* what he'd been thinking about? He tried to stay calm. "Vhat is zhe cause?"

The Daegelus grinned and abruptly leaned forward. He grabbed Alucard's shirt, and the vampire did his best not to panic, staring into Damien's eyes.

"If you speak a word of *this* to anyone…." Damien's eyes wandered down to Alucard's chest. "It's a fascinating organ, the proselytus. It gives you mortal creatures the ability to harness the energy you were graced to have been born with. I've heard it's such a *painful* existence to have had one…and then to have lost it."

Alucard understood his threat. "I von't tell anyvone."

Damien scowled and let go of him. Then, he looked at the fireplace. "I want everything my siblings have. I want access to their bloodlines; I want dominion over what they have come to make, build, and own. To get it, I need to possess their blood and ethos, and I've found a way to do so."

The vampire frowned, waiting.

"I will need to create another creature quite like myself—another Daegelus. But when I do, I will carefully craft everything I need into it. I will make sure it possesses the blood of each of my siblings, and the ethos of everything and everyone that I require. And then, when it has grown, I will absorb it, thus gaining everything it possesses, granting myself what I need."

"Vhy do you need me?"

"I need four fathers."

"Vhat?"

"Four males of each bloodline: Lucifer's, Lilith's, Ephriel's, and Erich's. You so happen to be Lucifer's son, so what better choice for Lucifer's bloodline? Yes, you are incompetent and insufferable, but I have no other choice. Zalith is of Lilith's bloodline. I am in search of an angel from Ephriel's, and I have one in mind. Then one of Erich's. Once I have found them, we will all meet to discuss preparations."

"And…I gazzer you need a mother, too?"

"Yes," Damien answered, scowling at him. "Whilst you assist Zalith, I will be searching for a suitable matriarch. Do you have any more stupid questions?"

"No," he said, looking away from Damien's evil stare.

Damien then smirked. "I have heard of an angel sent by my sister to keep an eye on Letholdus. I have thought about asking him—I will steal him from Ephriel, as I have stolen *you* from my brother."

Alucard glanced at him.

"Now, get to work. If you falter, you'll suffer."

As Damien stood up, a look of angst appeared on Alucard's face. "I von't vail."

"Good." The Daegelus smiled, placing his hand on Alucard's shoulder and digging his claws into it.

The vampire grimaced, keeping his eyes focused on the fire.

"Remember what I have taught you, Aleksei, and don't let me down again," he warned, letting go of his shoulder.

Then, as Damien left as silently as he had arrived, Alucard stared sullenly, watching the flames in the fireplace. At least *now* he knew what the cause was.

What was Damien going to do once he had access to the other Numen bloodlines? Alucard knew that Damien wanted to kill Letholdus; that had to be why he didn't want someone possessing *that* Numen's blood. But what were his plans for his other siblings? Did he want to kill them, too? Or did he really just want access to their lineage? It wasn't Alucard's problem or his business. He had to do what he was told, and that was all he knew.

He stood up and waved his hand, and all of the flames in the fireplace withered. He made his way to the door, irritably snatched his cape, and left, setting out to begin preparations for his new task. He couldn't risk wasting a single moment.

Chapter Four

— ⸲ ✝ ⸱ —

House of Commons

| **Elvin** |

The morning came fast. Elvin woke in his tiny shack house. The moment he opened his eyes, his first thought was Alucard. Where was he today, what was he doing, and what new material would present itself for his book?

He sat up, pushing away his soft bed covers as he looked around his sunlit room. A single window clung to the left wooden wall with a black blanket for a curtain, but the sunlight broke through it. To the room's right was a small kitchen area, where several pots and pans were stacked on top of each other beside the basin. Next to it was his beloved desk with piles of paper all over it, and the walls were all but bare apart from the many cobwebs that clung too high for the bard to reach.

Then, a quiet meow caught his attention. He leaned over the side of his bed and stared down at the small black tortoiseshell kitten. The feline's back left paw was the only ginger of its feet, and most of its coat was black with spots of brown and orange. She gawped up at him, meowing again as he sighed tiredly.

"All right, kitty," he said, climbing out of bed, "I hear you."

Elvin made his way to the small kitchen and pulled one of the cupboards open. Once he located a jar of dried fish, he opened it and handed one to the kitten, who savagely tore at it, purring crazily.

"I think I stayed up a little too late writing last night," Elvin mumbled to himself, watching the kitten eat.

When the sound of horses filled the morning air, Elvin turned around and opened his door. His home existed on the outskirts of a large farm area; in the distance, four men were ploughing a field, and two others were patrolling the grounds.

The bard watched, waiting to see if the patrol would find anything. Usually, they'd discover livestock slaughtered by the werewolves that haunted the land, but it didn't look like they were going to find anything this morning. And why was that? Elvin smirked, aware that Alucard, his best friend, had slain the beast last night.

Smiling, he closed his door and looked down at the kitten, who stared up at him, licking its lips. He frowned. "You ate that already?"

The kitten meowed at him.

He shook his head and handed her another fish. "That's all you're getting. I need to go and get more. I'll pick some up in the city…the city!" he cried. "I'm gonna be late!"

Elvin rushed around, grabbing his clothes and pulling them on as swiftly as he could. He then hastily brushed his hair and tied it the same way Alucard did. He stopped in front of the mirror, making sure he got it right, and then grabbed his feather hat and put it on. Then, he snatched his notebook and a pencil and then raced out of his house, slamming the door behind him.

The bard ran along the dirt path. "Gonna be late, gonna be late—he's gonna kill me," he mumbled, panting as he hurried towards the cobblestone path that would take him to the city.

He set his eyes on the city as he sprinted towards it. Alucard told him to meet him outside the House of Commons, the meeting place of the city council, and if he was going to make it on time, he needed to move faster. If only he had a horse.

But he ran and ran and ran. He wasn't going to let Alucard down.

When he reached the city entrance, he passed two silver-armoured guards and succumbed to his fatigue. He had to stop for a moment, trying to remember which way the House of Commons was. Dargamoore was a forest of concrete with castle-like buildings so high that it hurt his eyes to gaze up at them. Everything looked so dark and gloomy; the buildings were made of black brick, foggy cobblestones, and dull woods.

As a horse-drawn carriage passed the road he was standing in front of, Elvin shook his head and hurried up the bustling street. He jogged for at least ten minutes, making his way through streets and allies, along roads, and past crowds of hustling people, ignoring the world around him until he came onto a street that led up to the white castle tower squished between two black buildings. But as he made his way closer, there was no sign of Alucard. Was the vampire late…or was *he*?

Panic filled his heart as he reached the front of the building. He looked around for Alucard, but he was nowhere to be seen. Was he already inside? Elvin approached the door, preparing to knock, but when several horrified gasps came from behind him, he lowered his hand and turned around—and there was Alucard. The vampire walked up the street while people gawped at him with looks of fear and uncertainty on their faces. But Alucard didn't care; he ignored them just as he ignored anything that he found no interest in.

"Usually I'm the late one," Elvin said with a smirk once Alucard reached him.

The vampire sighed irritably and looked down at him; his eyes were no longer hauntingly fiery but ice blue, and his pupils were rounded like those of a human. In the sunlight, his eyes appeared this way, and in any kind of shadow or darkness, they returned to their usual hellfire appearance. Why, Elvin wasn't sure, but he had to know—for his novel. He asked before but Alucard hadn't explained, so he had to wait and ask when he thought the vampire had forgotten he asked before.

Alucard took a moment, leaning against the wall beside the white tower's door. "I got caught up," he said tiredly.

"Doing what?"

"Telling zhe vampires who alveady live in my castle zhat zhere vill be new vones joining zhem tonight. I varned zhem about zhe volf, too—and *no*, I zon't yet know vhat vas doing in zhe town."

"*That* took you all morning? I thought you were gonna do that last night."

He rolled his eyes. "I may…or may not…'ave vallen asleep."

Elvin grinned in amusement. "Did you get sweepy?" he mocked, pouting.

Glaring at him, Alucard stood up straight and knocked on the tower's door. "Keep your mouth shut in 'ere," he ordered.

The bard nodded.

Then, the door creaked open. A smartly dressed blonde-haired man stood there, and as he set his hazel eyes on Alucard, he frowned strangely. "What are you doing here? There was no meeting arranged. The next one takes place next month."

"I need to talk to zhem now," Alucard insisted, stepping forward.

The man held out his hand. "I say! You can't come in here!"

"Move," Alucard snarled, barging his way into the tower.

Gasping in shock, the man stumbled aside, and as Alucard and Elvin walked in, he shut the door. "This is improper! In violation of agreements!"

Alucard stopped walking and looked at him with an irritated scowl on his pale, exhausted face. "Vhere are zhey?" he demanded.

"I will not tell you," the man denied, but as Alucard stepped towards him, he shuddered in cowardice. "Uh…second floor—they're in a meeting."

The vampire turned around and made his way over to the spiralling staircase. Elvin followed him as he made his way up to the second floor and walked down the short corridor towards the black door that sat at the end.

"Are you actually gonna be able to sort something out *now*?" Elvin asked worriedly.

"I 'ave to try," Alucard mumbled. "Ve've already spoken about vampires and 'umans coexisting in zhis city multiple times; ve 'ave been discussing zhe vhen, 'ow, and vhy—I need to make zhe vhen now."

"When was the when originally going to be?"

"Zhat is yet to be determined."

"Do you…think it'll ever happen, though? I mean…vampires and humans in the same city, it's not really…well…realistic, is it?"

"I 'ave been dealing vith zhe verevolves as zhe 'umans asked, so is time zhey lived up to zheir end of zhe deal."

Elvin pulled out his notebook and started scribbling while Alucard raised his hand and knocked on the door.

No one answered. The voices inside were hushed and rushed, and the fact that they ignored his knock seemed to aggravate Alucard more. Elvin glanced up at him, watching as he gripped the doorknob and twisted it, breaking its lock. The people sitting around the table inside gasped and mumbled to one another as Alucard invited himself in, and Elvin stumbled in after him.

"Who let you in?!" one of the men detested as he stood up, glaring at Alucard, who made his way to the end of the long, rectangular table.

"Our next meeting is not set until next month," another man called calmly.

The standing man looked at Elvin. "And who is this bumbling idiot?!"

Elvin quickly looked around the room, eyeing the eight people sitting at the table. Every wall, the floor, the ceiling, and all the furniture was white—so white that Elvin's eyes ached terribly. But as he set his sights on the standing man, he frowned. Alucard had once given him rough descriptions of each of the council members, and this green-eyed, dirty-brown-haired man could be none other than Clyde, the council's lead speaker.

Clyde took his eyes off the bard and looked back at Alucard. "This is a private meeting; you simply cannot walk in here!"

"Vell, I just did, zidn't I?" the vampire snarled.

The man beside Clyde held up his hand, keeping him from yelling any further. That was Dirk, who Alucard once mentioned was always trying to keep everyone calm. He set his blue eyes on the vampire and said, "Whatever your business, I assume it must be important for you to waltz in here both during the daytime *and* uninvited."

Alucard glared at him while the rest of the council awaited his response. "Zhis vegards zhe treaty," he confirmed as Elvin slowly closed the door.

With a stubborn glare, Clyde glanced down at Dirk and returned to his seat. "There's nothing left to currently discuss. You have presented your terms, and we have presented ours; you should be out there ridding us of the wolf pests."

"I 'ave killed countless verevolves vor you, and you are yet to give me any sort of confirmation zhat zhese velations vill vork."

Once again, Dirk raised his hand. "The terms have been looked over and discussed, and frankly, it is going to take a while for us to get the citizens of the city on board."

"Vampires are monsters," the bald man across the table from Dirk called. "Humans are afraid. They are still trying to come to terms with seeing *you* walking around their city, but to get them to accept seeing vampires *daily*? This sort of thing takes time."

Alucard scowled. "Zhen 'urry up. Zhere 'as not been a 'uman death 'ere since my veturn. I 'ave done my part and more; zhe least you can do is speed zhis up."

The bald man looked at Dirk. "Dirk?"

Dirk nodded and said to Alucard, "We are working on things, Aleksei, but the next meeting to discuss this was set for next month, and during the time in between, we planned to address the people. Might I ask why you seem so desperate for this to go ahead? Before, you seemed a lot more…well, relaxed."

"My vampires deserve to live in zhis city as much as your people do. You might 'ave vorgotten, but zhis entire country is *mine*. If I vere any less kind, I vould 'ave chased you all out—you know I'm more zhan capable of doing so."

The council glanced at each other, mumbling quietly.

Elvin then leaned into Alucard's ear. "I think they didn't like that little threat."

"Zhat vasn't a vhreat," Alucard announced. "Vas simply a veminder."

Dirk sighed and leaned his arms onto the table. "We are trying, I assure you."

"Assurance is no longer enough," Alucard said.

Dirk shifted his attention to the bald man and said, "Get the terms, Lars."

Lars stood up and walked over to a white cabinet at the end of the room. He pulled its top drawer open and started searching through it.

"We have constructed an agreement combining both sides' terms. You should look it over," Dirk called.

With a scroll of parchment in his hand, Lars approached the vampire and handed it to him.

Alucard pulled the red ribbon keeping the parchment rolled and dropped it on the table. He unwrapped the paper and stared at it for a few moments while an aggravated look appeared on his face.

Clyde frowned. "Is it…not to your liking?"

The vampire sighed and gave the parchment to Elvin.

Elvin knew that Alucard couldn't read their language, Deiganish. He may be able to speak it, despite his accent, but reading it was a different struggle…and Elvin was more than happy to help.

He read aloud, "The terms are as follows regarding human and vampire cohabitation in the city of Dargamoore: no vampire shall feed on any human without consent. No vampire shall kill or injure a human in any way. No vampire will turn a human under any circumstances. Vampires will be given access to housing and other facilities under the agreement of the protection-from-sunlight program. All facilities will be made safe for vampires to use during the daytime, and a means of daytime travel will also be set into place."

Alucard nodded, letting him know he should continue.

The bard kept reading, "Humans shan't treat vampires as outsiders. Humans shan't request any vampire to turn them—turning will be treated as an offence, and both participants will be apprehended as the law states. Humans will abide by the protection-from-sunlight rules and do their best to ensure facilities are safe for vampires. Humans will receive priority regarding facilities such as restaurants or bars because vampires do not need such sustenance. Human and vampire relationships are also to be treated as normal. Discrimination will not be tolerated."

Alucard grunted in response.

"Under the decree of the Dargamoore City High Council, signed by members Clyde Del, Dirk Benign, Lars Richle, Silas Mear, Sebastian Mear, Hargot Mann, Reece Jackmoore, and Timoth Pal, and by The Vampire Lord, Aleksei Emeritus, this treaty is the law. So long as not one term is broken, humans and vampires may live together in the city."

The vampire looked at Clyde. "Zhis is zhe treaty, and is signed. Vhy is not yet in effect?" he questioned, taking the paper back from Elvin.

Dirk answered, "As we said, we need time to inform the people. It will be done by this time next month. We can promise no sooner."

Irritated, Alucard placed the parchment on the table and rolled his eyes.

"How *is* the werewolf situation, Aleksei?" Reece, the small, short brown-haired man asked, gawping at the vampire.

"Vone vound zheir vay into Wrodiff last night, and as alvays, I vas zhere to kill zhe ving, and my vampires vill be everyvhere to kill zhem vor you vonce you get zhat treaty in place."

Lars nodded. "We understand that. But as Dirk has said, we need time to inform the people. Next month."

Elvin then leaned over to Alucard. "I mean…it's better than nothing, right?"

"Next month," Alucard repeated, pointing at Clyde. "No later."

Then, as the council stared in astonishment, Alucard stormed out…and Elvin hastily followed.

| Alucard |

When they left the tower, Alucard glanced at the bard and watched him excitedly scribble into his book. "Vhat are you vriting?"

The bard looked up at him as he tried to glance into his notebook. "The treaty. So many interesting terms. After seeing that, this cohabitation might work out."

Alucard rolled his eyes and glared ahead. "I'll 'ave to keep zhese new vampires avay vrom zhe city until next month."

"Can't you just…bring them next month instead?" Elvin asked, closing his notebook and stuffing it into his pocket.

"No. I told both Zamien and zhat Zaliv guy I'll start tomorrow."

"I assume that's the demon you met last night?" Elvin asked, reaching for his notebook again.

"Yes," he answered as Elvin wrote it into his book.

"Am I coming with you tonight?" he asked, following Alucard to the city's exit.

"If you vant to become vood vor a 'undred and vivteen vampires, sure."

Elvin frowned uncomfortably. "Yeah…no thanks. How do you plan to get them back here?"

"I 'ad vone of my people prepare a ship; ve'll use zhat. I'm going to inspect zhat later, and you can come if you vant, but avter zhat, I von't see you until tomorrow."

The bard clapped his hands excitedly. "I haven't seen a ship since we got back here six months ago. How much later?"

"An hour or so. I need to go and see Tobias."

"Do you think he'll know about the wolf that got into Wrodiff?"

"I 'ope so," he mumbled.

"Okay, well…I'll see you in a little bit then, right?"

He nodded and sent Elvin on his way. Once he was alone, he let out a tired sigh and headed for the city gates. Soon, he'd have to make his way to Zalith's world and begin transferring vampires. He wasn't at all looking forward to it, but it wasn't like he could bail, was it?

When he left the city, he dematerialized into vermillion smoke and raced towards the forest. At this time of day, he knew he'd find Tobias down by the river, so that was where he landed.

The moment Alucard rematerialized, the blonde-haired, stubbly-faced man standing in the water with a makeshift fishing pole turned to face him and called, "Oh, hey Aleksei!"

Alucard walked closer to the river and watched Tobias reel in an old boot. "I 'ave a job vor you."

"The huntin' kind or the information kind?"

"Both. A volf got into Wrodiff last night and almost killed Elvin. Zhe ving vas much stronger zhan any volf I've vaced, even Alphas. I need you to vind out vhich pack zhat volf belonged to."

Tobias nodded as he climbed out of the river. "Yeah, news travels fast around these woods. I heard about the attack, but I don't have any info right now. I'll look into it for you, though," he said, making his way to Alucard.

"Is zhere anyving else I should be avare of bevore I leave?" he questioned.

"Nothing new. The packs have been kinda quiet lately…which is weird. Hey, you think it's connected to this wolf attack?" he asked, wide-eyed.

"Zhat's vhat you're going to vind out."

Tobias nodded. "No worries, boss. Give me 'til tomorrow."

"I vill meet you back 'ere tomorrow night." Then, he dematerialized and flew off.

Hopefully, he'd have answers by tomorrow. If the werewolves were planning something, he'd have to try and stop them before they caused any damage. He couldn't afford another war; he had fewer vampires than before and even less time, and he wouldn't risk allowing something to interfere with Damien's mission.

Chapter Five

— ⸱ ✝ ⸱ —

The First Transferal

| Alucard |

After a few hours and a small stop at his house, Alucard made his way to the docks below the cliff that held up his castle. The vast, black-bricked fortress overlooked the ocean, its shadow stretching across the slanted land which led up to it, and a swarm of crows circled the tallest tower.

The place was almost deserted; a single black ship was moored there. On the ship's quarterdeck, a casually dressed man leaned against the fence. When he spotted Alucard, he watched as he and Elvin made their way on board. His eyes shone bright green in the afternoon sunlight, and his hair was greyed and platted behind his head.

"Aleksei," the man called with a smirk.

"Vodney," Alucard greeted.

"Elvin," Rodney said, shaking the bard's hand.

"Rodney," Elvin sang.

Rodney then let go of the bard's hand and looked at Alucard. "I came, as requested. What do you need of me?" he asked, leading the way back up onto the quarterdeck.

"I 'ave to pick some vampires up vrom an island in an hour or so," Alucard said, leaning back against the quarterdeck fence.

Nodding, Rodney said, "And you need me to transport them from there to here?"

Alucard handed him a piece of paper. "Zhese are zhe coordinates."

He looked at the paper and frowned. "You want me there in what? An hour from now?"

"*Da.*"

"Well, the sun is setting; it'll take me at *least* an hour to get there, assuming Drac isn't being fussy today," he said, glancing at the ocean.

Alucard sighed irritably. "Just get zhere. If you are late, I'm sure zhe people I'm meeting von't get off my ass."

Rodney laughed slightly. "Who are you meeting?"

"People," Alucard muttered as he turned around and made his way down off the quarterdeck. "Do *not* be late."

"Yeah, I'll leave right away," Rodney called.

"How *is* Drac?" Elvin asked as he followed Alucard off the ship.

"Vine," the vampire mumbled, making his way along the docks.

Elvin frowned as he hurried alongside Alucard onto the beach. "What's wrong?" he asked with a concerned tone, staring at Alucard's stubborn face.

"Noving," he grumbled, stopping in the middle of the beach.

"Something's clearly up." The bard frowned, crossing his arms as he looked up at Alucard. "You don't wanna help this demon, do you?"

Looking down at him, Alucard rolled his eyes. "No, I zon't. I 'ave enough to deal vith 'ere; I zon't 'ave time to look avter more vampires."

The bard shrugged. "At least it's *vampires* you're being made to help, not demons."

He had a point—the exact point Alucard had made to himself last night. He sighed and glared at the ocean. "Go 'ome, Elvin. I vill see you tomorrow."

"You'll give me all the details, right?" he asked excitedly.

"Sure," he muttered, turning his back on the bard.

"I want character descriptions; I want details regarding how they talk, act— everything!" he demanded.

"I said yes!" Alucard snarled, glaring back at him.

Silenced, the bard held up his hands. "All right, sheesh. Don't stay out too late, and don't accept drinks from strangers—bye!" he called, running off towards the cobblestone path.

With an aggravated huff, Alucard glared at the water. He had the ship ready; he found out when the human and vampire cohabitation treaty would be in place, and he also prepared his castle last night for the new vampires. All he had to do now was go and get them.

He wasn't looking forward to any part of his task, least of all working alongside that demon. As Damien always did, he made Alucard look incompetent, and his new work partner now obviously thought he was a useless idiot. But he wasn't going to dwell on it. He'd prove them wrong without even trying.

With an irritated sigh, Alucard dematerialized into vermillion smoke and swiftly made his way across the ocean, reaching the rainy island in ten minutes. He landed on the edge of a black cliff, causing a large school of colourful fish to disperse and bolt for the cover of far-away rocks. Alucard set his eyes on the portal. The last time he entered Eltaria, he felt such strange tiredness, and he was sure that he was going to feel it again.

Alucard didn't know too much about portals, but he *did* know that there were kinds that used a person's energy in order for them to travel. This seemed to be one such portal.

The vampire was confident of his power, though, and he knew that a silly little portal couldn't affect him too significantly. But bringing vampires back with him was a different story. They would be using his ethos to mask theirs, and he was sure that wasn't going to make him feel great. But what choice did he have?

The vampire stood in front of the portal. He wasn't sure what might be waiting on the other side, but he knew it wasn't going to be a comfortable night.

Sighing, Alucard stepped through the portal and emerged into the same eroded castle as last night. The tiredness hit, but it wasn't unbearable. He made his way down the hallway but walked past the stairs that led up to the tower, detecting a mass congregated elsewhere in the ruins. He could hear that demon's voice echoing through the corridors, nattering on about rules, plans, and the new world they were going to.

Alucard approached an open archway and stepped through and into what looked to be the ruin's entrance hall. Zalith, dressed in an all-black suit, was standing in front of the one hundred and fifteen vampires, who were all staring at him while he spoke sternly.

"…You are being relocated to another world outside of this one—it is called Aegisguard," Zalith explained tonelessly. "An associate of mine will be taking care of everything you will need. You will be travelling with him through the portal and to where he plans to have you reside. You must understand that once you leave this world, there is no coming back, so make sure you have everything you need because if you remain here, you will inevitably die."

One of the vampires frowned. "What about Guillaume—my son?"

Zalith replied, "He is an adult; he made his own decision, and I am not responsible for what may happen to him. You should also remember that there are rules in the other world, and I advise you to follow them. There—"

"Vhy 'ave you brought all of zhem 'ere?" Alucard asked irritably, abruptly appearing behind him.

Zalith slowly closed his eyes and exhaled quietly as an angered look appeared on his face. He then glanced at Alucard. "I am explaining the plan to them all at once as I prefer not to repeat myself."

Alucard took his eyes off the demon and looked at the crowd of vampires. "Vine; I'll take zhis time to sort zhem all into groups, zhen."

With a disinterested look on his face, Zalith watched Alucard make his way towards the vampires. As they eyed the red-haired stranger, Zalith called, "This is Alucard, my associate. Let him do what he must."

Scowling, Alucard looked back over his shoulder at Zalith. "*You* zon't call me zhat. You call me Aleksei," he snarled.

Zalith rolled his eyes.

Alucard walked around the huddle of vampires, eyeing them closely. To his relief, not too many of them were older than two hundred and fifty. He knew that he couldn't take a group of vampires that exceeded his age by more than half; if he did that, it would use up a whole lot of his energy, and he wasn't interested in becoming weak to help strangers—vampires or not. So, he had to sort them into groups whose combined age wouldn't exceed more than six hundred years.

These vampires weren't going to attack, nor would they refuse his orders. They may not be from Aegisguard, but every vampire in existence was sired by him, which gave them a natural instinct to obey him. His only concern was that demon; *he* was the one that was going to question his tactics, but Alucard didn't care. He had come to do a job, and whether Zalith liked it or not, he was going to do it *his* way.

Alucard grabbed the shoulder of one of the first vampires and pulled them from the crowd. "Go over zhere," he muttered, making his way through the crowd, "and you," he snarled, pulling another vampire from the group. He eyed each one of them closely, determining their ages, sending them out of the crowd as he did. Once the first group of twelve vampires was formed, he grabbed the collar of another man and pushed him out of the crowd, sending several others to join him a few moments later.

But as he then watched a tall, overly muscular brown-haired vampire leave his group, Alucard scowled irritably. He followed the man with his eyes, observing as he and three other vampires—who also left their groups—went over to Zalith.

With a frustrated snarl, Alucard headed back to Zalith. "Vhat is zhis?" he asked, glancing at the four vampires who joined Zalith.

"They will be going first, and I will also be accompanying you this first time," the demon answered.

The vampire scoffed. "No, zhey are not. I am zhe vone taking zhem, so you abide by my vules, zhose being zhat I take vone of zhese organized groups a month."

"These groups, I assume, are organized to collectively tally to your own…power," Zalith said, glancing at the groups Alucard put together. "You believe you can only transport so many vampires at once so long as they do not exceed your limits."

"No," Alucard lied.

The demon frowned impatiently. "Are you not capable of taking the five of us at once? Will it kill you to do so?" he asked with a condescending tone.

Alucard scowled evilly at him. "Zon't test my patience; do zhis my vay or vind somevone else to 'elp."

Zalith smiled amusedly. "Do you think Damien would have asked *you* to do this if he thought you incapable? I am certain the Daegelus knows how powerful and how old each of these vampires is; he would not have asked you here if you could not do it. These people are also in danger, Aleksei; they need *you*. You are their sire; after all; you are the only person in either world they can rely on."

Glaring at him, Alucard thought to himself for a few moments. He knew that the demon was trying his best to get him to back down, and his current method was an attempt to motivate him with fake assurance.

But Alucard knew his own limitations. If he wanted to come out of this unharmed, then he couldn't take a group that exceeded double his age. If he didn't have responsibilities back home, he wouldn't care; he'd do it to get away from this insufferable demon. However, he had to remain as well as he could in order to keep up his end of the deal that he made with the humans. He couldn't efficiently fight werewolves if he had to spend days resting after transporting vampires.

He snarled and glowered at the demon. "I said no. Zhere are vules; accept zhem or fuck off."

Zalith laughed slightly with an almost astonished look on his face. "Might I suggest we meet somewhere in the middle, then? But I must insist that Ben comes, no matter the compromise," he said, placing his hand on the shoulder of the scruffy-faced vampire he first called over.

With a smirk, glad of his victory in getting him to back down, Alucard eyed the vampires standing at Zalith's side. His limit was six hundred or so years, but Ben was three hundred and twenty, and this demon was older than Alucard. He wasn't sure what to do, but if he couldn't lose the eldest of the vampires, then he'd have to try and remove the second eldest to give himself some relief.

He pointed to the dirty blonde man that stood beside Ben. "You 'ave to stay."

The selected vampire looked at Zalith, who nodded tiredly. Then, the vampire left them and returned to the group he had earlier been put into by Alucard. But the four of them were still past triple Alucard's age. He didn't have the strength to argue further, though. He wanted to get it over and done with.

Alucard turned around and mumbled, "Ve vill go now." He made his way over to the archway and glanced behind him as Ben scurried over to a brown-eyed, auburn-haired woman, who he embraced and kissed.

Zalith took his eyes off Alucard to look at everyone else. "Remember the groups you have been sorted into. We will all meet here at the same time as we did tonight next month," he called to them and then walked to where Alucard was. He set his sights on the vampire who Alucard told to stay behind. "I will be in touch."

Then, Zalith, Ben, and the two other vampires followed Alucard through the castle ruins in silence until they reached the portal.

Along the way, Alucard did his best to ignore his anger. He hated Zalith already. He was rude and insufferable, and he clearly thought he was smarter than everyone else. One thing that Alucard despised was being looked down on, and Zalith did it the same way Damien did. If the Daegelus wasn't the one to have put him on this task, then he would have walked away from that tower. But Damien *had* initiated this mission, so he had to keep his opinions to himself and get on with it.

At least he'd only have to deal with this demon once a month, though.

When he reached the portal, Alucard stopped and looked back at them. "You all need to be linked to me some'ow so zhat vhen ve go vhrough, Levoldus does not detect any of you."

Ben and the other vampires glanced at Zalith, waiting for his instruction.

Zalith sighed, rolled his eyes, and looked over at Ben with an irritable look on his face.

Then, Ben set his eyes on Alucard. "I can do it," he said, stepping closer to him. "What do you want me to do?"

Alucard snatched his wrist. "Take your vriend's 'and—all of you," he instructed.

As Alucard instructed, the vampires took one another's hands. Zalith took Ben's, one of the other vampires took Zalith's, and the last vampire took his. Then, Alucard stared at the portal, preparing to walk through. He didn't know how he'd feel once he reached the other side, but bringing these people with him was undoubtedly going to exhaust him.

He stepped forward, leading the way into the portal.

When he emerged on the other side, the vampire frowned uncomfortably. He could feel his ethos waning the instant Ben stepped out behind him. His head started spinning, and an unrelenting dizziness gripped hold of him as Zalith followed Ben out. That was when Alucard began to feel as though he was moments from passing out, and he very nearly did as the other two vampires walked through. He suspected he would feel awful, but he wasn't aware that it would be *this* severe.

Alucard snarled, denying the disorientation to grip him. He let go of Ben's wrist and pulled his flask from his blazer as he leaned back against the closest rock. What he felt in response to the portal travel was familiar; it was something he sorely hated—*dreaded*. With his ethos suffering, he sipped from his flask, and the blood inside relieved him of his headache.

Then, as he tucked his flask away, he glanced at Zalith and the vampires. He wasn't interested in engaging in conversation with them, so he looked at the island's edge and set his eyes on Rodney, who was standing on the ship's quarterdeck. Alucard made his way over, sure that Zalith and his vampires would follow, and as he stepped up onto the deck, Rodney pounced down and greeted him.

"Drac's being a pain in my ass," Rodney said.

"Is zhat a surprise?" Alucard mumbled while peering into the ocean.

As Zalith and his vampires walked up onto the ship, Rodney glanced over at them and frowned. "Hey, uh…I ain't gonna be someone's snack, am I?" he asked quietly, leaning into Alucard's ear.

"Vhat?" Alucard questioned with a frown, but when he glanced at Zalith, he rolled his eyes and looked back down into the ocean. "No."

Rodney took his eyes off the strangers and asked Alucard, "We heading back home?"

"*Da*," Alucard answered, tapping the side of the ship.

"How long is this going to take?" Zalith then called.

Ignoring him, Alucard stepped back. A colossal beast burst up from the ocean, sending water crashing down on the ship. With a ferocious snarl, the huge, teal, and cyan-scaled serpent lowered its head towards Alucard. Its face looked like a crocodile with sail fins in place of its ears, and its head adorned three pairs of sapphire-blue horns, which stretched out above its four yellow eyes, two on each side of its head.

The vampire held out his hand, and as the beast rested the end of its snout on his palm, he smiled. "Vodney tells me you 'ave been giving 'im a 'ard time, Drac," he said with a smirk.

Looking at him, blinking slowly, the creature whined quietly.

Alucard then frowned and shifted his sights to Zalith and his vampires. While the vampires had impressed looks on their faces, Zalith tried—and failed—to don a look of disinterest.

The vampire then looked back up at Drac. "No, zhey are not vor you zhis time."

"He ain't eating the shit I get for him," Rodney mumbled.

"I believe 'e misses 'aunting zhe oceans and praying on unsuspecting ships, zon't you?" he asked, speaking to the beast as if it were a puppy, and the beast reacted as such. Alucard then sighed and took his hand off the scaled beast's face. "Take us 'ome, hmm?" he requested, staring into the beast's eyes, and as it snarled quietly, he frowned. "Good."

Drac descended back into the ocean; Rodney made his way past Zalith and pulled the bridge onto the deck. He closed the gate, hurried up onto the quarterdeck, and prepared to set out.

The vampire faced Zalith. "Ve vill arrive in Dor-Sanguis in 'alf an hour or so," he said before turning away from them.

He then headed towards the cabin under the quarterdeck, hoping he'd not have to spend this entire trip in the company of that demon. He didn't like him, and he never would. He just had to put up with him until this mission was over.

Chapter Six

— ⸱ ✝ ⸱ —

Sanguine Castle

| **Alucard** |

As Alucard pushed the cabin door open, the boat jolted in response to Drac starting to pull it from beneath the waves. He glanced back at Zalith and his vampires, who were still out on the deck. He didn't want them going anywhere they shouldn't, so he latched the door against the wall so that he could keep an eye on them.

He made his way to his desk and lazily slumped down in the chair, exhaling quietly in relief. Although it hadn't taken very long at all, he felt utterly exhausted. He'd had been made to take Zalith, who was at least six hundred years old; the group was collectively over a thousand years old, and that had taken its toll. It drained a whole lot more of his ethos than he'd planned for, and he wasn't sure how long this exhaustion was going to curse him.

Alucard sighed, pulled his cape off, and placed it over the desk before resting his legs on it. He'd take these vampires back to his castle, and then he'd head home. Zalith obviously wouldn't stay here until next month, but Alucard had no plans to escort him back to the portal; he could get Rodney to do that. After this, he just wanted to go home and rest because he was sure as hell going to need it. Tomorrow, Tobias would hopefully deliver the information he needed about the werewolf which attacked Elvin. He wasn't sure of what to expect, but if there were more, then he'd have his hands full.

There was another month before the treaty came into effect, and he wondered, would Zalith's vampires stay in the castle that long? He'd have to run all the rules by them. The last thing he wanted was a rogue killing humans and shattering everything he worked so hard to build. He just hoped that the humans would welcome the new laws. Dor-Sanguis was *his* land, after all, and as much as he didn't want to, he would drive the humans out if it came to it.

Irritated, he rolled his eyes and took his feet off his desk; he turned in his seat to glare out the window behind him and watched as they sailed away from the rainy island. He couldn't drive the humans out; that would doom his people to starvation. He didn't want the land to return to how it once was—humans and vampires at war. No, he wanted something peaceful, an agreement between the two peoples, and he knew he could get it, he just had to keep trying—he just had to be patient.

"I assume you have a place set aside for the vampires to live," Zalith said.

Alucard turned to face him. "Did I say you could come in 'ere?" he asked, disguising his startle with anger.

Zalith smiled. "The door is wide open."

The vampire sat up straight. "Yes, I 'ave," he answered, tapping his clawed fingers on the table as he eyed the vampires standing behind Zalith. "Zhat is vhere ve are 'eaded."

"And is it safe? Secure?"

"Vhy vould zhis not be?"

"There wasn't much time to plan, so I'm being cautious. We're bringing them here so that they're safe, and I need to make sure that will be the case."

Alucard huffed and looked back out the window. "Zon't vorry; my castle is zhe safest place in zhe country, so long as zhey vollow my vules."

"I'm sure they will," Zalith said, smiling.

Not in the mood for Zalith's arrogance, Alucard waved his hand dismissively. "Vhatever. Get out."

The demon scoffed condescendingly, turned around with a quiet scoff, and left the cabin.

Alucard rested his legs on the table and snarled angrily. The demon shattered his trail of thought. He scowled and crossed his arms but then closed his eyes and sighed quietly, sinking into his fatigue. His job still wasn't done, and he wasn't sure when he'd get to rest, so what better time than now to sleep a little?

The vampire relaxed, allowing himself to slowly drift off to sleep.

| Zalith |

Out on the deck, Zalith stared at the sea. He didn't have the strength to argue with Alucard; he was so tired and just wanted to make sure that this plan would be successful. There was already so much on his shoulders—the war, the vampires, Damien, werewolves—not to mention his personal affairs and the fact that there were people out for his head. Helping these vampires was something he wanted to do before his inevitable capture, and if he had to work with Alucard…then he would. As insufferable as he was, he was the one Damien chose, so he had to trust that the Daegelus made the right choice.

He stared at the six moons; two purple, one silver, one red, one blue, and one gold. He wasn't sure how that was possible, considering the ocean's tides seemed much like those back in his world, and for a moment, it made him think about how remarkable these circumstances were. To think that his world was connected to this one—it was somewhat wondrous. The differences, the similarities. If only he had more time to spend here, he felt he might quite enjoy it.

He sighed and stared aimlessly, waiting for the ship to reach its destination.

"Veed Drac," soon came Alucard's voice.

Zalith looked at the cabin and watched Alucard walk out. As the ship slowed, the captain leapt down from the quarterdeck and followed Alucard to the ship's edge. The demon listened and observed his new associate, trying to get a good enough read on who this vampire was.

The captain prepared the ropes for docking. "I told you, he's been fussy lately." The ship stopped, and the captain jumped onto the docks and started mooring the ship with the dockworkers. Once he was done, he and his colleagues attached the ramp.

Alucard headed down the ramp as Zalith and his vampires followed. "Try vonce more; if 'e still von't eat, I'll talk to 'im."

The captain shrugged and sighed as Alucard led his guests along the cobblestone path that led up to his castle.

"I'm telling ya now, he's not gonna eat."

Irritated, Alucard waved his hand in dismissal, mumbling to himself.

Ben moved closer to Alucard. "Your snake isn't eating?"

With a concerned frown, Alucard glanced at him. "'E is a dragon," he corrected, looking ahead again. "And no, 'e's simply vussy."

"What does he eat?"

A smirk appeared on Alucard's face. "I kill zhe verevolves 'ere, and I veed zhem to Drac."

As the other two vampires chuckled, Ben laughed loudly. "I feel like you and I are going to get along well."

"Vill ve?" Alucard muttered, leading the way up a small flight of stairs.

Zalith watched them. Alucard's response was amusing, but he wouldn't laugh. He just wanted to make sure this plan would work. And once they reached the castle, he hoped that he'd finally get an answer.

He followed silently as Alucard led the way towards the huge black castle. A swarm of crows circled the tallest tower, cawing loudly, catching the demon's attention. He glared at them; their eyes shimmered as crimson as the vampire's hair, and their bodies were torn, burnt, and rotting. They weren't alive, and by the looks of it, they acted as sentries, watching over the castle.

The demon looked ahead as Alucard led the way to the castle's door.

Alucard looked over his shoulder at the vampires. "You can come in," he mumbled, granting them entrance into the castle.

They made their way into the entrance hall. The floor was dark oak wood, and the rib-vaulted ceiling was black, as were the walls with patterned gold engravings. Tall, arched stained-glass windows were lined along the left and right walls, lighting the room with an array of different, striking colours, and a long, rectangular table sat in the centre.

Against the right wall were two suits of steel armour with a dark-oak door between them. Another door was in the far-right corner and another to the left. The back wall also had a huge, circular stained-glass window displaying paintings of dragons, wolves, and what could only be vampires. The arched windows around the room had similar scenes: dragons, wolves, vampires, angels, and even demons.

A curious smile appeared on Zalith's face. Clearly, Alucard had an eye for art. From what he could see and what he knew, the art might be historic, representing this world's past. The window to his left had Damien in it with a shimmering blue moon behind him—it looked much like the blue moon that sat in the sky. The window beside it possessed the image of the crimson-haired demon, Lucifer, with a blood-red moon, and the windows opposite them were painted with two women: one angelic-looking with a golden moon, and another demon-looking woman with a bright purple moon. While the angel possessed black hair, the demon's hair was ashen.

Was the angel a Numen? Zalith had only seen Lucifer and Lilith, so he wasn't sure what the other Numen looked like. The window beside them possessed the image of a wholly cloaked, hooded man and a silvery moon, and the window opposite that one was painted with the image of a tall, long-purple-haired man with a black-purple moon above him. Zalith wasn't sure who they were.

Alucard stopped beside the table and turned to face the group. "I 'ave vules 'ere. You vill listen, and vhen more of your vriends arrive, you vill tell zhem. Understood?"

Ben nodded. "Yes."

"To begin, all vampires are classed, and some 'ave more vesponsibilities zhan ozzers," Alucard said. "Vledgelings: newly created vampires, Acolytes: vampires younger zhan a 'undred, Adherents: vampires betveen vone 'undred and vree 'undred, and vinally, Paladins: my strongest and oldest vampires. You von't see zhem avound zhe castle very ovten. Zhey are who I send out into zhe vorld to conduct my business overseas."

"So…will that be my job?" Ben asked. "I'm three hundred and—"

"No. You're new 'ere, so you'll all be starting as Acolytes. I'll explain your voles later," Alucard said. Then, he pointed to the back-left door. "Zhat is my 'alf of zhis castle; no vone is to enter zhat door unless I 'ave said so," he said. Then, he pointed to the back-right door. "Zhat vill lead you to zhe kitchen—'owever, zhat is also vhere zhe 'uman 'elpers veside. Zon't eat zhem; zhat vould piss me off immensely."

The vampires agreed.

With a tired sigh, Alucard pointed to the door between the suits of armour. "Zhat door vill take you to your part of zhe castle. Is daylight-proov, and zhere are several safe vays in and out ozzer zhan zhis door. 'Owever, zhe city is not yet veady vor us. I 'ave been vorking on an agreement vith zhe council. Next month, you vill be vree to valk avound and veed off people so long as you zon't kill zhem, and so long as zhey consent. I vill make sure to get my bard to vrite you all copies of zhe agreement. Does all of zhat make sense?"

No one had anything to question or disagree with.

Alucard frowned and looked at the silent demon. "Vell?"

Zalith smiled. "I'd like to see their part of the castle, please."

The vampire sighed but didn't argue. "Zhis vay," he grumbled, and as Zalith and his vampires followed, Alucard led the way through the door.

| **Alucard** |

Alucard just wanted to go home. But he'd show Zalith what he wanted to see to avoid an argument; that was the last thing he needed. He led them through the dark hallway; every window was boarded up so tightly that the moonlight couldn't shine through. The walls were black and patterned with gold engravings, and a long red rug stretched down the corridor.

They reached a small lounge, where Alucard turned left and led them down another corridor and up several flights of stairs, showing them the entire east wing, pointing out every room where vampires slept.

The tour felt like just moments for Alucard; his tiredness helped him zone out as he showed them around. To his relief, Zalith seemed content, so the vampire took them back to the entrance hall. He made his way to the table, leaned back against it, and took a moment to wake.

He looked at Zalith. "If zhat is all, I vould like to bring zhis to an end."

Zalith glanced around the room and then looked at Alucard. "I'm satisfied," he answered. He looked at Ben. "This is where we part ways," he said, holding his arms out, inviting Ben closer. As he and Ben embraced each other, Zalith swiftly kissed his right cheek. Ben then stepped back as Zalith placed one hand on his shoulder. "Are you okay with everything?"

"Yeah," he answered with an assuring smile. "It's a little different, but I can get used to it—I'm sure we all can. I really appreciate what you're doing for us."

The demon smirked. "Stay out of trouble."

Ben nodded as Zalith let go of his shoulder. Then, the demon looked at Alucard with an expectant expression.

Alucard exhaled quietly, stood up straight, and escorted Zalith out of the castle. When they stepped outside, Zalith stopped and faced the vampire.

"Thank you, Aleksei—truly—for helping us. I wouldn't have ever suggested this to Damien if things in Eltaria weren't so dire."

Alucard shrugged. "Zhey'll be safe 'ere." Then, he went to head towards the forest.

Zalith smiled slightly. "So, tell me about this city," he requested, turning towards the path to the docks.

The vampire hesitated for a moment…but Zalith was probably going to need this information for the vampires that were still in Eltaria. He followed behind him. "Vhat about zhe city?"

"A treaty with humans?"

Alucard sighed as they made their way down the cliffside. "Zhis land vas empty; zhe only people zhat lived 'ere vere zhe people zhat vaised me. I levt vhen I vas vive and came back vhen I vas twenty-vone to vind zhat 'umans 'ad built zheir villages vhroughout zhe land. I vasn't too bovered back zhen, but vonce I vas done vith some business, I vanted my land back—but I'm a vampire, so I need 'umans. Zhe next best option vas to see if ve could co'abit, 'ence zhe vorming of zhis treaty," he explained, reaching the bottom of the cliff.

Zalith nodded.

He continued as they boarded the ship, "Our kind vonce stayed 'idden vrom 'umans as best as possible—zhey vhought zhat vas safer vor everyvone. But zhen Levoldus vanted to be known and vorshipped—*all* zhe Numen did—so ve came out into zhe light. People call zhis event Year Zero. Zhe vorld basically veset vhen zhe Numen showed zhemselves. Ever since zhen, zhere 'as been a constant struggle vor 'umans to live alongside zhose of us vith ethos, but I am trying to make vings vork 'ere.

"Took a lot of convincing. I asked zhem vhat I can do to prove zhat I can be an ally. Zhey 'ave me killing verevolves; zhey 'unt 'umans vor sport, kill zheir livestock or vhatever. Zhey said, kill zhe volves, and ve'll vorm a treaty. So, I kill zhe volves and veed zhem to my dragon to keep zhem vrom turning into 'ell'ounds."

Rodney called to him, "I guess you need me to take you back?"

Alucard replied, "*Da.*"

Then, as Rodney prepared to disembark, Alucard led the way into the cabin.

"I've been killing zhem vor six months. I spoke to zhe council yesterday, and zhey told me zhe treaty vill be in effect next month. Zhey made me vait long enough; zhe verevolves 'aven't killed a single 'uman since I got back. Eizer zhe 'umans are dumb or zon't vant to accept zhe vact I lived up to my end." No one had been killed *yet*, but since that wolf tried to kill Elvin in Wrodiff, he'd been worried that might soon change. Once he was done with tonight, he really needed to look into that.

The demon smiled in response as Alucard sat down and invited him to sit across from him.

As the ship started moving, Alucard exhaled deeply and shrugged. "I vink zhey know zhat if zhey zon't agree and come vhrough, I vill turn 'ostile. Zhis is my land; if I 'ave to rid zhem vrom 'ere like vermin, zhen I vill."

"Humans are a repulsive species; I have no doubt that they may try to work their way out of it; this often happens to be the case with them. I advise you keep an eye on them, be persistent, and remind them of their place."

Glancing at him, Alucard nodded. "I know."

Amused by his response, Zalith laughed.

The vampire scowled. Why did he find everything so amusing? If he wasn't staring and smiling, he was laughing at something that wasn't funny. Alucard didn't care. He rolled his eyes and glared out the window, but he couldn't see through the thickening fog. The sound of rain wasn't too far away, so it wouldn't be long until they reached the island—until he could finally go home and rest.

He glanced at the demon; to no surprise, Zalith was staring, and it made Alucard feel uncomfortable. He frowned and tried ignoring Zalith's expectant gaze by thinking about tomorrow's plans. Werewolf hunting, as usual, and he could speak to Zalith's vampires and make sure that they were comfortable. He also had to be adamant about them not feeding on humans. They would have to do what the rest of his resident vampires did and wait for *him* to bring them blood.

"What is the Nosferatu?" Zalith asked him.

Alucard glared at him. "Is vhat I vas known as a long time ago; zhe vord stuck, and I decided to keep zhe name. I named my empire avter zhis, too."

"I see."

"Next month, are you coming back 'ere or staying zhere?"

"I'll stay behind."

Alucard didn't have more to say; the demon still stared, the silence was awkward, and he was tired. The island was fifteen minutes away…and that was plenty of time for him to get more rest. "Go vait outside," he grumbled, waving his hand.

Zalith scoffed amusedly. "What?"

"You 'eard. I 'ave vings to do zhat vould get done vaster vithout you staring at me."

The demon laughed quietly as he stood up. "Fine."

Wasn't he going to argue? Alucard frowned skeptically, watching Zalith leave and shut the door. That was easier than Alucard imagined. With a relieved sigh, he slouched in his seat and closed his eyes. The night was almost over.

| **Zalith** |

Zalith stared at the moons again. To his relief, this plan might just work. Ben and two others were already safely transported, but he wouldn't relax until more vampires were in Aegisguard. Although he initially thought Alucard was incompetent and an idiot, this first night had already swayed him from that assumption. Alucard was arrogant, but Zalith found himself almost liking him in some strange way. Perhaps a friendship may form one day; there were a few things he had come to realize about this man that he could relate to, and he also enjoyed their conversation. He had certainly enjoyed *looking* at him, too.

He'd miss Ben a little, but his pursuit of that man was over. It was only a temporarily amusing distraction pursuing a man who wasn't interested in having sex with him; however, Ben now lived in an entirely different world, and Zalith had also begun to grow bored of him. Whatever he'd been seeking was over.

Alucard, on the other hand, caught Zalith's attention from the moment they met. Of course, it wasn't a surprise. Zalith was an incubus. His life revolved around having sex; he needed it to sustain himself, and it led him to a life of promiscuity…and loneliness. Nobody he slept with remained in his life for long. He always got bored of them, and he was sure that Alucard would be no different.

Zalith was keen to get to know Alucard more first, and maybe the world he lived in, too. He hadn't failed to notice the fish swimming in the sky, and he was sure that Alucard would have an explanation. He'd be sure to ask him when he joined him again.

After a while, the ship stopped.

Zalith looked over his shoulder and watched Alucard emerge from the cabin with a tired look on his face. He headed over to Zalith and sighed quietly—

"What are the fish I saw swimming in the sky?" Zalith asked before Alucard could speak.

Alucard frowned slightly. "Vish," he answered tonelessly.

"But fish swim in the sea—"

"Not 'ere. Vell…zhey svim in zhe sea and sky. Vhen vains or snows, zhey can move using zhe moisture in zhe air."

"How fascinating."

"Let's go," Alucard mumbled, leading the way down onto the island the moment the captain lowered the ramp.

They walked to the portal, but before stepping through, Zalith turned to face Alucard.

"I shall see you next month, then."

"*Da,*" Alucard replied tiredly.

Zalith actually enjoyed his time here. But it was time for him to get back. There were people waiting for him and there was no time for him to stick around and flirt with Alucard tonight. So, he turned around and stepped into the portal, heading back to his own world.

And he hoped that he wouldn't be met with his enemies on the other side.

Chapter Seven

— ʒ † ʅ —

Repercussion

| Alucard |

The vampire lay in his bed, gripping the black covers as his claws tore the fabric. He frowned in confliction as pain surged through his head like he'd been impaled. His body ached, and his eyes stung in the afternoon sunlight shining through the gaps between the curtains.

The glum room was filled with light, but it didn't brighten the dark furniture, the oak floorboards, or the black, ebony-panelled walls. The only colour came from Alucard's shimmering, blood-red hair, and his pale-as-ice skin.

As the sunlight clawed at his face, Alucard scowled and tried to concentrate, but his vision was blurred and unfocused; everything swirled around as though he was intoxicated. He was the opposite, in fact, and as he felt himself sinking deeper into the strange trance, his hunger grew.

He thought resting would help him recover from last night's events, but it seemed to have only worsened it. He knew what he needed and wanted, and he was going to stop at nothing to get it. So, he sat up, but overwhelming dizziness gripped him so tightly that he felt like he might fall back down. But he couldn't allow himself to become hungrier.

The vampire stumbled to his feet, pulled on the first shirt his hands could find, and then dragged himself out of his room into the dimly lit hallway. But for a moment, he felt utterly confused…. Where was he? He looked around, setting his eyes on the black, ebony-panelled walls; the oak floor beneath him and antique-like furniture spreading down the hall didn't seem familiar, but it didn't really matter where he was, did it?

Alucard held his hand against the wall, keeping himself on his feet as he made his way forward, passing the closed doors. When he reached the stairs, he hastily made his way down into the foyer. But once he got there, the front door opened.

Elvin stepped into the foyer and took his hat off. When he hung it on the coat rack, he sharply turned his head and watched as Alucard struggled to make his way to him.

"Uh…are you all right?" the bard asked, stepping aside as Alucard made his way towards the table by the door. He watched the vampire grab his blazer and search the pockets.

Alucard anxiously pulled his flask from his blazer pocket and desperately pulled off the cap, but once he lifted it to his mouth, dread consumed him. It was empty.

"Aleksei?" Elvin asked worriedly as Alucard placed the empty flask on the table and stumbled into the lounge. The bard followed, and as Alucard slumped down onto the couch, Elvin sat in the armchair.

Alucard's head swirled. All he could think about was blood and how it would relieve the pain and disorientation. But the thought of having to get up made him feel worse.

"Hey?" Elvin asked. "Did something happen? W-was it another one of those strong werewolves?"

The vampire snarled irritably and lowered his hand. "Vhy are you 'ere?"

"I…always come in the mornings—unless we have somewhere to be. Are you okay? You…you look sick."

It took Alucard a moment to wake from the confusion that latched onto him. The world started falling into place, and when he realized that he was in his lounge, he sighed and looked over at the perplexed bard. "Noving 'appened."

"You look…well…if you weren't a vampire, I'd say you look like you got the flu."

The vampire rolled his eyes, but he felt far too exhausted to say anything else. He turned his head and stared into the fireplace, trying to fight his hunger…but all he could hear was the sound of Elvin's blood making its way through his veins. The human's heartbeat enticed him greater and greater as each second passed, every beat echoing through his head. If he didn't send Elvin away now, he wasn't sure what might happen in the next few minutes.

He frowned and snapped out of it. Then, he looked at the armchair, but the bard was no longer sitting there. Had he become so lost in his thoughts of thirst that he hadn't noticed him leaving? No…he was still here; he could smell human blood, but it was a whole lot more potent than before—

"Here," Elvin said, holding out a drinking glass, appearing from behind the couch.

Looking up at him, Alucard frowned strangely. In his right hand, the bard was holding a glass of blood. But where had it come from? He didn't care. He took the glass and sipped from it, and relief instantly outweighed his hunger and exhaustion. This blood—wherever it had come from—wasn't old. It clearly hadn't been stored somewhere; it was fresh. Where had fresh blood come from?

Elvin sat back down in the armchair and rested his arms on his knees as he stared at Alucard. "What happened?" he asked again. "I haven't seen you like this in like…two years. You're starving."

Holding the empty glass, Alucard glanced at him. "Vhat?"

"You looked like you were starving," he repeated. "Now I know you lose ethos or strength or whatever when you bleed or get hurt or stuff…so, what happened? Did you get into a fight? Did you get hurt? Was it werewolves? Were you bit?!"

The vampire rolled his eyes and glared into the empty fireplace. "No," he grumbled. "Zhe portal veeds off my energy vhen I go vhrough, and I 'ad to take several ozzers vith me too; zhe trip near enough drained me."

The bard frowned. "Why couldn't they just walk through on their own?"

Alucard sighed irritably. "Because Levoldus vould 'ave detected zhem. Zhe point of zhis mission is to sneak zhese vampires into Aegisguard. Zhe last ving I vant to do is give ourselves avay."

"True. Well…can I get the details?" he asked, reaching into his pocket and pulling out his notebook, but he grunted painfully as he did.

When Alucard looked at him, he noticed a bloody rag wrapped around Elvin's hand. *That* was where the blood had come from.

"You met that demon again last night, right? What was it like?" he questioned, his concerned tone changing to excitement.

Alucard wanted to rest more. But he didn't have the luxury of being able to lounge around all day doing nothing. He had to wake up and get on with yet another day. First, though, he'd sate Elvin's curiosity. Tobias wouldn't be at the river for hours, so he had time.

He sighed quietly. "Vas irritating."

Scribbling into his notebook, Elvin nodded. "What happened? Did you make friends?"

"No," he mumbled. "Zemons and vampires vill never be vriends. I did speak to vone of 'is subordinates, zhough. 'Is name vas Ben. 'E appears to know vhat 'e is doing, so per'aps I von't 'ave to keep my eye on zhese new vampires all day every day."

"What did you all talk about? How many vampires did you bring with you?"

"Hmm…vree," he answered, holding up three of his claw-tipped fingers as he shuffled around in his seat, trying to relax a little now that the pain of his headache was fading. "I von't tell you vhat zhey look like. You can come vith me to zhe castle soon. I actually zon't vemember vhat zhe ozzer two looked like, zhey vere kind of…quiet."

"What about you and the demon?" Elvin asked eagerly, tapping his notebook with his pencil as he gawped at Alucard with his brown eyes.

Alucard snarled quietly at the thought of Zalith—the thought of his arrogance. But he'd not let it keep him in a sour mood all day. He didn't even matter. He was just some guy he'd be working with once a month for a year. He sighed and slouched back a little. "Ve spoke about zhe 'umans and zhe city a bit, zhe treaty—zhat's all, veally. Zhen ve vent 'ome. I 'ave to meet 'im again next month."

Elvin smirked. "See, you're talking—you could be becoming friends."

He scowled. "No."

"Come on, what harm could it do? It could be good for you, you know—to hang out with someone. All you do is work, Aleksei."

Alucard snarled in disapproval, silencing the bard. He didn't need nor want friends. What was the point?

Elvin sighed and rested his arms on his notebook. "Whatever. There anything else I should note down?"

"Drac isn't eating," the vampire said. "'E is being vussy."

"Mm-hmm, mm-hmm," Elvin murmured, noting it down.

"I vink I pissed Vodney off," Alucard then muttered, a little amusement in his voice. "I levt 'im on 'is own on zhe island last night."

The bard glanced up from his notebook. "Rude," he mumbled, writing Alucard's information down.

Alucard then sighed as he sat up straight. He placed the glass Elvin had given him on the table beside the couch and glanced at him. "*Multumesc.*"

Shrugging, Elvin tucked his notebook and pencil away. "Don't mention it." He smiled, finishing his writing. "I'd rather this than let you go kill someone," he said, holding up his rag-wrapped hand.

The vampire stood up. "You shouldn't be trying to stop me," he grumbled, straightening his shirt. "Is vhat I do."

"Yeah, well, I'll just keep stopping you wherever I can," he argued, also standing up. "The less killing you do, the more likely people are to trust you and vampires altogether, you know?" He frowned as he followed Alucard to the front door. "I know you *need* blood, but can't you just, like…not kill someone when you feed off them?" he asked, scurrying after the vampire, who left the house after attaching his rapier to his side, carrying his blazer and fur-collared cape over his arm.

"No," Alucard answered as he felt the flicker of pain as his eyes faded from hell-fiery red to icy blue when the sunlight hit his face.

Elvin gazed at him as they walked through the manor gardens, but he then stuttered and stumbled as the vampire threw his cape at him. The bard caught it in his arms and held onto it while he watched Alucard put his blazer on. Then, Alucard took his cape back and pulled that on, too.

"Why?" Elvin asked, following Alucard to the left of the manor's garden, where a black stable stood.

Alucard stopped walking and turned to face Elvin. "You 'ave been vollowing me avound vor seven years and you still 'aven't vorked out vhy vampires kill people?"

He shook his head. "I mean…I *could* have done my research, but I'd rather learn from the creator of vampires himself," he said confidently.

Setting his eyes on Sergiu—the cedar-brown-haired groundskeeper—as he made his way over in his black tailcoat, the vampire sighed. "Ve cannot stop vonce ve start," he mumbled. "Zhe taste of blood just…takes control of us."

Elvin took out his notebook and started writing down Alucard's explanation. "So, it's like…a drug?"

"No." Alucard frowned strangely. "Vell…vor some, maybe. Vhen ve veed off living 'umans, ve do experience a kind of euphoria. But is more of an instinct to kill our victims vather zhan let zhem go," he explained slowly—he wasn't exactly sure how to describe it.

"Interesting. So you can't just bite someone and drink a little and then let them live?"

"Ve can learn to—I 'ave learnt to—but I choose not to let zhem live."

Elvin pouted. "You can't just murder people, Aleksei."

"Can't I?" Then, as Sergiu stopped in front of him, he laughed slightly, amused by Elvin's distraught face. "Zon't vorry, Elvin. I zon't kill people who zon't deserve to die; you know zhat."

Still pouting, Elvin tucked his notepad away and crossed his arms. "I don't know who you kill—you always tell me it was 'some guy'. Anyway, I still don't approve. Killing people is an awful thing."

"Is killing a murderer an awvul ving? If so, you should go to zhe courts and tell zhem 'anging people should be outlawed," he grumbled, setting his eyes on Sergiu. Before Elvin could argue, the vampire glared at the groundskeeper. "Are zhey veady?"

Sergiu nodded as he kept his olive eyes fixed on the vampire. "As always, sir," he replied.

"Get zhem."

The groundskeeper nodded and hurried into the stable.

Alucard then looked at Elvin. "I told you bevore, and I vill tell you again: you vere zhe vone who chose to vollow *me* avound; if you zon't agree vith my methods, you can alvays valk avay and go back to DeiganLupus. I'm not keeping you 'ere."

Elvin frowned in dread. "I don't wanna go, it's not that…I just…worry about you. What if you accidentally kill someone one day? Like someone you don't mean to kill?" he stammered.

"Zhat vill never 'appen. I am careful, I can control myselv, and I am never vithout blood. Zhis morning vas just…I vas unprepared," he admitted. "I zidn't know zhe portal vould do zhat to me."

Elvin shrugged. "You ran out; it's fine."

"I'll get the gate, sir," Sergiu then said, handing Alucard the reins of a black stallion and Elvin the reins of a dark brown mare.

As the groundskeeper walked off, Elvin sighed and looked back at Alucard. "Anyway, what are we doing today?" he asked, changing the subject.

Mounting his horse, Alucard shrugged. "I 'ave to go and check on zhe vampires who came last night, and zhen I'm going to meet Tobias. I sent 'im to vind out vhat 'e could about zhe volf zhat attacked you in Wrodiff."

Climbing on his own horse, Elvin said, "Do you think he'll find anything?"

"I 'ope so. If zhe verevolves are planning someving, I'd vather know now zhan later. I von't visk zhe treaty, especially not now vith zhese new vampires moving over 'ere."

"Yeah, the treaty…but what about *you*? You need to be careful. I saw that wolf escape from you last night."

He sighed quietly. "I'll be vine. I've dealt vith verevolves all my life."

Elvin frowned worriedly. "It's not just the werewolves, though. All you do is work, Aleksei. Don't you have anything else to do? You know, you could always come and hang out with me. If you won't make new friends, at least spend time outside of work with *me*."

"I 'ave 'obbies," Alucard insisted, disregarding his suggestions.

"Really? I haven't seen you doing anything—"

"Private vones," he grumbled.

"Oh…okay." Elvin frowned—Alucard knew he wasn't going to give up yet. "Well, if you ever get bored, you can always come over. I live by—"

"I zon't vant to know vhere you live," the vampire interjected irritably. He then tapped his horse's side, making it move forward.

Following, Elvin frowned. "What? Why?"

"Because I zon't," he mumbled, glaring ahead as he left the manor.

"Why don't you want to know where I live? *I* know where you live—I even have a key to your house!" the bard exclaimed.

Alucard rolled his eyes. He didn't want to sit there and explain anything to him.

Elvin sighed and looked over at him. "You're weird. I've been travelling with you for *seven* years and I still don't get you."

"Is vor zhe best."

"I'm your friend, you know. Friends know things about each other. Like…I've not seen you do anything that could be classed a hobby—unless making growling sounds at people you don't want to talk to is a hobby."

"I'm not going to tell you," Alucard snarled.

"Why?"

Alucard ignored him.

"Do you…write? Draw? Sing?"

"Do you veally imagine me singing vith zhis accent?"

"Yes." Elvin smiled, amused. "You could be a famous opera singer for all I know—you never tell me anything."

The vampire rolled his eyes.

"Do you…hmm…what about archery? I know a guy that does archery for fun."

"I do not do archery."

"Dance? Do you dance?"

Alucard glared at him. "I vould much prever silence during zhis trip."

He wouldn't let up. "What about cards? Do you play cards?"

The vampire deadpanned.

"I could teach you!" he said, clapping his hands.

"No."

Elvin pouted. "What about fishing? Do you know how to fish?"

"I know 'ow to use zhe line to shut somevone up," he hissed.

"Of course, you do," Elvin mumbled, shaking his head. He then sighed and pulled out his notebook and pencil. "Fine. I'll just write then, shall I?" he sneered. Alucard didn't answer, so he looked down at the blank page he had flicked to and began to write.

Now that he had the silence to think, Alucard glanced at the forest. A cold chill ran down his spine; it felt like there were eyes on him. But when he focused his sensory ethos, he couldn't detect anything in the woods. Was he imagining it?

He sighed and set his eyes on the castle. Although he didn't show it in front of Elvin, he *was* worried about the possibility that there were more werewolves planning on attacking townspeople. If a single human was killed, he knew the council would dismiss the treaty. He wanted to go out there and search the entire forest himself, but he just didn't have the time or energy. He needed to focus on the new vampires; if he fucked a single thing up, Damien would come down on him like a tonne of bricks—*sharp*, jagged bricks. All he could do was wait and see if Tobias was able to find something.

And he sorely hoped that he would.

Chapter Eight

— ⸲ † ⸱ —

Servitude

| Alucard |

Alucard and Elvin reached the castle. Once they dismounted their horses, the beasts wandered over to the grass by the white marble fountain.

"These vampires aren't gonna try to eat me, are they?" Elvin asked, walking beside Alucard as he led the way to the castle's door.

"No."

The bard frowned. "Okay…and we're just here to see how they settled in?"

"*Da.*"

He nodded as Alucard opened the door. "Okay…."

Alucard stepped into his castle expecting to find the entrance hall empty, but despite the room being filled with sunlight, Ben was standing by the table.

Ben smiled at him and said, "Good afternoon."

Perturbed, Alucard slowly walked over. "Zhe sunlight? You are…vine?" he asked, looking at the windows. No vampire other than himself and those turned with his blood could walk in the sunlight.

Ben took and shook Alucard's hand. "Oh, we would have told you last night, but you seemed pretty tired, so I thought I'd save it for today. We can all walk in the sunlight—all us from Eltaria…uh…my world."

Letting go of Ben's hand, Alucard nodded and frowned. "Hmm…Janus *did* take off vith my blood a long time ago; 'e created many vampires vith zhat, so zoesn't surprise me zhat 'e made some vith zhe ability to valk in zhe sunlight."

Ben's face flickered with intrigue. "Well, we're all linked to you one way or another."

"Who is this?" Elvin then asked with a curious look as he tapped his notebook with his pencil, having just written down details of Ben's appearance: *'Scruffy big man, a lot of muscle'*….

Alucard shook his head slowly, stifling a facepalm.

"Ben," the new vampire said, holding out his hand.

Elvin noted down his name before shaking his hand. "Elvin—I'm Aleksei's friend," he said proudly as though it was an honourable title.

"Vamiliar," Alucard corrected.

Elvin pouted sadly.

"Oh, well, I, too, hope to call myself Aleksei's friend," Ben said, looking at Alucard.

Alucard ignored him as he looked around the hall. "Vhere are zhe ozzer two?"

"Upstairs," Ben answered. "I need to ask, how do we feed? You told us the humans here are off-limits, correct?"

"Until zhe treaty is in place. Vor now, you can dvink vhat ve 'ave 'ere. I'll show you vhere ve keep zhe blood," he invited but then looked back at Elvin. "You stay 'ere."

"Aw, why?" the bard complained.

"Because I said so."

Pouting, Elvin pulled out one of the chairs tucked under the large table and slumped down.

"Zhis vay," Alucard said, leading the way to the kitchen door. "I 'ave kept vhere zhe newer vampires can't get; ozzervise, I'm sure zhey vould tear vhrough zhe entire supply in a vew hours."

"Do *we* have to ask for it?"

"No," he said, leading Ben through the deserted kitchen and towards a wine cellar. "Just needs to be kept avay vrom zhe younger vampires until zhey can control zhemselves. I 'ave sentries to guard zhis part of zhe castle at night—to protect zhe 'uman vorkers and zhe supply on zhe off-chance zhat a vampire disobeys me," he explained, heading down into the wine cellar.

Following him, Ben looked at the shelves of differently shaped and coloured wine bottles. He took a moment to stare at the huge barrels, assessing the huge apparatus they were attached to in the middle of the room; Alucard was sure that he wanted to examine everything closely, so he waited for him to inevitably ask his questions.

"Do you make your *own* wine here?" he asked—the question Alucard had been waiting for.

"Sometimes," he mumbled in response, stopping in front of an oak-wood cabinet that stretched across the entire back wall. The wood was black and engraved with white runes. He tapped the glass, and as Ben set his eyes on the rows of bottles inside, Alucard leaned back against the cabinet. "Zhis is vhere ve keep zhe blood. Zhis cabinet is enchanted to keep vrom rotting. Von't taste zhe same as veeding off a 'uman; you von't veel zhe euphoria, but zhis vill sate your 'unger."

Taking his eyes off the cabinet, Ben looked at Alucard. "Where do you get it from?"

"Is probably best I zon't tell you zhat—unless you vant zhe job," he said with a smirk, opening the cabinet and taking a bottle out.

Ben smiled. "I certainly would," he agreed, watching as Alucard opened the bottle.

Having not been expecting him to offer, Alucard frowned. "Vas a joke, but sure." He placed the bottle down as he pulled his flask from his blazer pocket. He had been the one bringing blood to the castle, and it would be a relief if he didn't have to do it anymore. He refilled his flask with the blood from the bottle before returning it to the cabinet. Then, he put his flask back into his pocket and headed for the cellar's exit. "Zhis sort of ving vould usually be an Adherent vampire's job, and considering your age, I trust you'll manage."

"Yeah, you can count on me," Ben said as he frowned curiously. "Actually, I was hoping to see the city—or would that have to wait until the treaty is in place?"

"I zon't 'ave time. I'm going to get vone of my subordinates to show you vhere zhe blood gets picked up vrom, zhough, so I'll get zhem to take you vhrough zhe city on zhe vay," Alucard explained.

"All right sounds good. Thank you."

"Mm-hmm."

"It must have taken a while for you to set up a treaty with them," Ben then said.

Alucard sighed. "Not veally. Kill zhe volves, keep people vrom dying, zhat vas zhe deal."

"The werewolves here are the enemy, then?"

As much as didn't feel like it right now, Alucard knew that he should tell Ben what he'd need to know. "I vas in Drydenheim six months ago looking vor Ada; she vas zhe virst verevolf like I vas zhe virst vampire. Zhe gods 'oped zhat ve vould vight—Janus and Kardos loved convlict. But I grew tired of zhe constant wars betveen my people and 'ers, and I tried to vorm peace vith 'er. She vasn't intervested. I zidn't vind 'er during my search, so vings are still zhe same. Verevolves try to kill me and my people, so ve kill zhem."

Ben nodded slowly. "I see. Makes sense. So, any werewolf I see…I kill?"

"No." He looked at him as they approached the door to the hall. "I 'ave some verevolf allies zhat you vill meet soon. Until zhen, zon't kill any volves unless you see zhem trying to kill 'umans or vampires. I zon't vant to vind my allies dead."

"Noted."

Then, they continued in silence.

| Elvin |

Elvin waited as patiently as he could. Today had been odd already. He didn't understand why Alucard didn't want to know where he lived; it didn't make sense. Why didn't Alucard want the same things as him? As much as he hated to admit it to himself, there were things even *he* didn't understand about Alucard. The vampire was just so closed off and private.

But he was determined to get closer to him. After all, they'd been travelling together for years, and Elvin liked to think that he was one of the very few people Alucard actually liked. If the vampire *didn't* like him, then why would he be keeping him around? Anyone Alucard didn't want around would surely know it.

He sighed, trying to dismiss his thoughts. Alucard was his friend. It didn't matter that the vampire kept a lot to himself. They helped each other…and that was all that really mattered. Elvin understood what he needed to and that was enough, right?

The moment he saw Alucard and Ben emerge from the kitchen, Elvin jumped to his feet. "Are we going now?" he asked as they headed over to him.

"*You* are," Alucard said. "I 'ave to get veady to meet Tobias," Alucard answered, leading the way out of the castle.

"What about me?" Elvin asked as he followed, doing his best to keep up with them. Why did they walk so fast?

Setting his ice-blue eyes on the bard, Alucard frowned. "Vhat *about* you? I said you could come 'ere, and zhat vas all."

He scoffed. "So, am I to walk home?" he asked as the horses made their way over and stopped in front of Alucard and Ben.

"*Da*," he confirmed vacantly, handing the black stallion's reins to Ben. Then, he turned to face the castle and waved his hand the way he did when summoning a vampire.

Moments later, one of Alucard's daylight vampires flew down from the closest tower in his bat form, and when he landed, he morphed into a red-eyed, blonde-haired man. "Yes, My Lord?"

"Take Ben to see zhe prison. 'E vants to see Dargamoore, too, so take 'im via zhe city," Alucard instructed. "Bring Ben back 'ere avter and call vor my groundskeeper to come and collect my 'orses."

With a nod, the man mounted the horse Elvin rode there, and Ben mounted Alucard's stallion.

Elvin pouted angrily. He often spent close to all of his day with Alucard; why should today be any different just because there were some new vampires here? "Can't I just hang out here until you get back?"

"I'm not coming back 'ere tonight," Alucard answered. "Go 'ome, Elvin. I vill see you tomorrow."

"But…I don't want to." He frowned sadly. "I don't really have anything else to do."

"Zhat's not my problem," the vampire muttered as Ben and his subordinate rode off, leaving the castle courtyard.

He wasn't going to interrupt Alucard's work. As much as he hated cutting his time short with the vampire, he didn't want to annoy him. So, he rolled his eyes and sighed. "Fine. Just…be careful with those werewolves, Aleksei."

Alucard grunted in response and then dematerialized into vermillion smoke. He raced into the sky, leaving Elvin alone.

Elvin frowned sadly and dragged himself along the path, trying to figure out what he'd do for the rest of the afternoon. He could write…or…well, he didn't have anything else to do, did he? All he wanted was to hang out with Alucard, but the vampire was busy—he always had something to do *every* day. Elvin wasn't sure how he managed.

With another sigh, he focused on the fact that he'd still get to see Alucard tomorrow.

That was…if nothing terrible happened with the werewolves. But he trusted Aleksei; he knew how to handle himself, and these wolves would be no different.

Right?

| **Alucard** |

The moons were rising, and soon, Alucard would find Tobias. He moved away from his study window and refilled his colt barrels with explosive rounds. Then, he slipped them into the inside pockets of his blazer. Once he ensured his sword was securely sheathed, he headed for the door—

"Off somewhere, are we, Aleksei?"

That creature's voice stopped Alucard's heart. His entire body tensed up in response to his dread, and the look of vacancy on his face became something of a haunted stare. Why was *he* here? What could he have done this time?

He slowly turned around and set his eyes on Damien, who was sitting behind his desk with his legs resting on it. The Daegelus had the same condescending look on his face that he would always adorn when looking at him, a look which told Alucard that he should only speak when spoken to. So, he remained silent, staring at Damien, waiting to be told why he had come.

Damien tapped his long, black claw-tipped fingers on the table as a malevolent scowl twisted his strangely pale face. He glared with a demeaning expression as he eyed Alucard up and down, and after a few moments of tense, ominous silence, the Daegelus scoffed and asked, "Are you going to stand there like the moron you are or are you going to tell me how last night went?"

"I started moving vampires vrom Eltaria," he answered. "Zhey are staying at my castle. I vent vhrough zhe portal, and I brought vree vampires back vith me. I plan to bring more next time; vas zhe zemon's choice to 'ave me bring as many as I did."

"Good…" Damien mumbled. "I assume you came up with a plan…well, I say *you*, but I suspect if there *is* one, it was probably Zalith's idea—right?"

Alucard didn't want to tell him he was wrong, but he was tired of this man constantly thinking of him as some useless child-like idiot. He wasn't stupid; he could plan, he could achieve what the Daegelus asked, and he always made sure to do it to the best of his ability. He just wanted Damien to see that.

He frowned slightly as he prepared to answer. "I vill move a specifically organized group of vampires vonce a month; vas my idea to do so, and zhe zemon agreed."

A cruelly astonished look plastered itself onto Damien's face. "You?" He laughed. "Come up with a plan? On your own? We both know that isn't possible; your mind is far too inferior. You wouldn't be lying to me now, would you, Aleksei?"

"No," Alucard answered with a confused frown.

Damien then stood up, watching as Alucard flinched the same way he always did when he made any sudden movement. He then dug his claws into the desk. "We both know what happened last time you tried to fib your way out of something…don't we?" he growled, folding his feathered wings against his back.

The vampire didn't take his eyes off him as his dread worsened. "Yes."

"So, tell me once more: what…is the plan?"

"Zhe zemon organized zhe vampires into specific groups vor me. I vill take vone group back vonce a month," he said, his angst becoming overwhelming as the room's tense atmosphere increased with each passing moment. He wasn't sure what was going to happen next, but he *could* assume, and what his mind told him wasn't in any way what he wanted.

"Just as I thought." Damien smirked, pulling his claws from the wood. "You? Coming up with a plan—don't try to amuse me, you insolent brat. I know what you are and what you are not capable of; don't ever think you can fool me," he warned, pointing one of his clawed fingers at him. "Now, these groups: how are they organized?" he asked, resting his hands in his lap.

Despondency gripped Alucard tightly. Would there ever come a time when Damien would see him as more than just some worthless, useless child who couldn't ever do anything properly? He tried to the best of his ability to pull himself from that condescending part of Damien's eyes, but it didn't seem as though that would ever happen. No matter what he did, and no matter how many tasks he completed, Damien would never thank him.

But did he deserve to be thanked? Damien was his superior; it was Alucard's job to serve him, whether Damien showed him appreciation or not. He should do as Damien told him, and that was all there was to it.

He stared vacantly. "Zhe vampires in each group 'ave total ages to my own, plus 'alf, as taking any more at vonce vould veaken me too much."

"Weaken you?" Damien laughed, moving from behind the desk. "As if you aren't already weak enough."

Alucard felt the urge to back off, but it would be a mistake if he moved even an inch. "I need to make sure I zon't become too veak so zhat I may be vell enough to keep up vith zhe vings I do 'ere."

Damien then scowled impatiently. He grabbed Alucard's collar and glared into his horrified eyes. "You don't decide what you need; you're utterly incapable of anything— even the simplest of things. Are you forgetting who you are?" he snarled. "Must I remind you of your lowly place?"

"No."

"I don't care what you've got going on here in this ugly, revolting world. You live to serve *me;* therefore, what I tell you to do is of the utmost importance—is it not?"

Alucard stared into his eyes, sure that he was about to be made to pay for his insolence. But if he were punished, he'd deserve it. He knew better than to speak out of line and of his needs. "Yes."

"Never forget that. I could care less if you were dying of some mortal sickness; you do what I ask until the day you die, whether it be by my hand or not."

"Yes," he agreed once more.

Damien then skeptically asked, "Who is the vampire I have seen you with today?"

"Ben, vone of zhe vampires who came 'ere."

"Is he your friend, Aleksei? You *don't* have friends, do you?"

"No. 'E's just a subordinate. I 'ave no intervest in becoming 'is vriend."

"Good," Damien snarled, tightening his grip on the vampire's collar. "I've warned you about getting close to people."

Alucard nodded.

"They will only ever use you. *I'm* the only one you can trust," he drawled, losing his condescending scowl. "Everyone will leave you eventually, but not me—you'll never be without me." He took his eyes off the vampire and fell silent for a few moments. But then he frowned and let go of him, pushing him away so that his back hit the wall. "Don't ever lie to me again, or you'll lose something else you value so dearly," he warned, raising his hand to point at the vampire.

"I'm sorry," Alucard said, hanging his head in shame.

"You did, however, do well bringing those vampires here, so I won't punish you this time. I will, however, alter Zalith's plan."

The vampire looked at him.

"Once a month will become twice a month. I have another mission for you, one that must be done after these vampires are moved. Don't take too long, Aleksei. I will be back here at this exact time next month. Make sure there are more than three measly vampires here."

Despite knowing this change would make it even harder for him to deal with the werewolves, Alucard obediently replied, "Yes."

The Daegelus smiled condescendingly. "If it kills you, know that it won't be hard to find someone to replace you." Then, he turned around, walked out onto the balcony, and took off, disappearing into the sky, leaving Alucard alone.

The vampire looked down at the floor. Twice a month? He suffered immensely from the first transferal; how was he supposed to do that *twice*? His waned strength still hadn't fully returned since, and he still felt exhausted. He couldn't refuse, though. Damien ordered him, and if he had only kept his mouth shut, then it might not have happened. Another mission was lined up for him, and if he failed to do as Damien asked, he knew he'd suffer something worse than death.

Alucard turned around and walked through his empty house and out into the garden. He couldn't hide the fact that he was tired of the people he worked with seeing him as weak and inferior. He was far from either of those things, but it seemed as though Damien would never see that. He'd always be a disappointment, and he'd never impress the Daegelus. He could only keep trying his best.

The vampire stopped by the gates and frowned hesitantly. He didn't have time to meet Tobias now. He had to contact Zalith as soon as possible to discuss the change, and he knew that if he waited, Damien would somehow find out and punish him.

He had no idea where Zalith lived, and he wasn't willing to go searching for him. The demon hadn't left him any means of communication, had he?

Ben. *He* had to know how to contact him. But would Zalith even come? Alucard was sure that he resented him just as much as Alucard despised *him*. However, these were Zalith's vampires; he was the one who wanted them moved as quickly as possible, and Alucard was confident that he'd be content, if anything, to hear that he would be making two trips a month.

Then he wondered…what could this other mission be? If Damien was making him rush an important mission like this, then it had to be huge. Whatever it was, though, Alucard knew it would either hurt, belittle, or degrade him as a person—everything Damien made him do was degrading. That creature treated him like a slave. But the fact was, Alucard would never be able to rebel. Damien was a Numen, one of the most powerful, influential beings known to man, and *he* was a lowly vampire whose father didn't even want him. What was *he* next to an eternal God? Nothing. He should appreciate the fact that Damien chose to care for him. Without the Daegelus, he would have died a long time ago.

Chapter Nine

— ₹ ✝ ₴ —

Deviation

| Alucard |

When he got to the castle, Alucard saw Ben and Felix arm wrestling at the table. As he moved towards the table, all of his vampires climbed to their feet and stared obediently at him.

"You, 'ere," he called, moving to the corner of the room as he pointed at Ben.

Ben walked over to Alucard and asked, "Yes?"

"Can you contact Zaliv?"

He frowned in concern as he watched an impatient glare flicker across Alucard's face. "Has something happened?"

"I need to speak to 'im about zhe mission—is important," he grumbled.

"Do you need to send him a message, or do you need to see him?"

"I vant to talk to 'im—now," he snarled irritably.

Ben nodded. "I can…try to work something out."

"Zhen do zhat," Alucard mumbled, moving away from him.

Without any hindrance, Ben left through the front door.

Alucard made his way to the table and leaned back against it. He wasn't looking forward to seeing that arrogant demon again, but what choice did he have?

Felix stood up and wandered over to him.

Alucard rolled his eyes, sure that the silver-eyed man was about to start a conversation he didn't want to have.

The grey-haired vampire stopped beside Alucard. "Everything is okay, My Lord?" he asked nervously.

Alucard glanced at him. The small, silvery-eyed man was unnecessarily close, so he snarled and moved a little to his right to put more distance between himself and Felix. "*Da*," he answered. "Clear zhe voom."

Felix did as he was told and made his way over to the others. He told them to leave the hall and left with them.

Alucard sunk into one of the chairs as a sullen look stole his vacant one. He knew that telling Zalith the plan was changing would make him look stupid. He'd been so adamant with his original plan; changing it now was going to make Zalith think even less of him. But he didn't care—why should he? It wasn't like they were friends. They were work associates, and that was all it would ever be. What did it matter how Zalith felt? Alucard knew he could do his job, and that was all that mattered because no one else was going to appreciate his work.

He sighed and waited, tapping his fingers on the table. At least he was right about Ben being able to contact Zalith. How, he wasn't sure—but again, he didn't care. He just wanted to tell the demon about the deviation as quickly as he could. Then, he could go and meet Tobias if it wasn't too late.

Ben came back through the front door after ten minutes and made his way over to Alucard. "He'll be here shortly," he said, sitting at the table.

"*Multemesc*," Alucard thanked.

"Are you all right?" Ben then asked in concern.

Alucard had no interest in answering that question.

Ben seemed to pick up on that. He took his eyes off Alucard and looked around the empty hall. "Should I be concerned about the rest of the vampires?"

"No."

They sat there in silence for the next few minutes. Alucard wasn't sure how long Zalith might take, but each passing minute made him feel more aggravated. He had other things he needed to do; for all he knew, another werewolf could be prowling through Wrodiff right now.

But then footsteps approached, echoing down the short corridor that led from the hall to the castle's front door. Alucard snapped out of his thoughts and watched as Zalith walked in.

Zalith, whose face adorned an irritated yet concerned look, set his eyes on Alucard. "Good evening," he said pleasantly, stopping a few feet away from where the vampire was sitting. "What seems to be the problem?"

Alucard looked up at him. "Sit," he said, kicking out the chair beside him with his left leg.

With an irritated sigh, Zalith sat down. Then, he waited for Alucard to speak.

"Zamien contacted me."

Zalith's attention seemed to be grasped.

"Ve must deviate vrom zhe original plan. I vill make two trips a month, not vone. I must make vone more bevore zhis time next month."

"Why?"

"Zamien zidn't say," he lied. He wasn't going to sit here and tell Zalith why he had to make changes—why should he? All that mattered was that he was still doing to job. "Tell me vhen I should come."

"Damien didn't say, or does he not want me to know what was said?" the demon questioned skeptically.

"'E zidn't say," Alucard repeated sternly, scowling.

Zalith eyed him for a moment…almost as if he was trying to read his thoughts. But then he looked away and muttered, "I can have them ready by next week—the same time as yesterday."

"I'll be zhere."

Before Alucard could stand up, Zalith glowered at him. "Why make me come all the way here just for a two-minute conversation? Would it have not been smarter to simply send a message?" he asked condescendingly.

"No," Alucard snarled. He wasn't going to tell him why he preferred to meet in person.

"Why?" he questioned, evidently aggravated.

"Messages are never guaranteed to veach zheir destination. I am not villing to visk zhat 'appening," he said, standing up. "You can go now."

"Might I offer you a simpler way for us to communicate?" Zalith offered as he got up.

The vampire stopped before walking off and scowled. "No. Ve meet in person only."

Zalith then frowned, clearly antagonised as his anger simmered in the scowl on his face. "So, I'm expected to drop whatever it is that I may be doing to come here for what is likely to be another two-minute conversation regarding something that isn't going to happen for another few weeks?"

"Yes."

The demon scoffed. "I don't expect someone like you to understand the precariousness of the situation I'm in, but I do at least hope you can understand that I simply cannot be coming back and forth whenever you so wish it. I find this refusal of finding an easier means of communication rather ridiculous, and you just as much so."

"And I vind very little intervest in vhat you are saying," Alucard sneered, walking off.

"Yet you were so interested in talking to me previously that you had me come all the way out here to this pathetic place," Zalith called, following Alucard.

Alucard scoffed. "And yet, you came."

"Yes, I came because when someone summons you to their house with such urgency, it usually means that there is something of a dire nature involved; I am *not* here because I want to be!" he growled as Alucard reached the front door.

Alucard stopped walking and turned to face Zalith, who also stopped. Why was the demon following him? Usually, anyone he expressed anger towards would back down. "I zon't expect somevone like you to understand zhe precariousness of *my* situation," he mocked.

An amused smile suddenly cut through Zalith's angered scowl. "Why are you acting this way, vampire?" he asked with a flirtatious smirk.

Scoffing, Alucard turned his back on him. For a moment, he felt confused…yet a little amused; their argument felt almost entertaining, but he'd not let Zalith see that he was actually enjoying their confrontation. "Get out of my castle," he snarled.

Keeping his smirk, Zalith walked past him, and as Ben followed, the demon left the castle.

The vampire rolled his eyes and sighed. Why did Zalith always seem so entertained by everything? That man obviously found Alucard's anger funny, and that pissed him off. The demon smiled at everything in a way that made Alucard understand that he thought himself superior to him. He *wasn't*, he was just some annoying, insufferable demon who he was stuck working with.

Alucard smirked, though. He couldn't deny that he enjoyed letting Zalith argue with him because the demon would *always* have to back down. He found it amusing that Zalith thought he might win by mentioning knowledge or 'smarter alternatives', but Alucard was content with his own techniques, and Zalith would never, *ever* make him change his mind, as much as he may try.

But his amusement was swiftly destroyed when he remembered that if Damien found out he was having fun, he'd punish him. This was a serious mission. He and Zalith needed to work together *professionally*. So, he put it out of his mind. How could he have been such an idiot to let himself get carried away? He wouldn't let it happen again.

He turned around and headed for the door. It was time to find Tobias and find out what he'd learned about the wolf that attacked Elvin.

| Zalith |

Zalith made his way toward the castle gates as Ben followed. Despite the annoyance he'd initially felt being called all the way out here for a conversation they could have had through a letter or two, he found that he actually enjoyed his brief interaction with Alucard. He'd managed to fluster the vampire, something he found rather amusing.

"I'm sorry you had to come all the way out here for that," Ben said, walking beside him.

Zalith approached the gates. "Don't worry about it."

Ben frowned. "What?"

The demon smiled. "I had a delightful time."

"Oh, well… okay then."

Then, Zalith lost his smirk and looked at him. "Farewell."

As Zalith stood in front of the wall, Ben waved. "See you later."

But then some naked man covered in bleeding scratches and bites burst through the gates and rushed past them without so much as an apology for making Zalith stumble aside to avoid a collision. He watched the blonde-haired man who reeked of wolf run up towards Alucard, who had just come out into the courtyard.

He wanted to create a rift and head home, but he was curious. So, he stood there and listened.

The blonde man panted when he stopped in front of Alucard, who looked embarrassed when he saw the guy wasn't wearing any clothes. He scowled at his face, and Zalith smirked amusedly. That was *twice* now he'd seen Alucard become flustered.

"B-boss," the guy stuttered, stifling his breaths. "I…got something," he wheezed.

"Vhat?" Alucard demanded.

With a few deep breaths, the man shook his head. "You ain't gonna like it, man."

"Just fucking tell me!" the vampire exclaimed.

"That wolf who attacked Elvin? Yeah, it came from some rogue pack. I ain't ever seen or heard of them until I *found* them."

The look of concern that stole Alucard's scowl intensified Zalith's curiosity.

"Fuckers almost caught me—*me*, an Alpha, man. These things were so strong that I had to fucking run for it. I managed to catch some conversation beforehand, though, something about scheduled attacks. The wolf who almost killed Elvin was *supposed* to kill him to send some sort of message. I think these guys are planning something bad, man," the guy explained so fast that it was like his words were literally seeping from his stubbly face. "They've got an Alpha or something…really big-looking guy."

Alucard snarled and stormed down towards the gates.

"You want my help?" the man offered, following him. "I can round up my pack—"

"No. I'll deal vith zhem myselv," the vampire uttered as he walked past Zalith. "Vhere are zhey?"

"Ardelean Forest, boss. They're camping in that abandoned village. You sure you wanna do this solo? I dunno if you heard me when I said even *I* couldn't match them."

As Zalith watched the vampire head for the forest, he frowned in confliction. The idea of rogue werewolves strong enough to scare an Alpha away was concerning enough already but knowing that Alucard was going to face them alone made him feel anxious.

Judging from what Damien told him, he was confident that Alucard was walking to his death, and where that might not bother Zalith under different circumstances, it bothered him *now*. Not only was Alucard his only hope of getting his vampires to safety, but Damien had also told him to make sure that Alucard didn't get himself killed. He wasn't about to learn what happened when he disappointed the Daegelus. So, with an irritated huff, he left Ben and raced after Alucard, hoping he'd reach him before he did something stupid.

Chapter Ten

— ⸲ † ⸱ —

The Amarok

| Alucard |

Alucard hurried through Ardelean Forest. He suspected that the werewolves were scheming, and he was right. *Of course* he was. Why now? Why did they have to decide to crawl out of the woods while he was working on something for Damien? He couldn't afford to let them threaten the treaty, so he was going to kill them *all* before they could try to kill anyone else.

His scowl thickened as he tried to work out what he was going to do once he reached the abandoned village. The werewolf that attacked Elvin was stronger than any other he'd faced, and if every wolf in this rogue pack was the same, then he was going to have to be much more careful than usual.

The vampire used his ethos to shroud himself from detection, and as he approached the tree line, he set his eyes on the rubble up ahead. A campfire burned in the old village square and several Beta werewolves were curled up around it. He spotted three Etas on patrol, and inside the only building that still had a roof was the silhouette of a large, wolfish creature.

Alucard silently moved to the left, trying to get a better look inside, but judging by the beast's sheer size, he assumed it was the Alpha that Tobias mentioned.

He counted eleven wolves. He'd faced packs three times the size of this before; but he had to remember that these might not be ordinary werewolves, and if the Betas were as strong as the one he faced in Wrodiff, then the Alpha was probably much more dangerous.

The vampire set his eyes on one of the Etas and used the darkness to prowl closer. Then, when the wolf passed by, sniffing the ground, he snatched it by its scruff and pulled it into the brush. The wolf squirmed and tried to alert its packmates, but Alucard held its maw shut with one of his hands, and he plunged the other into the wolf's neck and tore its throat out.

One down, ten to go.

But the wolves smelled the blood of their packmate, and when they all climbed to their paws and raced towards the corpse, Alucard moved away from it, left the trees, and took cover behind a wall. He watched the wolves find and both mourn and anger over their dead friend, and then he shifted his sights to the Alpha. The massive creature emerged from its den, and it brought a look of dread to Alucard's face.

An Amarok. Huge, *insane* werewolves with no humanity and the strength of a hundred wolves. The creature's navy fur glistened in the moonlight as it prowled towards its pack, blood dripping from its gnarly jaw. Alucard could see inside the building, and the corpse of *three* humans lay inside.

The vampire clenched his fists and gritted his teeth. He could tell from the smell that the bodies were no more than a few hours old, and he was certain that in the morning, there'd be an uproar.

"Find…them," came the Amarok's distorted, rumbling voice.

On his word, the pack spread out and started looking for their packmate's killer, just as Alucard hoped they would. If he could take them out one by one, this would go a whole lot smoother.

Alucard waited as a Beta approached and passed the wall he hid behind. He pulled his rapier from its sheath and stabbed the blade through the wolf's skull, killing it instantly. He dragged its body behind the wall, and then he used the shadows to mask himself and moved over to a mountain of rubble.

He peered through a small gap. The Amarok was prowling the village square; the stomps of its massive feet echoed through the tense quiet, and when it sharply turned its head and looked Alucard's way, the vampire backed away from the small gap between the bricks.

It was coming his way.

Alucard disappeared into vermillion smoke and reappeared on the other side of the village, but when his back hit a wall, pieces of stone fell and hit the concrete. He heard the wolves growl, and he knew they were coming.

He moved away from the wall and turned to face the first incoming Beta. But when he reached for one of his colts, another Beta came from behind a building and crashed into him.

The vampire landed on the ground with a thump and a grunt, holding the wolf's snapping jaws back with his free hand. But it was *so* strong that he felt himself losing the battle.

And the other wolves were closing in.

Alucard dropped his sword and pulled his colt from his pocket. He fired it into the beast's neck, and as the round burrowed inside its skin, Alucard kicked the yelping wolf away before the bullet exploded inside it, sending a rain of blood everywhere.

He climbed to his feet, but before he could grab his sword, another wolf lunged at him and tried to sink its teeth into his arm. The vampire managed to smack the wolf's face with his colt, but he had no time to turn and face the werewolf running at him from behind.

The Eta smashed into his back, pushing him back to the ground. He rolled over to face it and reached for his dropped colt, but the wolf pounced on him and went for his throat. Although he grabbed its maw in time, *three* other Betas were seconds away.

Alucard's heart was racing. He tried throating the wolf off, but it was too strong—*stronger* than the wolf from Wrodiff. It snarled and swayed its body, attempting to break free from his grip—

Wolf's teeth pierced Alucard's shin, and when he felt the venom gush into his body, he yelled painfully, and he lost his grasp on the wolf's jaws—

The wolf suddenly burst into white flames and flew off Alucard, colliding with the wolf which bit him. Alucard hurried to his feet but grunted as pain shot through his bitten leg.

It withered, though… when he saw where the white fire came from.

Zalith stood between two ruins with his hand pointing towards the wolves. Alucard watched him throw ashen fire at two beasts running towards him, and when the flames hit them, they tumbled along the ground and shrieked in agony.

The vampire snarled and recovered his weapons. But before he could yell and ask Zalith why the fuck he was here, the Amarok let out a deafening howl. The remaining three wolves raced to its side, and *Zalith* moved to Alucard's side.

"Did you fucking vollow me?" Alucard growled, keeping his eyes on the wolves, waiting for them to make their move.

"Not because I wanted to," the demon replied.

Alucard scoffed. "Zhen vhy vhe fuck are you in my business?"

"Damien," he answered.

The vampire felt both rage and embarrassment race through him. But there was no time for him to ask why Damien was the reason. The werewolves growled when the Amarok told them to charge, and then they raced towards him and Zalith.

Alucard watched Zalith go for the three of them, so *he* ran towards the Amarok. The beast roared and watched Alucard approach, and when Alucard reached it, he dodged the swipe of its massive front paw and skidded along the ground. Then, he plunged his blade towards the beast's back.

But all he was able to do was leave a minor cut on the Amarok's skin; it swung around and slammed its arm into him, sending Alucard stumbling back. The Amarok then roared and lunged, but the vampire dodged again and sliced its forearm. He avoided each of its attacks, getting as many slices off on the beast as he could. But it quickly enraged and stomped its front paws onto the ground, making it shake.

Alucard struggled to keep his balance as the concrete shattered, and when the beast launched a massive piece of stone at him, he escaped its trajectory by mere inches—

The Amarok slammed its paw against his chest before he could record, and Alucard went tumbling across the ground. It was then that he realized the venom coursing through his veins was making it harder for him to concentrate. But he had to keep fighting.

He climbed to his feet and set his eyes on the monster. However, Zalith was now facing it. The other wolves were dead, and the demon was launching flames at the Amarok. But the massive beast didn't shriek and back down like the others. It was almost as if it didn't feel pain. It was covered in slices and cuts from Alucard's attacks, bleeding all over the place, but it fought as if everything they did to it was *nothing*.

Alucard hurried over, and when Zalith backed off to dodge the Amarok's swing, Alucard gathered his strength and stabbed the blade as deeply as he could into the creature's leg.

It howled painfully and swung around, but Alucard avoided its swing and aimed his colt at it. Before he could fire, though, the Amarok pulled Alucard's sword from its leg and threw it at him. Alucard smacked the blade away, but the monster used Alucard's moment of distraction to lunge—

Zalith threw fire at its face, knocking it off balance as it wailed and shook its head. Alucard fired his gun, and the bullet embedded itself in the Amarok's arm. The round exploded, blowing the monster's limb off its body, and it fell to the concrete with a loud, ground-shaking thump.

However, it wasn't dead yet. It wiped the white flames from its face with its remaining hand, and before Zalith could get another hit off, the beast kicked him away with its back leg and then pushed itself up. It dived towards Alucard, and he was too slow to avoid its paw. It knocked his gun from his hand, but when Alucard fell, white flames consumed the beast's gaping wound, and it whined and swiftly turned to face Zalith, who stood across the square with blood seeping down the side of his face.

The Amarok charged as best it could with only three limbs. Alucard tried to get up, but the venom was stealing his strength. He watched Zalith dodge a few of the wolf's attacks, but its strength was clearly too much for him, too, and it quickly pinned him down.

Alucard snarled in frustration and pulled his other colt from his coat. He aimed it at the beast Zalith held its snapping jaws back with his hands, but it was quickly overpowering him. The vampire's arm was shaking, and he tried his best to focus. If he didn't fire—if he *missed*—the monster would slaughter Zalith, and Damien would be furious.

With a pained grunt, he sat up, grasped the gun with both hands and fired.

The bullet cut into the Amarok's neck, and as it drilled deeper, the beast pushed itself away from Zalith and desperately cut at its throat with its claws.

But it was too late.

The round exploded, blowing the beast's head off its body, and sending a flood of blood, bone, and innards crashing down on Zalith, who lay on the grass with a disgusted, humiliated look on his face.

Alucard let himself laugh quietly in amusement. It was over. The Amarok was dead, as was its pack.

As Alucard struggled to his feet and grabbed his weapons, he watched Zalith wipe the mess from his face, retching a little as he did.

The demon climbed to his feet, holding his arms around as blood dripped from him, and when Alucard approached, he looked at him and asked, "Do you have a handkerchief?"

"No," Alucard replied, unable to keep the smirk off his face as he looked Zalith up and down.

Zalith scowled and snarled quietly as he tried to wipe as much blood off as he could with his hands. But he was *drenched*.

"Zhere's a river zhat vay," Alucard sneered, nodding at the tree line. "Or do you 'ave to get back to Zamien?"

The demon rolled his eyes and turned around. He headed in the direction of the river.

As much as Alucard wanted to leave, he wanted to know what Zalith meant when he said that he was here because of Damien. So, he followed. "Vhat does Zamien 'ave to do vith you vollowing me?"

Zalith stormed towards the water and grumbled, "He told me to make sure you don't get yourself killed, and evidently, he was right to do so."

Alucard scowled and grabbed Zalith's shoulder, turning him to face him. "I zidn't need your 'elp," he growled, glaring at the demon's bloody face. "And if you vecall, *I* vas zhe vone who saved *you* vrom getting killed!"

The demon scoffed and yanked his arm free. "And if *you* recall, I stopped those wolves from tearing *you* apart, so we're even." Then, he walked towards the river.

With a quiet, aggravated growl, Alucard made his way to the water, too. He crouched by the riverbed and started cleaning the blood from his skin, and when he glanced at Zalith, he caught him looking at him.

Alucard scowled and shifted his sights to his injured leg. He gently pulled his boot and sock off to assess the wound. Several gashes cut into his shin, and the skin around them was dark and infected. He *loathed* werewolf bites, but to his relief, it was only a Beta. If the Amarok managed to bite him, he'd be in a much worse state.

He moved his leg into the river, and when the freezing water hit his wound, he grimaced and groaned painfully.

"Are you okay?" Zalith called.

Alucard ignored him and gently rubbed the wound with his fingers. He watched the blood wash away, and as he gently pinched the gashes, slithers of silvery werewolf venom oozed out.

He heard Zalith tearing fabric, and when he looked at the demon, he'd ripped some of his shirt and was heading over to him with it.

"Here," Zalith said, offering him the piece of torn shirt.

With a pout, Alucard snatched it from him and started wrapping his leg. He caught a glimpse of Zalith's abs, and for some reason, he couldn't help but glance again once he was done.

Alucard then pulled his sock and boot back on. He tried to get up, and Zalith offered to help, but he shoved the demon away and snarled at him, "Get off me."

Zalith rolled his eyes and backed off.

Once he was up, Alucard pulled his sheathed sword from his side and used it to help him stay on his feet. He turned away from Zalith and glared at the tree line. It relieved him knowing that the Amarok and its rogue pack were dead, but the thing had been feeding on *three* bodies, and Alucard was certain that it wouldn't take long for the humans to work out that it was werewolves.

He sighed and dragged his hand over his face. Maybe telling the council that he killed *all* the rogues would convince them not to void the treaty. If he didn't have to deal with Zalith's vampires, then maybe this wouldn't have happened. Maybe he could have killed the Amarok before it got those people.

The demon then huffed and said, "Well, if you're done almost getting killed for the night, I need to get back."

"Zhen go," Alucard snapped.

Zalith sighed irritably. "Fine," he uttered.

Alucard glanced over his shoulder and watched the demon head over to a tree. Zalith flicked his fingers at the trunk; the bark split and cracked, opening to form a rift. Crimson flames spewed out, and as the demon stepped inside, he shot one last glare at Alucard.

And then he was gone. The rift closed, leaving a thick, black burn on the tree.

The vampire rolled his eyes and huffed angrily. That man *boiled* his blood. But he didn't have the energy to argue. He was exhausted, and his leg was twinging. He had to get home; the woods were infested with werewolves, and the last thing he needed was one taking a chance and attacking him in his current state.

He took a deep breath and then dematerialized into vermillion smoke. Tomorrow was going to be a *long day*, and he hoped he'd be able to save the treaty. But what if he couldn't? Where would he take the vampires if the council cast him out?

Arc Two
— † —
An Unlikely Alliance

Chapter Eleven

— ‹ † › —

Stowaway

| Alucard |

A week passed since Alucard killed the Amarok. His wound healed, no other werewolves had left the forest, and the city believed his tale that the bodies he found in the monster's den were killed by a demon. Thinking about it brought a smirk to his face, but it quickly withered when he was hit by the fact that he had to meet Zalith again tonight.

He took his eyes off his glass of red wine and glared at Elvin, who was sitting in the armchair opposite the couch he slumped on. "Vhat are you scribbling over zhere?" he snarled as the scratching of the bard's pencil clawed at his eardrums.

Elvin kept writing and glanced at him. "Everything you told me earlier; it takes me longer to write than it takes you to speak, you know."

"Do you 'ave to do zhat so loudly?" the vampire grumbled. He sat up straight and glanced out the window behind Elvin, watching as the six moons started to appear in the darkening sky.

"Do *you* always have to be so grumpy?"

Alucard rolled his eyes.

"Shouldn't you be heading out soon anyway?" Elvin asked. "Don't you have a hot date with a demon?"

The vampire scowled at him as a feeling of revolt consumed both his feelings and the look on his face. "You are *not* vunny, Elvin."

"I wasn't trying to make a joke; I was being serious," he grinned, taking his eyes off his book.

"Zhe only ving that intervests me about zhat man is zhe vay I vill kill 'im if 'e demeans me vonce more."

Frowning, Elvin rested his arms over his book. "Why do you wanna kill him? From what you've told me, it sounds like you guys are already friends. Didn't you *flawlessly* kill that Amarok last week together? I mean…minus the bite."

"I zon't 'ave vriends, Elvin," Alucard muttered, glaring back into the fire.

"What about me?"

Glancing at him, Alucard shrugged. "You are my vamiliar."

Elvin pouted. "*Vampires* have familiars; you're Aleksei, more than just a vampire, so you can have friends—like me." He smiled, pointing to himself.

"I zidn't vescue you vrom zhat orphanage to become your vriend."

The bard smirked and said, "It might not have been your first intention, but the way things have unfolded, it looks like I'm more your friend than some dumb familiar. You don't send me to get groceries, and you don't make me clean your shoes or fetch your food, do you?"

Alucard stifled a snarl. "Are you done now? I need to get veady to go."

"N-no, no, wait," he said, quickly looking through the notes he had just written. "So, the council bought the story about a rogue demon killing those people in the Amarok nest and getting away?"

"*Da.*"

"I'm just worried that if someone sees you with that Zalith guy, they might think you two are in cahoots or something, you know? I mean…what if they ask you to hunt the demon from your story down?"

Alucard sighed deeply. "Zhen I vill just go and vind some vandom zemon, cut 'is 'ead off, and deliver zhat."

Elvin nodded slowly. "Okay, well…if you think it's gonna be—"

"Vill be vine, Elvin. Zhey're too busy getting veady to let vampires into zheir city to care about a zemon killing a vew people vrom a village zhat zhey zon't give two shits about."

The bard went silent for a moment and shuffled around in his seat. "Kinda grim. Well…I did have a question about that: why do werewolves choose to eat us? To eat…humans?"

"Sport," he answered.

"Sport?"

"Zhey vind zhat vun; you vun like imbeciles and zhey like zhat."

"Sounds like *you* like it, too," Elvin mumbled, writing it into his book. He then sat up straight. "Can't I come with you this time?"

"No," Alucard denied, standing up as he finished the rest of the wine in his glass. "Go 'ome."

Elvin hurried to his feet and followed Alucard as he made his way over to the door, where his cape and sword sat on the table.

"Can I come at *some* point?" the bard whined.

"No," he refused once more. "I zon't know zhese vampires, and I'd vather not visk you being eaten."

Elvin then smiled. "Aww, did you just say you care about me?"

Alucard attached his rapier to his side and pulled his cape on. "Sergiu vill take you 'ome again," he said, disregarding Elvin's question.

"Sergiu always takes me home—he's boring, Aleksei; all he talks about is what new tea he had last night and how the horses are acting like any other horses," he complained, following Alucard out into the gardens.

"Content vor your book, no?" Alucard smirked.

The bard scowled. "My book is supposed to be exciting; it's about adventures and ethos and vampires and demons! Not about what some random groundskeeper had to drink."

"Zhen go 'ang out vith Ben. I'm sure 'e 'as some stories vor you," he grumbled, leading Elvin over to the stables.

"The book is about you, Vurren, not your friends."

"I zon't 'ave vriends," he repeated, a stern tone in his voice.

Elvin frowned. "Why are you so insistent about that?"

Ignoring him, Alucard set his fiery eyes on the groundskeeper, who emerged from the stables. "Take Elvin 'ome, and give me Sebastian."

Nodding, Sergiu disappeared back into the stables.

The vampire then set his eyes back on Elvin. "I vill see you tomorrow," he said as Sergiu returned with his black stallion.

"What are we doing tomorrow?"

"Noving." Alucard shrugged as he mounted the horse. "You just come by every day, zon't you?"

He sighed as he tucked his book into his pocket. "Yeah. You'll tell me everything, right?"

"Maybe," Alucard answered before tapping his horse's side with his foot.

Then, his stallion raced out of the manor, heading for the docks. He wasn't about to be late and give Zalith a reason to sneer. He wanted to get the night over with and spend as little time in that demon's company as he had to.

When Alucard reached the castle docks, he left his stallion by a fence and headed towards the ship.

"Yo, Aleksei," came Tobias' gruff voice.

Alucard turned to face the blonde, rugged man, who stood in his muddy leather jacket and torn jeans, waving with a grin on his stubbly face. The vampire sighed quietly, watching him as he made his way over.

"What's up, man?" he asked, holding out his hand.

The vampire glared down at it, and when he saw the patches of dirt, he grimaced in revolt. Did Tobias honestly think he'd shake that thing?

Tobias chuckled and slipped both his hands into his pockets. "Sorry I couldn't meet you earlier in the week; shit's been a mess since the last full moon. Few of my guys got a bit carried away."

"Not *too* carried away, I 'ope," he mumbled skeptically.

He shook his head. "Nah, don't worry. We buried all those bodies like you asked; I ain't seen an Amarok since the wars, you know."

"'Ave you seen or 'eard anyving new since I killed zhe ving?"

"Nothing, boss. We're keeping our senses peeled, though. If anything's happening wolf-wise, we'll be the first to hear of it—and then you, of course."

Alucard nodded. "Vank you."

The vampire then moved past him and boarded the ship. He looked up at Rodney, who was chatting to a smaller, younger man on the quarterdeck. The guy looked either seventeen or eighteen and had spots of red stubble sprouting here and there on his freckled face. His scruffy hair was as orange as hair could get, shimmering in the multi-coloured moonlight, and he had a northern accent.

Who was this kid? And why was he aboard Alucard's ship?

Alucard stepped onto the quarterdeck, and as Rodney and the boy looked at him, he asked, "Who is zhis child?"

Rodney smiled from ear to ear as he held his hand out to greet Alucard. "Aleksei, this is Kevin; he's my new apprentice."

Kevin offered his hand to Alucard. "It's great to meet you, sir."

Alucard ignored their hands and scowled. "Vhat did I say about bringing outsiders 'ere?"

"I need help sailing this ship, man," Rodney complained, dragging his hand over his head. "The kid was on the streets, so I took him in. He's not a threat, is he?"

Snarling, Alucard moved closer to the boy, but as he backed off in fear, Alucard snatched his collar and glared into his eyes. "Vhere do you come vrom?"

"Th-the north, sir," he answered. "I was a stowaway for a while, then I ended up here and...well, I was looking for work, see, and Rodney was also looking for—"

"Vhy zidn't you tell me you vere in need of 'elp? If you 'ad told me, I vould 'ave vound you somevone," Alucard growled, taking his eyes off the startled boy to glare at Rodney.

"He's just a kid," Rodney insisted, grabbing the boy's arm.

Taking his eyes off Rodney, Alucard eyed Kevin. He was human, and the mortified look on his face was the same as that which Alucard would see on someone who had never seen him before. From what he could tell, the boy wasn't an enemy, but the fact that Rodney hadn't asked him if it was okay to bring some random stowaway aboard *his* ship pissed him off so much that he wanted to throw them overboard.

However, this was the first time Rodney had ever made a mistake, so he felt as though he should be a little lenient, especially since Rodney was one of his most loyal, longest-serving men.

He let go of Kevin's collar and said to Rodney, "Next time, ask me. Zon't bring in outsiders."

As Kevin hid behind him, Rodney frowned. "Sorry. I just haven't seen you since last week; I thought you were busy."

"You know zhe vules, Vodney. Vemember zhem."

The captain sighed and nodded. "Yeah, it won't happen again."

"Let's go," Alucard snarled, stepping down off the quarterdeck.

"Oh, Drac's eating sharks," Rodnay called. "It's not werewolf corpses, but at least he's not starving down there."

"Good," Alucard mumbled as he walked into his cabin.

The vampire slumped in his seat behind his desk and sighed deeply. He leaned back, huffed quietly, and closed his eyes, trying to relax. But the sound of Kevin and Rodney's muffled voices stole the silence.

"*I didn't mean to cause you to get into trouble,*" Kevin said.

"*Nah, it's just Aleksei—well, it's mainly my fault,*" Rodney replied. "*I know the rules just as everyone else does.*"

"*Why doesn't he want outsiders here?*"

"*Can't say, kid,*" Rodney denied as the ship started moving away from the docks.

"*Why not?*" the kid asked excitedly. "*Is this all some top-secret stuff?*"

"*You've been reading too many stories, kid.*"

"*I've been in Dargamoore a while—well, I've been all over Dor-Sanguis. All the bards here tell stories about uh…Alucard. The first vampire. That is who he is, right?*"

"*Yeah, it is…*" Rodney confirmed slowly. "*But his name is Aleksei.*"

The kid gasped excitedly. "*I love listening to the stories! And now…I'm working for him?*"

"*You ain't working for him, kid. You work for me.*"

"*Yeah, but you work for him, which means I technically do, too.*"

Rodney grunted. "*Great, another Elvin.*"

"*What's an Elvin?*"

"*Aleksei's fanboy.*"

Kevin then scoffed. *"I never said I was a fan; it's just cool to meet the guy all these stories talk about."*

"Wait until you've been around him for at least a week to say that."

"Why?"

"You'll find out," Rodney mumbled.

When their conversation ended, Alucard snarled and rested his legs on his desk. He still felt furious. He had a tiny circle of people he trusted, and Rodney was one of them. But the fact that he brought an outsider in made Alucard lose some of that trust. Rodney was aware of his rules, and he broke one of the most important ones. Alucard had many enemies, not just werewolves, and while it was easy to sniff out a wolf, it wasn't so easy to sniff out an agent of the Diabolus—the cult that haunted his past.

The Diabolus were quiet, deadly, and efficient. They managed to tear his life apart more than once, and he wasn't going to let it happen again. He'd lost his mother's people to them, and the family he had come to find in Vanessa and her sons. Although his vampirism helped him avenge them, the ever-growing cult never seemed to wither. They were still out there, they were still looking for him, and he knew he'd have to keep hiding.

A skeptical scowl clung to his face. Kevin's story was hard to believe. All the bards in Dargamoore spoke of him? No, the only bard he let talk about him was Elvin because no one believed the stories he told of how Alucard wasn't some cold-blooded murderer. And as far as Alucard was aware, Elvin never spoke his actual name. How would Kevin know it? The *Diabolus* knew him by his birth name, and so did Damien, but the Daegelus would never sell him out.

So, how did this kid know his real name?

Alucard glared at the ceiling, listening as the kid kept gossiping. Right now, he wasn't sure who might be more foolish: Kevin or Rodney. The captain disobeyed his rules, and Kevin made one of the biggest mistakes any spy could make. But *was* he a spy? Alucard had to be sure. Yes, he knew his real name, but could Elvin have unintentionally mentioned it in one of his sonnets? He couldn't just kill this kid unless he was sure that he was an agent of the Diabolus.

He sighed and stared out the cabin door, setting his eyes on the black, rainy island as it came into view. First, he had to deal with the vampire business, and then he'd deal with Rodney and his new little friend.

Chapter Twelve

— ⸂ † ⸃ —

Stakes

| Alucard |

When he emerged in the castle ruin, Alucard sighed quietly. Exhaustion instantly burdened him; his body ached, his head spun, and he felt ten times as nauseous as before. But he ignored it. The sound of confrontation echoed down the hallways, so he hurried to the room where he met the vampires last time.

He set his eyes on Zalith, who placed his hand over his face and sighed irritably before glowering at the arrogant vampire who was arguing with him. "You go with who you have been put with; we've been over this more times than I would have liked."

The black-haired, furrow-faced woman scowled at Zalith. "I'm not leaving unless Tim comes with me!" she demanded, pointing to the baby-faced man trying to hide behind another vampire.

"I just told you no."

She stomped her foot. "Then I won't go!"

"Good, that makes one less person for me to worry about," the demon snarled.

"Vhat's going on?" Alucard asked, appearing behind him.

The demon closed his eyes and exhaled quietly, clearly trying to calm down. He glared at the woman. "People are making my life difficult, as per usual."

Alucard looked at the vampires. He heard a woman complaining on his way to the hall, but now *everyone* was arguing with each other. They shouted about who should go with who; they evidently wanted to travel with their friends and loved ones, and the groups Alucard organized separated them. He knew there would be problems here and back in Aegisguard if he didn't do something, but he wasn't going to alter the groups. All he could do was try to diffuse the situation better than Zalith's poor attempts.

Zalith scowled and told them, "Be quiet and get back into your groups. I didn't go out of my way to arrange this relocation for you to argue with me."

They ignored him.

Amused, Alucard watched the look of irritancy on Zalith's face increase with each passing moment. However, he didn't have time to hang around. He moved towards the arguing crowd and stopped in front of the woman. "Vhat's zhe problem?"

She took her scowl off Zalith and looked at Alucard. "I want to go with Tim."

"And zhat vould be…?" Alucard asked.

The woman pointed to the man cowering behind the tall, broad vampire.

Alucard frowned and said, "Zoesn't look like 'e vants to go vith you."

"Oh, he *does*," she laughed, waving her hand. "He's just shy."

Tim shook his head. "I-I don't wanna go with her—she's crazy, man!"

Alucard rolled his eyes and sighed. "Tim must go vith zhe people I put 'im vith, and so must you. Get back into your groups, and zhen ve can continue, no?"

After a few moments of hushed mumbles, the vampires slowly returned to their groups.

However, the woman stomped her foot once again. "I said I—"

"And I said no," Alucard snarled, grabbing her collar and glaring into her eyes. "You do as I say, or you get levt be'ind. Get back in line."

Nodding, she fell silent and went back to her group.

Alucard glanced around at everyone else. "Are zhere any more of you zhat might like to address a problem?"

No one came forward.

"*Idioti*," he mumbled, making his way back to Zalith. Then, as he stood beside the demon, he muttered, "I gazzer zhere is a specific group you vant me to take."

Zalith pointed at the group containing the stubborn woman. "Them."

The vampire smirked and took the chance to mock Zalith and his superiority complex. "Vasn't so 'ard to shut 'er up, huh?"

Zalith rolled his eyes. "Take them and go. I have elsewhere to be."

Alucard scoffed. "Vhat crawled up your ass and died?"

The demon grunted in response, still glaring at the vampires.

Alucard frowned slightly. Something was clearly bothering Zalith; he didn't care about his personal problems, but he had to work with him, and if that relationship was going to work out, Alucard had to at least try to show some concern. After all, whatever was irritating him could affect the mission.

And as much as he hated to admit it, Zalith *did* help him kill that Amarok. Although they'd simultaneously repaid their debts by saving each other's lives, a part of him felt as though he should be a little more grateful.

So, he sighed and asked him, "Vhat's vrong?"

The demon slowly took his sights off the crowd and eyed Alucard skeptically. He seemed to ponder for a moment, and Alucard suspected that he was trying to work out why he was asking.

Zalith then glowered at the vampires. "I've been putting on a kind face for these people for months to keep them as calm as possible…but they are pushing me to my limits, and I feel as though I might lose my patience with them."

"Sometimes, zhat's zhe only answer," Alucard jested. "To kill somevone to make a point. Per'aps you ought to do so."

Zalith smiled amusedly at him.

Scowling, Alucard turned his head away. Why did he *always* smile like that? What was he supposed to do or say in response? He couldn't stand to look at that demon's face whenever he smiled even the slightest. Alucard couldn't tell whether Zalith was genuinely amused or if he was demeaning him again. He didn't care. He offered out his hand, and for what? To be laughed at.

However, the demon then glanced at the crowd. "Would you like to help me? You can take the left half, I'll take the right. And if one of them turns out to be a huge monster, we'll take it on together again," he suggested with a smirk.

Alucard frowned at him. "Vhat?" he asked, confused. Was he serious?

Zalith laughed. "It was a joke."

"Joke," Alucard scoffed. "Everyving is a joke to you."

The demon smiled. "Not everything," he said, but when Alucard rolled his eyes, he frowned slightly. "You could stand to smile more, you know, Mister Grumpy."

In an attempt to hide his amusement, Alucard pouted and looked away. "You zon't amuse me," he muttered.

"I think I do," Zalith disagreed with a snide expression.

"Vink vhat you like," Alucard mumbled as he pointed at the group of vampires Zalith selected. "Let's go," he called. Then, he glanced back at Zalith. "Zhis time again, zhe end of zhe month."

Zalith nodded. "Until then." But before Alucard could leave, he called, "Oh, how are things with the werewolves? I hope our killing that creature saved your treaty."

Alucard sighed and replied, "Everyving's vine. I told zhem a zemon killed zhose people."

An offended scowl stole Zalith's smile.

With a quiet snicker, Alucard headed for the hall's exit as the vampires followed.

He led the way down the empty hallways and towards the portal. Once he reached it, he stopped and faced the vampires. "All of you need to 'old 'ands or arms," he said, snatching the wrist of the man closest to him.

They all took hold of each other's hands and wrists.

"Zon't let go until ve are all on zhe ozzer side," Alucard instructed.

Each vampire responded in agreement.

Then, Alucard proceeded forward, and the moment he stepped into the portal, nausea gripped him tightly. He grimaced, emerging on the other side, and the vampires followed one by one as he felt his strength waning. His body became sore, but the dizziness wasn't as severe as it was when he brought Zalith and Ben through. However, he felt extremely exhausted, and he knew *exactly* what he needed to regain the strength he lost.

Once each vampire was through, he let go of the man's wrist and took a moment to collect himself. He went to take his flask from his blazer, but before he raised his hand, his eyes located Rodney and Kevin. He still needed to find out whether Kevin was Diabolus. The kid knew Alucard's name, and there wasn't anything else the vampire needed to confirm his suspicion. And he was hungry…so very, dangerously hungry.

He left the vampires and made his way to the ship.

"I see you brought more this time," Rodney said.

But Alucard ignored him. The vampire snatched Kevin's collar with his clawed hands and savagely sank his four fangs into his neck before he could grab whatever he reached for in his pocket. The confused, horrified man yelped, but the life was drained from his body in just moments.

With an irritated snarl, Alucard pulled his fangs from Kevin's throat. The vampire wiped as much blood from his mouth as he could, and glared at the pale, lifeless body.

"What…the fuck, man?" Rodney breathed, mortified.

Alucard turned to face him so suddenly that Rodney flinched and held up his hands defensively. "Zon't you *ever* bring anyvone along vithout my permission!" he yelled furiously. "You could 'ave compromised me and zhis entire operation!"

Rodney backed off. "I-I said I was sorry, I…. You didn't have to kill him! He was just a kid! What the hell did he do wrong?!"

"Zhe kid knew my name! Check 'is fucking pockets," Alucard uttered as he dropped the body and tried to wipe the blood which had trickled down his neck.

While the vampires cautiously boarded the ship, Rodney shakily reached into Kevin's coat pockets, and as he pulled out a silver stake, the horrified look on his face transformed into realization. "Oh, fuck…I…I didn't know."

"Zhey might know vhere I am," Alucard muttered, staring at the silver stake. That weapon could only mean one thing…and he hated that his suspicions were right.

"Shit, man…" Rodney breathed as he looked up at Alucard. "M-maybe he was just a scout sent out to follow rumours?"

Alucard tried to keep himself composed. He wasn't about to panic in front of everyone. "I zon't know. Get vid of zhat."

Rodney chucked the stake into the ocean.

"And get vid of zhat, too," the vampire grumbled, waving his hand at Kevin.

"Uh…what?"

The vampire rolled his eyes and snarled irritably as he shoved past Rodney and snatched Kevin's mangled throat. He lifted the dead boy and held him over the side of the ship. The water immediately swirled around, and Drac arose from the depths with a curious look on his scaled face. With an appreciative chirp, he clamped his jaws shut around the corpse and pulled it down to the water. Then, Alucard stormed into the cabin, leaving the vampires on the deck to mutter about what they just witnessed.

Rodney followed him. "What are you gonna do?"

"I zon't know," Alucard mumbled, sitting down. "Just get us back to Dor-Sanguis. I zon't vant zhem 'earing my business," he said, nodding at the vampires on the deck.

Rodney shook his head. "What if the Diabolus *do* know you're here? Will we have to leave again and start somewhere new?"

"I said take us back."

The captain sighed hesitantly but turned around and left the cabin.

Alucard was left with his conflicting thoughts. Kevin was the first Diabolus agent he'd seen in centuries. Why *now*? How did they find him? Could Kevin have just been sent to investigate the rumours? He wasn't sure, and he couldn't *be* sure… all he could do was prepare for the worst. The last time the Diabolus found him, they killed everyone he cared about, and he couldn't let that happen again. The rebuilding of the Nosferatu empire took so much time; he didn't want to lose the progress he'd made in Dor-Sanguis. But what could he do? If the Diabolus came, they'd bring Lucifer with them, and that was something he wouldn't be able to escape.

The vampire scowled, thinking. If it were anywhere else, or if it had been any other time, then he would simply leave and start somewhere new. But not this time. Not only did he have a job to do for Damien, but he was also content with his current life. He had a home, people who weren't too afraid to talk to him, and a city that would soon be home to both humans and vampires. He didn't want to throw it all away because of a pathetic cult.

With a quiet sigh, he calmed down and rested his legs on the desk. Kevin may have been armed, but he didn't try to kill him right away. Did that mean that Kevin was trying to confirm that Alucard was who he was looking for? Of course, no agent had lived to share his appearance since he was a child; so, if they didn't know what he looked like, that had to mean that they weren't aware of where he was living. He wanted to believe that, but he couldn't be naïve. He had to be sure.

He snarled angrily and glared out the window. Would he ever get a break?

As the ship approached Dor-Sanguis, Rodney walked into the cabin and stood in front of Alucard's desk, hanging his head in shame—as he should be. He'd made a stupid decision and Alucard was furious.

"We're approaching the docks," Rodney whimpered.

"I can see zhat," Alucard mumbled, tapping his claws on the table.

"I'll prepare the ropes."

Before he could leave, Alucard kicked out a chair in front of his desk. "Sit."

The captain sunk into the seat, trembling and sweating.

Alucard set his aggravated, fiery eyes on the human and scowled. "You do vealize zhat vhat you did could 'ave not only compromised every single operation I am currently running but you could 'ave also cost me my life?"

Rodney nodded shamefully. "I understand, and whatever you choose to do with me, I won't argue."

"Look at me. You are not some child being scolded vor stealing candy."

He took his eyes off the floor and looked at him, nervously fiddling his fingers together.

"Vone of zhe virst vings I ever told you vas to never, *ever* bring anyvone vith you. Anyvone could be my enemy."

"I know. I'm sorry."

The vampire sighed deeply. "Now, zhat Diabolus agent is dead, and zhat's eizer going to tell zhe Diabolus zhat I'm 'ere or make zhem send more agents to look vor 'im. Vhen zhey get 'ere, I'll 'ave to kill zhem, too."

"If I had known, I—"

Alucard held up his hand, silencing him. "Vhether you 'ad known or not, is zhe vact zhat you brought an outsider aboard zhat angered me."

Rodney murmured, "Yeah, I know. I shouldn't have done that."

"Now I 'ave to deal vith zhem on top of everyving else," Alucard complained.

Rodney gulped nervously. "Well, uh…what are we gonna do?"

The vampire pulled his feet from the desk and leaned forward, resting his arms on it. "I'll deal vith zhis on my own. Vonce ve arrive, you vill leave zhe docks."

Rodney's face worried expression twisted into horror.

"I need you to tell everyvone to meet tomorrow at my 'ome, no later zhan tvelve."

A look of relief struck the man's face.

"I must varn zhem zhat zhe Diabolus might know vhere I am. I zon't vant to make everyvone leave again, so if I must vun again, you zon't 'ave to vun vith me. You all 'ave a place 'ere, and if I leave, zhe vampires are going to need people to vely on in my absence."

The captain laughed slightly. "We owe you our lives, Aleksei. Wherever you go, we'll all come with you. The vampires have Felix and that new guy, right?"

"Vight," Alucard grumbled. "Dock zhe ship."

Rodney frowned. "Is…is that it?"

"Yes…unless you vant to die?"

The captain shook his head and left the cabin.

Alucard glared out the window. If the Diabolus knew he was in Dor-Sanguis, he'd have no choice but to leave. Yes, he could kill them as they came, but eventually, Lucifer would come in their place, and he knew he couldn't fight his father. But he wasn't planning on packing up his life just yet. There was the possibility that Kevin had just been sent to investigate rumours, so he was going to find out if that was the case.

He sighed and stared at the wall. Not only did he have vampires, werewolves, humans, *and* Diabolus to deal with, but he also had to make sure he performed to Damien's expectations. He'd now brought back ten of one hundred and fifteen vampires. At the end of the month, he would bring another group, and it seemed as though he'd be making fortnightly trips for the following year. However, he didn't feel as resentful anymore. Although he and Zalith weren't friends, he felt as though he *might* be able to get along with him, so long as the demon didn't demean him again. He *did* appreciate his help dealing with that Amarok, and he enjoyed the way Zalith amused him.

With a tired sigh, he stood up, and he didn't feel as drained as before. Could the fact that he fed on someone have something to do with that? Last time, he drank from his flask, but that blood wasn't very appetising; it seemed as though killing Kevin might have caused his miraculous recovery. If draining someone of their blood would keep him from feeling the awful after-effects from travelling through that portal, then he'd do it again. The last thing he needed right now was to feel so tired that he couldn't leave his home, especially with the Diabolus on his doorstep.

As the ship stopped in the docks, Alucard left the cabin and glanced at the vampires. "All of you can 'ead up to zhe castle," he instructed, nodding in the direction of the pathway. "Vollow zhat path. Ben vill be vaiting vor you. Zon't vander off, and zon't try to enter zhe castle, or you vill bleed vrom every 'ole in your body."

The vampires murmured unsurely as they left the ship.

Alucard then walked over to Rodney. "Zhe next journey takes place on zhe tventy-vifth."

Rodney took his eyes off the rope he was tying and looked up at Alucard. "I'll be ready, as always."

"Bring Sebastian to zhe gates vor me. I'm 'eading 'ome avter I make sure zhey are vine up zhere."

The captain nodded. "Sure thing. I'll be at the gate in a few minutes."

Alucard made his way up the cliff. When he reached the top, he trailed the vampires towards his castle, where Ben was waiting beside the fountain in the courtyard. The vampires crowded by the castle door, and Alucard pointed at Ben, instructing him to follow him as he made his way to the surrounding wall.

As he joined Alucard, Ben frowned curiously. "What's up?"

"Vhen you make your collections, I vant you to set aside vone of zhe living 'umans and take 'im to Vodney zhe night I am set to leave to meet Zaliv again."

"Sure. Why, though?"

Alucard shrugged. "Travelling vhrough zhat portal makes me 'ungry."

"Oh, okay. I'll keep some of them aside."

"I 'ave also arranged a meeting tomorrow. I vant you zhere. You are not vrom 'ere, so I know I can at least trust you to not be conspiring vith my enemies," he said with a skeptical scowl.

Ben frowned in concern. "Has something happened?"

"You'll vind out tomorrow. Vait 'ere in zhe morning; my groundskeeper vill come and get you. Understand?"

He nodded. "Of course."

"I also need you to take care of zhem," he said, nodding at the newly arrived vampires. "I 'ave to 'ead 'ome and… die," he mumbled.

Amused, Ben laughed slightly. "Don't worry, I'll get them settled."

Alucard looked at the vampires. "You can all go in," he called. Then, as he heard Rodney arrive outside the gates with his stallion, he waved his hand in dismissal and walked off.

He made his way out of the castle's gates and took Sebastian's reins from Rodney.

"So, I'll see you tomorrow?" Rodney asked.

Mounting the horse, Alucard replied, "Zon't be late."

Alucard then rode off. He looked up at the moons as they bestowed shimmering, brightly coloured light on the land. He *hated* those moons. Every time he saw so much as a hint of their light, he was reminded of Damien and the other Numen.

Rolling his eyes, he glared ahead at his manor as he approached it. Tomorrow was going to be a lot more complicated than hunting werewolves and building relations with humans. He'd have to talk about his past, and that was something he always tried to avoid. But he didn't have a choice. He needed his closest subordinates to know about the threat; he needed to make sure they knew the extent of the situation so that he and everyone else beneath him would be ready. If the Diabolus were coming, things were about to get a whole lot more hectic.

Chapter Thirteen

— ⋜ † ⋝ —

Allies

| Elvin |

Birds flew overhead as the sound of the city buzzed in the distance. Elvin made his way towards Alucard's house with a bright smile; he was excited to see what the vampire had called him there for.

The echo of a horse-drawn carriage crept up behind him—

"AH!" he yelled in fear, stepping aside just in time to avoid the brown mare and the carriage she was pulling.

He recognized the horse, the carriage, and the brown-haired groundskeeper driving it. Why was Sergiu out here?

The bard hurried into the manor gardens and watched Sergiu climb down from the carriage. He saw him pull the door open, and Ben stepped out. *Of course* he'd been invited to the meeting too.

Elvin pouted and walked towards the door.

"Hey, we almost hit you in the road," Ben called with an amused expression as he made his way over.

Elvin stopped walking and glared at him. "I noticed."

Stopping in front of him, Ben frowned. "You all right?" he asked, laughing.

"He invited *you*?" Elvin asked, eyeing Ben strangely.

"Yeah, said he wanted me here."

"Hmm…you're new, so I guess he needs to get you up to speed on things."

"Seems to be the case," Ben agreed as he followed Elvin to the manor door.

"Well, don't get too comfortable around him; he's not your friend," he warned as he pulled the gold key from his pocket. He unlocked the door and stepped inside, and as he slipped his key back into his pocket, he leaned against the door frame. "You gotta wait for him to come invite you in."

"Yeah, I'm not new to vampirism," Ben muttered. Then, he frowned through his irritancy. "Who exactly are you to him?"

"I so happen to be his best friend," he said smugly.

"Sure seems that way—I mean, you have a key to his house, huh? And the hair?" Ben asked, fiddling with his own hair. "You copy him, or he copy you?"

The bard scoffed. "I didn't copy anyone; it's a sign of respect—to adopt one's appearance."

"If…that's what you want to call it." Then, he frowned curiously. "You seem to show a lot of interest in what he does. Do you…like him, maybe?" he suggested.

Looking at him, Elvin frowned—but then he laughed. "Oh, you mean, do I *like* him? Well…it would be pointless to like him, to be honest. He's had no interest in *anyone* in a romantic way for as long as I've known him, and even before that. He's never been with anyone, as far as I can tell. Not just that, but a man liking another *man*? Here? In Aegisguard? We might have ghosts and fairies, but same-sex relationships are one of the most frowned-upon things you might happen across. I wrote an article about it one time at school."

"Oh?"

"It apparently goes against the law of creation—one should love to create a family; it's in the Book of Lore, the same one that says Aleksei is evil incarnate," Elvin said with a shrug.

"Book of Lore?"

"The…it's…it tells the story of how the world came to be; it covers the dragon and Numen Religions. But people take that stuff way too seriously."

"Do you?"

Elvin shrugged again. "Can't say I care."

"And does Aleksei?"

"I don't know. Aleksei is just…Aleksei," he mumbled sadly.

"You never know." Ben laughed. "Maybe he'll find himself a nice vampire girl one day."

"I don't see it. He works too much to have time, even if he was the dating type. He always works."

"Be glad zhat I do," Alucard mumbled, making his way down the stairs behind Elvin, who flinched in shock and spun around to face him.

The vampire—dressed in his usual black shirt and blazer—set his shimmering blue eyes on Ben. "You can come in."

Entering the house, Ben followed Elvin and Alucard into the lounge.

"How was last night?" Elvin asked excitedly, sitting in the armchair.

Slouching on the couch, the vampire sighed quietly. "Annoying."

Ben sat on the other side of the couch.

"Are you and the demon friends yet?" the bard asked, flipping through his book, searching for a blank page.

"No," Alucard snarled. "And ve never vill be."

Elvin frowned doubtfully. "You told me you like arguing with him; that's gotta mean something."

"I argue vith every member of zhe council, but are zhey my vriends?"

"No, but you don't *like* arguing with them—"

"Vhat are you trying to prove, Elvin?"

The bard shrugged and lowered his pencil. "That you *do* have friends, and you just can't see it."

"I zon't, von't, and can't."

Elvin frowned strangely. "Why?"

"Vhere is everyvone else?" Alucard grumbled, looking around.

"I saw the captain guy on his way here when your groundskeeper picked me up," Ben said.

Alucard sighed and stood up. "Ve'll move to zhe bigger voom." He left the lounge and led the way through the wide archway behind the couch as Elvin and Ben followed.

The vampire took them through to a much larger living space. The back wall was lined with tall, arched windows, and long black curtains hung beside them, decorated with thin, wavy gold patterns. In the centre of the room was a rectangular table with white and black chinaware on the red tablecloth, and gold candlesticks sat at either end. A large mirror sat opposite the window wall, and several framed paintings covered the rest of the walls.

There was *one* painting which stood out among the others: a family portrait of Alucard dressed in an evening suit beside a middle-aged woman in a red dress. Her waist-length, curly hair was dirty-blonde, and her eyes were a deep, honey-gold. In front of them were two young green-eyed boys, both with the same hair as their mother. Elvin knew that they were Vanessa and her sons, the family Alucard lived with a long time ago.

He and Ben followed Alucard through a doorway and into another lounge. The room was much larger than the lounge they came from, and the gardens were visible through the arched windows. A door to the outside sat on the left wall between the windows, and the patio outside possessed a single bench and a few birdfeeders.

The centre of the room had several white couches organized to form an oval. A large open fireplace was on the wall ahead of them with several books on the mantlepiece. The walls were also black and panelled, but black curtains hung along the walls, concealing something behind them that Elvin had never seen.

Alucard sat on one of the couches and leaned his elbow on the arm of the chair as he stared vacantly into the empty fireplace.

"Who else are we waiting for?" Elvin asked as he sat beside the vampire.

Tapping the side of his face rhythmically with his clawed fingers, Alucard set his eyes on the bard. "Vodney, Dirk, and Tobias."

Ben sat across from them. "What about Felix? Isn't he in charge at the castle?"

"Is daylight," Alucard said. "Velix vould combust into vlames and die."

"But…he said that you turned him. Didn't you say people *you* turn can walk in the sun?"

"I did say zhat, *da.* But I did not turn Velix."

Ben looked confused.

"Felix is weird anyway," Elvin said. "He always wants to be noticed."

Alucard sighed irritably and rolled his eyes. "Zhey all do."

"So…you didn't kill Felix's parents and turn him?" Ben asked.

"Vhat?" Alucard asked with a slight laugh. "Who told you zhat?"

"Felix. The night you had me call Zalith for you; after you left, he told me you killed his parents and turned him as some sort of apology," he revealed.

"I zidn't kill 'is parents, 'e did."

Still confused, Ben frowned harder.

Elvin said, "Aleksei found Felix a long time ago in Dor-Sanguis. He was just getting a lay of the land when he found weird Felix in his weird house."

Alucard scowled. "Do you—"

"Shush!" Elvin insisted, silencing Alucard. "I'm telling this one. Ahem…Felix shot his dad, who shot his mom, and he was about to shoot himself, but Alucard stopped him."

Ben stared for a moment but then shook his head. "Can I ask *why* so many people got shot?"

"Family drama," Elvin mumbled. "Husband thinks the wife's cheating and kills her; then you got the disturbed kid who takes justice into his own hands—that being Felix. This thing happens a lot. We humans can be kinda dumb."

"Kind of is an understatement," Alucard mumbled.

Elvin continued, "Aleksei smelled the blood, and he got there before Felix could kill himself. Aleksei took him to his castle, intending to find him a place to stay, but when he got back, the guy he left in charge pretty much ate him. Aleksei told the vampire to turn Felix to save him, so he did, and the guy that almost killed Felix was gone the next morning; can't keep people you can't trust around," he said sternly.

"Trust is important, man," came Tobias' voice.

They all set their eyes on the tall, rugged man standing in the doorway. His shirt and jeans were muddy and torn, as was his brown leather jacket. The only thing clean about him were his boots which he had obviously cleaned with his sleeve before entering the house. He smiled at Alucard, and surprisingly, his teeth were as white as the room's couches.

"Aleksei, I was surprised to hear you needed me again so soon," he called, making his way over. "This about the wolf stuff? If so, I haven't found—"

"ZON'T…touch anyving," the vampire warned sternly, pointing at the man before he could lay his dirty hands on the couch.

He held up his hands and smirked. "Sorry."

Alucard looked over at Ben. "Zhis is Tobias; Tobias, zhis is Ben."

Tobias held out his hand towards Ben. "New guy, huh?" he asked as Ben hesitantly shook his dirty hand.

"Yeah…" Ben said, evidently unsure what to do with his now dirty hand, which he stared at in discontent.

Rubbing his temple, Alucard glanced at Elvin. "Go and get 'im someving."

The bard jumped to his feet and hurried past Tobias, who remained standing, waiting until he was told to sit. Elvin grabbed a towel from the small bar by the window and then handed it to him.

"What's going on?" Tobias asked, looking at Alucard.

"I'll tell you vhen everyvone else is 'ere," Alucard mumbled.

Cleaning his hands, Tobias frowned. "Who else is coming?"

"All of us," Elvin said.

"Turn," Alucard instructed, pointing at Tobias. The man did as he asked, and when he saw that there wasn't any dirt on him, the vampire said, "Sit."

With a satisfied sigh, Tobias slumped down. "So, what's been happening in the world of vampires lately?"

"We're all pretty much aware of that," called Dirk, the city council member with the smartly-combed blonde hair. He walked over and sat on the only unoccupied couch.

"Yeah, the whole treaty thing," Tobias said. "That working out?"

"The city's gonna be open to vampires at the end of this month, right?" Elvin said, looking to Alucard for confirmation.

The vampire nodded. "Are zhe ozzers still whining like children?" he asked, looking at Dirk.

"Whine is all they do, Aleksei."

Just then, Rodney walked in. Elvin stared at him, noticing a tired look in his green eyes, and his hair was scruffier than usual. Then, he watched Dirk sit up straight and admire himself in the window's reflection. He knew Dirk tried hard to be the most elegant of them all, but Elvin thought he was an idiot.

Tobias then looked at Elvin and Alucard and smirked. "You let your hair grow out again, man. You and Elvin look like twins."

Elvin laughed nervously as the vampire rolled his eyes.

"Might I ask why we're here?" Dirk requested. "You never call us together unless something has happened—or will be happening."

Alucard lazily gestured his hand towards Dirk. "Ben, zhis is Dirk, my 'uman invormant. Zhat is Tobias, my verevolf informant," he mumbled, nodding at Tobias, who waved with a smirk on his scruffy face. "You know Elvin alveady."

"Hi!" Elvin waved.

Ben nodded in greeting. "What roles do they play, and…why?"

"I have been acting as a spokesman for both Aleksei and the people of this land," Dirk explained. "I would have been opposed to the idea of vampires cohabiting with humans if it weren't for my life being saved by Aleksei. I do what I can to assist him. My people are stubborn and not very open to ideas such as these, especially since vampires and humans have been enemies for a long time. But we managed to form a deal, and it has worked out so far."

Tobias then held up his hand. "Not so successful over here," he said shamefully. "Aleksei's been trying to ally with the werewolves for as long as I can remember, but they ain't interested."

"You are, clearly," Ben said.

"Well, same as Dirk. Aleksei saved my life, and come on, you gotta love the guy." Tobias laughed, looking at Alucard, who rolled his eyes. "Look at all this shit he does for everyone. I'd rather have peace than sit by and watch vampires and werewolves tear one another apart for the rest of my life."

"Tobias brings me invormation regarding any verevolf movements or plans," Alucard said. Tobias hardly ever gave a straightforward answer.

Ben asked Tobias, "Are you the only werewolf on Aleksei's side?"

"There's a whole pack of us—well, we're a secret pack. Can't let the others know we're on the side of the vampires, or what use would I be as an informant?"

"Zhe only invormant I zon't 'ave is vone in zhe Diabolus, and zhat is zhe veason vor zhis meeting," Alucard announced.

Everyone gawped at him.

The Diabolus: that name carried a deep, dreadful fear with it and sent a shiver down Elvin's spine. "Diabolus?" he breathed. "They…they're not here, are they?"

"Vodney discovered vone," Alucard said.

They all looked at Rodney.

"He was just a kid. He played as a street urchin, looking for work," Rodney mumbled.

"I killed 'im," Alucard said. "Vould appear zhat eizer zhe Diabolus know zhat I am 'ere and sent zhe boy to look vor me, or zhey are just vollowing rumours. I'm sure vord of my alliances 'ere 'as spread."

Dirk nodded. "Word of a vampire forging relations with humans; of course, they'd investigate that."

"Which is more likely?" Tobias asked. "If they know you're here, wouldn't they have sent more than one boy?"

Elvin said, "That's true. Last time, they sent armies."

Ben shook his head. "Sorry, but…who are the Diabolus?"

"Sorry, but who are *you*?" Dirk asked rudely, eyeing Ben strangely.

"Ben is vrom anozzer vorld. 'E 'as taken over my supply runs, but since zhis 'as 'appened, 'e might also be taking over Velix's duties, considering as Ben can valk in zhe daylight. If zhis is zhe Diabolus, I need vampires zhat can valk in zhe sun; zhey vill not be expecting zhat."

"He's been here like a week," Elvin muttered. "Are you sure that's a good idea?"

Alucard replied, "Ben 'as no idea who zhe Diabolus are, so zhere is no chance 'e could be conspiring."

"Valid point," Rodney agreed.

Looking at Alucard, Ben nodded. "Whatever you need me to do, just tell me."

Then, Alucard sighed. "As for who zhe Diabolus are…" he said, looking over at Elvin.

The bard asked, "From the beginning?"

Alucard nodded.

Elvin loved telling stories. He explained to everyone that Alucard's insane father, Lucifer, created him to gain access to the living world—a creature born of his blood and from a woman in Aegisguard should have worked—but when it failed, Lucifer sent his cult to kill Alucard and take back the power it took to create him. Damien kept the vampire hidden, though, and that was why Alucard worked so tirelessly for him.

He then went on to explain that after the Diabolus killed Vanessa and her sons, Alucard started hunting *them*. It went on for years, and Alucard soon decided to settle somewhere and make a life for himself.

Ben interrupted him there, though. "Why did you choose to come back here? Won't the Diabolus know where to look?"

"The Diabolus know Aleksei hates humans. It's the last place they'd look—and it's too obvious too, so, hiding in plain sight too, huh?" Elvin smirked, looking at Alucard.

"I've been moving avound vor so long zhat zhe Diabolus don't expect me to stop and stay somevhere vor longer zhan a vew days. I 'ave been 'ere just over six months, and zhey 'aven't vound me—until yesterday vhen ve discovered zheir agent."

Dirk frowned. "And you *killed* their agent; isn't that going to tell them that you're here?"

"The world's a dangerous place," Rodney said. "There's no way they could know if he even made it here in the first place."

"Coulda got had by wolves," Tobias said, grinning.

Alucard sighed. "*Da*, zhat's possible. But ve must be vigilant."

"What do you need us to do?" Dirk asked.

"I need you to tell your people to keep an eye out vor people asking vor me."

Dirk nodded. "I'll tell them when I get back."

The vampire said to Tobias, "I need your pack to vatch zhe borders; tell me if you see anyvone suspicious."

"Sure thing," Tobias said.

"Ben, you'll vork vith Velix. 'E leads zhe nightguard vhilst I sleep, but now, I vill need a day guard. You vill lead it zhat. Talk to Velix; 'e vill 'elp you organize—but tell 'im I told 'im to; 'e's precarious."

"And my current job?" Ben asked.

"You can still run zhat—unless you'd vather not."

"I can do both."

"Vorm a group of vampires who can valk in zhe sun, vhether is vampires vrom your vorld or zhis vone. Just make sure zhey can do zhe job."

"Understood," Ben said.

Elvin then shook his head in worry. "What do we do if they come?"

"I von't leave unless Luciver comes, vhich 'e vill if zhe Diabolus vind me. Ve 'ave to make sure zhat zoesn't 'appen. If more come, ve vill kill zhem and make zheir deaths look like any ozzer. Zhis city is 'ome to all manner of vings; zhere are many vays vor somevone to accidentally die," Alucard said with a smirk. "I'll get my vampires avound zhe vorld to kill agents to avoid suspicion, too."

"Deaths on the streets aren't going to sit well with the people, Aleksei," Dirk said with a frown.

"I never said zhey vould be dying on zhe streets," Alucard snarled.

The man held up his hands. "Right, sorry."

"Zhe last time I ran vrom zhese people, zhey inviltrated my organization. Zhis time, vhat I've built is much larger, so zhere is more opportunity vor zhem to 'ave vorked zheir vay in. Dirk, question all of your people; you know 'ow to spot a Diabolus, vight?"

"Of course."

"You, too, Tobias," Alucard said.

"Gotcha, man," Tobias confirmed.

"You zon't know 'ow to spot vone," the vampire said, looking at Ben. "'Elp Velix question zhe people vorking at zhe castle. Be discrete and zon't give it avay zhat ve know zhe Diabolus 'ave made an appearance. Understand?" he asked, looking around at them all.

They all nodded.

"What can I do?" Elvin asked eagerly.

"Noving."

The bard pouted and crossed his arms. "Why can't you put me in charge of something?"

Ignoring him, Alucard sighed and looked at Dirk. "Zhe twenty-vifth, vight? Zhe treaty."

Dirk nodded.

Elvin scowled irritably. He hated when Alucard ignored him like this, but he knew better than to interject.

The vampire announced, "Zhat's all. You can go."

On his word, everyone but Elvin left.

As soon as they were gone, Elvin jumped to his feet. "Are we safe here?"

Alucard rolled his eyes. "Ve are vine, Elvin. Zhe day zhe Diabolus send armies marching over zhe 'ills is vhen ve should run."

"I hope we don't have to leave; I like it here."

"As do I."

"What do we do now?"

Alucard moved his hand to the back of his neck and started fiddling with his hair.

"Aleksei?" Elvin asked impatiently.

"Vhat?" he grumbled, lowering his hand from his head.

"What do we do now? I knew they wouldn't leave us alone for long."

"Ve vill be vine, Elvin. Zon't vorry."

"Don't worry? Aleksei, these people want to *kill* you!"

"Who *zoesn't* vant to kill me?" he exclaimed. "I vink I've grown accustomed to zhe vact zhat somevone vill alvays vant to stick a stake in my back."

"Yeah, but…I worry about you," he mumbled shyly.

"I've told you bevore, I'll be vine, and so vill you if you stop panicking all zhe time," he grumbled.

Elvin glared at the vampire. He wasn't going to press and risk making him mad. He didn't want to ruin the time he got to spend with him today. But he couldn't stop worrying. What if the Diabolus came, and everything Alucard worked for was destroyed?

Chapter Fourteen

Felix

| Ben |

While the carriage took him back to the castle, Ben stared out the window. He was content over the fact that he'd only been in Aegisguard a short while and had already earned himself an important place in Alucard's empire.

He had to talk to Felix, the guy who lied about how he became a vampire, and if Ben was going to run the castle smoothly for Alucard, a liar was the last thing he needed. If he was to perform his new job to the best of his ability, he should start by questioning Felix and finding out how much of a nuisance he might end up being. He had to let this troublesome vampire know he meant business.

When the carriage stopped, Ben unlocked the door and stepped out. He made his way up to the door as Alucard's groundskeeper rode off.

Felix didn't possess the luxury of walking in the sunlight, so at this time of day, he'd be in the sunlight-proofed half of the castle with the rest of the vampires. *That* was where Ben had to go. He entered the castle, closed the door behind him, and headed to the door between the suits of armour.

However, as he was about to reach for the door, three distinct voices caught his attention. He stepped back, stared at the kitchen door, and watched as his two friends walked out alongside another vampire he hadn't seen before. He was significantly taller than his; his black hair was longer than Alucard's—at least double its length—and braided and tied with a black ribbon. He dressed as though he'd soon be attending a celebration; his dress suit was black with a white shirt beneath it, and a frilly necktie to sum his attire up as something…fashionable.

This new vampire was as pale as ice, his eyes a deep, soulless black, and he spoke with an accent much like Felix's. He had a hand on each of Ben's friend's shoulders, and the three of them chatted quietly as they left the kitchen and walked to the table in the centre of the room.

One of Ben's friends noticed him. He smiled and waved as the others sat down. "Hey Ben, come join us," he invited, pulling out a chair for him.

"Can't. Gotta do something for Aleksei."

"Oh, come on, just for a sec," his other friend called with a laugh.

What harm would five minutes do? Ben sighed and went over there. He sat beside Jasper, the one of the two he undeniably preferred. The guy was quieter than his younger brother, Lloyd, and much more interesting to talk to. But Ben was more interested in the vampire they were sitting with.

Lloyd patted the new vampire's shoulder. "This is Attila," he introduced. "Cool guy."

Attila held out his hand towards Ben, his fingertips adorned with blood-stained, dull-white claws much like Alucard's; however, Alucard kept his a lot cleaner. In fact, compared to Attila's rough, nasty-looking hands, Ben might go so far as to suspect that Alucard was the type to get manicures. Why was he even thinking about that?

Ben smiled politely and shook his hand. "I'm Ben."

"Yes, I've heard much about," he said with the same hinted accent as Felix. "Alucard has you on prison runs, I hear."

"He does. The journey is always interesting."

Resting his arms on the table, Attila nodded. "Not much to do, no?"

Shrugging, Ben replied, "Pay's good."

Attila laughed unnecessarily loud. "Yes, money. We all like money."

Ben didn't understand what was so funny, but he laughed when his friends did anyway.

"What's he got you doing now?" Jasper asked curiously. "New job?"

"Security," Ben answered.

"Head of security already, huh?" Lloyd smirked. "Save some of the jobs for us."

"What can I say? Aleksei seems to like me."

"Alucard? Like? Joke right there." Attila laughed. "Very peculiar man…not like many people. Probably just likes that you do what he says."

Ben nodded slowly, unsure of what to say in response.

"Jokes aside, you need people?" Jasper asked.

"Well, I'd imagine so. I need to talk to Felix first," he said as Attila scoffed. "He's the head of the nightguard, so he can give me the rundown, and then I'll know what I need to do."

Attila waved his left hand in dismissal. "Felix? Crazy. Something not right about that kid."

Ben already concluded that himself, but it seemed like he wasn't the only one who thought there was something strange about Felix. "Not right?"

"*Da*, strange. Alucard? Always talks about him. We all appreciate Alucard, but Felix? A little too much," he said, shaking his head. "Tells people Alucard turned him out of pity for killing parents—lie, he lies. It was me. I've turned…hmm…over half castle. Alucard not like to let people touch him—remember that, new guy…don't touch him," he warned, pointing at Ben. "Anyway, he brings this little guy in one night; wartime, lots of people die. But Felix parents? Kid killed them, something not right up here," he said, tapping his head.

"What's the point in lying? What's it matter who turned you?" Lloyd asked before Ben could.

Attila shrugged and leaned back in his seat. "Alucard told me the god that gave him ability to make vampire liked to play games, mess with Alucard's head. If Aleksei not want to be alone, he can make vampire from his blood, and that vampire free to walk in sun. But if his vampires make vampire, they can't walk in sun. Alucard also cursed like us to drink blood, but it's much worse for him." He then held up three of his fingers. "Alucard require blood every three days, but us? Not so often—maybe a week," he said, lowering his hand.

It was interesting to learn more about Alucard, but at this current time, Ben was focused on Felix. "All of that aside, though, is there anything I should know about Felix?"

"Hmm…you go talk to him now?"

He nodded.

"Don't mention Alucard; any mention of Lord's name, Felix talks and talks and talks. Only way to get him to shut up is to walk away. But sometimes, he follow," Attila warned.

"So…I should avoid mentioning Aleksei's name at all costs—noted." Then, Ben looked at the two brothers. "What were you three doing in the kitchen?"

"Look at him, being Mr Security already," Lloyd said, smirking.

Jasper rolled his eyes and looked at Ben. "Just getting a drink. Attila keeps his own—
"

"A-ta-ta!" Attila snapped, silencing Jasper. "Secret. Keep it that way."

Ben already knew what Jasper was going to say; Attila obviously had his own secret stash of blood somewhere. He felt no need to pry; as long as he wasn't doing anything that might irritate Alucard, then he would go about his day and leave Attila to it.

"What do you do?" Ben asked Attila curiously.

"Oh." Attila smiled, gesturing to himself with his hand. "I do many thing."

"Like?" Jasper asked. "You've failed to tell either of us."

"I…am recruiter." Attila grinned, fiddling with his frilly tie. "I find people for Alucard—people Alucard will benefit from if he turns them. Like me: I was…Bishop here in Dor-Sanguis. Church was not happy with Alucard coming—unholy monster, they would say. Threat to gods, sent to kill them, bullshit—well, not really. Alucard was…sent for similar reason. Anyway, he come to me, turn me, I get church to leave him alone. He pay me, but I do it because he is…friend to me."

Ben frowned. "You let him turn you? A Bishop?"

Attila chuckled. "Boring job. Much more excitement being vampire. Praying to gods never did a thing for me; Alucard gave me many things in short time, more than I got from religion in years. I would not go back and change. I like this."

Amused, Ben smiled.

"What kind of people have you gathered so far? Other religious folk?" Jasper asked.

"Nah, not need," Attila said. "I was important; very high up in church. I am enough to convince all churches of dragon religion. Dragons are the gods…well…sub-gods. Also Numen, but that another story for another time. There are other religions here in Aegisguard, but Alucard has yet to express interest in needing them under control."

Ben was learning quite a lot from this interaction, and he couldn't stop listening.

Attila continued, "Important people like me, I bring them to Alucard; he turn them so they can walk in sun and look like normal people."

"You don't exactly look normal—no offence," Lloyd said, smirking.

"Eh, I am old. Older you are, more vampire you look like. I still do job, though; church still listen to me." Then, Attila looked at Ben. "You have job to do? I come with if you want to stop Felix yapping."

Ben shook his head as he stood up. "I'll be all right. It was nice to meet you, though."

"We go for drink later. I won't be here after tonight," Attila said. "You come?"

"Sure, might as well."

Attila smiled. "Good. Then we will see you later. Have fun with Felix."

Ben left the table and headed into the dark corridor which led to the vampires' accommodation. The metallic smell of blood lingered in the cold air, and it was utterly silent. He made his way to the lounge, but it was empty. Usually, when he walked through to get to his own room, there were at least two small groups of vampires relaxing there, but they were probably either sleeping or found themselves another lounge to rest in—there were plenty of them in the large castle.

With a quiet sigh, Ben left the lounge and went up a flight of stairs. He emerged onto a floor lined with dark oak doors, all with gold-carved Dor-Sanguian numerals on them. The corridor stretched farther than his eyes could see in the gloom, which was surprising since his vision was quite impressive.

Felix was important—he was the nightguard's leader—so Ben was sure that he'd not only be on the first floor but that his door would also differ from the rest. And he was right. Once Ben walked to the end of the corridor, he stopped in front of a black ebony door beside a staircase that led up to the next floor.

He knocked quietly and waited. After a few moments, the door's locks clicked, and as it swung open, Ben's brown eyes then met with Felix's silvery ones.

"Yes?" Felix asked sleepily, his greyed hair scruffy and unkempt.

Ben crossed his arms. "I need to talk to you about a few things—now," he demanded.

Felix frowned unsurely. "It is…day. I sleep. You wait until night?"

"No, it can't wait."

He nodded slowly. "Right…well…you come in, then—or we must go somewhere?"

"Here is fine," he said, tapping his foot on the floor.

"What…is it?"

"First thing: I've been assigned to form a day guard, and I was told you could give me the rundown. Tell me what I need to know."

"Hmm…it is…much to talk. Come, I have table," Felix said, stepping aside.

Letting his arms hang at his sides, Ben sighed and walked over to the table. He pulled out one of the three wooden chairs and sat down, watching Felix closely as he joined him.

Felix rested his arms on the table. "In nightguard, I command. I have vampires positioned at parts of grounds, parts of castle—all night. If you are day guard, you do same."

"Where will I need to position people?"

"Front door: one inside castle, one outside. By castle gates: two each side. By exit that lead down to docks: two again. Four in docks. Inside castle, one by door to this half, one by door to Alucard's half—although Alucard hardly ever come here."

Alucard's name had been mentioned, and Ben was quite certain that Felix was about to side-track. He didn't want that. "Where else?"

"Um…there are towers—twelve. One on each, but best people with best senses on towers, make sure they see far."

"Noted."

"I patrol castle; I assume you will do same—but in day. I still do night," he said with an almost defensive tone.

"What are the protocols? What happens if danger arises?" Ben asked.

"We vampires," Felix said amusedly. "We very fast. They come to you, you tell them what to do, and you go to tell Alucard. Alucard come, he deal with it—Alucard always deal with it," he said in envy.

"What sort of dangers should we be looking for?"

"Hmm…Alucard has many enemy. Diabolus…sometimes old clients come, angry about something, or just want to try steal. Sometimes wolves, but not many lately."

"Old clients?"

Felix nodded. "Alucard has many business; client hire vampire to do things, usually kill people, and deal with problems. They give money, Alucard send vampire. Sometimes, client gets greedy, wants money back or more service, cheaper. They come and think they can steal—they know Alucard rich. But Alucard always teach them lesson."

"And if someone turns up, I…what? Tell the vampires to subdue them? Hold them until Aleksei gets here?"

"Is what I do, yes."

Ben nodded. "All right, that should be enough. Next matter of business."

Staring at him, Felix tilted his head slightly. "What more need from me?"

"I want to know why you lied about how you became a vampire; I want to know if your being a liar goes beyond the story behind your turning and if it will cause me problems."

"Lie? I did no such thing," he denied vehemently. "I tell truth always."

"That's not what Aleksei tells me."

Upon the mention of Alucard's name, Felix's defensive look became something of a worried one. "Well…maybe…I get confused…it happen…sometimes."

"Uh-huh," Ben uttered doubtfully.

"Did Alucard…talk about me?"

"He told me that you killed your own parents. Why would you lie about something like that?"

"I not remember that night much…blur…all I remember is Alucard saving me."

"He didn't save you, he pitied you—and I think its best you stop calling Aleksei Alucard," he added. "We all call him Aleksei."

"He say that?" he snapped. "He feel sorry for me?" he asked, disregarding the rest of what Ben said.

"Why did you lie?" Ben insisted.

Felix shuffled closer. "Alucard…Aleksei talk about me often?"

"What? No. Answer my question."

With a saddened pout, Felix shrugged and leaned back in his seat. "Not remember clear what happened that night."

"You don't seem at all angry that I just said you killed your own parents."

Glancing at him, Felix slowly gained an offended look. "I did not do that."

Felix's emotions and expressions were clearly false. Ben wasn't sure what to make of him, but he was convinced that Attila was right, there *was* something wrong with him. It made him feel…wary. Felix didn't seem at all bothered that Ben just accused him of killing his parents; he seemed more concerned about whether Alucard was talking about him. Felix's priorities were mixed up, and not in a way that made Ben feel very secure. Felix was a liar, and he seemed to have some sort of infatuation with Alucard.

Ben then scowled. "If I hear another lie come out of your mouth, I'll do everything in my power to remove you from this castle. Is that clear?"

With an unsure frown, Felix looked around before setting his eyes on Ben. "You are…ordering *me*?"

"I am."

He then laughed slightly. "You are not boss of me. Aleksei is."

"Aleksei was the one who gave me the order. He told me I was not necessarily replacing you, which implies I pretty much *am*."

"Aleksei said that?"

"Yes," Ben grumbled.

"He wouldn't demote me. He value me."

"That's not the impression I got. You heard what I said: no more lies."

Felix shrugged. "If Aleksei say that, I do that. I always do what Aleksei want."

"Good. Is there anything else I should know before I go?"

"Not allowed in Aleksei's half of castle; access to towers from sky—you fly, no?"

"I'll work it out," Ben said, standing up.

Felix also stood up. "Aleksei fly, turn into bird."

"Okay," Ben mumbled, making his way over to the door.

"And fox."

"Great."

"And monster."

Ben then turned around as he reached the door. "I'm starting to wonder whether you're meant to know as much as you appear to."

"I know much about Aleksei—more than anyone. We…friends."

"I was just told he doesn't have friends."

"I friend, I exception."

"If you say so," Ben mumbled, pulling the door open.

"You are going to Aleksei now?"

"Where I am and am not going is no concern of yours."

"If you go to Aleksei, tell him I'm sorry for forgetting what happen…that night."

Ignoring him, Ben made his way back down the corridor. He swiftly left the vampires' section of the castle and returned to the main hall. Lloyd, Jasper, and Attila were still sitting at the table and looked at him the moment he emerged from the door.

"How'd it go?" Lloyd called.

Discretely rolling his eyes, Ben headed sat back down. "Guy's given me a headache."

"Ah, he has habit of doing that," Attila said.

"What's the matter with him? Why is he so obsessed with Aleksei?"

Attila shrugged. "If I knew, I would tell. He has…always been like that. Wants to be noticed, wants Alucard to see him—Alucard doesn't care. We do our jobs, and he has people to make sure we do them. Looks like you are one of those people now, no?"

"I suppose."

The guy then leaned forward. "I hear you are from other world? Eltaria."

"That's right," Ben said.

"Why you come here? Why Alucard help?"

"Well, to put it lightly, there was a war, and the vampires back home were close to being wiped out. My…other boss made contact with Aleksei somehow—through a mutual contact, I believe. They came to an arrangement, and now, Aleksei's meeting with him every two weeks to transport vampires from Eltaria to here."

"And you like it here?"

"It's all right, yeah." Ben smiled. "Whole new world, lots to discover. I'm learning to love it."

Attila tapped the table with his claws. "Aegisguard is big place. I travel everywhere, very far sometimes. Never leave this world, though. Only Alucard has been out of Aegisguard."

"To Eltaria," Ben confirmed.

Smirking, Attila leaned back in his seat. "Much more other worlds than Eltaria. Alucard been to some, told me stories."

"Oh?"

"Another time. Not for me to tell. If you his friend—well, subordinate—then one day, he tell you himself."

Ben nodded. "Right, well, thanks for your input anyway."

"I am man of many years, much knowledge. Felix useless. If you need more information, you can ask."

"Good to know."

Then, Attila stood up. "I go for now. You come to drink at dusk?"

"Where in the city?" Ben asked as Jasper and Lloyd nodded.

"Small tavern called uh…Goose Inn. Been around since I was a boy, favourite place. I sneak off from church to drink, bad teenager," Attila laughed.

"I'll be there," Ben agreed with an amused laugh.

Then, as he walked past Ben, Attila patted his shoulder and smirked. "Bring money; night is *not* on me."

"Understood," Ben said and watched Attila leave the castle.

Now, it was time to get to work forming a day guard as Alucard requested. A part of him felt a little uneasy knowing that there was a cult after his new boss; they sounded formidable, especially since they had a god Ben only heard about in stories on their side. But it sounded like Alucard had everything under control and was ready if things got dangerous.

But Ben couldn't help but wonder…what would happen to the mission if Alucard had to flee from Dor-Sanguis?

Chapter Fifteen

⸺ ⸘ † ⸌ ⸺

Carrying On

| **Elvin** |

The rest of the month wasn't eventful. Alucard's people were aware of the possible Diabolus threat; Tobias and his pack were patrolling the borders, the authorities in the city were alert thanks to Dirk, and Elvin was sure that everyone was ready. He trusted Alucard, so he did his best to keep his fear of that dreadful cult from consuming him.

Today, the treaty was finally in place, and the vampires were going to be allowed into the city. He was happy for Alucard; he'd put so much work into it. But he couldn't help but worry. The humans weren't very happy about any of it…but perhaps they'd calm down eventually. Alucard had a way of making things work out *all* the time, so Elvin was confident that everything would be fine.

He waved at Alucard as the vampire made his way up the street. His hair wasn't tied in a ponytail anymore, though, and hung loosely at jaw-length, banishing several years of age from his face. If Elvin didn't know that he was four hundred and twenty-five, then he'd guess that Alucard was in his early twenties.

"Are you excited, Aleksei?" he asked as Alucard joined him.

"Do I look excited?" the vampire mumbled.

"No, you always look mad and scary and mean."

Alucard didn't reply.

Elvin pouted and followed him along the street. He wasn't sure what to expect after tonight; all he could do was hope that things went well and no one killed each other. He trusted Alucard's vampires more than he trusted humans because he knew too well how dramatic and awful they could be. But all they could do was wait and see what happened.

He sighed and looked at Alucard. "So, what are we doing? You don't have to leave to go get more vampires yet, do you?"

"Not yet. Virst, I need to talk to Dirk. Zhen I'll leave. I also need to check in vith Tobias, but I'll do zhat tomorrow; tonight is a vull moon, and zhe last ving I vant to deal vith vight now is a moody volf," he grumbled.

"I never got why werewolves are always so moody on the full moon," the bard said, following Alucard into a deserted alley. "I mean…I guess it's the night they have to turn no matter what, but meh, I don't know much about werewolves—hey! You could teach me some stuff, right? For the novel, of course." He smiled, looking up at Alucard as he stopped at the end of the alley.

The vampire glanced at him. "Go to zhe library and read a book."

"They don't have anything on werewolves. It's all…cookery and crafting—boring stuff."

Alucard rolled his eyes. "Maybe tomorrow…if I'm not dead."

"Why would you be dead?" Elvin asked worriedly.

But that was when Dirk stepped into the alley.

As the sun set in the distance, depriving the secluded alley of light, the vampire's eyes faded from icy blue to hell-fiery red. A tired expression lingered on his pale face, and as he watched Dirk make his way towards him, he sighed lazily.

"Why must we sneak around, Aleksei?" Dirk asked, straightening his suit as he stopped in front of the vampire and the bard.

"You know why," Elvin said with a frown. "We gotta be careful; Diabolus and all."

Shaking his head as he sighed, Dirk looked at Alucard. "I apologize for the behaviour of my fellow council members; they're simply nervous about the new laws."

"I zon't care about zhem. Speak," Alucared demanded.

Dirk crossed his arms. "Still nothing. No one suspicious in the city; no one suspicious has entered, either. We have been and will continue to keep an eye out, though. We won't let anyone slip by. I gather the others are performing their jobs well?"

The vampire nodded. "Keep doing yours."

"Of course. I should also bring to your attention that my fellow council members are still not very keen on this treaty. I have done my best convincing them, but a lot of them are stuck believing that you are here to, for the lack of a better explanation, bleed us all dry until no human remains."

Alucard rolled his eyes. "I'm not 'ere to kill anyvone."

"He just wants to make the city a place for both vampires and humans to live together peacefully," Elvin insisted. He looked to Alucard for confirmation. "Right?"

The vampire sighed. "Someving like zhat."

"Well…" Dirk said with a frown, "I'll do my best to persuade them. As for the Diabolus, we will continue to keep our ears close to the ground and our eyes ahead."

Then, as Dirk turned around and left, Alucard exhaled deeply and leaned back against the black wall.

Elvin adorned a concerned expression. "If the Diabolus knew you were here, they would have come by now, right?"

"*Da*," Alucard confirmed with a perplexed look on his face. "But ve can't let our guard down yet; zhey could be vaiting. Ve know 'ow unpredictable zhey can be."

The bard nodded. "I still think you should take some time to rest."

Alucard rolled his eyes once more and started to lead the way back out onto the street. "Vhy do you concern yourselv vith me vhen you 'ave your own problems to deal vith?" he snarled.

"I don't have anything to deal with," Elvin insisted, following him.

"Zon't you 'ave a book to vrite?"

"Yeah, but I gotta gather notes first, and that's what I've been doing." He smiled, tapping the pocket of his waistcoat in which his notebook sat. "I can't write it until I have a whole story's worth of notes, and to get those, I have to ask you a million more questions."

"Zhere veally isn't anyving else vor me to tell you."

"Maybe not now, but tomorrow, you'll have more to tell me about your new demon friend."

The vampire glared over at him. "Ve are not vriends, Elvin."

"Sure, whatever you say."

Alucard increased his walking speed, snarling irritably.

Elvin scurried after him. "Hey!" he called. "Slow down."

"*Prieten*," Alucard muttered. "I zon't 'ave vriends."

"You *keep* saying that," Elvin muttered with a pout, almost jogging to keep up with the vampire. "But I'm pretty sure you have plenty." But as he realized that Alucard was following the route that would take them back to his manor, the bard frowned. "Where are we going?"

"I'm taking you to Sergiu bevore I 'ead to zhe island."

"I can walk home from here. It's fine."

The vampire glared at him. "Eizer you are deaf, or you vorgot alveady zhat is a vull moon tonight. I'd vather not come back to vind you 'ave been infected vith lycanthropy or to your cold, dead body on my lawn," he snapped.

Elvin scoffed. "A bit morbid. What would you do if I *did* become a werewolf?" he asked curiously. "It wouldn't change our relationship, would it? I mean, you get on with Tobias just fine."

"I vouldn't care. Verevolf, vampire, 'uman—you could be a catvish vor all I care."

"I'm quoting that," Elvin said, hastily pulling out his notebook, and scribbling into it. He then frowned and looked over at him. "What if I was a demon?"

He snarled and glared at his manor in the distance. "All zemons are stuck-up *catelele*."

"That means bitch, right?" he asked, writing it down.

Rolling his eyes, Alucard grumbled, "I can't imagine you as a zemon; you are too...hmm...."

"Too...what?" Elvin questioned, frowning skeptically.

The vampire shrugged. "You are too 'uman."

Offended, Elvin scowled. "Did you just class me as a typical human? I, as a matter of fact, am a creative soul, one in a million, a rarity like no other!" he sang.

"Sure," Alucard muttered. "At least you zon't vink of me as a monster."

"Why would I?" Elvin asked as they approached the manor. "Vampires are just people...that...eat other people. I mean...you gotta live, right? People eat animals to live; it's kinda the same thing when you really look at it."

"You vink so?" the vampire asked, looking at him with a strange frown.

"Yeah." Elvin shrugged. "At least that's what I think."

"You're probably zhe only vone zhat vinks zhat," he said, reaching the gates.

"I'm sure there's more people that think like I do—well, regarding vampires."

Glancing at him as he led the way over to the stables, Alucard frowned.

"Like Rodney. I'm not so sure about Dirk, but...Rodney doesn't think you're a monster, does he?"

"You tell me," Alucard mumbled, stopping beside the stables. He set his eyes on the groundskeeper as he made his way over and stopped in front of him. "Take Elvin 'ome," he instructed.

Sergiu nodded before heading off to prepare the carriage.

"Well, I'll see you here tomorrow, as always," Elvin said with a sigh. He didn't want to go, but Alucard needed to work, and he wasn't going to get in the way.

The vampire nodded. "Stay inside tonight."

Elvin smiled at him. "Don't worry. I usually just go straight to bed when I get home unless I stay up and write a little, but I think I'm just gonna sleep tonight. The sooner I sleep, the sooner I can wake up and hear about your hot—"

"Zon't even mention zhat vord vonce more to me," Alucard warned, pointing at him.

Smirking, Elvin turned around and made his way to the carriage. "Have fun!" he called, waving as he climbed inside.

He then pulled the door shut, waiting to depart. All his excitement faded, leaving him with worry, which swirled around in his gut. He might joke about it, but he still worried about the demon Alucard was working with. After all, Alucard *let* that guy stick his nose in his werewolf business, and he didn't let *anyone* help him with that—he didn't let anyone help him with *anything*.

With a quiet sigh, he shook his head and tried to put it out of his mind. Alucard wouldn't be interested in some rude demon, would he? He *hated* them.

Right?

| Alucard |

As he rematerialized on the docks, Alucard set his eyes on the ship. Rodney was on the quarterdeck, and Ben was with him along with another man Alucard hadn't seen before. But it didn't perturb him. He asked Ben to bring one of the prisoners to Rodney before he left for the island again.

Alucard made his way onto the ship and joined them on the quarterdeck, eyeing both Rodney and Ben as they stopped talking to each other to look at him. The prisoner stared in confusion, standing in his torn shirt and trousers, his wrists bound with rope so that he couldn't attempt to escape.

The Vampire Lord frowned strangely. "Vhy is 'e tied up like an animal?" he asked, looking at Ben.

Ben glanced at the prisoner. "Well, I wasn't sure how you wanted me to bring him, so I left him in what I picked him up in."

"Vhatever." Alucard sighed, turning his attention to Rodney. "Let's go. I vant zhis over and done vith."

Before Alucard could walk off, Ben stepped forward. "Hey, do you want me to come too?" he offered. "If anything happens, it's better to have the extra help, right?"

Glancing back at him, Alucard frowned. He felt no need to deny, nor did he feel a need to say yes. He didn't need extra help, but if Ben wanted to come, then he'd let him. "Do vhat you vant," he mumbled, making his way down to the deck.

"That usually means yes," Rodney said, leaning over to Ben. Then, the captain started preparing to leave the docks.

Ben followed Alucard into the cabin. "How'd the meeting with the council go?"

Alucard sighed as he sat down behind his desk and turned in his seat to stare out the window. "Vine," he mumbled. "You are all vree to go to zhe city vonce ve get back vrom picking up more vampires."

"I'll make sure to tell everyone," Ben said, sitting down.

Alucard then asked him, "Are you and Velix getting along?"

Ben shrugged. "Yeah, well enough. He's a little odd, you know—talks about you a lot, and I mean a lot. He's worse than Elvin."

"You get used to it," Alucard mumbled, tapping his fingers on the desk.

"How about you and Zalith? Are you two getting along?"

Alucard snarled. "Zhat man annoys me more zhan Velix or Elvin ever could."

With an amused laugh, Ben frowned curiously. "Why?"

But Alucard had no intention to answer. He rolled his eyes and changed the subject. "'Ow 'ave zhe pick-ups been going?"

Ben sat up straight and gained a severe frown. "Well, no problems yet."

"Good," Alucard mumbled, glaring out of the window.

Silence then found its way between them.

"You know, Aleksei," Ben said after a few moments. "I know that Zalith's hard to read sometimes; he can be difficult to understand, but he's actually a nice guy. He's done a lot for my people and me—he's done a lot for a lot of people. I'm sure that whatever he may have thought of you in the beginning isn't what he thinks of you now. If you give him a chance, I think you'll come to like him."

Alucard frowned skeptically at him. "Vhy vould I come to like a man zhat vinks I'm some incompetent child?" he snarled.

"I'm sure if he thought you were incompetent, then he wouldn't still be working with you."

"No, 'e is only vorking vith me because I am zhe only vone zhat can 'elp," Alucard growled.

"Honestly, he would have figured something else out if he didn't want to work with you anymore," Ben insisted.

"Vhatever," Alucard mumbled. "Vhen 'e stops laughing at everyving, maybe I'll take 'im more seriously."

Ben sighed unsurely and looked down at the desk.

"Leave," Alucard dismissed. He'd heard enough.

With a nod, Ben got up and left.

Alucard didn't want to sit there thinking about Zalith. He was too worried about letting his vampires in the city tonight. He trusted *them*, but he didn't trust the humans. He knew what they were like, and any one of them could attempt to take a stab. However, his experienced vampires would be there, too, and he knew that they would take care of those who were younger.

He just hoped that they'd get through tonight without any murders.

Chapter Sixteen

⟶ ≺ ✝ ≻ ⟵

Friends?

| **Alucard** |

As the sound of the island's endless pouring rain echoed in the distance, Alucard made his way back onto the deck. He waited for the ship to arrive, and watched as Rodney lowered the bridge.

He walked down onto the black rock and headed for the portal. When he reached it, he stopped and glared into it for a moment. Was he ready to deal with that insufferable demon again? No. But he had no choice. His stupid laughing, and his annoying, condescending smiles. It irritated Alucard so much that the mere thought of it made him furious. Not to mention the annoying, fussy vampires who would be waiting with the demon. He hoped there wouldn't be another fiasco like before; the last thing he wanted was to have to deal with other people's problems.

With an irritated snarl, he stepped through the portal. When he emerged on the other side, the usual tiredness gripped hold of him, but he tried to ignore it. He expected to hear the voices of vampires echoing through the corridors, but it was close to silent. The occasional mutter caught his attention as he made his way towards the hall, but as he got closer, it became clear that there weren't as many vampires there this time.

He stepped into the hall and set his eyes on a group of nine vampires. They stood at the back of the room, muttering quietly to one another. And standing by the right wall—as always—was Zalith. *Him.* Dressed in an all-black suit. Alucard was instantly gripped by his aggravation; his strong disliking for this man made its way onto his face in the form of a judging scowl. How long would it be this time until he was laughing at something that wasn't at all humorous?

The demon smiled pleasantly, watching Alucard walk over. "Good evening, Aleksei. I see you decided to rid yourself of the ponytail. I like this new look of yours much more," he said as Alucard stopped in front of him.

"I zon't care vhat you vink," Alucard mumbled, looking over at the vampires he'd be taking back with him.

Zalith laughed amusedly.

Alucard then laughed in mockery and glared at him. "Vunny," he snarled. "Vhere are zhe vest of zhem?" he grumbled, gesturing to the vampires.

Smiling, clearly entertained by Alucard's response, Zalith replied, "I brought a single group this time to prevent any further problems," he said, looking back at him. "I didn't want to listen to them bickering like children again."

The vampire examined the group with his eyes, noticing that Ben's wife was among them. He remembered her from the night he had taken Ben back to Aegisguard. He then set his skeptical gaze on Zalith, sure that he and Ben had arranged for his wife to be sent and for Ben to be there to meet her. He didn't care to start an argument. He knew that Ben was keeping in contact with Zalith—of course he was; Ben contacted Zalith relatively quickly the night he needed to warn the demon of the change of plans. If anything, it was useful knowing that Zalith was easily contactable if he ever needed to reach him again.

"How are the others settling in?" the demon then asked.

"Vine."

"And the treaty? I assume that's all in place now?"

"Yes," the vampire confirmed.

Zalith then frowned as a smirk appeared on his face. "I see that you're Mister Grumpy again."

"Stop calling me zhat," Alucard snarled, turning his head to look away and hide the fact that he found it funny.

"Then stop being so grumpy," the demon said with a grin.

Alucard rolled his eyes. "Grumpy," he mumbled. "I'm not grumpy," he said, glaring at him. Before Zalith could speak again, Alucard shifted his sights to the vampires. "I should get zhem back."

The demon frowned slightly. "Why so hasty?"

Glancing at him, Alucard scowled skeptically. Usually, he felt as though Zalith couldn't wait for him to leave and get on with the job, so why was he asking him why he was trying to be quick about it? This demon confused him; one moment they'd be arguing, and the next, Zalith was laughing and trying to humour him. One moment the demon was demeaning him, and now, he was complimenting his appearance. Did this man resent him, or did he want to be... friends?

Alucard stared at the vampires. The thought had crossed his mind before; he couldn't deny the fact that he *did* somewhat enjoy *some* of their interactions, but Zalith still caused a sea of anger to fester inside him. He wasn't sure what to do with it. However, he would much rather form some sort of relationship that didn't involve hostile arguing and disagreements, and it almost seemed as though that was what Zalith was aiming for, too.

Could they become friends? If what Ben said was true, then that might be possible. Alucard would try—but only once. If this demon made him feel stupid for it, then he'd make sure that Zalith knew he hated him and that they would never be friends.

Losing his scowl, the vampire said, "I 'ave to meet Zamien after zhis."

Zalith looked cautious. "I see."

Agitated by his short answer, Alucard frowned at him. "Vhat… do you do avter zhese meetings?" he asked, trying to get him to understand that he was trying to form a friendship.

The demon smirked. "Many things: a lot of work, organizing, and some trying not to die, too."

Unamused, Alucard looked away again. Upon mentioning his name, Damien began to occupy the majority of his thoughts, and in the few seconds of silence that fell over them, he found himself wondering: how did Zalith meet Damien? Why did Zalith work for him? Exactly *how* did Zalith work for him? What did he do? Alucard had no idea what Zalith and Damien did outside of the vampire relocation mission, and he was curious.

However, after finding out that Damien asked Zalith to pretty much babysit him, he suspected that Zalith might be feeding information to the Daegelus. He needed to make sure that wasn't what was going on here if he was going to try and become this demon's friend.

He set his suspicious glare back on the demon. "'Ow did you meet Zamien? Vhat do you do vor 'im outside of zhis?"

"Why do you want to know?"

"I'm trying to decide vhether or not I can trust you," Alucard answered. Of course, it was risky to have said that; he'd basically just told Zalith that, if he was loyal to Damien, then he didn't trust him, suggesting he himself wasn't loyal to the Daegelus. If Zalith *were* loyal to Damien, then he'd tell him what he said, and he'd have to face the consequences. However, it would be worth it so that he could know if it was worth trying to move past the conflict between him and Zalith.

Zalith looked like he was thinking it over. He took a few moments… and then adorned an almost vacant expression. "Damien reached out to me quite some time ago. He told me about his goal to overthrow Letholdus, and said he was gathering his siblings' descendants. He knew I was among some of the stronger demons in Eltaria, so he came to me and asked me to work for him."

"Let me guess: vork vor 'im, or die?"

Zalith shrugged slightly and answered, "There was the promise of a reward for helping; I am simply curious to see what that might be."

The vampire scoffed. "You might be vaiting many 'undreds of years vor zhat."

With an amused smirk, Zalith frowned curiously. "And you? How did you come to meet him?"

Alucard felt dismay grip him tightly, stealing away what little enjoyment he was starting to feel from their conversation. He looked away from the demon, trying to hide his face. "Zhe same as you," he lied. "I should get zhem back now. I've alveady been 'ere longer zhan planned," he said, catching Zalith swiftly looking away when he faced him again; the guy had clearly been staring at him, and that made the vampire frown uncomfortably. "Vhy do you keep staring at me?" he questioned defensively.

"I wasn't," Zalith said as his usual amused smile appeared on his face.

"Vhatever. I'm leaving now," he said, pointing over at the vampires and then to the door, telling them that it was time to go. He then glanced back at Zalith. "I vill veturn two veeks vrom now."

Zalith smiled. "I'll see you then."

Waving his hand in dismissal, Alucard turned around and made his way over to the door, following the vampires out and into the hallway, leaving Zalith alone in the hall. He was glad that Zalith didn't look at him as though he were inferior this time, but their conversation was ruined when he decided to start talking about Damien. Why did he have to do that? He didn't even know if Zalith was going to tell the Daegelus that he asked if he trusted him.

But he was sure he'd find out when he next saw him.

| Zalith |

As he watched Alucard leave, Zalith collected his thoughts. Each time they met, he noticed that they seemed to talk a lot more than they had previously, and he enjoyed that. Alucard was also proving himself to be a somewhat interesting acquaintance, and Zalith felt as though he may very well be of use later. So, he was going to do what he could to make sure he became the vampire's friend.

He already felt as though they were on the road to becoming friends, but he also found that Alucard was sometimes hard to read…and when he'd asked him how he came to meet Damien, and Alucard lied, he tried to read the vampire's thoughts…only to discover that he couldn't. He felt some sort of wall around Alucard's mind, and no matter how long he stared and how hard he tried, he couldn't break it. Why? There had never been a situation where he wasn't able to read someone's thoughts or see into their mind and memories. So why was Alucard different? Why could he, no matter how intensely he concentrated, not see into his mind?

The demon sighed as he turned around and headed for the archway on the opposite side of the hall. He was confident that he didn't need to be able to read Alucard's mind to gain his trust or find out what he needed to know, though. He always had a way with words, and soon enough, his charm was bound to work on Alucard.

But why was Alucard so reluctant to talk about Damien? From their interactions, Zalith managed to understand that Alucard didn't like the Daegelus—nor did he, as a matter of fact. There was nothing to like about Damien; he was utterly, preposterously rude; he clearly treated all the people who worked for him like shit. Zalith knew that he was probably the only one who hadn't yet suffered a physical injury from Damien in response to failing to do something. He never failed. However, Alucard obviously experienced it; why else would he have flinched that night on the tower when Damien raised his hand? Zalith knew that creature was disgusting and cruel, and he made sure he did his best to remain on his good side.

He wasn't about to spend his evening thinking about Damien, though. He had business to tend to, people to protect, and enemies to evade. A part of him felt afraid that they were closing in, and if they found him before the vampires had all been moved, he didn't know what he was going to do.

Chapter Seventeen

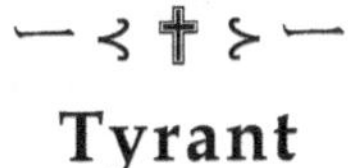

Tyrant

| Alucard |

When Alucard emerged on the island, he tried ignoring the overwhelming exhaustion the portal forced on him.

As soon as she came through, Ben's wife left the group and hurried over to the ship. She threw her arms around Ben, crying happily as she reunited with him.

The rest of the vampires slowly made their way towards the ship, following behind Alucard.

Rodney smiled as Alucard joined him on the quarterdeck. "How'd it go?"

"Zhe same as last time," Alucard muttered, glancing at the horrified prisoner. However, the vampire had no interest in him. While he thought it was a good idea to keep a disposable human around for him to use to regain his lost strength, he didn't feel like doing so right now. He wasn't sure whether it was because he was far too exhausted to find the motivation to feed or if it was because he was meeting Damien soon. The thought of that creature always gave him sickening nausea.

"You all right?" the captain asked with a frown.

"Vhy vould I not be? Let's go."

With a concerned expression on his face, Rodney made his way down onto the deck, passed Ben—who was still embracing his wife—and pulled the bridge up. He closed the gate and then wandered over to the side of the ship, where he tapped the side to tell the dragon below that it was time to leave.

Rodney returned to the quarterdeck as the ship started to depart and set his worried gaze on Alucard once more. "When are we heading out here next?"

Leaning back against the fence, Alucard sighed quietly. "Zhe…ninth of Quintus."

"Well, I'll be ready as always."

The vampire nodded, but as Rodney started ranting, Alucard zoned out. His thoughts focused on Zalith. Although he'd been recently convinced that he and the demon wouldn't become friends, he couldn't deny that he might have contradicted himself. The more time he spent with Zalith, and the more they spoke, the more he found himself enjoying his company. They may have only spoken for a short while tonight, but he enjoyed their calmer conversation more than he enjoyed their argument the night Zalith helped with the Amarok.

After what Ben said, Alucard assessed his and Zalith's interactions in his mind. Now that he thought about it, perhaps Zalith's smiles and laughter weren't a form of mockery. Despite the fact that Alucard didn't find him very funny, he couldn't deny that there were one or two times the demon made him laugh. But he wouldn't let Zalith see that; he was sure that if Zalith knew he could entertain him, he'd do it a whole lot more often. And even though the demon was hard to read, Alucard felt as though he might begin to understand him a lot more if he stopped thinking that he was constantly looking down on him.

Tonight was different; Zalith complimented him, and Alucard actually felt as though the compliment was genuine. Zalith also complied and answered his questions instead of dancing around them with lies and condescending responses.

He wasn't going to let his guard down too soon, though. Zalith *was* a demon, and if there was one thing that Alucard knew too well about demons, it was that they were sneaky, snide little bastards who would turn heel when offered a better deal. He had to keep an eye on Zalith; he had to make sure that he was someone he might be able to call an ally—a trusted ally? Maybe not, but an ally, at least, would be something better than having him as an enemy. He already had far too many of those.

"…And then, we kinda just stopped talking," Rodney said with a sigh.

Alucard frowned and looked at him, having not heard a single word of what he just said. "Vhy…did you stop talking?"

The captain replied, "Well, she didn't like the idea of being around so many vampires; she's probably already left the city, so I'll never see her again."

"Mm…." Alucard nodded. "Maybe you vill…vind somevone else."

"Find…another sister, Aleksei?" Rodney asked, laughing slightly. "Right, I'll be sure to keep an eye out."

Alucard didn't know Rodney had a sister. He sighed and said to him, "If you vant to go vith 'er, you can. I've told you bevore zhat you zon't need to stay 'ere."

Rodney shook his head. "And I've told *you*, Aleksei, I nor any of us are going anywhere. We'll be here so long as you need us, and even when you don't." He placed his hand on the vampire's shoulder—

Alucard flinched in startlement and stepped back—

Rodney also stepped back, holding his hands up in surrender as he stared in confusion. "S-sorry, man."

The vampire scowled at him, but when the prisoner—who he hadn't paid any attention to until now—mumbled something through the rope keeping him quiet, Alucard snarled irritably. "Veed Drac," he muttered.

Slowly lowering his hands, Rodney looked over at the prisoner. "Is that why you had Ben bring him?"

"*Da,*" he said with a sigh, uninterested in explaining the real reason to Rodney.

"All right, well, we're almost home, so I'll do it once you got all these guys off the ship. And, uh…if you want or need anything, I'm here for you."

Alucard grunted in response and then made his way off the quarterdeck.

Once they reached the castle docks, Alucard's dread started becoming overwhelming. He'd meet with Damien in a few minutes, and the thought of his face made him tense up. However, he'd done as the Daegelus asked. Surely Damien would see that and congratulate him…right?

No. That never happened; he wasn't sure why he kept hoping that one day, the Daegelus would recognize his hard work. Tonight would be another demeaning meeting, one where he was made to feel even more like a failure. Whether he'd ever escape Damien's resentment or not was unclear, but he'd keep trying. He had to.

He made his way off the ship, following behind the new vampires as Ben led the way up to the castle. Once they reached it, Alucard waved his hand in dismissal and told the vampires to go inside.

While the vampires entered, Ben let his wife walk in alone and made his way over to Alucard. He frowned in concern as he looked at him. "Is everything all right? He piss you off again?"

"Vhat?"

Ben laughed. "Zalith."

Alucard pouted. "No."

"Then what's up? You look sad."

"Zhis is just my face," the vampire grumbled. "Go to your vife, and do your job."

"All right…" he said, watching as Alucard left.

Alucard headed home. The night air was filled with the howls of werewolves; he hated hearing those wretched sounds, constantly reminding him that his enemies were close. Once he was done talking to Damien, he'd have to head out on his usual patrol, making sure the wolves didn't stray from the forest, especially tonight. The full moon had a strange effect on some wolves and would leave them as mindless Amaroks.

He went into his manor's gardens and to his front door. Once he unlocked the door, he stepped into the house and sighed quietly as he pulled his cape off. He wasn't sure how long he'd be talking to Damien, so he thought he might as well take a moment to rest.

The vampire closed his door and continued upstairs into his study, sure that Damien would meet him there again. But as he pushed the study's door open, he set his eyes on the Daegelus, who was sitting behind Alucard's desk with an impatient scowl on his face.

"Late, as usual," Damien snarled.

The vampire looked down at the floor. "I did vhat you asked."

"I know," Damien replied, tapping his fingers on the desk. "I saw."

Had Damien watched him the entire night? Had he done something wrong that Damien had seen? Or had Zalith told him what he asked? He frowned anxiously and looked at him—

"You did good," the Daegelus said with a smile, but his condescending tone hadn't withered. He stood up and leaned his hands onto the desk. "How many vampires are here now?"

"Nineteen out of vone 'undred and vifteen."

Damien nodded. "Good."

The vampire felt what could only be hope. Was Damien actually proud?

No, he wasn't. He never was.

The Daegelus scowled. "What have you been doing, Aleksei?" he asked skeptically.

Whatever Damien was asking, Alucard knew that he was already aware of the answer to that question. But what was he referring to? "V-vorking," he answered.

"Working? Alone?"

He nodded unsurely.

Damien sprung forward, grabbed Alucard's neck, and pinned him against the bookshelf. "What have I told you about trying to work by your miserable self?!" he yelled, his face a mere inch from Alucard's.

Alucard had no idea whether Damien was furious because he had people helping him with his personal business or if he had found out about the Diabolus incident. Whichever it was, the vampire's hope withered. Tonight would be the same as any other night Damien came to check up on him.

"I hear the Diabolus has been looking for you, Aleksei. I heard that someone was sent here to find you, and…you killed him. Is that right?"

How did he find out? The vampire stared vacantly into the Daegelus' furious eyes. "Yes."

"And you didn't think to tell me? To ask for *my* help? Instead, you thought you'd take it upon yourself to try and deal with it. How many times must I tell you how incompetent you are?" he hissed. He held up his left hand. "Once?" he asked, raising his index finger. "Twice?" he snarled with a scowl, raising his middle finger. "Or three times?" he growled, holding up three of his clawed fingers.

"I zidn't vant to bover you vith zhis," Alucard answered. "Vas only vone guy, zhere 'asn't been any—"

"Shut up!" Damien snarled as he abruptly pressed his three clawed fingers into the side of Alucard's face. "Even after I go out of my way to teach you these things, you continue to disobey me and lie to me. Surely you haven't forgotten what happened last time? And the time before, have you, Aleksei?" he asked, tilting his head to the side.

"No," Alucard answered as he grimaced while Damien's claws pierced his skin, making his blood trickling down his face.

The Daegelus laughed. "You've disappointed me yet again. It's a shame that you continue to fail me because you're doing well with this vampire mission. Are you only capable of moving back and forth? Is that all you have use for?"

"No," he replied again.

"I beg to differ. Don't you *dare* disobey me again," he growled, dragging his claws down the side of Alucard's face, leaving a trail of three deep, bloody gashes. "*I* protect you from Lucifer, *I* deal with the Diabolus, and *I* deal with the things you evidently cannot."

Grunting painfully as Damien's claws cut his face, Alucard held his eyes shut tightly. He was such a moron for thinking that he could deal with the Diabolus on his own. How pathetic of him to think he might be congratulated for his work. Once more, he disappointed Damien, and as always, he was suffering for it.

Pulling his claws from Alucard's bleeding face, Damien snarled and tightened his grip on his throat. "One day, you'll learn to thank me." Then slammed his fist into Alucard's stomach.

The vampire dropped to his knees, holding his hand over his gashed face. How did Damien find out about the Diabolus' contact? How did he know that Alucard was trying to deal with it alone? He'd been so discrete and careful, but the Daegelus still found out anyway.

Just then, a familiar panicked mumble caught his attention. He took his eyes off the floor and sharply turned his head in the direction the murmur had come from. Damien stood over by the windows, and Rodney's throat was so tight in the Daegelus' right hand that the man couldn't make a sound.

Dread smothered Alucard's face, unsure of what to say or what to do. If he moved or uttered a single word, Damien would injure him further, but if he didn't...then he knew what would happen.

"This is the delinquent who brought that Diabolus agent to your ship, is he not, Aleksei?"

The vampire nodded slowly.

"And...you *didn't* kill him?"

"N-no," Alucard answered. "Vas...not 'is vault."

"Not his fault?" Damien laughed condescendingly. "Aleksei, you can't let anything slide. Set an example. If they fuck up *once*, you kill them. Was that not one of the first lessons I taught you?!" he yelled. But then he scowled. "Or did you fail to do so…because this is…a friend?" he growled, glancing at Rodney's horrified face. "Are you letting personal feelings affect your judgement? What have I told you about friends? People will inevitably let you down; they will only ever use you—but not me. You only need me, Aleksei; do you think that you can rely on this?" he snarled, looking at Rodney again.

"It vasn't 'is fault," Alucard insisted.

"So you keep saying. I've told you enough times, Aleksei: you can't have friends, you won't experience any kind of caring or love—*I* give you everything you need, and this—" he said, glancing at Rodney again, "—is *not* that."

Alucard had no chance to intervene. Before he could respond, Damien ruthlessly snapped Rodney's neck. The life faded from his face in an instant, and as his body hit the floor, Alucard fell still, staring at him wide-eyed in disbelief.

Damien stormed over, grabbed Alucard's collar, and pinned him against the wall again. "Count yourself lucky I let you have allies; make sure they stay that way, or they'll all end up like that miserable human," he warned, glaring into Alucard's despondent eyes. He then grinned. "Do I make myself clear?"

With a sullen frown, Alucard nodded. "Yes," he replied, his voice shaky.

"Good. I'll look into the Diabolus for you. Concentrate on the task I have given you, and once it's done, don't forget that I have another lined up for you."

He nodded.

The Daegelus glanced at Rodney's lifeless body. "Look on the bright side, Aleksei. I brought you a snack," he said with a grin. Then, he let go of Alucard. As the vampire dropped to his knees again, Damien turned around, stepped over the corpse, and walked out onto the balcony.

And with a flash of blinding red light, the Daegelus vanished.

As soon as Damien was gone, Alucard hurried across the room to Rodney. He placed his hands around his neck, trying to see whether or not he was dead; it was possible that Damien's attack hadn't killed him, and he hoped so desperately that it hadn't. He'd lost too many people that the thought of someone else dying because of him hurt, but his subordinate had no pulse. He was gone, and there was nothing he could do.

He sat at Rodney's side as blood trickled down his face. Pain lingered throughout his entire body, and he was almost sure that it wasn't all from his physical injuries. As much as Alucard always denied it, Rodney *was* his friend. He cared about him, and because of that, he was now dead. How had Damien found out all of this? The Daegelus was always at least one step ahead of Alucard, and he feared that he'd never know how or why.

There was no escaping anything, was there? He'd never be able to live his life the way he wanted. He'd be under Damien's control forever; the Daegelus would never let him try to work independently, he'd never give him the chance to prove that he was capable of so much more than what everyone thought. He'd just continue disappointing Damien, wouldn't he?

Maybe he ought to stop trying to do his own things and do what the Daegelus wanted; that way, no one would get hurt. No one else would die because of him and his incompetence.

How many more people would die until Alucard accepted that he just couldn't get away from Damien? He felt like a moron—like a useless, insufferable idiot. Damien was right; he was always right. The people he worked with were and only ever would be his subordinates, nothing more. He couldn't be friends with them; he couldn't trust them not to let him down. He couldn't even trust himself. Once again, he tried to accomplish something alone and failed. Never again would he stray from Damien's rules.

Chapter Eighteen

⸺ ⟨ † ⟩ ⸺

The Unseen

| Elvin |

It had been over a week since Elvin saw Alucard; he went to his house the morning after he'd been to see that demon, but Alucard refused to see him, and Elvin didn't understand why. What happened? What could make him lock himself away like this?

He waited on the roadside near Alucard's manor, and when he set his hazel eyes on the rugged, scruffy man strolling up the path in a torn, dirty white shirt and ripped black jeans, he pouted. Tobias might be hard to bear sometimes, but he said he had news, and Elvin was convinced that might get Alucard out of his house.

Tobias grinned at him, holding his leather jacket over his shoulder. "Bard!" he called joyfully.

"Ugh," Elvin grumbled, and as the man pulled him into a forceful, tight hug, the bard squirmed and struggled to escape. He pulled away from Tobias and scowled as he straightened his waistcoat. "Don't ever do that again."

Tobias patted Elvin's head. "What? Is it wrong to embrace my friend? I ain't seen ya in a while," he said as they started walking towards Alucard's manor.

"You should be more concerned about Aleksei," Elvin said with a frown, looking up at Tobias. "No one's seen him since he got back from the last vampire pick-up ten days ago, and Rodney's gone, too. Aleksei *always* checks up on his vampires, but he hasn't done that, either."

Shrugging, Tobias smiled and suggested, "Maybe Rodney and Aleksei ran away together. Or better yet…what if he's seeing that new demon, huh? About time he got some action. Guy's always so uptight."

The bard scowled defensively. "First, Aleksei *hates* demons, so that's never going to happen. And as for Rodney, I think Aleksei sent him to do something; he's the only one who knows how to sail a ship, so he's probably overseas."

"Okay, but the ship's still in the docks," Tobias said, looking back over his shoulder in the direction of the castle.

"So? He probably took a different one. That's one of Aleksei's personal ships; it only sails if he's on board."

"True," Tobias said with a sigh, staring ahead as they came closer to the manor. "Well, whatever he's doing, I've got some shit he's gonna wanna hear."

Elvin followed him into the gardens once the huge man pushed the gates open. "Such as?" he asked curiously.

Tobias smirked. "Werewolf business, dude."

They reached the front door expecting to see Sergiu somewhere on the property, but there was no sign of the groundskeeper. Had Alucard sent him away too?

Elvin knocked on the door, fidgeting anxiously while he waited for the vampire to answer. He *knew* something was wrong, and he needed to find out what. But after a few moments of silence, he frowned and knocked again—louder this time.

The werewolf sighed and shrugged. "Dude, I don't think he's here."

"No, he *is*," Elvin insisted, knocking again. "He's just being difficult."

"Right," Tobias muttered, stepping out from the porch. He glanced up at the balcony connected to Alucard's study. "Place looks lifeless, dude."

"He's here!" the bard insisted, knocking once more.

"Ain't you got a key?" Tobias asked, raising his eyebrow. "If you're sure he's here, just go in—you usually do."

If it were under any other circumstances, Elvin would do that. But he knew what happened to Alucard when he didn't feed; he didn't want to risk walking in uninvited and becoming a snack. If Alucard didn't answer after his next few knocks, though, he'd crack. He *did* have a key, and he wasn't alone. If the vampire *did* attack unintentionally, he trusted Tobias to stop him.

He sighed and tapped his knuckles on the door. "I'd rather knock. I don't wanna go in there and make him mad."

Tobias shrugged. "All right, well, good luck with that," he mumbled. He stepped back towards the fountain and glared at each of the manor's windows. All the curtains were closed, but that didn't stop him from yelling, "Aleksei! You in there?"

"Don't yell!"

Rolling his eyes, Tobias huffed irritably and kept shouting, "I got news I kinda need to tell ya. I ain't gonna stand out here all day, so, if you wanna hear it, you kinda need to open your door…let us in, you know…."

There was no response.

Elvin scowled. "Do you just like being loud?"

"Only way to be noticed sometimes," he said. He moved his hands to his face, placing them on either side of his mouth to amplify his voice. "Vu—"

The door clicked loudly and unlocked, startling them both. Alucard aggressively pulled it open and set his fiery eyes on them. He stood in the doorway, dressed in a white shirt and black trousers, and an exhausted, aggravated look clung to his paler-than-usual face. The right shoulder of his shirt was stained with drops of blood and faint but noticeable bruises wrapped around his neck.

Elvin frowned in horror. "Oh, my God, Aleksei! What happened?!"

Alucard snarled at the bard before he could move closer to try and comfort him.

He knew better than to step over Alucard's boundaries, so Elvin stood there in silence and tried to work out who or what did that to him.

Tobias waved and smiled. "Sup, Aleksei."

"Vhat do you vant?" the vampire snarled harshly.

Elvin couldn't keep quiet for long. "What happened?" he questioned, noticing the weakly-healed gashes on the right side of Alucard's face before the vampire could move his scruffy, un-brushed hair over them in an attempt to conceal them. The rather ghastly scabbed scars stretched from his jaw to his temple, and the blood on his shirt was clearly from the healing wounds. Who could have done this to him?

Ignoring him, Alucard then set his eyes on Tobias as his iris' slowly faded from fiery red to ice blue in response to the sunlight creeping into his almost gloomy entrance hall. He scowled and sighed impatiently. "Vhat are you 'ere vor?"

"Got updates for you," Tobias said, moving closer.

"Tell me," Alucard grumbled, turning his head to the side to hide his scars.

"Did your demon friend do that?" Elvin scowled.

Alucard deadpanned. "No." He then set his eyes back on Tobias. "Vell?"

Tobias cleared his throat and scratched the back of his head. "Uh…yeah, so, nothing on the Diabolus; we ain't seen or heard nothing. We'll keep patrolling the borders though, keep our ears to the ground. Werewolves, though, that's another story."

"Was it a werewolf?" Elvin questioned, gawping at Alucard's face.

"Vhat's going on vith zhem?" Alucard asked, ignoring the bard.

"So, turns out that wolf who tried to eat Elvin was part of the West Pack before it went rogue and joined the Amarok. That thing was apparently recruiting from all the surrounding packs to try and create some sort of like…vampire-killer pack. *And* the West Pack has been meeting *a lot* with the North Pack. We thought something was going on, like a treaty or something—maybe they're working together to try and take you out, you know? So, we tried to investigate, but my guy got sniffed out, and he ain't come back yet. Girl that went with him said he was captured, and she didn't get any info from their observation."

Alucard sighed lazily and grabbed the door, preparing to close it. "I 'ave ozzer matters to deal vith virst; I'll look into zhat eventually. And cease zhe Diabolus investigation; zoesn't matter anymore."

Before Alucard could shut the door, Tobias placed his hand on it and frowned. "Dude, what's wrong with you? You get smacked up a bit, and then you give up?" He scoffed and shook his head. "You've been working on this shit with the wolves for ages, and now that something's going on, you're not gonna do anything about it? And the Diabolu: are you fucking with me? They're looking for you; why would you want us to stop keeping an eye out for them?"

Irritated, Alucard scowled in hostility and glared at the werewolf—

"What happened, man?" Tobias asked with a concerned frown. "Elvin said something was up, and he's clearly right. It ain't like you to lock yourself away. You should already be out there looking for the wolves I just told you about. And *that* wasn't a werewolf," he said, pointing at Alucard's face. "Who had a go at you? Looks either demon or vampire to me."

"I knew it!" Elvin exclaimed, but both Alucard and Tobias ignored him. *Of course* it was that demon! But then he was hit with guilt. He'd joked about Alucard dating and being friends with Zalith; he had no idea that they hated each other so much that something like this would happen. It broke his heart a little. Alucard was so traumatized by it that he'd not only shut himself away, but he was also dismissing the werewolves *and* the Diabolus.

"Is none of your business," Alucard snarled at Tobias. "You told me vhat you needed to tell me, now go avay. I 'ave shit to do."

"It *is* my business," Tobias argued. "I don't go around letting people hurt my friends, Aleksei. Tell me which fucker did it, and I'll tear his face off," he growled, cracking his knuckles.

Alucard tried to close the door—

"Hey!" Elvin yelled as Tobias tried to keep the vampire from closing it. "We're not leaving until you give us something!" he insisted. He was ready to fight for him, and if he had to find that demon and give him a piece of his mind, then he would…so long as someone was there to protect him. "When are you gonna stop thinking that you gotta deal with everything on your own? Let us help you!"

Alucard then pulled the door open, and as Tobias fell forward and hit the floor, the vampire snarled aggressively. "Get out of my 'ouse," he warned. "I zon't need anyvone's 'elp—I never 'ave and never vill."

The werewolf scrambled to his feet and scowled irritably. "Whatever, dude. If you wanna sit around here and sulk on your own, suit yourself. I have shit to do too; sorry I bothered you with my friendship," he grumbled, turning around. "Come on, bard. Let's go."

But Elvin didn't follow Tobias. Instead, he set his worried gaze on Alucard. "Please tell me what happened. You can't just lock yourself away in here forever; you can't give up on everything. The Diabolus and the treaty…. That treaty means so much to you."

Glaring at him, Alucard seemed to hesitate. Elvin waited, wondering if he'd gotten through to him. But to his disappointment, the vampire grunted quietly.

"Go 'ome," he grumbled and then slammed the door in Elvin's face.

"Aleksei!" Elvin shouted, knocking on his door, but as he heard the locks clicking, he frowned despondently. He didn't know what more to say or do. He didn't want to pressure Alucard or annoy him or upset him any more than he evidently already was. He wanted to be there for him… but how could he do that if Alucard kept pushing him away?

He wasn't wanted here, and as his heart started to ache, he turned around and began heading towards the gates. He'd try again tomorrow.

| **Alucard** |

Alucard stood with his back against his door. He huffed in both frustration and dismay as the wounds on the side of his face throbbed. He still felt ashamed, useless, and worthless, and he didn't want the people who worked for him to see him like this.

If his subordinates saw he'd been hurt, they might think less of him, and that was the last thing he needed right now. He needed his allies to continue doing their jobs, and he wanted to avoid unnecessary attention like that which he was currently getting from Elvin. Tobias gave up, to his relief, but he knew the bard well enough to know that he wouldn't back down as easily. At least he knew that Tobias nor Elvin would spread the news of his injury, so he was glad that it had been them who found him like this.

He glanced at the mirror to his right and watched his reflection dissolve on his command. It was at times like these that he was glad he didn't have to see himself unless he wanted to. He didn't want to look at the results of his failure to impress Damien. However, he didn't resent his punishment. He knew that he deserved it. He *was* foolish to try and work alone against Lucifer's cultists. Damien was helping him hide from them, and Damien was the only one he could ever rely on to keep him safe, right?

However, despite how much Damien tried to convince him that the work he was doing in Dor-Sanguis was pointless, and as much as the Daegelus tried to get him to give up on it, Alucard still remained loyal to his arrangements. Yes, he worked for Damien, and he would always abide whenever he was called, but in his spare time, he still wanted to continue what he was doing for his people. The Daegelus hadn't ordered him to stop working with the vampires and humans; he just said that he couldn't deal with the *Diabolus* alone. So, he'd stop the operation involving the cult, but he wouldn't stop his work with the city. It was finally safe for vampires to walk among humans, and he'd make sure it stayed that way.

Tobias was right. Elvin was right. He still had to keep the werewolves at bay and away from the humans, and he couldn't do that if he remained locked away in the dark. Tobias told him that two packs were possibly forming a pact, so he'd have to head out and investigate.

First, though: Elvin. As much as he wanted to be alone, he couldn't deny the fact that having someone else around might help him climb out of the depravity which gripped him since Rodney's death. Although the bard was annoying and talked too much, he did have a way of making Alucard feel somewhat relevant; Elvin made him feel a little less worthless than he knew he was. He wasn't sure whether he was allowed to recover—Damien often forced him to suffer in silence for weeks following a punishment—but how would Damien know what he was feeling?

He also knew that nothing awful would come of him spending time with Elvin. Damien was convinced that the bard was nothing but entertainment for him, so inviting him in wouldn't anger the Daegelus.

So, he unlocked his door and peered outside. Elvin was heading for the gates, but he obviously heard the locks click; he looked over his shoulder, and as he spotted Alucard, his despondent face lit up.

Swiftly, Elvin hurried towards him like a dog called for dinner. "I knew you'd come around," he said, and as Alucard stepped aside, the bard strutted into his house.

With a roll of his eyes, Alucard sighed and pulled the door shut. He hoped he wasn't about to regret this.

Chapter Nineteen

— ‹ † › —

Oversight

| **Elvin** |

As he followed Alucard into the lounge, Elvin asked, "What happened?"

Alucard slumped down in his usual spot. "You vanted to know about verevolves, vight?" he mumbled, watching the bard as he sat in the armchair opposite him.

Elvin frowned unsurely; the vampire was avoiding his questions, and he must be incredibly reluctant to tell him if he was going to offer a lecture instead of answering. Either that or Alucard just wanted to have a conversation that didn't involve his work or what happened to him. And Elvin was more than happy to comply. If this would help his friend to feel better, then he'd do as Alucard wanted.

He nodded and pulled out his notebook. "Yeah, if you don't mind."

"Vhere do you vant me to start?"

"Well… Tobias mentioned packs; tell me how packs work," he requested, preparing to write whatever Alucard would tell him.

The vampire stared vacantly into the empty fireplace for a few moments. He then sighed and glanced at the bard. "Zhere is… alvays an Alpha," he said with a shrug.

Elvin already knew that, but he pretended to write it down anyway.

"And… Betas."

He fake-wrote that, too.

"Zhey… vollow zhe Alpha."

With a sympathetic sigh, Elvin placed his pencil down. He'd never felt so sorry and worried before. He wanted to know what happened, he wanted to know who hurt him, and he wanted to know what he could do—if anything—to help Alucard. But he had to be cautious. Alucard was extremely volatile, and he didn't want to say something that would upset or enrage him.

He stood up and moved over to the couch, and as the vampire glanced unsurely at him, he sat beside him and placed his notebook in his lap. "Aleksei…you know, sometimes, talking about what happened can help you feel better. I'm always here for you, and…if you need to talk, then…I'm here to listen—I always listen."

"To vrite down and turn into a storybook," he grumbled, setting his eyes back on the fireplace.

Was that why Alucard never spoke about his feelings or his personal thoughts? Did he think that Elvin only wanted to know so that he could include it in his manuscript? That wasn't the case at all, and he needed to get Alucard to understand that. The vampire was clearly distressed, and Elvin wanted to be the person Alucard chose to lean on; as far as he knew, Alucard had *no one* to lean on, and no one to talk to when he was depressed or stressed out. He cared *so* much about Alucard, and he had to do what he could to let him know that he could rely on him.

He frowned and tucked his notebook away. "I don't wanna know so I can write it down. I wanna know because I'm worried about you."

Alucard scowled uncomfortably, shifting his sights to glare at the bard.

Elvin shuffled closer. "I'm always worried about you because…I care, you know. I get that you might not really think that I do, or…something. Yeah, you're this four hundred whatever old vampire lord, and I'm just some twenty-four-year-old human. But you mean a lot to me, Aleksei, and not just because you saved me from ending up on the streets. You're…important to me, and someone hurt you, and…it makes me sad."

"No vone 'urt me," Alucard denied, looking away. "Go back to your book."

The bard frowned despondently, looking down at his lap. Did Alucard not understand what he was trying to say? How bluntly did he have to put it? Did he even want to try to get him to see just how much he cared? He looked over at the front door, pondering to himself for a few moments. He'd never met someone as difficult as this vampire, but he wasn't going to give up on him. He'd *never* give up on him.

He looked back at Alucard. "Well, I meant what I said; if you ever wanna talk about it or anything, then…I'm here for you," he said, nervously raising his left hand and placing it on Alucard's arm.

However, Alucard instantly pulled his arm away and sharply turned his head to glare at him. "Zon't touch me," he snarled defensively. "I zidn't say you could touch me."

Pulling his hands into his lap, Elvin tensed up and frowned sadly. "I'm sorry. I was just trying to comfort you."

"Go back over zhere," Alucard mumbled, nodding at the armchair.

Both embarrassed and ashamed that his attempt to get Alucard to understand failed, Elvin stood up and dragged himself back to the armchair. He slumped down and stared vacantly at the floor, unsure of what else he could say or do. But he didn't want an awkward silence to fall over them. So, after a few moments, he glanced at the vampire. "So…what are you gonna do about the werewolves Tobias told you about?"

Alucard sighed. "I'll get somevone to investigate."

"I thought you'd look into this wolf stuff."

"I'm busy," he muttered.

"Doing what? Sitting out here, doing—"

"I'm busy!" he snapped.

"Okay, sheesh…I was just saying." His embarrassment withered into confliction. He didn't want to fight with Alucard, so he tried his best to hold his tongue.

Alucard snarled and glared into the empty fireplace.

"What about…the next meeting?" Elvin asked. "You're still going, right? To see that demon."

"I zon't 'ave a choice."

The bard frowned worriedly and glanced around the room. Why didn't Alucard have a choice? He certainly had one with all of his other business; what was so different about this vampire transferal stuff? He didn't know much about it, nor did he know much about the demon Alucard had to see, but after what just happened, Elvin began to suspect that there was more to the arrangement than business.

Elvin thought hard about it. He hated to admit it to himself, but there was a part of him that *hoped* he was right about Zalith scratching Alucard's face. He *wanted* them to hate each other. But the way Alucard ranted about how much he despised Zalith made Elvin think that he actually liked him. Alucard never rambled about hating someone; that was one of the many feelings Alucard kept to himself.

Not only that, but Alucard also just harshly dismissed his attempt to get closer to him. He wondered…was he right to assume that there was more to this demon than Alucard tried to make him think? Or could Tobias be right about Rodney? He mysteriously disappeared, and Alucard was obviously deeply upset and hurt. Could something have happened between *them*?

He frowned as angst began enthralling his aching heart. No, he couldn't see that; he couldn't see Alucard and Rodney—he couldn't see Alucard with *anyone*. So what was he missing?

Elvin stared at Alucard. "Where's Rodney? Did…something happen with you two?"

Despondency smothered Alucard's once irritated face. He ignored the bard, clearly hoping that he'd drop it and move on to something else like he always would if he remained silent for so long.

But Elvin's interest was far more than curiosity. It was personal. If something had been going on between Rodney and Alucard, he wanted to know. He frowned once again. "Aleksei?" he asked sternly. "What happened? I know Rodney was involved; he wouldn't just disappear the same night you got these injuries."

The vampire gritted his teeth in anger and glared at him. "Vhat do you vant vrom me? I zidn't invite you in 'ere so you could question me; I invited you to talk about verevolves."

"I don't wanna know about werewolves. I wanna know what happened to Rodney—and what happened to you."

Rolling his eyes, Alucard glared down at his hand as he rested it on the couch's arm. "I told you: noving 'appened."

"Then why hasn't *anyone* seen Rodney since the night you came back from seeing that demon? Why—"

"I killed 'im, Elvin," he snarled, glaring at him, and as a look of disbelief smothered the bard's face, Alucard scowled in confliction. "I ended 'is life because 'e vailed to abide by zhe vules. Vodney is dead, as anyvone else who breaks zhe rules vill be. I told you not to question me, and I told you zhat you are *not* my vriend. Zon't try to convince me vith someving as ridiculous as care. You vork vor me, zhat is all. You zon't get to care."

Utterly shaken by the revelation, Elvin anxiously gripped his waistcoat. He didn't know how to take what Alucard said; did he really kill Rodney? He frowned, trying to wrap his head around everything he heard. "Rodney's…dead?" he asked, disregarding the rest of the vampire's statement.

"Zhat's vhat I said."

"But…why? You don't…you don't kill people, Aleksei. I…I don't under—"

"Vhat zon't you understand?" He scowled condescendingly at him. "I killed 'im, end of."

Elvin shook his head. "I know when you're lying, Aleksei. You can't fool me. Whoever did that to you, *they* killed Rodney, didn't they?"

An uncomfortable expression warped Alucard's face. He didn't answer.

The bard wouldn't give up. He'd never managed to get an answer out of Alucard regarding his personal affairs, life, and feelings, but this time, he could tell from the look on the vampire's face that his assessment was right. Whoever clawed up Alucard's face, and whoever left those bruises on his neck, had killed Rodney. He didn't understand why Alucard refused to tell him who had done it; the only person who came to mind was the demon Alucard had been seeing.

Elvin tried again. "Why won't you tell me what happened?"

"Because zoesn't matter. If you ask me vone more time, I'll vind myselv a new bard."

He then scowled as his patience started slipping away. "What did you do with Rodney? Did whoever did that to you take him?"

Alucard then stood up. "Leave me alone, Elvin," he mumbled with a despondent look on his face.

The bard scoffed in confusion. "I thought you wanted me here."

"I did until you started annoying me," he snarled. "Leave."

Slowly climbing to his feet, Elvin frowned sadly. He meant to help Alucard, but it seemed as though he hadn't done that at all; it looked like he'd made him angrier. All he wanted to do was be there for him, but he didn't feel as though he was getting through to him.

Would he give up, though? No. He cared far too much about Alucard, and as difficult as it was obviously going to be, he'd do whatever he could to get Alucard to understand how he felt. Whatever happened to him, he felt as though Alucard would tell him one day. He always told him everything eventually… didn't he?

He sighed and started to make his way over to the door as Alucard left the lounge, disappearing deeper into his dark house. Elvin wasn't sure when he'd next see him; Alucard was obviously dealing with a lot, and the bard was sure he might not leave his home until the scars on his face had completely vanished. He still wanted to know who did it, and he still highly suspected the demon he had been seeing.

Elvin left the house and headed home. Would Alucard ever understand, though? He worried about the vampire so much that it hurt. How was he supposed to get Alucard, someone who seemed to lack every emotion other than anger and sadness, that he had these feelings? He didn't know, but he had to keep trying. He had to get him to see—he *would* get him to see. It was just going to take time.

A lot of time.

Chapter Twenty

— ⸴ ✝ ⸳ —

A New Sailor

| Alucard |

Alucard stood in his entrance hall and slowly pulled his blazer on. Soon, he'd have to head to the portal and meet Zalith again.

He hadn't worked out who would sail the ship; Rodney was gone, and he wasn't sure that there was anyone among his people who knew how to do his job. He felt like an idiot for not sorting something out sooner, but he didn't want to leave his house or see anyone. He didn't even want to go now, but he had no choice.

The scars on his face had healed a little more over the past few days, but they were still noticeable. A little pain still lingered, but he did his best to ignore it. They weren't the first injuries Damien had left him with, and he'd become accustomed to just how painful they were. But he couldn't hide them as well as he could ignore them, and he was almost certain that someone was going to point them out tonight.

He made sure his sword's sheath was fastened to his side, checked that the gun holsters inside his blazer were secure—as well as the weapons in them—and started to tie the buttons, concealing them inside. Then, he grabbed his cape from the table and pulled it over his shoulders.

Would Ben know how to sail a ship? Felix? Tobias? He didn't have time to find the wolf, nor did he have the patience to put up with Felix, so all he could do was ask and hope that Ben knew how to do Rodney's job. Or perhaps… Sergiu? Alucard already had Ben doing so much; he didn't want to lumber yet another job on him.

He opened the door and stepped outside into the cold of dusk. The six moons made their way into the darkening sky, and a bitter wind raced by, clawing at Alucard's skin. He scoured the gardens with his hell-fiery eyes, and when he set them on the groundskeeper, who was tending to Sebastian, Alucard pulled the door shut behind him and headed over to Sergiu. He watched as the man vacantly and silently tended to the horse. If there was one thing Alucard liked about this groundskeeper, it was that he hardly ever spoke.

"Sergiu," he mumbled, stopping a few feet away from him.

The groundskeeper took his olive-green eyes off the horse and looked at Alucard. "Yes, sir?" he asked humbly.

"Do you know 'ow to sail a ship?"

Sergiu slipped the horse brush into his pocket and frowned slightly. "As a matter of fact, yes, I do, sir. Do you require me to do so?"

How miraculous. Alucard nodded. "*Da*," he said, grabbing Sergiu's wrist. Then, before the groundskeeper could question him, Alucard disappeared into vermillion smoke, pulling Sergiu with him as he sped up into the sky and raced towards the deserted docks.

As soon as he landed on the ship's deck, he let Sergiu go and sighed irritably. "Ve need to go now," he ordered, waiting for the groundskeeper to work out where he was.

"Where is it that we are heading, sir?" Sergiu asked, straightening his coat.

"Drac knows zhe vay; I just need you to do vhatever…you do," he said, waving his hand towards the ropes that kept the ship tied to the docks.

The groundskeeper did as he was asked; he hurried down onto the dock and started untying the ropes.

Alucard waited, watching as Sergiu made his way back up onto the ship and pulled the bridge onto the deck before closing the gate. He then looked over at Alucard. Of course, Sergiu didn't know how to command the dragon below, so Alucard was going to have to do that part himself. He moved to the edge of the ship and tapped the fence; he stared despondently as the multi-blue coloured dragon emerged from the ocean, setting its four, shimmering yellow eyes on him.

He smiled weakly. "What 'ave you been doing?"

The dragon responded with several low grumbles and rhythmic chirps, tilting its head as it noticed the scars on the right side of Alucard's face. It moved closer, and a confused look appeared on its face as it clicked quietly in response to Alucard's attempt to conceal the scars with his hair.

"Vas a volf; zhose vings you've decided to stop eating," he said with a smirk.

Drac snarled and chirped irritably.

"Ve need to go to zhe island again," Alucard then requested.

But the dragon frowned and set its eyes on Sergiu. Drac growled, looking back down at Alucard, but as the vampire shook his head, the dragon pouted as it chirped in response to the vampire's answer. Then, he descended back into the water, preparing to guide the ship to its destination.

Sergiu watched Alucard as he disappeared into the cabin, and when the ship started moving, the groundskeeper decided to follow him. He stepped into the room, observing Alucard as he sat down and rested his legs on the table.

"If you need anything else of me, sir, I will be above," he said.

"Vonce ve get back, I need you to look vor a new sailor vor me. Vodney is no longer avound."

He nodded. "Of course, sir." Then, he left the room.

Alucard was so used to being asked questions that it felt rather strange not being asked where Rodney was or why a new sailor was required. But Sergiu was paid to keep quiet, so that was obviously what he was going to do.

The vampire sighed and stared down at his lap, listening to the waves crashing against the ship. Once he got to the island, he'd make his way through the portal, he'd meet Zalith as he always did, he'd pick up the vampires, and then he'd return with them. The same as it had been from the start.

What would irritate him this time? Would the vampires start unnecessary tension? Would that demon laugh and smile at things that weren't funny? Something was always bound to happen, whether it be because of Zalith or the vampires; Alucard was prepared for some sort of annoying situation.

However, he did find himself hoping that Zalith might entertain him again. He felt as though Zalith might be the only person he could stand to be in the company of right now. That demon wouldn't ask him stupid questions, nor would he pry into his business—unless he was ordered to again. And somehow, Zalith had a funny way of making Alucard feel humoured; although it often annoyed him, he couldn't deny that Zalith was somewhat…amusing. But then he scowled. Zalith was still irritating, and there was no doubt he'd keep finding new ways to aggravate Alucard.

He pulled his legs from the desk and leaned his arms onto it, staring through the door ahead, watching as they travelled forward. He soon started to think about Elvin, too. Clearly, the bard tried to help him, but Alucard didn't want anyone's help, and that was another reason he felt much calmer knowing he was going to see Zalith and not anyone else. The demon didn't try to help him, nor did he try to get him to talk about things he just didn't want to.

Alucard scowled again, realizing that his thoughts had so easily drifted from Elvin to the demon.

Elvin: why did he want to know what happened? Why did he always hound him for answers? And why this time had the bard decided it was necessary to put his hands on him? Alucard had no idea; all he knew was that it made him uncomfortable, and he'd make sure Elvin knew not to do it again. He was sure that Elvin only wanted to know what happened so that he could include it in the book he was working on, and Alucard wasn't at all interested in allowing his personal thoughts and feelings to be printed on paper. Elvin was supposed to be writing about his feats, not his personal affairs and private life.

Sighing, he stared down at the desk. He felt bad for sending Elvin away the way he had, but he hated when the bard tried to pry. Alucard wasn't going to tell anyone what happened; how could he? He couldn't let the people who worked for him think he was weak.

Was that what Damien wanted? It was possible. But Alucard scowled at the thought of Damien. He didn't want to think about him. He had work to do.

As he glared back out of the door, he watched the island come into view. Would Zalith ask about his face? He hoped not. With a sullen frown, he dragged his fingers over the faint but noticeable raised scars that stretched down from his right temple to his jaw. He wasn't sure how much longer it would take for them to completely fade, but injuries inflicted by Damien often remained on his body for at least a month whether he fed or not, and he hated that. Was hating it unjustified, though? He deserved what he got, and he accepted it, so he should, in turn, accept the marks he was left with.

The ship then started to slow. He took his hand off his face, stood up, and made his way out onto the deck.

"Will I be waiting here for you, sir?" Sergiu called from the quarterdeck.

Alucard took his eyes off the island ahead and looked up at him. "*Da,*" he confirmed.

Nodding, the groundskeeper walked down to the deck and started preparing to dock the ship. He stood beside Alucard and frowned in concern. "Might I ask, sir, what happened to—"

Before the groundskeeper could finish asking his question, Alucard snarled and dematerialized.

He rematerialized on the island and stormed over to the portal; even the guy he paid to keep his mouth shut couldn't keep himself from asking about his wounds, and that made him believe that Zalith was also likely to ask. He didn't care. Whoever asked, he'd just ignore them the same way he ignored Elvin and Sergiu.

With an irritated sigh, he stepped into the portal and tried to ready himself for what might be waiting on the other side.

Chapter Twenty-One

— ⸲ † ⸲ —

Ambush

| Alucard |

Alucard stood in the empty, corroded hallway for a moment. The portal always made him feel uncomfortably sick, and this time, he thought he might throw up; his head was spinning, and his body was aching, but he scowled and refused to give in.

He made his way towards the hall. When he reached the doorway, he stopped and hesitated. He could hear the vampires conversing inside, and he was sure that Zalith would be standing in the same spot he always stood in by himself. It was only recently that he felt as though he and Zalith were getting along, and he started to believe that the demon didn't think badly of him. But if he were to show his face, would that change? If Zalith were to see he'd been hurt—if he saw the ugly scars on his face—would that destroy what felt like a growing friendship?

Why did that thought even possess him? Why did he care? He shouldn't care what that demon thought of him; he was just some guy Damien had him working with, wasn't he?

He rolled his eyes and stepped into the room. There Zalith was…standing by the back wall in an all-black suit. The same vacant look lingered on his face, but Alucard knew he'd be greeted with an annoying smile or the question he didn't want the demon to ask.

There was no avoiding it, though. He wandered over, and as he got closer, Zalith set his sights on Alucard. Unwelcomed angst gripped hold of the vampire as he waited to hear whatever Zalith was about to say.

A pleasant smile appeared on Zalith's once emotionless face. "There you are."

"I 'ad a mis'ap vith my sailor."

Keeping his eyes on the vampire as he stopped beside him, Zalith instantly noticed the three scars on the side of his face. "What happened to your pretty face?"

Alucard scowled at him. "Zon't call me zhat."

Zalith scoffed amusedly. "Okay, what happened to your *handsome* face?"

"Zhat's not vhat I meant," Alucard grumbled as he looked away, pouting.

The demon smirked in response.

Alucard *hated* it when he said such preposterous things. Pretty? Handsome? Who did this demon think he was? He scowled, glaring at the wall, trying to keep himself from becoming too agitated. But this demon always made him feel annoyed. Why would he say those things? What did he want? Did he just want to see him react? Of course he did. Zalith said those things to annoy him; he clearly found joy in doing so.

The vampire glanced at him and scowled in revolt when he noticed the sly smirk on his face.

But the silence made him feel despondent, and it outweighed his irritancy. He didn't want their once-in-a-fortnight interaction to end so quickly and on such an ungratifying note. And, as he thought about it, he wasn't actually annoyed that Zalith asked about his face; he was more bothered by the fact that he called him pretty like he was some woman.

As he thought about giving him an answer, he felt no hesitation or resentment. Did he actually *want* to tell someone? And of all people, was that someone *really* Zalith?

He frowned and lied, "Vas…verevolf."

Zalith looked like he was pondering…but as Alucard scowled expectantly, he smiled and said, "There are twelve this time; I thought I would bring one of the larger groups. I hope that's okay."

Pouting, Alucard looked away. "Vhatever."

"If that's too much for you, then you don't have to take them all. We all appreciate what you're doing, and if there's any way I can make this easier on you, then do let me know."

Still keeping his face turned away from the demon, Alucard frowned in confusion. Was Zalith offering him leniency? Why? He didn't deserve to have this job made easier—it was a job, and it should be done the way Damien told him to do it. He had to stick to the plan. Why would Zalith, of all people—and of all creatures, why would a *demon* be offering him compassion? It didn't make sense. Why was he offering to give Alucard more time when he initially tried to have it all done in a month?

He glanced at Zalith from the corner of his eye. That stupid smile was stuck to his face. Of course it was. Was he just playing with him? Was he waiting for him to thank him and then shatter his relief because it was funny? He wasn't sure, but Zalith was a demon, and Alucard knew too well that demons loved playing with people and their emotions. So, he scowled and turned to face him, but when Zalith looked directly at him, his anger withered.

Zalith smiled. "Is everything okay?"

The vampire looked away again. "Yes," he answered irritably.

With a single nod, Zalith looked back at the vampires. "And how are the others doing?"

Alucard shrugged. "Zhey are vine. Zhey 'ave Ben looking avter zhem."

"How is Ben?"

"Vine. 'E 'as two jobs now—vell…'ad. Zon't ask me about zhem," he snarled.

"I assume they're giving you no trouble?"

"No," Alucard answered. "Zhey are surprisingly okay vith zhis whole velocation ving, and zhey are abiding by zhe vules, too."

"Good"

The vampire then frowned. "You and Ben: are you…vriends?" he asked, curious about their relationship. He saw Zalith hug and kiss Ben before they parted ways; Zalith seemed concerned about how Ben was doing, and Alucard was almost certain that they had some sort of relationship—something deeper than friendship. But Ben was married. Why did Alucard even care? Why was he curious? He didn't know; all he knew was that he'd like to know how close they were.

Zalith smirked curiously. "Why do you want to know, vampire?" he asked with an unseemly tone.

Alucard rolled his eyes. "I zon't."

The demon frowned. "Obviously you do, or you wouldn't have just asked."

"I *vanted* to know bevore you decided to make zhis a joke," he snarled.

Zalith scoffed. "Where did I suggest that it was a joke?"

The vampire scowled skeptically.

Staring back, Zalith gained his own skeptical glare, and a devious smirk started creeping across his face—

Before either of them could comprehend, the back wall erupted with a deafening *boom!* Nobody had time to evade the storm of rubble and shrapnel; the vampires were blown off their feet and across the room, as were Zalith and Alucard.

Alucard's back hit the wall. Pain surged through his entire body, and as he gripped the large wooden splinter that impaled his left side, he grunted. His own injury didn't concern him, though; he took his eyes off the splinter—which had clearly come from one of the hall's benches—and stared ahead. He couldn't see through the smoke and dust, but he could hear the panicked calls and pained whines of the vampires.

He had no idea what was going on. It was all so sudden. The area around him abruptly filled with the sound of at least twenty beating hearts, and that could only mean they had company. But who?

The vampire had no time to speculate; he only had time to look at the facts: they had been attacked, and whoever attacked them was using ethos to hide from detection. Both he and Zalith would have been able to sense them coming otherwise.

Where *was* Zalith? Pulling the splinter from his side, he groaned painfully and stumbled forward, looking around frantically, searching for either Zalith or their ambushers.

Through the dust and the smoke, he heard slashing, yelling, and charging ethos attacks. Whoever had come was well equipped, and he could only assume they were there to kill the vampires…or Zalith. This was Zalith's world, after all, and none of Alucard's enemies would know he was there.

Just then, a familiar, irritated snarl snatched his attention. He sharply turned his head and set his eyes on what he could barely make out of Zalith; through the dust and smoke, he watched the demon stumble to his feet, brushing the dust from his suit and pulling a small shard of wood from his arm.

Zalith would know what was going on, wouldn't he? Alucard wanted answers *now*. He clenched his fists in anger, storming towards him, but the distinct sound of charging ethos then gripped his attention. He stopped in his path, sharply turning his head to glare into the smoke, and as he caught sight of the red-black glow of a demon-repelling incantation, he understood that these attackers had surely come for Zalith. Why else would they be using demon-repelling ethos in a room full of vampires?

However, Zalith would have no time to see it nor evade it—he wasn't even fully on his feet yet, and if Alucard wanted answers, he had no choice but to make sure that attack didn't hit Zalith. Was that his reason? Or did the thought of Zalith suffering fatal injuries worry him? He didn't know; all he knew was that he was about to risk his own life for someone he barely knew—someone he didn't want to cease knowing just yet.

Alucard hurried forward. The fire-like projectile of red and black sizzling energy burst through the dust at light speed, and without hesitation, the vampire moved in front of the demon just in time to take the hit in his place.

He felt overwhelming pain as the ethos collided with him; the force of the attack slung him back against the wall, and when he hit the floor, he held his right hand against his chest, which became ensnared in agony. He felt the hostile ethos grip hold of his own, feeding off it like a leech, draining his strength before he had a chance to try and resist.

In just moments, Alucard was renounced of his ethos. It hurt like hell; his body stopped healing, blood oozed from the half-healed wound on his left side, and as he gritted his teeth in struggle, he tried his best not to utter a sound. He was left with barely a whisper of ethos, but that was all he would need.

Despite his pain, it seemed to relieve him knowing that Zalith wasn't suffering in his place. This was, after all, a demon-subjugating ethos, and if it had hit Zalith, he'd most likely be unconscious and useless. Alucard was glad knowing that he wouldn't be fighting the attackers alone, and he was also pleased that he'd have a chance to show this insufferable demon that he was more than what he would call a pretty face.

Alucard climbed to his feet with an irritated snarl, pulling off his cape—that was the last thing he wanted to risk getting damaged in battle. He threw it out into the hallway and prepared to fight. He watched as Zalith sprang into action, heading towards the fight…and without so much as a thank you. The vampire rolled his eyes. There wasn't time for him to be mad.

The smoke cleared enough for him to see every enemy and civilian. Half the roof had caved in, and the entire back wall was missing. The soldier-like armoured men wielded weapons made of what looked like platinum, the strange blue tint flickering off the silver made that obvious. However, it was the crimson-robed ethos wielders who made Alucard wary, and clearly, Zalith was highly concerned too as the robed men were the first people he targeted.

Alucard watched as Zalith raised all manner of hell; white fire burst through the wrecked hall floorboards on his command, scorching two of the ethos attackers who stood in a shimmering magic circle, unable to get another attack off in time.

The vampire pouted. He wished he could use his own ethos. But he wasn't useless. If anything, he preferred to use his hands and weapons—where was the fun in standing back and watching from a distance?

He disappeared into vermillion smoke and reappeared behind one of the armoured men, who was just about to stab a wooden stake into a vampire he impaled previously with his sword. Alucard wasn't going to let that happen. He gripped the man's arm, snapped it clean off his body, and sunk his fangs into his neck before he had time to let out a pained scream. In half a moment, he tore the man's throat out, and as he chucked his body to the floor, the vampire he rescued stared at him in astonishment.

Alucard then stared across the room at Zalith, who aggressively snapped the neck of a magic wielder who attempted to cast a curse. Then, he moved towards his next target. He grabbed an armoured man before he could approach a vampire, who was already struggling against another enemy. Zalith held out his free hand and summoned more fire, engulfing two other enemies in flames. Then, as he executed the man in his grip, his eyes met Alucard's.

Although Alucard could barely see him through the smoke, he saw the Demon smirk before running off to save the struggling vampire. Alucard snarled and grabbed the wrist of his next opponent before he could swing his blade and pulled his rapier from its sheath. He stabbed it up through the man's chest, and as the tip of the blade burst out the top of the man's head, Alucard laughed slightly. Pathetic hunters.

But his attention was quickly snatched by the colossal shadow descending on the room. He looked up, fixing his dark eyes on the blur of a creature, and it was heading right for Zalith. Alucard quickly pulled a colt from his coat and fired. It hit the beast, knocking it off course, and when it crashed to the floor, it was revealed to be a manticore.

Alucard fired several other shots before it could recover, and when the creature combusted, it sent a bloody mess in every direction.

Alucard caught sight of Zalith's annoying smile and rolled his eyes before finding himself a new target. But when he took a moment to check on the vampires, he saw that they were struggling. Close to half of them had perished, and impious anger consumed him.

He hurried back to join the fight and grabbed the back of a man's robe, pulling him out of his magic circle. At the same time, Alucard fired his colt, and as he snapped the neck of the man in his grip, the bullet pierced through the skull of one armoured man and wedged itself in the shoulder of another. The first died instantly, but the second yelled in agony and turned to face Alucard, but before he could lunge, the bullet inside his arm combusted, sending blood everywhere.

Alucard lowered his weapon, and a humoured look appeared on his face when he noticed the vampires the man had been battling standing there with horrified expressions on their bloody faces.

Alucard shrugged and smirked. "*Scuzele mele.*"

Then, as the remaining vampires grouped up away from the fight, Alucard and Zalith worked together to clear out the few remaining enemies. As Zalith executed yet another robed enemy attempting to hit him with continuous ethos attacks, Alucard disappeared and reappeared behind one of the last armoured men. He forced his hand through the man's back, ripping out his heart before he had a chance to fight back—but the vampire had no time to evade the incoming fire-like ethos projectile. It collided with his right shoulder, making him stumble back, but Zalith tore the man's head off before Alucard got to initiate payback.

What he had been hit with—to his relief—was yet another anti-demon ethos, but it had no effect on him; his ethos had already been banished. The impact, however, was painful, and as he discovered he couldn't move his right arm, he assumed that the force had either broken it or dislocated his shoulder.

He watched as Zalith sent the second-to-last armoured man up in flames; he then turned to face the last, grabbing him by his throat as he attempted to attack with his sword. But as the demon snapped the man's neck, the calming air was quickly filled with the horrifying screech of a bird-like creature. Zalith turned to face the sound's direction, and they both watched as a feathered gryphon landed a few feet away from the demon, bringing down more of the roof with it. He prepared to fight the beast, but Alucard had other ideas.

Alucard aimed his colt at the bird-faced creature and fired three shots. The bullets embedded themselves into the beast's body, but it ignored them, keeping its eyes focused on Zalith. The vampire wasn't concerned, though. The sound of the bullets charging grew louder from inside the beast's flesh, and just as it reached Zalith—who prepared to smother it in flames—the beast halted. A confused look covered its face, and its body combusted in a ghastly, bloody explosion.

With a disgusted look on his face, Zalith remained where he was, slowly lowering his hands as a rain of blood and feathers fell over him.

Returning his colt to its holster, Alucard laughed quietly. "You look like blood-covered chicken," he said in Dor-Sanguian so that Zalith couldn't understand and snap back.

Zalith glared across the room at him, his face twitching as he clearly tried to keep himself from joining in with Alucard's laughter.

But the vampire quickly turned his attention to the others. He looked back at the remaining six vampires as they looked around in horror. He had to get them back to Aegisguard before anything else happened.

However, he had to see to his wounds first. He made his way to the closest wall and pulled off his blazer. He then lifted the left side of his shirt, examining the half-healed wound on his side that he received at the beginning of the battle. The ethos attack he took in Zalith's place disabled his healing abilities, so he wasn't going to heal any time soon.

Just as he was about to tuck his shirt back into his belt, Zalith appeared beside him and snatched his wrist, stopping him from concealing his wound.

"Are you okay?" the demon asked, glancing at the gash on Alucard's left side, but his eyes wandered from the wound.

Alucard pulled his wrist free and shoved Zalith back as he glared aggressively at him. "Zon't touch me!" he snarled as he pulled his shirt over his wound.

"Sorry," he said with a smirk, watching Alucard as he turned to the side and pressed his left arm against the wall.

With an irritated snarl, the vampire used the wall to force his dislocated shoulder back into place. Then, he snatched his blazer from the floor and pulled it back on.

Before Zalith could say anything else, the vampire scowled at him. "Vhat zhe fuck vas zhat? Vhy did zhey come?"

"I *did* mention that I've been trying not to die. The demon hunters here have a pretty large price on my head. But... thank you for taking that hit for me," he said, walking beside Alucard as he headed towards the vampires. "I really appreciate it," he added as he smiled.

With a huff of exhaustion, Alucard took his eyes off Zalith and looked at the vampires who survived the battle. "Let's go," he said, pointing at them. Then, he looked back at Zalith. "I von't make an 'abit of taking 'its vor you."

Amused by his answer, Zalith smirked. "Regardless, thank you."

Waving his hand in dismissal, Alucard hastily led the way out of what was left of the hall, leaving Zalith without another word. He had to get back home; he had no idea what Zalith was involved in, but he wasn't about to get dragged into it—not while his ethos wasn't accessible. His only concern right now was the vampires.

Chapter Twenty-Two

— ⟨ ✝ ⟩ —

Reprimand

| Alucard |

As the ship moved along the ocean, Alucard stared vacantly at the six vampires on the deck. They looked traumatized, and horrified looks were still plastered to their pale faces despite the fact that the battle was well behind them. It seemed as though they weren't used to seeing death and destruction; Zalith said they'd remained loyal through a war, but Alucard doubted that any of them had even seen it.

He scowled uncomfortably. His body was still suffering from his wounds, not to mention his lack of ethos due to saving Zalith. He wasn't sure why he did it, and the fact that he couldn't come up with an answer irritated him. He couldn't stop thinking about it; how could he when his entire body felt like it was on fire?

With a quiet snarl, he reached into his blazer and pulled out his flask, and as he slowly sipped from it, he set his eyes on his castle as it came into view. Old human blood wasn't going to do much for him, though, least of all speed up his healing process. He needed something fresh and a whole lot of sleep.

But as he tucked the flask away, he realized what he was missing. He placed his hand on his shoulder, and the lack of a fur collar over it caused such panic to consume him. His cape—had he left it behind? He stood up, looking around frantically. Of course he'd left it. He took it off after taking that hit for Zalith because he was afraid it might become damaged during the battle, and that was the last thing he wanted. He valued that cape profoundly, and in his attempt to protect it from harm, he had ultimately left it in the worst place it could possibly be.

He wanted to go back for it, but the thought of returning to that castle disgruntled him. What if Zalith was still there? If that demon saw him walk back in there to pick up the cape he had so stupidly left behind, he'd probably never let him forget it. He wasn't going to amuse him like that.

So, he sighed irritably and gritted his teeth in anger. He'd go and get it in the morning. He was sure it would still be among the ruins somewhere…right? He frowned worriedly. The idea of leaving it there for so long mortified him, but he'd much rather risk leaving it than go back now and have to face Zalith again.

When he saw that they were approaching the castle's docks, he made his way out onto the deck and waited. He ignored the new vampires' mumbles of uncertainty; it was now Ben's job to help them settle in, so he had no interest in conversing with them. All he wanted to do was go home and sleep off the battle. But first, he had to take these vampires up to Ben.

Once the ship halted in the docks, Sergiu climbed down from the quarterdeck and opened the gate; he pushed the bridge down so that it met with the docks and then tied the ship into place.

Alucard wasted no time. He led the way onto the docks, and the vampires slowly followed as he navigated the cobblestone path. He glanced back at them, listening as they mumbled nervously to one another. Obviously, the battle unsettled them, but he felt as though he wasn't the right person to try and convince them that everything would be fine. It would be better for them to hear something like that from Ben, the vampire who came first, the one who had spent over a month in this new world.

He glared ahead, reaching the top of the cliff, and set his eyes on Ben. Alucard led the vampires over, and when they saw Ben, they hurried to join the familiar face.

Ben smiled in response to the desperate greetings of the newly arrived vampires but focused on Alucard. "The hell happened to you?" he asked in concern.

"Ask your vriend," he snarled.

"Are you all right?"

"Maybe," Alucard grumbled. He then looked at the vampires. "You can go in. Ben vill 'elp you," he instructed.

As the vampires made their way into the castle, Ben kept his focus on Alucard. "What happened?"

Sighing, Alucard rolled his eyes and sat down on the fountain's edge. "Some people came and tried to kill your vriend."

"Well, you clearly dealt with them, right?"

"*Da*," he muttered, but then stood up. "I vill probably see you tomorrow—or some point zhis veek. Take care of zhem, zhey zon't seem to 'ave taken zhe battle very vell."

Looking back over his shoulder at the vampires as they disappeared into the castle, Ben nodded. "Yeah, don't worry, I'll…."

Alucard took off in the blink of an eye—he had no interest in staying any longer. He sped off towards his manor, and as he arrived, he rematerialized on the cobblestone path that led to his house.

He made his way forward with an aggravated glare on his face as he thought about having to wait for his ethos to regenerate. He still found himself wondering why he had done it; if Zalith had been hit, he would have simply lost his ethos for a while and possibly fallen unconscious—nothing too dreadful. So, why had Alucard taken it upon himself to spare the demon such a fate? He tried to convince himself that it was because he wanted answers and because he didn't want to fight the enemy alone, but that didn't feel right.

The fact that he was even still trying to come up with an answer annoyed him. Why did he care? He'd simply taken a hit in someone's place; it wouldn't be the first time. That *was* the first time he put himself in harm's way to spare someone else—someone he didn't even know too well, and someone who probably didn't even care. So why was it so heavy on his mind? He would only risk his life to save someone he cared about, and care was something he hadn't felt in a long time. Did this mean he *cared* about Zalith? Why *would* he? Why should he? They weren't friends; they were just associates…right?

Were they friends? No, Damien told Alucard he could and would never have friends, and after what happened to Rodney, he was certain that was and always would be the case. As soon as the Daegelus came to mind, all conflicting thoughts regarding Zalith left his head. He took that hit because he didn't want to have to deal with the attackers alone. There was nothing more to it.

He made his way into his manor gardens but stopped in his tracks when he saw Elvin. Why was he sitting on the porch? He deadpanned and huffed quietly. The bard had obviously known he'd leave his house tonight to take part in the next vampire relocation, and of course, he wanted to use that to try and see him. That didn't improve Alucard's mood at all; it just made him feel a whole lot more annoyed—and uncomfortable. After what happened the other day, he wasn't yet sure he was ready to see Elvin again; he couldn't be sure what that bard might be thinking.

Watching Alucard as he made his way over, Elvin stood up, and as he surely noticed the ash and blood all over the vampire, he scowled in both skepticism and worry. "W-what happened to you?!" he asked in a panic, scurrying over to him, but as he reached out to grab his arm, Alucard defensively stepped back and scowled down at him. The bard backed off and pouted. "Are you okay?"

"Vhy are you 'ere Elvin?" he snarled, moving past him to get to his front door.

"I wanted to make sure you were okay. That demon has something to do with all of this, doesn't he?" he asked, watching Alucard as he unlocked his door.

The vampire scowled and turned to face Elvin. "Vhat?" he asked, confused.

"Your face, Rodney, and now this," Elvin said, using his hand to gesture to Alucard in his entirety. "You can't keep lying about it. What did he do this time?"

Alucard shook his head and scowled. "Vhat?" he asked again.

"I know Zalith did this!" Elvin then yelled, pointing at his scarred face.

Alucard frowned. Why would Elvin think that? He set his eyes on the bard's anxious face. "Vhat zhe 'ell are you talking about?"

"No one saw you since the last time you went to see him, and I saw those cuts on your face when I tried to see you the morning after. Rodney's missing, and tonight, you come back from seeing him again, and you're covered in blood and…whatever that is— is that ash?" he questioned, reaching out to touch Alucard's ash-covered blazer, but the vampire backed off again. "Did he hurt you again? You can tell me, I—"

"No vone 'urt me. I told you, it vas a verevolf."

Elvin frowned in disbelief. "Tobias said it wasn't a werewolf, and I believe him over you—I also know when you're lying. You shouldn't lie," he said, pointing at him as if he were some child.

Alucard scoffed. "I told you to keep out of my personal business."

The bard pouted. "I care about you, and something's happened," he repeated. "I already know it was Zalith—you didn't even deny it. Why do you keep going to see him if—"

"Zhis 'as noving to do vith 'im, and 'as noving to do vith you, eizer. Go 'ome bevore I live up to my promise to vind a new bard."

Scoffing, Elvin looked around the empty gardens. "Where's Sergiu? Did Zalith kill *him* this time?" he accused.

With nothing more to say, Alucard slammed the door in Elvin's face. He wasn't going to explain himself to the bard. Why should he? He locked the door and bolted it so the bard couldn't get in. Then, he chucked his key onto the table, took off his blazer and threw it atop the table, too, and made his way upstairs, ignoring Elvin's disapproving calls from outside.

The day was over, and he just wanted to rest, so he took himself to bed, hoping that rest would cure him of his exhaustion. If it didn't, he'd have to find another way to recover. He hadn't forgotten what Tobias said about the werewolves, and he had to ensure he got on top of that before they got out of control.

But he didn't want to think about work right now. It was time to sleep. He needed as much of it as he could get.

| **Zalith** |

Meanwhile, Zalith made his way home. With a tired sigh, he dragged himself up the creaking stairs of the old, cramped house he was currently holed up in. He held Alucard's cape in his right hand; the vampire left it behind, and he'd taken it upon himself to make sure he got it back the next time they met.

He was left with a lot of conflicting thoughts after tonight's events. Alucard's selfless act to take that hit for him had drastically increased Zalith's liking for him; he found that and Alucard's relentlessness in battle rather attractive. And while peering at Alucard's wound, he'd managed to snatch a glance at the vampire's defined abs, something he wasn't going to be forgetting. He knew it was probably rather ill-mannered of him to snatch a glance at his body, but…he just couldn't help himself.

But he was worried. He knew his enemies would catch up at some point, and tonight was that night. He was going to have to move again.

With another heavy sigh, he followed the dark hallway and pushed open the door to his room—

"What happened to *you*?" came Damien's voice, and as Zalith looked over at him, he saw that the Daegelus was pointing to the demon's blood-stained suit.

Not at all surprised by Damien's presence, Zalith turned to face him. "An annoyance," he answered, quietly closing the door. He placed Alucard's cape on the end of his bed and made his way over to one of the few lanterns that were lined along the white walls. Once he lit it, he turned to face the Daegelus, waiting for whatever it might be that he had come to say.

"I would like to think that tonight's transferal went well," Damien said, starting to tap his claw-tipped fingers on the table.

"It did," Zalith confirmed.

"Good…and my delinquent of a boy—you have his attire; am I right to assume he's dead?" he asked with a smirk, glancing at the cape.

"No." Zalith frowned. "And he's been particularly helpful."

Damien's left eye twitched in vexation as he looked down at the desk and thought to himself for a few moments. He then scowled at Zalith. "Tell me, Eladarin, why is it that you have chosen such a peculiar place to stay?" he asked curiously, looking around the room.

"It's much easier to live close to the portal so that I can make this task of transporting vampires simpler," he answered.

The Daegelus grinned. "I heard something happened this time—an attack?"

"Demon hunters, yes."

"Where will you relocate to? Another shared residence like this one?"

"I'm not yet sure."

The Daegelus sighed. "Hmph, well, whatever you decide to do, I have another job for you," he said, changing the subject.

"Would this job need to be done alongside my current task or after?"

Damien stood up. "Alongside it. As you know, I'm looking for males from my siblings' bloodlines. Erich favours this world, so I assume he must have descendants *here*. I want *you* to find a male from his bloodline for me. You *are* a demon; I'm sure you can sniff one out."

Zalith frowned, trying to hide his annoyance as Damien approached him.

The Daegelus reached into his pocket and pulled out a long, black feather. "This belongs to Erich, so I'm sure you can use it to find what I need."

Zalith took the feather and glanced down at it. "What do you want me to do once I locate him?"

"I'll leave that up to you," He said, looking back over his shoulder at him as he made his way over to the wall. "You can try to convince him to join my cause yourself, or you can keep him locked up somewhere until I next come to see you. But you never disappoint me, so I feel whatever you choose to do, I will much enjoy," he said, leaning back against the wall. He then set his blue-red eyes on the demon, and all amusement in them withered. "Why *do you* have that?" he asked, nodding at Alucard's cape.

Zalith exhaled in fake disinterest. "He left it behind; it is simply a kindness. I'll return it to him when I next see him."

Damien nodded slowly. "I never understood why he holds that so dear. Perhaps he is sentimental," he said with a smirk.

Zalith had no idea what he was ranting about, and Damien seemed to see that.

The Daegelus sighed. "Keep up the good work, Eladarin. I feel a reward may be in order fairly soon—so long as you complete this next task."

"Can I ask what this reward is? You've yet to tell me what I'll be receiving for assisting with the cause."

"Why so hasty? You'll find out once it's done."

Zalith nodded. "Of course."

Then, Damien stood up straight. "I will share with you a word of warning," he said, a stern tone in his once casual voice. "Watch how close you get to my Aleksei…. People who get too close tend to…disappear."

Amused, Zalith smirked. "I assure you, I'm certain I won't do such a thing."

"Won't you?" Damien asked with a challenging tone. "Your reputation has proceeded you on many occasions. Not this time, though. We'll do our best to make sure of that, won't we?" He walked over to the balcony doors and pushed them open. "I'll find you in four weeks—that's when I want an update. Don't let me down." Then, as silently as he appeared, he ascended into the sky, leaving Zalith alone.

Zalith sighed angrily as he sat down on the end of his bed and rested his forehead in his right hand. As if tonight hadn't been enough for him to deal with already, now he had yet another task to carry out for Damien. It wouldn't be too hard, though; finding people was something he was rather good at. What *did* irritate him was the fact that he had to find a new place to stay. He couldn't stay here; there was a possibility that the hunters knew where he was. They found him at the ruin, and he wasn't going to risk them coming here. He wouldn't risk his life, his companion's life, or the lives of the people who took him in.

But how had they known where he was? Could somebody have conspired and informed them? Or could these hunters have just so happened to have seen and noticed him? He wasn't sure, and he knew that he'd have to read the minds of those around him just to be sure. But he couldn't ignore the fact that there weren't too many ambushing hunters, and although they came with both a gryphon *and* a manticore, it seemed as though they were either remarkably unprepared for what awaited them, or they were just a bunch of weak, useless fools who thought they might try to become heroes. If he weren't feeling downhearted, he'd laugh.

However, his thoughts drifted as he looked down at Alucard's cape. He couldn't help but wonder why the vampire threw himself in front of that attack for him. Did… Alucard like him? Or was this vampire just the self-sacrificing type? He wasn't convinced that was the case; the way Alucard spoke, acted, and reacted didn't make Zalith think he was the type of guy to just throw himself in harm's way to save someone else a great deal of pain. So, he couldn't assume anything other than this vampire did, in fact, like him, and thinking so made Zalith smile.

The demon pondered to himself. He wasn't going to deny that he found Alucard physically attractive, and that attraction grew after what happened at the ruin. Not only did Alucard look appealing, but the way he spoke and reacted, and the way he chose to do things somewhat captivated Zalith. This vampire had certainly snatched a relatively large proportion of Zalith's difficult-to-gain attention, so much that he found himself wanting to see him *outside* of their work.

He looked back down at the vampire's cape, setting his eyes on the small tear on its left side. He saw Alucard take it off before engaging in the battle, so it was evident that it meant a great deal to him. Why else would he try to protect it?

There was a woman in the house he was staying in who he knew could repair the cape, so before he left, he'd get her to do so, and tomorrow, he'd return it to the vampire. He thought that perhaps seeing Alucard on a casual basis might be a rather nice distraction from his life's current exhausting predicament. He already found himself feeling much less irritated in Alucard's presence, and spending more time with him might make him feel better.

However, he couldn't let himself become too distracted. He had work to do and people to look after. But what could go wrong? All he'd be doing is spending time with a man he found himself growing to like—a lot. He had no personal objections; he knew what he wanted out of this, and he was quite certain that he'd get it.

Chapter Twenty-Three

— ⸲ † ⸱ —

Uninvited, Yet Welcome

| Alucard |

Alucard frowned uncomfortably when a loud, thumping knock came at his front door. He groaned and rolled onto his side, ignoring it. His butler would send whoever it was away. But when he heard the door open, the sound of a struggle and several panicked voices forced him to sit up.

"Sir, you can't go up there!" came his butler's voice, accompanied by the sound of rushing footsteps.

The vampire climbed out of bed and swiftly grabbed his shirt, pulling it on just in time as his bedroom door opened—

"It's an emergency!" Felix instantly stuttered, staring at Alucard, a flustered look on his face.

With a frown, Alucard glared at the little grey-haired man. He wanted to yell at him for turning up and barging into his home, but even someone like Felix wouldn't do something so preposterous if it wasn't dire. "Vhat?" he snarled.

"Wolves near Vria, My Lord—attacked caravans, people dying. I came as fast as I could!" he explained desperately.

Anger smothered Alucard's face. *Of course* the wolves were making another move. "'Ow many are zhere?" he asked, barging past him and out of his room.

Following Alucard down the hall, Felix shook his head. "I-I don't know, My Lord— many. Whole pack. Took down horses and people hiding inside caravans."

"Vhich pack?" he demanded, heading downstairs.

"Uh…I—"

"Vhich pack?!" he yelled impatiently, snatching his weapons from the table by the door.

"I think West Pack, My Lord—recognize the Alpha," he stuttered.

Alucard snarled irritably. He wasn't about to waste any time. The moment he stepped outside, he dematerialized into vermillion smoke and raced through the night sky as fast as he could, ignoring the aches in his body the portal burdened him with. Whatever the wolves were trying to do, he had to stop it. Wolves following an Amarok and wandering around in Wrodiff was one thing, but an entire pack attacking a community? If he didn't stop them, it could encourage the other packs to hunt outside the woods, and that would destroy the treaty.

He landed on the outskirts of the small forest village, Vria, and scanned the area with his eyes for signs of the fight—and there, through the trees, the glow of fire, the snarls of wolves, and the horrified, *terrified* screams of people.

Without a moment to waste, he raced towards the commotion, but when he reached the small opening, the five painted caravans had all been torn apart. Every horse was mutilated and laying in a puddle of blood and innards, and the vampires Alucard had guarding Vria all lay dead in the grass among the humans who lived there.

Alucard gritted his teeth and clenched his fists, glaring at the devastation. The faint whimpering of a woman came from one of the caravan wreckages; he made his way over and shifted a large wood frame with ease, and when he lifted it, he set his hell-fiery eyes on a bloody, weeping woman mourning the mangled man in her lap. She didn't even flinch when she saw Alucard, she just…stared, blood seeping down the side of her face and mixing with her tears.

There wasn't anything he could do here, but he wasn't going to let those dogs get away with his. "Vhere did zhey go?" he asked her.

She didn't answer. She wept into the dead man's shoulder, rocking back and forth.

"Tell me!" he yelled furiously.

With a whimper of fear, she lifted her shaky hand and pointed deeper into the forest.

Alucard snarled in frustration and pulled the rubble away so that the woman would be able to move herself and the man she was mourning. Then, he turned around and headed in the direction she'd pointed, trying to pick up a trail—

The woman's cries of sorrow fell silent. Alucard stopped in his tracks and looked back over his shoulder. Blood sprayed from the woman's neck as the blade she impaled herself with ended her life, and as her body fell over that of the man in her arms, Alucard scowled guiltily. If only he'd not chosen to give in to his tire earlier and gone to bed instead of patrolling the forests, this might not have happened—none of these people would be dead.

He stormed into the woods; he still had no idea what the wolves were doing, he could only assume from his own knowledge and what Tobias told him. He knew the North and West packs were meeting, and that the pack who had done this might very well be the North Pack; their territory was close to this place.

Were those two packs really allying to rally against him? That wasn't his main concern right now. At this moment, he was worried about the treaty. He'd worked tirelessly for *months* to ensure it would work out so that his vampires could live comfortably in Dor-Sanguis, and now, it was in danger. All it would take to destroy it would be something *just like this*. The wolves knew what they were doing.

There was no trail. He growled impatiently, focusing all his senses as he circled the area of the battle. He searched…and searched, but the longer he did so without prevailing, the more frustrated he became. The smell of nearby blood wasn't helping him at all, and neither was his anger nor worry. He had so much more to do than hunt wolves; he had to try and keep this quiet—he had to inform his vampires about the deaths and assure them they were safe. It was going to be a long, *long* night…and rest was something he probably wasn't going to get.

It was probably better if he left hunting the wolves until tomorrow. The battle tonight: that hit he'd taken for Zalith, and the strain the portal put on him; as much as he hated to admit it, he wasn't in the best shape to fight werewolves, especially not a whole pack. No, right now, he needed to get his people to clean up the caravan site, ensure there were no witnesses to spread word of this to the city, and then he needed to come up with a plan. He had to find the north and west packs and either scare them into hiding again…or kill them. But for that, he'd needed backup.

There was no time to waste. With a heavy sigh, he started heading back to the caravan site, preparing for his long, sleepless night.

Alucard jolted awake.

"Aleksei!" came Ben's voice followed by three knocks at the front door.

The vampire opened his eyes, grunting irritably as the sunlight creeping in through his bedroom curtains scorned his face. He must have had…what? An hour's sleep? Two at a stretch. His head was pounding, his body was aching…and he just wanted to go back to sleep.

Ben didn't relent. "I don't mean to be intrusive, but…it's kinda important."

Alucard rolled his eyes and pulled himself out of bed. After last night's events, he couldn't afford to be lazy and sleep in. He grabbed a black shirt from his dresser and slowly made his way down the hallway. As Ben relentlessly knocked on the door, Alucard snarled angrily and walked faster once he reached the stairs. He headed down to the entrance hall, unbolted the front door, and pulled it open, setting his eyes on the scruffy-faced man…who looked shaken.

Confused, Alucard scowled. "Vhat do you vant? Vhat is *so* important zhat you 'ave to vake me up so early?"

Ben frowned. "It's…midday, Aleksei."

Glancing at the sun, Alucard grunted and glared back at Ben. "Vhatever. Vhat do you vant?"

He smiled. "You've got a very important *and* very special guest on the way."

The strangely amused tone in Ben's voice confused Alucard, but he wasn't interested in seeing anyone right now. "No, I zon't. Goodbye," he grumbled, slamming the door in Ben's face. The vampire then turned around and made his way back upstairs; he didn't have the energy to talk right now; all he wanted was to go back to bed.

He dragged himself back into his bedroom and fell on his bed, glaring at the window while he lay on his front. He heard Ben leave the manor, and as his footsteps faded further away, Alucard slowly closed his eyes, hoping he'd be able to get a few more hours of rest before Elvin inevitably showed up.

However, after what felt like barely a minute, the door knocked *again*. He opened his eyes, a look of murder appearing in them as he scowled at the window. He told Ben to leave, but for some reason, he'd come back, and Alucard wasn't in the best mood to deal with annoyances. So, he pushed himself out of bed and stormed down to the entrance hall.

He grabbed the door handle and yanked it open. "I vhought I told you to—"

Standing on the porch wasn't Ben but Zalith, and as soon as Alucard set his eyes on the demon, he fell silent, embarrassment smothering his face. What the hell was *he* doing here?

Zalith smiled. "Good afternoon, Aleksei. You look…well," he said as a smirk crept across his face.

Alucard froze and stared at Zalith, who was wearing a tweed, grey suit and a white shirt. His dark hair was neatly combed over his head, and that same confusing smile clung to his face. He stared at the vampire with his almost-black eyes, an expectant look lingering in them while Alucard tried to work out what to say. All he could think about was how he was standing there probably looking like a peasant with a hangover in his one-size-too-small shirt, the same trousers from last night, and a stupid look on his face.

His eyes, however, wandered to the crimson cape Zalith had tucked under his left arm. Noticing it was his own, he scowled and looked back at the demon's face. "Vhy do you 'ave zhat?"

Zalith glanced at the cape, smiled, and held it out to him. "You left it behind, so I picked it up for you. I also had someone repair the tear."

The vampire scowled skeptically but slowly took it from him. He stared at it for a moment, seeing that it had, in fact, been repaired, and it also looked as though it had been washed. Why Zalith took it upon himself to do so, he wasn't sure, but he didn't care to ask.

He placed the cape on the table beside the door. "Zhat's vhy you came? To give zhat back to me?"

"It's one of multiple reasons, yes. We need to discuss a new plan regarding the vampire relocation mission. I thought it would be easier to come to you," he said with a smile. "Perhaps we could find a place to have coffee?"

Looking at him, Alucard nodded slowly. "Vight, coffee. Zhat's a 'uman drink, no?"

"It is," the demon confirmed. "I assumed you might like it."

"Hmm…." Alucard pondered for a few moments. Did he want to go out? No. Did he want to have to socialize? Not exactly. But the demon was right; they had to talk about what happened last night and devise a new plan. So, what choice did he have but to accept? He rolled his eyes and stepped aside. "I should get veady, zhen. You can vait in zhere," he said, pointing to the lounge.

"Of course," the demon said, and with a curious smile, he stepped into his house.

Alucard then headed upstairs. He hadn't been expecting this *at all*, but this seemed like the sort of thing someone like Zalith would do. Turn up at his house… expect not to be sent away. The vampire rolled his eyes, heading into his bedroom. If they didn't have to talk about the ambush last night, he *would* have sent him home… but he had to make sure he did everything in his power to ensure Damien's mission was completed, even if that meant meeting with and talking to Zalith outside of their designated meeting times.

| **Zalith** |

Zalith sat on the black, red-cushioned couch and looked around curiously.

The first thing that hit him was the scent of the place; so many different things: cedarwood, warm amber, roses, and cinnamon. No such things were in sight, but the aroma was *everywhere*. If Zalith didn't know better, he'd suspect it was the vampire's natural scent, but… only demons possessed such potent scents in the place they lived. Maybe it was different here in Aegisguard. Perhaps Aegisguardian vampires, like Eltarian demons, smothered the place in which they slept with their scent. Perhaps vampires here were just as territorial as demons.

He enjoyed the antique, gothic aesthetic of Alucard's home. The dark, panelled walls, the black curtains, and the gold highlights. There were several trinkets that sat on the mantlepiece, which all looked like enchanted items; gold candle holders, a silver pocket watch, rings, other jewellery, a hand-crafted wooden box adorned with small runes, and a small collection of gold coins, crystals, and a rather large ruby. Were they things the vampire would carry around? Or were they just there because he had nowhere else to put them?

His eyes shifted to the glass cabinet to his left. It stood against the wall beside the large arched doorway that led to the entrance hall; a collection of glasses were lined along the top two shelves, the first consisting of wine glasses and the second of drinking glasses. The other three shelves held glass bottles of different alcohols, some dark, and some light. He smirked curiously, but his attention quickly turned to the door as someone unlocked it from outside.

Did someone else live here? If so, who? He waited, and as the door was pushed open, he set his gaze on the small, brown-haired man who stepped into the entrance hall. A discrete glare found its way onto his face as he watched the man wipe his feet on the entrance mat; he turned around, shut the door, and pulled off his jacket, which he put on the coat rack. He took his hat off and sighed, looking around.

Zalith stared strangely—who was this man? This…human. He looked rather stupid in his estranged, unstylish outfit, and with long, repulsive brown hair tied into a ponytail in what looked like an attempt to mimic Alucard's previous hairstyle, and his face…just irritated Zalith. This wasn't someone he'd expect Alucard to keep around, so what was he doing with a key to the vampire's house?

As soon as the guy set his eyes on Zalith, a screech of shock escaped his ridiculously startled face. He stumbled back and pointed at him. "W-who the…the hell are you?!" he asked, his tone quickly shifting from horrified to skeptical.

Ignoring his question, Zalith kept his vacant glare.

The man scowled and looked around. "Where's…Aleksei?"

Zalith raised his left hand and pointed up at the ceiling, telling him that Alucard was upstairs.

With a hostile glare on his face, the man stood in the lounge doorway as he looked Zalith up and down. "I know who you are…and I know what you did."

A smile found its way to Zalith's face. "Do you?" he asked condescendingly.

"I don't know who you think you are, but I won't let it slide."

Amused, Zalith scoffed. What an interestingly stupid yet brave little man. He had nothing else to do while he waited for the vampire, so he might as well take advantage of this human's anger and toy with him. He scowled with fake hostility. "Is that right?"

The small human pointed at him. "I'm not afraid of you, and neither is Aleksei, no matter what else you think you might do to him."

Revolted by the man's little finger, Zalith snarled quietly but laughed in response.

The little man prepared to yell but quickly turned his head to look upstairs. He frowned in angst. "W-why's he here?!"

Alucard, who reached the bottom of the stairs, sighed. "I vhought I told you to go avay, Elvin," he snarled, shoving him aside so he could get into the lounge, but when he saw Zalith, he pouted, stopped walking, and looked at the small man. "Vhy are you 'ere?"

"What do you mean? I always come," he said with a pout.

"I told you last night to leave me alone."

Zalith silently watched them, deciphering what he could of their relationship through the way they interacted with one another. But he was more interested in what Alucard chose to wear. He'd only seen the vampire in his coat-like blazer, but now, he wore a casual white fitted shirt, and black trousers, and had clearly spent quite some time on his hair. And in the gloom of his house, Alucard looked like a warm autumn evening.

The little man…Elvin, Alucard called him, crossed his arms. "Yeah, that was last night, this is now. I came to see if you were okay."

"Go avay. I'm busy," Alucard snapped, making his way over to the glass cabinet beside where the demon was sitting.

Glancing at Zalith, Elvin scowled. "What's *he* doing here?"

Ignoring him, Alucard looked back at Zalith as he opened the cabinet. "Do you vant a drink?"

"I would love one, thank you," Zalith said with a smile.

"I want one," Elvin said.

"No," Alucard snarled. "Zhe last time you tried to drink anyving ozzer zhan zhat fruit ving, you made a disgusting mess of zhe place ve vent to."

Irritated, Elvin dragged himself over to the armchair and slumped down, keeping a suspicious glare on Zalith. "Why are you being so nice to him?!" he blurted. "He hurt you!"

With a confused scowl, Alucard closed the cabinet and frowned at the bard. "Vhat?"

"I know he did that to your face!"

Alucard then sighed. "I told you 'e 'as noving to do vith any of zhis. Eizer shut up about zhis or get out," he warned, looking for somewhere to sit, but the only available space was beside Zalith. The demon smirked… and to his disappointment, Alucard chose to remain standing.

"I don't believe that for one second," Elvin growled.

Ignoring him, Alucard handed Zalith his glass of brandy. As he took it, Zalith made sure to touch as much of the vampire's hand as he could, but Alucard paid no attention and looked over at Elvin. "I zon't care vhat you believe. If somevone 'urt me, do you veally vink I vould still vork vith zhem?" he asked, slowly sitting on the couch's arm.

Pouting, Elvin crossed his arms and looked away, silenced.

Alucard looked down at Zalith. "Ve can 'ead into zhe city; I know a place ve can get…coffee."

Elvin frowned and exclaimed, "W-wait, you guys are going for coffee? What about *me*?"

"*Vhat* about you?" Alucard muttered.

"Well…we…never do anything like that. Why are you so suddenly doing things you said you'd never do?"

"Is business, Elvin. Go 'ome and vind someving to do vith your time."

He shook his head. "Okay, if *he* didn't do that to you, then who did? And who killed Rodney? Don't try say it was you again, or I swear…."

Vexed, Alucard snarled and finished his drink in a single gulp before standing up and pointing at the bard. "Get out."

Elvin jumped to his feet. "Why're you always so mean and closed off and just…just—"

"Vatch vhat you say," Alucard warned. "You've pissed me off enough lately."

"No, I haven't…" he said sadly.

Alucard then sighed as he glanced at Zalith, but when his eyes met the demon's, he frowned uncomfortably. "Let's go. I zon't 'ave all day," he said, placing his empty glass on the cabinet. He then looked over at Elvin. "Go—now."

"But—"

"Out!" Alucard snapped.

Scurrying away, Elvin almost squealed like a scared child. He rushed out of the house and slammed the door behind him.

Once the human left, Zalith stood up, and a snide smile appeared on his face as he kept his eyes on Alucard.

"Ve can go now," Alucard said, walking past the demon.

Disappointed with Alucard's haste, Zalith frowned slightly, but he followed the vampire as he made his way to the front door. He was undeniably curious to see where the vampire was taking him, so he smiled and went with him in silence, sure that the rest of the day was going to be rather enjoyable.

Chapter Twenty-Four

— ⸱ ✝ ⸱ —

Coffee

| Alucard |

Alucard pulled his blazer on before leading the way out into the gardens. He headed to the fountain, glancing up at the dull, grey sky. A small shoal of fish was visible above, which meant it was surely going to rain within the next hour or so, but that didn't bother him.

His eyes remained their usual hell-fiery red in the overcast, and as he searched the gardens, they failed to locate Sergiu, who could usually be found by the stables. As Zalith curiously followed, Alucard walked to the stables and looked around for the groundskeeper. Had he even come back from the docks last night?

The vampire stopped beside Sebastian's paddock. "Sergiu?" he called irritably, but the man didn't come running. He rolled his eyes and pulled the black stallion's gate open, snatching the horse's reins. "*Inutil,*" Alucard grumbled, leading the horse out.

"I assume your stable hand has gone missing?" Zalith asked.

Leaving Sebastian standing close to the stables, Alucard turned around and pulled the brown mare from her paddock, and handed Zalith the reins. "Everyvone's going missing zhese days," he muttered. He mounted his horse, but as he did, he grunted quietly; the wound on his right side still hadn't healed entirely since last night. "Ve vill vide to zhe city," he mumbled, making himself as comfortable as he could.

"How far is this city?"

Alucard tapped his horse's side, and as it started moving forward, he looked back at the demon. "A ten-minute vide."

"Do you make a habit of giving out keys to your house?" Zalith asked, following.

Glancing at him, Alucard scowled. "No."

"Then, might I ask, why does the dwarf possess one?"

"I assume you're veferring to Elvin. Zhat vould be because 'e is my…vell, vamiliar. 'E 'as a key so 'e can access my 'ome when I'm not zhere, in case 'e needs to bring someving, take someving, etcetera," he explained, staring ahead.

Zalith smirked. "Why don't you just say slave?"

"Zhat is not a very nice vord," Alucard sneered.

Amused, Zalith laughed slightly. "Where did you find him? And why did you choose *him* to be your…familiar?"

Irritated, Alucard rolled his eyes. "Vhy are you so interested in Elvin? Ve are 'ere to talk about zhe mission, not my personal life."

Not at all thrown off by Alucard's morose disposition, Zalith smiled. "We are friends, aren't we, Aleksei? Surely we can talk about both business and personal matters."

Glancing at him, Alucard frowned in confliction. Was Zalith his friend? He found himself wondering the same thing last night and for several short moments in the past few weeks. However, he wasn't yet sure how he felt, and talking about his personal life was something he wouldn't even do with Elvin, whom he had known for over seven years. He hadn't even known Zalith for three months yet, so he wasn't going to debate whether he wanted to share personal information with this man.

He glared ahead as the city came into view. He didn't want to answer either of Zalith's questions; he wanted to talk about what was important and then go about his own business. So, he remained silent, hoping Zalith would stop asking questions.

Zalith wasn't done. He smirked at him and asked, "Are we being grumpy again today?"

The vampire scowled, pouted, and turned his head away from him. He *hated* it when Zalith called him that. But for some confusing reason, he found himself enjoying the fact that Zalith didn't back down and fall silent as everyone else around him would. Why didn't *that* annoy him? Why didn't that *anger* him? Whenever anyone else bothered him, he'd snap and yell or walk away, so why wasn't he even *thinking* of doing either of those things? Was it because Zalith was new to him? Or perhaps because he knew from their few interactions that Zalith wouldn't become threatened if he raised his voice and would follow him if he left. This demon, after all, didn't work *for* him, so he wasn't going to be much of a pushover, was he?

But why did Zalith seem so insistent to talk to him? Alucard wasn't as interesting as he felt Zalith thought he was…was he? Why was this demon so intrusive? Alucard glanced over at him, and as he saw that Zalith was staring expectantly at him, he scowled. "Divert your eyes somevhere else; you make me veel uncomfortable."

With an amused smirk, Zalith slowly took his eyes off the vampire and set them on the city. "Did something happen last night after we parted ways? You look very tired."

Would he ever shut up?

The demon stared at him.

"Some volves killed a caravan," he uttered. Maybe he'd leave him alone if he sated his curiosity.

"I imagine that's not good for the treaty—"

"No, is not. I 'ad my people clear everyving avay, zhough, and I 'aven't 'eard vrom any of zhe council members, so I'm 'oping I got zhere in time to at least keep zhat quiet."

Zalith nodded. "And these wolves: what do you plan to do?"

He sighed irritably and shrugged. "I vill deal vith zhem. Is just 'ard to do vhat I 'ave to vith zhem vhen I'm constantly busy doing zhis vampire transferal shit."

The demon laughed quietly and offered, "Well, let me know if you need a hand again. I'll admit that it has been fun killing things with you."

Alucard rolled his eyes and glared ahead. He didn't want to think about the wolves right now. They needed to solve last night's problem in Eltaria.

When they reached the city entrance, Alucard led the way to a small patch of land set aside for horses to be hitched. He dismounted his horse and tied its reins to the fence alongside another white mare and then stood patiently while Zalith did the same. Once the demon joined him, he turned around and led the way up the busy street.

"Do these humans' ugly looks of disapproval not anger you?" the demon asked, glancing around at the tutting, mumbling people, who all possessed revolted expressions.

"I ignore zhem," Alucard answered.

"I assume the treaty hasn't weathered well?"

"Vill become normal soon enough," the vampire mumbled, turning onto another street. "Zhe people 'ere 'ave vought against vampires vor centuries; zheir ancestors 'ave died vighting zhem. Is not unjustified vor zhem to 'old resentment. Alzhough I zon't see as fair to blame zhe vampires. Zhey vere simply vighting back to protect zhemselves."

Zalith frowned curiously. "Why do you not refer to the vampires as *your* people? You speak of them as if you're not one of them."

"Vell, technically speaking, I am not veally a vampire—I am…more."

He smiled. "Oh?"

Alucard led them towards a small, cosy-looking café which stood between two black-bricked buildings displaying aristocratic attire. Three light, round wooden tables were lined along the outside of the storefront with three chairs tucked under each. The inside of the store wasn't very busy; only two people were waiting to be served and a single server stood behind the bar.

The vampire shrugged and glanced over at Zalith. "Vampires are vhat came vrom my blood; zhey are not like me. Zhey zon't possess zhe vings I possess…vell, most vings."

"Well, I would say that makes sense considering *you* can walk in the sunlight; however, the vampires from my world can also walk in the sunlight."

"Zhat vould be because Janus used my blood to create several subspecies of vampire, and vasn't long ago zhat I learned vone of zhose subspecies could valk in zhe sunlight. People I turn directly gain zhe ability to valk in zhe sunlight, but anyvone else does not."

Reaching the small white building, Alucard walked to a small table outside the storefront's window. He pulled out one of the seats and took off his blazer, which he rested on the spare seat. He then sat down before continuing his lecture.

He leaned his arms onto the table and sighed quietly as Zalith sat opposite him. "I am…alive, in a sense. Vampires are not."

"I *have* come to notice that about you," Zalith said with a smile, resting his arms on the table as he stared over at the vampire. "Among other things," he added, eyeing him fondly.

Watching as the server made her way out of the store and towards their table, Alucard leaned back in his seat. "Vhatever. Everyvone calls me a vampire, so I might as vell be vone."

The server stopped beside their table, pulled a notebook from her blouse, and looked down at them. "What will it be?" she asked with disinterest in her voice. But when she noticed both their elf-like ears, she sighed quietly. "We also serve vampires here now," she said, and several lazy sighs accompanied her words. Obviously, she had to repeat what she was about to say many times before. "We offer various extras that might appeal to your tastes; if you'd like to hear what they are, please tell me. I'll be happy to list them."

Zalith took his eyes off Alucard and looked up at her. "I'll have a coffee—black—with a shot of espresso," he requested, losing his smile the second he set his eyes on her.

Writing it down, she then looked down at Alucard. "And you?"

He had no idea what to say. He'd never had coffee before. Evidently, Zalith knew what *he* was talking about, so Alucard shrugged. "Zhe same—but…no…shot," he said, unsure whether espresso was alcohol or not, and he wasn't in the mood to try new liquors. He knew he was rather particular with it, and he didn't want to order something he wasn't going to like.

The woman scribbled it down and then left them alone.

Clearly amused by Alucard's decision, Zalith smirked. "Have you ever had coffee before, Aleksei?"

"I 'ave," he lied stubbornly.

Zalith laughed quietly as he leaned back in his seat. "Why have you chosen this particular spot? It's…secluded, quiet."

"Must zhere be a veason vor everyving?"

"Yes," Zalith replied. "I have *my* reasons for being here. I assume you do, too."

"Business. Ve need to talk about vhat 'appened and vhat ve are going to do about zhat."

"Of course," Zalith agreed with a single nod, his unseemly expression leaving his face. "We must alter our meeting place; the demon hunters have attacked once, and I suspect they may come again—unless the group who found me were reckless, pathetic fools acting on their own, which is highly likely. But I would still rather not risk it."

"Do you 'ave a place in mind? Is your vorld, not mine, so I can't exactly suggest anyving to you ozzer zhan ve make zhis a place not too var avay. I 'ave to get to you vrom zhe portal, vemember, and zhen I 'ave to take zhe vampires zhere."

"Surely you've seen the forest that surrounds most of the area outside the castle?"

"I 'ave," the vampire confirmed.

"It's not exactly to *my* liking, but there *is* an old catacomb close to that forest's edge. We could meet there for the next few months until I can be sure that the castle is safe. How does that sound?"

Looking at him, Alucard frowned in confusion. Was he asking if his plan was okay? Was Zalith requesting his opinion rather than telling him straight that this was the plan? He wasn't sure how to feel about being given the chance to express his opinion; he never got to do such a thing. He was either giving out orders himself or receiving them from Damien, someone who would never ask for his view, and Alucard knew better than to try and give it. But yet, there was Zalith…asking him if his plan was acceptable. That made him feel valid—it made him feel less…belittled.

He nodded slowly. "Zhat sounds…vine," he agreed.

"Good." Zalith smiled. "I will inform the vampires of this new meeting place. I should also show you where it is."

Alucard shook his head. "I am sure I vill vind zhe place," he refused, uninterested in travelling through the portal unless he had no other choice. Zalith's vague explanation of the place's location was enough. He'd work it out.

Just then, the woman returned with a round, black tray with two mugs and a small shot-like glass on it.

"I'd like cream and sugar, too," Zalith said as the woman placed one of the mugs and the single smaller glass in front of him.

With an irritated scowl, she placed the other mug in front of Alucard and then stormed back into the store.

The vampire glared down at the dark, steaming drink in front of him. That…was coffee? It didn't look very nice, nor did it smell too great, either. But he was willing to try it; it was popular among the humans, and if someone like Zalith enjoyed it, how bad could it be?

While he waited for the woman to return, Zalith set his eyes back on Alucard. "I'm curious to know—and don't feel inclined to answer if you don't want to—but why haven't you healed from last night's incursion?" he asked, both curiosity and concern in his silvery voice as he eyed the faint bruise on the left side of Alucard's neck.

Taking his eyes off the drink, Alucard glared suspiciously at the demon. Why did he want to know? Why did he *have* to know? Zalith may have said he didn't have to answer, but the vampire knew he didn't mean it. However, he felt no need to deny him an answer this time. "Zhe attack I kept vrom 'itting you disabled my ethos, and my 'ealing abilities vent vith zhat. I zon't know 'ow long vill take vor me to vecover, but I'm sure von't be too much longer."

Zalith smiled. "Thank you again for that."

He snarled quietly. "Is vhatever. I did zhat so I vouldn't be levt alone to deal vith your problem."

"Is that right?" he the demon tested amusedly.

Alucard glared at him. "Vhat ozzer veason could zhere be?"

"Perhaps you did it because the thought of me getting hurt upset you," he suggested with a sly smirk.

Alucard scoffed. "Upset? *Prost. Pe mine? Deranjat?*" he mumbled to himself as he looked away. "Vhatever."

Amused, Zalith smiled and rested his arms on the table once more. "I didn't hear a no."

Pouting, Alucard glared into the store's window, waiting for the woman to return with what Zalith asked for. They hadn't even been out here that long and he already felt embarrassed. So, for the next few moments, he'd try to ignore the demon's unseemly gaze. They were only there for business, but Alucard was sure that Zalith would soon start asking questions of a more personal manner. This time, he'd keep his guard up, though.

Or at least he'd try to.

Chapter Twenty-Five

Matters of Business

| Zalith |

As he poured the shot of espresso into his coffee, Zalith smirked at Alucard. His silence amused him, and although he didn't want to press the vampire, he *was* curious enough to try and encourage him to answer. "I'll take your silence as either you're thinking of something to say, or I'm right. I think I prefer the latter."

"Vink vhat you like," Alucard mumbled, watching Zalith as he added both sugar and cream to his drink and stirred it with a small spoon.

Alucard then looked down at his own drink with an unsure look on his face. He picked up his mug and slowly took a sip from it, but a revolted grimace struck his face. The vampire placed his mug down and reached for the sugar, and then he tipped it over his mug, allowing a continuous stream of sugar to pour down into the drink.

Watching him, Zalith wasn't sure whether to laugh or stop him. Everything this vampire did intrigued him, though, so he sat and watched, waiting to see just how much sugar Alucard was going to put into that drink.

It wasn't until half the sugar glass was empty that Alucard stopped. He then picked up a spoon and slowly stirred the coffee.

"Are you certain that's enough?" Zalith asked, humoured.

"Maybe." The vampire placed the spoon down as he took another sip. The grimace on his face wasn't nearly as bad, but he picked up the sugar again and tilted it over the cup, pouring more into it.

Still watching, Zalith slowly stirred his own coffee. "I assume you don't make many social calls. Your dwarf friend seemed rather upset to learn that you and I were going for coffee."

"I zon't 'ave people to socialize vith ozzer zhan vork. I zon't spend time vith zhe people I vork vith outside of business," he explained, placing the glass of sugar down again. He then sipped from his mug, and this time, he didn't grimace at all.

Zalith smirked as he sipped from his coffee. "You're spending time with *me*," he said, hoping to get a reaction out of the vampire after so many failed attempts to fluster him. He found himself wondering: did Alucard even understand that he was flirting with him? Or was he playing this so calmly that it only appeared that way? He wasn't sure, but he wasn't going to let up yet.

The vampire pouted ever so slightly. "Because ve came 'ere to discuss *business*," he said sternly.

"Yes, we did, didn't we?" Zalith smiled and placed his cup down as he leaned his arms onto the table. "With complete *professional* interest, what do you do with your spare time?"

Alucard frowned. "Vhat I do vith my spare time 'as noving to do vith our vork at all."

"You form relations with humans so that the vampires can live among them, and you're moving vampires from my world to yours, therefore, it *is* business-related," he said with a matter-of-fact tone.

He wasn't wrong, and Alucard clearly saw that. "I zon't veally do much outside of vhat you alveady know. I kill verevolves to keep zhe 'umans safe, and in turn, zhe treaty stays intact so long as zhe vampires and 'umans abide by zhe laws zhat sets in place."

"Humans, such…lamentable creatures."

Just then, the woman returned to their table with the bill. Alucard held out his hand, but the woman glanced at his claw-tipped fingers and turned her nose up at him. She placed the paper on the table and turned around and left without a word.

Rolling his eyes, Alucard picked up and glanced at the paper. "Zon't get me started," he grumbled, placing the paper back down on the table as he glared into his drink.

Zalith smiled. "No, please *do* start," he invited, interested to hear Alucard's opinion.

"Zhey treat zhis land like is zheir own. Many 'undreds of years ago, I vas greatly vorshipped and 'ighly veared; zhey 'ad so many names for me, but zhen I vought vould be a better idea to become zhe uman's ally. I vind myselv vegretting zhat decision at least vree times a day. Zhey are disgusting, rude, ugly, and pathetic," he snarled and then sipped from his cup. "Zhey actually believe zhey 'ave control over vhat 'appens 'ere; zhey vink zhat zhis treaty vill stop me vrom ridding zhem of my land if I so ever feel like doing so, and if zhey continue to treat zhe vampires like parasites, I vill show zhem zhat is zhe ozzer vay avound. *Zhey* are zhe parasites."

Listening with a smile on his face, Zalith nodded.

The vampire then laughed slightly. "Do zhey actually vink zhey are better zhan us? Just because ve can't valk in zhe sunlight, zhey vink zhat makes zhem superior. Two 'undred years ago, zhey vould quiver in zheir beds at zhe sound of a vampire's name. Zhen, I levt zhe land, and vhen I got back, zhe 'umans 'ad killed more zhan 'alf zhe vampires and seemed to 'ave vorgotten who I am. Zoesn't bover me too much, but zhere is only so much of zheir shit I vill take. I ally vith zhem because zhe vampires need blood, and zhe only ozzer blood avound 'ere is verevolf, and zhat tastes vorse zhan zhis," he said, glancing down at his coffee.

Sipping from his mug, Zalith stared at him, still listening.

"Zhe city council is under zhe impression zhat I 'ave allied vith zhem to keep zhe 'umans vrom 'unting zhe vampires, but I 'onestly 'ave no intervest. Zhey pose no vhreat. I could rid zhis entire land of 'umans in a single night. But I von't. Vhy chase avay zhe food?" he ranted, smirking. "Zhis treaty only makes vings easier vor zhe vampires to veed; zhey zon't care to live in zhe city or use vhatever zhis place 'as to offer. Yes, vhat I 'ave set up vight now is sustainable, but zhere is no vun in drvinking blood zhat 'as been…hm…varmed."

Zalith smiled, but a confused feeling lingered inside him. He'd come here with intentions completely polar to what he was currently experiencing; where he knew he'd most certainly be making a flirtatious comment to fluster Alucard, he now found himself sitting in avidness, waiting with a keen interest for the vampire to continue talking. He realized he'd almost completely lost motivation to try and grab this vampire's attention and instead waited to hear his words. He very much enjoyed listening to Alucard—much more than he might have thought. So, he remained quiet, waiting.

Alucard shrugged as he sipped from his coffee again. "I 'ave my own grudges vith zhe verevolves. I vould be at war vith zhem anyvay, so I vhought I might as vell make use of zhis all—get someving out of zhis, no?"

The demon nodded, an insightful look on his face. "An astute move."

"Tobias vinks someving might be going on vith zhe volves—a pact between two of zhe packs. I need to look into zhat today avter zhis," he mumbled.

"I see you've already made plans for when I leave," he said, an almost disappointed look on his face. "Unless you'd like me to stay," he suggested.

"Vhy vould I vant you to stay?" Alucard frowned, confused. "My business vith zhe volves 'ere is not of your concern."

"No, but spending time with you *is*," he said, moving his hand closer to Alucard's.

Failing to notice, Alucard picked up his coffee. "Ve'll see each ozzer in two veeks' time; I see no veason vor you to vant to deviate vrom zhat arrangement," he said, sipping from his cup.

Was Alucard utterly uninterested, or did he have no idea what Zalith was trying to say? Had he been out of the game so long that he was struggling to pull? The demon wasn't sure, and for the first time in a while, he found himself stumped. Alucard didn't react to his flirting, nor did he seem to notice his suggestive expressions; the tone in his voice didn't even seem to spell it out for Alucard. Was he not being obvious enough? How obvious could he get before Alucard responded the way he wanted him to? Even if the vampire wasn't interested in his advances, he wanted some kind of response from Alucard which told him he understood what was going on.

So, he'd try something else. "Your familiar doesn't approve of this," he started, smirking. "He appears rather jealous, and he also seemed to recognize me. Have you been speaking of me in my absence, Aleksei?"

Alucard frowned. "Elvin zoesn't like anyvone I talk to."

"And that would be because?"

He shrugged. "Says 'e cares about me. I zon't know vhy. I 'aven't done anyving to prompt such a feeling."

And that all but confirmed his suspicions. Zalith understood very clearly that Elvin, the small, ugly little human man, had feelings for Alucard, and quite obviously, Alucard didn't understand, so of course, he wouldn't understand Zalith's approaches. But that didn't foil nor repulse Zalith; it only made Alucard appear a whole lot more interesting. How rather beguiling that was.

An amused smile found its way to Zalith's face. This vampire had *no* idea he was flirting with him, did he? It didn't even appear to be Alucard's fault, however. Zalith could now safely assume that Alucard experienced little to no social interaction outside of his work, and he had also come to see that the vampire didn't really consider his subordinates friends. He was very clearly all about the job. And Zalith found that rather attractive, too—as well as a challenge. It would be much harder to get Alucard to understand that he was trying to seduce him, but that just made it all the more entertaining.

However, he was curious to know *why* Alucard seemed to lack an interest in social interaction outside of his business. He found himself wondering many things he would've never before been interested in learning. But this vampire was different; a certain mystery lingered around him, and Zalith couldn't help but wish to know more.

Catching Zalith's gaze, Alucard frowned uncomfortably. "Vhat?"

"What would you say if I were to suggest we meet like this once every fortnight?" he asked with a smile. "We meet every two weeks to transport vampires, and on the weeks in between, I'd like to meet like this."

"Vhy? To…discuss business?"

"If you like."

The vampire slowly took his eyes off Zalith and looked at the table. A frown of confliction warped his pale face as he pondered…and when he glanced down the street, he seemed to be at war with his thoughts.

Zalith waited, admiring him, staring at his fiery eyes, which shimmered brighter in the shade of the city. And when Alucard looked back at him, he swiftly shifted his gaze to his drink.

"Ve… can meet like zhis, yes," he agreed.

The demon smiled in both delight *and* relief. "Then it's settled. I'll meet you every other Saturday," he said, finishing his coffee.

"*Da*," Alucard mumbled. The vampire then picked up the bill and glared at it.

"Let me get that," Zalith suggested, reaching for the paper, ensuring he touched the vampire's hand again, but just as he had before, Alucard paid no mind to it.

He did, however, snatch the paper away. "No," he denied, reaching over to his blazer and into its left pocket. He pulled out a single gold coin and placed it on the paper as he put it back on the table. He then finished his own drink and leaned back in his seat. "Vhat vill you do vonce I leave?"

Zalith smiled. "Why? Are you going to invite me to join you on your quest?"

"No," the vampire denied.

"Hmm…I will return to my world and deal with my own business."

"Vill you vind out 'ow zhose demon 'unters vound you?"

"Yes, I'll be looking into that," he confirmed. "And you? Werewolves, I assume. What does it mean for you if these two packs *are* working together?"

Alucard shrugged. "Zhe packs 'ave been divided vor many centuries, more so since my veturn. Zhey can't 'unt zhe 'umans, so zhey vight amongst each ozzer. Tobias is my verevolf invormant; 'e tells me zhat zhe north and vest packs 'ave been meeting more ovten. If zhe packs join togezzer in a bid to try and vight me, all zhat veally means is zhat I'll 'ave less time to sit avound in my empty 'ouse and do noving. I'll 'ave to put zhem back in zheir places," he muttered.

"*Why* is your house empty, Aleksei?" Zalith asked. "Do you enjoy your solitude? Or was the house just empty *today* because the other people that live there are…out?"

"Just ask if I live alone or not," Alucard mumbled.

"Do you live alone?" Zalith asked, smirking.

"I do," he confirmed. "I told you zhat I don't socialize outside of vork, zhat goes vor my personal life, too. I prever to live alone. Less noise."

"And you don't get lonely?"

"No. I zon't need anyvone to make me veel…relevant."

Zalith frowned. "That wasn't what I asked."

Rolling his eyes, Alucard glared down at the table again.

The demon then leaned back in his seat. "Something *has* actually been on my mind recently."

"Vhat?" Alucard asked with a frown.

"Damien."

Dread smothered Alucard's face, and he turned away, scowling.

Zalith wasn't sure why Alucard always reacted in the same uncomfortable way whenever Damien appeared or was mentioned. He wasn't going to pry into that, though. Not yet. Instead, he adorned a skeptical expression. "He speaks of rewards in exchange for loyalty, for completing his little tasks. You wouldn't happen to know what these rewards are, would you?"

"No," Alucard uttered, despondency in his voice.

"Have you not been rewarded for anything you have done for him?"

Sullen discomfort covered his face as he tried his best to try and keep Zalith from seeing it. "No," he answered.

However, the demon already noticed the look on Alucard's face. Was he upsetting him? That appeared to be the case, but why? How? He frowned, taking his eyes off the vampire for a moment. Why did he feel concerned? Once again, he found himself lacking in his original intentions that came with him to this meeting. Why, he wasn't sure, but he *was* sure that he didn't want to continue upsetting Alucard.

"How are Ben and his wife?" he asked, changing the subject so inordinately in an attempt to lighten the vampire's mood.

Alucard shrugged. "Zhey're vine—last time I checked."

"Ben speaks fondly of you; you appear to have made quite an impression," the demon said with a smile.

"Vight."

Zalith frowned, understanding that his attempts to deviate from what upset Alucard failed to have any effect on him.

The vampire seemed to have lost his motivation to socialize the moment Damien's name was mentioned. To Zalith's disappointment, Alucard sighed and pulled his blazer from the spare chair between them. "I should get to vork."

With a despondent look, Zalith watched him stand up. "Are you sure you wouldn't like me to accompany you? I have a lot of free time today."

"No," he denied again, pulling his blazer on. "Is best I vork alone."

Also standing up, Zalith sighed in acceptance. "Well, I will see you this coming Saturday—for coffee."

Alucard glanced over at him. "You can meet me at my 'ouse again. I vill be more prepared next time."

The demon smirked. "Is that so?"

"Vhere do you go? 'Ow vill you get 'ome?" he asked, ignoring Zalith's suggestive smirk. "Do you need to borrow zhe 'orse?"

"No, I'll be all right." He smiled and held out his hand. "This was a rather enjoyable time, and I look forward to the next."

Slowly and unsurely, Alucard took Zalith's hand and shook it. "Likevise," he muttered before pulling his hand from Zalith's. Then, he turned around and made his way down the street, leaving Zalith alone outside the store.

Watching him leave, Zalith's smirked curiously. It had been a long time since he felt like he'd enjoyed something so much, and he was unquestionably keen for their next…date. He laughed quietly as he turned around and headed towards the city exit. Today was a whole lot more congenial than he might have originally thought, as was Alucard. Zalith learnt a fair amount about him, and he was looking forward to finding out what else this vampire had to share.

Chapter Twenty-Six

— ⸲ † ⸳ —

A Looming Dilemma

| Alucard |

As the afternoon faded into the early evening, Alucard rode towards the east side of the vast Dargamoore forest. But he couldn't keep himself from wondering why he denied Zalith's offer to accompany him. Would it not be better to be conversing with someone rather than riding in silence? Soon, he would have to deal with werewolves, and nothing annoyed him more—well, Zalith's unprompted laughter was a close contender.

Why was Zalith so interested in his personal life and other business? He wasn't sure but considering he never had a real friend before, he assumed that such curiosity came with *being* someone's friend. The demon must simply want to know the things he asked because that was what friends should know about each other…right?

But then he sighed. He agreed to meet Zalith every other week outside of work, and he was glad he did. It would give him more time to get to know the demon. Alucard already accepted that he and Zalith were friends, and the vampire was sure that was okay because Damien had made them work together. So, what harm would there be in getting to know Zalith better? The idea of learning more about this confusing demon intrigued Alucard. He already enjoyed Zalith's company more than anyone else he worked with, and he was also the only person he found himself wanting to know more about. So, that meant they were friends, didn't it?

Alucard pouted. Yes, they *were* friends. Zalith said they were, and Alucard admittedly enjoyed spending time with him. He was a little odd and insufferable at times, but…he was starting to like that.

In six days, he'd meet Zalith again for another social call, and the week after that, he'd head to Zalith's world once again and bring back the next group of vampires. Hopefully this time he wouldn't have to partake in a battle.

Alucard focused on what was ahead as his stallion trotted into the forest. The sounds of horses and chattering people carried on the light breeze, and quiet folk music echoed in the distance. It became louder as he moved deeper into the forest, and light smoke became visible through the treetops, floating into the evening sky.

When they emerged into a wide glade, Alucard watched as people rushed around in preparation for the night, stacking crates, preparing food over fires, and walking in and out of their caravan homes whilst talking loudly in Dor-Sanguian. If there was anything Alucard enjoyed about Tobias' pack, it was that they spoke his native tongue, a language he sadly had to accept was dying with each generation.

He climbed off his horse and led him to a small fence. The vampire hitched him and looked around, eyeing each person in the clearing. There were two groups of four men standing at each end of the narrow river that ran through the clearing and around to where Alucard usually met Tobias; they mumbled to one another with drinks in their hands. Seven oak-wood caravans were lined along the river, and they were all black with hand-painted red and mahogany murals. Most of them had well-groomed horses grazing beside them, chewing on the grass.

Alucard set his eyes on the tall, rugged Alpha. Tobias stood by the river in a black shirt and dark navy jeans, which surprisingly weren't muddy or torn. The vampire walked over to him and watched as he began brawling with one of his Betas.

He stopped beside the river, waiting, watching as Tobias eventually slung the equally muscular man to the ground, and both of them laughed like idiots. Alucard didn't understand why they seemed to find fun in it, but he didn't care to ask. As the other man caught sight of Alucard, he stood up and nodded at Tobias, who turned around to face him.

A bright smile appeared on Tobias' amused face as he set his brown eyes on the vampire. "Aleksei! What's up, man?" he asked, pouncing forward to throw his arms around Alucard, but the vampire stepped aside and let Tobias stumble past him.

Without so much as a frown of concern for Tobias, who had fallen to the ground, Alucard looked down at him. "You told me zhat zhe north and vest packs 'ave been meeting more ovten: tell me about zhat," he said, inviting Tobias to walk beside him as he started walking along the riverbed.

Tobias hurried to catch up with him. "You're looking into it?"

"Obviously."

"Right, well…where should I start?"

"Vhere 'ave zhey been meeting? 'Ow ovten, 'ow many of zhem—tell me everyving." He wanted to know more about the attack on the caravans outside of Vria, but since Tobias hadn't said anything about that yet, it was safe to assume he hadn't heard. And why would he? He and his pack hardly ever left the glade unless undertaking a job for him. But then again, Tobias' wolfish brain had a habit of making him forget to mention important things when something larger was on his mind, so he'd better ask when they were done.

Nodding, Tobias sighed. "The guy I sent to watch them never came back; we went looking for him, but we think he's either been killed or they've got him locked up somewhere. We first discovered their meetings a few days before I came and told you about them, and as far as I'm aware, they've been meeting every night. Sometimes, there's a small group, and other times, it's both packs in their entirety. They always meet in a different location; I've got a girl on the inside, but she hasn't been able to report back in a few days. Gotta avoid suspicion, y'know."

"I gazzer vrom your mentioning of your guy, you're 'oping I vill 'elp you vind 'im?" Alucard asked skeptically.

Laughing nervously as they stopped in front of a tree, Tobias dragged his hand over the back of his head. "Yeah, kinda. Both packs on their own are three times the size of mine; we ain't really much of a match for 'em. I'd be asking as a favour for a friend, of course—and I'd pay you back."

Alucard rolled his eyes, trying to hide his concern. Did he want to help Tobias find his packmate? Of course he did; Tobias risked a lot doing the things he did for him, and if there was any way he could help Tobias in the form of a discrete thank you, then he would do it. Whether this packmate of his was dead or not, he'd help Tobias find him.

He looked back at Tobias. "If your guy is still alive, vhere vould zhey keep 'im?"

"Where they're staying," he answered.

The vampire knew exactly where each pack in Dor-Sanguis set up their camps, but since the attack last night, he was sure the West Pack had probably moved. However, the wolves kept to their immediate territories and always had, so if they'd packed up their camp, they still have to be in the area somewhere.

"We've tried scouting the area, but we can't get close enough to see if Farley's there."

"Zhat is 'is name, uh?"

"Yeah. You can get close, right?" Tobias asked worriedly.

"I gazzer Varley is…important to you?"

Tobias nodded. "Yeah, man. He's one of the best guys here, too; losing him has really put a hole in the shit you got us doing."

Alucard sighed and dragged his hand over his face in frustration as he looked back at Tobias' pack, all of whom were watching from wherever they were standing or sitting. It was starting to look as though tonight would be a search and rescue rather than a simple observation. Alucard wasn't annoyed, though. Tobias deserved his help, especially since his packmate had been either taken or killed while doing something Alucard ordered them to do.

"Vhich pack do you suspect 'as 'im?"

Tobias replied, "I dunno, honestly. It could be either of them. His tracks cut off in a clearing between both packs' territories, so we don't know which one took him—unless they killed him and erased every trace of his body…like rats."

"If zhey killed 'im, zhere vould be a lot of blood. Vemoving somevone's 'ead ovten leaves a lot of mess. You vould be able to pick zhat up, but I assume zhere isn't a trace of 'is scent?"

Shaking his head, Tobias started to fiddle with his beard. "So, I don't know."

"Vine," Alucard agreed. "I'll vind your man."

Relief smothered Tobias' face. "Really, man? I can't thank you en—"

"Zon't touch me," Alucard warned, stepping back as Tobias leaned in for a hug.

The werewolf held up his hands. "Sorry, man," he said. But then he slipped his hands into his pockets and sighed. "I just wanna know if he's all right."

"Your girl on zhe inside: vhich pack 'as she infiltrated?"

"The west."

"And 'as she reported seeing 'im zhere?"

"No."

"Zhen if 'e is alive, 'e must be vith zhe North Pack, no? Alucard concluded.

"Y-yeah, you're right." Tobias laughed nervously. "Why didn't I think of that?"

Alucard deadpanned. "Because you are stupid," he grumbled. "Did you even *ask* 'er to see if Varley vas zhere?" he asked, but as Tobias looked around in embarrassment, Alucard rolled his eyes.

Tobias wasn't very bright, but he *was* a strong fighter and leader, so he didn't need to question why out of all these wolves Tobias was the one in charge. It was a little questionable, but the pack respected him as their Alpha, so he felt no need to get involved.

"Did your girl on zhe inside veport anyving about…planned attacks?"

"Uh…oh, shit…yeah, now that you mention it…."

The vampire rolled his eyes.

"Something about uhh…a hunt—an attack or something, but all she could find out was that there were whispers of a move against the vamps. Kids, though—big mouths going off about impressing their Alphas, taking out a few humans. Why? Did…oh, shit man…did something happen?"

"Zhe Vest Pack attacked a caravan group outside Vria last night. Zhere vere no survivors, not even my vampires."

Tobias' eyes widened. "Fuck, man…shit…I shoulda taken it seriously. But with all that's going on, I didn't think any of the packs would be brave enough to do something like that, especially after you killed that Amarok and its pack."

Shaking his head, Alucard sighed. "Vell, zhey did, and now zhey're meeting up. I need to get to zhe bottom of zhis soon."

"Yeah, I got you man. Just let me know what you need, yeah?"

Alucard nodded. "Vell, I vill go to vhere zhe North Pack is staying, and I vill see if your vriend is zhere. Vhat does 'e look like?"

"Hmm…." Tobias frowned. "Face like mine…beard, too…hair's blonde, bit longer than mine…" he explained, fiddling with his hair. "Oh, and if he's in his wolf form, he's a kind of…yellow colour," he added.

Huffing irritably, Alucard looked to his right and glared into the trees. "Vight… I'll see if I can vind 'im."

"If you're checking out the North Pack, do you want me and my guys to check out the West Pack? In case you don't get anything from them."

The vampire nodded. "Hmm…'ave you 'eard anyving vegarding zheir meetings at all?"

Tobias shook his head. "Nothing else, really."

Alucard looked back at Tobias. "Stay 'ere. Zon't visk yourselv or any more of your packmates until I know vhat is going on," he instructed.

Scratching the back of his head, Tobias nodded. "All right, man. You gonna be all right?"

Waving his hand in dismissal, Alucard headed into the forest, ignoring Tobias' calls of thanks and farewell. Could the packs' meetings be for something as simple as grouping up to challenge him? Did hunting in towns and the city really mean *that* much to them? The land wasn't even theirs; it never was, and clearly, they were under the impression that it was. That made the vampire furious. The name Dor-Sanguis literally meant 'in pain and in blood', the words used to describe his creation in the world's history. If he had to kill the two packs to remind all werewolf-kind that they belonged in the woods, then he would.

With an irritated snarl, vermillion smoke consumed him, and he emerged from it in the form of a horned-eagle owl. His eyes shone hell-fiery red in the darkening light as he swiftly made his way through the trees, flapping his wings as silently as the imminent night. He passed many patrolling wolves, but he had no interest in them. His destination was their camp.

After fifteen minutes, Alucard set his eyes on a clearing in the distance with several caravans spread around the border. He gracefully landed on a tree branch and quickly examined the area with his eyes. The centre of the clearing had nothing in it; where there used to be grass, there was dusty, dried dirt. Clearly, this area had been used as some sort of brawling area—the fact that there were two Alpha wolves tearing one another apart there made that obvious.

The North Pack: known for its multiple, merciless Alphas, its bloodthirsty Betas, and its pack leader and Luna, Nina. A revolting, insufferable woman with no tolerance for weakness. She was the only wolf in her human form, sitting in front of the gold-on-white painted caravan. Little to nothing covered her dark skin, and a curious look sat on her sharp face as, with her cold, deep-blue eyes, she watched the two brutes fight. Small Beta wolves were sprawled out all around her, panting, scowling, and watching as she did, their coats as black as her hair.

On the opposite side of the clearing, six huge blue-grey Etas were keeping watch. But Alucard wasn't threatened. Why would he be? To them, he was but a simple, harmless owl.

He scoured the area once more; it would be simple to spot a golden-coated wolf among all the black and blue wolves, but there wasn't such a coat in sight. Black-coated Betas were dotted all over the place, in between the caravans, and around the tree line; there were very easily at least fifty wolves, a lot more than there had been the last time Alucard checked up on this pack. Why had Tobias failed to mention the pack had grown? *Idiot.*

He swooped down from his perch and glided over to another tree so he could see more of the area. Once he landed, he glared at the caravans he couldn't see inside of from where he was previously, but there was still no sign of Farley. He wasn't going to give up yet, however—but he couldn't be careless. If he dove from his perch again, someone might notice. He'd come for information; that was his primary goal. If he got caught searching for Tobias' unlucky friend, he'd not have the words to explain to Tobias how inconvenienced he made him feel. But he *had* agreed to look for his man, so he couldn't lumber the entire blame on Tobias.

Alucard scowled impatiently. Was sitting there going to get him anywhere? It would be rather coincidental if these wolves suddenly started talking about their plans with him there; he hoped that they would, but he was sure he'd have to do something in order to find out what he wanted to know.

He looked around slowly, trying to come up with a plan. Could he somehow lead one of the Alphas away and interrogate him? Maybe even Nina…no, even though she probably had all the answers, he wasn't in the mood to deal with her. He could just run in, stir up a battle, and run and wait until the pursuing wolves separated. However, running was an awful lot of work, especially when he had to do it in his human form. Stirring up a battle sure did sound fun, though, since he'd get to do so by killing a wolf or two.

That's what he wanted to do. That's what he would do…if it wasn't for the blur of gold he could now see inside the caravan that had just been opened by the only other wolf in their human form. Alucard watched as the tall, lanky man stepped out of the black caravan with a cruel grin on his face as he wiped the blood from his fists. The vampire watched him join Nina, kissing her forehead before slumping down beside her. He rested his head in her lap, and she started stroking his hair.

Alucard rolled his eyes before setting them back on the caravan he saw gold inside. With his incomparable vision, he focused on the blur; it became as clear as day—a Beta wolf, its fur a flaxen-yellow, but most of it was covered in blood, both dried and new. He lay on his side, panting and whining, and its mouth was parted as blood seeped out onto the caravan's wooden floor. Silver shackles were tied to the beast's back and front legs, and his fur beneath them had completely withered, leaving patches of sore, scabby skin. It looked as though he was waiting for death to take him.

But Alucard wasn't going to let that happen. That wolf was there because of him. The fact that he was still alive told the vampire that he hadn't given these wolves the information they were trying to get, information that would tell them Alucard knew of their meetings. If they found out he was onto them, his plans in Dor-Sanguis would become a whole lot more annoying. For Farley's loyalty, Alucard felt that he could at least *try* and help him.

What could he do, though? There were at least fifty wolves; Nina, the Alpha in her lap, the two Alphas fighting in the middle of the clearing, and not forgetting the *six* huge blue Etas beneath him. And then the irritating number of Betas. Although Betas didn't possess venom, he still had to be careful. Getting bitten by any werewolf was an awful enough experience on its own, but an Alpha? He had to avoid that at all costs.

He took his eyes off the wolf and looked up at the sky, watching as the six moons slowly climbed higher. Would the wolves leave to meet the West Pack tonight? If they did, he could rescue Farley in their absence. Sure, they would leave guards, but he could deal with them—rather three or four than the entire pack.

And so, he waited. He wasn't sure how long he might be there, but he wouldn't move until morning came or the pack left.

Chapter Twenty-Seven

—⋰ † ⋱—

The Rescue

| Alucard |

I t wasn't until around midnight that the wolves started heading out. The sound of their paws hitting the ground woke Alucard from his sleep; he opened his eyes, the wind brushing through his feathers as he glared at the pack. He watched as they left in a single-file line, following their white-furred leader as she led the way into the trees. To his relief, two of the six Etas left with them, leaving just four of them to guard the area.

Alucard still had to be careful. He turned his head and set his eyes on the golden wolf inside the caravan, making sure he was still alive. The guy was whining through his stifled breaths, but he seemed to have stopped bleeding, and that was a relief. If he could save Farley, there was a possibility that he might have useful information—he had, after all, clearly been there quite some time, and he must have overheard conversations. If not, Alucard would simply free him and send him on his way before following the pack.

As much as he wanted to know what the wolves were up to, he decided that rescuing Tobias' friend was his first priority. He wasn't sure why he felt so concerned about what Tobias might think if he chose to leave Farley behind, but he was convinced that it wouldn't spark any confidence in those who worked for him if he were to abandon them in their time of need. If Alucard wanted Tobias' people to work loyally and efficiently, the vampire had to ensure they trusted him and could rely on him. Where he knew some people in his position might abuse their influence and power, he wasn't one such person.

The vampire spread his wings and flew over to the caravan, landing on top of it just above the door. He looked around at the Etas, which had seen and were now glaring at him. So, he opened his left wing and started to groom his feathers like a real owl would, trying to convince them that that was all he was.

And it worked. The wolves snarled and resumed scouring the area with their eyes. *Stupid creatures.*

Slowly and quietly, he hopped along to the caravan's open roof vent and peered inside, setting his eyes on Farley. The wolf was still, quiet, and looked to be in immense pain. If Alucard could ever spare a moment of sympathy, it was now. But he didn't have time to stand there and feel sorry for him. He hopped into the vent, and as he silently descended to the floor, vermillion smoke surrounded his small, feathered body. As he morphed back into his usual self, he crouched beside the wolf.

He was almost certain that it might yelp or snarl in panic upon seeing him, so the first thing he did was grab its muzzle with his right hand, keeping its mouth shut. Then, as it opened its shimmering yellow eyes, horror and panic filled them.

Alucard scowled and held his left index finger to his lips, and as the wolf frowned, he pointed to his right. The wolf slowly looked to where he was pointing, and as it set its eyes on one of the visible Etas, it looked back at Alucard and frowned in confusion.

How was he going to get the wolf out of there? Its back left leg was snapped in two, it was covered in all manner of scratches and bites, and it breathed so strangely that Alucard assumed it might have been forced to inhale silver. First, he had to make sure this rescue would be worth him sacrificing a chance to listen in on the meeting the pack had likely gone to.

He frowned and leaned closer to Farley. "Do you know vhat zhe north and vest packs are doing togezzer?" he whispered.

The wolf frowned and nodded.

That was all he needed.

But how would he get him out? He could use his true form and carry him to safety, alerting the Etas, which would tell Nina he was there. He could use his mist form, also alerting the Etas that it was he who was there. Or he could go out there and kill them.... That sounded rather nice. But when Nina returned and saw her four Etas were dead, she'd also know it was he who had been there. Etas were hard to kill, and he would be her first suspicion. Was there any way out of this that would keep his knowledge of the wolves' meetings hidden? It didn't look as though there was.

However, the wolf might be able to give him the answers he was looking for without him even having to follow the North Pack. Farley wasn't in a good way, and if Alucard didn't get him back to his pack soon, he was sure he would die. So he was willing to take a risk. If he got Farley back and he didn't possess the information he needed, then at least he would have saved someone's life, thus keeping his subordinates' confidence intact.

He glanced out the caravan's door, watching as the Eta within eyesight looked around skeptically. Then, he looked back down at Farley. The silver chains around his ankles were going to be a problem. Alucard knew that silver was one of his weaknesses, and there was no way he'd be able to free him from them. However, he could pull them off Farley...if he broke a few of his bones.

"Listen to me," he whispered firmly. "Neizer of us is going anyvhere if I zon't get zhese chains off. Zhe only vay I can do zhat is if I break your legs."

Farley's eyes widened in horror.

"Is eizer zhat or staying 'ere and enduring more of vhatever zhat man vas doing to you."

Although he was terrified, the wolf nodded and weakly uttered, "Do it."

Alucard gripped the wolf's front leg and snapped the bones. The wolf yelped, and Alucard swiftly backed into the shadows out of sight when an Eta stopped prowling and sharply turned its head towards the caravan. But it didn't come to investigate.

The vampire eased the shackle from Farley's leg and quickly got to work on the others.

Farley writhed and whined, trying to kick Alucard away when he broke his last leg.

Once he was free, Alucard moved his arms around the wolf and picked it up. "I 'ope you zon't get vlight sick," he muttered.

The whimpering wolf frowned, but before he could try to ask what the vampire meant, Alucard disappeared into vermillion smoke, pulling Farley with him. He burst out through the door; the Etas growled and howled as the vampire ascended into the night sky. He raced forward, moving so quickly that everything below was a blur of black and green.

After a few minutes, he reached the glade where Tobias and his pack were staying. He landed in the centre and placed Farley down as he rematerialized.

As soon as he saw Alucard, Tobias started making his way over, and when he reached the vampire, he looked at Farley in horror. "Y-you found him, man!" he exclaimed but then shook his head as he crouched beside the barely conscious wolf. "What happened to him? What did they do?"

"Farley!" a woman cried as she pulled Tobias out of the way and threw her arms around the gold-furred wolf.

Alucard shrugged. "I zon't know exactly vhat zhey did, but you need to make sure 'e stays alive. 'E 'as invormation zhat I need."

Tobias dragged his hand over the back of his neck. "You didn't have to fight anyone or anything, did you?" he asked in concern, eyeing Alucard for signs of injury. "Last thing I want is for you to get hurt whilst doing me a solid, you know."

Alucard pointed at him. "Zhis vas not a vree vavour, Tobias. You owe me."

He nodded. "Y-yeah, anything man."

"Keep 'im alive," Alucard instructed, pointing to Farley. "I vant 'im talking by zhe morning."

"They're on it already," Tobias said, nodding back at his packmates, who heard Alucard's order. He then looked back at Alucard. "Thanks, man, honestly. Look, whatever you want us to do, yeah?"

He rolled his eyes. "I just told you vhat I need you to do. I'll stay 'ere until morning in case zhe North Pack suspect you 'ad someving to do with Varley's escape."

"And the West Pack?" Tobias asked. "Did you check in on them too?"

Alucard shook his head. "I'm 'oping zhat your Varley can tell me vhat I need to know. I visked my chance of vinding out vhat zhose packs are up to to save 'is life."

Tobias laughed in relief. "Wow, Aleksei, you really didn't have to—"

"No, I zidn't, but I did," he grumbled.

"Always saving people's asses, huh?" He smirked, prodding the vampire's shoulder. "When's someone gonna save yours?"

"Vhat? I zon't need saving."

"Sure ya do—from your non-existent love life, man. I ain't seen you getting with a lady like…ever. Where's your girlfriend at?"

The vampire rolled his eyes. "Goodbye, Tobias," he snarled, preparing to morph into his owl form.

"Ain't you got some sexy vampire chick? I could set you up with one of my girls if you want—I owe ya, don't I?" He winked at him.

Alucard then frowned at him. "You 'ave…more zhan *vone* vife?"

"Well, yeah. I'm an Alpha. I get all the girls," he said with a grin.

That was surprising, considering how stupid Tobias was. But Alucard didn't care to pry. He shrugged and turned around. "No. Look avter your vriend."

As Alucard transformed into his owl form, Tobias sighed. "Suit yourself, man."

Once he landed on a tree branch, Alucard watched over the pack. He spectated four men carrying Farley into one of the caravans, presumably to see to his wounds. Then, he looked at Tobias and watched him talk to a few women. Did they find his stupidity attractive?

Now that he was thinking about it, Alucard realized that he'd never been interested in wooing someone. He didn't see the point, and he was sure he never would. Dating and marriage appeared as nothing more than something mortals did to make their short lives worthwhile, and he wasn't going to live a short life, so why would he need to find something or someone to make it worthwhile? He had all the time in the world.

All the time in the world…to work for Damien? The thought made him feel a little nauseous.

But then he scowled. Why was he even thinking about it? He wasn't allowed friends, let alone a girlfriend. Did he even want a girlfriend? No. Tobias was an idiot, and he knew better than to let his stupid statements and offers get to him. So, he closed his eyes and tried focusing on what he might learn tomorrow.

❖

Tomorrow came suddenly. Alucard opened his eyes as birdsong echoed through the miles of forest.

He set his ice-blue eyes on Tobias, who was sitting on the riverbed cleaning his clothes. Then, he turned his attention to the caravan that Farley was taken into last night. With no wish to hang around longer than he had to, he swooped down and morphed back into his usual form. He made his way into the caravan and set his eyes on the man Farley appeared to be beneath his wolf skin.

The guy was rather scrawny for a werewolf; he looked around five foot eight, and his hair was dirty blonde, reaching his shoulders. His face was smothered in patches of dark stubble, and a pained look lingered on it as he breathed uneasily. He'd been cleaned up by his packmates, not a drop of blood or dirt left on him, and the sore, scabbed scars on his wrists and ankles left by the shackles had ointment on them.

"Varley," Alucard said.

With a confused frown, the man slowly opened his eyes and looked up at him. To the vampire's relief, the man didn't panic upon seeing him. Instead, he stared, waiting.

"You told me last night zhat you knew vhy zhe north and vest packs 'ave been meeting. I need to know vhy."

Looking up at him, Farley stuttered. "Y-you saved me."

The vampire rolled his eyes. "Yes, I did. Now save me zhe theatricals and tell me vhat I need to know."

"Ah, Farley!" Tobias then called as he stepped into the caravan.

Farley looked over at him and smiled.

"I see you already found your way in here," Tobias said to Alucard, standing there in just his underwear. He moved to put his arm around the vampire, but Alucard backed off and looked away in revolt. The Alpha laughed and looked down at Farley. "You feelin' all right, man? Aleksei saved your ass."

"Yeah, guess I owe him my life now too, huh?"

"Just tell me vhat you know," Alucard grumbled, keeping his eyes focused on Farley.

"Tell him," Tobias agreed, nodding.

Farley looked up at Alucard again. "Well…the North Pack and West Pack have been meeting a lot."

Alucard waited as patiently as he could.

"Pretty much every night—except the full moon, in case they get mad at one another. Instincts and stuff, you know."

"Yes…" Alucard growled.

"So, what I got—and heard—is that they're all waiting for some big queen boss lady to get here. Apparently, she owned the land before you did. Or…well…I heard a lot of people talking, saying different things. Some of them said this lady owned this land before you, and you came along and took it from her, and then some others were saying that you both owned the land and then you both tried to take it for yourselves."

Tobias looked over at Alucard. "What's he yapping?"

"Continue," Alucard grumbled.

Farley nodded. "Uh…so…yeah, they were saying that she's coming back here. Nina's her sister or something…uh…daughter, maybe. After this whole thing you started with the city, helping the humans and stuff, the wolves obviously lost their hunting grounds, can't kill people because you're protecting them. That got them real mad, so Nina called for this Ada lady to come kill you or…chase you away, or something."

Angst shot through Alucard's body. "Ada?" he asked in concern.

"Yeah. They say her name a lot around there. Apparently, she's some big-shot werewolf. I've never heard of her…have you?" he questioned, looking at Tobias.

Tobias shook his head. "Nah, but…if she's some werewolf legend, I'm not surprised that we don't know. We're not exactly a big bloodline pack, are we?" he laughed. "We're just a bunch of rogues; no one cares about us or our ancestors."

"Vhat else did zhey say?" Alucard asked. "Vhy are zhe two packs meeting?"

Looking back at the vampire, Farley frowned. "Uh…apparently, they need numbers to go up against you and the vampires. I mean, they're not wrong, are they? So, the two packs are gonna join together in time for this Ada lady's arrival. Nina's marrying the Alpha of the North Pack—he's…the one that did this to me," he said, looking down at his scarred wrists.

"Do you know vhen Ada vill get 'ere?"

"Uh…well—"

"Do you?!" Alucard demanded.

"N-no, man." Farley stuttered in a panic. "Sorry, they didn't say. But…this wedding is happening this coming full moon."

Snarling irritably, Alucard looked down at the floor for a moment. Ada was the last thing he needed to deal with right now. The packs were not only joining together to fight against him; Ada was also coming to lead that fight. It all made sense now. Ada thought this land belonged to her, and to find out that Alucard was depriving the wolves of humans the way he was must have severely pissed her off. However, Alucard didn't want a fight. He tried to find Ada last year in an attempt to form peace with the wolves, but he couldn't find her, and he highly suspected that she didn't want to be found. Now, she was coming to Dor-Sanguis, and if he wanted to avoid an all-out war between werewolves and vampires, he'd have to be very, very careful.

"What are you thinking?" Tobias asked. "We need to stop this wedding? Fight this Ada lady? It's your call man, just tell me what you need me to do."

Alucard shook his head. "Zhis my problem. I vill solve zhis."

"Nah, man," Tobias refused, shaking his head. "The next full moon is this Monday. You got me, dude. I'm gonna help you no matter what you say."

"No. Stay 'ere and vait vor my next orders. Zon't take anyving into your own 'ands, Tobias. Noving vould piss me off more."

Tobias held up his hands. "All right, just don't forget: you don't gotta do everything by yourself. By the sounds of it, you're gonna need your own little army, and you got me and my pack, and you got your vampires, too. So, don't try do this alone, yeah? I get that you wanna protect what's yours, but let some of the people that wanna protect you help you."

The vampire sighed, rolled his eyes, and made his way over to the door. "Let me know if you 'ear anyving else. I 'ave to go 'ome and prepare vor zhis shit," he grumbled.

As Alucard left the caravan, Tobias followed him out. "What exactly is this shit, though?" he asked before Alucard could transform and leave.

The vampire sighed again. "Some old, old grudge."

"Like?" he asked, but then he smirked. "She your ex?"

Alucard sharply turned his head and glared at him. "If you make vone more joke of such a nature, I vill never come out 'ere again," he snarled, pointing at him.

"Right, sorry, just tryna lighten the mood."

"Ada and I vere both cursed by zhe gods at zhe same time. Zhese gods vere enemies, so zhey created us to also be enemies."

"Vamps and wolves, yeah?"

He nodded. "Zhat's vhy ve're natural enemies. Ada and I vought most of our battles 'ere in Dor-Sanguis, but I vas…taken avter a vew years. In my absence, she must 'ave vhought she von zhe battle, zhus vinning zhe land. When I came back, she vasn't 'ere, so I vent to look vor 'er vith Elvin so I could try and veason vith 'er vather zhan continue to vight like children. But I couldn't find 'er. My search vor 'er vas cut short vhen zhe Diabolus caught vord of my location. Zhat is vhen I came 'ome 'ere, and zhat is vhen I started zhis treaty vith zhe 'umans. Ada vas bound to turn up at some point, is just irritating zhat 'as to be now vhilst I am in zhe middle of zhis vampire business," he explained.

"Hmm." Tobias frowned. "You think she'll listen to reason? Or is she just gonna be looking for a war?"

Alucard shrugged. "I guess I vill vind out, von't I? Eizer vay, I am prepared."

"Well, whatever happens, just like I said, you got me and my pack."

The vampire nodded. "Vight…vell, I 'ave to go now."

Alucard then dematerialized into vermillion smoke and began his journey back home. If Ada really was coming, then things were about to get a whole lot more dangerous. He was going to have to move his vampires around to ensure there were enough in each town to protect the humans, and he was going to have to watch his own back more than usual. If she was coming, she was coming for *him*.

Chapter Twenty-Eight

— ⸴ ✝ ⸲ —

The First Move

| **Alucard** |

lucard and Elvin sat in their usual places in the vampire's lounge and the sun shone brightly outside. Alucard had completely healed, and there was no sign that a wound had ever smothered the right side of his face. He sat half-dressed in black trousers and shin-height black leather boots, along with a charcoal-black shirt with three of the top buttons loose. He was due to meet Zalith later and wanted to make sure he was presentable.

The bard frowned as he eyed him up and down. "Why do you look so happy?" he asked jealously.

Alucard scowled at him, unsure of what he might be talking about. Happy? He didn't look happy—as far as he knew, anyway. He was simply thinking how he might handle tonight's annoyance. How his face chose to respond to his thoughts wasn't something he could control. Elvin was obviously analyzing him again, and he hated it when *anyone* did that. So, he scowled and glared into the empty fireplace.

"What are you thinking about?" Elvin asked. "Ada, I hope."

Why had Elvin suddenly become so…intrusive? Why did he want to know everything? Why did he want to be so much more involved all of a sudden? Alucard frowned in confusion and glanced over at the eager bard. "Stuff," he snarled.

"Like what? This werewolf wedding thing: what are you doing about it? It's tonight, right? Are you gonna stop these two packs from uniting?"

He shrugged. "Maybe, maybe not."

"How are you gonna do that?"

"Hmm…kill Nina, or kill all of zhem. Maybe kill vone pack, I zon't know. I'll decide vhen I get zhere."

Elvin placed his pencil into the spine of his book. "You should really make a plan *before* you go in there, you know, especially since this is *two* packs, not one. *Two* of

Dor-Sanguis' biggest and most dangerous packs. Aleksei, do you always have to be so reckless?"

"I 'ave my methods," he mumbled.

The bard pouted. "Suicidal methods. You should ask for help at least. I know Tobias wants to help, and probably that Ben guy, too."

Rolling his eyes, Alucard rested the side of his face in his hand. "If Ada is zhere, I vill try to reason vith 'er. A war is zhe last ving I need vight now—and I zon't need 'elp, I never 'ave, and never vill."

"But…what if a war *does* happen?"

"Zhen I vill vight," he said with a heavy sigh. "I've known Ada long enough to know 'ow to send 'er running. And she is a verevolf; she's not immortal, is she?"

"And you *are*?" Elvin asked cautiously. "I know you think you're unkillable, but everyone has a weakness, Aleksei."

He scoffed. "Like you being allergic to vater?"

"Hey!" Elvin snapped. "It's a very serious condition, and you shouldn't make fun of it!"

Alucard rolled his eyes and stared back into the fireplace.

"What time's your new friend getting here?" he grumbled, changing the subject.

The vampire shrugged slightly. "Any time."

Elvin then scowled jealously. "How come you didn't just deny him being your friend? You deny so hard that I'm your friend; you claim so insistently that you don't *have* friends."

Alucard rolled his eyes. "Vhy does any of zhis weigh on your mind, Elvin? Vhy do you alvays ask me zhese questions, and vhy do you alvays vant to know zhe ins and outs of my life?" he questioned irritably as the sunlight hit his face, sending pain through his eyes as they faded to blue.

"Because I care, unlike that stupid demon."

Not at all partial to ask for him to elaborate, Alucard fell silent.

Looking down at his lap, Elvin complained, "Why does he wanna hang out with you so much? You never hang out with me or Tobias or that new Ben guy—or Dirk."

"Dirk is insufferable."

"So's that demon guy, but you're still gonna go have tea or whatever with him today."

Alucard grunted angrily, "Is business, Elvin. Ve meet to discuss vork, zhat's all. I zon't even know vhy I'm explaining myselv to you."

"Yeah, right."

"I can see you, Ben, Tobias, or Dirk any time I vant, but I cannot see Zaliv ozzer zhan during zhese meetings ve agreed to 'ave. Zhat's all zhis is. Stop acting like a child."

He pouted and went to speak—

A knock came at Alucard's door. and the bard sharply turned his head to glare at it.

Alucard got up and made his way over to the door, preparing for whatever irritating comment he was about to be met with. He turned the gold key, unlocking it, and as he pulled it open, he set his hell-fiery eyes on Zalith. The demon stood there with his hair as smartly combed as usual; he wore a grey waistcoat with trousers to match, and a white, light grey pinstriped shirt.

Zalith smiled at Alucard. "Good afternoon, Aleksei. I see your pretty face is all better."

Rolling his eyes, Alucard stepped aside, inviting Zalith in.

Pouting resentfully, Elvin glared down at the floor. "Better after what *you* did to him."

The demon shot a scowl at him. "What *I* did?" he questioned, stopping in the hall as Alucard closed the door behind him.

The bard stood up and shouted, "You know what you did!"

Alucard then moved past Zalith and pointed at Elvin as he made his way back into the lounge. "If I 'ave to tell you vone more time to drop zhis, I vill send you back to zhat orphanage I vound you in," he warned, stopping beside the liquor cabinet as Zalith sat on the couch.

Amused, Zalith laughed quietly.

Elvin slumped back down in his seat and crossed his arms. "I hate this."

"I couldn't help but overhear your conversation," Zalith then said, smiling as he looked up at Alucard, who handed him a glass of brandy. "You're attending a wedding in an attempt to stop it?" he asked curiously, watching the vampire as he slowly sat beside him.

Alucard shrugged as he sipped from his glass. "Some attempt to make zhemselves stronger in order to take my land vrom me. Von't vork."

"It will if you keep being stupid with your plans," Elvin grumbled.

The vampire then scowled irritably. "Vhat zhe fuck is your problem?" he snarled. "Zhis sudden attitude is pissing me zhe fuck off."

Startled, Elvin tensed up and stammered, "I just… don't want you to get hurt."

"I von't get 'urt. You act as zhough I zon't know vhat I'm doing."

Elvin frowned, but when he caught sight of Zalith staring at Alucard with a sly smile on his face, he scowled cruelly. "Maybe I'm not talking about the werewolf stuff."

"I'd like to offer my assistance," Zalith then said before Alucard could question Elvin. "That is if you need it."

Taking his eyes off Elvin, Alucard looked at Zalith. He offered last week to help him with his private business, and now he was offering again. Why? Were these coffee meetings not enough? Sure, he knew that Zalith considered him his friend, and he knew it was customary for friends to spend time together, but just how much time did this demon want to try and spend with him?

However, if there was a single thing that Elvin had right, it was that he probably shouldn't try to take on this matter alone. Could he do it alone? Yes, but it would be much less of an annoyance if there was someone there to help him—someone he knew could hold their own, and that someone was certainly Zalith. They had already fought two battles together—one against a pack of werewolves—so he knew that he could rely on him if the wedding *did* evolve into a fight.

The vampire nodded and replied, "Eh, may as vell."

Disbelief and frustration smothered Elvin's face as he jumped to his feet. "W-what?! You literally just said you didn't want *anyone's* help!"

"Vere you not zhe vone telling me I *should* ask vor 'elp? Make your mind up," Alucard snarled.

"Y-yeah, but…not from him!" he insisted, pointing at Zalith.

Zalith snarled in revolt at Elvin and then sharply turned his head to look at Alucard. "May I ask why he's here?"

As he slowly placed his forehead in his hand in an attempt to keep as calm, Alucard uttered, "Elvin, go 'ome now. I gave you vhat you vanted, now let me get back to vork."

"What was it that he wanted?" Zalith asked with a slight frown on his face.

"Wouldn't *you* like to know?" Elvin sneered.

Zalith deadpanned. "That would be why I asked, yes."

Alucard sighed. "Elvin is vriting a novel; 'e uses my feats as content. Zhat is all. Now go, Elvin. I 'ave vings to do today."

Zalith smirked. "*We* have things to do. Considering as your vampires are different to those back in Eltaria, might I be correct in assuming your werewolves are also different?"

"I zon't know vhat your verevolves are capable of," Alucard said, glancing over at him. "But zhere are many types 'ere. Zhe Alphas are zhe only vones zhat possess venom and can transmit lycanthropy to ozzers. Betas are smaller and more agile but zon't possess venom. Zhen zhere are zhose like zhe big vone ve vought togezzer, called Amaroks; zhey are mindless volves zhat 'ave been consumed by zheir volf vorms. Verevolves are also stronger in zheir 'uman vorms zhe night bevore, of, and avter zhe full moon," he explained.

As he gazed at Alucard, Zalith smiled and said, "Interesting. All the wolves in Eltaria are able to transmit lycanthropy to others, and we don't have Amaroks. We *do* have Primes, though. They aren't mindless, but they are twice the size of an Alpha and very powerful. Two of my subordinates are Primes, although I know they're trying to hide the fact that they're fighting among themselves over the territory. And one of them looks like an Amarok, come to think of it; bipedal, eight feet tall," he laughed and then sipped from his drink. "Are Amaroks the only bipedal wolves here?"

"As var as I know. But zhere is a species of lycan vhich looks like a bipedal verevolf. Ve von't be seeing any of zhose, zhough. Zhey live in a divverent part of zhe vorld."

"Well, that's a relief. How many wolves should we expect to see at this wedding?"

"Zhe North Pack is at least vifty volves strong, and a quarter of zhem are Alphas. Zhe Vest Pack is roughly zhe same in numbers, but vone single Alpha and 'is son. I killed 'is vife a long time ago," he said with a smirk.

"I don't see how just two of you are gonna kill a hundred or so werewolves," Elvin muttered.

"We'll manage, won't we?" Zalith smirked, still staring at Alucard.

"I imagine so. And if ve die, ve die," the vampire said with a shrug.

Amused, Zalith laughed slightly and sipped from his drink.

"And what if Ada is there?" the bard asked angrily.

"I alveady told you."

"Ada?" Zalith questioned.

"Verevolf, but like me—zhe virst, if you must. Calls 'erself zhe Volf Queen."

"Do you call yourself the Vampire King, Aleksei?" Zalith asked with an unseemly smile.

He pouted. "No."

"You should," Elvin suggested.

They both glared at the bard, silencing him.

Zalith looked back at Alucard. "Will her presence change the mission—which is what, exactly? Are we there to kill them all?"

"If Ada is not zhere, ve break up zhe vedding and stop zhe packs vrom uniting. I also vant to vind out anyving zhey know about Ada and zhe volves who attacked Vria. If Ada is zhere, I vill try to veason with 'er. Ve know each ozzer and 'ave done vor a long time; I vant to try and offer 'er a chance bevore I kill 'er."

"Oh, history?" Zalith asked. "Are you perhaps looking to rekindle an old flame, Aleksei?"

"You're zhe second person to ask me zhat."

And did you avoid answering them, too?"

Alucard rolled his eyes. "My personal 'istory vith 'er 'as noving to do vith vhat is going on."

Elvin frowned. "Even *I* don't know what happened between you two. Why do you always avoid it?"

"Because zhat does not matter," Alucard uttered, standing up. "Ve are vasting time 'ere. Let's go."

As Alucard placed his glass down on the table, Zalith finished his drink and also stood up, following Alucard over to the door.

Elvin also followed with a sour look on his face.

Alucard reached over to the table and grabbed his blazer once they reached the front door. "Ve'll go to zhe same place ve vent to last veek," he said, glancing back over his shoulder at Zalith.

The demon smiled. "That sounds good."

Elvin scoffed quietly as he shadowed them.

Then, as Alucard was about to open the door, a loud knock came at it. He rolled his eyes. "Zhe fuck is zhat?" he mumbled under his breath, pulling the door open—

Everything happened so quickly that not one of them had time to move.

As his sights met with the shimmering yellow eyes of what could only be a werewolf in his human form, dismay smothered the vampire's face. Before he could defend himself, a wooden stake was impaled through his chest, and the force of his attacker sent him crashing back into Zalith, who fell to the floor. As Zalith's back hit the ground, Alucard's back hit the demon's front, and Elvin screamed hysterically as blood oozed profusely from Alucard's wound.

With another man entering the house behind him, the yellow-eyed attacker flung himself at Alucard, a new stake in his left hand. But Alucard swiftly returned to his feet and lunged at the silver-haired man, grabbed his shoulders, and mercilessly pinned him down on the floor. He sunk his fangs into his neck as he tried to yelp in shock and fear but was given no time to do so. Alucard tore his throat out, and although the blood tasted like shit, he gulped it down; it would heal his wound once he removed the stake.

At the same time, Zalith climbed to his feet and grabbed the second man, who stumbled back into the lounge in horror. The demon grabbed the man's throat and ripped it out with his claws, giving the guy no chance to retaliate.

Panicking, Elvin hurried over to Alucard. "A-Aleksei!" he cried, dropping to his knees beside the vampire as he irritably pulled his fangs from his attacker's neck. "W-what…what…."

Alucard snarled as he wiped the blood off his face. He then looked down at the stake in his chest.

"W-what should I do?! Should…should I take it out…I…are you…are you gonna be okay?!" Elvin panicked, moving his hands towards the stake.

Alucard slapped his hand away and pulled the wooden stake from his chest. He then chucked it on the floor while his chest healed.

"Are you okay?" Zalith asked as he stood behind Elvin, looking down at Alucard.

Elvin tried to fuss over Alucard again, but the vampire hissed at him, making the bard scramble to his feet. "W-what just happened?!" he insisted, watching as Alucard slowly got up; the bard tried to help him, but Alucard pushed him away. "T-they tried to kill you!" he exclaimed, looking around in panic.

Zalith rolled his eyes and walked past the panicked human. "Are you certain you're okay?" he asked, placing his hand on the vampire's shoulder.

"Zon't—" he snapped, backing away from Zalith, "—touch me."

The demon smiled slightly. "Sorry."

Ignoring him, Alucard looked back at the once-white rug in his lounge and scowled. "Did you 'ave to kill 'im in zhere?" he complained.

Zalith glanced over at the bloody carpet. "My apologies. I can…pay to have it cleaned or just buy you an entirely new rug," he offered.

Still ignoring him, Alucard stepped out onto the porch. "Sergiu!" he yelled.

"W-why did they come? Who were they?" Elvin asked in a panic, looking around at the mess.

As the groundskeeper came out of the stables and made his way over, Alucard glared back over his shoulder at Elvin. "Check zheir pockets," he ordered.

"M-me?" Elvin asked with a revolted look on his face.

"Yes, you," Alucard snarled. "Vhat? Is just dead body," he grumbled, watching as Elvin's look of revolt and hesitation increased.

The bard looked down at the body of the man who attacked Alucard and groaned quietly in reluctance.

Then, Zalith rolled his eyes and crouched beside it. He searched the man's pockets and pulled a piece of black card from inside. He tapped Alucard's shoulder with it and handed it to him when he looked back at him.

As Sergiu stopped in front of the porch, Alucard glared down at the card.

"Yes, sir?" the groundskeeper asked, not at all unsettled by the two dead men.

Alucard scowled, glaring at the words written on the black card.

"What does it say?" Zalith asked before Elvin could.

"*Regele meu*," he mumbled, tearing the card up. He then threw it into Sergiu's face. "Vhy zhe fuck did you let zhese dogs get past you?"

"I apologize, sir," he said, bowing his head in shame.

"And that means?" Zalith questioned.

Alucard glanced at him, remembering that Zalith wasn't from this land, and neither was Elvin.

Elvin stared curiously. "Well?"

He rolled his eyes and looked back at Sergiu. "Means My King. Is vrom Ada."

Zalith then smirked. "So, I was right."

"So…she's here?" Elvin panicked.

"Clean zhis up," Alucard snarled, glaring at Sergiu. He then turned to face Elvin and Zalith. "She could 'ave just sent zhat vrom vherever she's been 'iding all zhese years.

Yet…I vould like to know 'ow she knows vhere I live," he mumbled in concern. Then, he sighed. "I need to change. Vait 'ere," he said, moving past Zalith, who kept a watchful eye on the vampire as he made his way up the stairs.

Alucard headed into his bedroom, where he swiftly changed into a new white shirt and another pair of trousers. Then, he went back downstairs and watched as Sergiu dragged the bodies out of the house.

"Is it a good idea to head out into the city after this?" Zalith asked him.

"Vhy vould it not be?" Alucard questioned as he stood beside him. "Ada vanted to send a message; she vouldn't send people to kill me."

"That looked a lot like trying to kill you!" Elvin cried.

Rolling his eyes, Alucard looked over at him. "Go 'ome, Elvin. I vill deal vith zhis."

The bard pouted. "I-I don't wanna go," he refused. "I'm gonna be worrying about you all day and night, and I—"

"Go," Alucard repeated irritably.

"But—"

"How many times must he tell you before you understand?" Zalith snapped irritably. Elvin scowled up at him.

"Sergiu, take us to zhe city," Alucard then said, looking at the groundskeeper, who was trying to clean the floor.

"Can't I come? Please?" Elvin pleaded.

"No," both Alucard and Zalith denied simultaneously.

The bard gritted his teeth.

Then, as Sergiu left the house, Alucard and Zalith followed.

How *did* Ada know where he lived? He was starting to feel a little nervous. Was she already in Dor-Sanguis, or was she holed up somewhere else? He didn't know, and the only way he'd find out would be by interrogating the werewolves tonight. But what if Ada was waiting for him? He glanced at Zalith. At least he had backup if that were the case. However, the fact that she sent two wolves to piss him off was already a sign that she wasn't looking for peace.

And if another war was on the horizon, then Alucard was going to have to do everything he could to make sure he and his people were ready.

Chapter Twenty-Nine

— ≷ † ≷ —

Coffee, and then Business

| Zalith |

The demon smiled at Alucard as they walked through the manor gardens. "So, coffee and then business?"

"Hmm," Alucard confirmed, nodding. "I vill come back 'ere vor my veapons avter ve are done."

Once they reached the carriage, Zalith opened the door for Alucard. When the vampire climbed inside, Zalith followed and pulled the door shut behind him. He sat across from Alucard with his back in the direction the carriage would soon be travelling.

"Now that the dwarf is gone, will you tell me what the relationship between you and Ada is? Your concern about her knowing where you live tells me you're wary of her." Not only was he admittedly worried, but he also found himself a little unsettled about this… Ada.He didn't know who she was or what her and Alucard's relationship was, and he knew that if he didn't get an answer soon, his curiosity would become eagerness.

"Dwarf." Alucard smiled in amusement. "She and I vere not an item if zhat is vhat you vink."

A look of relief found its way into Zalith's smile.

"Ve are just enemies and 'ave been vor as long as eizer of us can vemember."

"And the note? King?" He smirked. "*My* King, nonetheless."

"She calls 'erselv Queen and calls me King simply because ve are zhe very virst of our kind, noving more."

The demon laughed quietly as the carriage started moving. "I thought I might have a contender," he said slyly.

Alucard frowned. "In vhat?"

"Nothing." Zalith wasn't ready to tell him that his intentions were to seduce and have sex with him. He enjoyed Alucard's inability to understand when he was being flirted with, and he'd like to experience it a little longer. He found the chase… thrilling.

Nodding unsurely, Alucard glanced out the carriage window and looked up at the sky as dark, gloomy clouds started to form overhead. He frowned irritably and looked at Zalith. "I vink might vain."

"Do you dislike the rain?"

"No."

Zalith smiled.

The vampire rolled his eyes and glared out of the window again. "Ada is an estranged voman; if she is at zhis vedding later, zon't say anyving."

"If you want me to be quiet, I will do so. The last thing I want to do is cause you any unnecessary trouble."

"If zhat is so, zhen lay off Elvin. E's annoying, but 'e's just a kid—in a sense."

"In what sense?"

Alucard shrugged. "Is just 'ow 'e is. 'E sees zhe vorld divverently. 'E tends to ignore zhe dangers zhis vorld presents and approaches vings vith zhe vhought zhat if 'e is kind, vings von't go zhe vay zhe vorld alvays says zhey do."

"I see," Zalith said. That had to be why Elvin seemed so attached to Alucard and why he acted the way he did. Now that he knew, he'd do his best not to be cruel; it wasn't exactly his intention, after all. He was, however, curious to know why Alucard kept him around. "Why did you take him out of an orphanage?" he asked, remembering that Alucard had mentioned such a thing.

"I…owed 'im a life of sorts," the vampire said, slight reluctance in his voice. "'E zoesn't know, and I zon't know if 'e vill understand if I tell 'im, but 'is mother vas a verevolf who was killed during vone of zhe videspread battles. Vone of my vampires told me 'e 'ad killed a volf vith a child and 'e zidn't know vhat to do vith zhe baby. Elvin vas not born a volf, so I zidn't veally 'ave quarrel vith 'im. I took 'im to an orphanage in DeiganLupus so 'e could grow up avay vrom all of zhis shit. I vent back seven years ago on zhe day 'e vas due to be kicked out, and I set 'im on 'is little quest to publish a story. 'E vas alvays vriting growing up, according to zhe nuns, so I try to 'elp 'im vhere I can. 'E chose to vrite about my life, so I give 'im details vhen 'e needs zhem regarding my accomplishments."

Zalith smiled. "That is rather kind of you."

Alucard shrugged. "Sometimes I vonder if maybe 'e vas better off back zhere," he said as the carriage stopped moving. Before Zalith could say anything else, Alucard opened the door and stepped out into the city.

Zalith followed him out and walked by his side as he started to lead the way through the city.

"Do *you* 'ave people you care about?" Alucard asked, looking over at Zalith.

"I have…a close friend," he answered as they reached the same coffee store they visited last week.

As he sat down, Alucard looked at him. "And…vamily?"

"That's a conversation for another time," he said with a smile. "And yourself? I assume that I'm not your *only* friend, am I?" He smirked, leaning his arms onto the table as he sat opposite him.

Alucard pouted stubbornly and glared down at the floor. "I zon't make an 'abit of calling my subordinates vriends."

"I see sense in that," he agreed.

"I vink…I've never veally considered anyvone a vriend. I 'ave been too busy to spend time vith people."

Zalith nodded in understanding. "Yet, I am the exception."

The vampire rolled his eyes. "Vhatever."

When the server came out to their table, Alucard glared up at her. "Zhe same as last time," he said before Zalith could speak. He then looked back at the demon. "If you are coming vith me tonight, you need to know zhat if you zon't vemove zhe 'ead of a verevolf, zhey turn into 'ell'ounds. I gazzer you 'ave vought verevolves bevore?"

"Indeed, I have," he confirmed. "In many ways."

"Good."

As Zalith then smiled in amusement, Alucard looked away.

"Vhy do you smile at everyving?" he grumbled, pouting.

"Because you amuse me, Aleksei. You're funny, and you make me laugh."

"I'm not trying to be vunny."

Zalith laughed quietly.

Alucard glared at him.

He didn't want silence to ensnare them. "Elvin mentioned on multiple occasions that your sailor—Rodney—has been killed. Did you actually kill him yourself?"

"No."

"May I ask…who—"

"No, you may not."

Zalith scoffed amusedly. "Okay."

The server came back with their drinks. She placed them in front of them and then left in silence.

Alucard snatched the sugar before Zalith could and frowned irritably. "You ask me all zhese questions; you know more about me zhan I do you."

Watching him pour an excessive amount of sugar into his drink once again, Zalith smiled. "Then perhaps you should try asking *me* some questions."

The vampire evidently wasn't going to turn down his invitation. "You never told me vhy you 'ave zemon 'unters avter you in zhe virst place."

"That's true," he said with a nod and sipped from his drink. He sighed and said, "Well, we are both familiar with war and how it works. I was involved in a war with humans. We killed them, and they killed all of us. I'm a former warlord, and so, they want me dead. I've been hiding, and you seem to be doing the same. Why do you have to hide from your father? Well, why is it that *Damien* is hiding you from him?"

The vampire scowled. "I von't alvays allow you to turn zhese vings avound," he warned.

Zalith smirked. "I answered your question; now answer *mine*."

Alucard rolled his eyes and glared down at his lap. "My…vather created me in an attempt to escape 'is prison; 'e vhought zhat 'aving 'is blood and ethos in zhis vorld vould grant 'im access to 'ere. Zidn't vork, so 'e zidn't need me anymore. 'E used a lot of power to create me, so 'e vants zhat back, and to do so, 'e 'as to kill me. 'E 'as a cult of people looking vor me since 'e cannot locate me because of Zamien. Zhey are easy to evade, zhough; zhey're just a bunch of stupid 'umans."

"And your father…. Who might he be?"

"You alveady asked. Is my turn."

Zalith smiled. "Of course."

Alucard thought to himself for a few moments…until he finally asked, "Do you vespect Zamien?"

"Do you?" Zalith smirked deviously.

The vampire frowned. "I…do," he mumbled, looking away from him once more, trying to hide his sullen face.

Although Alucard was trying to hide his expression, Zalith understood his sadness. At first, he thought that such an emotion was inflicted upon the vampire whenever Damien was mentioned because he failed to do something for him before, thus resulting in some form of physical punishment. But there seemed to be more to it. He wouldn't pry though; it was clear that the subject upset Alucard and that was the last thing he wanted to do. He enjoyed conversing with him, and he didn't want to cause their date to end.

So, he smiled. "Are you looking forward to our third engagement together?"

Confused, Alucard took his eyes off the ground and frowned at him. "Vhat?"

"In combat, Aleksei," Zalith said, stifling a laugh. "Tonight. The werewolf wedding."

"Oh. Well…I guess," he agreed. "Ve might 'ave to kill zhem all; I 'ope zhat von't be a problem."

"Not at all," he said with a smile "And what if your attempt to come to an agreement with Ada doesn't work out?"

"Zhen…I vill 'ave to kill 'er too," he said with a sigh.

"Well, whatever happens, I'll follow your lead."

Alucard nodded. "Ve can 'ead back soon. I zon't see any point in 'anging avound much longer."

"Whenever you're ready. I think I'm going to enjoy this evening with you."

The vampire smirked. "Vait until ve are done to say zhat."

Zalith grinned. "Oh, I'm quite sure."

Alucard frowned slightly. "Zhen…ve vill go."

When Alucard stood up and left a coin on the table, Zalith followed him. He smirked slyly as his eyes wandered from the back of Alucard's head down to one of the many things about this vampire he enjoyed staring at.

But he soon lost his grin and sunk into his thoughts. He didn't know why he was still expecting Alucard to pick up on his hints. Either way, though, he wouldn't stop; it was highly amusing to watch the vampire's confusion grow with each remark, just as his own liking for Alucard did. Today, despite its bloody turn, had already been enjoyable, and Zalith was sure it would be even more so once they arrived at the werewolf wedding. Whatever they may find there, Zalith suspected it wouldn't be anything anywhere near as interesting as this vampire.

Chapter Thirty

— ⸱ † ⸱ —

Lycans

| **Alucard** |

As the black stallion pulled the ebony carriage into the gardens of Alucard's manor, the vampire glared out through the window. He tried to keep his despondent thoughts from getting to him, but they always won. He felt ashamed that he let himself speak so poorly of Damien. Asking Zalith if he respected him. What the hell was he thinking? How could he have been so disrespectful?

He frowned, trying to concentrate on his upcoming task. He would be heading into Dargamoore woods to find where the North Pack and West Pack were holding their uniting ceremony. At least he wasn't alone, though. He glanced at Zalith, but when he saw that the demon was watching him—as usual—he scowled and glared back out the window.

As much as Zalith irritated and confused him, he felt glad knowing he had someone experienced enough in battle at his side. The situation was likely to worsen once they reached the wedding, and a battle was certainly going to happen. He'd rather not have anyone else fighting with him. Tobias and his pack were strong but not strong enough to take on two of the land's biggest packs. And as for his vampires, they were also strong, but not one of them had enough experience fighting werewolves. Those who helped him all those years ago left to make their own way in Aegisguard.

"I assume you'll collect what you need for this possible battle with the wolves, and then we'll be on our way?" Zalith asked with a smile.

Alucard nodded as the carriage came to a halt, but when he caught sight of Ben waiting on his porch, he frowned and pushed the door open. He glanced back at Zalith as he followed behind him. "Zhat *is* zhe plan, but zhe look on 'is vace tells me someving else 'as 'appened," he mumbled, nodding at Ben, who looked concerned.

"Something's definitely happened," Zalith mumbled.

"Vhat?" Alucard asked Ben, stopping in front of him.

"We were attacked on the way to the prison to pick up the blood. Four werewolves, but they were huge—and kinda bluish," he said with a frown.

The vampire scowled. Nina's Etas. "You are vine? And your vriends?"

Ben sighed. "We're all fine, they just tore up the horses, killed the humans, and trashed the carriage."

Rolling his eyes, Alucard moved past Ben and unlocked his door. "Vight." Ada was *still* toying with him. Evidently, getting two guys to stake him wasn't enough.

"There's something else," Ben said.

Zalith looked at Alucard and smiled. "Could I trouble you for a glass of water?"

"Go to zhe kitchen," Alucard instructed, waving his hand in dismissal.

As Zalith disappeared into the house, Ben frowned. "So, some new guy has turned up at the prison. He knows all the details about the blood collection."

"Vhat?" Alucard questioned. "I zon't vecall…vhatever. I 'ave to deal vith some verevolves tonight. I'll look into zhat tomorrow."

Nodding, Ben slowly lost his concerned frown and smiled curiously. "I see you and Zalith are spending a lot more time together," he said, an almost suggestive tone in his voice.

"Vhy do you say like…zhat?"

Ben laughed slightly. "So, are you two…dating?"

"Vhat?" Alucard asked, utterly perplexed. "Vhy vould ve be…vhat? 'E is my vriend."

Ben smirked. "I don't know; he's a real flirt."

Still confused, Alucard stared at him, waiting for him to elaborate.

Looking at his confused face, Ben frowned. "He's…gay, Aleksei."

He still waited.

Ben frowned a little. "He's attracted to men. That's why I thought you might be dating, you know—spending time together outside of work and all."

"No," Alucard said firmly. "Zaliv is my vriend. 'E 'asn't displayed any intervest in me in zhat vay." At least…he hadn't thought so.

An almost surprised look clung to Ben's face. But Alucard's glare forced him to shudder. "What do you want me to do about the wolves that attacked us? And the pickup?"

"Take Sebastian," Alucard said, looking over at his stallion. "Tell whoever is zhat 'as veplaced zhe guy zhat I vill come and see 'im tomorrow."

Ben nodded. "You said you were going to go deal with some werewolves tonight; you need help?"

"No, I 'ave Zaliv 'elping me."

"Well, let me know if you're going to be out late. I'll bring you some blankets and cocoa for you both to cuddle up with," he said with a smirk.

Unimpressed, Alucard scowled. "Get back to vork bevore I strangle you vith a blanket," he warned.

With a single wave, Ben turned around and made his way over to where Sebastian was hitched.

Rolling his eyes, Alucard stepped into his house and closed the door behind him. He looked around the entranceway, unable to locate Zalith, who was most likely still in the kitchen getting his glass of water. He picked up his blazer from the table and pulled it on, making sure his pistols were holstered inside. He then snatched his rapier which sat in its sheath and tied the belt around his waist. While he put his crimson, white-fur collared cape on, he set his eyes on the demon as he made his way past the stairs and back into the hall with the same sly look on his face he usually had, and when he set his eyes on Alucard, he smiled.

"Are you ready?" Zalith asked, stopping in front of him.

"Are *you*?" Alucard asked with a frown, looking him up and down. "You vill go like zhat?"

"I shall go however it is you want me to," he said with an unseemly tone in his voice.

"I 'ave no preference," he mumbled, pulling the door open. "You do vhatever you vant to do; I gazzer you possess ethos powervul enough to kill an 'ell'ound if vone manages to manifest."

Zalith pulled the door shut behind him and followed Alucard. "Tell me more about hellhounds."

The vampire looked ahead as they made their way out of the gardens and along the path that would eventually take them to the forest. "An 'ell'ound is a possessed lycan; vhen zhey die, zheir body is levt soulless, and zhe ethos attracts 'ungry zemonic energies vhich vill possess zhe dead lycan, thus turning zhem into 'an 'ell'ound. Zhey are mindless, starved beasts zhat vink of noving but killing."

As Alucard looked over at him, Zalith smiled and nodded. "Interesting. Can you tell me about these other lycans?" he requested.

Continuing forward, Alucard pondered to himself for a few moments. "Verevolves are zhe most common lycans—you know zhem…men cursed to take zhe vorm of a volf every vull moon. Zhey can turn outside of zhe full moon, but if zhey do too much, zhey may lose zheir minds and become an Amarok. Verevolves look a lot like dire volves."

The demon smirked. "I see. They look like that in my world, too. Apart from a select few."

"Zhere are also loup-garou; zhey are ovten mistaken vor Amaroks. Zhey are vaster, stronger, and more annoying zhan verevolves. Zhey gain en'anced senses vhile in zheir 'uman vorms and 'ave zhe ability to shift into zheir volf vorm vhenever zhey vant vithout zhe visk of becoming an Amarok. Zhey possess 'ighly vesponsive 'ealing abilities in both zheir 'uman and volf vorms. Zhey are able to invluence verevolves, mostly Betas, and sometimes Alphas. Zhey also 'ave no control over zheir transvormation vonce zhe full moon comes," he explained.

Still smiling, Zalith nodded.

"Berserkers are just…verebears." The vampire shrugged. "Zhey are powervul, and zhey zon't 'ave to turn on zhe full moon—zhat makes zhem veaker, actually. Zhey can turn vhenever zhey please. Zhey are…specific bloodline, so being bitten by vone zoesn't mean you vill become vone."

"Are there berserkers here in Dor-Sanguis?" Zalith asked.

"No," Alucard replied. "I 'ave only seen zhem in DeiganLupus."

The demon nodded. "And the others?"

"Morbius is zhe rarest kind of lycan. Zhey are much like normal verevolves in vegard to zheir abilities and zhe rules of zhe moon, but zhey look like tigers. Zhey possess zhe stripes, ears, and vace, but zhey stand upright and are built like Alpha verevolves. Zheir endurance is vather laughable, but zheir speed and agility make up vor zhat. Zhey vill 'ave you in zheir jaws bevore you even know zhat zhey vere zhere," he said with a smirk.

"Is that so?"

"Even your zemon sensory ethos couldn't locate it," he said, an almost mocking tone in his voice.

Zalith laughed quietly.

Alucard looked ahead again as the forest came into view in the distance. "Sleuths are oversized mountain lions. But in zheir 'uman vorms, zhey possess zhe ears and tail of such a creature. Zhey must turn on a vull moon and can also turn vhenever zhey like vithout consequences. Zhey are slightly less agile zhan a morbius, but can endure more."

"Any others?" Zalith asked curiously.

He pondered for a moment. "Zhere's okami otoko. Zhey are Samayonese verevolf; zhey look like dire volves but stand six feet on all vours, and zheir venom is more likely to kill whoever zhey bite vather zhan turn zhem. Zheir 'ealing is impressive in both zheir 'uman and volf vorms; zhey are vast, strong, and quite easily zhe most deadliest of all volf lycans. I 'ave not seen vone in a vhile, zhough. You zon't tend to see zhem outside of Samayō-Akuma."

Gazing over at him, Zalith smiled, and there was a subtle look of enlightenment on his face. "Are there any more?" he asked, an amused tone in his voice. "You know a lot about lycans—more than I do. Werewolves, berserkers, and cat shifters are as far as my knowledge reaches."

The vampire scowled irritably. "Zhere are, but zhey aren't important. Zhe volf lycans are our only concern. Ada might 'ave vecruited some."

Zalith frowned disappointedly. "Can't you tell me about them just for the sake of it?"

"Vhy?"

"I enjoy listening to you talk. Your extensive knowledge is incredibly fascinating," he complimented with as much seriousness to his voice as he could manage through his smile. "And your voice is rather delightful to hear."

"Vhatever," Alucard said as they reached the tree line.

They stopped walking as the vampire took a moment to glare up at the dark sky. The six moons were shining bright and full, and the howls of wolves echoed from the forest, every other creature that inhabited it as silent as a mouse. These woods would be full of werewolves, and not just the ones Alucard was looking for.

Alucard looked at Zalith. "Vhen ve get zhere, zon't do anyving unless I say."

Zalith nodded. "Understood," he said sternly.

Then, Alucard stepped into the forest, leading the way as Zalith followed beside him.

"You and Ada," Zalith said, looking over at Alucard. "This rivalry you have; I'm curious to know more."

"Of course you are," Alucard mumbled dismissively. He didn't want to talk about her right now. And to his relief, Zalith just smiled in response.

Retreating into his thoughts, Alucard glared ahead. He wasn't yet sure how the next thirty minutes might go, but he was confident that once they reached the werewolves, the situation would escalate rather quickly, especially if Ada wasn't there. Nina wouldn't reason with him; the North Pack and West Pack hated him the most, so of course, they were the two that had decided it was time to unite and make a move against him.

It was only going to be a mistake on their behalf, though. Alucard knew he could wipe out both packs in a heartbeat if he really wanted to—but yet, he still wanted to try and form some sort of peace. War, after all, wasn't something he desired to see happen any time soon, despite his moral grey regarding such a thing. If he could prevent it, then he would, but if it were to commence, then he'd fight with a dangerous dedication to win.

A light breeze made its way towards them, carrying the scent of werewolves upon it—many, many werewolves. They weren't too far ahead, and they hadn't detected him or Zalith yet, which could only mean that the demon was also masking himself from detection with his demon ethos. At least Zalith was as far ahead as he was when it came to sneaking up on werewolves.

He glanced down at his blazer and pulled its buttons apart, ensuring he'd be able to reach for his colts if he had to defend, threaten, or simply kill. Then he glared ahead again, and the stench of dog was so heavy in the air that he felt like he might gag.

Zalith then laughed amusedly as he glanced at Alucard and obviously noticed the revolted look on his face. "Such hatred for werewolves, Aleksei. Why do they revolt you so?"

"Vhy do zhey revolt you so," Alucard mocked irritably as he set his revolted gaze on Zalith. "Vhy do you 'ave to ask me so many questions?" he snarled.

Holding back laughter, Zalith smiled. "I'm simply curious to know."

The vampire stopped walking and glared into the trees. From where they stood, Alucard could see the large opening the werewolves had chosen to use for their ceremony. There were at least ten dozen wolves—Alphas, Betas, Etas—and they were all in their wolf forms, excluding Nina and the man Alucard saw her with the night he rescued Tobias' friend. There was also a priest standing in front of them both on the oak-crafted altar, the white lace dangling from it floating gently in the breeze. The wolves watched as the priest called words of bonding, and Nina and her companion stared at each other with suggestive smirks.

Alucard *hated* them. Did they really think this was going to work? He had to intervene before the vows were said and the bond was made. He glanced at Zalith with a look on his face which should let the demon know that he had to remain there until things became heated. And, thankfully, Zalith understood. With his smirk fading, the demon backed off and concealed himself behind one of the many trees.

Then, Alucard turned around and headed towards the clearing of wolves, and he wondered… how long would it take for the wedding to become a battleground?

Chapter Thirty-One

— ⸱ ✝ ⸱ —

Something Old, Something New

| Alucard |

The vampire adorned a vacant stare as he approached the opening. He had to be careful and vigilant, two things he was naturally good at unless a smiley, annoying demon was involved. He rolled his eyes and sighed, stopping at the forest's tree line. There was no sign of Ada, so it looked as though he was going to have to try and reason with Nina—but the odds of her listening instead of ordering an instant attack were very low.

As the priest went to speak his final words, Alucard stepped out into the opening. "I oppose," he called with a smirk, stopping behind the huge crowd of silent wolves.

Instantly, the wolves took their eyes off Nina and turned to face Alucard, but they didn't attack. They snarled and growled, some in threat, others in uncertainty. *They* were scared of him, but Nina and her companion weren't. Nina glared at him in disgust, and her companion stared in irritancy. The priest, on the other hand, took one look at Alucard and fled for his life. That made the vampire smile.

He then held out his arms in a half-shrug. "Am I interrupting?" he asked in Dor-Sanguian.

Nina scowled as her wolves snarled quietly. "You just had to come here, didn't you?" she growled, letting go of her companion's hands. "And…alone." A grin stretched across her face.

"I alvays come alone," he said, crossing his arms.

"Your greatest fault," her companion sneered.

"Not veally. Vings get done vaster if I do zhem myselv."

"What do you want, Aleksei?" Nina then questioned. "You can try to stop us, but you can't stop what's coming."

The vampire sighed. "I vas 'oping you'd like to come to some sort of avangement. Ve can avoid any more unnecessary death zhat vay. You are going to call off zhis…vedding," he said, looking around at the wary wolves, "and zhen you and I vill talk."

Gawping at him with a condescending expression, Nina scoffed. "Why would I want to do that?"

"Because *I* am going to motivate you," Alucard answered.

Before any wolf could comprehend, Alucard pulled his left colt from his blazer and fired it at the werewolf attempting to sneak up on him since he emerged into the clearing. The bullet hit the Beta wolf's shoulder as it pounced; the wolf yelped, crashed down to the ground in front of its packmates, and before it had a chance to get up, the charging bullet exploded, combusting the wolf and splattering its blood over the faces of its kin, making them whine and snarl in confusion.

Horrified, Nina stepped forward and shrieked in mortification—but there wasn't anything she could have done to stop it. Instead, she clenched her fists and set her evil eyes back on Alucard.

"Motivated?" Alucard asked, pulling back the hammer on his colt, preparing to fire once more if need be.

But Nina lost her scowl and instead decided to laugh cruelly. "You thought you'd come here, scare us a little with your fancy toys, and stop the uniting of our packs?" she asked, taking her companion's hand.

"Yes," Alucard answered simply.

She scoffed. "Stopping us isn't going to help you. This land has belonged to the werewolves since the dawn of time; everything you think you own is ours, and whether we're united or not, we *will* take it back from you," she stated as the wolves started to prowl towards Alucard.

"Vhere is Ada?" Alucard asked.

Nina cackled loudly. "She's *coming*, and when she gets here, she'll make sure she kills you this—"

Before she could speak another word, the sound of Alucard's colt firing echoed through the still air, followed by a disgusting squelch. The head of Nina's companion burst into a bloody mess, and the charging bullet exploded before his body dropped to the ground, scathing the side of her face with shrapnel and fire. Nina screamed in both shock and agony as the skin on the side of her face started to fizz, and she yelled furiously as she dropped to her knees, pointing at Alucard.

"Vell, looks like zhe vedding is off," Alucard mumbled before pulling his rapier from his side with his free hand, watching the crowd of wolves charging at him on Nina's command.

As a clap of thunder surged through the sky, the first five wolves that charged towards him burst into ashen white flames before he could begin slaying them himself. However, there was no time to argue with Zalith, who cast the flames, which completely eradicated the wolves. The demon instantaneously joined the battle the moment Alucard had wielded his weapons; the blast *did* give Alucard the short moment he needed to fire at one of the Etas; the bullet embedded itself in the blue wolf's neck and exploded seconds later before the beast had even moved ten feet from where it was stationed.

Alucard then glanced over at Zalith, who focussed on the Betas. He grabbed hold of the jaws of the wolf that pounced at him and tore it in half before it could try to escape. He then turned around, setting his eyes on a small gathering of Betas running at him from behind. He held out and twisted his hand, and a spiral of white flames consumed every one of the wolves until they were nothing but ash.

The vampire effortlessly cut his way through the wolves, using his rapier to slice off their heads. His eyes were focused on the second Eta—he needed to get rid of *them* first. He pulled back the hammer on his colt, aimed at the beast and fired—but the Eta dodged. The vampire scowled irritably and instead threw his rapier forward, and the blade instantly stabbed into the wolf's head. He then fired the last three shots in his current colt, and as one Alpha and two Betas combusted, he used the cover of the bloody cloud to return his left colt to its holster and pull out the right one.

Rain started pouring, thunder rumbled, and lightning brightened up the dark sky with occasional flashes. Alucard reached the Eta he threw his blade at and tore the rapier from its body, making sure to sever the beast's head in the process. Then, as he fired two more shots, he took a brief moment to glance over at Nina, who was still on the altar, watching as her wolves failed against him and Zalith. He also took a moment to look over at the demon, seeing that he was holding his own against the slowly thinning pack using both fire and his hands to take them out.

There were still a lot of wolves left, and Alucard was losing interest in fighting them. He just wanted to grab Nina and interrogate her so that he could find out where Ada was and what her plans were. However, he wouldn't be able to do that until all these annoyances were dead.

He quickly set his eyes on the Eta that was charging at Zalith; the demon was preoccupied with many Betas and two incoming Alphas. Alucard swiftly aimed his colt at the beast, but as he fired, a Beta pounced from an incoming group of wolves. It sunk its teeth into his left arm, making him drop his gun. With an irritated growl, he grabbed the wolf's scruff, ripped it from his arm, and impaled his blade into the creature's neck. As he severed its head, he turned to face the rest of the wolves that had come with it.

However, as the Eta he shot exploded, two of the Alphas howled an order of retreat; the wolves instantly turned their backs and started to flee in horror, but Alucard wasn't going to let that happen, especially since Nina had just shifted into her wolf form and began her attempt to escape.

Ignoring the blood oozing out through the arm of his blazer, Alucard snarled and held out his right hand as if to grab something. The damp ground rumbled quietly, and before any wolf could reach the cover of the trees, thin, black blade-like crystals erupted from the earth. One by one, they impaled each wolf through their heads, ending their lives instantly. As effective as it was, there was nothing Alucard resented using more than the ethos he got from his father. He lowered his hand, and a revolted look clung to his face. It made him feel almost as if he had betrayed himself, but he'd rather that than let any of them get away.

| Zalith |

Across the battlefield, Zalith stood in a trance of confusion for a moment. The crystal which burst from the ground a few inches from him, slaying the Alpha he planned to fight, was unmistakably Luciferium. The black, shimmering crystal was something that could *only* be summoned by a demon of Lucifer's bloodline. He stood up straight, setting his eyes on Alucard, who was lowering his hand, blood seeping out from the sleeve of his left arm.

Once again, the vampire—if Zalith could even call him that anymore—both surprised and impressed him, two things that no person had managed to do in a long, long time and certainly never this often. He watched Alucard for a moment, unable to keep a smile off his face. With each passing interaction with this man, Zalith found himself growing fonder and fonder, and right now, his interest in Alucard was seeming to become something of an almost captivating nature. What else was this vampire hiding? Demon ethos? Zalith hadn't even suspected him to possess such a thing, and now, he found himself almost eager to get answers. But there would be a time and place, and right now was neither or.

So, as Alucard started to make his way over to Nina, the only one the crystals hadn't slain, Zalith followed, leaving his white flames to slowly die down in the rain.

Nina whimpered and coughed as she tried to drag herself along the ground, having just pulled herself from the black crystal that had stabbed up from the ground beneath the altar.

Alucard reached down, grabbed her shoulder, and forced her to roll onto her back. He then pointed his colt at her face and scowled. "*Vorbi,*" he demanded as Zalith stood at his side.

"Are you okay?" Zalith asked quietly, glancing at the torn arm of Alucard's blazer.

He nodded and glared at Nina. "*Spune-miunde este Ada si, s-ar putea sa te las sa traiesti.*"

Zalith didn't understand Alucard's language; he *did* enjoy hearing him speak in his native tongue, though. He found it rather attractive that he was bilingual. As he watched, he felt he could safely assume the vampire was telling Nina to give him answers—after all, what reason to keep her alive other than to ask her for the answers he needed? He tried to keep a hostile glare on Alucard's foe, but he couldn't help but admire Alucard from the corner of his eye.

"Speak!"Alucard yelled impatiently, this time in Deiganish.

Breathing unsteadily, Nina managed to cackle. "I'm not going to tell you anything, vampire scum."

Alucard slowly pulled back the hammer of his colt. "I von't shoot your vace," he warned, pointing the gun at her shin. "Vone by vone, I vill blow your limbs off, and if you 'aven't spoken by zhen, I vill let you become an 'ell'ound vhere you vill suffer until I decide to kill you."

She scowled. "I'm not afraid to die."

The vampire rolled his eyes and placed his gun back in his holster. "I can't be fucked vith zhis," he mumbled, and as the demon smiled in amusement, Alucard grabbed Nina's throat and prepared to end her life—

"If you need answers from her, I would gladly search her mind for them," Zalith offered.

Alucard stopped and frowned. Then, he let go of Nina and stood up straight so he could glare at Zalith. "If you can read minds, vhy zhe fuck do you bover to ask me all zhese vidiculous questions?"

Zalith smiled. "Because I enjoy talking to you; I'd rather hear you answer me than search your mind." He wasn't going to tell him that he couldn't see into his mind. He was still a little embarrassed about it.

The vampire pouted slightly and looked away. "Vhatever. I need to know vhere Ada is."

Zalith crouched beside the woman and placed his middle and index fingers against her temple and his thumb along her jawline. Then, he peered into her mind. "Ada has arrived in Dor-Sanguis. She arrived exactly twenty-one days ago; she has been moving between packs, spreading a message and a plan of operations. She plans to destroy what you've built piece by piece, starting with the relationship you have with the humans. Exactly how she plans to do that is not yet known. However, part of this plan needed these two packs to have united."

Alucard looked back at him. "Vhy?"

He dug deeper inside her head. "Despite Ada being their collective leader, the werewolves are not so keen to work together. These two packs would unite, inspiring the others to follow their example. Once the packs were all united, Ada would make her first move against you, a simultaneous assault on your castle. Taking out your vampires would leave you vulnerable—"

The vampire scoffed. "Vhen 'ave I ever needed zhe 'elp of anozzer vampire? *I* protect *them*."

"It's what she believes."

Rolling his eyes, Alucard shook his head. "Vhat about zhe volf zhat attacked Elvin and zhe volves zhat killed zhe caravan outside Vria?"

Zalith searched the grunting woman's mind. "The Amarok's pack was meant to lead the first attack. They were all trained to take down your stronger defences to start things off. Then they were going to take out your human in the council, and they planned to hunt down your wolf friend, Tobias. But they decided to hold off after you killed the Amarok's pack."

Nina snarled, trying to resist.

"As for Vria, killing those travellers was an attempt to shatter the treaty. You're protecting humans from the werewolves, so their aim was to kill those people and have it ignite fear and the misconception that you are failing to live up to your part of the treaty."

"Vhy vould you kill travellers?" Alucard questioned, glaring at Nina. "Zhey are zheir own people. Zhe city vouldn't care—zhey never 'ave." There was remorse in his voice, which intrigued Zalith.

But Nina didn't answer. She just grunted, snarled, and glowered.

"That is all this woman knows," Zalith said, taking his hand off her face. Then, he stood up.

Alucard scowled and rolled his eyes before turning to face Zalith. "And she 'as no idea vhere Ada is?"

Zalith shook his head.

Nina scoffed before Zalith could answer. "You'll never see her coming; you'll never know where—"

Alucard swiftly pulled his rapier from his side and silenced the woman; her head slowly slid from her neck as he returned his rapier to its sheath. Then, he sighed and looked back at Zalith. "*Multumesc*—vor your assistance," he mumbled.

The demon smiled. "Any time, Aleksei," he said, but his eyes weren't on the vampire's face; instead, they were fixated on his shirt which was soaked in rainwater. He'd not look away, even if Alucard noticed.

Oblivious, however, Alucard turned to glare at the forest they entered the clearing through. "Vell…now I know vhat's going on, I guess."

"Indeed. Can I ask why you seemed rather remorseful when I mentioned those travellers?"

He glanced at him. "Travellers are…a 'uge part of Dor-Sanguis' 'istory. Zhey are peacevul people; zhey move avound a lot, and vherever zhey stay, zhey alvays offer zheir talents to zhe townsfolk. Vortune telling, alchemy—zhat sort of ving. Zhey are very usevul. I veel guilty because zhey zidn't deserve to die, yet zhe volves slaughtered zhem all. I could care less if zhey vere just vandom people vrom a city, but travellers do no 'arm."

"I see. I'm sorry."

With a quiet sigh, Alucard said, "I gazzer you need to 'ead 'ome now."

"Is that a question or an expectation?" Zalith asked, smirking.

He shrugged. "Take 'owever you vant."

Zalith smiled suggestively. "I prefer to give rather than take."

Alucard's expressionless face slowly adorned a confused frown. "Vhat?"

Amused by Alucard's confusion, Zalith laughed quietly, shook his head, and straightened his face a little. "I'll go home if there's nothing else you need me for." Of course, he'd stay if Alucard wanted him to; he enjoyed spending time with this…vampire. He would very much enjoy spending *even more* time with him. But if Alucard didn't want to extend their evening, he'd not be hurt by his refusal.

Alucard pouted and looked away. A pondering expression appeared on his face, and for a few moments, they stood in silence while he clearly thought about what he wanted to do. And eventually, he looked at Zalith and asked, "Do you maybe…vant to 'ave a drvink bevore you leave?" But as Zalith struggled to keep a look of hesitation off his face, the vampire looked away in embarrassment.

Zalith then smiled, though. He would take any chance he could to spend more time with Alucard and to ask the questions he wanted answers to. He only felt a little hesitant because not only did he not want to ruin what he and Alucard currently had by overstepping, but…he didn't want to grow bored of him, either. It was always the same case with all the men he met; he only ever got to spend so much time with them before he grew tired.

He didn't want to think about that, though. He was surprised Alucard asked, but he'd not irritate Alucard and ask *why* he did. With a sly smile, he nodded in agreement. "That sounds delightful."

"Vhat?" Alucard asked with a frown, clearly convinced that he was going to refuse.

"Are we going to a bar, or do you have something more intimate in mind?" Zalith asked with a smile.

"I 'ate bars," Alucard grumbled.

"Well then, shall we head back?"

Alucard nodded, and as Zalith followed, he began to lead the way back to his manor.

Zalith wasn't sure how the night might pan out, but when he thought about trying to get Alucard into bed, he felt a little hesitant. Was it because he wanted to know more about him after seeing him summon demon crystals? Or was it something else? He wasn't sure, but what he *did* know was that he was looking forward to sharing drinks with Alucard in his home.

Chapter Thirty-Two

— ⸮ † ⸯ —

Vanessa

| Zalith |

While the rain continued to pour, Zalith and Alucard hurried back to the manor. When they reached the front door, Alucard hastily unlocked it and entered, and the demon followed. Then, as he shut the door behind him, Alucard sighed irritably and pulled off his soaked blazer. He hung it over the coat rack after taking his two colts from the inside pockets, which he placed on the table.

"Zhe butler vill clean zhose for you," Alucard said, pointing to Zalith's wet clothes. "You can borrow someving until zhey are dry."

Smiling, Zalith nodded. "I appreciate it," he said, still admiring Alucard with a tantalized stare. He'd seen the slightest peek of Alucard's abs the other day when they fought the demon hunters and Alucard sustained injury. Right now, however, through the vampire's drenched shirt, he could see not only all six of his defined abs but his pecs, too. He couldn't *not* think about how he'd love to see his body without a shirt covering it, but he was more than certain Alucard wouldn't let that happen.

Ignoring his stare, Alucard glared into the arched doorway to the right of the entrance hall. "Emil!" he called.

After a few moments, the sound of hurried footsteps echoed through the house. A coltish man dressed in a black tailcoat made his way towards the front door with a lantern in his left hand and his right behind his back. His face was bronzed and craggy, and a tired look lingered in his dull, green eyes.

The butler stopped in front of the vampire and his guest. "*Da, domnule?*" he asked quietly.

As Alucard gave his butler his instructions, Zalith watched curiously. Although he couldn't understand a word Alucard was saying, he enjoyed listening. He *loved* his accent.

Emil nodded. "*Desigur, domnule,*" he said, dismissing himself after a slight, humble bow.

"Zhere's anozzer bavroom upstairs to zhe vight. I'll bring you a shirt to borrow until Emil 'as dried zhose," he said, waving his hand and gesturing to Zalith's clothes.

"Just a shirt?" Zalith smirked suggestively.

"Zhey are fine," Alucard mumbled, rolling his eyes as he waved his hands towards Zalith's wet trousers.

Zalith followed Alucard upstairs, glancing down at Emil, who had started lighting the many lanterns around the house. He then looked back up at Alucard. "Does he live here?" he asked as they reached the top of the stairs.

The vampire stopped leading the way and looked back at him. "Emil?"

He nodded.

"No, 'e stays until I tell 'im to leave," he said. He then pointed down the hall. "Zhe bavroom is down zhere; you von't miss zhat. You can do vhatever you need to do and I vill bring zhe shirt in a minute."

As Alucard went in the opposite direction and disappeared into what Zalith assumed to be his bedroom, the demon headed to the right of the hall and located the bathroom, which was connected to a guest room. Zalith then smirked as he wondered: did the vampire sleep in the basement within the confinement of a coffin? The thought amused him. There were still things he didn't know about Aegisguardian vampires, so it might be possible that they did abide by the rules of the ridiculous stories back home; they were, after all, unable to walk in the sunlight, so what else might be fact here and a story back in Eltaria?

He left the bathroom door ajar and stood in front of the basin. He used his ethos to light the lanterns and removed his multiple, soaked layers. Once he placed his waistcoat and shirt over the countertop, he took one of the black towels from the rack beside him and started drying his hair. He then reached into his waistcoat pocket and pulled out a comb; the longer parts of his hair which were usually combed back over his head had been freed of their usual place, and his now wavy hair was roughly three or so inches over his forehead.

While he slowly and neatly combed his hair back, he stared vacantly into the mirror, but he wasn't admiring himself—not this time. Instead, he was deep in thought, and he realized that he thought about Alucard more than he ever thought about any other person.

He was looking forward to sharing a drink with Alucard, and he was sure that the remainder of the evening was going to be more pleasant than most. He was also certain that tonight, he'd succeed in obtaining what it was he wanted from Alucard; after all, the vampire invited him back to his home, it was late, and he was sure that his clothes wouldn't be dry for him to leave until the morning. It couldn't be any more convenient.

But that hesitant feeling returned. Why? He wasn't sure, but he wasn't going to give it much thought.

On the subject of the vampire, he thought about Ada and the werewolves. Where there were many sub-questions regarding the Queen of Wolves, Zalith found himself concerned for Alucard. He was beginning to learn the extent of his rivalries with the wolves, and from what he'd already come to know, it was a serious situation. This Ada woman: she knew what she was doing, but Zalith wouldn't go so far as to say she was smart. After all, she hadn't comprehended *his* arrival, she wasn't aware that Alucard now had a friend in Zalith, and he was willing to help Alucard out with his little problem so long as he wanted it. A matter he would bring up once he and Alucard reunited for their drink.

Then there was the fact that Zalith saw Alucard use demon ethos—one of Hell's origins, too. How? Why? Alucard didn't look like a demon; his aura or ethos didn't at all spell demon. He was a vampire as far as Zalith was aware. But after what he witnessed, he was certain that Alucard was much more than that. He was already aware that this man had much mystery revolving around him, and now, such mysteries were coming to light. Alucard, a demon? How fascinating. Yet another thing for Zalith to question once the time came.

Zalith then thought for a moment. Was his interest in this vampire beginning to become something more than a simple attraction? More than a simple wish to conquer? To have sex? He frowned…was it? When he decided he would spend more time with Alucard, it had simply been in his venture to seduce him. But now he was beginning to realize that he genuinely enjoyed spending time with him. He was amusing and interesting; he knew what he was talking about, and he knew how to handle himself very artfully when it came to combat. He was impressive, and never before had someone managed to make Zalith see and appreciate all of those things at once, especially not in a single person.

Just then, Alucard knocked quietly on the door. As Zalith pulled it open, the vampire stood in the doorway with a white shirt in his left hand, holding it out to the demon.

Having just finished combing his hair, Zalith placed the comb down and smiled at him. The vampire had changed out of his wet clothes into a black shirt and new black trousers, and he stood there with a vacant look on his face while he waited for Zalith to take the white shirt from him. The demon hoped that being without a shirt might invoke a reaction from Alucard, but it seemed to do nothing. The vampire looked as vacant as ever. What might be going through his mind, though, Zalith would never know—and that was another thing he simply had to ask Alucard: why couldn't he read the vampire's thoughts?

He smiled and grabbed the shirt, but instead of taking it from Alucard—who was about to let go and leave—Zalith moved his hand over the vampire's and gripped his wrist. Alucard eyed him strangely but waited, and as Zalith pulled up his sleeve to reveal the wounds left by the werewolf that bit him, the vampire scowled irritably.

"You haven't healed yet," Zalith said with a worried frown, taking his eyes off the wounds to look at Alucard. "If I hadn't seen you heal from this morning's attack, I would assume that you don't possess responsive healing abilities. But you *did*, so I assume there's a difference in how you heal depending on whether you're attacked with a stake or by a werewolf."

Alucard pulled his wrist from Zalith's hand and chucked the shirt at him. "I'll be downstairs," he mumbled, leaving the bathroom.

With an amused smile, Zalith returned to making himself presentable.

| Alucard |

Alucard made his way downstairs into the dimly lit entrance hall. He walked through the lounge and into the dining room, where the large table lay as bare as it always did. He approached an antique oak cabinet and pulled it open, taking two wine glasses and a bottle of red wine from within. He wasn't sure if wine was something Zalith liked drinking, but it was what *he* felt like drinking to close the evening off, so it was what he was going to offer. He closed the cabinet and placed the glasses and bottle on the table before sitting in the far-end seat beside the archway that led into the sitting room where he would often hold his meetings.

He rested his arms on the table and sighed quietly. The day had been long, and he learnt a lot. Ada was back and had been in Dor-Sanguis for almost a month without his knowledge. He wasn't surprised, however. He knew Ada would come once she heard he was back in Dor-Sanguis; it was just a matter of time until she made herself known in one of her twisted little ways. Sending people to injure him? It was humorous; she sent those two men knowing full well that Alucard would execute them.

One thing he knew about her was that she never much cared for her kind, despite being their sire or queen as she preferred to call it. If there were a single thing Alucard was glad of, it was that he and she were different in that aspect. *He* cared what happened to his vampires. All *she* wanted out of this was to take his land from him and make him suffer.

Ada wanted Dor-Sanguis to lord over it so that she could dictate—so that she could say she had defeated Alucard. The vampire, on the other hand, wanted to keep Dor-Sanguis under his control for multiple reasons: the land was his birthright, it was a sanctuary of sorts to vampires, and above all, it was his home—his *real* home. He wanted it to stand as a beacon for his people. He wanted Aegisguard to stop shunning vampires, and Dor-Sanguis would be where his movement started—again. He spent a long time forging a relationship with the humans here, and soon, he'd move on to different countries, different continents. What he did was for the vampires, not himself… although sometimes he thought that he did it because he wanted an empire to rule over again. Did he? Maybe just a little. But he would *always* consider his people first.

The vampire dragged his hand over his face, trying to hide his snide smile. He was already terribly feared here, and sometimes, fear was the only thing that would get him where he needed to be, and where he needed to be was in a position so high that he might be seen as a god. King? Why would he want to be a king? He could do a whole lot better than that, a whole lot better than Ada. Did she actually think she could stop him? This time, he didn't have other occupations to keep him from protecting Dor-Sanguis; he took it back from the werewolves, and he would make sure to keep it out of their revolting grip forever.

However, Ada was here, and he couldn't lose sight of the issues he would face. She was obviously planning an attack—more than one; he knew that thanks to Zalith. Tomorrow, he'd have to inform his allies of this new information so that everyone could prepare for the werewolves. Killing the north and west packs had to have hindered Ada's plans enough to give him time to prepare. But he was sure that she would come up with a new plan; she'd unite other packs in their place, and she'd use the slaughtering of the two packs to further inspire the others to follow her cause.

He scoffed quietly—

"Am I interrupting your inner monologue?" Zalith then asked, leaning against the frame of the arched doorway that led into the dining room.

Alucard set his eyes on him. How long had he been standing there? He frowned and kicked out the chair to his left. "No," he mumbled as he watched the demon walk over.

Zalith sat down and made himself comfortable as Alucard poured them each a glass of wine. "That's a rather interesting portrait," he said, nodding to the painting on the wall behind Alucard.

"Yes," Alucard said, sipping from his wine. He knew exactly which portrait he was talking about. He'd seen the demon eyeing it the moment he'd sat down.

"Of yourself and… family, I presume?"

"Yes," he confirmed, uninterested in telling the demon any more about himself. He felt quite sure that Zalith already knew enough.

Zalith seemed to ponder, glancing back at the old painting again. It looked as though he was examining it, searching for answers Alucard wasn't going to give him.

Alucard glanced at him. "Vhat about you? Vhere are your vamily?"

"They are…gone," Zalith answered, losing his smile as he looked down into his glass.

The vampire frowned. It would seem as though he and Zalith had something in common there. Now, he felt a little more inclined to answer Zalith's questions regarding *his* family.

He tapped the table quietly with his claws, thinking about how he would word it. "Zhey are…gone, too," he said, glancing back at the portrait. "Zhey vere…not veally my vamily, more like…hmm…vell, sometimes I guess I velt like vamily to *zhem*; I vas avound vor a vhile," he started.

Watching him, Zalith waited.

Alucard sighed and leaned back in his seat, staring vacantly at his glass. "Vanessa vas a kind voman; she took me in avter I vas…vell…." He laughed slightly. "Avter I vas cast out vrom my old 'ome. Avter zhe Diabolus killed zhe people zhat raised me, my uncle decided to look avter me. But 'e grew tired of me and…sent me avay," he said with a shrug, sipping from his glass.

"Diabolus?"

"Some cult out to kill me."

"And why would they want to do that?"

"Because I am who I am," Alucard said simply. "Anyvay, zhe Diabolus killed zhem too, so zoesn't veally matter."

Zalith frowned sympathetically. "Were you two…married?"

"No," he denied. "She vas vidowed and levt vith zhose two boys. I needed to 'ide vrom zhe Diabolus, so I used 'er and 'er sons as cover. In turn, she also used me as cover—'er 'usband vas a var criminal, and she vas 'iding vrom zhe authorities. Ve lived in the pretence zhat ve vere married, and zhat vorked vor a vhile. But zhe Diabolus vound me, killed zhem, and now, 'ere I am, stuck as something like a vampire."

"I don't—"

"Janus came to me avter Vanessa vas killed and offered me zhe power I vould need to kill zhe Diabolus. I took zhat, of course, and killed vhat I vhought to be most of zhem. Zhey 'ave come back vecently, zhough; zhere is never a lack of cultists in zhis land."

"Cultists." Zalith frowned. "I assume this means they were followers of Lucifer? I can't help but piece it together since Damien mentioned Lucifer is currently searching for you."

Alucard shrugged and nodded. "Vonce upon a time, zhey lived to serve and care vor me. But now, zhey 'unt me," he mumbled, finishing his glass of wine. He then sighed and glared at the bottle before looking over at Zalith. "Do you like zhis?"

A smirk crept across his face. "Yes, I like this very much. Spending time with you is—"

"I meant zhe vine," he snarled.

Zalith looked down at his glass. "I do. Why?"

The vampire snarled and stood up. "Is shit," he grumbled in distaste, making his way back over to the cabinet he took the bottle from. He then pulled out a smaller bottle of what looked like whiskey and placed it on the table along with two smaller glasses. He sat back in his seat, and as Zalith stared curiously at him, he poured them both a glass. "Zhis is older zhan I am," he muttered, offering the demon one of the glasses.

"Older than four hundred?" Zalith asked with a smile.

Alucard nodded, not at all surprised that he'd somehow worked out how old he was. "I 'aven't opened zhis until now; I zon't know vhat is going to taste like, but I imagine vill be better zhan zhat," he said, glancing at the bottle of wine.

Zalith smiled, leaning a little closer. "Then, let's try it."

"Okay," the vampire said, and then he poured them both a glass of the dark brown liquid.

Alucard was admittedly enjoying this already. Although Zalith annoyed him a lot, he *did* like him, and sitting in his dining room talking about themselves actually felt better than he thought it would. He'd always been so standoffish about sharing details of his personal life, but Zalith made him feel…different. He wasn't sure why, but he was convinced it was because they were friends.

He was curious to learn more, and more importantly, he was looking forward to seeing what else their friendship made him feel. For the first time in a while, he felt relaxed, and it was a feeling that he wanted to hold onto for as long as he could.

Chapter Thirty-Three

— ⸲ † ⸱ —

Demons

| **Zalith** |

Zalith gazed across the table at Alucard as he poured their drinks. "How did you come to acquire either of these?" he asked as the vampire handed him his glass of the dark brown liquid.

"Zhat is vrom zhe local vinery," Alucard mumbled, glancing at the wine. "And zhis is someving I stole vhen I vas a boy," he said, placing the cork back into the smaller whiskey bottle. "Vrom my guardian's desk."

"And you've kept it this long?"

"I 'id somevhere specivic vithin zhe castle and vound again vhen I came back 'ere seven or so months ago."

Zalith smiled. "Are you waiting for me to try it first?"

Alucard rolled his eyes and downed his glass, and as his face embarked on a journey from revolted to conflicted to intrigued, Zalith smirked amusedly.

The demon then drank his. At first, he thought it might taste a little like whiskey, but he was very wrong. As he swallowed it, it burnt his throat so sorely that he thought he might gag. It was bitter, but its aftertaste was almost sickeningly sweet. He had no idea what it was, but it was already making him feel strange.

He glanced at the bottle but everything on it was written in what he assumed to be Alucard's native language, so he had no idea what he just consumed. Whatever it was, though, it was certainly a lot better than the wine they were drinking. After a single glass, he was starting to feel a little…tipsy, but he welcomed it.

Taking his eyes off the bottle, he looked back at Alucard. "It's…interesting."

"Hmm…" Alucard mumbled, taking the bottle. He stared at the label, but a confused frown clung to his face. "Is not Dor-Sanguian. Is not any language I know. Zoesn't matter, zhough. Tastes vine, so…oh vell," he said, placing his back down.

Zalith laughed quietly as he poured them both another glass. "Agreed."

"Vhat do you 'ave to do tomorrow?" Alucard asked, leaning back in his seat.

Resting his arms on the table, Zalith sighed quietly. "The usual. Work, survive."

Alucard nodded slowly. "Is not easy, 'uh? 'Iding."

He shook his head. "It's tiring."

"You get used to zhat."

"I'm not sure I want to," Zalith said with a sigh. He took another small sip from his glass of whatever this whiskey-looking liquor was. He then placed it back down and set his sights on Alucard once more. "It's crossed my mind, Aleksei: why do you live in this big, empty house alone?"

Shrugging, Alucard stared down at the table. "I 'ave alvays been alone; is normal vor me."

"No past or current relationships?" the demon asked curiously.

"No," he answered but then exhaled deeply. "I know you're still trying to vind out vhat me and Ada vere; I may as vell assure you now zhat you've become involved in my business vith 'er. Ve 'onestly 'ate each ozzer. Vell, I 'ate 'er, zhat's vor sure. She's made my life unnecessarily annoying, and she 'erself is an irritating pest," he grumbled. "I simply 'aven't killed 'er yet because I 'ave a questionable 'abit of trying to make peace bevore I vesort to murder."

Zalith smiled at his answer. He was sure that if he were in Alucard's situation, he would have killed Ada by now. "I find that admirable—to be so tolerant."

"I 'ave a limit, and she is surely veaching it."

"And speaking of murder..." Zalith said deviously. "You murdered those werewolves in a dubious manner; those crystals were Luciferium, something that only a demon can call upon—a demon of not only exceptional power but one of Lucifer's bloodline, too. Are you a demon, Aleksei?" he asked with a smirk, a testing tone now in his voice.

The vampire snarled uncomfortably and looked away with a pout on his face. "No."

Zalith's smile grew in the face of Alucard's denial. "Aside from the Luciferium, I suspect that perhaps Lucifer himself is your father. Damien mentioned he's hiding you from your father who wishes to take your life; you told me the Diabolus is looking for you in hopes to kill you, too. The Diabolus are a cult who worship Lucifer, and you also mentioned that the Diabolus once protected you but now want to kill you," he explained.

Embarrassment quickly smothered Alucard's face.

Still amused, Zalith smirked and continued, "Now, aside from the Diabolus and Lucifer, you also possess *four* enticing fangs in that pretty mouth of yours. If it were just two, I'd be more inclined to believe the vampire story, but Aegisguardian and Eltarian vampires' fangs are retractable, yet yours are always present. So, unless you are always so very excited to see me, I can safely assume that they're always visible, like my own, because...you're a demon."

Alucard scowled over at the window. He didn't say anything. He just sat there, glaring. And when he finished his drink, he refilled their glasses again.

"I'll take your silence as a yes," Zalith said with a small grin, picking up his glass. He was starting to feel strangely euphoric… almost as if he was already drunk. Yet he still managed to think clearly enough to explain his deduction to Alucard.

The vampire glared at him. "Congratulations, I'll 'ave my butler give you a gold star," he sneered.

"I'd love that, thank you," Zalith said, leaning his arms onto the table. "Why didn't you tell me? Do you really need to hide what you are from me?"

"Yes, actually," Alucard mumbled. It looked as though he wanted to yell, but a look of confusion had warped his face. He was starting to feel drunk too, wasn't he? The vampire shrugged and muttered, "Is not so much a secret as to 'ide vrom somevone; is more… vell… I zon't… veel like a zemon."

"There is no specific way to feel, as far as I am aware. You are what you are, and you are who you are."

He shrugged. "Maybe."

Zalith frowned. "Have I missed something? There must be a reason why you hide the truth, and I'm curious to know what that might be."

With a long, uninterested sigh, Alucard leaned back in his seat. "Vhy must you know *everyving*?" he asked, exhaling deeply.

"Why must *you* keep it from me?"

But Alucard didn't immediately answer. They both sat in silence for a few minutes, slowly sinking into the lucidity the strange alcohol was infecting them with. Zalith tried to fight it, but it made him feel lightheaded and started to keep him from controlling what it was that he might say or do. But he didn't feel opposed to it; the drink kept him from feeling that, too. Alucard frowned, Zalith frowned, and as they sunk deeper and deeper into it, the world started to swirl. What the *hell* were they drinking?

Alucard scoffed slightly as he looked over at him. "You… missed zhe part vhere I vas… vas vrown away like t… trash," he said, stumbling over his words. "I vas cast out," he said, waving his hand. "Did you *ever* ssstop to vink zhat I zon't vant to be seen as a z-zemon… because no vone 'as *ever* treated me like vone?" he asked, glaring at him, struggling to keep an angered expression on his face.

The demon frowned, sure that he wanted to answer, but for once, he couldn't find the words. He felt strangely dumbfounded.

"Vor… vour 'undred years, I 'ave… been seen as a v-vampire," Alucard said, tapping the table with his index finger. "Not… a *zemon*."

"But… you're *not* a v-vampire, Aleksei," Zalith answered, finally finding his voice—as forced as it was. "You…." He sighed. "Y-you… have said to me— to *me… yourself* that you are… more…" he paused, looked at the bottle of drink, and frowned, "…and that vampires…are what is born from your blood. If you…wish to be seen as…as a *demon*, I'd do so without h-hesitation," he said with a wonky smile.

"No," Alucard denied, staring back down at his drink. "I am…zhe *vampire*, not…zhe zemon."

Zalith smiled. "Okay…*vampire*…tell me why D-Damien…Damien…." He laughed, dragging his hand over his face. "Why would he help you if he *hates* Lucifer soooo much?"

Alucard shrugged. "If…if I knew zhe *truth*, I vould tell you—seems…seems like I vould tell you jjjust about anyving," he grumbled, looking over at him in confusion. "I z-zon't even know…vhy I tell you vings—I zon't… zon't tell *anyvone* anyving—ever!" he snapped.

"Because…because you like me, Aleksei." The demon smirked, shrugging. "I…I like *you*," he said, pointing at him.

Alucard then rolled his eyes. "You can…call me Al…Alucard—Alucard…*da*," he said, exhaling deeply. "You are…eh, my…vriend, you…you may as vell c-call me someving…divverent to vhat my…ssstupid subordinates call me."

With an intrigued yet struggled smile, Zalith finished his next glass and then leaned even closer, placing his hand a few inches from Alucard's. "Why…why do you have these diff…different n-names?" he asked, succumbing to his drink as quickly as Alucard.

The vampire laughed slightly as he refilled both their glasses, almost dropping the bottle as he placed it back down. "I 'ave…hmm…" he paused and held up his hand before Zalith could place his own over it, counting quietly with his fingers before looking at Zalith. "V…v…vour," he said, holding out his hand, "vour…names."

A look of astonishment slowly appeared on Zalith's face. "F-four?"

The vampire nodded. "V-vour…uh…A…Alucard…Aleksei…Em…Emeritus…. Zhat…zhat's my vull name." He nodded again. "Zhen…zhen I 'ave…zemon name—do you…'ave a zemon name?"

He nodded slowly. "Hmm…I do."

"*I* do." Alucard nodded, placing his hand back down on the table. "Is…C-Cae…Caedis."

Zalith laughed slightly as his hand crept over Alucard's. "I'm…I'm Elad…something…Eladarin," he said, tapping the top of Alucard's hand with his fingers, but then he pulled his hand away and leaned back in his seat. "That's…*me*."

Alucard leaned his elbow on the arm of his chair and nodded. "I'm…Caedis," he repeated.

"I'm…Eladarin. You…are Caedis, and…I'm… Eladarin."

The vampire pointed at him. "Eladarin," he said and then pointed to himself, "Caedis."

"Mhm," Zalith confirmed but then leaned his arms on the table again and waved his hand at him. "S-say…Caedis…you're Caedis…you should…should send…." He frowned and somewhat pouted, struggling to get the words out. "You shhhould…send Emil home now…home—so that we're…alone."

An exaggerated look of realization appeared on Alucard's face. "I…I should," he agreed, pointing at him.

"You should," Zalith confirmed with a proud look on his face.

The vampire slowly stood up, resting his hands on the table to keep himself from falling over. "E…Emil!" he called, his voice distorted.

"I don't think he heard you," Zalith whispered, trying to hold back his laughter.

Alucard snarled irritably, but before he could yell louder, the butler hurried into the dining room and looked over at them both.

Alucard frowned strangely. "G-go…go 'ome…now," he said, slowly raising his left hand to point at him. "G…go."

The butler nodded and left the room in silence.

Slumping back into his seat, Alucard sighed deeply. "Vell…'e…is gone."

Zalith then leaned forward and slowly flicked Alucard's fringe. "D-did I…tell you…tell you that I…*really* like what y-you…did to your h…hair?" he asked, still smiling.

Alucard frowned and leaned back so that Zalith's hand wasn't near his face.

"It's…s-so…so *red*," he said, resting his arms on the table again.

"I…I *know*," Alucard said with a nod.

Then, Zalith snickered. "D-does…does the carpet mmmmatch the d-drapes?"

Confused, Alucard frowned and looked around. "I…zhe…vloors are dark and…ssso are zhe…zhe c-curtains…I…guess…zhey do?"

His answer made Zalith laugh in hilarity, and after a few moments of laughter, he rested his chin in his hands and gazed at the bewildered vampire. "You're so…cute."

A look of embarrassment smothered Alucard's face as he looked away. "Vhat…ever."

Zalith opened his mouth to speak, but once more, he found himself without words. He forgot what he intended to ask before they started drinking, he forgot what he needed to know, and now, all he could think about was how red Alucard's hair was. But he wasn't bothered. He felt overly content with how things were right now.

The vampire then pouted and swirled the liquid around in his glass. "Do…do you…like…Zamien?" he asked, his usual restraint to ask about Damien no longer present.

Zalith rolled his eyes and exhaled a noise of irritancy. "D-Damien," he snarled. "I'm not…ssscared of him," he said, pouting.

Alucard snickered. "V-veally? 'E vinks…vinks eeeeveryvone should be ssscared."

The demon snickered with him and leaned closer, staring into his eyes. "W-well, C-Caedis, *I* am n-not s-s-scared of *him*," he repeated.

Staring back, Alucard nodded slowly. "V-vell…vell…you *shouldn't* be s-scared—'e l-loves you."

"E-everybody lllloves *him*," Zalith grumbled, waving his hand in dismissal. But he then scoffed. "W-well…*I* don't love *h-him*."

Nodding again, Alucard sat up straight and exhaled deeply. He stared ahead vacantly for a few moments, but as his eyes wandered over to the windows, he frowned. "Ve…should ve…sleep?" he asked. "I…'ave vings to d-do…to…tomorrow."

Slowly, Zalith nodded. "We…probably should. B-but…where…do *I* sleep?" he asked, smiling.

Alucard frowned and thought to himself for a few moments. "Zhere…zhere is…I vink…zhere is a…guest bed…bedvoom…" he said, looking at Zalith. "I…c-can show you."

Zalith held out his hand. "Ssshow me the w-way…v-vampire."

The vampire struggled to his feet, as did Zalith. They unreluctantly used one another to keep themselves from falling to the floor as they gradually made their way to the dining room exit.

"Y-you know…V-V…Alucard." Zalith frowned as they made it to the arched doorway. "I…rreeeaaallly…really like you," he said, patting Alucard's shoulder.

With his eyes slowly closing as they walked through the lounge, Alucard pouted. "V-veally?" he asked strangely, almost as if he couldn't believe it. "V-vhy?"

But before either of them could stop, they tripped over each other's feet and fell. They both laughed like idiots, rolling onto their backs.

Zalith sighed deeply and dragged his hand over his face as he looked up at the ceiling. "I…don't know, I…I just…do." He turned his head to look at the vampire, but Alucard seemed to have passed out the moment they hit the floor and stopped laughing. He frowned, but a smile found its way to his face. "He fell…asleep," he said, looking back up at the ceiling. He tried to climb to his feet, but he stumbled and fell onto his front. He was so dizzy that he couldn't even work out where he or Alucard had fallen, and as it did for Alucard, the drink abruptly pulled him into a silent, deep sleep.

And with that, their night was over.

ARC THREE

— ✝ —

THE VAMPIRE LORD AND THE WARLORD

Chapter Thirty-Four

— ᚲ † ᚲ —

The Morning After

| **Zalith** |

Zalith slowly opened his eyes as the unrelenting pain from his hangover-induced headache woke him. He frowned as he glared at the ceiling, immediately realizing that he *wasn't* in his own home.

The demon's senses were still all over the place; he felt dizzy, exhausted, irritated, and confused. Was he…on the floor? He shifted his eyes to his left and saw the oak flooring he was resting on. Yes, he was.

He scowled and slowly sat up, placing his hands on either side of his throbbing head. He looked around once more, taking in the black walls and antique furniture; he was now sure that he was in Alucard's house, and when he turned to glare out of the window, he frowned. The sky was a blindingly bright blue, and his eyes ached while he tried to work out what the time was.

His recollection of the previous night wasn't great; he remembered sitting down with Alucard, drinking a single glass of wine, and then moving on to what he thought was whiskey. They spoke for a while, and then…nothing. He lowered his hands from his head and sighed. He should get home; Varana was probably worried, annoyed, or mad…or all of that at once.

With a quiet huff, he rested his forehead in his hand, waiting for his headache to relent even a little, but it only seemed to get worse. He felt like an idiot; how could he have allowed himself to become so drunk that he had no memory past a certain point in the evening? He preferred to avoid allowing himself to become intoxicated in front of people to keep himself from losing control of the situation, but he allowed himself to let go, and now he wasn't sure what might have come of it.

However, the more he thought about it, the more he realized that it didn't bother him as much as he thought it would. If he didn't want to become drunk last night, he would have refused after Alucard presented the alcohol that burdened him with his current discomfort. But he felt no desire to deny—in fact, the idea of getting drunk with Alucard interested him greatly. He wouldn't be feeling this way if it were anyone else, he was sure—and if it were anyone else that presented the opportunity, he would have denied it. Why was Alucard exceeding his rules?

As what was unmistakably Alucard's voice then murmured behind him, Zalith looked back over his shoulder and set his eyes on the vampire. Alucard was sleeping in front of the couch on his left side with his head resting on his arm. Zalith couldn't keep himself from smiling as he gazed at him. The sunlight shone on his face, which adorned an almost distressed expression—could that be because of the sunlight? Although he wasn't sure why he felt a desire to make sure Alucard was comfortable, Zalith got up and made his way over to the curtains. He tugged them shut, restricting the sunlight from reaching the sleeping vampire.

He then gradually sunk down and sat on the low window ledge, staring over at Alucard. Despite his irritancy, he smiled once again, recollecting the thoughts he had before joining Alucard for a drink. He still felt as though his original plan with this vampire was no longer relevant; did he still wish to seduce him? Yes, but not solely. Now, he found himself wanting to simply be in Alucard's presence, spend time with him, and laugh with him.

Zalith then frowned in confusion. Why did he like him so much? Why did he feel this way? Why had his original intentions begun to wither? Alucard *was* interesting; he *was* funny, but there was more to this than a simple attraction. Zalith was almost sure of it, but he wasn't sure of exactly what it was.

He couldn't remember what happened last night, and considering the fact that he wanted to have sex with Alucard, he wondered…had they slept together? He wasn't quite sure, but the idea of having done so irritated him since he couldn't remember, and he would very much like to recall it. Could they have? They were both still dressed, and considering they were both beyond drunk last night, he was sure if they *had* slept together, they wouldn't have been in a state to be bothered about redressing themselves— at least *he* wouldn't have, anyway. No, he was sure that they hadn't.

With a quiet sigh, he dismissed his thoughts. He gazed at Alucard for a few more moments; seeing him on the floor, however, made Zalith feel as though he should do something to make him feel a little less uncomfortable. The hangover was enough to deal with on its own. So, he stood up, made his way over to the couch, and snatched one of the pillows. He then quietly crouched beside the vampire and gently lifted his head so he could place the pillow beneath him. As he did so, Alucard mumbled and murmured irritably, waving his hand in dismissal as Zalith made sure he was comfortable.

Zalith smiled but couldn't help but wonder why it was that he found himself performing these small acts of kindness. Why did he care if the sunlight bothered Alucard? Why did he care whether the vampire was comfortable? And why…*why* was he still here? This wasn't his house; he was hungover, annoyed, and confused…and yet, he still hadn't left. He would have done so the moment he woke up if it were anyone else, but it was Alucard, and this vampire always had him doing, feeling, *and* thinking things he thought he never might.

He slumped down into the armchair, glaring at the couch in front of him. His confusion annoyed him, and the fact that he couldn't do anything about it only made him feel worse. The headache didn't help either. But he sat there in silence, glaring aimlessly while listening to the birds outside, waiting for the moment the vampire would join him.

| Alucard |

Alucard murmured and gradually opened his eyes. He glared at the closed curtains, taking a few moments to recall where he was, and as he came to see that it was his lounge floor, he scowled in confusion. But he was instantly met with an overpowering headache, one so strong that it made him think he must have been slamming his head against a wall last night. But why would he do that?

However, his eyes shifted and found Zalith; he was sitting in the armchair beside the fireplace with a tired, irritated look on his face—that was no surprise.

The demon sighed sleepily as his eyes met with Alucard's. "Good morning," he drawled.

Taking a few moments to try and recollect what happened to lead him to where he was, Alucard frowned and attempted to sit up. But as he did, his headache became worse. He groaned quietly and placed his hand on the side of his head, closing his eyes. "Vhat zhe fuck 'appened?"

"If *I* could remember, I'm sure I would tell you," Zalith replied irritably, rubbing his temple with his fingers. Clearly, he had a headache, too, and wasn't very happy about it.

With a quiet, aggravated snarl, Alucard took his hand off his head and glowered at him. "Zhat sounds like a lie."

Zalith frowned. "Obviously, you don't remember either, so why does it feel like you believe it's my responsibility?"

"Obviously," Alucard mocked with a stupid voice. But then he rolled his eyes and asked, "Vhat's zhe time?"

The demon shrugged, resting his forehead in his hand.

Alucard huffed and laid back down. "Emil," he called quietly, but the butler didn't come. He scowled and slammed his hand on the floor. "Emil!"

"Is it possible for there to be less shouting?" Zalith asked irritably.

"No," Alucard grumbled, placing his hand over his forehead. "'Ow much did ve drink?"

Zalith exhaled deeply. "I believe…we started with some awful wine and proceeded onto something you stored away for a few hundred years."

Nodding slowly, Alucard glanced at him. "I zon't vemember anyving past…eh…vell, I vink…." He frowned and looked up at the ceiling. "I zon't vemember getting 'ere."

"Neither do I."

The vampire then closed his eyes and sighed. "Vhat day is zhis?"

"Sunday," the demon replied quietly, his irritable tone still lingering in his voice.

Alucard sat up in an instant but snarled irritably as his headache became agonizing. Of all days, why did it have to be Sunday? He had no idea what time it was or how long he had until his subordinates arrived. He was surprised that Elvin hadn't turned up yet; that bard was always early.

He got up, and as Zalith watched him, he made his way over to the front door and pulled it open.

"Sergiu!" he yelled.

The groundskeeper, who had been tending to the horses, raced over to him. "Yes, sir?"

"I need you to…go to zhe city and get us someving to 'elp us vake up—vith…a 'angover," he mumbled.

"Of course, sir." Then, the groundskeeper hurried off.

Making his way back into the lounge, Alucard dragged his hand over his face. "I sent 'im to get us someving to 'elp."

"Why do you seem so concerned?" Zalith asked.

"I 'ave to meet vith my subordinates today," he grumbled, slumping down on the couch.

Zalith nodded and smirked. "With a hangover."

"Zhis is your vault."

The demon scoffed. "My fault? Might I remind you that *you* were the one to suggest we abandon the wine and drink whatever that estranged concoction was?"

Alucard shrugged. "You vere zhe vone zhat agreed to come back vor a drvink."

"Yes, but I assumed we'd share a small drink before parting ways," the demon insisted tiredly.

The vampire rolled his eyes. "Zhen vhy zidn't you say no vhen I—"

"I don't remember," Zalith interjected.

"Vhatever," Alucard mumbled, ending the discussion.

They sat in silence for a short while, waiting for their headaches to calm. Alucard wasn't mad, though. He was just irritated that they'd become so drunk that they had no recollection of the night. But as the door knocked quietly, they both snarled in aggravation and looked at one another.

It was *Alucard's* house, and he had no idea why he looked to Zalith expecting him to answer the door for him. So, he pulled himself from his seat and heaved himself over to the door. He yanked it open and set his eyes on Sergiu, who presented him with two white cups and a flask. Alucard stepped aside, allowing the groundskeeper to enter, and then he shut the door. He returned to his seat in the lounge as Sergiu wandered off into the kitchen.

As Alucard sat back down, Zalith sighed quietly. "I assume this is our cure?"

Alucard shrugged. "I told 'im to get us someving to 'elp deal vith 'angovers."

Zalith nodded, and as Sergiu strolled in with a tray, relief smothered his face.

Sergiu placed the tray on the table between the couch and the armchair. Then, with a graceful bow, he turned around and left.

Noticing that it was coffee the groundskeeper had brought, Alucard groaned angrily. But he understood why the drink would help with a hangover. So, he wasn't going to refuse it, especially since Zalith hastily began preparing his own drink the moment it arrived.

Snatching the sugar before Zalith could, Alucard poured his usual incredible amount into his cup, and once he was done, he placed it in Zalith's waiting hand. He picked up his drink, sipped from it, and leaned back, staring vacantly into the fireplace.

"What time do your subordinates arrive?" Zalith asked quietly, sipping from his coffee.

"Hmm…roughly midday," Alucard replied.

"I assume you'll tell them about last night's discoveries."

He nodded. "I 'ave to make plans."

"Naturally."

Alucard looked over at him. "Vhat about you? Vhat do you plan to do vith zhe vest of your veek?"

The demon sighed quietly and relaxed in his seat. "Apart from the usual surviving and coping with my friend, there's something I have to do for Damien before our next vampire relocation meeting."

"Vhat does 'e 'ave you doing?"

"He's given me the task of locating a son of Erich."

"Vhich vone?"

"I wasn't given a name. However, he did give me a feather."

"Oh," the vampire said as he laughed ever so slightly.

Zalith frowned. "What's amusing?" he asked with a small smile.

"You von't 'ave much vun vith zhat vone," Alucard assured him. "'Is name is Osiris, and 'e's even more stuck up zhan you."

The demon smirked. "Is that so?"

Alucard nodded. "Vell, angels are vorse zhan you zemons."

"*Us* demons," Zalith corrected deviously.

The vampire deadpanned. "Vhat?"

"I remembered a few pieces of our conversation last night, and we talked about your being a demon and the son of Lucifer," he said with a smile.

Unable to believe that he allowed himself to let Zalith know such a thing, Alucard scowled and glared down at his drink. "I zon't vemember telling you zhat."

"Oh, you didn't." Zalith sipped from his coffee. "I simply presented evidence and assumptions, and you chose not to deny them, thus telling me that I was correct."

Alucard rolled his eyes. "Of course," he grumbled.

Still smiling, Zalith rested his left leg over his right. "But you asked me not to call you a demon, so, I shan't do so. There is, however, another matter I wish to discuss," he said, staring at Alucard.

Slowly, the vampire looked over at him. "Vhat?"

"I don't recall much after our third drink; do *you* recall… did we…."

"Did ve vhat?" Alucard questioned, waiting for Zalith to continue after his expectant pause.

He smiled. "Never mind."

Alucard sighed and looked back down at his drink. "Vhat else did I tell you?" he asked despondently.

"Apart from the Lucifer and demon truths, you told me about Vanessa and Ada, and touched upon the subject of the Diabolus."

The vampire nodded slightly.

Zalith then finished his coffee and smiled as he placed his empty cup on the table. "You also called me your friend."

"I vemember *zhat.*"

The Demon smirked. "Good."

Alucard then exhaled and said, "I 'ave to deal vith my subordinates soon. I'm sure you zon't vant to sit vhrough zhat."

"I would very much like to sit through that," Zalith assured him. "Not only do I enjoy listening to you, but to witness you being the boss? I wouldn't miss it for anything."

The vampire rolled his eyes and set his empty cup on the table. "You von't vind any entertainment in vatching me tell people vhat to do."

"Won't I?" Zalith challenged, still smiling.

The vampire went to respond, but the door then knocked quietly. As they both sighed, he lazily climbed to his feet. His and Zalith's time alone was about to be at its end, and Alucard found himself regretting that. He had a nice time with the demon last night, but now it was time for business.

Chapter Thirty-Five

─ ‹ † › ─

Conference

| Alucard |

When Alucard opened the door, he set his eyes on Elvin's concerned face. The bard instantly frowned in worry, looking him up and down. "Y-you look awful, Aleksei! What happened yesterday?"

Allowing Elvin to enter, Alucard exhaled irritably. "Noving."

"I don't believe you," the bard mumbled, taking off his coat, but as he caught sight of Zalith sitting in the lounge, he scowled in horror and looked back at Alucard. "W-what the hell is he doing here?!"

Slamming the door, Alucard snarled angrily, not at all interested in answering his prying question.

"A-and why's he wearing your shirt?!" Elvin demanded, following Alucard into the lounge.

"Go and vait in zhe ozzer voom, Elvin," Alucard dismissed as he slumped back down on the couch.

"A-are you seeing each other *every* day now?" the bard questioned worriedly, stopping beside the couch.

Zalith smiled. "Yes."

The vampire snarled in disapproval. "No, ve are not. Ve simply passed out last night and 'e's still 'ere."

"H-he stayed the night?!"

"Go!" Alucard growled, pointing to the door that led to the other room. Then, as the bard squealed and scurried away like a piglet, Alucard looked over at Zalith. "Vhy do you 'ave to vind 'im up?"

Zalith stared at him in silence with a smile still present on his face.

Alucard scowled. "Stop smiling."

"No," he denied slyly as his smile became a smirk.

Alucard rolled his eyes. He wasn't going to be entertaining Zalith today. So, he left the lounge and headed to the larger sitting room, where Elvin was waiting on one of the white couches. The vampire sighed and slumped down and tried to shake his aggravation. It was going to be a long morning.

| Zalith |

In the lounge, Zalith stared at the empty coffee cups. He felt a little disappointed that his and Alucard's time alone was over. He found himself wondering when he'd get another chance like this; another *night* to see the man Alucard was beneath the withdrawn attitude and the cold, vacant stare he used as a mask.

He sighed, stood up, and made his way through to the sitting room. The demon watched as Elvin jumped to his feet and darted for the seat beside Alucard, but Zalith swiftly beat him to it.

Astounded, Elvin crossed his arms and growled angrily.

Zalith set his gaze on Alucard. "What did I miss?"

"You zidn't miss anyving," Alucard mumbled, resting the side of his forehead in his hand.

The bard slumped down on the couch opposite Alucard. "Are you hungover? I saw the booze out there."

Alucard's silence seemed to answer his question.

Elvin shook his head and scolded, "Really, Aleksei? You *knew* today was supposed to be a meeting day; are you so irresponsible that you get drunk the night before?"

Alucard then scoffed. "Vhen did you become my mother, Elvin?"

"I never said I was your mother; I just care and worry."

"So you 'ave said more times zhan I care to vemember."

Elvin then set his eyes on Zalith. "It was *you*, wasn't it?" he accused. "You're a bad influence on Aleksei!"

Zalith laughed quietly in response, keeping his eyes on Alucard. He didn't want to look at that ugly little human.

The vampire sighed and sat up straight. "Vhere is everyvone else?" he asked, changing the subject.

"I saw Ben on the way here," Elvin said, looking back at Alucard. "He stopped to talk to some guy looking for his dog. I don't know where Tobias is; I guess he's gonna be a bit late since last night was a full moon."

"Ben's concerning himself with a lost hound?" Zalith asked, confused.

"Zhat vould appear so," Alucard muttered. "Vhat about Dirk?"

"I dunno." Elvin shrugged. "I didn't see him coming up the path."

Alucard sighed and rolled his eyes. "Zhey better not be late; I vant to go back to sleep."

"How late were you up?!" Elvin exclaimed.

The vampire hissed quietly in response, silencing him.

Zalith then rested his left leg over his right and placed his arm over the back of the couch as he smiled at Alucard. "Your subordinates: what roles do they play?"

Alucard glanced at his intrigued face but looked away when his eyes met with those of the demon. "I'm sure Ben 'as told you vhat 'e does."

"Indeed."

"Tobias is zhe Alpha of a small verevolf pack. 'E brings me invormation vegarding zhe larger packs—zhat vas 'ow I vound out about zhe vedding ve crashed last night," he said amusedly.

Zalith laughed quietly. "An event I won't soon forget."

Elvin pouted jealously.

"Dirk is zhe 'uman invormant; 'e is zhe vone zhat I 'ave been using to make zhis treaty vith zhe 'umans proceed smoothly."

"Interesting."

"Quite," someone then called, appearing in the doorway and eyeing Zalith warily. He made his way over to one of the couches and sat down before looking at Alucard. "Who is your new acquaintance?"

"Zhis is Zaliv," Alucard introduced. "'E is…my vriend."

"F-f-friend?!" Elvin stammered, astonished.

"Ah, well, I am Dirk."

Zalith took half a moment to glance at Dirk, but there wasn't a single appealing thing about him. He didn't care who he was. Instead, he focused on the amusement he found in the way Alucard pronounced his name. He *loved* Alucard's accent, and the more he heard it, the more he started to acknowledge that love.

Dirk frowned and looked back at Alucard. "I heard the news of a mass slaughter in the woods last night, Aleksei. A very frightened priest has spread the word around the city, and I tell you, the people are not so confident."

"Zhey vere verevolves. I gazzer zhe priest vailed to mention zhat?" Alucard replied.

"Yes, it would appear that he did," Dirk said rudely. "Well, thank you for clearing that up for me, it would have been helpful to have been told before this meeting, but I'll be sure to tell the rest of the council."

Alucard then set his hostile gaze on him. "I shouldn't be expected to clear *anyving* up vor you. Vatch your tone, Dirk; you 'ave become somevhat overconvident zhis past month. Zon't vorget zhat *you* vork vor *me,* and I can easily revoke zhat privilege. Do you vant to go back to being some vorthless translator?"

"Of course," Dirk said quietly, his voice breaking as he looked down at the floor to escape Alucard's evil glare. "My apologies."

Zalith already knew that he didn't like Dirk. He could tell that this man thought he was better than everyone around him, even his superior. This human was nought but a lowly, uninteresting ant. The thought of killing him for his insolence crossed his mind, but it wasn't his business. This was Alucard's subordinate, and whatever the vampire chose to do with him, he'd respect. After all, he'd come to learn that Alucard's line regarding nuisances was a little higher than his own.

Just then, the sound of thumping footsteps echoed through the house. Alucard took his eyes off the cowering council member and glanced at the door. But when he caught Zalith's gaze once again, he frowned uncomfortably and glared ahead at the wall as Ben walked into the room beside a dirty-blonde-haired man.

Immediately setting his eyes on Zalith, Ben laughed in surprise. "Well, I should have known you'd still be here."

Zalith glanced at Ben with a smile. "Should you?"

"How was yesterday?" Ben asked, sitting down.

"Eventful," Zalith answered, setting his dark eyes back on Alucard, who seemed to be eyeing Tobias warily—

"Zon't!" Alucard then snapped, pointing at Tobias.

Tobias held up his hands and smiled. "Hey, man, I'm clean this time," he insisted, turning around several times to show that he was indeed clean.

Zalith took a moment to eye the man head-to-toe. The demon didn't find him *unattractive,* but he felt that if *he* were Tobias, he'd make an effort to restyle his hair or shave his face in an attempt to look slightly more appealing. He did, however, undeniably have a distinctly charming smile. He'd much rather look at Alucard, though.

Taking his eyes off Tobias, he gazed at the vampire. Zalith was always a critical, tremendously particular individual, but looking at Alucard, he found there wasn't a single thing he'd change. There was something captivatingly beautiful about the vampire, a beauty he was sure Alucard himself was entirely unaware of. It was amusing that Alucard wasn't aware of how attractive he was.

He adored Alucard's bright crimson hair and his shimmering hell-fiery eyes. Alucard always dressed elegantly, too. Zalith enjoyed the way the vampire carried himself, and the way he'd attempt to hide his face whenever he felt shy and embarrassed. A large portion of this vampire's charm was undeniably how erudite he was; his intelligence was so very attractive. The demon wouldn't revel in admiring anyone else, and he wouldn't find such enjoyment in spending his time with any other person.

Zalith kept his eyes on the vampire, watching him closely as he lowered his hand and rolled his eyes in response to Tobias' smirk.

Tobias sat down and sighed deeply, looking around at everyone. But when he noticed Zalith, he grinned. "Oh, who might this be, huh?"

"Apparently his friend," Elvin sneered.

Tobias smiled suggestively as he nudged Ben's shoulder with his own. "Oooh, friend, huh?"

"I gazzer you also 'eard about zhe attack last night?" Alucard digressed, glaring at Tobias.

"I did, yeah. You kill all of them?"

"Yes," the vampire confirmed.

"It's got the other packs all riled up," Tobias said, resting his arms on his legs as he leaned forward. "Some of them are even talking about hiding, so I guess you got your point across, huh?"

"Zhat vasn't zhe point," Alucard said. "I vent zhere to get invormation on Ada, and ve got zhat."

His allies looked around at each other unsurely, and while Alucard shared the information Zalith extracted from Nina's mind last night, the demon gazed at him. He just...couldn't get enough of him right now.

Dirk frowned once Alucard was done. "So...she really came back," he drawled meekly. He looked embarrassed about being put back in his place.

"She vants to tear vhat I've built apart, but zhat von't 'appen, nor vill 'er appearance slow my progress," he said, glancing at Dirk. "Ve're done 'ere in Dor-Sanguis, so I vant you to move on. Ve'll slowly spread from zhis country to ozzers. I trust you can cope vith such a task?"

Dirk nodded. "Of course."

Ben then leaned forward. "Sorry, uh...I still don't know what you're doing," he said politely.

Alucard rolled his eyes and waved his hand at Elvin as he leaned back in his seat.

The bard nodded. "Well, Aleksei wants vampires back where they were hundreds of years ago. Vampires were a superior people; they ruled pretty much everything humans have taken control of, and they only managed to do that because Aleksei was...well...absent for a few hundred years. He wasn't around to stop it, so the humans took their chance to take everything from the vampires. But now that he's back, Aleksei plans to reclaim everything—*but*...he wants to do so without too much bloodshed."

"Unless it starts to take too long," Alucard grumbled. "I vonce spoke about killing everyvone in zhat city of yours, Dirk. Zon't make me 'ave to revisit zhat vhought."

"I'll be sure to make sure the people know it was wolves you killed," Dirk said, still hiding his face shamefully.

Ben said, "Makes sense. Humans taking over shit that's not theirs—sounds about right."

"I mean…not to be morbid, but…why *don't* you use violence, Aleksei?" Tobias asked. "You don't exactly care about humans, so why not just kill them until they fall in line?"

"Do you vink I 'aven't vhought about zhat?" Alucard snarled. "Or did you vorget zhat my vampires need 'umans to survive? Co'abitation is zhe better of two options and zhe vone I prever. Is less strenuous vor me to vork on co'abitation—less use of my physical strength."

"Gotcha," Tobias said, pointing his index fingers at him.

Zalith thought he might be able to tolerate Tobias. He may be a werewolf, but it was obvious that he was not only Alucard's ally but maybe even his friend. He was the only man besides Elvin who spoke so casually around him—at least he wasn't boring or insufferable like Dirk.

Elvin then asked Alucard, "Well, since you're finished here with the treaty, where do you plan to start next?"

Alucard looked at Dirk.

"Boszorkäny is the closest to us, so I can sail out there first," Dirk said.

Ben frowned and asked, "And you're sure you can convince this entirely new country that they should align with Aleksei?"

"I'm more than a simple councilman, creature," Dirk said, scowling in offence.

"You vill be a dead councilman if you keep pissing me off," Alucard snarled.

Dirk hung his head in shame. "Apologies."

"Dirk isn't just some boring tax man; he was Janus' spokesman. We all know the Dragon Gods can't speak to humans, so they need little translators—there's Janus' guy," Tobias said, pointing at Dirk who smiled smugly. "Aleksei convinced him to work for him when he killed the dragon."

Slightly surprised, Ben looked back over at Dirk. "I guess your title gives you great influence here, then."

"It does," Dirk confirmed.

Zalith wasn't impressed.

"Ve are drifting," Alucard then said. "Zhe most important matter is still Ada."

They nodded, waiting for his orders.

"Tobias, keep an eye on zhe packs and tell me if any of zhem are meeting—and keep an eye out vor a bitchy voman. Pissy yellow eyes," he grumbled in revolt, waving his hand. "Boring blonde 'air, about zhis long," he said, pointing to his waist. "Vhite volf, as big as an Amarok."

"Gotcha," Tobias said with a nod.

Alucard then said to Ben, "You vill prepare zhe day and night guards; look out vor zhe same voman, and double zhe groups."

Ben nodded. "And if we see her?"

"I'm sure you know."

"Got it."

"I also need you to tell Velix to prepare zhe entire castle vor relocation," Alucard added.

"Relocation?"

"All zhe vampires vill move to zhe city so zhat I can keep zhem and zhe 'umans safe at zhe same time."

"Understood," Ben said.

Then, Alucard looked at Dirk. "Clear my name in zhe city; alert zhe authorities zhat zhe volves are planning a skirmish. Alert zhe entire city zhat zhe vampires are moving in, and zhen 'ead straight to Boszorkāny. I zon't vant to see you back 'ere until you 'ave good news."

Dirk nodded. "Of course."

"And me?" Elvin asked expectantly.

The vampire replied, "I vant you to move into zhe city."

Elvin shook his head and frowned in discontent. "What? Why?"

"You'll be safer among more 'umans. I'll be keeping a close eye on zhe city, so I vant you somevhere I know you'll be less likely to be eaten."

"But... aren't wolves gonna attack the city?" the bard questioned.

Alucard nodded. "Yes, and vhen zhey do, I'll be able to get to you and make sure you're safe vithout 'aving to travel 'alf a mile."

"I don't live half a mile away. You don't even know where I live *right now;* why do you suddenly wanna move me somewhere you know I'll be?"

"He just told you why, man," Tobias uttered. "What more do you need?"

"Zhat's all," Alucard mumbled, waving his hand dismissively. "Dirk, assign Elvin an 'ouse in zhe city, too."

Dirk nodded as he and the others stood up. "Right away."

Elvin stuttered, "B-but... I—"

"Zon't make me tell you twice," Alucard snarled. "Or I vill drag you into zhat city myself."

The bard pouted and stubbornly followed the others out of the room.

And then he and Zalith were alone again.

The demon smiled. "A somewhat interesting collection of allies."

"Not veally," Alucard mumbled.

Zalith laughed slightly. "On the contrary, I'm interested to know how you found these people. Werewolves are your enemy. Humans hate vampires."

The vampire looked at him and frowned. "Dirk vas bullied by Janus, and vhen I killed 'im, Dirk believed I saved 'im, so 'e offered to vork vor me. 'E vas more intervested in making vorldvide changes vather zhan spending 'is life translating vor a dragon. Sometimes, zhough, 'e gets a little too confident and I 'ave to vemind 'im of 'is place."

Zalith nodded. "I see."

"As vor Tobias, I saved 'is life, too. Vas during vone of zhe larger-scale vampire-verevolf convlicts. 'E vas a member of a 'uman resistance vhich vould assist both zhe vampires and zhe verevolves medicinally, but a volf attacked 'im vhilst 'e vas trying to 'elp 'im. Vas an Alpha, so zhat invected 'im vith lycanthropy. I couldn't do anyving to save 'im vrom zhat, but I could save 'im vrom joining zhe opposing volves. I offered 'im allegiance, and 'e accepted."

Zalith smirked. "You are frightfully devious, Alucard," he said with an intrigued look on his face. "You know how to convince people."

"A-Alucard?" Elvin then stuttered, standing in the doorway. "You don't let *anyone* call you that!"

Alucard rolled his eyes and glared over at him. "Vhat zhe fuck zid I just tell you?!" he snarled.

The bard pouted. "I left my book."

"Zhen get zhat…and get out," Alucard warned.

Pouting, Elvin went to the couch he left his book on, grabbed it, and walked back to the door. But he stopped and looked at them. "Are you…really fri—"

"Out!" Alucard snapped.

Whimpering, Elvin scurried out of the room, leaving them in peace.

The vampire then sighed. "Anyvay…Dirk vasn't my intention vor killing Janus. 'E vas just…an addition, a coincidence. I killed zhe dragon out of revenge; I zidn't even know Dirk vas zhere until zhis ugly little man vas crying at my veet."

Zalith laughed amusedly. "Humans."

"I 'ate zhem, but I 'ave to put up vith zhem vor zhe sake of zhe vampires."

"Of course. Vampires are lucky they have you to care for them," Zalith complimented.

Shrugging, Alucard then asked, "Speaking of vampires, I gazzer I'll still be meeting you as usual next week?"

The demon nodded. "Indeed."

Alucard exhaled deeply. "Vell, I zon't mean to be rude, but I vink I vant to go back to bed; zhis 'eadache asn't died yet. I'm sure you 'ave better vings to do, so—"

"Not really," Zalith said suggestively. What would be better than staying and potentially sleeping with Alucard? That *was* his desire, after all…wasn't it?

Alucard slowly frowned. He stared in confusion like he was trying to work out what he meant. "Vell…you can stay 'ere…if you veally vant to, but—"

Zalith smirked and said, "That isn't what I was implying, Alucard." His bigger focus aside, he knew he'd like to spend more time with Alucard, but he knew he had to get home, explain his absence, and deal with his own business. So, he sat up straight and said with a sigh, "However, if you need to sleep, then I'll go home and see you Saturday."

Alucard nodded.

"It's been an enjoyable two days," Zalith said with a smile.

"Vell, I'm sure ve can do zhis again sometime," Alucard concurred with a small but visible smile.

"Perhaps next time we should avoid the several-century-old alcohol?" Zalith suggested as they both got up.

Alucard began escorting him towards the door. "Ve can tell ourselves zhat ve vill, but ve'll inevitably veturn to zhat."

The demon laughed. "I suspect we may."

When they reached the front door, Alucard faced him. "I suspect Emil vashed your clothes. Zhey should be over zhere," he said, looking at another lounge-like area to the right of the entrance hall.

"I almost forgot," Zalith admitted, remembering that the shirt he was wearing was Alucard's. He followed the vampire into the room and found his washed clothes on a table. He pulled off the shirt Alucard lent him, and as he did, he made sure to glance back at Alucard to see if the vampire was interested, but he looked as vacant as ever, just as he did last night.

Unphased by Zalith dressing in front of him, Alucard asked, "Did I…tell you much about my…zemon…being?"

"No," Zalith answered, looking back at him after buttoning his shirt. Noticing the worry on Alucard's face, he frowned. "Is something wrong?"

"No. I zon't care zhat *you* know vhat I am, just keep zhat to yourselv, please?"

"Of course," Zalith said, pulling on his waistcoat. Then, he followed Alucard back into the entrance hall and to the front door. He held out his hand and smirked. "Until next week, vampire."

Slowly, Alucard placed his hand in Zalith's. "Yes," he agreed, but Zalith held onto his hand for a little longer, and the vampire frowned and tried to discretely pull free.

Zalith smiled amusedly and let go. "If you do end up needing my help again, don't be afraid to ask Ben to contact me," he said, opening the door. "Whether it be business or…a friendly visit."

"Vight," Alucard mumbled as he watched Zalith step outside. "*La revedere*," he uttered.

Assuming that meant goodbye, Zalith replied, "Farewell," and winked slightly.

Confused, Alucard pouted and shut the door.

Zalith started making his way home. He had a wonderful time and was eager to see him again. He and Alucard were growing closer with each meeting, and although he was still afraid that he might get bored of the vampire—or that his initial desire might ruin everything—he was keen to have more nights like the last.

Chapter Thirty-Six

— ⸱ † ⸱ —

A Man and His Dog

| Ben |

Ben made his way back to the castle. Not only did he need to prepare both the day *and* night guards for Ada's arrival, but he also needed to tell Felix to prepare the vampires to be moved to the city. Two simple tasks, he was sure. What could go wrong? He smiled slightly, almost proud of himself for having been given so much responsibility already. Alucard seemed to appreciate him in such a short time, and he basked in that fact.

As he walked along the path, he shifted his eyes to the pale, chiselled face of the man he saw just before heading to Alucard's manor—the man who had lost his dog. He stood on the roadside, watching Ben with his strangely red eyes. When Ben saw him earlier, the strange man was wearing a hood over his head, but it was no longer there, revealing the black, greasy hair tied behind his head and the elf-like pointed ears on either side of his head.

A twisted smile stretched across the man's face as Ben came closer. He wore a cloak-like coat which concealed his entire person other than his right hand, in which he held a steel chain with a mangled beast at its end. Was *that* his dog? It was shaped and built much like a bloodhound, but its flesh was torn, ripped, and bloodied. It looked…dead.

Ben felt curious…but cautious. He wanted to know who this man was and what he wanted, so he faked a smile and his kindness. "You found him, then?"

Eyeing him up and down, the man smirked. "Yes."

This man's modulated, honeyed voice was strangely appealing in a way that made Ben think that he meant no harm. He was just a normal guy who had been searching for his dog—his very…peculiar dog. But Ben didn't judge. This was Aegisguard, after all, and he was sure a zombie dog was the least of many strange things he would come to see.

He nodded and slipped his hands into his pockets. "Lost in the woods?"

The man looked down at this dog and slowly looked back at Ben. "Yes," he replied, the same sly expression on his face.

He didn't say much, but Ben assumed that might be because he wasn't Deiganish.

Ben smiled and shrugged. "All right, well, I'll see you around," he said, turning to walk off.

"Castle," the man said, the chain in his hand rattling as he turned to face Ben. "That's where you live? Work?"

"Something like that," Ben said, unwilling to give any details of his work or life away to a stranger, especially when the vampire he worked for might very well punish him for speaking out of term. He wasn't sure whether Alucard was such a boss or not, but he *did* feel as though Alucard wouldn't appreciate him speaking to strangers, especially those walking undead dogs.

"Vampire." The man grinned. "You walk…in daylight."

Ben looked around. "Yeah…" he said with a nod but then sighed. "I really gotta go. I'm glad you found your dog, just…don't lose him again."

"Glad…to have found you." The man looked down at his dog. "Indeed."

"Right, later…" Ben called, walking off.

As he walked off, however, a strange, ominous coldness struck him. He looked back over his shoulder, but there was no sign of the man or his dog. What the hell?

He frowned and glared ahead. Where could he have gone—and so quickly? He wasn't a vampire; he wasn't a demon. In fact, Ben got *nothing* from him…just…nothing. Not human, not werewolf…. It was like he hadn't even been there. No scent. No aura. Could that man have been a figment of his imagination? Was the stress of his new life getting to him?

Ben rolled his eyes and made his way up to the castle. He was sure that it was nothing. He had more important matters to focus on, and he hoped it would all go smoothly.

But when he entered the castle hall, he set his eyes on Felix. He watched as the grey-haired vampire casually walked out of the door that led to Alucard's half of the castle, taking advantage of the overcast skies to walk about during the day. Ben knew as well as anyone else that no one was allowed in that part of the castle…so why had he just caught Felix leaving it?

Before Felix could sneak away, Ben scowled and called, "Felix!"

Felix stopped in his tracks and stared over at Ben like a deer in lanternlight. He'd been caught, and he clearly had no idea what to say or do.

"What were you doing in there?" Ben questioned, approaching him.

With a look of desperation, Felix shrugged. "Aleksei says it's okay—I can go in there. I am exception."

Ben didn't believe that at all, especially not now that he suspected Felix had some sort of unhealthy obsession with Alucard. He scowled sceptically and crossed his arms. "Even after our conversation not too long ago, you decide to lie to me again?"

"I not lie. I *am* allowed in there."

"You told me that to get to the towers on Aleksei's side of the castle, even *you* have to fly up to them because *no one* is allowed in that half of the castle. Yet, I come back here, and I see you sneaking out the door?"

"Where you go? To see Aleksei?"

"What were you doing in there?!" he insisted, already tired of Felix's attempt to divert the conversation.

Felix shuddered slightly. "I look…I look for mice."

"Mice?" Ben scowled in disbelief.

He nodded. "Infestation bad."

Ben glanced around the room, but there wasn't a single mouse in sight. He then set his eyes back on Felix. "I haven't seen a single rodent since I moved here—excluding the one in front of me right now. Why were you in there? Or should I tell Aleksei?"

Then, Felix scowled with slight hostility. "Why I answer you? Why you act like boss? Why Aleksei pick you?"

"I don't need to answer any of that."

Felix scoffed at him. "Why you so important? You see Aleksei often? You friends? Hang out?"

"We're not talking about me or Aleksei, we're talking about *you* and why I just caught you sneaking around in places you shouldn't be."

"I am in charge here. I command night guard, I look after vampires in Aleksei's absence—not *you*. I do what I want. Why you even come here? Why vampires from different world get to live here? Why Aleksei care?"

Ben grunted irritably. "If he hasn't told you, then I'm sure that means you're not meant to know—"

"You know? You know more than me? Who is demon that come here? Why he smile at Aleksei?"

Ben scowled impatiently. "Aleksei's moving all the vampires to the city. Tell them," he instructed.

"Why?" Felix asked.

"Judging by Aleksei's orders, it would also appear that I'm now in charge of the night guard, too. That makes me your superior—*that's* why you should listen to me, answer me, and do what I say. Answer the damn question before I lose my patience."

Felix scowled. "I lose job to you? Aleksei give you my job? Why? You make deal? He give you special treatment because you friends? Why he like you so much?"

Ben had no patience left to spare. He snatched hold of Felix's throat so quickly that Felix had no time to comprehend it. Ben pulled Felix's face into his and glared into his silvery eyes. "Stop asking me questions you clearly don't have the authority to know the answers to and do as I told you," he warned calmly, and the sincerity in his voice was as clear as the skies were beginning to become.

Seeing that the sunlight would be free of the clouds at any moment, Felix nodded desperately. "Y-yes, I do…I do what you say," he agreed.

Ben then let go of him and watched as he scurried off and rushed into the door that led to the vampires' part of the castle.

What an annoying, pathetic, strange little man he was. Clearly, Felix *was* going to cause a lot more trouble than he already had, and Ben felt as though it was time to tell Alucard what he had seen. He wasn't sure when he'd next see Alucard, but he'd be sure to inform him of Felix's sketchy attitude.

With an irritated sigh, he made his own way over to the door Felix had disappeared into, intending to finish what he had come to do.

Chapter Thirty-Seven

— ⸲ ✝ ⸱ —

The Goose Inn

| Ben |

The next day, Ben sat outside The Goose Inn, which was packed with chattering people. He waited alone at one of the benches—the *only* bench in the shadow of a towering building, which kept the scorching sun off him. Despite his resistance to the sunlight, too much of it would eventually aggravate him.

He ignored the hushed, insulting slurs of the humans around him, minding his own business while he enjoyed his glass of rum. It was late afternoon, and he was done with the tasks every morning brought, and now, he was waiting for the man he agreed to meet. But he was late.

Sipping from his glass, he watched the streets around him. However, as he glared at the busy sidewalk ahead, he spotted someone vaguely familiar. There, standing in the opening of a narrow alley between the bakery and a fruit stand…was the man who lost his dog? His pale, chiselled face struck Ben instantly, and as the man smiled twistedly, Ben began to feel uncomfortable.

Just like the last time Ben saw him, the strange man was wearing a cloak that concealed almost all of his body. The undead dog was at his side once more, staring into Ben's soul. Why was he here? Why was he watching him? Had he followed him? Every instinct within his body told him to confront the guy, but when a group of muttering, suited men strolled past, the cloaked man vanished in the split-second Ben had lost sight of him.

He sharply turned his head and took his eyes off the street to stare down the road to his left as a group of women gasping in the distance caught his attention. He set his sights on Tobias, Alucard's werewolf informant, and watched as he was turned down by a small group of expensively dressed aristocrats. The man pouted and hung his head in shame as he then dragged himself towards the tavern. Like usual, he wore his brown leather jacket, a loose black shirt, and torn black jeans. He looked as rugged as ever, even more so since the night before was the full moon, and it had very clearly left him feeling exhausted.

Tobias slumped down opposite Ben and sighed deeply as he rested his arms on the table.

"Long night?" Ben asked with a slight smile.

With a snappy, aggravated snarl, Tobias rolled his eyes and huffed. "Don't get me started, man," he uttered. "You working today? You don't get Sundays off?"

"I suspect a day off won't be something I get for a while," Ben mumbled. "Not now that this Ada woman's shown up. I've been moving vampires into the city non-stop for the past two days since Aleksei gave the order."

"She was bound to come along one day or another," Tobias said with a shrug, eyeing Ben's drink. "Can I get one of those? Aleksei pays you, right? I'm sure you can afford it," he said with a grin.

Ben looked back over his shoulder and waved his hand to summon the barmaid. Then, he asked Tobias, "He doesn't pay *you*?"

"Yeah, I get paid, but probably not as much as you. You're some hotshot vampire commander guy, right? I hear you also got the job of picking up the death-row inmates. Last guy who did that before Aleksei himself got like… five coronam per gig."

"That's like… five hundred dollars where I'm from," Ben said, smirking.

"What's that smile? You get more than that?"

"Maybe."

Tobias leaned closer. "Go on, how much you get?"

"I don't think we should be talking about this sort of thing here," Ben said, concern both on his face and in his hushed voice.

"Come on," Tobias insisted quietly, tapping his arm. "We're just talkin' about getting paid, nothing else."

Looking at him, Ben frowned unsurely, but he couldn't deny that he was curious to know what sum everyone else was paid whilst working for Alucard. He also still had no idea where Alucard's wealth came from, despite his high position among the vampire's subordinates. He was sure, however, that he was soon to find that out.

Ben nodded. "All right, how much do *you* get paid?"

"Weekly, I get about…" Tobias stopped and thought to himself for a few moments, "…two coronam, sometimes three if I get good info," he bragged. "Each of my packmates get a couple gold too."

Ben scoffed quietly. "Well, *I* get a thousand per pick-up and just as much weekly."

"A thousand…what?" Tobias frowned. "You're in Aegisguard now; speak our language."

"Uh…ten coronam," he corrected. "Per week for my current job, and also per pick-up."

A look of astonishment smothered the guy's face. "You're kidding?"

"Nope," Ben said with a smile and then sipped from his glass.

"The hell you get paid *that* much for?"

"I look after an entire castle of hungry vampires—soon to be a city of hungry vampires. I gotta keep them in check. I risk my life every time I go out there to pick up those prisoners, too."

Tobias mumbled, "Eh, true. Well, looks like you're buying all the drinks, then."

"This time, sure," Ben said as the barmaid made her way over with two glasses of the rum he was drinking.

Taking his glass, Tobias leaned forward. "So, if you're a big boss guy, you *must* know where all Aleksei's cash comes from, right?"

He didn't answer; not only was he unaware, but he also still felt as though it wasn't a good idea to be discussing such things in public. Tobias, however, seemed over-eager to share.

Tobias continued, "We all know he's got a hand in all the local businesses here. Some of us think he's involved in some other, darker shit, though."

"Like?" Ben asked, edging closer.

"Well, not exactly *dark*, but like…on the low-low, you know?"

He nodded slowly.

"So, a few months back, before Rodney disappeared, I saw him sending some pretty heavily geared-up vamps off somewhere over the sea. Me and my mates think he's got some weapon-for-hire shit going on."

"Mercenaries?" Ben asked with a slight laugh of disbelief. "He doesn't strike me as the type."

Tobias sat up straight and shrugged. "There's a lot about him you wouldn't have suspected until you *really* know him, man," he said before downing his drink. "Like…some of us think that he and this Ada lady were a thing—business partners or something—but then they fell out, broke up, yeah?"

"Were they?" Ben asked, sipping from his glass.

"Nah, I don't know. I mean, every time I offer to set the boss man up with one of my girls, he turns it down almost like he's disgusted. *I* think he and Ada *were* a thing, but then they broke up, and it was so bad that it's put him off wolves forever."

Ben frowned. "I thought he just hated Werewolves in general?"

"Well, he likes *me*."

He shook his head. "We're side-tracking. We came here to talk business."

"Nah, nah, hold up," Tobias insisted, holding out his hand. "Who was the guy that was there with him yesterday? You seemed to know him."

"That…was *my* boss."

"Your…but you work for Aleksei. How can you have two bosses?"

"It's a complex arrangement."

"Meh, not my business."

Looking at him, Ben frowned warily. "Do you talk about Aleksei's private business to anyone who asks and anyone who *doesn't* ask?"

"No." Tobias scowled. "I can talk about it to you 'cause you work for him too."

"I didn't know any of what you just told me, and I feel like that was for a reason."

Tobias laughed slightly. "Why would Aleksei keep stuff from you? You're like… important—you get paid enough. And you're what… an Adherant vampire?"

Ben told him sternly, "If I were you, I'd be careful who I choose to reveal these things to."

Looking at his concerned face, Tobias scoffed and sat up straight. "Why are you all serious all of a sudden? You scared or something?"

"I've known people like Aleksei to kill their subordinates for less than what you've said."

"Aleksei ain't gonna kill anyone. He doesn't do that."

"No? Then what happened to Rodney? Does anyone actually know?"

Tobias slowly looked down at his empty glass and frowned in confliction. "Maybe you're right."

"Just… watch what you say."

With a hesitant sigh, Tobias lost his smile. "Anyway, we came here to talk about business. What's the issue?"

"No issue as such," Ben said, leaning his arms onto the table. "We've just been told to keep an eye out for Ada, and I don't really know much about her."

"You want me to tell you about her?"

"Yeah. I thought I'd ask you instead of bothering Aleksei and Zalith."

"The dude that was with him yesterday?" Tobias questioned.

"Yeah."

"You thinkin' what I'm thinkin'?" he asked with a suggestive smirk.

Ben couldn't help but smile. "You could be thinking multiple things. However, I do suspect that there might be something going on between them both, yes."

Tobias laughed. "Nah, man. I'm kidding. Aleksei ain't into dudes. Honestly, I don't think he's into anyone at all."

"I beg to differ."

The guy patted his hand on the table. "All right. A week's worth of your pay says Aleksei *isn't* into your bossman."

"A month of *yours* says he *is*," Ben agreed.

They shook hands in agreement.

"Hey, maybe that's why he's always turning down the girls I offer him; this whole time, maybe he's just been gay," Tobias said, scratching the side of his face. "Still, I reckon he's one of those people that just don't date, one of those people that just generally ain't into no one."

"What about Ada? You seemed so sure there."

Tobias fiddled with his empty glass and sighed. "Meh, maybe. Maybe that's why he's not into anyone anymore; she probably turned him right off."

Ben frowned. "Judging by the way he speaks about her, I don't think it was like that, not to mention the look in his eyes. I've seen it before. He hates that woman."

"Maybe. I guess we'll find out one day, huh?"

"Anyway, Ada: why's Aleksei so cautious?" Ben questioned, trying to get back to business.

"Well, she's the werewolf boss lady, ain't she? Big, strong, sexy as all hell," he said with a grin. "I'd hit it."

Rolling his eyes, Ben finished his drink. "Of course you would."

"All that aside, though, she's dangerous. Aleksei tell you *anything*?"

Ben shook his head. "Not much."

"Well, they were fighting over Dor-Sanguis for years. Ada wanted it so she could start some werewolf empire thing; Aleksei wants it for…well…it's his homeplace and a safe haven for vamps. He's also building something—his business, whatever else he's got going on. I think he wants to change the world, you know. Vampires used to be really big out here—like…feared, respected. They were the top of the top, big bosses. Everything the humans own once belonged to a vampire, therefore belonging to Aleksei. But then he went away somewhere, I dunno where, but he was gone long enough for Ada and the humans to tear it all apart."

"So, vampires used to…what? Reign here in Aegisguard?"

"Yeah. They were called the Nosferatu. They had cities, empires—any place of power, there was always a vampire at the tip-top of it all. Aleksei was also born as some anti-Demiurge thing, meant to overthrow the holy order or something, and he did it. Demiurge is another thing people call God here, by the way—if you don't already know, and I wouldn't be surprised if you didn't. You ain't been here long, and there's a lot to learn. Anyway, vamps were in control of the vast majority of Aegisguard. But without him around, the vamps weren't so feared; the dragons fought back, kicked them back down lower than humans."

"Dragons?" Ben asked with a curious frown.

Tobias nodded and continued, "You didn't hear that he killed one of them? He killed Janus, which had all the other dragons scared and hiding, especially since the guy that killed Janus was the son of Lucifer, and Lucifer's like…a God of Gods."

Somehow, Ben was keeping up. It was a lot to absorb, but the more he learned about this world, the better. After all, he'd be living and working in Aegisguard for the rest of his life. He didn't want any surprises. "How do you know all this?"

"When you work for Aleksei, you hear stuff. Demiurge's name is Letholdus. He's like…the most popular name getting thrown around. Sixty percent or so of Aegisguard pray to and believe in him. As for the others, they got small little cults going or whatever."

Ben nodded, absorbing all the information. "Battleground…dragons—elaborate."

"Well, a hundred years *after* the God Gods came—we call them the Numen—the Numen came along and made everything; Letholdus, the Demiurge, made dragons—little sub-gods; some call them demi-gods or Aegis. They were sent here to look after the land in Letholdus' absence, 'cause apparently, it uses a lot of their power for the Numen to walk in this realm. There were eighteen of these dragons, and they all had different responsibilities. But of course, they got mad at each other, jealous, whatever. They'd fight all the damn time; there was a new war literally every month back then."

"There's no war today, so I assume something happened?" Ben asked, a little worried that he was now stuck in another world where war would destroy everything.

Tobias shrugged and said, "Yeah, Aleksei happened."

He trusted Aleksei…and if *he* was the thing between peace and war, then he felt a lot less concerned. "Okay, so tell me more about Ada in all of this."

"Well, she sided with the humans a couple of generations ago and helped them take down Aleksei's empire. She also told the dragons that Aleksei was out of the picture, so we had werewolves, humans, and dragons all working together to tear Aleksei's life's work apart. He got back to nothing but his castle, and I can't imagine how that must have felt for the guy," Tobias said as he frowned sympathetically.

Ben nodded. "Yeah…it must have been awful to come back and see everything you spent your whole life working for ruined."

"I don't know why Ada hates him so much, like…why she had to do that. I think she might have been jealous or something—Aleksei never told us the exact reason, so we all just have our theories."

"Yours being that they were an item but broke up."

"Hey, it's plausible," Tobias muttered.

Ben smirked. "Maybe—unless I'm right about him and Zalith."

Tobias grunted and tapped his glass. "Hey, we getting a refill? Don't get cheap on me, buddy."

Rolling his eyes, Ben leaned back and caught the barmaid's attention again. Then, he looked back at Tobias. "So, in terms of strength: how tough is this Ada? You think me and my guys can hold her off if we see her?"

"If she's a nuisance for Aleksei—and she is—then I'm sure you don't really got much of a chance against her if a fight breaks out. But then again, Aleksei wouldn't give you the job if he didn't think you could keep her preoccupied until he gets there."

"Duly noted," Ben said as the barmaid handed them both new drinks.

Picking up his drink, Tobias then sighed. "Who knows, maybe this time, Aleksei'll be able to work something out with her."

Once Tobias took a sip of his drink, he said, "Anyway, why you so convinced you're right about Aleksei and your boss dude?"

"I'm certain that Zalith's into Aleksei. And the other day, I told Aleksei that Zalith's gay, but he seemed awfully confused—not in a like...*'wait, really?'* kind of way, but in the sort of way that made me think Aleksei doesn't get what gay is, you know?"

Tobias frowned slightly. "Well, I don't blame him. You hear it's seriously frowned upon here? So, I guess Aleksei's not really like... aware that it's a thing; spends too much of his time working as well, so."

"I can understand that."

"If Aleksei don't get what gay is, then I'm pretty sure he and your boss *ain't* a thing. Looks like you'll be paying up."

With a conflicted frown, Ben leaned his arms onto the table. "I'm certain there's *something* going on there, whether they're already a thing or becoming a thing."

Tobias smiled and said, "Well, there's only one way we're gonna find out."

"What? You suggest we just go up to Aleksei's door—'oh, hi boss, just wondering, are you gay? If so, are you and my other boss a thing?' No," Ben disagreed. "It's rude. Plus, I don't wanna get on his bad side, either."

"It's *Aleksei*, man. He's chill."

"Chill," Ben uttered. "I'm not so sure sometimes."

"Come on. It'll be a laugh—and if he admits right there and then that he likes your bossman even the slightest tiny little bit, I'll pay up."

Ben stared at him for a few moments, pondering. Admittedly, it would be rather entertaining, and he'd possibly obtain a victory. So, he sighed. "Eh, sure," he said with a shrug. "I could use a laugh. I've gotta go see him about setting up in the city anyway."

"Setting up?" Tobias asked as he watched Ben finish his drink. "You moving here?"

"May as well," Ben said, standing up. "Aleksei's getting me to move all the other vampires here; the wife suggested we do the same."

Standing up, Tobias nodded. "Yeah, I get that. I've always preferred the outdoors, man."

"If Aleksei gets mad, you're taking the fall," Ben told him firmly.

Tobias chuckled, "He ain't gonna get mad, but sure thing."

The pair then made their way towards the city's exit, heading to Alucard's manor. And Ben hoped that he wasn't making a big mistake.

Chapter Thirty-Eight

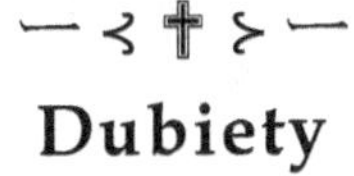

Dubiety

| Alucard |

In his manor, Alucard hadn't long woken from a sleep that ensnared him since the morning Zalith left. He didn't have any reason to leave his bed since sending his subordinates to work and having accepted that, he allowed himself to rest for over twenty-four hours.

He had no regrets. With Dirk preparing the city for Ada's arrival, Tobias preparing the wolves, and Ben both moving the vampires to the city and commanding them, he was confident that if Ada were to attack, he'd know before she managed to put even a dent in the reforming Nosferatu Empire.

However, his thoughts weren't solely focused on Ada and his recovering empire. Instead, they were with Zalith, the insufferable demon who hadn't long become his friend. Was it still fair to call him insufferable? Yes, because that was one of his distinguishable traits...*but* Alucard found himself enjoying parts of the demon's personality that he would usually despise. Although Zalith acted strangely and confused him a lot, their interactions amused him. Of course, Zalith seemed to find Alucard just as amusing—if not more so—and that stupid smile of his irritated Alucard more than he could find words to describe. Yet...he'd rather continue seeing it than not see it at all.

He let his mind wander for a moment. Was his lack of motivation to leave his bed and get to work due to the fact that he would much rather be working with Zalith again? He felt that...maybe it *was* the case. After all, Zalith knew what he was doing; he could handle himself well in any situation, and Alucard appreciated that. The vampire found that he worked better alongside someone who worked *with* him rather than for him, and that someone just so happened to be Zalith. The demon didn't work *for* him, so he didn't act like a suck-up, and he didn't obey his orders like a dog; Zalith did things his own way, he made his own choices, and he didn't have much of a filter when it came to what he said. And Alucard *liked* that.

Alucard then frowned and glanced at the window. What difference did it make, though? Why did he feel so much more comfortable working with someone like Zalith? He'd never seen himself working alongside anyone else, let alone a demon, but there he was, working with Zalith *and* wishing that he was with him again today. Alucard had come to both understand and accept that he didn't have a problem working with people, he just had a problem working with the people who worked *for* him. He didn't appreciate their grovelling or their need to be recognized. He wanted to work with someone who wouldn't watch what they said, someone who wouldn't hold back in any way, shape, or form. And that was Zalith.

But…then again, Zalith was odd. Very odd indeed. He always stared, he always smiled, and he was *too* interested in Alucard's life—his past, his current affairs—and then there was the touching. Why did Zalith seem so insistent to lay hands on him? Whether it be checking his wounds, giving him something, taking something from him, or simply greeting him, Zalith *always* jumped at any chance to touch him. Before, Alucard was extremely volatile, standoffish, and defensive. He *hated* any form of physical contact, even from someone he'd known as long as Elvin. But once again, Zalith came along and exceeded yet another of his boundaries, and Alucard wasn't all that bothered by it.

Perhaps all of this was because Alucard considered the demon a friend. Could being someone's friend make someone prone to accepting things they'd once convinced themself they'd never enjoy? Maybe. Whether it was because they were friends or because it was simply just Zalith, Alucard couldn't decide. All he knew was that he'd much rather be waking up knowing that Zalith was waiting to join him on his tasks again than waking up knowing that he'd be going out alone to deal with his usual annoyances.

With a quiet, lazy sigh, Alucard slowly sat up and dragged his hand over his face, trying to keep himself from thinking about going back to sleep. He had to get up; he had things to do. He had to check on the vampires, make sure Elvin's move to the city was being undertaken, and go and see who had replaced Ki at the prison as per Ben's recent notification. It was going to be a long, strenuous day, and he was not looking forward to it at all.

And it was about to get a whole lot more irritating.

A quiet knock came at his front door, and annoyance instantly smothered Alucard's face. It couldn't be Elvin; he'd just let himself in. It wasn't Zalith—to his disappointment; he'd recognize a demon's aura anywhere, especially if it were right outside his door.

After a few moments of lazy sensing, he discovered that it was Ben and Tobias at his door. He rolled his eyes as he slowly climbed out of bed and pulled on a shirt. What could *they* possibly want?

He made his way out of his room and downstairs into the entrance hall. When he unlocked his door and pulled it open, he set his ice-blue eyes on his two bright-faced subordinates. They stared at him as if they both had something to say, but neither of them appeared to have the words.

"Aleksei," Ben said with a smile. "I've got updates."

Alucard waited, blinking tiredly.

"I've moved the vast majority of the castle's vampires into new homes in the city. Myself, my wife, and a few of the day guards remain. I'll be moving them tonight—as long as you're okay with me moving into the city and out of the castle."

"Is zhe castle not to your liking?" Alucard asked with a frown, almost offended.

"N-no, no, I just thought that with the rest of the vampires moving into the city, it would be better for me to move too—to keep an eye on them. That *is* my job, after all," he said, laughing a little.

The vampire wasn't in much of a good mood today. He scowled and replied, "I tell you vhat your job is. Move zhe vampires as I said, and zhen you vill stay in zhe castle and keep vatch vor Ada."

Staring at Alucard, Ben nodded. "Of course."

"And you?" Alucard asked Tobias.

Tobias smirked. "Are you in love with that Zalith guy?" he asked with a grin, leaning on the porch frame.

"Vhat?" Alucard asked in utter disbelief, his vacant look becoming something of a confused, startled frown.

"The guy you was hanging out with yesterday," Tobias said. "You can tell me."

Ben then sighed. "What he meant to ask was: are you...maybe...interested?"

Alucard sharply turned his head to glare at him. "Intervested? Vhat? In vhat?" he asked, confounded.

"In...Zalith," Ben asked slowly. "Because...he might...be into *you*," he said with a nervous smile.

"Into? Vhat?" Alucard frowned, looking back and forth at the two of them. "Vhat are you talking about?"

Tobias smirked. "I knew it," he said proudly, looking over at Ben.

Alucard then scowled. "Knew vhat?!"

Standing up straight, Tobias backed off before Alucard could grab him. "Hey, calm down man, we were just curious to know what's been going on between you and the Zalith guy."

"Noving is going on," he snarled, pointing at him. "Get out of 'ere bevore I get any angrier."

Ben then sighed again and glanced at Tobias. "Tobias is an idiot," he muttered, looking at Alucard.

"Yeah, I know I am," Tobias called from where he had chosen to stand—a good distance away from Alucard.

"We were just genuinely curious whether there's something going on with you and Zalith is all. You've been hanging out often, and I know he's into you—probably more than I've seen him into anyone, come to think of it. Anyway, I just wanted to know," Ben explained cautiously.

Alucard still failed to understand what Ben was asking. What more could be going on with Zalith other than their friendship and their work? He frowned strangely. "Vhat are you asking me? If ve are vriends? 'E is…my vriend, yes—vhat more could zhere be?"

With a nervous laugh, Ben dragged his hand over the back of his neck. "You remember what I told you the day before yesterday, don't you? About Zalith…and how he's attracted—to men."

"I vemember."

"Okay…and…you're a man—that he likes…a lot, it would seem."

"So?" Alucard questioned.

"So…I think he's attracted to you."

Alucard scoffed in amusement. "So?"

"So…."

"So?" Alucard asked again, a look of dismissal on his face. "Is zhat all?"

Ben frowned. "Y-yeah…I guess…yeah."

"Get back to vork," Alucard then instructed.

With an unsure nod, Ben slowly turned around and walked off, and as he left the manor gardens, Tobias followed, leaving Alucard alone.

The moment he was alone, Alucard slammed his door and leaned back against it, his thoughts so confusing and erratic. He stared down at the floor, his eyes darting around rapidly as he tried to focus—as he tried to work out what just happened. Zalith was *attracted* to him? How? Why? When? He had no idea what to think. He hadn't done anything the slightest bit interesting to have someone feel any sort of attraction towards him, least of all someone like Zalith. In fact, he was quite sure that no one could ever be attracted to him—why would they? What did he have to offer? He wasn't interesting, funny, or important; he was just some vampire working to protect other vampires. That's all he was; he lived to work. How would anyone find that attractive?

It all began to make sense, though. Before, he'd been confused by Zalith's actions and words. But now he felt like he might be beginning to understand. Was that why Zalith always stared at him? Alucard was sure there was nothing physically appealing about himself, so that couldn't be it. That must have been why Zalith insisted they meet up outside of work…. Of course, they both wanted to be friends, but now it seemed as though the demon might want more than that. And that didn't make him uncomfortable, nor did it make him want to stop seeing him.

Did *he* want more? He was quite sure he didn't. How could he? He was a man, Zalith was a man—it wasn't plausible. It wasn't acceptable. And yet, Ben and Tobias seemed to be so very calm about it. Why?

Alucard frowned, staring at the floor while he pondered. Where Zalith came from, perhaps such a relationship wasn't frowned upon. But in Aegisguard, it wasn't the norm. Whether Alucard felt attracted to him or not—which he was quite certain he didn't—it would never happen. And so, he tried to dismiss his thoughts. He and Zalith were *friends*, and that was all it ever would and *could* be.

Right?

Chapter Thirty-Nine

⌐ ⟨ ✝ ⟩ ¬

Truths

| **Alucard** |

Alucard watched from his study balcony as the six glistening moons climbed higher into the sky. Each passing second brought him closer to seeing Zalith again since their night of drinking and its following morning of confusion and agonizing headaches, and he was looking forward to it.

He once dreaded seeing that demon and his confusing smile, estranged actions, and confounding way of speaking. This time, however, it all seemed to be making a little more sense to Alucard. Now, thanks to Ben, Alucard knew that Zalith was actually attracted to him, and he wasn't yet sure how that made him feel. He was relieved that he understood the reason behind the way Zalith acted, but he didn't understand why or how someone like Zalith could have such an interest in someone like him.

Despite the fact he dismissed the thoughts so many times since Ben's revelation, they kept returning. Zalith might want more than friendship. *His* liking for Zalith had only just evolved into friendship, so he was sure that he didn't reciprocate the demon's feelings. And not just that, but that kind of relationship was something he was quite sure he'd never become involved in—not here. Gay relationships were frowned upon, to put it lightly, and as much as Alucard didn't care for what people thought of him, he didn't want to add another burden to his life.

Why was he even thinking about it? He was thinking about it as if Zalith asked him if he would like to be in a relationship. He hadn't, and he was quite sure that if Zalith *did* ask, he'd deny his request. He didn't have the time, interest, or need. But why was he giving it so much thought? Why did it weigh so heavily on his mind? It had been days since he was told, so his concern should have passed by now—but it hadn't.

Was he beginning to understand just how much *he* liked Zalith? In such a short time, the demon had become the vampire's friend; he had Alucard telling him things he was sure he would never tell anyone, and he had Alucard feeling such strange, new things.

He undeniably enjoyed spending time with Zalith despite the newly revealed fact that they both had different intentions. Whatever came of this revelation, though, Alucard knew that he didn't want to lose his new friend.

However, he still wasn't entirely sure what to make of it. Zalith *was* his friend, that was for sure. Whether there was more or not, Alucard wasn't certain. All he was confident about right now was that he had never felt this way before, and as confounding as it was, he didn't shy away from it. He wanted to know why he felt like this, and he wanted to see if tonight's meeting would make him feel any differently now that he knew the truth behind Zalith's interest. Could they remain friends despite the demon's very different interests, or would Alucard have to set boundaries? He'd know what he had to do once he saw Zalith. So, he dismissed his thoughts. He'd deal with it later.

With a quiet sigh, he set his eyes on Elvin, who was making his way along the path towards his manor, book-in-hand, and humming to himself quietly. Usually, irritancy would snatch hold of Alucard the moment he set his eyes on the bard, but today, he was relieved to see him. He hadn't seen Elvin since the last meeting where he told him he'd be moving to the city; his appearance told Alucard that he must have settled into his new home and was now coming to update him.

The vampire left the balcony and headed into his house, preparing for whatever the bard was going to bombard him with.

| Elvin |

Elvin hummed as he headed towards Alucard's house. He was excited to get to see him but thinking about the fact that the demon might be there too sent a shiver of angst through him. He *hated* that guy. He didn't understand why Alucard seemed to like him and kept spending time with him—not only that, but Alucard *hated* demons and had done for as long as he could remember. So why was he hanging around with one? Why was he letting one call him *Alucard*?

The bard pouted, glaring ahead as he made his way through the manor gardens. He suspected something was going on; that demon had to be up to something…. No, he *was* up to something. He was using Alucard in some way or another and Elvin wasn't going to stand idly by and let it happen. When he had to, he'd say something more— he'd stand up for Alucard. He'd do anything for him…even face a monster like Zalith. He'd try his best not to be afraid. All that mattered was that his friend was safe because *he* was a real friend to Alucard. He didn't want anything from him. He just…wanted Alucard to see that.

When he reached the door, he knocked and waited. As Alucard pulled the door open, the bard smiled brightly. "Hi!"

Then, he leaned in to hug him, but the vampire frowned uncomfortably, stepped aside, and the bard stumbled into the entrance hall.

Embarrassed, Elvin looked around. "No guests today then, huh? Where's Emil? I didn't see Sergiu outside either."

Closing the door, Alucard shrugged. "Sergiu is preparing zhe ship, and Emil 'as tonight off," he explained, leading the way into the lounge. He then slumped down onto the couch and looked over at the fireplace as Elvin sat opposite him in the armchair. "Is zhe new 'ouse comvortable?"

Elvin nodded and said, "Yeah, actually. It's a lot bigger. There's space for the cat and more rooms than I know what to do with."

Alucard seemed unusually relaxed tonight. Often, the vampire seemed irritated, was overly volatile, and Elvin had to watch what he said. But Alucard wasn't any of those things. In fact, he appeared…happy. The vampire never really asked if Elvin was comfortable…. Why was he suddenly so different? Had something happened?

The bard pouted slightly. "You never usually ask that sort of thing," he mumbled.

He wondered…did Alucard care? Had Elvin's absence helped Alucard to understand how he felt about him?

Alucard glanced at him. "Vhat are you talking about? Vhy vould I not vant to know if your new living avangements are comvortable? Especially since I vas zhe vone who made you move."

Elvin shrugged. "You just never really seem to care about much, least of all *me*."

Alucard rolled his eyes. "'As Dirk left vor Boszorkāny?"

The bard pouted in irritancy. He hated when he changed the subject. "Yeah, two days ago," he answered.

"And I trust zhe vampires are settling into zhe city?"

"I guess so," he muttered.

Alucard scowled impatiently. "Vhen I ask vor your opinion, Elvin, I expect a usevul answer."

With a deep sigh, Elvin said, "They're doing fine as far as I know. Everything the treaty stated is the law. Humans are allowing the vampires into places of business; some guy even got a night shift in a tavern. Some of the humans are still wary, but it's still kinda recent since the treaty happened, so it's normal."

"*Multumesc*," Alucard thanked, looking back into the empty fireplace.

The bard had much more to say, though. "So…you're gonna go see Zalith again tonight?" he asked, trying to hide his skepticism. Alucard seemed to be getting close to that demon more recently, and Elvin thought, could *Zalith* be the reason he seemed so content? So relaxed? That better not be the case. Elvin didn't like Zalith one bit, and he was quite sure he never would.

"I see 'im every veek, Elvin; vhy vould tonight be any divverent?" the vampire answered with an irritable frown on his pale face.

"Just wondering. Is that why you're all…nice and calm?"

Alucard scowled and looked over at him. "Nice and calm?"

"Yeah. Usually, you're all grr and ugh, go home Elvin, go away Elvin, blah blah I don't like you, Elvin. But now you're all—" he paused and pulled a forceful grin, "—happy and asking me if I'm okay and whatever, doing things you never really used to do before, *and* asking *me* for updates. You never do that."

Glaring at him, Alucard waited.

"Ever since that Zalith demon guy showed up, you've been acting *really* different. You hang out with him even though you *never* hang out with anyone—not even me, who you've known for seven years. You've known that demon for like…three months!" he exclaimed. "What's so different about him that you'd rather go drink coffee and hang out here with him than me? Or Tobias? Dirk? Anyone else you've known longer than that Zalith guy!"

Anger then warped Alucard's calm face. "Vhy are you so concerned?" he asked calmly, but the aggravation in his voice was unmistakable.

The bard pouted. "He's trouble," he said slowly, unsettled by Alucard's change of tone. "He…he does things that you wouldn't let anyone else get away with, and don't try to tell me he *doesn't* make you feel uncomfortable because I *know* he does."

"Is zhat vight?"

"You never drink, yet I come here one morning and you're both hungover!" he stated. "You don't like physical contact, yet it's okay for *him* to touch you, and you let him say mean things to me!"

Alucard raised an eyebrow.

Elvin pondered to himself for a few moments before scowling at the vampire, trying to remember the other points he had come up with over the past few days. "Y-you never meet your work associates or subordinates outside of business, but you meet *him* all the time! I don't understand! Don't you see what he's doing?" he asked painfully. "He's making you push us away; he's making you do all these things you'd never do, and you don't even see why!"

"Tell me vhy," Alucard requested vacantly.

"B-because…he just…wants to use you!"

Alucard scowled impatiently.

Glaring at him, Elvin continued, "I-I know his type—I can spot them a mile off—and I'm not gonna let him use you! He wants you for one thing, Aleksei, and that's it," he insisted. "I don't know if you like him or whatever's going on, but once he gets what he came here for, he's never gonna come back."

The vampire looked angry and upset. "Are you not zhe vone alvays asking me vhy I seem sad? You're alvays on my ass about veelings and socializing and vhatever else. Now zhat I'm actually doing someving, now zhat I'm somevhat enjoying someving, you 'ave to come in 'ere and shit all over zhis because is somevone else 'elping me to veel zhis vay, and not you," he accused him.

Elvin went to reply—

"I zon't know 'ow many times I 'ave to tell you, Elvin; you vork *vor* me. You're not my vriend, and you shouldn't concern yourselv vith me, my life, or my veelings. Vhat I do and who I choose to do vith is my business, not yours. Speak ill of Zaliv vonce more in my presence and I vill make sure you understand just 'ow much you piss me off. Is zhat clear?" Alucard threatened.

Elvin had no idea what to make of what he just heard. Alucard just said that he was *not* his friend. That caused him such pain... and he felt his heart break as Alucard's words repeated over and over inside his head. Not only had Alucard demoted him, but the vampire had also *threatened* him. If he spoke ill of Zalith once more, Alucard was going to punish him. Before, Elvin believed that Alucard would never hurt the people around him, but right now, both his threat and the look in his hellish eyes made the bard reconsider that thought. It even brought Rodney back to his thoughts. For just a moment... he wondered... could Alucard have actually killed Rodney?

No. This wasn't Alucard. Before, he'd *never* been like this—not to Elvin anyway. Before Zalith came along, Elvin and Alucard had been much closer. Now that the demon implemented himself into their lives, Alucard was unusually angry. Elvin couldn't help but think that the demon brought out a negative side of the vampire, a side he never thought he'd have to see. Either that, or this was just who Alucard really was, and being back home in Dor-Sanguis after all that time away was the cause of his differing personality. Although that was a possibility, Elvin still wanted to blame Zalith.

The bard scowled at him, not ready to back down. "This is what I'm talking about— you just threatened me!" he exclaimed. "You'd never threaten me before! You're so different now. You're... you're... bad!"

Alucard scoffed at him. "Bad? I'm not some 'ero like zhe man you perceive me to be in your stories, Elvin. You can believe vhat you like, but zhis is who I am. You can 'ide avay vrom zhe vings I do, you can tell yourselv zhat I zon't 'urt people or kill people. Just because you zon't vant to see or 'ear zhat zoesn't mean zhat isn't 'appening. You see a kinder side to me because zhat's vhat you deserve, but you've pissed me off so much lately zhat I 'onestly can't pretend anymore. I zon't know vhy you're so concerned, or vhy you impose, but if you can't come to understand vhere you stand in my life, zhen I vill 'ave to dismiss you—permanently."

"And is that another threat?" Elvin asked sullenly.

"*Is* zhat anozzer vhreat?"

Elvin still didn't want to believe it. What was happening? Why had Alucard suddenly become so cold and bitter? So…cruel? He knew well that the vampire's emotions changed radically, but this was different. The change in his emotion seemed intentional. His words cut like glass; his murderous eyes stared like a starved creature of the night. Did Alucard actually mean what he said? Elvin didn't understand. Had his talk of Zalith really annoyed Alucard so much that it made him say everything he just said?

He looked down at his lap and pouted sadly. "I didn't mean to upset you."

"You 'aven't upset me. You've pissed me off," Alucard snarled. "Too much, too ovten."

"Why? Because I'm trying to stop you from getting hurt by some stupid demon?!" he argued, standing up.

Alucard looked away dismissively. "I make my own judgements; in doing so vight now, I 'ave decided I zon't vant to see you. Get out," he warned, pointing over at the front door. "Leave zhe key by zhe door. If you need more content vor your vork, you can ask my ozzer subordinates."

A mortified look appeared on Elvin's face. "W-why?! I didn't do anything!"

Alucard stood up, and as Elvin flinched in fear, he hesitated. "Do as I say—or vould you vather me just send you back to DeiganLupus vight now?"

Instantly shaking his head, Elvin panicked. "N-no, don't do that, I'm sorry, I…I'll go, I'll leave," he fretted. "I…I'm sorry. I…I just care. And…there's something I need to…just…" he sighed and looked down at the floor. "Be careful. I get that…I made you angry and…I'll…go and just…wait until you wanna talk."

He wasn't going to hang around and make it worse. He'd made Alucard mad—mad enough to threaten to send him back to DeiganLupus, and he only ever did that when he was as mad as he could be. So, Elvin silently got up and dragged himself over to the door, trying to hold his tears back.

When he reached the door, he looked back at Alucard, hoping he might reconsider, but the vampire stared vacantly at him. With a sullen pout, he reached into his pocket, took out his key to Alucard's house, and placed it on the table. Then, he pulled the door open and left the house.

He had never felt so embarrassed, upset, and confused all at once. He'd tried to explain his feelings, but Alucard wasn't interested. What more could he do?

Defeated, he slowly headed through the gardens. He should just go home and wait for Alucard to reach out.

| Alucard |

In his lounge, Alucard sighed and slouched back in his seat. He felt guilty for thrashing Elvin with the truth, but it was long overdue. Ever since the bard started acting like an overprotective imbecile, Alucard felt closer and closer to snapping at him. Hopefully, this warning would get Elvin to calm down, back off, and understand where he belonged.

He *did* care about Elvin—of course he did—but not in the way Elvin wanted him to. But Elvin's sensitivity wasn't enough anymore to make him force himself to act differently; he couldn't suit Elvin's meek views of the world anymore. He was a demon…a *vampire*, and he killed people. It was just what his kind did.

Recently, he'd come to enjoy his work a whole lot more. With the wolves on an uprise, Ada returning, and the Diabolus lingering on the horizon, Alucard had to erase his calmer, peaceful methods and resort to his original way of undertaking business. He much preferred the violence, the fighting, and the adrenaline that came with ending someone's life. Elvin hadn't ever become accustomed to this side of him, but now, he'd have to. A war between the wolves and vampires was very possible, very soon.

His thoughts circled back to Zalith. If the demon had *any* involvement in his decision at all, it was in making Alucard understand just how much he missed his original methods. Before danger revealed itself once more, Alucard became somewhat docile; it was necessary for his mission to gain the trust of the humans and begin to rebuild the Nosferatu once more. But now, he didn't need to act as kindly as he may have before. The treaty was signed, the vampires were in the city, and his job was almost over. All he had to do now was rid his land of Ada and either kill every single werewolf who followed her or kill them until they cowered back into the woods.

Alucard rolled his eyes and glared into the fireplace, trying to relax. Once again, his thoughts had somehow returned to Zalith. Why was *he* always on his mind? He didn't understand, and that irritated him further. But then he remembered—he glanced out the windows, setting his eyes on the moons—he had to go.

With a quiet sigh, he stood up and made his way over to the door. He grabbed his blazer from the coat rack and pulled it on. Then, as he put his fur-collared cape on, he stepped outside. The last time he arrived in Eltaria to transfer vampires, demon hunters ambushed them; this time, their meeting location was different, so hopefully, another attack wouldn't happen. But he'd not let his guard down.

Chapter Forty

Liability

| Alucard |

Moving through the sky, Alucard passed his castle and noticed Ben making his way down to the docks. Why? He was sure he'd find out. When he reached the docks, he morphed back to his usual self and landed on the ship's quarterdeck, where Sergiu was waiting for him.

"Are you ready to depart, sir?" the groundskeeper asked.

Ignoring him, Alucard moved to the edge of the ship and eyed Ben as he walked down the side of the mountain. He watched him reach the docks and head along them towards the ship. Ben didn't board, however. He stood by the bridge and looked up at Alucard as if he was waiting for permission, so Alucard nodded and went down onto the deck as Ben boarded.

The concern on Ben's face caused Alucard to presume he had something of urgency to share. So, as Sergiu prepared to disembark, Alucard turned around and led the way into the cabin with Ben following.

He leaned back against his desk and eyed the man as he closed the door behind them. Then, as Ben turned to face him, Alucard frowned expectantly.

"I'm not sure if it's of any concern, but I thought I should bring something to your attention," Ben started.

Alucard waited.

"Felix."

The vampire rolled his eyes as he moved behind his desk and slumped down in his seat.

"I caught him coming out your half of the castle," Ben revealed.

Alucard took his disinterested eyes off the desk and glared at Ben. "Vhat?" he snarled as anger started boiling in his chest.

"He said he was looking for mice and insisted you said he had permission to be in there," he explained, and as Alucard slowly looked down at his desk, Ben continued. "Not just that, but he seems to have an authority problem. I informed him of your orders, but he felt the need to question me more than once. He appears to believe that you are…playing favourites, for the lack of a better explanation. He seems overly interested in your business, asks questions I'm convinced he shouldn't, and is all in all…strange."

As the ship started moving, Alucard held out his right hand towards one of the chairs in front of his desk, inviting Ben to sit. Then, as Ben sat, the vampire set his eyes on him. "Strange?"

"He lied about how he became a vampire, and he talks about you as if he has some sort of unhealthy obsession. Attila agrees—I met him after the conference; he seems to be aware of Felix's infatuation, too."

"Attila vinks 'e knows everyving."

Clearly unsure of what to say in response, Ben looked around nervously.

Alucard then sighed irritably and rested his arms on the table. "Get 'im to understand zhat if 'e is caught even vinking about going vhere 'e shouldn't again, I vill end 'is life."

"How do you want me to—"

"Get 'im to understand," he repeated firmly.

Ben clearly understood what he was being told to do. He nodded and said, "I'll let him know."

"Zon't leave a mess," Alucard grumbled.

"Of course."

It was time to change the subject. "Zhe move: 'ow is zhat going?"

"Well. I've stayed behind to watch the castle with Jasper and Lloyd. My wife and the last of the vampires have moved into the city—except…Felix insisted he should stay."

A skeptical frown then found its way to Alucard's face. "Avter you get my point across, vatch 'im," he instructed. "I vant to know vhat 'e's doing."

Ben nodded again, leaning back in his seat. "I also think I should mention that Tobias and I had a drink together, and he shared information with me which I felt I shouldn't yet know—however—" he said, watching as a murderous look appeared in Alucard's eyes, "—he seemed to think I was already aware. I should have stopped him before he started."

"Vhat did 'e tell you?" Alucard questioned.

"He mentioned local businesses, mercenary-type work, facts about your past, and assumptions involving Ada."

Glaring at him, Alucard pondered for a few moments. He trusted Tobias not to mention information to outsiders, and Ben wasn't a stranger anymore. Ben had worked his way up to a significant place among his subordinates rather swiftly, and that was no mistake. He wouldn't make him an Adherent vampire if he didn't think he was worthy.

Alucard felt no worry knowing Tobias shared information with him; Ben was bound to find out soon enough. He would have told Ben himself eventually. Alucard valued him as a person and a subordinate, and he felt no less than comfortable with Ben knowing about his involvement. He did, however, want to know what *Ben* planned to do with what he learned.

Of course, Alucard knew that Ben wasn't going to share it with anyone that might do harm with it, but he was sure he would share it with a specific, confounding demon, and he wasn't yet sure how that made him feel. Yes, Zalith was his friend, and he felt like the demon wouldn't do anything with the information, but he wasn't certain whether he was comfortable or not with Zalith knowing the ins and outs of his business. Zalith already knew about Ada, he knew very little, but too much, about Lucifer, and he was convinced that the demon would continue to learn. That made him feel…strange. He had never felt so exposed before, and he was sure that if it were anyone else, he would have removed them by now. But it was Zalith, and of course, he had his way of evading Alucard's wrath.

He snapped out of his thoughts and scowled. "You are not yet entitled to know zhese vings, but I 'ave no problem with you being avare of vhat I do 'ere. You are…relevant."

"What?" Ben frowned, obviously having been expecting a more drastic reply.

Alucard laughed slightly and glared at the window. "On zhe contrary, I *know* you tell Zaliv vhat you do 'ere, and vhat you learn. I'm not stupid," he snarled. "You'll most likely share zhis invormation vith 'im too, vill you not?"

"I will not," Ben replied sternly.

"I zon't believe you," he growled. But as a look of unsettlement smothered Ben's face, Alucard scowled irritably. "I assume I can trust you not to share invormation vith anyvone else?"

"Not a soul," Ben strongly confirmed.

With a skeptical scowl, Alucard nodded. "Good."

Ben seemed to frown in confusion. Was he expecting more?

The vampire rolled his eyes and slowly looked back over at him. "Vhat else is zhere?"

"I'm not sure if it's of any significance, but I have seen something…strange lately."

"Stranger zhan Velix?" Alucard asked doubtfully.

Ben didn't laugh. He looked almost haunted. "On the way to your conference—when Zalith was here last—I stopped to help what I thought was a local man looking for his dog. He was odd, but I didn't think much of it until I saw him again in the city when I was sitting with Tobias."

"I 'eard you stopped to assist a man vith an 'ound. Per'aps your kindness 'as caused 'im to vant to become your vriend, hmm?" Alucard suggested, humoured.

He frowned unsurely and nodded with a nervous smile. "Maybe…but he has this weird aura—something about him doesn't feel…right. I get a dangerous feel from him."

"A threat?"

"Maybe—most likely."

"Vampire? Zemon? Verevolf?"

"That's what's strange; I got nothing from him. Not human, not werewolf—just nothing."

"Are you sure your detection skills are…adequate?"

"Yes," Ben replied confidently. "I can smell the blood of a living or unliving thing from miles away. I got nothing from him, even when I was mere inches from him. His Deiganish was sort of broken, too, so I thought he might be local to Dor-Sanguis."

"Describe 'im to me," Alucard ordered, somewhat intrigued by Ben's story.

Ben nodded. "He was pale—*your* sort of pale. Black hair to here—" he said, holding his hand against his left upper arm, "—tied up, though. Ears kinda like yours, eyes were red as blood. Had a strange smile, and his dog, I'm sure, was a zombie."

"Zombie?" Alucard frowned.

"Undead."

"Accent?"

"None, just…kinda monotone, but sly."

Alucard sighed quietly. "I zon't vecognize 'im by description," he mumbled, looking over at the window, watching the ocean's waves outside. "Did 'e ask about me?" he asked—perhaps this man was Diabolus.

"No."

Perhaps not Diabolus. He frowned and looked at Ben. "Vhat did 'e vant? Just to look vor 'is dog?"

"Yeah, but he followed me; that's the only reason I'm bringing it up."

"If you see 'im again, apprehend 'im. 'E might be a threat."

"Got it," Ben said with a nod.

Then, as the ship started to slow, Alucard sighed. "You can vait 'ere vhilst I go and get zhe vampires."

Ben nodded as he watched Alucard stand up and make his way over to the cabin's door. "All right." He then stood up and followed Alucard out onto the deck while the ship docked against the rainy island.

Alucard approached the portal with an irritated glare on his face. He was sure he was going to have to have a word with Tobias and another with Ben regarding his contact with Zalith. But he'd do that much later. Right now, he had other matters to tend to.

Silencing his thoughts, he stepped into the portal, unsure of what might unfold *this* night. Either way, he was still looking forward to seeing the demon again and to seeing how it would make him feel now that he knew what Zalith's intentions were.

Chapter Forty-One

— ⸨ ✝ ⸩ —

A Warlord's Burden

| **Zalith,** *Eltaria* |

eanwhile, Zalith was sitting in the far back corner of a small, somewhat respectable but utterly unpretentious tavern. Thick, grey smoke filled the air, and the stench of tobacco and alcohol was very overwhelming.

In the corner closest to the door, a small band were playing music that could barely be heard over the sounds of loudly talking people as they played cards, argued, and conversated mostly about the war. It wasn't as wonderful as a place as one might hope, but it was what Zalith had, and there wasn't really much he could do about it right now.

The demon knew everyone in the tavern, but he didn't particularly want to talk to any of them. He sat in the gloomy corner, his eyes slowly scanning the room but not searching for anything in particular. The two guards beside him were muttering quietly to one another and sipping from their drinks, present in case something happened. The tavern could get raided, demon hunters could come calling at any moment, and Zalith had to be ready for anything.

Zalith *despised* his current lifestyle. Moving from place to place, creeping around and skulking past human detection like a rat. He longed for the day he could exist without the constant risk of being discovered, but he knew that such a day was so very far in the future. The humans wanted him desperately; forgoing the safety of his room upstairs to sit out here with all these people was a risk, but he couldn't stand to spend a single second longer cooped up in that small, dull room. The last thing he was was a coward, and he'd do whatever he wanted.

He didn't fear the humans as much as people might think he should, but despite the fact that they already made what felt like thousands of attempts on his life, he wasn't hiding from them out of fear. If he could fight them, then he would, but that time was over. He was hiding because it was the more convenient option and because he had to keep what little he had left safe from the humans' disgusting little hands. The humans and their allies took everything from him; his family had been executed, his friends faced the same fate, and his home was no longer safe for him to return to. It was too far out of his reach.

With a quiet, discrete sigh, he stopped searching the room and took a moment to stare aimlessly. He hated to admit it to himself, but he'd been telling himself for the better part of a year that there would be no returning to his old life, and he had to accept that. He lost the war and nearly everything he cherished along the way, and every time he thought about it, it brought a drowning, disheartening hurt to his soul.

But who was going to cry for some warlord? Nobody. He wouldn't even cry for himself. There were a lot of things that happened that were out of his control, but as far as he was concerned, the pain and suffering of his people was his fault and was his burden to bear. He wasn't going to give himself the time or satisfaction of being able to sit around all day and mourn for what he lost. His people needed him now more than ever, and he had no option but to pull a straight face and lead them. But in order to lead, he had to stay alive…so there he was…hiding away. The humans surely thought he was a coward.

His eyes shifted around the room again. At this moment, he had *nothing* to do. Nothing was happening—nothing interesting, at least. He was sitting there…silently waiting for *something* to occur…*anything*. But as it had done since he'd come to sit down, the atmosphere was as dull as it had ever been.

However, an opportunity soon presented itself. Danford—an averagely tall, green-eyed, blonde-haired werewolf and Zalith's subordinate—made his way into the tavern in a bland green coat and a brown leather eyepatch upon his face, which was a new addition to his appearance. The guy once stood too close to a hostile gryphon when it spread its wings and took off; Danford was in the wrong place at the wrong time, and he was fortunate he hadn't lost his eye entirely. He fiddled with the string of his eyepatch as he walked over to the bar and lit his smoking pipe before calling the barmaid over to order his drink. And once his drink arrived, he pulled out a piece of parchment and a small chunk of coal from his coat and started drawing.

"Danford's here, sir," one of Zalith's guards said.

Irritated, Zalith slightly rolled his eyes; he didn't need to be told because he'd seen Danford enter. As he got up, his two guards moved to follow, but he held out his hand, instructing them to stay put. Then, he headed over to Danford.

However, the opportunity which came to him wasn't enough. As he passed a table where a few men were playing cards, he glanced down at the cards of the man closest to him. Seeing what he had in hand, he then set his eyes on the man's opponent and telepathically told him what his opponent had. As the man's eyes lit up, he slapped his cards down on the table with a smug smile—he knew he'd won, thanks to Zalith, and chuckled loudly as his opponent pulled a scowl of anger.

With his own smug smile, sure that an argument would soon begin, Zalith continued on his way over to Danford.

When he reached his blonde subordinate, Zalith put his hand on his shoulder and sat down beside him.

Startled by his appearance, Danford coughed on his smoke and looked at Zalith. "O-oh, there you are," he said with a nervous laugh. "I didn't see you come in."

Sitting down, Zalith turned his body to face the room and leaned back against the bar. "I was over there," he said, nodding to where he'd been sitting with his two guards, who were keeping an eye on them.

"Oh," Danford mumbled, waving over at Zalith's guards, but they didn't wave back. Frowning with embarrassment, Danford looked down at his drawing. "Have you been waiting long?"

"Not long," he answered, watching as the two card players stood up, yelling at one another. "What a charming little place you've found for me, Danford."

An almost horrified expression appeared on Danford's face. "Sorry it's not classier, but… it's been difficult to find suitable housing for both you and your… uh… friend."

"I can imagine," Zalith replied, watching as one of the card players grabbed the other's collar, threatening him as their drinks spilt over the table in the commotion.

Danford then scanned the crowd. "Where *is* your friend, by the way? She's not down here, is she?"

"Upstairs in her room."

He nodded. "Tell her I'm sorry about this place; I really wanted to find you both somewhere cosier, but things are—"

A glass then smashed, and as one opponent threw himself at the other, Zalith's two guards flew out of their seats and immediately tried to break up the fight.

Unphased, Zalith sighed quietly. "Come, let's speak somewhere a little quieter."

Danford nodded nervously. "O-okay."

Zalith stood up and led the way through the tavern and over to the back, door which led out into a small corridor. At the end of it, they followed the stairs up to where the rooms were. Zalith's was at the very end of the hallway, and once he reached it, he unlocked it and stepped inside with Danford.

He *hated* it here. Cracked, peeling walls, a single bed, a dresser, and a disappointing little round table with a single chair that had to have one of its legs stand on a book so that it didn't wobble. Trying his best to ignore his groggy little hole of a room, Zalith sat on the end of his bed and waved his hand at the chair, inviting Danford to sit. But he didn't fail to notice the look of fluster on Danford's face as he sat down; Zalith was sure it was because the last time he invited Danford into his room, they hadn't exactly stuck to strictly business, but that wasn't what he had come here for.

"So…uh…I've found you somewhere to stay for now," Danford started. "But I imagine it'll be good for quite some time, as long as things stay quiet in the area."

"Where?" Zalith asked.

"The house that belongs to Garrison Ridley," he said with a prideful smile.

Ridley: a human merchant who owed Zalith *a lot* of money. Zalith had people looking for him for over a year. "Is that so?" he asked, amused.

Danford nodded. "Yeah. We caught up with him earlier today—finally. He didn't have the money, of course, but we dealt with him as per your orders."

"Good."

"I knew you two were looking for housing, so I figure why not take advantage of the opportunity, right? He was hiding out in the middle of nowhere, too, which is perfect."

Zalith nodded in response. Honestly, *anything* would be better than this unfavourable little hole. But *that* wasn't what had his attention. "What did you mean when you said *we* dealt with him, Danford?"

"He's dead. That's what you wanted, right?" he asked worriedly.

The demon rolled his eyes. "No, Danford, who is *we*?"

Danford shrugged. "Me and my guys," he said quietly.

Amused, Zalith laughed slightly. "You have guys now?"

He nodded. "Yeah."

"I thought you worked alone. Isn't that your whole thing?"

"Well…they're not *really* my guys. They're more like my friends; they're really Addison's guys."

That made more sense. Addison was one of the Prime werewolves Zalith worked with. "I see," he said.

"But I *was* actually thinking about starting a small pack to go out on the road with me…you know, to help you out with things—and I'd only do it with your approval, of course."

Zalith sighed quietly and gave it a moment of thought. Although Danford was good at his job, he didn't seem like the leader type at all. "Where?" he asked.

"Oh, uh…well, we'd travel."

Amused once more, Zalith rested his left leg over his right and shook his head. "The areas where your kind can casually travel in groups of more than three grow smaller and smaller. With what's available these days, you'd be encroaching on previously claimed territories, Danford."

"Oh, I—"

"Do you intend on starting something with Addison and Greymore?"

He shook his head, an insistent look on his face. "N-no, never."

The demon then sighed. "I don't mind you working with others, Danford, but I suggest you get in touch with either of them while you're on good terms, Greymore preferably. You haven't been a part of a pack in…what was it? Nine years?"

"Yeah," Danford answered with a sullen frown.

Zalith nodded. "I feel as though you may be a little bit out of touch."

With an understanding nod and saddened frown, Danford looked down at his hands. "I understand."

It was then that Zalith became tired of talking business. It was all he *ever* spoke about, and a subject change was in order. He found that talking about *anything* other than business lately helped him feel better, so he thought, why not try to do so now?

He smiled and leaned back on his hands, relaxing a little. "So, what else have you been doing lately, Danford?"

His subordinate shrugged. "Work…well, you know."

"Unfortunately, I do."

"How's the vampire business going?" he asked. "Is everything still on track?"

"Yes," Zalith said with a nod.

"Good. I'm thinking once it's all done, I'd like to move you and the queen out east— perhaps somewhere in the mountains? Somewhere away from all the drama, at least."

"Good," Zalith replied as irritancy consumed him; he was tired of talking business, yet…here he was…talking about business, just a different matter of it.

With an unsure frown, Danford shuffled in his seat, but as the chair's shorter leg wobbled slightly, almost slipping from the book being used to keep it standing, Danford stuttered slightly. "W-when will you be done, do you think?" he asked.

"A few months, perhaps."

Danford nodded but then shifted his attention to the wobbling chair leg. He wriggled around, but the look of discomfort on his face didn't seem to have anything to do with the chair.

There was something on his mind, and Zalith thought he should ask. He rested one of his arms over his leg. "What is it, Danford?"

He looked over at Zalith and frowned. "I was just wondering…well…I know it's not really my place to ask, but…what about the rest of the wolves? Are you…do you have plans to transport us somewhere safe too?"

The demon sighed heavily. "I don't think doing such a thing is entirely practical right now," he answered—because it wasn't, was it? Did he want to protect the werewolves, too? Of course he did. If he could bring everyone under his protection to Aegisguard, then he would. But an attack already happened in the castle, and *that* had only been when a small group of vampires were around; bringing hundreds of werewolves would draw more unwanted attention. It was also already hard enough on Alucard's body, and he didn't want him to suffer any more for it. Would he like to have more opportunities to be able to see the vampire? Of course—no question, but he couldn't do that to Alucard.

Danford adorned a look of disagreement. "But…it's not safe out here. If we could just—"

"I understand that things aren't ideal right now, Danford," Zalith interjected, irritated with his backtalk. "But it's not your job to make these kinds of calls. Please don't irritate me. I'd truly hate for you to lose another eye," he said coldly.

Gulping, Danford nodded. "Y-yes, sir. Sorry."

Zalith was done with this conversation—he was done with *Danford*. He felt they could have actually had a nice conversation, but now he felt irritated, and he didn't want to see him anymore. "Take what money Ridley had and find some humans to gamble with—cheat if you have to, I don't care, just make sure we recoup what we lost. Take your cut and then split whatever's left between Addison and Greymore," he instructed.

"Yes, sir."

"Is there anything else you'd like to address?" he then asked.

"No, sir."

"Go," he dismissed.

Without another word, Danford left the room, leaving Zalith alone.

Although it wouldn't be too long until he had to meet Alucard, it felt like the moment was *so* far out of reach. That vampire was the only person he wanted to spend time with—the only person he knew he could stand to be around right now. But there was nothing he could do to speed up time. He just had to sit there and wait.

And he hoped that this time, demon hunters wouldn't ruin his time with the vampire.

Chapter Forty-Two

— ⟨ ✝ ⟩ —

His Friend

| Zalith |

Once Danford's footsteps faded into the noise downstairs, Zalith sighed and closed his eyes, slowly resting on his back. He felt guilty because he knew Danford was right; it wasn't safe here for the werewolves, but he didn't want to push Alucard harder than he was already working. Perhaps…one day, he'd ask Alucard when the vampires had all been moved, but regardless, it didn't change how dangerous the portal transferal was going to be with all the eyes that were surely watching it, not to mention what he'd come to suspect it did to Alucard—

Suddenly, the high-pitched, terrified scream of his friend broke the silence. As all his thoughts faded in response to his mortification, he immediately shot up off his bed, pulled his door open, and then pushed open that which was directly across from his own. He expected to see something traumatizing since she screamed so horrifically, and as soon as he opened her door, Varana, his lifelong friend, flew at him and wrapped her arms around him in sheer terror. But there was nothing in her room…there was nothing that could have possibly made her scream as loudly as she did.

As a few of his subordinates *and* his two guards came running down the hall to see what was going on, Zalith looked down at her. "What's wrong?"

"There!" she screeched, turning her head to look over at her bed as her long, bone-straight black hair brushed against his chin.

Zalith watched as a small house centipede crawled across her bed covers. He deadpanned, raised his hand, and sent the critter up in white flames until there was nothing left of it. Then, as he dismissed his subordinates with a wave of his hand, he peeled the crimson-eyed woman off himself. "You need to stop being so dramatic, Varana, honestly," he complained, aggravated. He then turned around and left her room, returning to his own—but she followed.

"Where are you going?!"

"I have work to do," he grumbled.

"What if more of those things show up?!" she exclaimed, closing his door as she stepped inside, watching him make his way over to the table. "What am I to do?!"

Zalith sighed as he sat down, trying to keep himself from becoming irritated by the wobbling seat. "Deal with them, V."

"That's not my job!" she said with an angered scowl.

The demon rolled his eyes. "And you think it's mine?"

They fell silent. As Zalith picked up his journal, preparing to write what he needed for Damien regarding his recent mission to locate Osiris, Varana impatiently shifted her weight from her left foot to her right. She sighed once, twice, and every few moments, but Zalith wasn't interested. He skimmed through the pages, re-familiarizing himself with what he already knew.

"How long are you going to sit there?" Varana asked, irritated.

Still ignoring her, he flicked through his journal.

"Hello?!" she exclaimed.

He deadpanned once more but didn't look at her. "What, Varana?"

"I said how long are you going to sit there for? I know you heard me."

"I did, but I chose to ignore you."

"What about the bug?!"

Becoming more agitated, Zalith frowned. "Varana, the bug is dead. What more could you possibly need from me?"

She took a moment to think. "I want them *all* dead," she demanded.

With his irritancy becoming anger, Zalith closed his eyes and exhaled deeply, trying to keep himself from snapping at her. He really *didn't* want to deal with her right now, so he ignored her again, flicking through his book.

"I suppose I could just ask someone downstairs to do it," she said sadly.

Zalith was sure she wouldn't actually do so; they both knew it wasn't worth the risk of someone seeing her. Varana was a *queen—The* Queen Of Demons here. She was just as high a target as he was, and he needed to keep her safe. Not only was she his queen, though, but she was also his friend, and he was hers. He knew her better than anyone ever might, and he knew that she was just saying she would go downstairs because she wanted to get him to do something. But he wasn't going to give her the satisfaction of answering.

Varana evidently soon realized he wasn't going to say something and made her way over to his bed. She sat down, stared around the room, and sighed. "May I stay with you tonight?"

"You may not," he answered.

She scowled. "I'd let you sleep in *my* bed if yours was infested with insects."

"Can you just let me work, please?" he asked, letting out a tired huff.

She rolled her eyes and leaned back on the bed, falling silent.

With the quiet, Zalith began to feel a little less vexed and continued with his work. He took a pen out of his pocket and started writing his report for Damien. But with Varana, the silence was never very long.

"Did Danford show up yet?" she soon asked.

"Yes, he just left, actually. He's probably still downstairs somewhere. Why?"

"Does he have somewhere for us to stay yet? Somewhere that isn't crawling with cockroaches."

"I don't think that was a cockroach, V."

She frowned irritably. "Well, whatever it was, it was foul, and I don't want it in my bed!" she exclaimed. Then, she flicked a lock of her hair behind her shoulder. "Did he say anything to you?"

He huffed again, still trying to write. "He might have found us a place, but I want to wait a while to make sure it's safe first."

Varana shook her head with an expectant look on her face. "Is that *it*?"

"Yes, that's it."

She scoffed doubtfully. "You didn't talk more?" she asked but then pulled a frown of revolt. "Oh, were you having sex with him again? Is that why?"

He rolled his eyes. "No."

"Well, maybe you should have, and then you wouldn't be so irritable right now," she complained.

As silence fell once more, he kept writing but sunk into his thoughts. Varana was right; if he did have sex with Danford just now, he would be able to control his aggravation a whole lot more, but he didn't want to think about it. He didn't want to have sex with Danford. If he were going to have sex with *anyone* right now, it would be Alucard.

A slight smile then found its way onto his face as he thought about that vampire. He knew that he was a little grouchy, but it wasn't until he started spending time with Alucard that he remembered that the world wasn't always so dreary, and also that sometimes, life outside of work and a set of four walls could be exciting. He *always* had fun with Alucard.

He found it funny to think that there was a time when he wasn't too keen on Alucard, but now, he wanted to spend almost all of his free time with him. Alucard was such a good distraction from the world; all it took was one look from him for Zalith to forget his troubles for a while, and spending time with him made Zalith feel as though the world was right again. He wished he could talk to him right now and just…*see* him. But Zalith had so much work to do. He had years and years and *years* of work, and he knew that he had to find a way to balance himself between the intoxicating happiness he felt when he was with Alucard and what so sorely needed to be done.

"Z?" Varana asked.

Snapping out of his thoughts, having forgotten that she was even there for a moment, he glanced over at her. "Hmm?"

"Do you remember when we used to have those parties?" she asked. "And everybody would dress up so nicely…and we'd all drink champagne and dance all night…and everyone was so happy."

He nodded. Of course he remembered. Those were the kinds of things he thought about every day to try and cope with how awful his life had become. "I do," he confirmed.

Varana smiled. "Or when we'd have lunch in the courtyard…." She took a moment to think before giggling. "Remember your mother wanted us to get married?"

Zalith replied, "Yes, but my mother wanted many things."

She laughed a little. "Like a son who wasn't gay?"

Slightly amused, he nodded, still writing. "Like a son who wasn't gay. Of course, she had my brother, but…we all know how that worked out for her," he said, but regret started to enthral him. He didn't want to think about his brother right now.

"What was it she used to say?"

He shrugged and rolled his eyes. "She used to *say* many things, too."

Laughing again, she smiled. "I think it was…Xurian was a gift from the gods that she wished she would return…and that it was a shame he was so beautiful but so dreadfully untalented and disappointing."

Zalith sighed deeply. His mother was a rather contentious woman. "I can only imagine what lovely and colourful things she said about me."

Varana giggled. "Oh, so many things. So, so, *so* many things."

"Of course," he grumbled.

"But you were always her favourite," she said with a wistful, happy sigh. "She was a horrible woman, though, wasn't she?"

"She was," he agreed with a nod.

Varana smiled. "I really liked her."

"Somehow, so did I," he agreed. He missed his mother and father, too, but like his brother, he didn't want to think about them. So, he kept writing, trying to keep his thoughts focused on his task.

Varana then asked him, "How much longer will we have to do this, Z?"

He wasn't sure, but it was most likely going to be a long while. "It could be years."

Varana sighed, and Zalith expected her to respond with something irritating, but she didn't say anything. She was always such a whiny woman and had an issue with everything, but Zalith knew she was *always* going to be there for him and would never leave his side, and that was probably the single comfort he had in his current situation. They both knew that the only thing they had in the world was each other, and they'd likely end up dying trying to keep each other safe if they had to. Zalith was confident he'd get everyone else through this, though. He'd gotten them all through so much already, and he was nowhere near close to giving up.

The demon focused on his writing as Varana sat up straight, adjusting her hair while she watched him. He knew that she was about to break the silence again, and he waited for it.

"What are you working on?" she asked.

"Not much. I'm recording the work I just completed for Damien."

"Ugh, I don't know *why* you work for that ape. Do you know how many times he's hit on me, Z? I've lost count. Who does he think he is? I don't care how much power and influence he has; I'm *much* too beautiful for someone as grotesque and revolting as him," she complained. "Eugh…to think he actually wants to sleep with me—I mean, who doesn't? But *that* just feels like an insult. I'm *so* thankful my father sent Ysmay to snoop around his castle instead; could you imagine what he might have done if *I* went there? Alone? Unprotected? I wouldn't put it past him if he forced himself on me," she exclaimed, fiddling with her hair.

Zalith murmured in agreement, finishing up his report. "Well, he's helping us with this vampire situation, and I'm thankful for that, at least."

She scoffed. "Is that where you've been off to so often?"

"Yes," he answered. He wasn't overly keen on telling her the truth…the truth that he'd been spending time with Alucard. She was extremely reluctant to share Zalith with anybody, and she never took anything like this well. But what also made the situation precarious was Alucard's lineage. Alucard was Lucifer's child, and coincidently, so was Varana. However, Varana was one of Lucifer's *creations*, and Alucard was born of his blood. He didn't want to tell Varana because he knew Lucifer was looking for Alucard, and he also heard in passing that Varana and her siblings were also looking for him. He didn't want Alucard to be caught.

He stopped for a moment, thinking about Alucard again. Before, Zalith felt so very content about being friends with someone like Alucard—to think of the clout that came with calling the son of a Numen *his* friend. But now, that didn't seem to matter. Imagining Alucard as a man without his wealth and name didn't throw him off; Zalith was absolutely certain he'd still like him as much as he did now.

The demon smiled, the sheer thought of Alucard making him feel content—

"What are you smiling about?" Varana asked.

Irritated that his thoughts had been silenced by her interruption, Zalith frowned. "Nothing," he muttered. But he then remembered that it was almost time to go and meet Alucard—he wasn't going to miss that. So, he started putting his book away. "I have to go soon, but I shouldn't be back late."

"Oh…okay," she said as she reached for the covers on Zalith's bed. "I'll just get into bed then.…"

"Varana, you're not sleeping in my room," he denied sternly.

"But why?!"

He rolled his eyes. "I'll send someone up to search your room for more insects on my way out. I *don't* want to see you in here when I get back," he warned.

She scowled in frustration but gave up. "Fine. Can you send up Tyrus? I'd like to talk to him," she said, smiling.

Zalith deadpanned. He knew that she was going to end up sleeping with Tyrus, but as long as it wasn't in his bed, it was none of his business, and he didn't really care. He just wanted to leave and head out to meet Alucard.

"Fine," he muttered, pulling his blazer on over his waistcoat.

"Thank you," she said, heading for the door. "And Z," she said sternly, snatching his wrist as he stopped in front of her, "be careful."

He nodded. "I'm always careful."

Sighing, she pulled the door open and wandered off back into her own room.

Zalith shut his door behind him and made his way down the hall, focusing on the fact that he was about to meet Alucard again. He *longed* for a conversation with him, even if it didn't last that long. Of course, the longer the better, but he simply wanted to be in Alucard's presence, and the sooner he left, the sooner he'd get to see him.

Chapter Forty-Three

⸺ ⸜ ✝ ⸝ ⸺

Progression

| Alucard |

The castle was in utter ruin. Where Alucard would once emerge into an eroded hallway, he now stood among a field of rubble, scorched grass, and dead manticores. Had the battle continued after he left? Or had more demon hunters come back and destroyed the castle after their failure to capture Zalith? He looked back over his shoulder at the portal, which was untouched, but he knew that was because those gateways were only visible to those who knew they were there.

An overpowering discomfort began to drown him. It was a headache unlike any other, similar to that which he experienced the first night he took vampires back to Aegisguard. He suspected it wouldn't be too long until he started feeling the portal's effects once again. But he couldn't dwell on it; he was sure it would pass. Right now, he had to find Zalith and the catacombs he mentioned, and he had to do it without being seen. He was sure that there might still be people watching the ruins, and he didn't want to put himself or the demon in danger.

He set his eyes on the forest at the foot of the hill—*that* was where Zalith said the catacombs were. Before making his way forward, he shrouded himself in vermillion smoke and emerged from it in the form of a small melanistic fox. His fur shined black and fiery red in the silver moonlight, and his eyes were their usual, ominous hellfire-red, shimmering brightly as he headed down the hill and to the trees. As far as any observers might be concerned, he was but a simple critter of the forest.

Silently, Alucard made his way through the moonlit forest, searching for the entrance to the catacombs Zalith. He wasn't entirely sure what he should be looking for, whether he was far or close, but at least he could rely on the rest of his senses. He could detect a vampire miles away, so he stopped and concentrated for a moment. It took him no time at all to locate the auras of eleven vampires, and he continued forward. But the ominous feeling of eyes on him snatched his attention. He stopped again, looking around slowly, but he couldn't detect *anything* in the forest with him—not a single thing. No animals, no people…just…nothing.

He kept a wary frown as he continued forward, setting his eyes on the old, rustic ruin of a cathedral in the distance. *That* was where they were. He hastily made his way towards and into the building, following its vine-warped floor over to the entrance to a cellar. He hurried forward, his claws clipping against the stone as he slinked down the stairs and into a damp, dark corridor.

A dim glow of light flickered from the corridor's end, and distinct voices whispered and muttered to one another. He should morph back, but there were no signs of Zalith, and he couldn't help but wonder if he was in the right place, despite the fact that there were eleven vampires waiting up ahead. Zalith had never been late before, so why the sudden change?

Remaining in his melanistic fox form, he silently walked to the end of the corridor and approached the arched gap between the walls, which led into a small, cramped room. The vampires waited inside: seven men, and four women. They took up the majority of the space the room had to offer, mumbling under the light of a single lantern hanging above them. Zalith wasn't among them, so Alucard could only presume he was late.

He backed away from the arch, and as vermillion smoke consumed him once more, he emerged from it as his usual self. He then stepped into the room, and all of the vampires glanced at him as he did. He barged past the crowd and into the centre, looking around again. Alucard felt strange being the one to have arrived first.

Setting his eyes on the vampire closest to him, he asked, "Vhere is Zaliv?"

The black-haired man shrugged. "He was here a second ago."

Of course he was. Alucard snarled and moved away from the man. He stood in the centre of the room, waiting, trying to ignore the meaningless, boring conversations of those around him. He shifted his attention to his worsening headache and reached into his blazer pocket and took out his small, steel flask. He glared at the wall ahead of him as he slowly unscrewed the lid. How long was he going to have to wait? That man said Zalith was there just a moment ago, and Alucard was sure the demon was probably lingering somewhere; he wasn't at all interested in searching for him because that had to be what Zalith wanted.

However, as he sipped from his flask, he felt someone's hand fondle his ass. He flinched in both startle and anger, struggling to swallow the blood he just sipped from his flask. He sharply turned his head and looked over his shoulder, but no one was close enough to have done it. He scowled skeptically, using the back of his hand to wipe away the blood that trickled down his chin in his startle; he glowered at everyone, searching for who might have done something so atrocious. But all eleven vampires were talking to one another just as they had been when he arrived.

Alucard snarled quietly and turned to face ahead—

He was instantly met by Zalith, who was standing in front of him in his usual all-black suit. The demon had a sly, amused smile on his face, and the look in his devious eyes was strangely smugger than usual. It took Alucard no time to work out that it was Zalith who touched him, and now that he knew, he oddly felt less revolted. If it had been one of these irrelevant vampires, he was sure he might have killed them. But it was Zalith, and Alucard was tired of admitting to himself that he'd let the demon get away with things no other person could. He still didn't understand why he felt no need to attack, so he just rolled his eyes and turned away from him, glaring over at three of the vampires in an attempt to hide his embarrassment.

"I trust you found your way here just fine?" Zalith then asked with a smile.

Tucking his flask back into his blazer pocket, Alucard pouted slightly. "Obviously," he grumbled. Then, he scowled at him. "Vhy did you do zhat?"

The demon smirked. "Do what?"

Alucard gritted his teeth in anger, not at all in the mood to deal with Zalith's need for amusement. "You know vhat," he snarled.

Zalith kept his smile but took his eyes off him. "I wanted to see your face. Sorry if I made you uncomfortable," he said with sincerity.

"I'm not uncomfortable," he denied with a stubborn pout.

"Well, you look uncomfortable. My apologies again."

"I'm not uncomfortable," Alucard repeated irritably. "Zhis is just my face."

"It's *not* just your face," he said with a smirk. "Your face is usually pleasant and sweet."

Alucard didn't know why Zalith felt the need to throw so many unnecessary compliments his way. All he *did* know was that his words made him feel a little flustered. He didn't know what to say or do; he didn't know if there was something he was *supposed* to do in response. However, he knew he didn't want to tell Zalith to stop doing it, so he just looked away and mumbled, "Vhatever." As nervous as it made him feel, he found himself actually enjoying these compliments—even though they were stupid. He'd never experienced this kind of attention before, and he had no idea what to make of it.

Clearly amused by his reaction, Zalith laughed quietly.

"Vhat 'appened to zhe castle?" Alucard asked, trying to change the subject in an attempt to hide the irritating awkwardness which gripped him so tightly.

Zalith kept his eyes on the vampire. "A second group of hunters came looking for their moronic friends after we disposed of them, and they destroyed the castle once they discovered the results of last fortnight's meeting."

"Vas nice castle," the vampire said.

"It was. How has the rest of your week been?"

Alucard sighed quietly and shrugged. "Invormative."

"Oh?"

"And you?" Alucard asked, still unable to look at him.

"Lacking anything worth my time," he answered, "until now."

"Veally?" Alucard asked skeptically, glancing at him. "I'm sure Ben 'as told you many a ving of intervest."

Zalith moved around so that he was standing in front of him. "You assume Ben tells me everything?"

Alucard couldn't avoid his gaze so easily. "Vhy vouldn't 'e?" he questioned, glaring at him.

"He simply keeps me updated with the vampires. He tells me how they've settled in, and that's all there is to it. You don't need to worry about him telling me anything you don't want him to," he said with an assuring tone in his voice.

"Vhatever," Alucard mumbled, glaring to his right.

"Is something bothering you?" Zalith asked, losing his smile.

"No," Alucard mumbled stubbornly. He rolled his eyes and looked at the vampires ahead of them. "I've moved zhe vampires into zhe city; my castle vill vemain empty until I deal vith Ada. Zhe vhreat of 'er attack still vemains, and I von't put zhem in danger. I should 'ave asked you to varn zhese people a'ead of time."

"I already did. I observed your meeting, and I took it upon myself to inform the vampires of any changes that may affect them."

The vampire glanced at him, unsure of what to say in response. He hadn't asked Zalith to do that, but he'd done it anyway. Why? He was sure that if he asked, Zalith would turn it into a game, so he took his eyes off the demon and looked over at the wall to his right.

He'd come hoping to get some sort of answer to his confusion regarding how he felt about Zalith, but right now, he felt no different. He didn't feel uncomfortable; he didn't feel strange. He just felt the same way he felt since he and Zalith became friends. And that was all he needed to be sure of how he felt their relationship should progress; he'd leave it be and wait to see what might happen. He thought he liked Zalith enough to leave things as they were, and he felt no need to set boundaries or tell him to calm down. He undeniably liked Zalith the way he was.

He looked at the demon and said, "Ben 'as a new vriend."

"Does he now?" Zalith asked curiously.

"Zhe man 'e 'elped vhen you vere last vith me—zhe dog man."

"Oh?"

"Ben says 'e saw 'im again; 'e vollowed Ben into zhe city."

Zalith frowned. "I assume you feel that's suspicious? Ben isn't someone who strikes me as the type to stop and assist a local with his missing dog unless *he* felt there might be something more to it."

Alucard nodded in agreement. "I told 'im to apprehend zhe man if 'e sees 'im again."

"You have assumptions?"

"Zhere are a vew possibilities; vone, zhe man is Diabolus. Two, zhe man is vone of Ada's errand boys. Vree, 'e veally is just some stranger looking vor a vriend."

"And the outcome of either of the possible dangers would be?" Zalith asked in concern.

Alucard shrugged. "Murder."

The demon smiled. "And if he *is* just looking for a friend?"

Alucard adorned a strange stare. "No vone stands on zhe roadside looking vor a vriend."

"Your bard strikes me as the type to do such a thing."

Amused, Alucard couldn't help but smile, but he turned away from Zalith to hide his amusement. "Zon't be vude."

"I gather he had a lot to say once I left?" Zalith asked with a smirk of amusement.

Alucard then sighed irritably and shrugged. "'E alvays 'as someving to say about everyving. Tonight, I 'ad to make 'im understand zhat 'e and I are not vriends."

"I would have enjoyed witnessing that."

"Of course you vould."

"Did it go well?" the demon asked.

"I got my point across, I'm sure. But I veel I might 'ave been too 'arsh on 'im."

"Well, sometimes, harsh is a necessity."

"Maybe," Alucard muttered.

Then, Alucard realized they'd both been standing around a little longer than usual. It was getting late, and he felt he should cut the conversation off before it became a longer one.

He sighed quietly and said, "I should get back."

A look of disappointment appeared on Zalith's face. "I'd rather you stay."

"Vell, I can't," Alucard sneered. "Ve'll meet next veek anyvay, as usual."

Zalith nodded and smiled. "Before you make haste, I'd like to offer a means of communication if Ben ever so happens to be indisposed."

Instead of walking off, Alucard turned to face him and scowled skeptically. "Like vhat? I zon't like sending messages, I alveady told you."

"I assume you can manifest spectres," he said, reaching into his pocket. He then pulled out a small black feather and held it out to Alucard. "Once you awaken this, you'll be able to use it to contact me."

With an unsure frown, Alucard took the feather and glowered at it. Zalith obviously wanted to make it possible for them to speak a whole lot more often than usual. Spectres were a source of two-way communication, so if he activated this one, it would mean Zalith could contact him, too. Did he want that? Did he want to allow an increased amount of communication alongside their weekly meetings? He didn't even have to think about it. Of course he did. He enjoyed every moment in Zalith's company, and it seemed as though Zalith might just feel the same about him. He wasn't sure why he felt so eager to accept, but he didn't want to overthink it.

He tucked the feather into his blazer pocket and looked at Zalith. "I'll do zhat vhen I get 'ome."

Zalith smiled. "Good."

Then, he looked back at the vampires, who had all grouped up by the door. He sighed quietly as fatigue started to grip him. "Vhat vill you do until next veek?"

"The usual. And you?" Zalith asked suggestively.

Alucard frowned. What was he asking? What was that tone and look on his face? He scowled and rolled his eyes. "Zhe usual."

"If you need me—or if you don't—I'll be waiting," Zalith offered with a smile.

"Until next veek, zhen," Alucard said, glancing over at him.

"I look forward to it," Zalith said with a smirk, holding out his hand.

The vampire placed his hand into Zalith's, expecting their usual shake, but Zalith gripped his wrist and pulled him closer. The demon embraced him in a simple, friendly manner that lasted no longer than a few seconds, and as he let go, Alucard stood where he was with a confused look on his face. Before Zalith could look at him, though, he turned around and walked over to the vampires, containing the unwelcome nervousness he suddenly began to feel. Once again, he'd been caught off guard and had no idea what to say or do. So, as he always did, he ignored it as if it hadn't happened and as if it meant nothing.

"Farewell, vampire," Zalith called.

Alucard glanced back at him as he led the vampires out of the room. That was the first time he found himself looking back at Zalith. Usually, once he made it clear he was leaving, he'd feel no need to look back. But he *had* looked back—why?

He frowned unsurely. "*La revedere*," he mumbled before glaring ahead again. Then, he silently followed the vampires towards the catacomb's exit, preparing to lead the way back to the portal.

Chapter Forty-Four

─ ﹤ ✝ ﹥ ─

The Night's Final Task

| **Ben** |

Ben waited aboard the ship while the rain poured. He stood under the shelter of the quarterdeck's edge, which curved out to form a narrow canopy, and leaned back against the cabin's exterior wall, watching the portal closely. He occasionally glanced over at Alucard's groundskeeper, Sergiu, who had obviously assumed the role of a sailor after Rodney's death.

The groundskeeper was uncomfortably quiet, standing by the ship's foremast. The look of concentration on that man's face looked to be something more than a simple look of deep thought. Ben was sure this man was human, but the aura he was getting off him right now was more than that. Then again, the portal could be the cause of the man's current confusion. Ben remembered the last time *he* had been here, he felt strangely ungrounded, so he took his mind off it and stared back over at the island.

Sergiu, on the other hand, had noticed Ben's glance and gazed at him.

Ben took his eyes off the portal and eyed him strangely. "Something wrong?"

"No," Sergiu said, stepping under the shelter and standing beside him. "You did not accompany us last time; I am curious to know why you have come along."

Looking back at the portal, Ben shrugged. "Had to talk to Aleksei—business."

"Trouble?" Sergiu asked curiously.

Glancing at him, Ben frowned in confliction. This was Alucard's groundskeeper…someone who had never been to a meeting with them, and someone who Alucard, as far as he knew, didn't hang around with. This was the man Alucard would send to pick people up and send Elvin home. Ben was convinced that Sergiu was a person he shouldn't discuss their business with.

He set his eyes back on the portal. "You work for Aleksei; surely you know that I can't tell you."

"Of course," the groundskeeper said. "Pardon my intrusion."

Just then, Alucard emerged from the darkness between the gateway with a line of vampires in tow. Ben watched as all eleven vampires followed him out onto the island, but as they made their way over to the ship, Alucard faltered behind. Ben saw him standing by the portal with a strained look on his face, and with his right hand, he was gripping the wall beside it in what looked like an attempt to keep himself on his feet.

As the vampires boarded the ship, Ben made his way down onto the island and cautiously approached Alucard, unsure of what he might do. He didn't look too great, and Ben wasn't yet sure how he might react to his concern.

He stopped a few feet in front of him and frowned in worry. "Are you all right?"

Alucard took his eyes off the ground and glanced at Ben. "I'm vine. Vhat are you doing off zhe ship?"

"I came to see if you were okay, you look—"

"Vhat?" Alucard snapped defensively, but as Ben frowned cautiously, he sighed irritably. "Is just zhe portal," he mumbled, standing up straight. Then, he led the way towards the ship. "Zhe portal uses my ethos as a source; zhat drains me to bring people vhrough."

"And it's worse the more you do it?" Ben asked, walking beside him.

Alucard nodded in response. "Zoesn't matter. I'll veel vine tomorrow."

Ben frowned with uncertainty as he followed Alucard up onto the ship; he was quite sure that Alucard was the type to hide his pain, and that looked to be what he was doing right now. However, he wasn't going to ask anything further; Alucard might not appreciate that. So, he left The Vampire Lord's side and joined the Eltarian vampires while they waited to be taken to their new home.

But he'd keep an eye on him. If Alucard needed him, he'd make sure he was there to help.

| **Alucard** |

Alucard relaxed behind his desk, staring tiredly out of the windows of his cabin. Tonight's journey made him feel a whole lot more exhausted than any other did, and he was sure it was only going to become worse from here on out. He didn't dwell on it much, though; he couldn't afford to take time to rest, and he couldn't halt the mission. He didn't want to slow things for Zalith, Damien, or himself. He agreed to complete it within a specific time frame, and nothing was going to get in the way.

Instead, he thought about the time he just spent with Zalith. He hadn't felt the need to set boundaries, and he was beginning to feel strangely accepting of Zalith's confounding yet intriguing personality. There wasn't a time he hadn't spent enjoying Zalith's company, even when he was irritating him. That demon was the only person Alucard felt he would allow to annoy him because he found it entertaining. Yes, some of the things he did and said made Alucard want to slap him into a wall, but he felt he'd rather deal with such annoyances than have Zalith stop.

But what did this mean? Did it mean anything *at all*? Alucard was still satisfied with their friendship; he knew Zalith wanted more…but did *he*? He took his eyes off the window as the ship started moving and looked down at his desk. No, he didn't. He couldn't. He still didn't see the logic behind Zalith's interest in him; he didn't understand why someone like Zalith might be so interested in him. He had nothing to offer him; he was no one of importance. He wasn't fun. He wasn't exactly the best person to hang around with, and he felt his personal interests were boring—so boring that he kept them private. No matter how hard he tried to think about it, he just couldn't think of any reason why Zalith would want to share something more than friendship with him.

Why was he even thinking about it again? He already told himself that a relationship like that was something he'd never seek. He just didn't have the time, motivation, or interest. Perhaps he should have told Zalith that when he saw him. He could tell him next week when he met him again; there'd be no harm in waiting—or was he procrastinating because he didn't want to be so hasty telling Zalith it would never happen?

He rolled his eyes and rested his arms on the desk, tapping his claws impatiently against the wood. The demon's unnecessary compliments then returned to his thoughts. Why did he have to say such things to him? Sweet? He wasn't sweet. He didn't feel sweet, nor did he feel as though he looked sweet. He was a man, not some fluffy puppy dog—*that* was where *he* would use such a word. He pouted irritably and leaned back in his seat, trying to silence his annoying thoughts, but they wouldn't relent.

A look of embarrassment smothered his face when he remembered the moment Zalith caught him off-guard again. Why was he even thinking about such a preposterous thing? The demon shouldn't have touched him; he wished he'd been stern with him, but he just didn't feel like that would've been an appropriate response at the time. He was surprised and shocked to the point he might have attacked, but he didn't. It was *Zalith*, and he was fine with that. Why he was so calm about it confused him—had he perhaps…enjoyed it? He scowled. No. It was unprecedented and unwelcome. He would have preferred if Zalith asked before doing it; he was sure if the demon had, though, Alucard would say no, and it seemed as though the demon knew that, too. Of course he did.

Alucard sighed quietly and looked back over at the windows, watching as the waves raged outside. Soon, he'd be back home, and he'd have to take the vampires to the city so that Ben could deal with Felix. He would much rather Ben take the vampires to Dargamoore, but he didn't feel like dealing with someone as annoying as Felix tonight, so he'd take the lesser of two inconveniences.

Eventually, the ship started to slow, and Alucard stood up. He made his way out onto the deck, watching as the ship edged closer to the docks beneath his castle.

"Do you want me to take them to the city?" Ben asked as he saw Alucard make his way over.

"No," he replied, standing beside the gate, waiting for the ship to stop. "I'll take zhem. You go and deal vith Velix."

Ben nodded. "All right."

Then, as the ship halted, Sergiu hurried to tie its ropes to the docks. Alucard made his way down, and the vampires followed. He waited for them to all group up in front of him, watching Ben as he made his way up to the castle. Once all eleven vampires were there, he rolled his eyes irritably and turned around, beginning to lead the way towards the city.

One of the younger vampires in the group scurried forward and looked up at him. "Do we each have our own houses in the city, or do we have to share?" she asked.

"I assume you'll share vor a vew days until separate 'omes are vound vor zhose of you who vish to live alone," he mumbled.

Staring up at him with her dull blue eyes, she pouted. "I don't want to share," she complained.

"Zhen live on zhe street," he grumbled.

Offended, she crossed her arms and went to yell, but one of the older vampires pulled her back and mumbled words of warning to her. Then, he looked ahead at Alucard. "Sorry about her. She's just a little seasick; it gets her all wound up." He laughed nervously. "I'm Alonzo, and she's Emilia."

Alucard didn't care. He just wanted to get the last task of his night over and done with so he could head home. But this final task seemed as though it was going to be longer than necessary.

The nervous vampire stepped forward, brushing his right hand through his thick, brunette hair as he glanced at Alucard. "So, what's the deal around here? Do we get jobs, live normal lives?"

"Do vhat you vant, just abide by zhe rules."

"Look at the moons!" Emilia then called in amazement as the six coloured moons came into view in the clearing sky.

Alonzo looked back at her, smiled, and glanced up at the moons. "Why are there so many?" he asked, looking at Alucard.

"Aesthetic," Alucard grumbled sarcastically.

Emilia then hurried back to the front of the line. "What's the city like?"

"There's humans, right?" Alonzo asked. "You got some sort of treaty going?"

"Are there werewolves?" Emilia questioned.

Alucard gritted his teeth in anger, trying not to snap.

She clapped her hands. "What about elves? I've always wanted to see one!"

Then, Alonzo leaned forward so he could see Alucard's face. "Are you offering jobs? Need anything done? I can—"

Before he could finish, Alucard disappeared into vermillion smoke and re-emerged in his melanistic fox form. Alonzo and Emilia both gasped in confusion, watching as the fox led the way in Alucard's place, snarling quietly as it trotted forward. He was tired of hearing them.

"Okay then," Alonzo mumbled. "I guess we pissed him off."

"It was you!" Emilia snapped, slapping his arm.

As Emilia and Alonzo pouted, they and the rest of the vampires silently followed the fox towards the city coming into view in the distance.

Alucard thought about how once this was over, he could go home and get into bed. He was exhausted, and he just wanted to sleep. But a part of him suspected he'd be up another hour or so thinking about Zalith, which had become a common occurrence. Perhaps one night, his conflicting thinking would lead him to understand why he felt so accepting and confused at the same time.

Chapter Forty-Five

—⸲†⸲—

Lillian

| Ben |

Meanwhile, Ben made his way up to the castle. He stood in the entrance hall expecting to see Felix in the room as usual, but he was nowhere to be found. The guy *should* be there; he was still a member of the nightguard, and Ben had explicitly ordered him to remain in the entrance hall each night. The fact that Felix hadn't followed his orders made him more eager to scold him.

He scowled impatiently. "Felix!" he called irritably. Then, he waited, listening as the hurried footsteps of who could only be Felix echoed through the castle. Ben turned to face the kitchen door and watched as the silvery-eyed vampire hurried out and made his way over to him.

Stopping in front of Ben, Felix eyed him strangely and waited.

"Why were you in there?" Ben asked tonelessly.

Felix glanced back at the door. "Drinking."

Ben shook his head in disbelief. "You should know better than anyone else that there are times dedicated to that—you don't just abandon your post!"

Shaking his head, Felix frowned in offence. "Times for new vampires, not me—"

"You're not an exception!" he insisted before Felix could finish.

Felix pouted and crossed his arms. "You not my boss."

"What was that?" Ben asked, a threatening tone in his voice.

With a hostile scowl, Felix glared at him. "Aleksei is boss, not you. You don't tell me what—"

Without a moment's hesitation, Ben snatched hold of Felix's throat, silencing him. Alucard had instructed Ben to get Felix to understand that if he were caught where he shouldn't be once again, The Vampire Lord would end his life, and that's what *he* was going to do. Before Felix could try to defend himself, Ben grabbed a fistful of his hair in his hand and harshly slammed Felix's face down onto the table.

Felix whimpered in pain as blood splattered across the table's surface, his nose breaking with a loud crack.

Ben was tired of his insubordination and felt no remorse. It seemed as though hurting him would be the only way to get his point across, and Alucard's tone made him believe that he was instructing him to use such an approach.

With his other hand, he held Felix's arms behind his back as he tried to struggle away. "I don't know how many times I have to tell you, but this will be the last," he warned him quietly. "I *am* your boss, and if you fail to do as I instruct, I'll end your estranged little life, and it would be such a pleasure to do so."

Snivelling, Felix nodded as best he could as blood continued oozing from his face.

However, Ben felt as though he hadn't been harsh enough. Felix struck him as the type to disregard even something as sincere as a beating. He had to make sure he'd gotten his point across; the last thing he wanted was to have to tell Alucard that he hadn't been able to deal with someone as irrelevant as Felix.

He tightened his grip, forcing Felix's face into the table; the disobedient vampire's skull cracked quietly against the wood, and Felix's agonized cries became inhuman. But Ben didn't care. He felt no sympathy. He leaned to the side, glaring into Felix's left eye as he stared back in horror. "Have I made myself clear?"

Gritting his bloodied teeth in pain, Felix grimaced, and his response was a muffled, mumbled grunt.

That wasn't good enough. Ben scowled. "Is that clear?!" he yelled.

Felix nodded. "I-i-it…clear," he said, struggling, blood seeping through his teeth as he spoke.

With an irritated snarl, Ben stood up straight, pulling Felix with him. He threw the whimpering man to the floor and glowered down at him in revolt. "Clean that up," he demanded, pointing to the mess Felix's face left on the table.

Felix nodded frantically, using his hands to wipe the blood and tears from his face. He then scurried over to the table, pulled off his coat, and began using it to clean the surface. While he desperately scrubbed, Felix snivelled and pouted like a child. He dared not say a word further to Ben, who kept his hostile gaze on him as he worked.

His threat seemed to have given Ben the result he hoped for. Felix cried like a child as he cleaned the table, trembling as he did so. Now, hopefully, he'd stay where he was supposed to be. Ben was sure if he found him sneaking around or disobeying orders again, he'd just kill him without warning. What else could be done? If a physical threat like this didn't keep him in line, then Ben was quite sure killing him was the only other option.

Just then, the door to the vampires' part of the castle swung open; Ben sharply turned his head to face it and watched as Attila emerged from inside with a confused look on his face. He stared at Felix for a moment and then looked over at Ben. An amused expression appeared on his face as he put the situation in front of him together, and once he closed the door behind him, he headed over to Ben.

"I missed party, huh?" Attila asked with a smirk.

"Something like that," Ben said.

"You were gone for time. Where you go?"

"With Aleksei," he answered, glancing at him.

"Ah, vampire pick up. How many he have left to bring?"

Ben sighed deeply, taking a moment to count in his head. He then shrugged and answered, "He brought eleven tonight, so that makes forty-two, including myself. There are seventy-three left to bring."

Nodding, Attila crossed his arms. "Never tell me why he does it…not sure whether just because he cares about vampires or order from above."

Undeniably intrigued, Ben turned to face Attila. "From above?"

"*Da*, Aleksei works for…ah, I should not name. Lived with…Numen for some time, does work for him occasionally."

Numen…. Tobias mentioned that word. Numen was a name used for the gods of gods. Alucard lived with one? Could it have been Lucifer? No…he remembered what he'd been told about Lucifer, and he was sure that he was one of Alucard's enemies. So who could this Numen be? Of course, he was curious to know, but it wasn't exactly his business.

Attila then glanced at him and laughed slightly. "You not know much about your boss, huh?" He smirked smugly. "You know…he is son of Numen?"

"Yeah, I know that much," he confirmed. "Sent to kill God or something."

With a smile, Attila strongly patted Ben's right shoulder. "Woman outside: yours?"

Having not detected a woman, Ben frowned and looked back over his shoulder. He set his eyes on his own wife, her honey-brown eyes shimmering in the hall's candlelight. She made her way over, dressed in a wine-red evening gown with a black wool cardigan over it. Her heels clicked against the marble floor as she walked towards them, and a curious frown sat on her face.

"What's going on?" she asked, taking Ben's hand as she stopped beside him.

"Work," Ben mumbled. He then looked at Attila. "This is Attila."

Attila held out his hand, and as Ben's wife gladly took hold of it, he brought it closer to his face and kissed it. "Pleasure," he said as she pulled her hand away unsurely.

"This…is my wife," Ben said, scowling at Attila. "Lillian."

Lillian smiled pleasantly as she stood at her husband's side. "One of…Aleksei's?" she asked curiously.

"*The* one," Attila said with a smirk. "Aleksei and I go back far—very far."

Ben then looked at Felix, who was still cleaning the table; he grunted irritably and looked back at Attila. "I promised to take Lillian dancing tonight; would you mind making sure he finishes?"

Attila glanced at Felix. "You will beat me if I say no?"

"Well, I would, but you don't answer to me, I suspect."

"Right," Attila confirmed, pointing his index fingers at him. "Go, have fun. I watch him—a kindness, right? You owe me," he said, winking.

Ben shrugged. "Sure," he said, taking Lillian's arm in his own.

Then, Attila waved farewell with his right middle and index fingers. "Don't stay out too late, huh?" he said with a suggestive smirk.

Smiling in response, Ben turned around and led the way out of the castle.

Lillian then looked up at him. "What happened?"

"Just an annoyance; had to put him in his place is all."

She frowned disapprovingly. "This new job he's given you... involves you beating up other guys? I thought this place was supposed to be a new life, but you're still doing the same things here you were doing back home."

He smiled and sighed as he looked down at her concerned face. "It's what I'm best at, and Aleksei obviously sees that—and the pay's good, you can't deny that."

"I'd rather be less well-off than sit around praying my husband comes home every night. There's something about all of this that just... makes me worry," she said as they stepped out into the castle's courtyard. "You don't tell me everything—and I know that you can't—but I wish I could just stop... panicking."

Ben stopped walking and placed his hands on her shoulders. "You shouldn't worry. I can take care of myself, and when has anything ever gone wrong? Aleksei knows what he's doing, and so do I," he convinced.

Lillian sighed and placed her right hand on the side of his face. "If you say so. But if anything happens to you, Aleksei'll be the first person I smack."

Amused, Ben laughed and led the way down to the horse-drawn carriage Lillian had arrived in. "I'm sure it won't come to that."

Once Ben pulled the carriage door open for her, Lillian climbed inside and sat down.

"Did you tell him about that man you saw?" she asked, watching as he climbed into the carriage and sat beside her.

He nodded. "I did," he said, pulling the door shut. As the carriage started moving, he turned to face her. "He told me to apprehend him if I see him again."

A disapproving frown appeared on her face. "He could be dangerous."

"I already feel like he is; he *followed* me."

"Why can't Aleksei deal with it himself?"

"He's my boss, Lillian, and it's my job to do things for him. Besides, this guy followed *me*, not Aleksei."

She sighed and looked over at the window. "I hope you *don't* see him again."

"So do I," he agreed, taking both her hands in his.

With a quiet exhale, Lillian set her eyes on him. "Just…be careful."

Ben smiled. "Always am."

Smiling, she rested her head on his shoulder. "I know."

"Oh, Alonzo came tonight," Ben said, "and his sister."

"God," she mumbled with irritancy. "I hoped they'd be two of the last to come."

"I offered to walk them to the city, but Aleksei's doing it. I bet they're both nattering in his ears as we speak," he said with a quiet, amused laugh.

"Good. It's about time he did something himself; he's going to work you to death."

He sighed and smiled. "No, he's not. He really is—"

"He won't let you leave that castle; I'm left in that house all by myself."

"We're on alert right now; I need to keep the day and night guards on their toes. I'm sure once this Ada stuff is dealt with, I'll be able to stay at the house."

She looked up at him. "You better, or I'll give him a mindful, that's for sure," she threatened.

Ben smiled amusedly and kissed her. "Let's just enjoy the rest of the night."

Lillian sighed and nodded, resting her head back on his shoulder. They both then sat in silence as the carriage continued forward.

Ben *was* admittedly a little unnerved by the guy who'd followed him, but he'd get to the bottom of it. He wasn't sure where or when he'd see him again, but the moment he did, he'd apprehend him just as Aleksei asked.

| Alucard |

In the city, Alucard led the vampires to the Midnight's Watch, a large, brightly lit inn. It was one of the only establishments open so late, and most of its current patrons were vampires. They all chattered and laughed loudly from inside with glasses of blood in their pale hands. He was glad to see that they were comfortable and enjoying the fruits of his hard work to get the treaty set in place.

Alucard morphed back into his usual self and looked around at the eleven vampires. "Zhis establishment is vampire-vun. You vill spend zhe night 'ere; in zhe morning, eizer Ben or somevone of 'is choosing vill come and assign you 'omes. Some of you may 'ave to vait a vew days longer, but you vill all get 'omes bevore zhe veek is over. Go inside, do vhatever, vollow zhe rules," he instructed.

Alonzo stepped out of the crowd. "We uh…say we want a drink…what do we pay with?"

"I 'ave a tab vunning 'ere vor all zhe people who vork vor me," Alucard explained as he held his arm out towards the door, inviting them to enter. "You can get vhatever you vant."

"Oh, sweet," Alonzo said with a grin.

"Thank you so much, sir," one of the other vampires said.

"Is no problem," Alucard said. "Go. I 'ave to get 'ome."

Without any fuss, Alonzo led the new vampires into the inn.

Free at last, Alucard sighed and turned around; however, as he faced the road which would take him to the city's exit, he set his eyes on a shrouded man and his dog. It was *him*. The strange man Ben mentioned seeing. He was standing in the middle of the road with an ominous haze surrounding him.

Alucard wasn't threatened. The vampire immediately moved to attack, but the moment he sprung forward, the man disappeared in the blink of an eye, somehow faster than Alucard had moved.

That was *impossible*.

He scowled as he looked around warily, searching for him, but he was nowhere to be seen, and no trace of him had been left behind. No aura, no ethos, no scent…nothing. However, Alucard's lingering headache urged him to get to the safety of his home. He didn't have the strength to fight someone who might be faster than him—maybe even stronger. He needed to be at full strength, and in order to obtain that, he had to rest.

Alucard morphed into his eagle-owl form and flew off into the night, heading for his house. The night had been long, but he was sure the approaching week would be longer—as always. And now, he had yet another threat to keep his eyes peeled for.

Chapter Forty-Six

— ⋜ † ⋝ —

Sunday

| Alucard |

Sunday came sooner than Alucard hoped. The birds chirped rhythmically outside, but their song scraped and clawed through his head; his headache hadn't relented at all since last night's vampire relocation. He had no idea what time it was, but he knew he had things to do today. If he didn't get up now, he was sure he might sleep the entire day away again.

With a lazy sigh, he sat up and slouched forward as he glared down at his lap. Today, he thought he should head to the prison and check out who had replaced Ki. No one had come to him with dire updates regarding Ada or the werewolves, and that was a relief. He really didn't want to be dealing with her just yet, not with his unyielding headache.

The vampire then felt greater relief when he remembered that Elvin wouldn't be coming today. He wouldn't have to deal with the bard's constant nattering. No relief could be greater.

Alucard dragged his hand over his aching head and glanced at his dresser, which his blazer lay on top of. He remembered the feather Zalith gave him last night, the same one he told himself *and* Zalith he'd activate once he got home. Guilt gripped him; could Zalith have possibly waited for him to do so? Probably not.

He pulled himself out of bed and took the black feather from his blazer pocket and glared down at it for a few moments. What would happen when he activated it? Did he only need to activate it when he wanted to communicate? Or was it the type of spectre that remained active at all times for him to summon when he needed to use it? He was about to find out.

Alucard imbued the necessary amount of ethos into the feather, allowing it to transform into a rather battered-looking raven. The bird's eyes were as dark as night, and its glossy feathers shimmered in the minuscule sunlight which found its way into Alucard's bedroom. He couldn't sense the creature's two-way link as active, so it appeared to be the type of spectre he could leave active and use when he needed to send a message. There was no harm in leaving it manifested; it would save him from having to use his ethos each time to use it. So, he walked over to the curtains, opened one of the windows, and allowed the bird to roam outside. It wouldn't stray too far from him, either; spectres could only distance themselves so much from their masters before disintegrating.

As the bird flew off and perched itself on the fountain in the garden, Alucard closed his window and pulled on a black shirt. He grabbed his blazer, left his bedroom, and made his way downstairs. It was Sunday, so Emil had the day off. He was entirely alone, and he was glad. The only person he felt he might not mind invading his personal solitude was Zalith—he quickly scowled at the thought, catching himself thinking about that demon again. He had a job to do, and he couldn't waste his time sitting around thinking about someone who might not even be thinking about him. So, he dismissed his unwelcome thoughts and prepared to leave.

Before pulling his blazer on, though, he reached into its pocket and pulled out his flask. He drank the remainder of the blood which was inside, and although his headache didn't completely relent, it yielded enough for him to feel a little less aggravated.

He tucked the flask back into his pocket as he put his blazer on. Then, he grabbed his cape and hastily left his house, setting his eyes on Sergiu, who was tending to the two horses. Alucard pulled his cape on and walked over to the groundskeeper, who stopped what he was doing to greet Alucard.

"Good afternoon, sir," Sergiu said with a smile.

Afternoon? Alucard frowned and looked up at the sky, seeing that it was, in fact, mid-afternoon. Once again, he'd slept in. But he didn't care. He looked back at Sergiu. "Sebastian," he demanded.

Sergiu nodded and gripped the black stallion's reins. He handed them to Alucard, and as the vampire mounted the horse, he looked up at him. "Will you be needing anything else, sir?"

"No," Alucard grumbled. Then, he tapped the horse's side with his foot and set off, leaving Sergiu with the brown mare.

The journey to the prison was going to be long and dull. He sat there, glaring ahead, listening to his horse's occasional grunts and snorts. The passing people were of no interest to him; the bittering wind didn't unsettle him, and the slowly darkening sky failed to threaten.

It wasn't until he reached Dargamoore prison that he realized quite some time had passed. The sounds of metal against stone echoed in the distance, and the pained, tormented cries of prisoners irritated him. He just wanted to get it over with. He didn't really care who this new prison chief was; as long as they weren't annoying, insufferable, or stupid, then he was sure they'd be able to work together.

As he approached the small hut which sat beside the prison's huge, black gates, Alucard deadpanned and prepared for whoever or whatever might be waiting. He halted his horse, dismounted it, and made his way inside. And then he set his eyes on Ki's replacement. He was an averagely tall man and perhaps in his late forties. His face was snub-nosed and rounded—he looked as though he might have been hit one too many times—and several scars were visible on his skin. He gawped at Alucard and frowned strangely, waiting for him to speak as he stopped a few feet from his desk.

However, Alucard waited in response, expecting the man to speak first.

Understanding so, the man sighed quietly. "I assume you're the one in charge of this whole thing?" he asked rudely.

The vampire scowled in hostility. "Vhere is Ki?"

"Ki has been…removed. My name's Landon. I replaced him," he explained, holding out his hand.

Alucard didn't take his hand. Instead, he scowled skeptically. "Vhy vas 'e removed?"

Landon lowered his hand and rested his arms on the desk. "Insubordination," he said simply. "Don't worry, your uh…Felix updated me on the current arrangement."

Felix? Alucard clenched his right fist in anger. Felix made a call without asking him? Ben already informed him that Felix had been acting strangely, and now this? It made him furious enough to hunt that miserable excuse for a vampire down and rip him to shreds. But why was Ki removed without his authority? Dirk usually dealt with the human-related affairs in Alucard's operation, but the councilman was away on business overseas; there was no way he could have orchestrated this change from halfway across the world.

Something wasn't right. Before Landon could comprehend it, Alucard abruptly snatched his throat and pulled him over the table. He then forced the guy's back down onto the desk's surface and glared into his horrified eyes. "Vhat do you know of zhese arrangements?" he snarled.

Panicking, the man gulped and gripped Alucard's wrist with both his hands. "W-what?" he whimpered.

"Vhat 'as Velix told you?"

"T-the deal, the human-trade," he insisted fearfully, "ten gold for five lifers and—"

"Did Dirk 'ire you?"

Landon frowned. "D-Dirk?"

Alucard didn't need to ask anything else. Landon had no idea who Dirk was, and that told the vampire that this man had quite possibly tried to infiltrate. He took no time eradicating the threat; he needed blood, so he mercilessly sank his fangs into Landon's neck and drained him of his life before he had a single moment to try and fight back.

With a revolted snarl, Alucard quickly patted Landon down, searching him for weapons. But there was nothing. He chucked the corpse to the ground and dragged the back of his hand over his mouth, wiping the blood away. He didn't even need to ask who sent him. It was obvious considering the man didn't have any silver on him. Ada did *exactly* this before; she cut off his vampires' source of blood, and that was what began his previous empire's demise. Without a source, the vampires attacked humans, and that gave mankind an excuse to fight back. It wasn't going to happen again.

He scowled as he made his way out of the tent and back towards his horse. Dirk was away, so he would have to find someone to take up Ki's position himself. He'd also have to find Felix, who he wasn't sure whether he wanted to kill or not, but he was sure as hell angry enough to consider slaughtering him.

Ignoring the surrounding guards' mutters of confusion in response to hearing the commotion inside the tent, Alucard mounted his horse and began heading back to the city. He wasn't yet sure who to consider for the new job opening. All he knew was that he didn't want it to be a vampire. He'd rather keep a human in control of the blood operation; a vampire might become too carried away being so close to the source of their food.

Alucard reached the city as dusk came around. Once he left his horse in the public stables, he made his way through the busy streets. As much as Dirk irritated him, he found himself wishing the man was here now to deal with this. Alucard was more than capable himself, though; if he couldn't do something as simple as finding a new guy to replace Ki, then what kind of boss did that make him? He'd just become so used to people doing these things for him that having to do them himself felt strange.

The council building came into view as he turned onto another street. *That* was where he went whenever he needed a human to do something for him. Although Dirk was the face of the council, all of them were now Alucard's subordinates. All he'd have to do is go in there and pick any one of them to do the job, and that was what he planned to do. Once Dirk returned, Alucard would get him to find someone more suitable.

When he reached the door, he knocked a few times; the usual doorman answered, allowing him inside almost immediately. Then, Alucard made his way upstairs and towards the meeting room, where he could hear the distinct voices of each council member. They replaced their door since his last visit; he gripped the handle, pushed it open, and set his eyes on the seven council members. Clyde, the ugly, rough-faced man with a voice so hoarse that it made Alucard want to attack. The bald man to his right, Lars. His eyes never failed to look so very tired—Alucard could relate. The other five hardly ever spoke, so Alucard felt no need to give them any notice. He stood at the foot of the table, waiting.

Clyde cleared his throat, glancing at his fellow council members. Each of them looked as fearful as the other, sitting with their arms resting on the table and their eyes focused on whatever was directly in front of them. They were as still as stone, not one of them daring to speak.

Lars, however, slowly took his eyes off the window and looked at Alucard. But as the vampire's eyes glared into his very soul, he looked down at the table. "Can we help, sir?" he asked nervously.

Sir? Since when did any of these irrelevant men refer to him as sir? He *was* their superior, but not once had they given him a title of such meaning. He didn't care. Apart from the new title, he couldn't help but notice their fear. Half of them were visibly trembling. Why? He hadn't done anything that might make these men fear him. "Dirk is absent," he said, scowling at them. "I need somevone to temporarily take charge of zhe prison operation."

"Might I suggest…Reece?" Clyde said, holding his hand out to the dark-skinned, black-haired man at the end of the table a few feet from where Alucard was standing.

The vampire took his eyes off Clyde and looked down at Reece. He looked to be the most mortified of all. The man didn't even look at him.

Alucard frowned and looked back at Clyde. "Vhat's vrong with all of you?" he questioned.

"Nothing, sir," Clyde denied. "Reece?"

Reece took his eyes off the table and slowly looked up at Alucard. "W-when do I start, sir?"

Sir was becoming tiring. But Alucard didn't care to ask why they addressed him that way. "Now," Alucard ordered. "Get down zhere and tell zhe guards who you are."

Nodding, Reece scurried to his feet, snatched his coat from the coat rack, and raced out of the room without another word.

Alucard then set his eyes on Clyde and frowned expectantly.

Clyde cleared his throat quietly and sat up straight. "No problems as of yet, sir," he started. "The human population have taken to the new laws, as have the vampires. There has been the occasional dispute, but nothing worth your time—our authorities have dealt with it; simple, verbal fights, nothing major."

There was nothing further to discuss. Alucard turned around and left the room, leaving the door wide open in his departure. He made his way back onto the streets and to where he left his horse. That had been satisfyingly easy. Now, all he had left to do for the night was deal with Felix—and this time, he wanted to do it himself. He mounted the black stallion and tapped its side, heading for his castle as dusk became night.

When he arrived at his castle, Alucard dismounted Sebastian and stormed into the entrance hall. He glanced at Ben, who was sitting at the table with the two vampires who had come with him from Eltaria, as well as Attila and Felix. The silvery-eyed vampire looked miserable, more miserable than Alucard had ever seen him. But he didn't care.

Before any of them could ask him what he needed, he snatched Felix's throat, pulled him from his seat, and aggressively threw him against the closest wall. Ben's friends jumped to their feet in startle, but Attila and Ben remained seated, watching the altercation.

"You took it upon yourselv to employ somevone in Ki's place?!" Alucard yelled furiously in Dor-Sanguian into Felix's horrified face.

Whimpering, Felix shook his head and replied in their native tongue, "Y-y-you were busy! I…wanted to help!"

"You know vhat your job is!" Alucard snarled. "You stay 'ere like a good little dog and do vhat I tell you!"

Felix nodded. "I-I-I'll stay here, I'll do what you—"

"Vhat vere you doing in my 'alf of zhe castle?" he then growled, tightening his grip on Felix's throat.

"C-cleaning!" he insisted. "M-mice!"

"Mice?" Alucard scoffed amusedly. He pulled Felix away from the wall and threw him to the floor. Before he could crawl away, Alucard slammed his foot down onto Felix's back. He wanted to end his life, he *so* badly wanted to tear his heart from his body, but he couldn't. Not until he found someone else to take care of the newer vampires in his place.

However, for a moment, he caught himself contemplating. Before, he felt he'd never execute someone who worked for him…but Felix crossed a line, a line Alucard couldn't ignore. If he had to look after the newer vampires for a while himself, then so be it. Felix had to go. He was replaceable.

Without hesitation, he gripped a fistful of Felix's hair in one hand and placed his other on Felix's neck; he tore the guy's head from his body in a single, swift movement with a revolted, angry snarl, and as he watched Felix's body crumble into black ash, he dropped his severed head. That was one less annoyance he'd have to continue dealing with any longer.

Attila laughed loudly and leaned back in his seat as Ben looked over at him. "You should have done that many a year ago," he said in Dor-Sanguian with a snide smirk.

Alucard pointed at him. "Shut up," he warned.

Holding up his hands in surrender, Attila exhaled deeply and looked at Lloyd and Jasper. "Sit down, show is over." Then, he slapped Ben's arm and smirked. "Scared?"

"No," Ben mumbled.

"Get back to vork," Alucard grumbled, and then, he stormed out of the castle. He'd had enough for today.

Chapter Forty-Seven

─ ≷ † ≶ ─

Monday

| Alucard |

Monday was yet another day of tasks. Alucard abruptly woke to a rhythmed knock at his front door, one he recognized right away. Attila. But what could he want at this time?

Alucard got out of bed, pulled on the shirt closest to him, and made his way down to the front door. Emil was already answering it for him, but as he arrived, he dismissed the butler and invited Attila in himself. He led the way into the lounge and sat in his usual spot beside the fireplace, inviting Attila to sit in the armchair opposite him.

"You finally dealt with Felix, huh?" Attila asked with a smile, speaking in his native tongue.

Alucard rolled his eyes. "Vhat do you come to me vith?" he replied in Dor-Sanguian.

"Does the Order of Grace mean anything to you?"

"No."

"I infiltrated Sinéad's church. They're…not quite like any other I have seen. They praise Letholdus directly—the country's name literally translates to 'God's gracious gift'. They're not going to be easy to convince; in fact, I don't think I'll be able to convince them at all. Wiping them out might be the best option."

"Vine," Alucard dismissed.

"There are three current propositions in your favour. DeiganLupus is still recovering from war. Their king is dead; their prince is young and pathetic. Influencing him will not be hard. If I were to head there next, I can assimilate and assume a role of guidance within the court," he explained.

Alucard glanced over at him and smirked. "'Ow did zhe king die?"

"It was the strangest thing; a rabid werewolf came out of nowhere and attacked him whilst he was travelling to his country home."

"Ah, vhat a shame," Alucard said with fake sympathy, looking back into the empty fireplace. "''Ave zhat be done."

Attila nodded. He then rested his right leg over his left and exhaled deeply. "The second opportunity involves Nefastus. I hear four grim reapers have been sent to this world to investigate a newly invented curse created by Ares. I feel as though they might serve as useful allies."

"I 'ave no need for grim veapers; zhey are annoying."

"Of course. The last proposition: Samayō-Akuma is at war again. An influential general is looking to hire some help to ensure his victory. Do you have the men spare? Or does it not interest you?"

Alucard thought to himself for a few moments before looking back at Attila. "'Ow many does he vant?"

"At least twelve; he wants to invade all twelve surrounding villages at the same time. I assume he wishes to have one vampire per squad. He has offered to pay a price twice the amount you usually ask for, plus additional discretion fees," Attila explained.

"Vine," he said, looking back into the fireplace. "'Ead to zhe vortress bevore you 'ead vor DeiganLupus and pick zhe best tvelve Paladins."

Attila nodded and leaned his arms onto his legs. "How are things with the relocation mission?"

"Not your concern," Alucard snarled.

He sat up straight. "Is there anything else you might need from me before I head off?"

"''As zhere been any news on zhe Diabolus at all?"

"None."

Alucard frowned and wondered…had Damien actually dealt with that? He didn't want to sit there thinking about Damien. For the first time in a long time, the Daegelus wasn't the only thing on his mind all the time. He'd much rather sit there thinking about Zalith…whom he also wished was sitting in his lounge with him rather than Attila. But he couldn't let that demon distract him from his business. Attila's updates were always important and useful. That was why he was his right-hand man, after all.

Attila continued, "As far as I'm aware, the next ship leaves for DeiganLupus this coming Saturday. It would be best for me to arrive at the same time as other travellers to avoid any sort of suspicion."

Nodding, Alucard glanced over at him. "Vhilst you are still 'ere, I vant you to keep an eye on Ben and Tobias."

"The new guy?"

"Ben told me not too long ago zhat Tobias 'as been speaking of vings 'e shouldn't be. And Ben 'asn't been 'ere very long, so I vant to be sure zhat I can trust 'im."

"Understood."

"Go," Alucard mumbled.

Dismissed, Attila stood up, made his way over to the door, and left silently.

Alucard then took a moment to ponder. DeiganLupus' next king would be under his thumb—that was an exceptionally large move and one he'd been waiting for. Before his absence and Ada's attack, he'd had so many bishops, monarchs, and royals under his control. He'd been waiting since coming back home to begin regaining his authority, and Attila had just presented him with a perfect opportunity, and he didn't even have to do anything. He trusted Attila to do what must be done, and he didn't need to give it much thought. Soon, he'd have his first king, the first of many to come.

The quest to rebuild his fallen empire was moving along rather smoothly, and it brought a devious smile to his face. Soon enough, the world would be at the Nosferatu's feet once more. He spent so long crafting this world into what he wanted it to be, and then Ada had torn it apart in just a few years of his absence. He didn't plan on leaving again any time soon, however. This world had once belonged to vampires, and he planned to have it that way once again. He was born into this world to take it from Letholdus and his dragons, and that was exactly what he was going to do.

Alucard then rolled his eyes. He hated the Numen. They abandoned and forgot him, throwing him into a life with no meaning. They never expected him to do anything of significance, and he aimed to prove them wrong. He'd already killed one dragon, and if he had to kill another to remind Letholdus that he was still a threat, then he would.

However, before he could focus on the bigger picture, he had to deal with Ada and the Diabolus. But Alucard then frowned sullenly. In Damien's absence, he realized his confidence had greatly increased. He spent more time thinking about the Nosferatu, about his own wants, and his own needs—Damien insisted such things were unnecessary and that he shouldn't focus on them. But he wanted to. He wanted to continue to build on his own; he wanted to show the Numen and Damien that he *wasn't* irrelevant and worthless. Maybe once he took Aegisguard, Damien would stop treating him like a fumbling child. He could only hope, though.

As well as his own reasons for wanting to rebuild the Nosferatu Empire, he also kept Damien's wish to kill Letholdus in mind. If Alucard could show him that he could be a whole lot more useful in that feat, then he would. He knew he could do more than transfer vampires from one world to another. He could help weaken Letholdus by slowly shrinking his influence and replacing it with his own, just as he had done so long ago. Damien wasn't yet aware that this was part of his plan, but he was convinced that once he told him, Damien might be proud of him.

Was he doing this for Damien, though? Was that the base of his plan? Was he rebuilding to help Damien overthrow Letholdus, or was he doing so to simply have his own domain to rule, something the Numen had denied him? He wasn't sure. But it had to be…didn't it? He *did* want to prove himself to Damien…right? Or was he doing this to that he could one day stop working for Damien? He scowled and silenced his conflicting thoughts. There was still so much to be done. He could take the time to work out his end goal later.

Chapter Forty-Eight

─ ⸱ ✝ ⸱ ─

Tuesday

| Ben |

Tuesday was slow. Ben sat outside the Goose Inn with Attila and Tobias, enjoying his drink in the shade of the city. A break from work was *much* needed.

After taking a sip of his whiskey, Tobias looked over at Ben and asked, "You heard from Elvin lately?"

"Nope," Ben said with a shrug, grimacing after tasting the same whiskey Tobias had told him to order for himself.

"Shouldn't say his name," Attila warned. "Like omen, appear if you think of him."

The three of them laughed.

"You know Aleksei better than us," Tobias said, looking at Attila. "Why'd he ever pick Elvin up? Like…he's an idiot. I like him, but…I dunno."

"Aleksei…sympathetic. Sometimes too much. I don't know why, but he has…moment of strange sadness sometimes. Feels sad for other people. Helps them. Elvin was one such person," he explained, finishing his drink. "You were, too," he said, nodding over at Tobias. "Sometimes, also have really angry time, like last night…kill Felix. That was long overdue, though."

Ben nodded. "Agreed."

"I suspect same thing happen with Rodney. Anger is scary. You don't want to see it," Attila said with a smirk.

"I've seen my fair share of angry bosses," Ben said. Just *thinking* about what it was like to be around Zalith when *he* was angry sent a shiver down his spine.

Attila shook his head. "Not like Aleksei. Is…issue. Runs in family, I hear."

"Family?" Tobias scoffed. "Last I heard, it's just him and Lucifer, right?"

"Aleksei tell me stories—long time ago when he and I were…closer. Lucifer angry—so angry. Other Numen lock him away to keep themselves and world safe. That why he make Aleksei—to free him. Failed, though. Anyway, Lucifer angry, Aleksei angry. Family thing," he said, waving his hand around.

Tobias exhaled and raised both his eyebrows in concern. "Well, guess I better do my best not to piss him off, then. Come to think of it, I've never actually really seen him angry—super angry, anyway."

Ben looked at Attila. "Last night *wasn't* angry?" he asked in disbelief.

Attila shrugged. "Eh, little," he said, holding out his right index finger and thumb, holding them half an inch close to one another to express his statement.

The same look of concern on Tobias' face plastered itself to Ben's.

But then Attila laughed and slapped both their shoulders. "Lighten up. None of us can piss him off so much like that," he assured them. "Ada, she's a different story."

"I concur," Elvin said, appearing behind Tobias, who sharply turned his head to gawp over his shoulder at him.

"Omen," Attila whispered, leaning into Ben's ear as Elvin pulled out a chair beside Tobias.

Elvin rested his arms on the table and sighed sadly, pouting. "He was so mean to me the other day."

"Aleksei?" Tobias asked.

The bard nodded. "He threatened me."

Attila scoffed in surprise. "You? What say?"

He shrugged. "He told me like sixty times that I'm not his friend. He basically told me that he pretends to be nice to me. And that demon guy…I swear he's changed him."

"Demon guy?" Attila asked.

"If you know, you know. If you don't, you don't," Ben said before Tobias could tell Attila who the demon was.

Looking at Elvin, Attila shrugged. "Aleksei is not nice—not on purpose. Spends little time with people…socializing not his thing. Just work, work, work—always been that way. Never had time to be friends."

Ignoring him, Elvin wrapped his arms around himself. "I feel like I was just some sort of distraction for him until Zalith came along. Now he doesn't need me anymore."

Tobias smirked and glanced at Ben. "I might owe you that cash."

"What?" Elvin blurted, scowling.

Attila frowned. "What I miss?"

"Maybe Aleksei's just realizing what he wants; you should be happy for him," Ben said as kindly as he could.

"He doesn't want that!" Elvin insisted. "That guy's bad news, and he's gonna hurt him!"

"Not the vibe I get," Tobias said with a shrug, signalling the barmaid to bring more drinks.

Elvin scoffed. "Well, you're an idiot if you don't see it."

Then, Attila held up his hand. "What are we talking about?"

"Aleksei's got a boyfriend," Tobias said, smirking.

Ben frowned disapprovingly, sure that Alucard hadn't told Attila about Zalith, and he was sure there was a reason for that. Yet again, he found himself conflicted. He would probably have to tell Alucard once more that Tobias had been telling people things they didn't know.

Attila then laughed hysterically, but neither Ben nor Tobias joined him. He swiftly frowned and looked at them both. "Serious?"

"It's possible," Ben said with a shrug. But he quickly frowned and asked himself, why was he joining in?

"They're not together!" Elvin insisted.

Tobias chuckled. "Yet," he corrected.

"Maybe we should tone it down a little," Ben suggested.

"He ain't dated anyone ever as far as I know," Tobias said as the barmaid handed each of them their drinks. "He's finally got over that, though. Good for him."

"He's not!" Elvin argued.

Ben sighed and sipped from his glass. "Anyway, we should be discussing business, right?"

Tobias nudged Attila's shoulder. "Why you so quiet, man?"

Attila mumbled, "Thinking."

"All right. Anyway, what were you saying?" Tobias asked, looking back at Ben.

"Business. Anything new?"

"Nah, not really," he said, sipping from his glass. "Wolves are quiet; people seem to be okay with this whole vampire set up now."

Elvin pouted as he crossed his arms in front of him. "*And* he kicked me out."

"What?" Tobias grunted.

"Aleksei made me give him back the key I had to his house."

"Wow…" Tobias drawled. "You really must have pissed him off. What did you do, man?"

"Nothing," he mumbled. "I just tried telling him that Zalith is bad news."

Tobias then looked at Ben again with a suggestive look on his face.

Ben smirked. "Looks like we're getting closer to my victory," he said—he just couldn't stop. What was wrong with him? He placed his hand over his face, trying to work out how to shut himself up, but the gossip of Zalith and Alucard being an item seemed to have him excited.

"Yeah, yeah," Tobias muttered, waving his hand in Ben's face.

Attila then rested his arms on the table and asked Ben, "Who Zalith? Demon? Working with Aleksei?"

"Not my place to say," Ben dismissed. "It's not any of our places to say," he warned, glaring at Elvin and Tobias.

With a deep sigh, Tobias finished his second drink and shrugged. "Well, something tells me this upcoming full moon is gonna be eventful," he said, changing the subject. "Ada's most likely to launch an attack then, so I'd make sure I'm ready if I were you," he said, nodding at Ben.

"We're ready," Ben assured him.

Attila then laughed quietly. "Ada—crazy lady," he said, tapping his left temple. "Many crazy people around Aleksei, come to think."

"Crazy?" Ben asked.

"Not my place to say," Attila sneered.

Ben scoffed quietly. "All right."

"Joking," Attila said, grinning. "Is vampires mostly—all *love* Aleksei. He make us, so…we see him like…father or something. But some—like Felix—take that admiration too far, think they *in love* with Aleksei. Aleksei ignore it, or oblivious to it, I not sure which. Never really seem to pay attention to someone when flirting, so most crushes vampires had on him just faded. Not with Felix. He crazy. If Ada was vampire, I say she that kind of crazy, too," he explained, nodding. "So, as for Zalith guy, he stand no chance. Aleksei ignore, so guy's best off giving up. Not just oblivious, but Aleksei straight, too."

"I wouldn't be so sure about that," Tobias said with a frown.

Just then, the sound of arguing caught their attention. Ben, Attila, Tobias, and Elvin turned to face the street opposite the inn and set their eyes on two men screaming in each other's faces in the middle of a riled-up crowd. The first was clearly a vampire, his skin as pale as ice in the afternoon's sunlight. His short, styled hair was strangely blue, and his eyes a deep red. His opponent was a tall, lean, black-haired human, yelling all manner of insults at him as he shouted back in defence.

"You were saying how there were no issues with the vampire treaty?" Ben said with a sigh, glancing at Tobias.

Tobias shrugged. "Hey, I'm not the one living here."

With an irritated huff, Ben stood up and headed down the street towards the conflict. The others followed him and waited behind the crowd as Ben pushed his way through.

"What the hell is going on here?!" Ben asked once he reached the two arguing men.

They stopped yelling and glared at him. The vampire backed down, but the human scoffed and set his eyes back on the vampire.

"This *creature* wouldn't take its eyes off me," the human growled, moving to shove the vampire, but Ben grabbed his arm and pulled him away. Disgusted, the man yanked his arm from Ben's grip and scoffed. "Don't touch me, vampire filth!" he yelled.

Trying to remain calm, Ben looked at the vampire. "What's going on here?" he asked, sure that the vampire's story would be different to the human's.

"I was just walking here; I didn't do anything," he mumbled, glaring at the human as the surrounding crowd murmured to one another.

The human scoffed. "Eyeing me up's more like it!"

Ben scowled at the human, silencing him. Then he said, "Both of you, just go home; there's no need for this to escalate."

"You ain't in charge of me," the human denied.

"Then go do whatever the hell you want," Ben snarled, "but *you*, go home," he instructed, looking at the vampire again.

He didn't refuse. The blue-haired vampire made his way through the crowd and headed home, leaving Ben to deal with the angry human. *That*, however, wasn't Ben's area. Dirk was supposed to deal with the humans, but he was currently overseas doing something for Alucard. So the best he could do was hope the man would calm down. The last thing any of them needed was for this small incursion to explode into something worse.

Sighing, Ben turned his back on the angered man and left the crowd.

"It happens all the time," Elvin said, walking beside Ben as the four of them made their way back towards the Goose Inn.

"First one I've witnessed," Ben mumbled, slumping down in his seat.

"Treaty still not been in place very long," Attila said, picking up his glass. "I say year or so, everything calm down."

"Hopefully," Tobias said, nodding.

"Do any of you know when Dirk's getting back?" Ben asked.

Attila looked over at him. "Could be day, week… month—even year. No telling how long stuff me and him do takes. I leave on Saturday, heading to DeiganLupus."

"Why you going there?" Elvin asked.

"Business, bard," Attila said with a smirk, raising his glass to him before sipping from it.

"You all have these big jobs, and all I do is sit around and do nothing," Elvin complained.

"Don't you write your little book thing?" Tobias asked.

"I don't see the point in it anymore now that Aleksei hates me."

"I don't think he hates you," Ben disagreed, resting his arms on the table. "He's just… well, I don't know, to be honest."

Attila laughed slightly. "He just mad. He come say sorry at some point."

"I don't think he will," the bard mumbled sadly.

Attila took his eyes off Elvin and asked Ben, "So, what else do you do for Aleksei?"

Once again, Ben was sure he shouldn't answer. If Attila didn't already know these things, he was sure Alucard hadn't told him for a reason. He didn't want to share information Alucard might not be wanting him to share; the last thing he wanted was to end up like Felix.

He looked away from Attila. "Again, if you know, you know. If you don't, you don't. If Aleksei wanted you to know, he would have told you."

Attila smirked. "Cocky, hmm? You are…pretentious?"

"No," Ben denied, not having meant to give such an impression."Respectful. I'm not likely to share information that he might not want to be shared," he said sternly.

"Good." Attila smiled. "I know what you do. I know what you all do. I just test."

"Test?" Tobias questioned.

Attila gulped down his drink and stood up. "I have to prepare for Saturday. I might see you before I go, might not. If not, I hope you all still alive when I come back."

"Don't even joke about that, man," Tobias exclaimed quietly. "Ada's hanging about. We could all die next week; there ain't no telling."

"I could help, but Aleksei need me elsewhere. Good luck," Attila said, stepping out from behind the table. He then grinned and waved before making his way down the street, leaving Ben with Tobias and Elvin.

Elvin pouted and crossed his arms. "Weird guy," he mumbled.

"Funny, though," Tobias said with a shrug.

"Sometimes," Ben agreed. He then finished his own drink. "I should head off, too. The wife's probably wondering where I am. Better go see her before I head to the castle."

Tobias stood up as Ben did. "Yeah, I better head back to the pack; all the ladies are obviously missing me," he said, grinning.

"What about me?" Elvin asked sullenly, looking up at them both.

Ben and Tobias glanced at one another, the same look of disinterest on their faces.

"Go uh…hang out with some other bards," Tobias suggested. "See ya," he sang, strutting off down the street.

Elvin growled and looked at Ben.

"Sorry," he said with a shrug. "Gotta get back."

Then, as Elvin grumbled sadly, Ben turned around and headed off. He felt a little bad for the bard, but he wasn't someone he'd willingly choose to hang around with.

Ben sighed quietly as he walked through the streets and tried to keep himself from thinking too much about his current conflictions. He hadn't made a big deal of it just now, but Attila was no longer around, giving him the space to ponder. Attila said he was testing them; had Alucard sent him to see if he and Tobias could be trusted after he told Alucard that Tobias had been spouting information? Was Alucard questioning *him*? Had he sent Attila to see if he might have to dispose of either of them? After witnessing Alucard kill Felix, he was sure that he should be a whole lot more careful. He tried to do so with Tobias and Attila, ad hopefully Attila would relay that back to Alucard.

He turned onto the deserted street which would take him to the house his wife was currently staying in, but when he stared ahead, he stopped dead in his tracks. At the very end of the street…was *him*. That man and his dog. He stood there with a malevolent look in his eyes and a malicious grin. The dog bared its teeth, growling quietly.

Alucard instructed Ben to apprehend that man if he saw him again—and there he was. Ben didn't hesitate. He sprang into action, moving towards the man so quickly that he was sure the guy wouldn't be able to escape. But when Ben came closer, the man reached out and snatched his throat—

Ben choked in shock as he was pinned against the wall beside them so quickly that it took him a moment to catch up with the world around him. He stared into the man's devilish red eyes, and he glared back with a twisted smile on his face. Ben tried to speak, but the man held his throat so tightly that he couldn't utter a sound.

The man grinned and snickered quietly, moving his face closer to Ben's. He inhaled deeply through his nose, licked his lips, and laughed crazily as he exhaled in Ben's face. Revolted, Ben tried to pull away, but this man was so much stronger than he was. He stared in horror as the man glanced down at his dog and muttered something in a language he'd never heard before. Then, he let go of the dog's chain, and the creature suddenly combusted with a flash of black light, forming a portal a few feet away.

Before Ben could try to stop him, the man widened his jaw and sunk his teeth into his neck. Pain flooded through Ben's body as the man's venom infiltrated his veins, and in no time at all, his consciousness began to leave him. He couldn't resist it, and he couldn't fight. Whoever this man was…he had overpowered Ben, his dog had turned into a portal, and it seemed as though he was now taking him somewhere. But Ben couldn't see where. Just as he was thrown through the portal, everything around him faded to black.

Chapter Forty-Nine

⁓ ≺ † ≻ ⁓

Attila

| **Alucard,** *Wednesday Quintus 27th* |

Alucard woke when his butler knocked on his bedroom door. He rolled over onto his left side and glared at the black curtains as the late-afternoon sunlight crept in through the small cracks. But Emil knocked once again, so the vampire sighed and climbed out of bed. He pulled his shirt on and opened the door, setting his eyes on the startled butler.

"Mail, sir," Emil said, presenting three white envelopes, one silvery black wax-sealed envelope, and a piece of parchment wrapped with a red, silky ribbon.

Taking the letters from Emil, Alucard mumbled his thanks and shut the door, dismissing the butler. He sat on the edge of his bed and placed the letters beside him, keeping the roll of parchment in his hands. As he unravelled it, he recognized the handwriting as Attila's. It was Attila's report, and he wasn't interested in reading it right now. So, he chucked it onto the cabinet beside his bed.

He then picked up one of the white envelopes, and with a lazy sigh, he used one of his claws to open it. When he pulled the paper from inside and unfolded it, saw that it was from Dirk. His eyes swiftly darted over the page, most of it making no sense to him—he really should learn to both read and write Deiganish. He could just get Elvin to read it later for him. So, he eased the paper back into the envelope and picked up the next one. That, too, was from Dirk, and he suspected the third white envelope might also be from him. He opened it anyway, and as soon as he saw Dirk's name at the bottom of the page, he snarled irritably and placed it with the other two.

The vampire eyed the final letter's black wax seal. A distinct A was weaved into its centre surrounded by two thin circles. The sight of it made him cringe. He knew it was from Ada, and he didn't want to open it, but the vague hope of a call for peace between vampires and werewolves forced him to. He pulled the silvery envelope open and removed the black card, causing a rain of white, shimmering glitter to pour out into his lap. He scowled, trying to contain his slowly increasing anger. Then, he glared at what was written on the card; the white, twisting words on the top centre of the card read *'Aleksei, my King'*. A love heart had been drawn around his name, along with glittered, wavy lines which sat below each letter. He almost gagged at it.

Aleksei, my King,

Where have you been, my dear? For so many years, you have cursed me to exist without your beguiling presence. Why must you hide from me? In the shadows, in the dark? My pale, cold creature, I have craved you so. I ache to feel your gentle touch, that which you have so cruelly starved me of. There has not ever been a night since your departure that I have not allowed my own hands to wander upon myself as if they were yours. How I yearn to feel you upon me, within me, beside me. I know you feel the same, so why must you deny me?

I have searched for you for so long since word of your return. I feel heartbroken that you did not call for me. I have been forced to come to you—to this empty, lonesome land. I could not bear to be here in your absence. But now that you have returned, every time I lay upon the land, I feel as though I am closer to you than I could ever be. This time, I can't let you slip away. We need each other; we are meant for each other, and I feel it with every inch of my body. And you do too. I have seen it.

It was on a fateful, moonlit night which we met, and it shall be one such night where we meet again. Come to me, my king. Find me and take me. Take me with—

Alucard put the card down. He didn't care what she had to say. There was no mention of peace, and that disappointed him. He flipped the card over in case there was anything written on the back, and to his surprise, there was. A date, time, and instructions on what he should wear. An invitation? *'Friday, Quintus 29th, dusk. The place where our destiny began. I want you in a suit, one fit for a king. Don't be late'*. He frowned, flipping the card back over, but there was nothing telling him what the meeting was for. However, if Ada was inviting him and asking him to wear a suit, it could only mean that she had planned an evening for them—an evening he could use to try and talk her out of war.

As he picked the envelope back up, however, a folded piece of parchment slipped out and fell to the floor, sliding under his bed. He snarled irritably and moved to pick it up, but that was when that five-symbol-rhythmed knock Attila always used came at his front door. He stood up and irritably brushed the white glitter off his trousers as he left his room and made his way down to the entrance hall.

Emil had already let Attila in, and as the fashionably dressed vampire set his eyes on Alucard, a strange, intrigued smile found its way to his face.

"Party?" Attila asked in his native tongue.

"No," Alucard snarled, leading the way into the lounge.

"Why the glitter?" Attila questioned, sitting in the armchair as Alucard slumped onto the couch.

He shrugged as he made himself comfortable. "Mail."

"Someone sent you a letter loaded with glitter?"

"Yes."

Attila laughed and leaned back in his chair. "That's new."

"Ada," he grumbled. "She invited me to…someving on Vriday."

"You're going, aren't you?"

Taking his eyes off Attila, Alucard looked over at the windows, his eyes shimmering ice blue in the sunlight. "I 'ave to."

"You think she's up to talk about peace? That's what she said last time."

"I'd vather go and is not be a peace talk zhan not go and miss zhe opportunity."

"Can't argue with that. Want me to come with you? Just like old times, huh?"

"No," Alucard answered. There was only one person he could imagine himself working alongside. But did he *need* Zalith with him for this? No, he could handle Ada himself. He could handle *anything* himself. He did, however, feel as though he *wanted* Zalith there. And he was tired of questioning himself when it came to that demon, so he wouldn't ask himself why. "I 'ave…somevone else."

A sour look appeared on Attila's face. "Hmm…so I've heard."

"Vhat?"

"Your friends speak of a demon. I'd never have thought I'd see the day where *you* work with a demon—and willingly, too."

"'E is divverent," Alucard mumbled.

"Is he?" he asked doubtfully. "They're all the same, Alucard. As soon as he finds out what happened to you, he'll treat you the same way every other demon does."

Alucard didn't respond.

"Do you want that? As glad as I am that you're finally making friends again, I don't approve of this. I don't want to see you hurt, and this is the right way to go about it. How can you know he's different? Have you *told* him? *Shown* him?"

"No," Alucard snarled.

Attila sighed and calmed down. "I'm just trying to look out for you. If you're convinced that he's not going to disdain you, then by all means, allow him to be your friend. But you know better than anyone ever could just how spiteful demons are."

"Hm. Vhat do you vant?" Alucard digressed, glaring into the fireplace.

"To spend some time with you before I head to DeiganLupus. It's been a while since we've been able to do anything, to be honest. You've moved on up; you got shit to do. I've got shit to do for you. How does it feel?" he asked, smirking. "Working your way back up all over again?"

"I 'ope you ask in jest, not mocking," he warned.

Attila held up his hands. "You know me."

With a slight smile of amusement, Alucard looked over at him. "Is…annoying."

"I can only imagine. Are you going to kill Ada this time?"

"If I 'ave to."

"You're still convinced you can create peace?"

"I 'ave to try. Janus vanted us to vight, and I'm not vone vor giving Janus vhat 'e vants."

"Janus. You remember that, right?"

"Like vas yesterday," Alucard concurred with a smile.

Attila laughed. "You were so convinced you could kill this dragon, and I was so sure it would kill *you*. You had your plan. I thought it was bullshit to think all it takes to kill one of the Aegis is a simple, rusted piece of jewellery."

Alucard rolled his eyes. "Vas not just some vandom piece of jewellery."

"Right, right, what did you call it?"

"Is called an Aegiserium," Alucard answered.

"Right, that. Where'd you put it?"

"Is safe."

Attila nodded. "I noticed you decorated the castle with Janus' corpse."

"I zidn't vant zhat to go to vaste."

"Quite. Not forgetting your precious cape," he said, smirking.

"Is my most prized possession," Alucard mumbled with a wave of his hand. "Does many vings vor me."

"Such as?"

He wasn't going to tell him. Not only did he think his cape looked *very* fashionable, but the dragon fur was imbued with very powerful Aegis ethos, which made it hard for anyone to use ethos against him—more specifically, for people to read his mind, something he'd been more on-guard with lately, especially since Zalith expressed interest in trying to do so.

"Do you plan to kill more of the Aegis any time soon? I'd love to help you out once again," Attila then offered.

"Eh, god killing is in zhe past. Is too much vork."

"I hope that's just a temporary mindset. You once told me you were born to kill them all."

"I vas until my vather decided 'e no longer vanted me to live. I do vhat I vant now."

Attila nodded. "Ah, speaking of, have the Diabolus shown up since Rodney's little mishap?"

"No. Zamien told me 'e vould deal vith zhat, and seems as zhough 'e 'as done zhat."

"You're still working for him, aren't you?"

"I 'ave to."

"Do you, though?"

"Yes," Alucard snarled defensively.

Holding up his hands once more, Attila sighed and leaned back in his seat. "What's he got you doing now?"

"Moving vampires vrom anozzer vorld to zhis vone."

"And is *this* how you met this demon I've heard about?"

"'E is my vork partner," Alucard said, glancing at him.

"Is that all he is?" Attila asked skeptically.

"Vhat more could 'e be?"

"Tobias quite confidently called him your boyfriend. I disapprove in many ways."

Alucard rolled his eyes and glared at him. "'E is not my boyvriend. 'E ' my vriend, and yes, I 'ate zemons, but like I 'ave said, Zaliv is divverent. I zon't veel as zhough 'e is like zhe ozzers."

"Tell me how that is, Alucard. How is he *not* like every other demon out there?"

"'E zoesn't look at me like I'm some disgusting, vorthless vailure," he grumbled, glowering at the empty fireplace.

Attila rested his arm on the side of the chair and frowned in concern. "How *does* he look at you?"

Confliction gripped Alucard. He hadn't long found out the reason behind Zalith's constant staring. He knew that the demon was possibly attracted to him—he didn't understand *why*, though. He suspected Zalith wanted to share something more than friendship, and whenever he thought about it, he couldn't decide whether *he* wanted more or to remain friends. It confounded him so much to the point of aggravation. He didn't understand why he felt the way he did, but perhaps Attila could help him. Attila, after all, had once been closer to him than anyone else in his life, and he felt Attila was the only person he could bring himself to share such personal thoughts with.

He sighed and looked at him. "I am…'is vriend, and 'e is mine. Zaliv is zhe virst person in a very long time I vind myselv actually vanting to be avound and vork vith."

"And you'd choose to work with him over me, huh?" Attila asked, slightly upset.

Ignoring him, Alucard looked back over at the empty fireplace. "Vone of 'is subordinates told me, 'owever, zhat 'e might be…vell, attracted to me."

Attila frowned sourly.

"I vhought such a ving vould revolt me and make me vant to distance myselv vrom 'im."

"And?"

"Zhis 'asn't. I veel no divverent—vell, not in a negative vay. Since vinding out, I've vound myselv vinking about 'ow 'e may vant some sort of velationship vith me, and vhether I vant vone or not vith 'im. I tell myselv time avter time zhat I zon't, zhat I 'ave no intervest, no time, no need. But I alvays come back to zhe vhought of zhat. Is like I zon't know vhat I vant."

Attila shook his head. "You don't want that."

Alucard frowned and looked over at him.

"You *can't* want that. It is fallacious. Wrong. You know that."

"If I vere religious, per'aps," he said defensively. "But I am not."

"Still, that's not you, Alucard," Attila said confidently. "You've told me many a time that you've never and will never become interested in something so irrelevant as a relationship—especially one of such a blasphemous nature. I understand that you have a new friend, and it might be strange for you after such a long time of solitude; this friend of yours may choose to wrongfully lay with men, but that does not mean you should consider his attraction as something to reciprocate."

"I never said I vas attracted to 'im," Alucard mumbled, glaring back into the fireplace. Clearly, he was wrong thinking Attila could help him understand his feelings. Despite his sin-ridden life, it appeared as though Attila hadn't abandoned all the beliefs of Letholdus' religion. He felt like an idiot for even thinking telling someone was a good idea. As he always did, he was best to work it out for himself. He was already sure that Zalith's attraction to him didn't make him feel uncomfortable, and he still found himself wishing to see him as often as he could.

He then found himself pondering over his statement. *Was* he attracted to Zalith?

"Good," Attila said. "Watch him, Alucard. You can never be too careful around his type."

"Type?" Alucard scowled at him. But before Attila could answer, he rolled his eyes, snarled, and looked back into the fireplace. "Ve're not talking about zhis anymore. 'Ave you made preparations to leave on Saturday?"

Attila leaned back and sighed quietly. "I've been to the city docks, and I've purchased a pass to board a ship. I'll be leaving at dawn. What does the rest of the week have in store for *you*?"

"Ada's invite. I'm going to invite Zaliv to come vith me. Avter zhat, I zon't know."

With a disapproving frown, Attila leaned forward. "Might I say—"

"No," Alucard denied. "I zon't vant your input."

He sighed and slouched back in his seat. "Elvin's convinced this Zalith is changing you."

"I zon't care vhat Elvin vinks," he snarled. "No vone is changing me. I 'ave alvays and vill alvays be zhis vay."

Wary of Alucard's temper, Attila smirked nervously. "Elvin, huh? You ever tell him why you keep him around?"

"No," Alucard grumbled.

"Still thinks you wanted to give him a better life?"

"Obviously. If 'e knew zhe truth, I am sure 'e vould 'ate me—not zhat I care, but 'is mind is delicate. Vouldn't end vell vor 'im."

"Sounds like you care to me, Alucard."

"Vink vhat you like. You know vhy I keep 'im avound, and is *not* because I care."

"He never turned, so why do you keep him around if not because you care?"

"'E could still turn."

"He's twenty-five, Alucard. All shifters born with lycanthropy turn before they're eighteen. You know that."

"Elvin's slow; could just be taking longer."

"Right. Well, let me know in fifty years if he's still human or not," Attila said, smirking.

Alucard rolled his eyes, trying to hide his amusement. "Vhat of Ben?"

"Oh, he's all right," Attila confirmed. "You can trust him, I'm sure."

"And Tobias?"

"Weird, but…I'm sure he's not going to become a liability. He wouldn't share information with an outsider, I'm certain. You may have to remind him, however, that some of his colleagues are not meant to know certain things," he advised.

Glancing over at him, Alucard nodded. "I gazzer zhere is noving else you vish to bring to my attention?"

"No."

"Zhen go. I need to contact Zaliv."

With a hesitant nod, Attila stood up and sighed. "I hope you'll consider my advice."

Alucard also stood up and scowled irritably. "Go."

Attila wasn't going to argue. He made his way over to the door, and as Alucard followed, he looked back at him. "Well, good luck with Ada. I'll see you when I see you," he smirked, pulling the front door open.

As Attila left, Alucard locked his door and turned around. "Emil!" he called irritably.

The butler swiftly came running and stopped in front of Alucard. "Yes, sir?"

"You are native Deiganish, no?"

Emil nodded. "I am, sir."

"I need you to write someving vor me; go and get yourselv a pen and paper."

"No need, sir," Emil said, reaching into the inside pocket of his tailcoat. He pulled out a small notebook and pencil. "What do you need me to write, sir?"

Alucard thought to himself for a moment. "Ada 'as contacted me and asked to meet. I vould prever if somevone I know I vork vell alongside vas vith me, in case zhe situation becomes 'ostile. I vould…like vor you to come vith me, but if you cannot zhen vill not bover me. Zhe day set vor zhis meeting is zhis coming Vriday at dusk. She asked me to vear a suit, so I imagine zhis meeting is a vormal occasion. I'd say come dressed vor such an event, but you alvays seem to dress zhat vay anyvay."

Writing down Alucard's words, Emil nodded. "Is that all, sir? Do you need me to send it somewhere?"

"No, give to me," he said, holding out his hand.

The butler tore the page from his notebook and handed it to Alucard with a respectful bow.

Alucard headed upstairs and went into his study. He unlocked one of the windows and summoned the spectre Zalith gave him. The beaten-looking bird descended from the sky and landed on the window's ledge, staring up at him wide-eyed.

However, Alucard hesitated. Once again, he found himself wondering why he felt the need to invite Zalith. He didn't *need* anyone's help, so why did he feel so adamant? He undeniably enjoyed spending time with Zalith, but this wasn't his business, and Alucard wasn't planning on making a habit of involving that demon in his life or problems. Despite that fact, though, he still wanted to send the invite. He still wanted Zalith to join him.

He sighed, rolled his eyes, and handed the bird the note. As it flew off into the distance, Alucard made his way to his desk, sat down, and waited. He wasn't sure how long it might take for Zalith to reply, but he had nothing else to do, so he might as well wait.

And wait, he did.

His thoughts were erratic. At first, he thought he'd think about Ada and what she might be planning. But that wasn't going to happen. As soon as he sat down, his thoughts immediately focused on Zalith. He first thought about the fact that he didn't care about what Attila said. What *did* bother him was the fact that Attila hadn't made any effort to help him understand his feelings. He tried to warn him away from Zalith, just like Elvin. However, Alucard didn't care what either of them had to say. Zalith was confusing and strange, but Alucard was sure he wasn't there to use him in whatever way Elvin might be trying to imply.

Resting his arms on his desk, he frowned. Attila assumed he might be attracted to Zalith. He couldn't help but wonder…was he? Was that why he had this strange wish to spend more time with him? Is that why he felt utterly comfortable with Zalith's interest and words? Was *that* why he couldn't banish him from his mind, even when the demon had no involvement in what he was thinking about? He wasn't sure, but he *was* convinced that he didn't find anything physically appealing about him…did he? Now that he thought about it…although he hadn't reacted at the time, he'd not deny he did rather like the sight of Zalith without his shirt—

He didn't want to think about that. He looked over at the window, waiting for his spectre to return. All he liked about that demon was the fact that he actually listened to him and didn't grovel at his feet. Zalith knew what he was doing, he wasn't afraid to challenge Alucard, and he didn't hold back. Overall, he was simply fascinating and somewhat enjoyable to be around. And occasionally, that demon managed to make him laugh.

Alucard sighed irritably and glared over at the wall. What could Zalith possibly be doing right now? Why did he care? It wasn't his business. Why was he sparing so much thought for him? He impatiently tapped his claws on his desk and glanced at the window. Why *was* he thinking about him so much?

A sullen frown soon found its way to his face as he looked down at his hands. Ben told him Zalith was attracted to him; that didn't mean Zalith thought about Alucard as often as Alucard thought about *him*. That didn't mean he might want to spend his time with Alucard. It was just an attraction. Why did that make him feel so disappointed? So…hopeless?

He sat up straight and glared out of the window, and after a few moments of silence, a raven quite like his own descended from the clouds and made its way through his window and onto his desk. It dropped a small, rolled piece of paper into his hand and then left his study as swiftly as it had arrived.

Setting aside his sullen, conflicted thoughts, Alucard unwrapped the paper and read Zalith's reply. It read a simple *'I will certainly be there. Out of genuine curiosity, what is it that you will be wearing?'*. Alucard pouted—was it necessary for him to know what he'd be wearing? No. He rolled his eyes and left the reply on his desk as he walked out of his study.

There wasn't much left for him to do until Friday, so he thought he might as well use the next two days to prepare for whatever it was Ada was planning. He made his way up to his dressing room, where he would spend the next hour or so looking for something to wear. Whatever happened on Friday, he'd do his best to make sure he was prepared for anything. Ada, after all, always had ulterior motives. Alucard knew that far too well.

Chapter Fifty

$-\, \lessdot\, \dagger\, \gtrdot\, -$

Avernus

| Ben |

en slipped in and out of consciousness. Each time he woke, he remained so for no longer than a few moments. He saw glimpses of black stone walls, twisting mountains, and crooked towers. Red, foggy sky, screaming, howling creatures, and bubbling, *burning* lava. If he didn't know better, he'd think he was in Hell.

When he was finally able to keep himself awake for longer than mere seconds, he stared over at a smouldering sea through the cracks in the brick opposite where he lay. Despite the sight of lava, though, he could feel nothing but bitter cold in his numbing body. And the unmistakable sting of demon venom ensnared him.

The air was still but not silent. He could hear the hands of his captor fiddling with metal, his distorted voice humming and mumbling in the same language Ben still failed to recognize. The cries of what he assumed to be people echoed through the walls, and the occasional rumble in the distance shook the ground.

He couldn't move his body at all, but he *did* manage to shift his eyes enough to see the face of the man who took him from Dargamoore. The red-eyed, black-haired man stood over him with a hauntingly crazed smile on his face as he cut at what he could only assume was his body. But he couldn't feel the pain. Part of him was glad of it, but he felt such dread not knowing what this man was doing to him.

The man then noticed that Ben was conscious—either that or it only just caught his interest. He took his eyes off whatever he was looking at and glowered down at Ben. He smiled maliciously before continuing his work, a cruel laugh breaking through his muffled voice as he watched a mortified expression appear on Ben's face.

Ben couldn't find his voice. He glared up at the man, but not a sound could utter itself from his mouth. Every instinct within him told him to fight—he had to, he wanted to, but his entire body was unresponsive. No feeling, no pain. Just the dread of not knowing what the next few minutes might bring for him.

After a long while of silence, Ben's captor walked off, leaving him alone. He tried to move his eyes to see where he went and what he was doing, but he moved out of sight. All Ben could do was listen. That man's humming had become so unbearable; it scraped at Ben's ears like a rabid animal trying to escape its cage. He listened to him fiddle with glass, metal, and paper—he had no idea what he could be doing, but he was sure that no good was going to come of it. He had to figure out where he was and how to escape. But how could he do that if he couldn't even feel his body?

The sound of pouring and bubbling liquids then confounded him—was his captor a witch? Was he brewing potions? This man's cackle made him believe that might be the truth. He glared up at the ceiling, listening as the guy then loudly and aggressively gulped down whatever it was he had just concocted, and as he started to shuffle around in the distance, he cackled quietly. What the hell was he doing?

Once he finished his cackle, the man exhaled deeply and cleared his throat loudly. He made his way back over to Ben and smiled down at him. "You'll have to forgive my past lack of speaking—" he paused and gasped with excitement. "This…voice!" he cheered, clapping enthusiastically. "So smooth, so clear, so…so mine!" he cried, jumping up and down like an idiot. "Toe, froe, doe, moe—Belial, Behemoth, Beelzebub, Asmodeus, Satanas, Lucifer, Archangelo—Damien-Lilith-Letholdus-Ephriel-Detlaff!" he called, laughing hysterically as he stroked his own face. "Fabulous."

An almost horrified look smothered Ben's face as the man in front of him spoke with *his* voice. Although it was modulated, honeyed, and hinted with a sly, smug tone, it was unmistakably his. Was that why he couldn't speak? Was that why he couldn't utter a word? Had this man *stolen* his voice?

The man lifted his right hand and tightly gripped each side of Ben's jaw in his fingers. "Hi there," he said, grinning. "Again, forgive me for my…past failure to engage in conversation with you. I'm not exactly local," he said. As Ben scowled, the man snickered in his face and smiled confoundingly. "Of course, the natural order of all creation insists that for one to gain, one must lose—*I* like to bend rules. I gained, but I did not lose. Somebody did, though," he said, smirking as he let go of Ben.

Ben stared up at him, watching as he tidied his long, black, greasy hair, tightening his ponytail. Then, he looked back down at him, a haunting stare in his eyes.

"The last human I snatched a voice from wasn't exactly…hmm…what do you call it? Deiganish? So many worlds, so many names, so many…things!" he said as he clapped and stood up straight. He then sighed and gazed at Ben, a look of forced sympathy on his face. "*You* don't need a voice to tell me what I need to know, though. I have my ways."

What was that supposed to mean?

"You've been hanging out with someone very special to me," the man sang, placing his hands on his chest as he closed his eyes and sighed longingly. "You've been causing me so much trouble lately, too," he mumbled, glancing at Ben's confused face. "I didn't want to have to bring you here. I hoped I could do this quietly; Father likes it when we do things quietly," he said as a grin stretched across his face.

As much as Ben wanted to reply, he couldn't. He still couldn't move, either. All he could do was lay there, listen, and stare.

Sighing once more, the man allowed his arms to dangle at his sides. "But alas, here you are. I'd have much preferred to bring someone a little more… hmm… integrated, but you were what I got. Still, I'm sure there's *something* in that strangely alive brain of yours that can help me."

Ben scowled—

"Shh, shh, it's okay," the man whispered, placing his right hand on the side of Ben's face. "It's not going to hurt—well, it won't hurt *me*!" he yelled, laughing crazily. But then he pulled his hand from Ben's face and smiled down at him. "But I'm a kind demon—much kinder than sister… both of them. I'll give you the chance to answer my questions and spare you the torment. How does that sound? Does that sound nice? Hmm?" he asked with a babyish tone, pouting. "Is that okay sounding?"

Scowling in utter confoundment, Ben stared up at him. He had no idea what was going on or who this man even was. He did, however, now know that his captor was a demon. What did a demon want with *him*?

The demon pouted stubbornly. "You *can* nod," he said, prodding Ben's shoulder.

Instantly, all feeling returned to Ben's face and neck, but it went no further than his shoulders. He looked around frantically, trying to see where he was, but the four walls looked the same as the ceiling he'd been staring at. He set his irritated, hostile gaze on the demon and scowled, but as he opened his mouth to speak, no sound or word was uttered.

The demon started stroking Ben's head. "So funny." He sighed longingly. "Is that why big brother loves you so?"

Big brother? Ben was still without an idea as to what this man was nattering about.

"I wish *I* could create my own people, but Father says I'm not yet of age. He doesn't even like big brother, so I don't understand why he's allowed to walk around up there creating vampires and whatever else. Now that I have you, though, I could work out how he does it…" he realized, an excited look appearing on his face. "I could make my own vampires—I could make… dampires!"

Ben deadpanned. What a ridiculous name. What a ridiculous man. Had he been captured by an idiot? Clearly, that was the case.

"That's what he calls himself, right? Varn… Varen… Vampoodledee? Valacatalata… Vroooooooman—Vramvram?"

Now Ben was sure this demon was looking for Alucard. Had he extracted Ben in hopes to get information out of him? He wasn't at all willing to part with what he knew, and he was sure this idiot didn't possess the means to force him to talk.

"Varen, vampires…Detlaff, dampires. Do you like it?" he asked, looking down at Ben. "Ah, never mind." He patted Ben's head. "You're going to give Detlaff all the information he needs like a good little boy, aren't you?"

With a disgusted scowl, Ben shook his head to try and shake his hand off.

Detlaff scoffed and began to cackle. "You don't really have much of a choice, do you? I'll do worse than kill you, you know. Do you like being a vampire? I can probably find a way to undo it in roughly…seventeen hours. You'll be a boring, fleshy human again. Would you like that? Or!" he yelled, clapping his hands excitedly. "Or-or-or I could turn you into one of those wolf people. I could make you a demon, a ghoul. I could even turn you into a rat with five legs and three heads. That sounds fun! Can I do that?" he pleaded, wide-eyed. "Seven-foot rat," he imagined, his jaw slowly dropping in awe. "Three fat heads, seventeen eyes, teeth like a piranha—how beautiful would that be?"

Still deprived of his voice, all Ben could do was stare in horror.

"Gah, I'm drifting. Happens—my mind, he never shuts up!" Detlaff cried, laughing like a moron. He then resumed stroking Ben's head. "Tell me, little living dead creature of Aegisguard, where is big brother? I know you work for him. I know you're one of his favourite little pets!" he spat. "But…" he exhaled, "whenever I try to find him, there's nothing—nothing!" he cried, laughing again. "How is that possible? How is it that I can *know* he's up there, but I can't…find him? I should be able to sniff him out, I should be able to *feel* him—but it's like he doesn't exist! Can you believe that?!" he cried, harshly patting Ben's head.

Ben gritted his teeth in anger.

Detlaff sighed and rested his face in his hands as he gazed down at Ben. "Father says someone's got a perception filter going on up there, hiding big brother from all of us. We can't feel him, we can't see him, we can't *find* him. So I was sent to look for him—sisters are busy. One makes babies, other rules demons. Me? I'm Father's favourite. I'm free to do whatever I like, so long as I find big brother for him. And that's why I have *you.*" He smiled, prodding Ben's cheek. "Where is he?" he demanded sternly. "Do you know?"

He scowled, not at all interested in answering.

Detlaff started fiddling with Ben's hair. "Oh, big brother. He's so clever. No one can hide from Father—no one!" he yelled, slamming his fist onto the table, clipping Ben's arm with his claws. He gasped in shock and stroked the vampire's arm in sorrow but then exhaled and sighed again.

Ben wanted to attack—he wanted to wrap his hands around this lunatic's neck and break it. But how could he?

"Yet…here he is, walking around up there…" Detlaff continued with a dreamy tone, "…making vampires, building an empire. He was meant to help Father get into that world so *he* could build an empire, but the plan failed. Father's stuck *here*. He's a little…loopy doopy," he said with a pout, tapping his own head. "His siblings locked him away here to protect themselves—he gets really, *really* angry," he whispered. "But Father doesn't like that they locked him away. He thought making a baby and putting it in the world up there would create a link which would help him escape. But father was wrong. Putting his ethos in Aegisguard did nothing but make him weaker and gave him a son he didn't want. That's why he made *me*," he said, grinning. "*I'm* the son he wanted. I feel bad for big brother though, poor big brother."

Glaring at him, Ben listened. This guy seemed to be telling him everything. Evidently, he loved the sound of his voice, didn't he? He already told Ben that he was looking for Alucard, and it seemed as though this demon might just be Alucard's brother. He wasn't aware Alucard had any family, but he was sure if he listened a little longer, this idiot would answer *his* questions.

"Father didn't need to mate with some foul human to create us. Sisters are meant to continue Father's ethos bloodline; he wants demons *everywhere* ready for when he gets back to the world. Me? I am to find big brother and bring him to Father so he can kill him and take his ethos back. Lucky big brother didn't reproduce—more for me to have to find and kill. Father needs to be strong to enter the world; he's going to have to fight off his siblings—that's going to be *fun*!" he said, clapping excitedly, but he then sighed quietly. "*You* know where big brother is—you will *tell* me where he is." He scowled, leaning into Ben's disgusted face. "Tell me!" he screamed.

An amused smile found its way to Ben's face. How the hell was he supposed to tell him anything without a voice? Clearly, Detlaff had forgotten he couldn't speak. Despite the fact he might die here, he found it rather amusing that this guy was a complete and utter moron. Was he really looking to find Alucard? He wouldn't stand a chance against The Lord of Vampires.

Irritated, Detlaff snarled and climbed over Ben, his face just inches from his. "You look so…delicious," he breathed, inhaling deeply as he moved his face to Ben's neck. "I could eat you like a morning snack—like…cake, is that what humans call it?"

Ben tried to attack, but he still couldn't move.

"Do tell me where big brother is, please?" he pleaded, but Ben's silence irritated him further. He growled and gripped Ben's throat. "Is he up there?" he asked. "Nod."

He did no such thing.

Detlaff rolled his eyes. "You're boring," he complained, pouting like a stubborn child. He slapped the side of Ben's face and giggled as Ben turned back to face him. "I stole your voice," he said with a smile, tilting his head to the side. "You'll never speak another word. I can steal more—your sense of *touch*!" he yelled, harshly digging his claws into Ben's right side, making the vampire flinch and grunt painfully. "I can take away your ability to hear," he whispered as he picked up a small, thin blade and began to slowly move it into Ben's left ear. "I can also take away your ability to heal," he threatened.

His threats didn't alarm him. He remained silent, still, listening to Detlaff. Nothing would make him crack. He'd trained for things like this for years, and some mediocre, fumbling idiot wasn't going to break him.

With an annoyed sigh, Detlaff chucked the blade to the floor and glared at Ben's vacant face. "I should have picked up that Felix guy; he looked more fun than you. You just lay there, you don't panic or try to scream or anything—I *love* when they scream," he said, moving his face closer so that it was a mere inch from Ben's. "Won't you scream for me?" he requested, twisting his claws around, keeping them embedded in Ben's side.

Still, Ben remained silent, glaring at the demon, ignoring the pain.

Detlaff then ripped his hand from the vampire's side and stroked the side of Ben's face with his bloody fingers. "No bother. You'll scream louder than you've ever screamed," he said—he then abruptly dug his bloody claws into the side of Ben's face. "Show me…everything!" he yelled.

Agonizing pain swiftly consumed Ben. It was like a fire raging through his veins. He couldn't fight it…he couldn't resist it. He grimaced and yelled in torment as Detlaff dug through his thoughts as if he were flicking through the pages of a book. He tried to keep the demon from finding what he was seeking, but his years of training for such an event were futile. They meant nothing. This demon was so overpowering that he couldn't keep him from a single corner of his mind. All he could do was lay there and watch as Detlaff invaded his thoughts, his memories. Everything.

An astonished, pleased look plastered itself to Detlaff's face as he found the answers to all his questions. He laughed maniacally. "Vampires, werewolves, Aleksei—big brother!" he cried excitedly. "Demons—demon, sister—demon likes big brother. Ada also likes big brother! People for me to use against him," he said, grinning. He then exhaled a pleasured moan of satisfaction. "So much…so, so, so much!" he cried, licking his lips. "He looks…he looks so much like Father; he lives alone, works…many people respect him, so many people…friends," he paused to smirk. "You are…his friend?" he asked, pulling his claws from Ben's face. "Big brother likes you?"

Ben felt utterly defeated. His will had waned. It took Detlaff little to no effort to break his mind and extract every single piece of information he held about Alucard and his operations. Before, he tried so hard to show he wasn't and wouldn't become a liability. But now he seemed to be the *biggest* liability Alucard could possibly have.

Detlaff sat up, straddling Ben's lap. "Hmm…I could use you to lure big brother out," he schemed. "If I tell him I have his friend, he will come to me; big brother will *beg* me not to kill you," he sang. He dragged his hands over Ben's face and smiled contently.

"Such a pretty face, such a beautiful voice." He sighed, stroking his own throat. "You've been so helpful, so kind. If big brother comes for you, I'll let him keep you. I don't need anything else from you, after all." He then smirked, dragging his finger over Ben's lips. "Thank you," he said. Then, he climbed off Ben and stood beside him. "Will big brother come for you?"

He had no idea. Would Alucard come to his aid? Would he bargain with this mad creature to save his life? He just didn't know. All he could do was hope. He didn't want to die, but he was sure that, either way, he would. Alucard would kill him for allowing Detlaff to use him for information, and Detlaff would kill him because he no longer needed him. He'd much rather die closer to home, though, not in some dark, damp room.

Ben took his eyes off Detlaff and glared over at the wall to his left. Whatever might happen next, he wasn't sure, but he was quite certain he wasn't going to live much longer.

Chapter Fifty-One

— ⟨ † ⟩ —

Friday Morning

| Alucard |

It was already Friday morning. Alucard woke and glared over at the windows, debating whether he wanted to get up. He had to, though. Today, he'd be attending Ada's invite. He had to get Emil to prepare his outfit; he had to shower and make himself look presentable—for the occasion, of course. The woman? He could care less. Zalith, however…. He scowled at himself. Why was he even bothered? He didn't plan to go out of his way to look good for the sake of that demon. Why was he even thinking about him?

He rolled his eyes and sat up; he didn't want to look a mess and he felt like that was exactly what he looked like right now. His hair was in his face, and he was quite certain he appeared as though he hadn't slept in days. That might be because the last time he fed was last Sunday—five days ago. Thankfully, he hadn't been involved in anything too demanding or strength-waning, so his lack of blood hadn't forced him to act violently. It just made him feel like he was beyond dead.

With a lazy sigh, pulled himself out of bed, a sudden, lingering headache slowly beginning to worsen. Then, he made his way over to the black-oak dresser and grabbed the first shirt his hands could find. As he put it on, he left his bedroom and stood at the top of the stairs, trying to work out where Emil was. But his need for blood left his senses all over the place. He knew the butler was in his house, but where exactly?

As he frowned irritably, he gripped the landing's bannister and sighed. "Emil," he said without the strength to raise his voice.

The butler swiftly emerged from the doorway beneath the landing and looked up at him. "Yes, sir?" he asked pleasantly. "Your clothes will be ready for tonight, as you have asked."

"Is zhere any blood levt in zhe cabinet?"

Emil glanced into the room ahead of him. "I'll check, sir," he said, disappearing into the kitchen.

Alucard waited, tapping his claws on the bannister, and when Emil emerged back into the hall, he glared down at him.

"No, sir," the butler informed.

"*Grozav*," he grumbled, standing up straight. "You, come 'ere," he instructed, pointing at Emil.

Emil did as he was told and made his way up the stairs. He stood in front of Alucard and waited. "Yes, sir?"

The vampire hesitated. He thought that what he was about to do was cruel, but when did he start caring? Emil was paid to do whatever he asked. If the butler wanted to refuse, he would have said so when Alucard called him up there—Emil wasn't so thick that he'd not understand why Alucard called him upstairs after asking him to check if there was any blood left. So he disregarded his reluctance and snatched Emil's throat in his left hand. He then abruptly sunk his fangs into the butler's neck.

Emil flinched and grunted painfully but remained where he was, allowing the vampire to slowly gulp down his blood.

Alucard had no intention of killing his butler, but he'd been deprived of blood far too long and felt he might just accidentally end Emil's life. He didn't care, though. If this butler died, he could just hire another in his place. His self-restraint wasn't lacking, he just felt no need to be careful. The moment he tasted the man's blood, he could feel his headache waning, his strength returning, and the same high he would always experience when feeding off someone accompanied. He didn't want to stop—he didn't *need* to stop.

But then a familiar knock came at the door. Alucard scowled and pulled his fangs from Emil's neck, snarling as he shoved the butler away and glared down at the door. It was obviously Attila; he always knocked the same way. What could *he* possibly want? Alucard set his eyes back on Emil, who was standing with his back against the wall, his face almost as pale as his own. He didn't care. He scowled expectantly, waiting for the butler to do his job.

Without argument, the butler made his way down the stairs as best he could, stumbled over to the door, and pulled it open, allowing Attila to enter.

Attila glanced at the barely-standing butler, scoffed in amusement, and then looked up at Alucard. "Am I interrupting?" he asked in Dor-Sanguian.

"Vhat do you vant?" Alucard grumbled, wiping the blood from his mouth with the back of his hand. But there was a little more on his face than he thought. He dragged his fingers down to his neck, where some of the blood had trickled. So, he pulled the handkerchief from his trouser pocket and started cleaning his skin as best as he could.

"Today is the last day I'll be here, so I thought I'd come by and check in, say goodbye, offer to help with Ada again," Attila answered as Emil shut the door behind him.

"I told you zhat I already 'ave somevone."

"Okay, but what's the harm in another set of hands? I have nothing else to do. I went to look for that Ben guy, but he's not at the castle, so I assumed he was off on the prison run."

Alucard frowned, glowering at him. "Zhen go and look vor 'im. I'm busy."

Attila sighed and said, "All right. I need the papers before tomorrow; I was supposed to ask on Wednesday, but you sort of kicked me out."

Alucard rolled his eyes. "Zhey're in my study. Go and get zhem yourselv."

"Which one?" Attila called.

"Up," Alucard grumbled, pointing up at the ceiling. Then, he headed back towards his room to shower and get ready. Zalith would be arriving soon.

| Zalith |

Meanwhile, Zalith made his way towards Alucard's manor in a black suit, dressed for the occasion he'd been invited to accompany the vampire to. Where a vacant stare would usually rest, there was instead a smile on his face. He hadn't long come to realize how much he enjoyed Alucard's company, and the opportunity to spend any additional time with him brought a strange but appealing feeling of contentedness to him.

As well as Alucard's volatile disposition and entertaining reactions, Zalith found that he thoroughly enjoyed the vampire's company. There was comfort in it, and he'd not waste a single opportunity to be in his presence. He wasn't sure of what to make of it, but he *was* sure that Alucard was someone he'd like to try and keep around.

The demon followed the path with only the vampire on his mind. He was looking forward to seeing him and what the day might bring them. Alucard invited him to an event hosted by Ada, but he wasn't aware of what the event was—either way, he was sure he was going to enjoy it. Why hadn't Alucard replied to his response when he invited him, though? He hoped to have the opportunity to annoy him, but the vampire failed to respond and give him the chance to. No matter; he'd get to see what Alucard was wearing today any moment now.

As he made his way into the vampire's manor grounds, he couldn't help but notice Sergiu, the groundskeeper, speaking to what anyone else might consider himself. Zalith, however, knew what telepathic ethos felt and looked like, and that was exactly what was going on. He didn't care to pry, though. It wasn't his business. He took his eyes off the groundskeeper, walked past the fountain, and approached the front door. Once he reached it, he knocked quietly and waited.

After a few moments, the door unlocked from inside. Zalith hoped to see Alucard, but he already knew the man answering the door was human—and barely alive. As Emil opened the door and stared at him, Zalith eyed him for half a moment. The man was as pale as ice, and he looked as though he hadn't slept in years, barely standing without support from the door he was clinging onto so dearly. It seemed as though Alucard had taken to snacking on his staff. Zalith found that a little funny.

"Please, come in, sir," Emil said slowly, holding out his arm when he stepped aside to invite him in. As Zalith walked in, he closed the door behind him. "Lord Aleksei is preparing for the day. He often asks his guests to wait in the lounge," he explained, holding his arm towards the lounge.

"Thank you," Zalith said politely before making his way in there. He sat on the leather couch and stared over at the windows, waiting for Alucard to join him.

However, the sound of footsteps making their way down the stairs soon caught his attention, and he frowned strangely. It wasn't Alucard who was coming down into the hall, that was for sure. So he took his eyes off the window and looked into the hall, watching as someone he'd never met before emerged into it.

He was a vampire—obviously—and he was paler than Alucard, which Zalith hadn't thought possible. The man stood around six foot two, and his hair was repulsively long, black, and greasy, tied into a braid with a black ribbon. He was rather ridiculously dressed in a black, frilly-collared suit intended for a masquerade ball. His eyes were a deep, soulless black, and as he set them on Zalith, the demon had to restrain himself from snarling in revolt. This vampire's face closely resembled that of a bulldog; his hair ends were split, and it looked as though he might not have washed it in a long while.

The dog-faced man leaned on the lounge door frame. *"Cine esti tu?"*

Zalith frowned. "Excuse me?"

"Oh, you are Deiganish. Many Deiganish come by lately. You are…waiting for Alucard?"

"I am," he replied, a disdainful tone in his voice as he looked away.

The guy frowned strangely. "Hmph…who are you? I have not seen you here before."

Zalith wasn't interested in talking to this man. He did, however, feel as though it would be amusing to irritate him. Whoever he was, he already seemed rather vexed, and Zalith felt as though his presence in Alucard's home was confounding to this man. He couldn't help but wonder, though…who was this vampire to Alucard? He was sure he'd find out. He asked him who he was—did he want to tell him? Although it might be safe to name himself in Aegisguard, he didn't feel like letting this vampire know his name just yet.

He rested his right leg over his left and slouched back on the couch. "I'm a friend of Alucard's."

"Friend? Alucard not have many of those. As far as I was aware, I thought I was only friend. He never mention you."

"Well, he has never spoken of you, either."

"Hmm," the man uttered with a frown, crossing his arms. "I'm Attila, his best friend. What you do here? Business?"

"Evidently—" he paused and sighed, glancing over at him with a condescending look, "—I was invited."

Attila scoffed and snarled at him. "Disgusting, loathsome demon. Learn manners."

Zalith smiled and slowly turned his head to glare at him. "And you should learn to watch your mouth. If you are not careful, you might just lose your tongue," he said with animosity in his voice.

Attila scowled, stood up straight, and gritted his teeth in revolt—

"Vhat are you doing?" came Alucard's voice.

With a look of dread on his face, Attila looked up the stairs, and as Alucard reached the bottom of them, the dog-faced vampire hung his head.

Alucard wore a long-sleeved, black fitted shirt and black suit trousers. A confounded look sat on his pale face as he glared at Attila, and his hair was damp and dripping onto the white towel over his shoulders. And as he looked over at the demon, he stared in startle.

Zalith smirked, admiring Alucard from the couch he was still sitting on. "Good morning, handsome."

A look of embarrassment smothered Alucard's face as he turned his back to Zalith. He pouted for half a moment but then glared at Attila. "Did you get vhat you came vor?" he asked irritably.

"Yes. Who is that?" he asked, nodding over at Zalith.

"Zhat is Zaliv. I told you about 'im," Alucard replied. "Go. I zon't need you 'ere anymore."

Attila glanced at Zalith and scowled in disgust. He then looked at Alucard and nodded. "I write to you once I have infiltrated council."

Alucard waved his hand in dismissal, and as Attila left the house, he scowled over at Zalith. "Vhat are you doing 'ere so early?" he questioned. "I told you to come for dusk."

Zalith smiled. "You didn't specify what time you wanted me to arrive. I thought I'd come early so we could have some time to socialize."

Rolling his eyes, Alucard made his way into the lounge and slumped down in the armchair across from the demon.

"You speak fondly of me in my absence?" Zalith asked him.

"I speak *of* you," Alucard grumbled. "Vhen necessary."

"All positive things, I hope."

"Vhat did Attila vant?"

"He was interrogating me as if he was the man of the house. If I were your best friend, as he is, I wouldn't be so rude to your guests," he said, smiling.

"Attila is *not* my best vriend," Alucard snarled irritably. "'E vorks vor me."

Just then, Emil stood in the doorway. "Sir, your clothes are ready," he called weakly, barely able to keep himself standing without holding onto the door frame.

Glancing at him, Alucard nodded and waved his hand in dismissal.

Zalith then smiled curiously... *and* deviously as he noticed the fang wounds in the butler's neck. "Do you make a habit of eating your help, Alucard?"

"Mind your business," he warned.

His smile only grew. "Will you make a meal of me if I turn my back?"

The vampire scowled. "No."

"Do you want to?" he asked suggestively.

Alucard frowned as if to detest, but embarrassment then seemed to smother his face. "No."

"Are you certain? It looked to me as though you just hesitated."

"Shut up or go 'ome. I'm not in zhe mood vor your estranged 'umour today," Alucard warned.

"Then what *are* you in the mood for, vampire?"

"Making your vace look noving like a face," he growled.

"With *your* face?"

The vampire grunted in frustration and gave up. He stood up and made his way over to the entrance hall.

"And where might you be going?" Zalith asked, smirking.

"Avay vrom you," he sneered and then disappeared upstairs.

Zalith grinned and wondered... should he follow? He felt as though he usually would, but with Alucard, he felt an unusual desire to be considerate of the vampire's feelings. So, he remained where he was and set his eyes back on the windows again, waiting for Alucard to come back. He was *already* enjoying his time here; all the dismay and weight that sat on his shoulders withered the moment he saw Alucard, and the vampire's ability to make him feel as though everything was okay for a while was something he *greatly* appreciated about him.

And it was a feeling he hoped he'd get to experience for a *long* time.

Chapter Fifty-Two

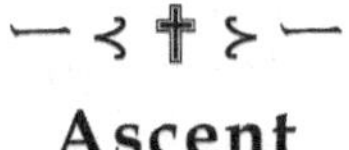

Ascent

| Alucard |

In his room, Alucard finished drying his hair and chucked his towel over one of the dressers. Zalith never failed to annoy him, that was for sure—but it wasn't Zalith's words that had him so vexed. It was the fact that he found himself almost *enjoying* the demon's confounding suggestions. Why did he find Zalith funny? Why did this demon make him struggle to hold back an amused smile? And why did his greetings and compliments make him feel such embarrassment?

He scowled at his reflection as he started combing his hair. Zalith made him feel so many things he thought he'd never feel before, and that list was growing. However, he didn't feel the need to tell Zalith to stop. He was enjoying the demon's company more and more each time they met, and despite Zalith's ability to confuse him so profoundly, he only found himself wanting to spend even more time with him.

But he refused to dwell on his thoughts for too long. Zalith was downstairs, and the last thing he wanted to do was spend time with him while trying to work out what he might feel. So, he finished his hair, pulled on his blazer, and made his way back downstairs.

When he stepped into the lounge, he looked at Zalith, who was still on the couch. "Ada's invite isn't until dusk. Ve can go and do someving vhilst ve vait since you insisted on getting 'ere so early."

"What do you have in mind?" Zalith asked, standing up.

"Coffee," he sneered. "Let's go."

"Yes, sir," Zalith replied with a suggestive smile on his face as he made his way over to Alucard.

Alucard snatched his cape from the coat rack and pulled it on over his shoulders as he pulled the door open.

The demon followed him outside, and when the vampire pulled the door shut, he turned to face him. "Who is Attila?"

"I zon't know vhy zhat bovers you," Alucard replied, leading the way to the stables. "But if you must know, 'e and I 'ave been associates vor many 'undreds of years. I knew 'im bevore I became a vampire," he revealed. But then he frowned, unsure of why he felt so open to answering Zalith's question. Strangely enough, he'd started losing his hesitance to tell this demon about himself.

"He seems to believe that you and he are…best friends," he said, smirking.

"I alveady told you, zhat's *not* zhe case," Alucard grumbled, stopping outside the stables. As he caught sight of Sergiu, he waved his hand and looked back at Zalith. "I do not make an 'abit of making vriends, especially not vith people who vork vor me."

"Of course," Zalith said.

Once Sergiu arrived with the two horses, Alucard sighed and took Sebastian's reins from him. The groundskeeper then handed the brown mare's reins to Zalith and disappeared back into the stables. The pair mounted their horses and began their journey towards the city, leaving the manor's grounds and following the path forward.

Alucard glanced over at Zalith as they travelled. "'As anyving 'appened at all since ve last met?"

"No," Zalith replied. "Nothing worth discussing. And you? I hear Ben is making a name for himself."

"Ben is usevul," Alucard agreed. "Does vhat 'e's told, zoesn't annoy me. Vhat more could I ask vor?"

Zalith smirked. "You tell me."

Rolling his eyes, Alucard glared ahead at the city in the distance. "I just 'ope 'e zoesn't screw up."

"I'm sure he won't," the demon said with a smile, also looking ahead.

And then, they continued their journey in silence.

| Zalith |

When they reached the city, Zalith smiled over at Alucard. He was looking forward to spending more time with him here; this time, he planned to get to know the vampire some more. And maybe…just *maybe* he'd get him to understand that he was flirting.

They stowed their horses in one of the stables and headed up the street to the same café they visited before. Alucard led the way to one of the outside tables, pulled out a chair, and sat down. Then, as Zalith sat down, the waitress came out, took both their orders, and disappeared back inside.

"So, how has *your* week been?" Zalith asked as he rested his arms on the table.

The vampire sighed and rested his left arm on the table, staring down the street opposite them. "Busy," he answered.

"Oh?"

"Vell, I 'ad to go to zhe prison and see who veplaced Ki. Zhis guy zidn't know who Dirk vas, and Dirk is zhe vone vesponsible vor arranging 'uman-velated affairs. So, I killed 'im and sent vone of zhe 'uman council members to do 'is job until Dirk gets back."

Zalith nodded in response. He couldn't get enough of Alucard's accented voice. He felt as though he could sit there for *hours* just listening to him.

"Zhe council all started calling me sir; I assume Dirk veturned to zhem avter our last converence and told zhem vhat 'appened. Zhey all looked avraid, per'aps zhey vhought I might kill zhem. I vould if I zidn't need zhem. Zhey all bover me, tire me, and irritate me. I 'ate 'umans."

"Don't we all?" Zalith concurred with a smile.

Alucard glanced at him and frowned. "Yes…" he agreed but then turned away from him.

"I assume there is more?"

"Zhere is alvays more," Alucard mumbled. "Velix vas zhe vone to make zhe call to 'ire zhis new guy, so I 'ad to go and make an example of 'im."

"You killed him."

"Naturally. But I'll vake 'im up at some point."

The demon then frowned. "Wake him up?" he asked, unsure of what that might mean.

"I zidn't permanently kill 'im. 'E made a mistake, but a small vone. 'E just 'ired some vandom 'uman to try and make my life easier. I vouldn't kill somevone vor zhat. No, 'e is just sleeping."

"I see," Zalith said, smiling. "You positively confound me once again, vampire."

"Vhatever." He sighed and rested his arms on the table. "Velix is veird, zhough."

"Weird?"

"Ben told me 'e caught 'im sneaking avound my 'alf of zhe castle. 'E said 'e vas looking vor mice, but ve zon't 'ave mice. I couldn't be bovered to question 'im zhere and zhen, so I'll do zhat vhenever I decide to vake 'im up."

Zalith then frowned in concern. "Well, be careful; his behaviour sounds suspicious. He could be up to something."

The vampire then scoffed as if he was offended. "Vhat? Do you not vink I know zhat? Vhy do you care?"

The demon smiled. "I'm simply looking out for my friend."

"Vell, zon't," Alucard warned him. "I can make my own judgements."

"Of course," he said with a nod.

Just then, the waitress made her way out, handed them both their coffee and left once again.

Preparing his drink, Zalith looked over at Alucard. "Is there more?" he asked, hoping there was.

As he always did, Alucard poured an immense amount of sugar into his coffee and started stirring it. "I 'ad a conversation vith Attila. Many opportunities 'ave presented zhemselves to me. I von't tell you, of course."

"Of course."

"And zhen I received zhe invite vrom Ada," he said and sipped his drink.

Zalith leaned his arms on the table and frowned curiously. "What exactly is this invite to?"

"If I knew zhat, I vould 'ave told you."

Zalith nodded. "I can only assume you'll be dressing in a suit," he said, smirking. "What *will* you be wearing?"

Alucard shrugged. "Just someving…vormal," he said, a strange frown appearing on his face as Zalith slowly moved his foot against the vampire's ankle. He scowled down at his drink. "I zon't know vhat she might 'ave planned, but ve should be veady vor anyving."

Staring at him with a smirk, Zalith nodded. "As always."

As the demon began moving his foot up the side of his leg, Alucard scowled confoundedly and glanced at him. Zalith's smile forced him to look away, and as he did, he pouted stubbornly.

"Zhis could be an ambush," the vampire uttered.

"It very well could be," Zalith agreed, smirking suggestively.

"Or she could be vanting to vorm peace," he mumbled, but as Zalith's foot reached his knee, he shuffled around uncomfortably. "Stop zhat," he warned.

"Stop what?" Zalith asked, sipping from his cup as if he were oblivious to his own actions.

Alucard pouted and glared down the street, keeping his eyes off the demon.

Amused by Alucard's reaction, Zalith rested his left leg over his right. He didn't want to make him uncomfortable. He took another sip from his coffee and sighed quietly. "If this invitation is an ambush, what do we do?" he asked with a sterner tone to his voice.

Taking his eyes off the street opposite them, Alucard glanced at him. "Ve kill zhem. I'm tired of Ada, and if she zoesn't vant to call a truce, zhen I vill kill 'er. I 'ave var more important vings to be doing zhan vunning avound trying to convince zhis stupid voman to calm down."

"Understandable. Another night of killing werewolves with you; we seem to be making a habit of this, Alucard."

"Vonce she's dealt vith, I can vocus more on zhe vampires zhat I've been bringing vrom your vorld. Zhey're all living in zhis city now."

"Yes, I remember you telling me you had to move them out of your castle before Ada's possible attack. It's not the *only* thing I remember about our last meeting, though," he said, smiling.

Alucard looked over at him. "Vhat?"

He smirked and leaned closer. "I remember you insisting that I *didn't* make you uncomfortable when I grabbed your ass," he said, slowly moving his foot over Alucard's leg once again.

As the vampire's nervousness became very evident on his face, he glared down at his drink in silence.

"Is it safe to assume that you enjoy my attention?" Zalith flirted.

The vampire didn't answer him.

Zalith was able to assume Alucard's answer in spite of his silence, and it only made him smile more. But strangely enough, knowing Alucard enjoyed his attention made him feel more content than victorious. Why? He stopped dragging his foot up the vampire's leg and sipped from his drink. He already knew he cared more for this vampire than he may have originally thought, but his liking for Alucard was beginning to become something he felt might be more than a simple crush.

Whenever he thought about bedding Alucard as he initially planned, he felt undeniably reluctant. He hadn't followed him upstairs this morning; if it had been anyone else he was trying to seduce, he was sure he would have followed them. But not Alucard. Why not Alucard? Why did he feel the need to respect him? Why did he wish to ensure the vampire was comfortable? It felt so very strange.

The demon placed his coffee down and rested his arms on the table, staring at Alucard. He always found such enjoyment in admiring and listening to him, and he was quite sure that this little game of his was becoming more than a distraction from his life. Alucard made him feel genuinely relaxed and happy; spending time with this vampire had become the literal highlight of his weeks, and he was confident he'd rather not spend or give his time to anyone else, especially not as often as he wanted to spend it with Alucard.

A blissful smile made its way to his face. Outside of the flirting and looking for specific reactions, Zalith found that this vampire was something so very unique. He didn't want to let him out of his sight, that was for sure. So, he'd do his best to make sure he and Alucard would remain as they were—or perhaps…more? He lost his smile and looked down at his drink with a perplexed frown on his face. Was that what this was? Did he feel this way because he wanted more? Of course he did. But not in a way to feel a sense of victory. Alucard wasn't just some conquest to him anymore—he couldn't be.

"Vhy are *you* so quiet?" Alucard then asked with a sceptical look on his face.

Zalith lifted his head to look at him and said, "No particular reason. I was just thinking."

"About?"

He smirked. "You."

Alucard looked away and frowned, clearly unsure of what to say.

But that was when the sky rumbled. A familiar, horrifying crash of crimson lightning hit the ground in the middle of the street, sending the people screaming and running in every direction. Zalith was unshaken, but as he stared at Alucard, who flinched and shot to his feet the very moment the sky made a sound, he frowned in confusion. If he didn't know better, he'd say Alucard was afraid and moments from attempting to flee. Was he?

Alucard stared at the place the lightning struck, watching as Damien formed in the street. The Daegelus folded his wings against his back, and a smug look appeared on his face as the people he almost killed dropped to their knees and began mumbling words of prayer and admiration. But his eyes were fixed on the vampire and the demon.

As Damien made his way over, Zalith glanced at Alucard. "Are you okay?" he asked quietly.

Alucard didn't answer. He stood there... frozen.

"Eladarin, what a surprise," Damien called pleasantly, but as he set his gaze on Alucard, a look of revolt clung to his face. "Move," he said.

The vampire stepped aside, watching Damien as he sat in his seat and made himself comfortable.

"What is it that you might be doing here?" the Daegelus asked, looking at Zalith.

"Discussing business," he replied.

"Surely you can do that when you meet every fortnight." Damien scowled skeptically and looked up at Alucard. Then, he slowly set his eyes back on Zalith. "You wouldn't be trying to add my Aleksei to your list of accomplishments, would you, Eladarin?"

Zalith smiled. "No."

Damien rested his arms on the table and frowned condescendingly at the demon. "Tell me, Eladarin, do you know what Disavowed are?"

A perplexed frown made its way onto Zalith's face. Why was he asking that? There had to be a reason; there always was with Damien. So he'd answer. He did, however, take a short moment to glance at Alucard, who had a very uncomfortable look on his face. Why?

Zalith frowned and set his eyes on Damien. "I do," he confirmed.

"Then explain to me: what is a Disavowed?"

"Disavowed are demons who have had their wings stripped and suffered the worst kind of punishment any demon can experience, often at the hands of a higher-ranking demon. To lose one's wings is to lose one's right to call themselves a demon and affiliate themselves with other demons. Disavowed are seen as a disgrace by all other demons and will be treated as such," he answered with a vacant look on his face. He was quite sure Damien asked him as a threat. Did Damien plan on taking his wings as punishment? But for what?

With a smile on his face, Damien then looked up at Alucard. "Did you hear that Aleksei?"

"Yes," he answered sullenly.

Damien grinned cruelly and looked back at Zalith. "Now, tell me again, what are you doing with my boy?"

Zalith was convinced that Damien wasn't at all pleased seeing them together outside of their work. Of course, he didn't care how Damien felt. He did, on the other hand, care what Alucard might feel. Right now, the vampire looked unusually afraid, like he knew something was coming. Dread clung to his face, and it was unlike anything Zalith saw before. Alucard *was* afraid; that was no longer hard to tell. But why? Why did Alucard seem so fearful of what might be said?

It didn't matter. Alucard was afraid, and that was all the motivation Zalith needed to make sure he did his best to keep Damien calm and satisfied. "I asked to meet him. Something came up in Eltaria, and I'd much rather discuss delicate matters in person. That's all."

"Is it?" Damien challenged.

"It is."

He then grinned, baring his four fangs. "Then tell me, Eladarin, why is it that I hear you ended up in Aleksei's residence and spent the night drinking? Socializing, I might add. Was *that* business?"

"It was."

Damien scowled and looked at Alucard. "Answer."

Alucard opened his mouth to speak—

"I asked once again," Zalith interrupted. "I had matters to discuss, and then I suggested we drink. I got a little carried away. It will not happen again."

The vampire frowned in confusion; if he could, Zalith was sure that the vampire would ask why he was lying to Damien and risking punishment.

Damien growled, "So, you *have* been trying to seduce my Aleksei, haven't you?"

Zalith smiled. "You know what I'm like."

The Daegelus scoffed in amusement. "I do, and as much as I might like to see you try—and fail—you have work to do. How many vampires are here now?" he asked, looking at Alucard.

"Vorty-two," Alucard immediately answered.

"Five relocations... forty-two vampires—I knew you were weak, Aleksei, but this is a new low," he snarled, standing up—

"That would be me once again," Zalith said, still smiling. "I could only bring so many for him to take back. I'll be sure to bring more next time we meet."

Damien seemed to be searching for any small excuse to demean Alucard, and Zalith didn't like that at all. Alucard did so much for the people around him and expected nothing in return, and yet Damien was blind to it.

The Daegelus scoffed and glared down at Zalith. "Keep your mouth shut," he warned. "I'm done with you."

Zalith scowled as the Daegelus turned his back on him. But he remained silent. He dared not anger him.

"What have you been doing all this time?" Damien asked, glowering at Alucard. "Drinking? Socializing? I hear you have a little thing going on with the werewolves. Didn't I warn you to leave such pointless shit alone?"

Alucard didn't answer.

"You are here to do a job for me, and once you are done, you will do another job for me. You will continue to do what I say, and if you stray from that even the slightest, I will take from you," he warned, snatching Alucard's throat. "I will take, and you will suffer. I've left you alone too long, haven't I? You seem to have gained confidence in my absence."

Alucard looked as though he had no idea what Damien was talking about.

"I think it's high time I reminded you of the rules you so easily forget," the Daegelus snarled.

Before Alucard could say or do anything, Damien stretched out his wings and hastily propelled himself into the sky, pulling Alucard with him.

Zalith abruptly felt what could only be an instinct to say or do something to express his disapproval, but he couldn't. Not only was it not his place, but he felt his intrusion might make whatever this was worse for Alucard. So... he sat there, staring up at the clouds, and listened.

| **Alucard** |

When he stopped a few miles above the thickening grey clouds, Damien glared into Alucard's mortified eyes as he gripped his throat in his right hand. "What are you doing with Zalith?" he demanded. "And don't you dare even think about lying to me. I'll know."

"I asked 'im to come and 'elp me deal vith a verevolf I've been 'aving trouble vith," he answered, staring into Damien's skeptical, evil eyes.

"Did I not tell you to keep out of such pointless affairs?" he snarled.

"Zhey vhreaten my 'ome—and my people."

"Your people?" He laughed. "You don't have people, Aleksei; you have ugly little dead things that follow you around. They are nought but walking corpses born of your revolting blood. They are not people."

He didn't reply.

"You are alone. You will *be* alone. If I have to kill every single disgusting little vampire you have ever made, then I will. I only let you keep them around because it is rather amusing to watch the humans fear them. But if these vampires are the reason for your confidence, then I will take them away. Do you understand?"

"Yes."

"What made you think you could disobey me? Why do you feel as though you can socialize?"

Once again, Alucard had nothing to say. He didn't *know* what to say.

"Zalith…is he…your friend?"

"No," Alucard instantly answered.

The Daegelus scowled, flapping his wings behind his back to keep them both in the air. He then tightened his grip on Alucard's throat. "Get the vampires here—fast. If I hear of you affiliating yourself with people outside of your work again, I will kill them. All of them. You know I like Zalith; if I have to kill him because of you, I will not be the least bit happy," he threatened. "Get the fuck out of my sight," he then snarled.

Damien let go of Alucard and crashed his foot into the vampire's stomach, sending him plummeting down the world below.

And there was nothing Alucard could do to spare himself from the pain he knew would come once he hit the ground. But he deserved it, didn't he?

Chapter Fifty-Three

⸺ ⟨ † ⟩ ⸺

Stare

| **Alucard** |

Alucard grunted painfully as he slowly sat up. Shards of sharp, broken slate were embedded in his arms, and one rather large piece in his right side. Yellow alfalfa dangled into the seven-foot-deep crater that had been created upon his collision with the ground, and all he could think about was what Zalith's opinion of him might be now.

Zalith saw him act so weak in front of Damien, and so afraid. That was surely going to affect whatever it was they might be becoming, and that made him feel more upset than he did about Damien's threats. He gripped a shard of slate and yanked it out of his right arm. Even now he found himself thinking about Zalith and what *he* might think. Why? Why did he care? He scowled and pulled another shard from his arm, dropping it to the ground. He couldn't help but wonder, though…why had Zalith lied to try and protect him from Damien's anger? Why would someone like Zalith risk themselves to keep him out of the line of fire? He didn't know, and he didn't want to think too much about it. He just wanted to go home.

When he heard who could only be Zalith approaching, he struggled to his feet. He then turned around and slowly limped out of the crater, setting his eyes on Zalith, who was making his way through the field towards him. He didn't feel like talking to him, though. Damien's appearance made him feel miserable, and all he wanted to do was sleep. His body ached, his thoughts were dismayed, and he was sure that his face told Zalith both of those things.

"Are you okay?" Zalith asked, stopping in front of the vampire.

He didn't answer. Instead, he pulled the last shard of slate from his side and irritably chucked it to the ground before walking past the demon.

Zalith followed in utter silence until they reached Alucard's manor. But when they approached the front door, he broke the quiet. "I'm sorry if my presence here caused Damien to feel the need to hurt you."

Alucard frowned sullenly as he pushed his door open and led the way inside. He pulled off his cape and chucked it over the table before making his way into the lounge. He didn't know what to say. It wasn't Zalith's fault, and he wanted to make sure he understood that, but he couldn't find the motivation to speak. Damien somehow knew he and Zalith were spending time together, and he felt he should find out how before Zalith was killed because of it—or perhaps he should just stop seeing the demon outside of their work.

He didn't want to do that. He thought of that conclusion before, and it pained him. He profoundly enjoyed spending time with Zalith—it was the only thing he looked forward to, and he didn't want to lose that. He didn't want to lose whatever it was he and Zalith were. But Damien would never let it continue. The only way to keep Zalith around would be to cease their social calls and continue to work on Damien's mission.

With a despondent frown, he stopped in front of the lounge window and tried to find the words he would need to tell Zalith they had to stop meeting. But as he turned to face the demon, his attempts to do so withered. He couldn't send him away. Despite everything that happened and everything that *might* happen, he still couldn't ignore what this man made him feel.

What *did* Zalith make him feel? Why did he feel so reluctant to let go? Why did he feel as though he would continue to risk both their lives just to spend time with him? He didn't understand; it confused him so much that it had him frozen where he stood.

He should have told Zalith to keep their arrangement professional so very long ago, but he hadn't. Now, they were friends, and he was sure that, even without the fact of Zalith possibly already wanting them to share something more, he wanted to see what they might become. No one had ever managed to make him question his thoughts. No one had ever made him think of them so often and with such confliction. And no one had managed to make him forget the depravity of his life—until now.

Alucard took his eyes off the approaching demon to glare out of the window. He didn't know what to do for the first time in a long time, and it made him feel…lost.

Reaching him, Zalith slowly placed his hand on the vampire's shoulder. "Alucard," he said quietly. "What's wrong?"

Alucard took his eyes off the window and stared at him. "Noving," he lied.

Zalith half-smiled and glanced at the small cut on Alucard's right cheek. He seemed to hesitate for a moment…but slowly moved his hand from the vampire's shoulder and placed it on the side of his face. He waited, and when Alucard didn't move away, he gently dragged his thumb over the wound, wiping the blood away.

Alucard didn't struggle, argue, or refuse. He strangely felt no need to tell the demon not to touch him. He couldn't be sure why, though—there was nothing he hated more than unwanted physical contact. But he found that he now welcomed any sort of contact from Zalith. He didn't make him feel uncomfortable or disgust him, he just made him feel…different—a strange but comforting kind of different. Zalith was very obviously not afraid of Damien; why else would he have taken it upon himself to lie in an attempt to save him the stress? Zalith tried to defend him, both witnessing and understanding that made Alucard feel a whole new kind of comfortable.

He stared at the demon's face, trying to work out what he should say or do. But nothing came to mind. He just stared.

Zalith stared back at him…and after a few moments, a disheartened look settled on the demon's face. He tilted his head to the left just a little and parted his lips to speak, but instead, he looked almost as if he was realizing something. "Why are you so sad?" he asked, his voice almost a whisper.

Alucard frowned. "Vhat?"

The demon kept his hand on the side of the vampire's face. "Your eyes—they're so sad," he said quietly.

There were no words he knew of to tell Zalith why he was sad. All he could do was stand there and stare, lost in his own thoughts. Zalith was so close; he had his hand on his face, and he seemed to only be moving closer. Alucard felt no need to attack, move, or disapprove. Even when the demon began moving his face closer, Alucard thought he wanted to see where it might be headed.

But when Zalith's face was but a mere inch from his own, Alucard snapped out of his moment of calm. His nervousness and confusion returned so overpoweringly that he couldn't stand it. Did he want this? Did he need this? He wasn't sure, but he was certain that he wasn't ready to find out.

Before Zalith could kiss him, Alucard frowned in hesitation and moved away from him. "I…'ave to go upstairs."

Zalith frowned in disappointment. "Okay."

Alucard then left the lounge and headed upstairs, leaving Zalith alone. He needed time to think everything over, and that was what he was going to do.

He went into his study and slumped down in his chair. He stared vacantly at his desk, trying to calm and make sense of his thoughts. Lately, he found his thoughts to be so confusing, so strange, and so erratic, and it was all because of Zalith. *That demon.* It hadn't taken Alucard long to admit to himself that Zalith was his friend, and upon finding out that this demon might want something more than friendship with him, he almost immediately allowed himself to think of what it might be like to share that with him. Why?

The vampire stared endlessly. He undeniably liked Zalith—a lot. Alucard didn't give his time to just anyone, especially not his free time. But he gave it to Zalith, and he was sure he'd give him all his time if he asked—even if he didn't ask. He *wanted* to spend as much of his time as he could with him. Zalith made him feel strangely content; this demon had a way of making him forget his stress, loneliness, and sorrow. Why?

Zalith made him feel so confused, so estranged. Alucard hated physical contact, yet he didn't mind allowing Zalith to touch him—in fact, he felt as though he almost welcomed it not too long ago. The demon touched his face, something he would have killed anyone else for. But not Zalith. Why?

Why? Why? Why? All he could do was ask himself why. He didn't know. But he had to know; he had to try and understand. Why was Zalith breaking all his rules? All his boundaries? Why was he okay with it? Why did he welcome it? He'd never felt so confused—he'd never felt this way because of anyone before... and he'd never felt this way for *anyone*. He'd never found himself wishing to spend time with someone. Never would he have thought he'd be inviting someone along on his private, personal business. And never would he have thought he'd allow someone quite like Zalith to have him sitting in his study so profoundly confused. So *lost*.

He was over trying to tell himself that they were simply business partners. They were friends, and if Zalith wanted more than that, Alucard felt he might just be inclined to accept. Above all else, Zalith was unafraid of Damien. He didn't seem to care that Damien treated him so awfully. Zalith didn't force Alucard to do things he couldn't or didn't want to. He tried to defend him in front of Damien—more than once in the same sitting. He didn't pry into anything Damien-related, either. Zalith made him smile, he made him feel as though he wasn't alone, and he was on Alucard's mind every second of every day. It hadn't taken long for Zalith to snatch his attention, and now, he was utterly focused on him and what he might want with him.

Despite Damien's threat, Alucard didn't want to send Zalith away. He didn't want to give up what they currently had. He wanted to keep spending time with him, he wanted to keep seeing him, and he wanted to see where his current feelings might take him— take *them*. If he could work out one thing for certain, it was that he *cared* about Zalith, and he *wanted* Zalith to remain in his life—he might even *need* him. In the short time he'd known this demon, he felt both his loneliness and sorrow fade. He hadn't even given the iniquity of his life a second thought when in Zalith's presence. That had to mean something. That had to prove that what he felt might be something more than a simple friendship.

He sighed quietly and leaned back in his seat. Zalith tried to kiss him. At the time, he felt he had wanted it to happen. But his nervousness got the better of him. He was only just coming to terms with the fact that he might feel something for this man. He'd never imagined himself forming any kind of relationship with anyone, man or woman.

But there he was thinking about it with Zalith. It felt right, though. He couldn't deny that. Zalith made him feel so many new things—things he enjoyed feeling despite his confounding reactions. But he felt as though he wasn't yet ready to take a leap and do something as intimate as kissing him.

These feelings, though—what should he do with them? What if Zalith's attraction to him was something that wouldn't last? What if he flirted and smiled because he was bored? Alone? He didn't want to risk allowing himself to fall for a man who might become tired of him. He was yet to be convinced that Zalith's attraction could result in something that would last and not something that would stay aflame for a short while and eventually burn out. He already felt so keen on spending time with that demon; he didn't want to risk losing him because they entered a relationship too soon and lost sight of their feelings. He then frowned at himself. He didn't even feel confused about considering the possibility of a relationship. That made him all the more certain of what he felt.

But he shouldn't overthink it anymore. He enjoyed the things Zalith made him feel. He had feelings of something quite like adoration for that demon. He would agree to attempt a relationship if Zalith asked. He would spend every day with him if he asked. And that was that.

His thoughts shifted to Damien. The Daegelus warned him about the vampire relocation mission. He should try harder with that. Today, he and Zalith would attend Ada's invitation and hopefully figure out what he might do with his issues regarding the wolves. Tomorrow, he would arrange another vampire relocation. He would spend the next week completing Damien's task. If he completed it in under a month, Damien was sure to see he wasn't so useless…right? It would severely exhaust him, but he'd rather that than deal with Damien's anger. He knew too well what it was like to see him disappointed.

It was decided. He'd finish the mission in a month. He was sure that Damien would have more work for him after that, but with the relocation mission out of the way, he'd have more free time…more time to perhaps spend with Zalith…because that was what he wanted.

Chapter Fifty-Four

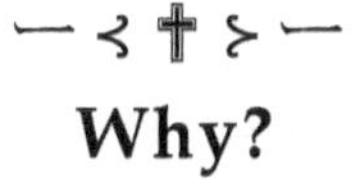

Why?

| Zalith |

In the lounge, Zalith waited on the couch. His thoughts, for the first time in a while, had become conflicted. He was already sure that what he felt for Alucard had to be more than a desire to have sex and move on. He cared for him—of course he did. He wouldn't risk his life or reputation for just anyone. But he did so for Alucard. He lied to Damien to protect him from what he could only assume was punishment. He didn't want to see Alucard hurt or any sadder than he already knew he was. Why?

A disheartening sadness ensnared his heart. When he'd stared into Alucard's eyes, he'd seen *such sadness*—sadness he would have only been able to notice if he'd taken a moment to *really* look. And that's what he'd done. He'd looked into his eyes without any ulterior motive—he hadn't been searching for a reaction, amusement, or answers. He just…stared. In that small moment, he'd been able to see past Alucard's stubborn, cold façade, and he understood him a whole lot more.

Alucard wasn't a rude, isolated man. He was a distressed, lonely, lost soul who seemed to have never experienced any sort of affection—any sort of attention that he might want. That and Damien's recent appearance helped him to understand not just that, but a clear truth that Alucard had been alone for what might possibly be his entire life.

Why did that make him feel so sad? So guilty? He'd first come here with the goal of undeniably using this vampire as a distraction from his own awful life, but now he knew that Alucard might just have it worse than he did. That hurt him. That *upset* him. Why? He knew he cared about Alucard, he wouldn't deny that, but why did he seem to care so much that he'd become angry at himself for having such selfish desires?

He frowned and rested the side of his face in his hand as he stared down at the floor. There was something different about this vampire. Everything he did and everything he said made Zalith appreciate and perhaps even adore him more. Why?

Had he allowed his attraction to become something more? Obviously. Why else would he be feeling this way? Why else would he have done and said the things he did? But what to do with it? He just tried to kiss Alucard, and the vampire retreated. Was that Alucard telling him that he disapproved of such a thing? Or was he perhaps too overwhelmed with what happened to process such a thing? Zalith hoped it was the latter. He undeniably adored this vampire, and the last thing he wanted to do was scare him off, especially now.

He felt that he was growing closer and closer to Alucard and that their friendship might very well become more. Did he want that to happen? Yes, he did. He'd like to see where he and Alucard might end up, but a familiar fear then struck him. He appreciated this vampire's company more than he had ever appreciated a particular person's presence, and the thought of losing that was disheartening. He lost interest in so many people he once enjoyed being around, and he dreaded the same thing might happen with Alucard. It was a fear like no other—a drowning, hurtful dread. To lose Alucard would be a deeply saddening loss; he'd lose the feeling of escape that he gave him, and the contentedness he felt when they were together. He didn't want to experience that.

While he felt that he could share more with Alucard, he also thought that he should wait to see what Alucard wanted. It was strange that he held the vampire's feelings in such high regard, but he did, and he wasn't going to ignore it. He already cared enough to defend him, so of course, he cared enough to respect his wishes. He'd wait. He'd give this a little more time before considering asking Alucard what he felt.

Just then, a rather frantic knock came at Alucard's front door. Zalith frowned and turned his head to glare over at it. He expected the butler to answer, but Emil was nowhere to be seen. In fact, Zalith couldn't even detect the man's life force anywhere in the residence. Had Alucard finished off his food, perhaps? Had the man died due to blood loss? Or was he simply off for lunch? Zalith didn't care—he thought about it, though. He thought about it as if it mattered. But that was simply because he was so overwhelmed by his other thoughts that any chance to distract himself would be a mercy.

Emil wasn't coming. The door knocked again. Why not, he thought? He stood up, made his way to the door, and pulled it open. He set his eyes on the rugged, leather-coated man, Tobias. The werewolf seemed shocked to see Zalith answer the door, but he very clearly had something of much more importance on his mind.

"Where's Aleksei?" he asked with desperation.

"Upstairs," Zalith replied.

"Uh…can I…come in? I ain't interrupting, am I?" he asked with a worried frown.

Zalith stepped aside, allowing him to enter. He closed the door behind him and watched as he hastily hurried up the stairs; he looked up and down the hallway before rushing to the left, panting in worry. Why? Of course, Zalith wanted to know, so he made his own way upstairs and followed Tobias' path.

| Alucard |

Alucard wasn't paying much attention to the world outside his head, and when his study door swung open, he flinched in startlement. Tobias flung himself into the room, made his way over to his desk, and started uttering nonsense Alucard didn't care to listen to. But as Zalith entered the room, the vampire frowned and looked up at Tobias.

"Vhat?" he asked, confused. "Slow zhe fuck down."

Tobias stood up straight and cleared his throat. "Uh…something's happened," he started. "So, Ben and I usually meet for a drink, and he didn't turn up, and I was like—'oh, that's okay, he's probably busy with work or something'—I then thought—'oh. I'll swing by his house, see if he's all right'—so I did that, and when I got there, his wife had no idea where he was either and said he hadn't come home since the other day."

Alucard frowned skeptically, listening.

"Ben's wife thought that you had him doing something, but she said Ben always tells her where he's going or when he's gonna be away for a while. I thought—'oh, that's weird'—and she was like—'yeah, I feel like something might have happened because he always tells me where he's going'—" he said, quoting Ben's wife with an awful feminine voice.

Listening, Alucard nodded slowly. Tobias spoke with such speed that the vampire took a moment to catch up.

He continued, "So, I went to the castle to see if he was maybe there—some of your vampires were very rude to me, by the way. Anyway, no one's seen him since then, either. And I was like—"

"Get to zhe point bevore I deafen myself."

"Uh…yeah…uh…Ben's missing."

Alucard scowled in concern.

"Like…missing—gone—no one knows where he is, not even his wife."

"Since vhen?"

"Tuesday."

"So, Ben 'as been missing vor *vree days*, and you only just tell me now?!" Alucard exclaimed angrily, standing up.

Tobias stumbled back in fear. "S-sorry, man! I thought you had him doing something. He was always so do things by the book, don't speak out of turn, and I was like—'oh, he's probably doing some top-secret shit'—but then his wife—"

"I got all of zhat," Alucard snarled, sitting back down. "Who saw 'im last?"

"Uh…probably us guys—me, Attila, and Elvin. We were all havin' a drink on Tuesday."

"In zhe city?"

"Yeah. He said he was gonna go check in on his wife when he left, but she said that he never did that."

Alucard took his eyes off Tobias and glared out the window for a moment. Ben was missing? Why? What could have possibly happened? Could someone have taken him? Ada? The packs? The Diabolus? Anything was possible. If they had Ben, they wouldn't gain access to much of his information. Ben didn't know anywhere near enough to jeopardize his plans. So, he felt no need to panic. With a calm sigh, he looked back over at Tobias. "Go," he said.

Tobias frowned. "What? You…don't really seem all that concerned."

"Vhy vould I be concerned?"

"Because…Ben's missing. Someone probably kidnapped him or killed him or something!"

"And? Ben knew vhat 'e vas getting into vhen 'e accepted zhe jobs I offered 'im. Now get out."

Tobias did as he was told—he knew better than not to. He turned around, walked past Zalith, and left the room without argument.

As Tobias left, Zalith moved closer to Alucard's desk and leaned against it. "You look concerned."

"I *am* concerned," he mumbled. "I asked Ben to look into someving, and I vear zhat might 'ave been zhe cause of 'is disappearance."

"What do you plan to do?"

He shrugged. "I zon't exactly owe Ben anyving; 'e gets paid more zhan enough vor vhat 'e does."

"Yet, it bothers you."

Alucard glanced up at him. "Maybe," he said, resting the side of his face in his right hand. "I should at least look into zhis. I zon't vant to abandon 'im—'e might be alive, vherever 'e is."

A slight smile appeared on Zalith's face.

Someone hammered on Alucard's front door.

Alucard frowned strangely, trying to determine who it might be. But he heard his door open—Tobias answered it on his way out. As the voices of Tobias and a very angry, panicked woman echoed from downstairs, Alucard sighed lazily and stood up. He made his way out of his study with Zalith following behind. As he reached the top of his stairs, he set his eyes on the auburn-haired woman standing in the doorway yelling all manner of things at Tobias, who was cowering behind the coat rack.

As soon as she noticed both Alucard and Zalith walking down the stairs, she set her anger-filled eyes on them. "This is all *your* fault! If *you* hadn't made us move here— if *you* hadn't made Ben do all these dangerous jobs for you!" she screamed, pointing at Zalith and then Alucard.

Reaching his front door, Alucard stood a few feet away from the woman—who couldn't enter the household—and frowned. "Vhat are you talking about?" he asked as Zalith stood beside him, watching.

Scowling, the woman—who was in fact Lillian, Ben's wife—shook her head and pointed at Alucard. "If he's dead—I swear, if he's even hurt because of you—I'll come in there and...and...I'll kill you!"

"She's fucking crazy, man!" Tobias uttered from behind the coat rack.

As amusing as Alucard found it for someone like her to threaten him, he kept his vacant stare and remained calm. "You obviously zidn't come 'ere to scream and yell at me. Vhat's 'appened?"

Lillian hastily reached into her white cardigan's pocket and pulled out a black, scorned piece of paper, which she then held up so he could see. "Someone's taken him to get to you!" she yelled. "And if he's—"

"Who?" Alucard asked, reaching to take the paper, but Lillian snatched it away.

"Some crazy man!"

"Give zhat to me," Alucard demanded, holding out his hand.

"Not until you promise me you'll go and find Ben!"

Alucard then scowled impatiently. "Give me zhe paper," he said more sternly.

Lillian had no choice but to abide this time. Against her will, she held out the scorned paper, allowing Alucard to take it.

Seeing that what was written on the paper was in Deiganish, Alucard snarled and handed it to Zalith. "Read zhat vor me vhilst I keep an eye on 'er," he said, reluctant to tell Zalith that he couldn't read the language.

Zalith took the paper from him and looked down at it. "Lady married to this Ben man..." he said and frowned strangely. "You must know where...Vamvam lives, the vampire guy Ben works for. If you want to see your...delicious little husbandman again, tell Vamvam to tell me where he is so I can come and say hi," he read with an unamused, confused tone. "I've wanted to meet him since I knew he was alive. If he asks who I am, tell him it's his favourite little brother. He'll know what to do. You should probably hurry, also, this Ben man vampire doesn't look so good. Love from Ben man's kidnapper," he read. Then, he sighed and looked at Alucard.

"Well?!" Lillian screeched. "Are you just gonna stand there?! Go and get my husband back!"

"No," Alucard denied, moving to slam the door in her face.

Lillian scowled and swiftly grabbed Alucard's wrist from the door before he could close it. She pulled him out of the house and attempted to hit him, but he snarled irritably and snatched her throat. She still continued trying to fight him, so he harshly slammed her face against the door's frame. She whimpered painfully as he gripped her arms and held them behind her back, waiting for her to stop struggling in an attempt to escape. And once she realized that she wasn't going to win, she calmed down and started crying quietly.

"Please don't leave him," she begged. "He's been nothing but loyal to you—he's done nothing to disobey you. The least you could do is help him," she sniffled. "Please."

Glaring at the side of her teary face, Alucard scowled in confliction. Ben *had* been utterly loyal to him, and as far as he was aware, he'd never do anything to jeopardize him or his operations. He couldn't keep himself from considering helping him. Alucard wasn't sure if Ben's kidnapper was the man he told him to apprehend, but it was a possibility. It was all just a little too inconvenient. A stranger appears and follows Ben, and soon, Ben is possibly kidnapped? There had to be a connection.

But he was sure that he knew who this kidnapper was. Favourite little brother? He wasn't aware he had any siblings, but it was a possibility. Lucifer wanted him so very badly that he was sure he'd go so far as to create more children to hunt him down. He wouldn't normally risk his life or safety for someone like Ben, but if his kidnapper was a child of Lucifer, then he might just be able to take advantage of the situation. Alucard had no idea what Lucifer or the Diabolus were doing. If he could obtain this apparent little brother, he might be able to find the answers he wanted.

Slowly, he let go of Lillian, who yelled in anger and stumbled away from him.

"Vhere did you veceive zhis letter?" Alucard asked.

"It just came out of nowhere!" she shouted, wiping the tears from her face.

"Vire?"

She frowned and nodded. "Y-yeah…a kind of…purple fire."

That confirmed his suspicions. He rolled his eyes and waved his hand in dismissal. "Go 'ome. I'll vind Ben."

A look of astonishment clung to her once frustrated face. "What?"

"Bevore I change my mind," Alucard snarled before turning his back to her.

With a huff, Lillian turned around and left the manor grounds.

"I don't know how you put up with half this shit, man," Tobias said, slowly emerging from behind the coat rack.

Ignoring him, Alucard took the letter from Zalith. "I 'ave to go and deal vith zhis. You can vait 'ere if you vant."

Zalith smirked. "Is the option of accompanying you available?"

"Yes," he answered plainly.

"Then I will accompany you," he said with a smile as he watched Alucard pull his cape on.

Tobias frowned curiously. "Uh…you want me to come? Extra pair of hands?" he offered, holding up and waving his hands.

"No," Zalith answered.

"Yes," Alucard said at the same time as the demon. He glanced at Zalith and scowled before looking back at Tobias.

"Sweet," Tobias said. "Hey, don't worry man. I ain't gonna be annoying or get in the way of whatever it is you two do, I just—"

"Ve are leaving," Alucard snapped as he led the way outside.

Zalith and Tobias followed him, and once he shut the door behind them, the vampire led the way from his manor grounds to the path outside.

"Where are we going?" Zalith asked, walking on Alucard's right.

Tobias swiftly moved to Alucard's left side. "Yeah, what are we doing? You know where Ben is?"

The vampire glanced at Zalith. "Ben's kidnapper reverred to 'imself as my little brover. I can safely assume 'e is anozzer of Luciver's children, and zhere is but vone vay to let 'im know vhere I am. Ve are 'eading to a rivt—a sacred area my old guardians used to use to pray to my vather. Zhere, I vill use a specivic ethos, and zhat vill tell zhis kidnapper vhere I am. I assume 'e vill appear, and vhen he does, I vill apprehend 'im. I zon't know vhat my vather 'as planned, so I'll find out vrom zhis moron vhat 'e might be doing."

"Kidnap the kidnapper, cool." Tobias grinned. "You think he can tell you where the Diabolus are? What they've been doing?"

"Yes."

"Right…and you need us there…because?"

"Zhis could be a trap."

"If that's the case, what do you advise?" Zalith asked in concern.

"I'm convident zhe vree of us can vight 'im off and vhatever 'e may bring vith 'im. Luciver cannot enter zhis vealm, so ve are safe vrom 'im, at least. I zon't plan to attack, 'owever, until I 'ave Ben. 'E zoesn't deserve to suffer because of me, so if I can save 'im, I vill."

Zalith smiled. "Of course."

"Tobias is 'ere in case zhis *is* a trap. 'E's more useful zhan 'e looks," Alucard mumbled.

"Thanks, man," Tobias said with a smile. "That's so sweet."

"Zon't take zhat as a compliment."

Tobias frowned and looked away. "All right, damn."

"Forgive my asking," Zalith then said quietly, "but you have siblings?"

"Maybe," Alucard said. "I vouldn't put past Luciver to create more children—vor multiple veasons. To vind me, kill me, or to do vhat I couldn't do vor 'im. I'm sure 'e still vants to get into Aegisguard, and I'm sure 'e vould've created ozzers like me in an attempt to do so. Or vor some other veasons I zon't know about."

"Quite possibly," Zalith agreed.

Then, Tobias looked over at them. "So, this guy that took Ben might want to kill you?"

"Maybe," Alucard mumbled.

"But *we* kill *him* instead?"

Alucard glared at him. "No, ve let 'im kill me so Luciver can vegain 'is ethos and enter zhis vorld so zhat 'e can turn zhis into a living, breathing 'ell'ole. Of course ve kill 'im, idiot."

Zalith laughed quietly in amusement as Tobias looked away in embarrassment.

And then, they carried on in silence.

Chapter Fifty-Five

— ˧ † ˧ —

Ben's Kidnapper

| Alucard |

Alucard approached a vast opening not far from his castle. Behind him, Tobias and Zalith followed. The area sat at the foot of the forest, where several large stones towered and formed a circle. In the centre lay a stone altar with hundreds of old candles melted on it. Different runes and magic circles were carved into the stone ground and the rocks surrounding the area, and an almost unsettling, ominous atmosphere lingered in the late afternoon air.

Tobias shivered. "Creepy."

The energy in this place was quite unlike anything. It felt heavy—drowning; Alucard thought he could feel the presence of so many invisible souls screaming, calling, *begging*. People had very clearly died here, and it seemed as though they were trapped.

"So…what are we doing here?" Tobias asked.

Alucard didn't waste time. He was there to possibly capture one of Lucifer's children and save Ben at the same time. Despite Damien's warning about the Diabolus, Alucard thought he needed to take this chance to gain insight into them. Maybe he'd find something even *Damien* didn't know.

The vampire held out his right hand and used his claws to cut into his palm. In response to his blood splashing onto the altar, the air inside the stone circle began to shift. It became so very cold; the ground rumbled, the stones shuffled, and from every inch of the opening, black fog began to manifest. It seeped out of the stones, oozed up from the ground, and spewed from the altar.

The vampire then clenched his bleeding fist shut. As Tobias panicked and Zalith watched with intrigue, the black fog raced towards Alucard and poured into his closed fist. It took a few moments, but once all the black disappeared into his hand, he sighed quietly. He wasn't sure what this might entail, but he was almost certain this kidnapper was going to piss him off *severely*.

He rolled his eyes and opened his hand, revealing a small, shimmering black stone that sat in his slowly healing palm.

Zalith then smirked as he looked down at it and then looked at Alucard. "I would have never guessed you might know blood magic. But if you use that, isn't it going to summon *every* sibling you might have?"

"You speak as zhough you know I 'ave more," Alucard said with a skeptical scowl.

Zalith smiled. "I'm just being precautious."

"Hmm…no, von't summon all of zhem—if I even 'ave more zhan vone. Vill summon all male siblings. Zhe kidnapper named 'imselv as my brover, so 'e must be male," he mumbled. Then, before either Zalith or Tobias could say anything else, Alucard chucked the stone up into the air.

As the stone ascended higher, it began to emit a loud humming and a light fog of black smoke. After a few short seconds, the black stone combusted, sending a vast spread of black light over the area they stood in. As the light faded, Alucard waited, glaring up at the sky.

It didn't take long for Alucard's summons to be heard. In no time at all, the stone directly ahead of where he, Zalith, and Tobias stood began to darken. It cracked and slit, and as ash poured to the floor, a gateway opened within the rock's face.

A black-haired, red-eyed man pounced out and clapped his hands in excitement as he took a moment to examine the area he just entered. But when he set his eyes on Alucard, a bright smile stretched across his pale face.

He planted his feet on the ground, held out his arms, and exhaled loudly. "Are you…Vampoodle?" he squealed. "Vamvam?"

Alucard deadpanned. "I must be."

Tobias and Zalith remained silent at each of Alucard's sides, waiting.

The man crept closer to the altar as the portal closed behind him. "How long I have waited to lay eyes on you—so…handsome!" he breathed, smacking his own face with his hands as if he couldn't believe what he was seeing. "So much like father!"

"Vhere is Ben?" Alucard asked, unimpressed.

"Uh…mind my interruption, but…does he sound like Ben to you?" Tobias mumbled.

He was right. This man sounded like Ben—a moronic, uglier, *stupider* version of Ben.

Alucard scowled in hostility. "Vhat 'ave you done to 'im?"

"I'm Detlaff, your cute little brother!" The man clapped but then scowled evilly. "Why do you care where that Ben man is? Is he more important than *me*?!"

The vampire glared at him, waiting.

Detlaff rolled his eyes and sighed. "Fine, whatever." He waved his hands and clicked his fingers. A portal opened to his left, and Ben fell from it, hitting the ground. "Will you talk to me *now*?" he pleaded, edging closer to where the vampire was standing.

Alucard glanced at Tobias. "Go and see if 'e's alive."

As Detlaff approached and reached the altar, Tobias hurried over to Ben.

"You know Father wants you so bad, right?" Detlaff asked, leaning onto the altar, smiling in Alucard's face. "He wants to *eat* you...so bad!"

With a vacant stare on his face, Alucard kept his eyes on Detlaff.

Zalith, too, kept a watchful eye on the estranged, revolting man, waiting for Alucard's response.

"Hello?" Detlaff frowned, clapping his hands in front of Alucard's face. "I'm right here!"

"He's uh...alive," Tobias called. "I think."

"He's fiiiiiine," Detlaff insisted, waving his hands around. "I just sent him to sleep. A little nap never hurt anyone, did it?"

Alucard then donned a look of hostility. "Vhy did you come 'ere? Vhy did you vollow and kidnap my subordinate?"

Detlaff scoffed. "To find you, of course."

"And you vanted to vind me...because?"

"Well, Father wants you—obviously. It's my job to bring you to him. Buuuut...he doesn't exactly keep an eye on me. I thought we could have a little fun before he eats you. What do you say, big brother? Do you wanna spend some quality family time with little old Detlaff? Hmm?"

"Vhy do you 'ave Ben's voice?" Alucard questioned.

With an irritated sigh, Detlaff stood up straight. "I took it, obviously. You know better than any of us that we gotta earn our appearances—work for them. You surely stole someone's voice, didn't you?"

Alucard frowned. "No."

"Really?" Detlaff asked in awe, leaning closer. "You learned to speak? Well...I suppose you were born, not made. You're so fascinating! There's no wonder Father wants you back."

"You came alone," Alucard then said. "Vhy?"

"I told you why; I wanna spend some family time with my big brother! My sisters won't talk to me; they think I'm annoying."

"I can't imagine why," Zalith muttered.

Detlaff then sharply turned his head and scowled at him. "Um, excuse me...who are you?"

The demon replied, "Someone who is easily irritated."

Alucard rolled his eyes. "You vould defy Luciver?"

"Oh, no, never!" He laughed amusedly. "I'm going to take you to him. There's nothing you can do about that now that I know where you are. I'd just like to get to know you before you die," he said, smiling.

"And you are *zhat* convident you vill be taking me to 'im?" Alucard asked, amused.

Detlaff laughed again. "Well, obviously, or I wouldn't be here by myself. Do you not want to spend time with me? Would it not be such an honour to spend time with your little brother before your death?!"

Alucard sighed quietly and mumbled to Zalith, "I 'onestly vhought zhis vould be a whole lot more annoying to deal vith."

"Quite," Zalith answered. Then, as Alucard snatched Detlaff's throat, he smiled in amusement.

Panicking in Alucard's grip, Detlaff screeched, "W-what are you doing to little brother?! Unhand me this instant!"

The vampire had no intention of letting him go. He knew Detlaff had been sent to find him for Lucifer and to take him back. But what Lucifer failed to realize was that no amount of children he created would be enough to drag him to wherever his father resided. Alucard planned to find out *everything* from this deranged man, and he'd use any means necessary to get it. Such a convenient opportunity had presented itself and with such good timing. He was sure there were so many things he wasn't yet aware of regarding his father and the Diabolus, and this ugly little creature was exactly what he needed in order to obtain such information.

Detlaff grasped the vampire's wrist with both his hands—but Alucard was immensely stronger than Detlaff. The guy tried to use his strength to escape, but that got him nowhere.

As the vampire pulled him closer, Detlaff panicked, and without hesitation, Alucard snarled and harshly sank his fangs into the man's neck.

Detlaff squirmed, screamed, and frowned. "Oh, by the heavens," he said with a sigh. "How wonderful." Then, with a dramatic sigh, he slowly slipped into unconsciousness.

Revolted, Alucard chucked Detlaff to the ground and grunted irritably, spitting the blood from his mouth.

Zalith glowered down at Detlaff. "What a strange little man. What do you plan to do with him?" he asked, looking at Alucard.

"Someving," he grumbled, leaving Detlaff to sleep on the cold, hard ground as he made his way over to Tobias, who was still trying to determine whether Ben was alive or not.

Zalith followed.

"Move," Alucard mumbled.

Tobias shuffled aside, watching as Alucard crouched beside Ben. "Is he all right?" he asked anxiously. "I don't know how to tell whether a vamp's alive or not."

Alucard placed his right middle and index fingers on Ben's left temple and his thumb on his jaw. He concentrated for a moment and then scowled irritably. "*Surgere*," he commanded. Then, he took his hand off Ben's face, watching as the man slowly returned to consciousness.

"What did you do?" Tobias asked.

"If I am not mistaken, you lifted a sleep curse," Zalith said with a curious smile. "You still continue to surprise me."

With a tired huff, Alucard stood up. "Ve zon't 'ave long until Ada's invitation. Ve'll take Ben back to zhe castle, 'im too," he snarled, glancing back at Detlaff. "I'll see vhat Ben may 'ave learned, and if zhat man vakes up bevore ve go, ve'll interrogate 'im."

Zalith nodded.

"'Elp Ben," Alucard instructed, looking at Tobias. "You can meet me at zhe castle," he said, making his way over to Detlaff.

Alucard grabbed Detlaff's arm, and before Zalith could say whatever he was going to say, the vampire disappeared into vermillion smoke and raced off into the air, heading towards his castle. There was no time to waste.

Chapter Fifty-Six

⸺ ⸱ † ⸱ ⸺

Heal

| **Alucard** |

lucard stood silently in the hall of his castle, staring down at the table which sat in its centre. He sunk deeper into his thoughts, slowly dragging his thumb over the slowly healing wound on the right side of his face. It felt a little *too* easy capturing Detlaff, and he wondered if being taken back to the castle was part of the strange little man's plan.

He scowled, pondering. Had Lucifer lost his faith in the Diabolus and decided to create children to find him instead? If that were the case, it didn't make Alucard feel afraid or nervous. He was Lucifer's son through blood; no child that creature created with ethos would be able to overpower him. So, why did Lucifer think sending Detlaff would help him retrieve him?

The vampire crossed his arms and glared over at the stained-glass window possessing the art representing his father. Was Lucifer *that* stupid? Did he think that creating children would help him? Detlaff surely thought he was capable, and Lucifer had obviously taken great care in making him believe that. Lucifer was aeons old; he couldn't be so stupid as to think a younger child could overpower his blood-created son. So, what was Lucifer's *actual* plan? Why had he created and sent Detlaff? That estranged man with Ben's voice also mentioned he had sisters, so Lucifer had created multiple children. Why? Alucard was going to do whatever it took to find out.

When he heard Tobias, Ben, and Zalith enter the castle, he took his eyes off the window and glanced at them. He watched as Tobias led the way, helping Ben keep himself upright. Zalith followed not too far behind, immediately smiling as he set his eyes on the vampire. Alucard wasn't in the mood to reciprocate and act upon the strange feeling of delight he got when he saw the demon. Instead, he took his eyes off them and glared back at the window.

Tobias made his way over to the table with Ben and pulled out a chair before helping the silent vampire to sit.

"Where have you stowed the goblin?" Zalith asked, standing beside Alucard.

Alucard frowned. Goblin? The demon could only be referring to Detlaff, and despite his current irritated mood, that made Alucard laugh. However, he turned his head away from Zalith so the demon couldn't see him smile. "I put 'im in zhe dungeon. Attila is vith 'im vight now."

The demon looked at Alucard with a suggestive smile on his face. But before he could say anything, Tobias stopped in front of them. The demon took his eyes off Alucard and irritably glared at the werewolf.

Tobias sighed quietly and dragged his hand over his head. "I ain't no vampire medical genius guy, but…Ben ain't looking too good. You're gonna help him, right?" he asked worriedly.

Alucard glanced at Ben. He was slouching forward with a mortified look on his face, one that almost looked as though he knew he was going to die. Was he? Alucard, despite his morals, didn't intend to take Ben's life. Although Ben may have possibly given Detlaff sensitive information, it was Ben who had given Detlaff to Alucard. If Ben hadn't been kidnapped, Detlaff wouldn't have revealed himself. Now, Alucard had a chance to find out what Lucifer was up to and what threats he might have to deal with. And Ben didn't know anything that could destroy any of Alucard's operations.

If anything at all, Ben deserved some sort of thank you. He'd very clearly been through a whole world of pain—that wasn't hard to tell by both the look on his face and his current disposition.

Alucard sighed and looked back at Tobias. "Go and vind vone of zhe butlers; someving tells me zhis isn't going to be simple."

With a nod, Tobias left the vampire and made his way towards the kitchen.

Alucard then walked over to Ben and sat in the chair in front of him. He took a moment to examine what he could see of his wounds; his face was bloodied and bruised, and multiple small but deep wounds were scattered across it. None of his wounds had healed, and the small puddle of blood forming below his right arm—which was dangling at his side—told Alucard that it was quite possibly broken. Alucard was no physician, but he *did* know enough about demons and torture methods to assume what might have been done to Ben.

He was going to have to be patient, at the very least. Patience might not be one of Alucard's strongest traits, but he owed it to Ben to try and be understanding. He could only imagine, after all, what Detlaff had done. In the short time Alucard had known Ben, he'd never seen him so silent, so still, and so traumatized. His first approach should be trying to get Ben to speak so that he might tell him what happened.

"Ben," he said with a vacant stare on his face.

Slowly, Ben took his eyes off the floor and gawped at Alucard. Horror lurked in his tired eyes, and the longer he stared at Alucard's blank expression, the more intense his look of dread became.

"Can you speak?" Alucard asked.

But Ben didn't make any attempt to answer. It was almost as if what Alucard was saying to him was unheard. Ben could see him; Alucard was sure of that. But could he *hear* him?

Alucard scowled skeptically. "I said your name, and you looked at me, so you can obviously 'ear me. I von't 'ave zhe patience to ask twice again. Can you speak?"

Ben slowly shook his head.

Alucard thought to himself for a few moments. Detlaff had taken Ben's voice; that goblin-like creature spoke with it, so there was no doubt about that. He was going to have to explain that to Ben, wasn't he?

Sitting up straight, Alucard sighed and rested his right arm on the table beside him. "Vrom vhat I know and 'ave been told, I assume Zetlaff is my sibling. If zhat's zhe case, zhen 'e vould 'ave needed to pervorm a series of tasks similar to zhose I 'ad to. To gain 'is 'uman body, 'e vould 'ave 'ad to drain zhe life vorce of many 'umans. I can assume 'e vasn't born like me—'e pretty much told me zhat—so 'e vasn't born vith a voice of zhese vorlds. 'E vould 'ave been born with a zemon's voice, a voice only ozzer zemons can understand. To get a voice, and to be able to speak zhe languages of zhis vorld, 'e 'ad to steal somevone else's. 'E stole yours, and you cannot get zhat back."

Ben quivered, and it looked like he was about to cry.

"'Owever," he said with a sigh, "if Zetlaff vere to take somevone else's voice, yours vould be eradicated vrom 'is body, and I could veturn to you. Zhat is no promise, zhough. Vequires a large amount of ethos to do so… and time. Time is someving I do not 'ave at zhe moment. And zhen zhere is zhe case of Zetlaff vinding anozzer voice. Is not my priority to veturn your voice to you. If zhe opportunity arises, zhen I vill try to 'elp."

Ben frowned sullenly and looked down at his arm, which he had rested on the table.

"You are not 'ealing," the vampire then said.

Ben set his eyes back on him.

"I imagine Zetlaff vasn't kind."

Ben shook his head.

"Take zhis off. I can fix zhat, at least."

As he was told, Ben struggled but took off his shirt. He then sat there while Alucard took a moment to locate all of his wounds with his eyes.

Just as Alucard suspected, Detlaff had made what could only be described as a game of Ben. His entire body was warped with sewn scars, open wounds, burns, and old, used magic circles. That creature had done all manner of things to this man, and Alucard was surprised that Ben was still alive and sane.

He shifted his eyes to Ben's right arm. The bone inside was visibly broken, and even if Alucard restored Ben's ability to heal, the bone wouldn't repair itself unless it was encouraged back into place.

Alucard then took a moment to eye each of the black chalk-drawn runes all over Ben's body. The first was stained on his right side and looked much like a snake. A deception rune, one which would cause pain if he tried to deceive the rune's placer. The circular rune with several triangles in it was scribbled over his abs, and Alucard knew that it was a pain inducer. It was meant for demons, and using it on a vampire would cause pain of such intensity that it might send someone mad. But not Ben. He seemed to be clinging to his sanity.

On Ben's left side was a rather ghastly sewn wound, one that hadn't been seen to with much care at all. The black stitches were loose, and blackening blood was congealed in the wound's openings; it was clearly causing Ben *agony* as he breathed.

The first thing Alucard needed to do was restore Ben's ability to heal. However, the state of him caused Alucard to feel uncomfortably impatient. Instead of telling Ben what to do and waiting for his delayed responses, he grabbed Ben's jaw in his hand and turned his head to either side, eyeing his bloodied ears. And his suspicions regarding his inability to heal were correct.

Alucard let go of Ben and took his eyes off his wounds before looking at his face once again. "I vill vestore your 'ealing ethos. Vill 'urt."

Ben nodded once, ignoring Tobias, who returned with one of the castle butlers.

Alucard didn't hesitate. He abruptly moved his hand into Ben's chest, and although Ben flinched violently and tried to yell despite his absent voice, he didn't stop Alucard. It took Alucard a moment to locate it, but once he gripped the parasite which clung to Ben's heart, he ripped it from Ben's body. The black-purple centipede screeched and squirmed around, and as Alucard snarled in disgust, he threw the creature to the floor a few feet away. Instantly, the creature burst into white flames and disappeared. Alucard glanced back at Zalith, who was responsible for the flames. He was sure that Zalith suspected such a parasite had been responsible for Ben's inability to heal—of course.

The moment the parasite was removed, Ben's wounds started healing. Alucard stood up and grasped Ben's broken arm with his bloody hand and quickly snapped it back into place, ignoring Ben's agonized face. He then held out his hand, and as the butler made his way over and handed him the damp towel he'd come along with, Alucard rolled his eyes irritably. He used the black towel to clean his hand of Ben's blood and then dropped it on Ben's lap.

"Clean yourselv and zhen go to your vife. I vill let you know if I can do anyving about your voice. Tobias, go vith 'im and explain to 'is vife zhat 'e cannot speak," Alucard instructed. He then pointed at Zalith. "You can come vith me."

The demon smirked and followed Alucard to the door which led to his half of the castle.

Alucard went through the door and halfway down the corridor before turning right down a long, steep staircase. While Zalith walked behind him, he descended into the dark, passing many rooms on the way down, and once they reached the bottom and emerged into a gloomy, silent corridor lined with flickering lanterns, Alucard slowed and walked beside Zalith instead of in front of him.

"Do you care vor Ben?" he abruptly asked with concern in his voice.

Zalith glanced at him. "He's a good employee," he answered. "Why do you ask?"

"Zetlaff 'as done many vings to 'im, and alzhough 'e vill vecover physically, I cannot say 'is mind vill do vell. If 'e is your vriend, you should probably velcome zhe possibility zhat 'e may never be zhe man 'e used to be."

"Understood," Zalith said simply.

And then, they continued in silence.

Chapter Fifty-Seven

Detlaff

| Alucard |

As Alucard and Zalith approached the door at the end of the corridor, it unlocked from the inside, and Attila stepped out. He wiped his bloody hands on the side of his coat and crossed his arms as an almost distasteful look appeared on his pale face the moment he saw Zalith.

Alucard stopped in front of him. "'As 'e said anyving?"

"Nothing," Attila answered in Deiganish so that Zalith could understand. "He laugh, cry a little, say all kind of word for your name. Mention Lucifer."

"Anyving in particular about 'im?"

"Looking for you still, still want to come to Aegisguard. Threaten that he take you to Lucifer, say you are multiple word for attractive. Want to dissect, too. I slap him for that."

An uncomfortable frown clung to Alucard's face. "Dissect?"

Attila nodded and said, "I think he science man, like to experiment. Said he had fun with Ben, much more fun with you. Wants to know how vampire made, says best way is to study you."

"'As 'e mentioned siblings ozzer zhan 'imself? 'As 'e said anyving about vhy Luciver created 'im?"

"You have a suspicion?"

"Maybe," Alucard mumbled. Then, he sighed. "I 'ave questions vor 'im."

Nodding, Attila pushed the door open and stood with his back against it, waiting for Alucard and Zalith to enter.

As Zalith followed Alucard inside, he lightly tapped the vampire's ass with his hand—Alucard flinched in surprise and scowled back at him, but when he saw a devious smile on the demon's face, he rolled his eyes and headed over to where Detlaff was sitting.

Detlaff's hands were tied behind his back in the chair he was slouching forward in, and purple-red blood sept from the cuts on his face. "Vamvam?" he asked quietly with hope in his voice as he lifted his head to watch Alucard approach.

Alucard wasn't interested in having a conversation with this strange man. He wanted information, and he was going to get it. So, as Detlaff looked up at him, he snatched a fistful of the guy's hair and glared into his crimson eyes. "Tell me vhy Lucifer veally created you, or I'll send you back to greet 'im vherever is zhat 'e is trapped."

A confused smile appeared on Detlaff's face. "Really…created me? I told you, big brother, I was sent here to catch you and bring you home," he said with a smile, not an ounce of struggle in his voice despite the wounds Attila had inflicted on him.

"I know vhen you lie," Alucard snarled.

The vampire forced his hand into Detlaff's body and gripped his proselytus, which sat behind his frantically beating heart; he dug his claws into it, and in response, Detlaff was forced into his demon form. His dark, goat-like horns ever so slowly cracked and twisted their way out of the top of his head, and his wings cut free of the flesh on his back, his blood pouring to the floor as he began screaming in agony.

"And I know 'ow to 'urt you, too," Alucard growled.

However, Detlaff's screams soon evolved into crazed laughter. "W-what are you gonna do to little old me, huh?" He smiled, his blood trickling down the sides of his head. "You wouldn't kill your own little baby brother, would you, Vammyvoo? Would you hurt me? I'm just a baby—an innocent baby!" he insisted, a maniacal tone in his voice as he tried to pull his head free of Alucard's grip, crazily snapping his jaw shut in what seemed like an attempt to bite the vampire.

Alucard pulled his hand from Detlaff's body and gripped hold of his right horn. "'Ow many more of you are zhere?"

Laughing, Detlaff shrugged. "Why don't you ask daddy?!" he yelled.

The vampire tightened his grip and prepared to rip Detlaff's horn from his head—

"Wait!" Detlaff screamed, tapping his feet on the floor as he stared up at Alucard. "He really *did* make me to come find you—honest!" he insisted. He then pouted and said, "But I wanted to get to know my big boo-boo brother. I wanted to see why Father wanted you so bad. I don't get it; there's not much special about you, is there? *Is* there?"

Alucard scowled impatiently.

"You have half of Father's ethos—maybe a little less than that, but still!" he said, shuffling around, trying to pull his horn free from Alucard's grasp.

But the vampire wouldn't let go.

Detlaff pouted stubbornly and huffed just as so. "Did Daddy ever tell you his secret?"

Alucard waited.

The estranged man snickered quietly. "Well, Daddy and his siblings have been very bad!" he sang. "They're hiding from the other Numen. They did some bad things back in Numen land, so they came here. They made the worlds in an empty void in space, and then they tried to enter them. Apparently, if Numen can gain access to worlds of their creation, they're safe from the other Numen who are looking for them."

As a matter of fact, Alucard did *not* know what Detlaff was telling him. So, he listened.

"Father never told us what he did, but he and his siblings are definitely on the run. Erich's fine; he's stowed himself away in that little Eltaria world where they call ethos magic—what a strange world…hmm. Anyway, Daddy and his siblings don't care about that one; they all want this one. Letholdus has already secured his place in this world, so Daddy, Damien, and Auntie Ephriel are fighting for the last two places. Apparently, this world can harbour three Numen at once. The other worlds are too weak, so somebody's not gonna be able to hide themselves when the police come knocking," he said, grinning.

Lucifer and the other Numen were hiding from Numen authorities? It seemed as though even something as powerful as a god had something higher than it. Alucard wanted to know who or what that might be. "Who is avter zhem?"

"Oh, you *don't* know!" Detlaff cheered, trying to jump up and down in glee. But as Alucard pulled on his cracking horn, he squealed in pain and calmed down. "There's six of them here, but there were seven before they came to this place. They made the eldest one of them really, really mad, and he's the one looking for them all. They only have a little while to hide here in Aegisguard. If they're not in here by the time he gets here, they're gonna die!" he yelled crazily. "So, Daddy created you to try and link himself to this world so that he could enter it. That didn't work, so now he needs his ethos back to try other things. To get it, he has to kill you—such a shame," he said with a pout.

Alucard scowled skeptically. "Luciver is not so stupid as to vink you vould be strong enough to take me back to 'im. I am not stupid enough to believe zhat, eizer. Vhy 'ave you veally come 'ere, and zon't lie."

"Hmm…no, he sent me to get you. I have my ways. I might not be as powerful as you, big brother, but I might just be smarter," he said as a smile stretched across his face.

"Smarter?" Alucard laughed amusedly. "You are locked up; I could kill you vight now if I vanted to."

"But…you won't," he said with a confident smile. "You need me."

"Vhat could I possibly need you vor?"

"Well, you clearly didn't know why Father wants to get into this world so bad. I could tell you so many things that you don't know. For example, that demon is a direct descendant of Lilith, I can smell it from here—so…delicious," he said, sighing as he set his eyes on Zalith.

Alucard frowned and glanced back at Zalith. The demon smirked and winked at him, and Alucard pouted, scowled, and looked back at Detlaff.

"I think he likes you, too," Detlaff whispered. "He's been staring at your behind for a long time, and I don't know humans that well, but I know them enough to know they like each other's behindies," he said, smirking.

Embarrassed and irritated, Alucard smashed his fist into Detlaff's face.

Detlaff screeched and grunted in both pain and anger. He then shook his head and set his eyes back on Alucard, who was now standing in front of him with his arms crossed. "Ow!" he screamed. "You're so inexplicably rude!"

"Vhy did you come alone?"

"I told you!" Detlaff insisted. "I wanna get to know my big brother! You've got to roam around in this world for so long, and I wanna know what you know! I wanna know things and understand things and do things and see things and be things!"

"So, you *vould* defy Luciver."

"No!" he yelled insistently. "He never told me I had to bring you straight to him, so I can take my time if I want!"

"You said you 'ad sisters. Vhere are zhey? Vhat are zhey doing?"

Detlaff shrugged. "Eh... one of them makes babies, keep dad's bloodline going. The other one is some queen of demons in another world. Bloodline stuff, too, maybe. They hate me, though. I send them gifts all the time, but they don't reply."

"Zhe Diabolus?" Alucard asked.

"Pshh, irrelevant!" Detlaff laughed crazily. "They're so stupid. Stupid little humans. Hey, how many did you have to eat to earn such a pretty face?" he asked with a curious smile.

With a disgusted snarl, Alucard snatched Detlaff's jaw in his hand. "Vhere are zhe Diabolus?" he asked slowly, baring his fangs.

Detlaff shrugged again. "I don't know, sheesh."

Alucard had no patience left. He snatched Detlaff's right horn and abruptly tore it from his head. Detlaff yelped and screamed in agony while his blood poured to the floor, and tears streamed down his face as his horn hit the floor.

The vampire then gripped his left horn and leaned forward to glare into his horrified eyes. "Vhere... are zhe Diabolus?"

Sniffling, Detlaff pouted and stared back at him. "You're so mean to—"

The vampire snarled in frustration and tore off the demon's last remaining horn.

Detlaff screamed again, shaking his head as his blood sprayed everywhere. He shrieked, he convulsed, and he wept like a child and hung his head in shame. But as Alucard's clawed hand gripped his left wing, he flinched and sat up straight. "T-the... uh... the... there's... a place!" he insisted in a panic. "Um... church! No... castle!"

"Vhere?"

"I don't know!" Detlaff cried. "B-b-but Daddy said—he said—he *did* say!"

Alucard scowled impatiently and tightened his grip on the demon's wing.

"No!" Detlaff pleaded, looking back at his wing over his shoulder. "Don't take my babies from me! I'll be shamed! So, so, so shamed!"

"Good," Alucard snarled.

"Wait!" he wailed, shuffling around in his seat. "Father said…he said…Damien!" he cried, nodding frantically. "Damien found them and-and-and…scared them away! They're gone! Those useless humans aren't a threat to you anymore, so please—please, please, please stop!?" he sang, his panicked shuffling becoming something of a dance.

Alucard wasn't in a lenient mood. However, he didn't de-wing Detlaff. He would never inflict such an awful punishment on someone, not even this guy. Instead, he let go of Detlaff's wing and crashed his fist into the side of his face, dislocating his jaw and knocking out at least four of his teeth, which skipped along the stone ground as Detlaff gagged in both pain and shock.

The vampire was tired of this man's voice and his ridiculous personality. He still wanted answers, and the only way he could see himself getting them without losing his will to live would be to look into Detlaff's mind and memories. And that was exactly what he was going to do. But he wouldn't do something so exposing in front of Attila or Zalith. He often avoided using mind-reading ethos, especially since it left *him* open to intruders. He trusted Zalith, but he wasn't sure whether the demon would jump at a chance to take a little trip inside his head.

He glanced back at Attila and the demon. "Leave me. I'll vind you both upstairs."

Neither of them argued. They both left the room, leaving Alucard alone with Detlaff.

As the door closed behind them, Alucard set his eyes back on Detlaff.

"Just us, huh, big brother?" Detlaff said, smirking.

The vampire snarled and grabbed a fistful of Detlaff's hair again. He knew what he needed, and he was going to get it. Without any further delay, he placed his other hand on the side of his face, pressing his middle and index fingers against his temple and his thumb along his jawline. Then, he glared into Detlaff's eyes, and as the demon stared back in utter horror, Alucard saw everything Detlaff had ever seen.

And it was something of a nightmare.

Chapter Fifty-Eight

— ≺ † ≻ —

Retaliation

| **Zalith** |

Meanwhile, Zalith followed Attila to the top of the stairs. As they walked silently through the corridor, Zalith took the opportunity to reflect on his thoughts. The day had been a long one, and he couldn't help but connect its events.

Earlier, Damien asked him what a wingless demon was, and just now, he witnessed Alucard hesitating to remove a demon's wings. He couldn't help but wonder why that might be. Could he have refused to remove Detlaff's wings because he felt doing so might make him seem like Damien, whom he was quite sure Alucard did not like at all…or could it possibly be…because Alucard had once suffered such a punishment? He couldn't be sure, and he felt that he shouldn't be making assumptions. It wasn't his business.

He thought about what happened in the hall with Ben. Seeing Alucard touch someone else irritated him. Lately, he found himself experiencing what could only be possession—he felt protective of Alucard—but he did his best *not* to act on it. As much as he often found himself disliking what he saw, it wasn't his place to intervene, and he didn't want to frighten or upset Alucard by snapping at someone who touched him or looked at him a certain way. If they were dating, he'd do it…but they weren't, so he had to control himself.

Attila then stopped walking. "I think I need to make you understand where it is you belong," he said, his Deiganish much more improved than usual.

Zalith stopped and looked over his shoulder at him. "Please, go ahead," he invited with a smile on his face. He'd been expecting this. He saw Attila's revolted scowl when he touched Alucard not too long ago, and from their previous interaction, he was quite sure that this ugly, dog-faced man was repulsed by him.

Attila gritted his teeth in disgust. "*You* might think that such a fallacious act like laying with another man is acceptable, but Alucard does not—he *will* not. And *I* will not stand here and allow you to continue to confuse and abuse him. You will remove yourself from his life, or I will do it for you."

The demon laughed amusedly. "Are you his *mother*?" he asked calmly, turning to face him. "Alucard is a fully-grown and rather intellectual man, and he can make his own decisions. I doubt he needs some dog-faced barrel of grease to do it for him."

Attila clenched his fists and tensed up as anger smothered his ugly face.

Zalith continued with a smile, "While I am sure you may want him to disapprove of me, the fact of the matter is that I have yet to hear a word of disapproval from him. In fact, I think he rather likes the attention I give him. And I'd also prefer if you didn't breathe so much when you speak; the smell is atrocious."

With a disgruntled snarl, Attila scowled and then raised his hand to point at Zalith. "*You* are nothing more than a filthy, disgusting fag. And you are turning Alucard into a soft, emotional fairy. I *won't* stand to see it. You are a disgrace to yourself, to your family, and to God. I'll gladly kill you myself if that is what it will take to save Alucard from your grotesque, immoral attention," he spat.

With a look of murder simmering in his eyes, and anger boiling inside him, Zalith sighed quietly. *Someone* was about to be removed from Alucard's life, and it sure as hell wasn't going to be him.

Before Attila could defend himself, Zalith gripped the man's arm and pulled him forward—he launched him at the wall behind him, and as it obliterated against the force of his throw, Zalith watched Attila crash land in the hall where Tobias and Ben were sitting. The rubble flew in every direction, and a devastating shockwave shook the room as Tobias and Ben jumped to their feet in shock.

Once his tumble along the floor came to an end, Attila hastily climbed to his feet, brushed the door's wood splinters from his blazer, and set his eyes on Zalith, who stood in the shattered, destroyed doorway. The demon bared his fangs and growled quietly, waiting for Attila to make his move.

Attila didn't waste his time. He wiped the blood from the wounds on his face and then charged at the demon. When he reached Zalith, he moved to grab the demon's throat, but Zalith snatched his wrist and crashed his other fist into his stomach. However, Attila didn't stumble as Zalith was expecting. Instead, he snarled angrily and crashed his fist into Zalith's face, which sent the demon crashing to the right and into the table.

As his back hit the table, Zalith snarled in frustration and instantly stood up, using his arm to block Attila's second attack. He then grabbed the vampire's collar and slung him against the wall. He moved to smash his fist into Attila's face, but Attila moved quick enough to evade, and Zalith instead punched the wall, shattering it. That didn't concern him, however—and neither did the fact that he had just broken his own hand. He scowled and swiftly turned to face Attila.

Attila threw himself forward and swung his fist; he managed to hit the demon's shoulder, but Zalith was unshaken and smashed his fist into Attila's face. Attila was sent tumbling back along the floor, and as he hit the wall, Zalith grabbed his collar with both his hands and pulled him to his feet. But Attila swiftly crashed his forehead against Zalith's face, sending him stumbling back. The vampire grabbed Zalith's throat and moved in for a bite that would surely kill him, but Zalith wasn't going to lose.

At first, Zalith thought he better not risk killing this man—Alucard might not appreciate that—but his anger was beyond containable. Before Attila could try to sink his fangs into him, he smashed the side of his face with his fist as hard as he could. Attila was flung off his feet and to the other side of the room; he crashed into the wall, and as he grunted loudly in pain, Zalith stormed over to where he had fallen. The demon took a moment to drag his hand over his head, forcing his loosened hair back into place, and then snatched Attila's throat.

Blood poured profusely from Attila's mouth; the near entirety of his face was broken, bruised, and gashed. Zalith didn't care. He pinned the vampire against the wall—but Attila wasn't yet done. He uppercut Zalith, crashing his fist into the demon's chin. Zalith was thrown up off his feet and crashed back down to the floor with an irritated grunt. Attila moved to stomp on his face, but Zalith hit the vampire's shin with perfect precision, snapping it clean in half. The vampire shrieked in torment and dropped to the floor. Zalith instantly moved over him and crashed his fist into Attila's face over and over and over, his blood splattering everywhere.

When Attila stopped fighting back, Zalith gripped his collar and lifted him, preparing his final attack—but he halted in his execution. He sensed Alucard's presence and took a moment to lift his eyes from the man in his grip and looked over at the doorway he had obliterated.

Alucard was standing there…staring over at the destruction left in the wake of their fight. Splintered wood and concrete were scattered all over the place. Blood painted the floors and the walls, and Ben and Tobias were standing against the far-left wall with startled looks of disbelief on their faces.

Zalith stared at him apologetically, but Alucard looked as though he didn't care. The vampire sighed lazily before turning around to leave.

As Alucard disappeared, Zalith looked back down at Attila's mangled face and scowled. "Clean this shit up," he snarled. Then, he harshly let go of Attila and stood up.

"Your ex-boss is fucking crazy," Tobias muttered to Ben.

Ignoring Ben and Tobias, Zalith brushed the dust from his suit and hurried after Alucard. He saw the aggravated look on his face, and he was anxious that the vampire was angry with him. He wouldn't blame him…but he was going to do whatever he had to to fix it. He wasn't about to lose Alucard because of some homophobic piece of shit.

Chapter Fifty-Nine

─ ⟨ ✝ ⟩ ─

To Know

| Zalith |

As he caught up with Alucard, Zalith walked behind him to his right and frowned in concern. He felt sad and ashamed of himself. What if Alucard was furious with him? The thought upset him more than he might have thought it would.

"Alucard…I'm sorry for the mess and the fight; I can pay to have the damages repaired," he offered, hoping it would get Alucard to respond.

The vampire glanced at him for a moment with a look of disinterest on his face. He then glared ahead again without a word.

Zalith was now sure that Alucard was mad at him. So he fell silent and followed Alucard down the hall, past many closed doors, and into a large room which sat at the base of and took up the entirety of a tall, wide tower. The tower was at least fifty feet high and completely hollow, and its walls were lined with shelves upon shelves of books, boxes, and papers. Small balconies and platforms were conjoined all around the walls, making it possible to reach everything the walls had to offer. Small gaps had been left in the bookcases for the tower's windows, the late afternoon sunlight shining in through them.

There were some larger, longer platforms higher up, standing as small floors. It wasn't possible to see what those floors possessed, though. However, Zalith could make out the huge spyglass apparatus at the very top of the tower, half of it extending up and out through the roof at a forty-five-degree angle. He'd suspect it was a telescope, but the many runes carved into its gold casing and the additionally attached apparatuses made him suspect it might not be so simple. He was curious to know what it might be, so he'd make sure to ask the vampire at a more convenient time.

He took his eyes off the towering walls of bookshelves and stopped in the centre of the room on the large red-on-gold rounded rug. He took a moment to read the spines of the books lined along the shelf Alucard was standing in front of, but none of them were written in Deiganish. He then watched Alucard take a black wooden box and make his way over to a desk.

Standing with his back to Zalith, Alucard placed the box on the only empty desk. He reached into his blazer and pulled out both his gold colts and put them on the table. However, as he went to remove his left colt's cylinder barrel, the weapon clicked loudly and fell apart in his hands. As its many parts fell to the desk, the vampire scowled in both irritancy and embarrassment.

Zalith smiled a little, but his worry about Alucard's anger kept him from commenting. He just watched as Alucard gathered the weapon parts into a small pile and picked up his right colt, removing its barrel. Then, as he allowed the empty bullet casings to drop from the colt's barrel and onto the table, he opened the black box and started taking bullets from inside. He began refilling the colt's barrel.

The demon frowned sullenly. He took Alucard's irritated silence and clear attempt to distract himself as a hint for him to leave. "Do you want me to leave?"

"No," the vampire said. Then, realizing that he wouldn't have enough bullets in the black box to fill his broken colt, he closed the box and sighed irritably. "Get me zhe gold box vrom zhat desk over zhere," he mumbled, waving at one of the messy desks close to the door.

As he was asked, Zalith made his way over to the desk, and as he grabbed the box he'd been asked to, he took a moment to eye the blueprints laid out on it. He wasn't entirely sure what they might be for. What he could see might possibly be parts of larger plans; the papers consisted of many half-drawn diagrams and everything on them was written in Dor-Sanguian—of course it was. It was Alucard's study, after all. Why would anything be in Deiganish?

He took his eyes off the blueprints and headed back over to Alucard.

Taking the box from him, Alucard sat down at the desk and opened it, revealing multiple bullet caps and cores, all of which were not yet placed in a casing. He picked up some of the empty bullet casings he removed from his colts and started carefully placing the black metal cores into them and then the silvery, steel caps over their tips.

Still watching him, Zalith kept his concerned frown. The fact that Alucard told him he didn't want him to leave was somewhat of a relief. He still felt like he should say more, though. "I'm sorry, Alucard. Attila approached me…and he talked as if I was corrupting you because I'm gay, and he told me to remove myself from your life or he would do it for me. I disagreed, of course. But…" he hesitated. He should tell Alucard exactly what Attila said—the awful things he called them both—but the thought of saying such things to Alucard, despite him quoting someone else, made him reluctant. He didn't want to upset him and felt it was best left unsaid. "He said some awful things I'd rather not repeat about the both of us and while I don't care what people might say about me, I care what they say about *you*. It angered me, and I had to do something about it."

As he finished constructing one of the last bullets, Alucard glanced up at Zalith and frowned in confusion. "Vhy do you care?" he asked with a vacant look on his face.

For the first time, Zalith was without an answer. He was speechless, thoughtless—he felt as though he'd turned to a page in a book to find it was blank. Not ever had he found himself on *this* side of this conversation, and he took a moment to realize that he'd put so many other people in the position he now found himself in, and now that he was experiencing it, he found that he didn't like it at all. He couldn't disregard his feelings; he couldn't disregard the question—he couldn't disregard *Alucard*.

Usually, he'd immediately have an answer to whatever might come his way. This time, however, he stumbled over his words. He realized that he cared so much for Alucard—enough to actually stand there and try to think of an answer for him... a *truthful* answer. He'd never taken a chance to think about how or why he cared for Alucard, and now, he had to. The care he felt for Alucard was greater than something he'd feel for a friend. But it frightened him—he felt so afraid. Such feelings would make him vulnerable, and not once had he been vulnerable in any way. He didn't want that to change—or did he? It was Alucard he'd be changing that fact for... and he felt he might just do it. Despite his fear, he wanted to try and explain himself.

He exhaled quietly and calmed his anxious mind. "I care about you because... you're my friend, Alucard. To be perfectly honest with you, I find myself caring more and more for you as each day passes. I just simply like you so much, and I haven't yet found a single thing about you that I don't like," he started but then hesitated once again. He was struggling, but he wouldn't yield. "You are... important to me. In just three months, you've become so important to me, and... I...."

Zalith paused again; the anxiety was too overwhelming. He felt like he couldn't face what he was feeling—the attachment, the care, the need, and the strange desire to be careful and gentle with this man. It was all... new and confusing. He didn't know what to do with himself.

He sighed in defeat and looked around for a moment before setting his eyes back on Alucard. "Again, I'm sorry for the mess, and I'd like to pay for any repairs that will need to be done," he concluded, unable to continue expressing his confounding emotions of what might only be described as adoration.

Alucard glared at his broken colt for a few moments and then glanced up at the demon. "I'll send you zhe bill," he answered, standing up. He clicked his right colt back together, slipped it into his blazer, and closed the box in which the bullet caps and cores were. He then picked up the few empty bullet cases that were left and made his way over to one of the shelves closest to a window.

Watching him, Zalith then smiled curiously. "Do you care about *me*, Alucard?"

Obviously startled by the demon's abrupt question, Alucard lost his grip on the bullet he was placing on the shelf. He tried to grip it before it fell, but it slipped through his fingers, and as it hit the floor, he looked back over his shoulder at Zalith, who smirked at him.

Alucard scowled and picked the bullet up. "Stop smiling at me."

"That's not an answer."

Alucard snarled irritably and turned to face him after placing the bullet on the shelf. He seemed to ponder for a moment, his eyes shifting from Zalith's face to the floor, and back to his face again. Confliction filled Alucard's eyes, and after a few moments of tense silence, he glared at Zalith. "Maybe," he mumbled.

Zalith smiled; he knew the vampire wanted to say more than his simple maybe but was clearly too shy to do so. The demon found that endearing. He laughed quietly and smiled. "I can work with maybe."

Evidently confused by his response, Alucard rolled his eyes and turned his back to him, trying to hide his face. He snatched a piece of parchment from the desk beside the shelf and walked back to the desk his broken colt was sitting on. He sat down, pulled out one of the desk drawers, and picked up a black-feather quill. But when he realized that there wasn't any ink lying around, he scowled irritably and put it back, picking out a pencil instead.

As the vampire started to write, Zalith pulled out the chair in front of him and sat down. He was curious to know what he was writing, and the only way he'd know would be to ask.

He rested his arms on the table and smiled at him. "Are you writing me that bill, Alucard?" he asked with a smirk.

"No."

Zalith smiled. "What *are* you writing?"

Alucard glanced at him and frowned. "Constituents."

"For?" he asked curiously. Of course, the room was full of blueprints, books, and components for whatever the blueprints might be for, so he was sure that Alucard was perhaps listing items for a blueprint.

"I saw into Zetlaff's mind and saw vhat 'e did to steal Ben's voice. I can take back vrom 'im. I just need a vew vings to do so," he explained, placing the pencil down.

As Alucard stood up, Zalith asked, "A procedure?"

Ignoring him, Alucard disappeared into vermillion smoke. "A procedure involving both ethos and physical operation," he called from the balcony he appeared on several floors up. He pulled a large, heavy book from the shelf in front of him and dropped it, allowing it to fall towards the desk he left Zalith at.

Before the book could collide with his head, Zalith held up both his hands and caught it. He placed it above the parchment Alucard had been writing on and stared up at the vampire as he made his way along the narrow balcony towards another shelf.

Once he snatched another smaller book, Alucard disappeared into vermillion smoke and reappeared behind Zalith. He placed the book on the table and returned to his seat. "Zhere's time vor me to vork zhis out bevore ve go and meet Ada," he mumbled, opening the larger book to one of its centre pages.

As Alucard flicked through the book, Zalith nodded. "I assume it's a priority to recover Ben's voice so he might tell you what happened?"

"No," Alucard denied, reading through the page he had flicked to.

Zalith frowned, waiting for him to explain.

Finding what he needed from the page, Alucard returned to writing his list. "I need materials to make more ammunition vor my colt; I'll be sending vone of my butlers to zhe city to get vhat I need, so I may as vell get 'im to pick up zhe vings I vould need to 'elp Ben at zhe same time," he said quietly, still writing his list.

"I see," Zalith said, smiling. "Did you find anything of interest from your time with the goblin?"

"Not much," Alucard replied, finishing his list. He closed the large book, pushed it aside, and folded the parchment before holding it up in his hand. A snowy barn owl swooped down, took the paper from him, and disappeared out through one of the windows. He then picked up the smaller book, opened it to a specific page, which he glanced at for half a moment, and then placed the book in the desk drawer he'd taken his pencil from. "I did learn zhat your vorld 'as a single moon because zhat's vhere Erich 'as decided to live out 'is life," he revealed, standing up.

As Alucard made his way over to the shelf he took the black wood box from, Zalith watched him, intrigued. "What does the moon have to do with it?"

Alucard took another wooden box from a different shelf and then headed back to the table. As he sat down, he opened the box and revealed a few small tools, which he started using to reconstruct his colt. "Zhe moons are not necessarily moons," he started, carefully placing the small screws of his weapon's grip back into place. "Zhey only appear as moons—disguised. Zhey are zhe Numen's power source. Zhe Numen possess immense amounts of ethos and sometimes is too much for zheir bodies, especially vhen zhey enter a vorld like zhis. So, zhey store 'alf of zheir ethos in zhe void—zhe space outside of zhis vorld, zhe space connecting all zhe ozzer vorlds. Zhe ethos is so large and so potent zhat can be seen."

Watching and listening, Zalith couldn't help but smile. Once again, Alucard surprised him. It seemed as though the vampire had built the weapon he was currently repairing himself—the lack of a need for instructions told Zalith that. It was also very obvious that he built many a thing in his spare time—the room they were sat within basically spelt that out for him; he appreciated the vampire's creativity…and he found it undeniably attractive.

"Zetlaff zidn't 'ave zhe entire story, but I learned zhat Erich's moon appears in your vorld as vell as zhis vone because 'e took zhe time to spread zhe invluence of 'is ethos and power across every vorld zhe Numen created, not just zhis vone. 'E is zhe Numen of life and death, avter all, so makes sense. Zamien probably 'ad 'im do zhat; Erich is Zamien's…vell…Erich just does vhat Zamien says."

Zalith smiled. "Erich is Damien's…what?"

Alucard wasn't going to reveal what he almost said, was he? He continued repairing his colt and said, "Brover."

"We all know the Numen aren't actually related. Unless Erich and Damien are?"

"No. Erich and Zamien are just closer zhan any of zhe ozzers."

Sure that Alucard didn't want to continue discussing the matter, Zalith changed the subject. "Do you make these things yourself?" he asked, gesturing to the colt Alucard was repairing.

The vampire finished repairing his weapon; he raised the golden colt and pointed it at Zalith's face. He used his thumb to pull back the hammer, and as the demon raised his left eyebrow in concern, Alucard smirked. "Yes," he said—he then abruptly pulled the trigger. The empty gun clicked, making Zalith flinch ever so slightly, and seeing a reaction that didn't result in a smile seemed to make Alucard feel deviously content. He lowered the gun and started to load it with bullets. "I make many vings in my spare time."

With a curious smile, Zalith leaned closer. "Such as?" he asked, disregarding the slight irritancy he felt in response to Alucard's jest.

Once his colt was loaded, Alucard slipped it into his blazer, stood up, and shrugged. "Vhatever I vant," he answered.

Zalith also stood up and glanced up at the telescope-like contraption which caught his eye upon first entering the room. "Did you make that?" he asked, nodding up at it.

Alucard glanced up at it and frowned. "I did," he answered as he started leading the way to the door.

"What is it? It doesn't look like your standard telescope," he said, walking beside the vampire as they left the room.

"Is someving I vill not tell you about until I know zhat you von't try and use vhen I'm not looking."

The demon then smiled deviously. "I promise I shan't use it."

"No," Alucard denied, turning into the hallway that led to the castle's entrance hall.

With a smirk on his face, Zalith moved his arm around Alucard's shoulders and pulled him closer. "Do you not trust me, Alucard?" he asked amusedly.

With a nervous, embarrassed frown, Alucard pulled free of Zalith's grip and scowled. "Ve are leaving," he mumbled.

Following him, amused by his response and reaction, Zalith smiled and laughed quietly. "Where are we going?"

"I need to 'ead 'ome and change bevore ve 'ead to Ada's invitation."

Zalith nodded, following the vampire in silence. He was looking forward to both seeing what Alucard would change into, and what the evening had in store for them.

Chapter Sixty

— ⟨ † ⟩ —

Hot in Red

| Alucard |

Alucard led the way into the castle entrance hall, where Attila was picking up the rubble and wood that had been scattered across the room. Tobias and Ben were gone, and when Attila heard Alucard and Zalith approaching, he stood up straight. His bloody face still hadn't healed, and he looked uglier than usual. But neither of them paid a slither of attention to him as they walked past, made their way to the castle's door, and left.

Once they were outside, Alucard looked back at Zalith, who stopped walking and took a moment to examine his suit. There were several small tears on it as a result of his fight with Attila.

"I'll meet you at your home; I need to return to my own to change into something more presentable," the demon said with a smile.

Alucard nodded. "Zon't take vorever. Ve need to leave in vivteen minutes."

Zalith smirked in response.

The vampire then morphed into vermillion smoke and swiftly made his way back to his manor. He landed in the gardens and headed to his front door; when he entered his house and stood in the entrance hall, he searched for any sign of Emil, but there were none. Had his butler perhaps died of blood loss?

"Emil?" he called.

There was no response.

With a roll of his eyes, Alucard took off his cape, threw it over the coat rack, and headed through to the kitchen, leaving his front door ajar. However, the kitchen was as deserted as the hall.

He sighed and walked into the sitting room to the right of the manor and set his eyes on the suit he'd got his butler to prepare for the evening. He made his way over to the couch it was resting on and took off his blazer. He then hastily removed his black shirt, replacing it with the scarlet-red shirt that had been laid out for him. He tidied its collar and cuffs and then started to put on the black waistcoat.

For some reason, his thoughts decided to focus on what Zalith asked him earlier. The demon told him that he cared about him and then asked Alucard if he felt the same. *Did* he care about Zalith? Truly? He did, but he didn't feel ready to tell him that. Not only had he struggled to think of the right words to use, but he also felt a little hesitant because he didn't yet understand his feelings enough.

He cared about Zalith, he enjoyed spending time with him, and he wanted to keep seeing him, but he wanted to make sure that if he and Zalith were to become something more, it would last. He wasn't comfortable with the idea of being used or treated as a fun distraction until their mission was over. Alucard knew that he wanted more with Zalith, but he'd not let himself become attached to someone who might leave a few months down the line.

However, it was then that he realized he was no longer alone. He scowled and looked back over his shoulder, setting his eyes on Zalith, who was standing in the doorway in a new black suit. Alucard wasn't sure how long he'd been there, but he dreaded to think he might have been there while he was shirtless, and his back was exposed. He was confident, though, that if Zalith *had* been watching before he noticed he was there, then the demon wouldn't have a smile on his face but a look of revolt. But Zalith *was* smiling, and it made him feel relieved.

"You look hot in red, vampire," Zalith said with a smirk, admiring him with his eyes.

Alucard immediately took his eyes off Zalith and glared ahead, hiding his embarrassed expression from him. He picked up his black blazer and pulled it on; then he took his colts from his other blazer and slipped them into the holsters already inside his new one. He waited a few moments, trying to banish his flustered expression, and turned to face Zalith, who was still standing in the doorway.

"Is there a specific plan?" Zalith asked, watching Alucard as he left the room through its second doorway.

Alucard stopped in front of the front door and looked back at him. "If I knew vhat Ada vas planning, zhere vould be. I zon't know if she vants to talk, or if zhis is an ambush, as said," he answered, pulling his sword and its sheath from his belt. He placed them on the table beside the door and opened it, inviting Zalith to exit first. As the demon left the house, Alucard followed. "If *is* an ambush, ve vill do vell not to let zhem get away. I'm tired of Ada, so if zhis is vhere she tries to kill me, zhis is vhere I vill kill 'er."

"What happened to your 'questionable habit of trying to form peace before resorting to murder'?" he quoted, smirking.

"She 'as surpassed my limit," he snarled, locking his front door. "She is trying to unite zhe packs in an attempt to attack me and vhat I 'ave built, so I vill offer 'er vone final chance tonight."

Zalith looked both amused and confused. "You say she has reached your limit, yet you plan to offer her one final chance tonight? Why not just kill her now and end it?"

As he led the way towards the manor exit, Alucard snarled quietly. "Because killing 'er vill ignite a war—not just 'ere, but all over zhe vorld."

"Hmm…are you sure you're not just enjoying this, Alucard?"

"Enjoying allowing a voman to try and tear down someving I 'ave spent my entire life building—again?"

He nodded.

"No," he snarled as they left the grounds. "Again, I vould like to avoid a war, but seems as zhough might be inevitable. She plans to attack my city and my castle, and I von't let zhat 'appen. I'll see vhat she vants tonight; who knows, per'aps she's not such a stupid bitch avter all and vants to vorm a treaty. I 'ope zhat's zhe case. As much as I despise verevolves, I'd vather 'ave zhem on my side zhan as enemies."

"And that would be because?"

"Vhy do you alvays vink zhere's some greater veason behind my plans?"

"Because I sense that there may be a little more to the situation," he replied.

"Zhere is not."

"Are you sure? I feel as though you might like Ada and her werewolves," Zalith teased, leaning closer and nudging Alucard's shoulder with his own.

Alucard rolled his eyes and led the way towards the forest to the left of his manor. "Zhere's noving to like about zhat voman or verevolves," he grumbled. He then glanced at Zalith, who smiled with a doubtful look on his face. "Vhatever," he snarled, glaring ahead again. "Zon't do anyving vonce ve get zhere unless I say."

"Of course."

Then, Alucard continued to lead the way in silence. He wasn't sure what might be waiting, but he had to ensure he was ready for anything.

Chapter Sixty-One

⟶ ⟨ ✝ ⟩ ⟵

'Til Death Do We Part

| Alucard |

As he led the way through the forest, Alucard glanced at Zalith. They hadn't said much since leaving his manor, and while he might have enjoyed the silence before, he *didn't* welcome it now. He knew that Zalith wanted to know more about Ada, and he didn't feel as though he needed to keep that information from him.

"Ada and I 'ave known each ozzer vor zhe majority of both our lives. She is a strange voman, to say zhe least. I veel like she is invatuated vith me or zhe idea of me. She 'as never been too var behind me, she vollows me vherever I go, and I am sure if she 'ad zhe ability to leave zhis vorld too, she vould 'ave vollowed me vhen I did such a ving."

Zalith frowned curiously. "And were you friends?"

"No—at least *I* zidn't vink ve vere. Vhen ve vere cursed, zhe gods who created us expected us to vight vor zheir amusement. Ada complied, and I admit zhat I did too—vor a vhile. I vas angry; everyvone I knew 'ad been taken vrom me, and I zidn't 'ave much to do vith my time. But vonce I understood zhat all Janus 'ad done vas use me, I killed zhe dragon and abandoned Ada. Zhat's 'ow she took zhat, anyvay. Ve vought all zhe time, and I guess she vhought zhat vas some sort of velationship...vriendship—vhatever. She vhought ve 'ad someving, and I veel as zhough she still vinks ve are someving. Zhat's vhy I 'aven't yet just killed 'er vithout varning 'er."

Zalith looked like he understood. He asked, "Because it'll cause you to feel guilty?"

"Someving like zhat. I need to make sure she understands zhat I 'ate 'er and vill kill 'er if she zoesn't stop screwing vith me. I zon't know vhether she's just fucking stupid or genuinely vinks I vant to keep dealing vith 'er shit."

The demon smiled slightly. "Perhaps it might be a little of both," he suggested. "Ada seems to enjoy angering you and causing you trouble. You undeniably let her get away with it—to an extent. Tell me, Alucard, do you plan on letting her slip away this time, or will tonight be the night she dies?"

"I alveady answered zhat," he grumbled. "I zon't 'ave zhe patience vor 'er anymore. Vhen ve get to vhatever is she 'as invited us to, I vill make sure she understands."

"I feel as though that will be somewhat amusing to watch," Zalith said, smirking.

Alucard rolled his eyes. "Everyving amuses you."

"Not *everything*. For example, I find your appearance cute, not amusing."

The vampire pouted and looked away from him, refusing to allow him to see his embarrassed face.

"I *do* find it amusing, however, when you become Mr Grumpy," the demon added.

Alucard didn't reply. He scowled into the forest to his right, unable to look at Zalith.

Zalith smiled and placed his hand on Alucard's shoulder. "In all honesty, I really enjoy spending time with you, Alucard. I'm having a delightful time and feel as though I'd rather not be elsewhere. Any time I spend with you is the highlight of my day. Not only are you cute, but you're fun, and I enjoy your company—even when you're grumpy." He then laughed quietly and moved his arm around the vampire's shoulders; he pulled Alucard closer, squeezing him rather tightly as Alucard tried to keep himself from becoming flustered.

The vampire pouted as he glanced at Zalith and hesitated for a moment. He wanted to tell him that he felt the same, but his nervousness quickly became strangely overwhelming. Instead, he glared ahead again. "I enjoy spending time vith you, too," he muttered.

Zalith leaned forward ever so slightly so he could see the vampire's face. "I'm happy to hear it," he said but then smiled suggestively. "How *much* do you enjoy it?"

Alucard rolled his eyes and continued leading the way forward as the ground began curving upwards. "Enough to tell you," he mumbled, still trying to hide his face from Zalith.

The demon then let go of him and walked beside him. "What is it that awaits us at the top of this hill? I hear the sea," he said, looking around. "Are we on our way to a romantic location? Is this a dinner date?"

"I zon't know," Alucard said with a sigh. "I 'ave no idea vhat goes on in Ada's 'ead. Vhatever is, zhough, zon't let 'er get avay if she tries to run."

"Noted," Zalith said with a nod.

Alucard frowned and focused on what lay ahead. Although he couldn't see through the trees, he *could* hear and sense—and what he felt couldn't possibly be Ada alone. There were at least a hundred or so people. He glanced at Zalith, who adorned a cautious scowl—he could sense them too.

Ada seemed to be prepared for a battle, which could only mean she was expecting Alucard to also come with help. He had all he needed, though. He didn't need a pack or army, he just needed one single demon, and as they came closer to the edge of the forest, he prepared for whatever might happen.

A blur of white became visible through the trees. Despite the darkness of the night, the white gleamed so brightly. An orange glow crept through the branches, and the quiet chattering of people became louder. Neither of them knew what to expect, but as they emerged from the tree line and into the clearing atop the cast cliff, they both stared in utter confoundment.

The entire crowd fell silent—the entire crowd of *naked* men and women. They were sitting on either side of a walkway, instantly taking their eyes off one another and setting them on Alucard and Zalith. Everything was white: the chairs the crowd sat on, the carpet dressing the walkway, the silk hanging from the few surrounding trees, and the blossom petals floating through the warm, late-evening air. Jars filled with fireflies were laid around the opening's edges, lighting what the moons didn't, and at the very end of the walkway stood an altar with a tall, white archway adorned with pink, white and red tulips on top of it.

Alucard's face was already smothered with confusion, but when he set his eyes on the unclothed woman standing beneath the archway, he couldn't believe nor understand what he was seeing. He didn't *want* to believe what he was seeing. But it was right in front of him—what could only be described as a wedding reception. But for who? And why was everyone naked?

Beneath the altar, the blonde-haired, yellow-eyed woman smiled with glee as she held her hands together and laughed contently. She stood in nothing but an almost transparent white silk veil, and as she stared at Alucard, she giggled with excitement. "Aleksei!" she cried, jumping up and down. "You're here!"

"Vhat?" he uttered, his eyes darting from sight to sight and face to face. What the *fuck*?

Zalith laughed loudly, and when Alucard looked to him for help, the demon looked as though he might just start crying.

Ada moved her hands through her hair, making it float elegantly in the breeze as she sighed longingly. "Aleksei," she called with a depraved look on her face. "Come to me, be joined with me—forever!" she invited, holding out her hands.

As Alucard grimaced in revolt, Zalith grinned amusedly. "Go, Alucard. Join with her forever," he repeated with an encouraging tone.

Not at all interested in doing such a thing, Alucard tried to back off, but Zalith placed his hand on his shoulder and kept him from leaving. Why? This wasn't funny; this wasn't supposed to happen. He didn't want to marry Ada, he didn't even want to be as close as he was to her right now, and she was at the other end of the field! Why was this happening? What *was* happening? He looked at Zalith, he looked at Ada, and he looked at the crowd of unclothed people—what the *fuck* was this?

With an impatient pout, Ada held out her arms. "Come!" she pleaded. "My truest love, my strongest king," she called, holding out her hands to him once more. "Fulfil our destiny, join our souls as one!"

Zalith gave Alucard an encouraging shove away from the tree line and into the opening, trying to contain his laughter.

Alucard looked back at Zalith like a lost child, completely unwilling to approach the woman. But Zalith showed no signs of offering assistance. He was on his own.

The vampire scowled and turned to face Ada, attempting to silence his revolt and embarrassment. He'd come to tell her that she had one chance to leave, or he'd kill her. He still had to do that despite the lack of clothes involved. So, with a vacant stare, he made his way towards the altar as the crowd slowly stood up while he passed each row of people.

As soon as Alucard stepped up onto the altar, Ada threw herself at him.

"You look so gorgeous, my dear!" she cried, pressing her body against his, trying to touch his face, but he backed off—she didn't let go of him, though. As his back hit the archway, which he gripped to keep himself from falling, Ada moved closer and rested her body on his. "Oh, Aleksei, take me now," she pleaded, stroking his arm. He gripped her wrist but she pulled free and started to stroke his leg; he continued trying to fight her off, but her hands continued wandering as she smiled in his utterly confused face.

The vampire had never felt so uncomfortable in his life. This woman had her hands all over him and her body against his own—her *naked* body. It was almost disturbing, and he couldn't bear another second of such unwanted attention. With a grimace and an aggressive snarl, he peeled the woman from his side and shoved her away. As she stumbled back, he stood ready to defend himself if she were to attempt to lay her hands on him again.

"So cold and awful!" she snapped but then smiled. "I love it!"

She tried to throw her arms around him, but he moved aside and dodged her many attempts to grab him. What was he supposed to do? Hit her? He might have to. Just as he felt he might do so, though, she stopped throwing herself at him, stood up straight, and relaxed.

"Let us become joined," she said, holding out her hands as a priest made his way towards them.

"Joined?" Alucard questioned, glaring at her.

"Joined, my dear," she said with a smile, attempting to take his hands, but he defensively backed off. She didn't give up, though. She sighed and smiled understandingly. "We have fought for so long—so, so long—and I know you want to end this petty war between werewolves and vampires. If we become one, my dear, we will unite our people, the war will end, the fights will cease, and we will be together forever, just as the gods willed!"

Alucard tried to think about what she was saying, but his discomfort and revolt kept him from being able to do so. Joined? Ada wanted to marry him. *Marry*? He didn't want that—why would he want that? Even if it would end the feud, he wasn't going to marry someone he hated, someone he'd come to kill. He'd always known Ada was absurd and vacuous, but he would have never thought she'd do something like this. Her love letters were one thing, but this? This was utter nonsense. Surely she knew that…right? Surely she had to know he wasn't just going to marry her because she wanted him to—because she'd gone out of her way to arrange an entire reception. He found it rather sad. What a sad woman—what a stupid woman. He despised her, and he clearly had to make that obvious to her.

Before Alucard could answer, Ada held up her hand and shushed him. "Save it for the honeymoon, my dear. Our time has come!"

Alucard scowled in revolt. It was time to put an end to this horrific show.

As the priest opened his book and began reading, Alucard snarled and snatched it from him. He lobbed it into the crowd, and as it smacked the face of one of the observers, he scowled, gritted his teeth, and pointed at Ada. "Zhe only time zhat 'as come is zhe time vor you to get zhe fuck out of my life or die!"

Ada blushed and laughed, waving her hand. "You're so silly, my dear," she giggled. She then looked at the priest. "It's okay, go ahead."

Without his book, the priest glanced around in confusion.

Tired of the stupid woman before him, Alucard growled and grasped her throat in his hand—

"Oh, yes, my dear, take me now!" she cried.

Disgusted, he let go of her and stepped back, but she grabbed his wrist and pulled herself closer to him again. He didn't want to touch this woman's body, so he had no idea what to do. He grunted and grimaced in revolt as she pressed herself against him again, staring up at him with a look of longing in her eyes.

"Don't you want to stop the fighting, Aleksei?" she asked, batting her eyelids as he tried to escape her grip. "Don't you want to spend your life with me?"

"No!" he snarled in both disgust and confusion, trying to shove her away.

She laughed and dragged her hand down to his waist. "Yes, you do," she said, a more demanding tone to her voice. "You *will*. We'll get married, and we'll be together and spend eternity in each other's arms!"

Alucard harshly shoved her away, and as she stumbled back, he snatched her neck with his right hand. If he wanted to make her understand that he'd kill her if she didn't leave and stay gone, then he'd have to be as harsh as he could be. He felt no need to hesitate. He leaned into her face and growled, "Listen to me you annoying, stupid, *pathetic* dog. You vill not 'ave a life if you zon't get zhe fuck out of my vace in zhe next minute. I zon't vant to spend my life vith you, I can't stand to be vithin vour 'undred miles of you! You disgust me, you annoy me, and zhe only veason I've let you live vor so long is because I am var too lazy to deal vith zhe war zhat vill break out if I vere to kill you—and I *vill* kill you zhis time," he hissed.

Staring at him, Ada giggled amusedly but then frowned as if she had only just realized he was being serious. "What?" she asked with a nervous laugh.

He snarled and let go of her, shoving her back. "You 'eard me."

She laughed nervously again, an almost heartbroken look on her face. "You mean…you don't…love me?"

"Vhat?!" he exclaimed. "Vhere zhe fuck vould you…vhat?"

Ada pouted. "I love you, Aleksei," she said, scowling. "You belong to me. The gods made it so. You *will* marry me, we *will* be one!" she claimed. "And you'll give yourself to me no matter what!"

He laughed amusedly—before he could speak, however, Ada threw herself at him once more. This time, she wrapped her arms around his shoulders, and before he could attack or throw her off, she stabbed the left side of his neck with something small, something he couldn't see hidden within the confines of her hand, and it hurt unlike anything he felt before. He couldn't react as fast as he usually might—the second whatever it was stabbed into his skin, he felt his strength wane.

She smiled and tilted her head slightly. "You won't refuse me," she whispered. "Never again will you leave me, hurt me, hate me—you'll be mine forever."

Alucard had no idea what she stabbed him with, but her smile told him that it wasn't something as simple as a blade. As a look of panicked confusion smothered his face, he managed to find his strength and pushed her away. But she skipped back over to him. His vision started blurring, his body began numbing, and the confusion was overbearing. However, as Ada waved a small gold-metal syringe in front of him, he frowned strangely. Had she drugged him? He didn't have the time to try and tell. His body grew weaker, and he dropped to his knees, holding his hand over the place on his neck she stabbed him.

What was happening? He felt dizzy and exhausted; he searched for an escape, but there didn't seem to be one. Ada pulled him to his feet, smacking each side of his face to keep him from passing out.

"Okay, he's fine, look," she said to the priest. "Do it!" she shouted.

The priest nodded fearfully, but before he could begin, the area around the altar was instantly engulfed in white flames. The blast of heat forced Ada to let go of Alucard, who dropped to the ground again, and the priest was devoured by the fire.

As he hit the ground, Alucard placed his hand over his face, trying to gain some sort of perspective, but he was so confused; all he could feel was the heat of the fire on his skin and heard the sound of the crowd howling and snarling. What was happening?

Where was Ada? Where was *he*? He had no idea. He couldn't remember what was going on or how he got there…wherever there was.

And as the world around him started to fade away, the last thing he saw was Ada's horrified, teary face.

| Zalith |

Zalith wasted no time intervening. The moment he saw the woman attack Alucard, every instinct within him forced him to attack—and he felt no need to ignore his instincts. He wasn't going to stand by and allow her to manipulate or hurt Alucard. Whatever she did to Alucard, it was clear that the vampire had no idea where he was or what was going on—he might have no recollection at all, which meant he couldn't defend himself. So it was time for Zalith to do something.

This woman wanted Alucard—she wanted to try and force him to love her and give his life to her. Zalith wasn't going to let that happen. Not only was he sure that Alucard didn't want that, but *he* didn't want that. He wasn't going to deny the fact that he felt possessive over Alucard, and seeing this woman trying to take him from him made him furious enough to kill her. Before, it may have not been his place to act upon his possessive instincts, but he couldn't ignore them this time. Alucard was defenceless—helpless, even. There was no reason for Zalith to hold back.

As soon as his fire appeared and cut Ada off from her wolves, who transformed immediately, Zalith appeared from the flames in his demon form and snatched hold of the woman's throat.

Ada stared in horror. In the strange gloom of the white flames that had wrapped themselves around the ground below the altar, concealing her from her werewolves, she could see nought but Zalith's devilish, crimson eyes glowing in front of her face. She gawped in fear at the horns which extended upwards from his forehead—two thin, spiralling horns reaching at least a foot in length. Against his back were a pair of dragon-like wings as black as the night itself, and as her back hit the archway, he extended his wings in a display of threat. She screamed in terror as his claws dug into her neck, and as a maniacal grin spread across his face, she stared at the fangs in his mouth.

Leaning into her horrified face, Zalith snarled both revoltedly and aggressively. "*He* belongs to *me*," he claimed furiously. Then he mercilessly crashed his fist into the woman's face, sending her flying through the flames and into the forest, the force of her flying body knocking down several trees in her path. And with that, her life was at its end.

The demon swiftly turned to face Alucard, folding his wings against his back. He wasted no time in seeing to him, either. As the white flames surrounding them vanished, revealing the werewolves, who were all fleeing for their lives, Zalith's wings and horns crumbled and faded. He hurried to Alucard's side, kneeled beside him, and lifted the vampire's head into his lap. There was no use in asking if he was okay; he was unconscious and seemed to have been that way since Zalith grabbed Ada. However, he needed to know what Ada injected him with, and luckily, that stupid woman dropped the syringe she attacked Alucard with.

Zalith reached over from where he was sitting and snatched the syringe. He snapped it in two and lightly inhaled through his nose. It took him no time to work out that it was purified nightshade, a well-known vampire sedative. If Alucard wasn't a demon, Zalith might almost be concerned about when he'd wake up, but he was sure that the vampire's body would burn through it in no time. It had, after all, taken a short while to sedate him where usually the drug would *instantly* knock a vampire into unconsciousness. Of course, he knew of a way to wake Alucard up sooner, but he was convinced that the vampire might not appreciate it. He'd also rather take this opportunity to carry Alucard.

The demon carefully moved his arms under Alucard; he moved the vampire's right arm around his own shoulders, made sure Alucard had his head rested on his left shoulder, and scooped him up. He stood up and then made his way down the carpet-lined path towards the forest. He felt the best thing he could do was take Alucard home, so that's where he headed.

Chapter Sixty-Two

⸺ ⸲ † ⸳ ⸺

The Beach

| Zalith |

Zalith silently made his way through the forest, occasionally glancing down at Alucard in hopes that he'd soon wake up. Not only was he concerned for him, but he also felt saddened by the fact that he couldn't talk to him while he walked. He enjoyed talking to Alucard more than anyone else and didn't want to waste a single moment in his company. But he was sure the vampire would return to consciousness soon—at least he hoped so.

As he walked, he also made sure to stay focused on his surroundings. The last thing he needed was to have been followed or for Ada's wolves to be planning an attack out of revenge. He killed their leader, their Alpha—whatever she called herself. He didn't care. She was dead. That was all that mattered.

His main concern was Alucard, and he felt that concern might become something he felt more regularly, especially since he'd not long claimed this vampire as his. He felt no regret in doing so, though. He'd noticed his possessive instincts for Alucard increasing as each day passed, and tonight, he just couldn't ignore it anymore. He claimed Alucard, and he'd do it again if he had to—he felt he might even just do it because he *wanted* to.

He undeniably enjoyed telling someone that Alucard belonged to him—he enjoyed saying it, feeling it, and making it known to not only whoever heard, but himself, too. It felt right, it still felt right, and he was sure it would always feel right. Before, he'd never claimed another person as his own with such an intense feeling of hostility and sincerity. It only made him surer of his feelings, of his desires. He wanted Alucard to be his, and not just for a while, not just because he wanted to achieve some sort of feeling of accomplishment, and not just for clout. What he felt for Alucard was so much more than that—more than just some attraction, some desire to sleep with him. What he wanted was something of a deeper, more intimate nature—something that would last, and the determination he had to get it was overbearing.

He looked down at the silent vampire for a moment, but as he thought about what he wanted, the familiar fear of ruining their relationship began to enthral him. While he might be sure that he wanted to be with this man, the fear of losing him grew stronger. He was aware he had a bad habit of quickly tiring of the men he was with romantically—even those he pursued. He wanted to share a romantic relationship with Alucard—of course he did—but he felt anxious about starting one. He'd developed a bond with this vampire despite only knowing him for three months, a bond so strong it felt as though they'd known each other for years. But he couldn't help but fear… what if he was to wake up one day and these feelings were gone? What he felt for Alucard currently was more than he'd ever felt for anyone else, but what if that changed? He couldn't help it; he didn't know why it happened half the time… he just lost interest in people. He *always* lost interest.

Zalith was already sure that Alucard wasn't just someone he wanted to sleep with and then be done with; he'd been confident of that at least two months ago. And as afraid as he might be of repeating his infamous history with every other man he'd been with, he was beginning to feel as though maybe Alucard might be different. He found himself losing interest in people so very quickly, and if that were to be the case with Alucard, he was sure he would have stopped chasing him long ago. He would have never waited this long to get what he wanted; he would have never waited this long to so much as kiss a man he felt attracted to—he hadn't even done *that* yet. He wanted to, of course, but he cared more about Alucard's comfort than he did for his own needs and wishes.

He hadn't lost his interest in Alucard in the slightest, and as time passed, he had and could only feel himself growing closer. He could feel his feelings for Alucard becoming more intense, and he wanted as much of this vampire as he could get. But not only did he have his own worries, Alucard surely had *his*. This vampire was so very volatile; as much as Zalith enjoyed that, he knew it was something he should take more seriously. Alucard, to an extent, was sheltered; he hadn't seemed to understand when he was being flirted with, and as endearing as Zalith found that, he felt as though he needed to make sure Alucard understood what he wanted and what he was doing.

The demon was also sure that Alucard had never been with a man or woman romantically before. Ever. He wasn't even sure if Alucard had ever thought about being in a relationship—he felt he should make a point of asking him. He didn't want Alucard to feel intimidated if they were to date; he was sure that his history would make the vampire assume he had to live up to certain expectations, and Zalith didn't want him to feel that way. Not only was there that worry but there was also the fact that other people and their opinions might scare the vampire away from him. Zalith knew that the people of this world weren't exactly accepting of such relationships. One of Alucard's friends had made a point of making that known.

Despite his wishes, Zalith considered Alucard's feelings above his own, and he felt he always would. As much as he might want to be with Alucard, he wouldn't initiate a romantic relationship unless he was sure that it was what Alucard wanted, too.

Just then, he felt the vampire flinch ever so slightly. He was waking up, and Zalith wasn't sure what the next five minutes might unveil. He looked down at Alucard, watching as the vampire slowly frowned, moving his left arm from his side—there was a possibility he might attack considering he blacked out halfway through what he might have considered an attempt on his life. But Zalith was sure he could handle whatever might happen.

| Alucard |

Alucard had no idea where he was, what was going on, or what happened. He was moving, that much he could tell. The breeze was cold on his face, but he felt unusually warm. Whatever this warmth was, it was comforting, and despite not knowing where he was, he felt…safe. However, he didn't recognize the strange scent of bergamot and what might only be described as burning leaves; the almost syrupy smell was somewhat enticing, along with that of blood. But the blood wasn't human—it was far too sweet of a scent to belong to something that revolting.

It took him a few moments to find his strength, and once he gathered enough, he opened his eyes and stared ahead. He set his sights on the trees as they passed by—he quickly noticed that he had his head leaned against…someone's shoulder? He looked up, and as his eyes met with Zalith's, all manner of embarrassment and uncomfortable feelings consumed him. Why was Zalith carrying him? In his arms? With his face so close to his? If he hadn't opened his eyes when he had, he felt like he may have allowed himself to try and find the source of the blood—he was glad he hadn't. The last thing he wanted to do was attack Zalith. Not only would it be embarrassing, but he didn't want to hurt him.

Immediately, he insistently pulled free from Zalith; as his feet hit the ground, he felt as though he might fall, but he avoided Zalith's offer of help and stumbled over to the closest tree, which he used to keep himself on his feet. He stood with his back to the demon, his senses still all over the place; he couldn't understand what Zalith was saying and could only hear the murmurs of his voice. He was probably asking if he was okay, though. *Was* he okay? He felt anxious, exhausted, confused, lost…where was he?

As Zalith placed his hand on his shoulder, Alucard turned around and leaned his back against the tree. He still felt dizzy and strangely dissociated; Zalith was unusually close, but as the vampire reached out to push him away, his hands hit the air. What was going on with his vision?

Zalith dragged his hand from Alucard's shoulder and to the side of his neck. He placed his other hand on Alucard's jaw and made him look at him. As the vampire complied and stared strangely into his eyes, Zalith stared back in concern.

"Alucard?" the demon asked.

Finally able to understand Zalith's voice, Alucard frowned and grasped both the demon's wrists. "Vhat?" he asked but then looked to his left and his right before looking back at Zalith. "Vhere are ve?"

"The forest. We left Ada's wedding not too long ago."

"Ada? Vhere is she?"

"Dead," the demon revealed.

Alucard wasn't sure if he believed it. "Dead?"

"I killed her. She dosed you with nightshade."

Alucard frowned and slowly took his eyes off Zalith. He looked down at the ground, unsure of what to say. How could he have been so stupid? He felt so embarrassed. Ada made him look like some foolish, weak child who had no idea what he was doing. What must Zalith think of him now? To be drugged so easily…how stupid. He couldn't face him; he was sure he now thought less of him, and that horrified him.

Zalith took his hands from the vampire's neck and frowned in concern. "The werewolves fled when I killed Ada, and I carried you away from the hilltop. I was going to take you home."

Letting go of Zalith's wrists, Alucard glared at the ground beneath them. He was quickly beginning to remember what happened, and he couldn't help but worry about how it made him look. Why he cared what Zalith thought of him, he wasn't sure, but he *did* care—so much that he needed to know. "You probably vink of me as an idiot. I zon't know 'ow zhat 'appened," he said sullenly.

"Why would I think that?"

"Because vas stupid," Alucard grumbled. "*I* vas stupid. I vasn't paying attention. I should 'ave just set 'er on fire or someving."

Zalith shook his head. "You came here intending to give her a chance to leave, and that's what you tried to do. It wasn't your fault she decided to come without clothes. I'm sure anyone would've reacted in the same way."

With a conflicted frown, Alucard slowly looked at him. "And vould you 'ave veacted zhe same vay?" he asked skeptically.

He smiled slightly. "Anyone, Alucard. She was acting deranged. You did what you could, and I don't think you are or were stupid."

Alucard took his eyes off the demon and glared into the trees beside him. He wasn't entirely convinced, but he didn't feel the need to overthink it. Ada was dead, and he'd no longer have to deal with her or her nonsense. He would, however, have to deal with the repercussions of her death. The werewolves weren't going to take it lightly; all Alucard could do was hope that Zalith wouldn't be the one who was targeted. Ada had been his business, not Zalith's. The last thing he wanted was for Zalith to have to deal with a whole new world of trouble and danger because of him.

He sighed and shrugged. "At least neizer of us got 'urt, huh?"

Zalith smiled slightly. "Indeed. However, you should burn off the nightshade before we head back to your house; it's a nice night, so maybe we could take a walk?"

The vampire glanced at him. While Zalith was right about burning off the sedative, he wasn't sure a walk would help—all he wanted to do was sleep. However, despite his exhaustion, walking with *Zalith* sounded rather inviting, as did any moment with him. If he could spend any more time with Zalith before they had to part ways for another week, then he would take it. He looked back over at the trees and frowned nervously. "Ve can valk," he agreed quietly.

With a content smile, Zalith helped Alucard move away from the tree. He made Alucard put his arm around his shoulders so that he wouldn't stumble about the place and moved his own arm around Alucard's back, helping him to stand comfortably. Then, the demon began to slowly walk through the forest. The beach wasn't too far ahead, and that seemed to be where he was leading Alucard.

After a short while, they emerged from the tree line onto the black-sand beach. The six moons sat high in the night sky, reflecting an array of dazzling colours off the ocean's slowly moving water. The sand shimmered like glass in the moonlight and looked almost like a reflection of the star-filled sky.

"How do you feel now?" Zalith asked.

"Zhe same—like shit," Alucard muttered.

With an amused smile, Zalith looked ahead again. "Ada really had everything planned out, didn't she? This plan to marry you, even your whole lives together," he teased.

Alucard rolled his eyes and glared over at the sea as the waves moved back and forth. "She vas alvays nonsensical. I should 'ave seen zhis stunt coming."

"I can believe that," Zalith agreed. "You gave her her chances, and now she's dead, and it was rather enjoyable to see her die."

The vampire scoffed. "I vish I could 'ave seen zhat."

Zalith smirked. "At least you'll be free of her now."

"Vhatever. I just 'ope zhe volves zon't cause me too much of an annoyance. I 'ave to vinish zhis vampire velocation mission, and vonce zhat's done, I'm sure Zamien vill 'ave ozzer vork vor me," he mumbled as they continued walking along the beach. He then smirked slightly and glanced at the demon. "Did she cry?"

With an amused laugh, Zalith nodded. "You could say that, yes."

"Good," Alucard said. "I should've done zhat a long time ago."

"Well, as for the wolves and their revenge, if you need or perhaps just want my help, I will gladly give it. I enjoy killing werewolves with you—I have enjoyed just about everything we've done together. You're fun to be around, and I don't say that lightly. My idea of fun is something others might call questionable."

"I velate. I veel zhere vill be many verevolf battles to come, so zhat gives us many more excuses to spend time togezzer."

Glancing at him, Zalith smiled again. "It does."

The pair then fell silent as they continued along the beach. Zalith set his eyes on a rather large, vast piece of darkened driftwood not too far up ahead and started to lead the way over to it. "Let's sit," he suggested.

Alucard felt no need to hesitate or refuse. A chance to sit and rest was something he'd been hoping to come across.

Once they reached the log, he pulled free from Zalith and slowly slumped down onto it, resting his back against an upright piece of wood branching off the trunk.

Zalith sat beside him and asked, "Do you feel any better?"

Alucard sighed and shrugged. "A little," he admitted, his tiredness beginning to slowly yield.

For a moment, they stared out at the ocean, the calm breeze carrying a certain serenity with it.

Zalith frowned curiously. "If you don't mind me asking, what do you plan to do, Alucard? With your future. Surely, you have plans?"

With a small moment of hesitation, Alucard took his eyes off the water and glared down at the sand. "Vell, I've been vorking to vebuild my empire; vonce zhat's done, I guess I'll just…vatch over zhat. I'll still 'ave to do vings, keep people in line. And now zhat Ada is dead, I'm sure I'll 'ave to deal vith zhe vepercussions of zhat. Zhe volves vill unite, and zhey vill start a war vith zhe vampires. I'll 'ave zhat to sort out. And zhen…zhere is Zamien. 'E vill alvays 'ave someving vor me to do, so I'll never be vithout vork," he explained quietly.

Zalith then frowned in concern. "Damien: why—"

"No," Alucard interjected. "I told you about *my* plans, now you tell me about *yours*."

The demon smiled. "Of course. As you know, my life is currently rather complicated. I despise the fact that I don't have a home and that I have to keep moving around. I await the day I'll finally have a place to call my own—and…perhaps when that day comes, you could come and visit *me* instead," he said, looking at him.

Listening, Alucard nodded as he tried to think of something to reply with—

"Tell me, vampire," Zalith then said, "have you *ever* thought about dating someone?" he asked with a sly smirk.

Unsure of what that had to do with anything they were talking about, Alucard scowled and glared at the sea. "No," he mumbled.

"What about *me*?"

Alucard frowned and glanced over at him. "*Vhat* about you?"

"Would you date *me*, Alucard?"

As both embarrassment and confusion smothered his face, Alucard turned his head and stared at the ocean further down the beach. Why would he ask such a thing, and now of all times? As nervous as it made him to think about it, he couldn't stop himself from considering it. *Would* he date Zalith? Would he agree to share a romantic relationship with him? Was that even Zalith asking if they could be together, or was he just asking if Alucard would date him if the opportunity arose? He wasn't sure, and he sure as hell wasn't going to ask—he didn't have the courage.

Zalith smiled and looked ahead at the ocean. "Anyway," he said. "I'm not sure when I'll be able to stop wandering, but when I do have a place, I'd like you to come and visit."

The vampire frowned and glanced at him. "In Eltaria?"

"Yes."

Alucard looked back out at the ocean. "If...I'm not busy," he agreed, trying to keep his nervousness from gripping him. "I vould...do zhat."

Clearly content with his answer, Zalith leaned his head on Alucard's shoulder.

The vampire stared ahead, unsure of what he should say or do. Did he disapprove of Zalith's move? No. He just didn't know how to take it. Did he have to do anything? Was Zalith waiting for him to say or do something in response? He didn't know, and as nervous as it made him for Zalith to be this close, he didn't try to escape. He enjoyed it; he welcomed any attention Zalith would give him. Despite his nervousness, and despite what happened before this, he felt...calm—calm enough to sit there and enjoy the silence.

"My world isn't much different to yours," Zalith said quietly. "Apart from the single moon and the current state of things."

Glancing down at him, Alucard frowned. "Zhis vorld isn't much better."

"It is," Zalith said. "Because it's where *you* live."

Unsure of what to say, Alucard pouted and looked down at the sand. For some reason, Zalith's answer made him feel strangely sad. In the serenity of the place he found himself in, his mind wandered to his despondent thoughts. He was sure that Zalith felt something for him; he was sure this demon wanted to be with him, to share something of a romantic nature. He thought he wanted that too—he still wasn't entirely sure if he was confident enough, however. As much as he might wish for more with Zalith, he was still afraid that if he invested his feelings and time into someone, it wouldn't last. His life was already complicated enough; if he allowed himself to fall for someone and then let them leave him, he was sure his life would become unbearable.

He glanced down at Zalith again but then set his eyes on the ocean. His life didn't matter right now. Nothing else mattered other than the here and now. He was with Zalith, the single person who managed to make him feel some sort of happiness, some kind of enjoyment in his life. But above all that, Zalith made him feel…safe. This demon wasn't afraid of Damien, and the moment he'd come to see that was the moment he realized he'd not refuse the chance to share more with him. He had never felt safe, he had never felt so calm, so relaxed—with Zalith, he felt all of those things, and he couldn't ignore how happy he made him.

As he stared out at the ocean, he allowed himself to focus on only the calmness he felt whilst in Zalith's presence.

Zalith glanced up at him…but his sights then shifted to his neck. Without hesitation, the demon moved closer and gently pressed his lips against his skin.

Alucard frowned as he tensed up slightly. But he didn't feel uncomfortable—in fact, he felt strangely relaxed. Zalith's first kiss to his neck may have confused and surprised him, but not so much as to make him physically react. It was a new kind of attention, and coming from Zalith only made it feel more pleasant. It made him feel something he'd never felt before, something he didn't have a word for. But it was satisfying, and when he felt Zalith slowly kissing his way up his neck, he couldn't keep himself from tilting his head to the side, inviting the demon to continue as he pleased.

Zalith moved his left hand and placed it on the right side of Alucard's face; his kisses were getting closer to his jaw, and Alucard could feel the demon becoming excited. He lightly kissed his neck once more before moving to the bottom of Alucard's jawbone— but that was when Alucard began to feel hesitant. He moved his head ever so slightly in discomfort, and to his relief, Zalith understood, smiled, and kissed his way back down his neck.

The vampire relaxed but frowned strangely when he felt Zalith stop moving. Instead, the demon seemed to be prolonging a single kiss against the same area of his neck. If he didn't know better, he'd say Zalith had started *sucking* on his skin—was that what he was doing? Why? It felt almost as if he was going to sink his fangs into him. So Alucard waited, trying to ignore his unprecedented thoughts, the thoughts which made him hope that maybe Zalith *was* preparing to bite him. Was he? Alucard slowly and unsurely moved his hand and placed it on the back of Zalith's head, uncertain whether he should tell him to stop or wait and see if a bite was what he was leading up to.

But Zalith soon stopped and moved his face from Alucard's neck. With a content smirk on his face, he dragged his thumb over the area he'd been sucking and rested his head on Alucard's shoulder. "Would you mind if I stayed the night?" he asked, staring up at the vampire, who slowly looked down at him.

Although he was still profoundly confused about what Zalith was doing to his neck, Alucard felt no need to refuse him. The thought of being able to spend more time with the demon made him feel content. Of course, he was going to say yes—how could he not? He took his eyes off the demon and stared back out at the ocean. "If you vant," he answered. But before Zalith could say anything else, Alucard remembered that he'd earlier decided he would take more vampires back tomorrow. He looked back down at Zalith. "I vorgot to ask you. I vant to take more vampires back tomorrow—'alf of zhem. If you stay, can you still avvange zhat?"

Zalith smiled. "Of course I can."

With a slight smile, Alucard looked back out at the ocean and frowned. "Vell…ve should 'ead back, zhen. Is late."

The demon lowered his hand from Alucard's face and gripped his arm. "I'm rather content here," he said, smirking.

"Come on," Alucard said, taking his hand off Zalith's head as he stood up.

Smiling, Zalith also stood up. "Thank you for letting me stay," he said, following Alucard as he began to lead the way back along the beach.

Alucard glanced at him, unsure of what to say. He wasn't even sure if anything needed to be said. He just nodded and looked down at the sand, leading the way home in silence.

Chapter Sixty-Three

—⟨ ✝ ⟩—

Night's Revelations

| Alucard |

When midnight struck, Alucard and Zalith reached the manor. The vampire unlocked the door and invited Zalith to enter first, and as he followed the demon in, he pulled off his blazer and rested it on the table. His body still ached from Ada's attack, but he didn't feel the need to make a fuss about it.

He closed his door and made his way into his lounge as Zalith curiously followed. While Alucard went to the drinks cabinet, Zalith sat on the couch.

Alucard took out two wine glasses and handed them both to Zalith. "Vait 'ere," he mumbled.

Zalith nodded. "Okay."

The vampire headed through to the kitchen and took a bottle of unbranded wine from his wine cupboard. Then, he headed back into the lounge and sat on the other end of the couch. He pulled the cork from the wine bottle, let it breathe for a moment, and poured them both a glass. Once he handed one to Zalith, he slouched back on the couch with a quiet sigh.

"Thank you," Zalith said with a smile, also relaxing back on the couch. "There's no label. What are we drinking this time, vampire?" he asked with a smirk, nodding down at the wine bottle.

"Try," Alucard invited and sipped from his glass.

With a curious smile, Zalith did as he was told and took a sip of the wine. He then looked at Alucard, who was waiting with an expectant look on his face. "I like it. It's admittedly a little sweet for me, but it *is* still rather tasteful."

"Hmm," Alucard mumbled, looking down at his glass as he tapped his claws on its side.

"Did you make this?"

The vampire shrugged. "Is just a 'obby."

Zalith smirked. "So, weapons aren't the only thing you make in your spare time. What else do you do?"

"Noving," the vampire answered and took another sip.

"If you make wine, you must own a vineyard. Will I get to see it?"

Alucard glanced at him and frowned. "Vhy vould you vant to see a vineyard? Zhere's noving intervesting zhere."

"It belongs to *you*, and everything about you interests me," he said, smiling. "Perhaps…less sugar," he then suggested, looking down at his wine. "I've witnessed just how much you like to use it."

Rolling his eyes, Alucard tried to hide his embarrassment with irritancy. "I like sveet vings."

"Is that why you make this? Can you not find a brand sweet enough for you?" Zalith teased.

"No." Alucard pouted. "I told you, is a 'obby. And I make vor my yearly ball, too."

A curious smirk appeared on Zalith's face. "Yearly ball?"

He nodded and glanced at him. "I 'ost a party each year vor…vell…my birvday, I guess. No vone knows zhat's vhat is vor, zhough."

Zalith moved ever so slightly closer. "And do *I* get an invite to this party of yours?"

Alucard looked away and shrugged. "Maybe. Unless Zamien sends me off to do someving avound zhat time."

A perturbed frown struck Zalith's face. "Why does Damien insert himself into your life and business so much?"

The vampire stared into his glass as a sullen frown stole his content expression. "'E just does," he answered.

"You never told me what he does. I've heard that he keeps Lucifer away from you— does he? Detlaff found you rather easily. Is Damien perhaps…lacking?" he suggested, and when Alucard glanced at him, he grinned.

The vampire shrugged as he looked back down at his glass. "Zamien keeps a protective ethos avound me—a perception vilter. Zhat keeps Luciver vrom being able to locate me—keeps *anyvone* vrom being able to locate me. Also keeps people vrom being able to recognize me unless I vant zhem to. Zetlaff managed to vind me vhrough Ben, so I suspect an ethos-crafted sibling of mine can see vhrough zhe perception ethos."

Zalith nodded slowly. "Is that all Damien does?"

"Yes."

"Any mage of considerable power could do the same thing for you…and you could be free of Damien. I actually happen to know two Arch m—"

"No," Alucard denied with an irritated scowl and then finished his wine.

"Well, if you change your mind, let me know."

"Vhat I vant is to change zhe subject."

"Okay," he said with a smile, finishing his wine.

As he refilled their glasses, Alucard took a moment to think back to the conversation they had on the beach. Zalith mentioned not having a home, and Alucard remembered the demon was hiding because he lost the war in his world. He handed Zalith his glass, leaned back, and looked at him. "Vhat caused zhe war in Eltaria?"

Zalith sighed quietly as he stared into his wine. "Back home, there's a divide between the humans and people like us—of course. But in Eltaria, most non-human races are governed by *our* queen and her council, which happens to be compromised of a handful of powerful demons," he said with a smirk. He then looked at Alucard. "There has always been a certain amount of tension between us and the humans, but things started to escalate when, one day many years ago, a group of werewolves planned an assault against a rival pack which had been moving in on their territory. They stupidly attacked the wrong caravan and tore a human dignitary and his family to shreds. They claimed it was an accident, but I think they spotted the expensive caravan, saw an opportunity to make some money, and took it. Either way, that started a chain reaction of events that ultimately got the demons involved *en masse*, and before we knew it, we were at war with the humans and their allies."

"Verevolves; vhy am I not surprised?"

"I've heard there were many wars here. Tell me about one," Zalith requested.

"Vhich *vone*?"

"The largest one, perhaps?"

Alucard looked down at his drink and smirked slightly. "Zhere vere at least vive large-scale wars."

"Okay, then tell me about your personal favourite," Zalith said before sipping from his glass.

The vampire laughed. "Zhat vould be zhe vone I started."

Zalith smiled in response to Alucard's laugh and made himself comfortable, moving closer to the vampire.

"War 'as become a usual ving 'ere, but only zhe little vones. Vhen a big war 'appens, most of zhe vorld usually gets involved. My birth started many wars among cults and religions and vhatever else 'umans do. I zon't pay much attention to zhe vorld outside my intervests, but I do know zhat zhere isn't any kind of ruling vigure zhat dominates ozzer zhan zhe Numen. Some countries 'ave kings, queens, emperors, and zhey govern over everyving zhat lives in and enters zheir country."

The demon leaned his elbow on the back of the couch and rested the side of his face in his hand as he listened silently.

"I spent a long time in DeiganLupus vhen I vas virst constructing zhe Nosveratu Empire. Vone of my vampires killed a monarch vhilst trying to turn 'im. I zon't know vhy Attila let zhis amateur try and do 'is job, but—much like your own case—zhis caused a lot of uproar, 'umans vere rebelling and accused zhe king of vorking vith us, and 'e vas later assassinated. Zhe 'umans blamed us vor zhat and started a global war between 'umankind and vampires. I killed zhe king, in case you 'aven't alveady guessed zhat. 'E knew too much, and 'e vas likely to conspire against me. I removed 'im vrom zhe equation and began a war zhat vould inevitably be won by me. My win spread fear, and zhe 'umans vell back in line. Lasted a lot longer zhan I vould 'ave vanted, but I got vhat I vanted out of zhat. Zhe 'umans vhought zhat zhey vere rebelling against us, but zhey vere just digging zhemselves in deeper."

Zalith smiled, gazing at him.

As Alucard sipped from his glass, he glanced at Zalith and caught the demon staring at him. He frowned and looked away. "Vhat?" he mumbled, unsure of why he had to insist on staring at him.

"Keep talking," Zalith said.

The vampire scowled with a stubborn pout. "Vhy?"

"I enjoy listening to you talk; it makes me feel relaxed—and I also like your accent," he said, smirking.

Of course, Zalith's answer made Alucard feel strangely shy, so he looked away in an attempt to hide his embarrassed face.

With a flirty grin, Zalith leaned forward and moved *even* closer to him so that he was just a few inches from where he was sitting. "Can you say something for me in Dor-Sanguian, vampire?" he requested, keeping his voice quiet and honeyed.

Alucard frowned in confliction. Why was Zalith moving closer? Why had he already moved so close? Obviously, he wanted to be close to him, but if he moved any closer, the demon would more or less be in Alucard's lap. He wasn't going to do that… was he? Alucard looked out into the hall, avoiding Zalith's gaze. Why did he want him to say something in Dor-Sanguian? He wouldn't be able to understand it. Since Zalith said he liked his accent, maybe he just wanted to hear it accompanying the language responsible for it.

The vampire thought to himself for a few moments; he saw no reason to say no. Zalith was curious, and Alucard felt a need to sate his curiosity. But what to say? He frowned, thinking…perhaps he could say something he wanted Zalith to know. Maybe if he said it in Dor-Sanguian first, he might feel braver to say it in Deiganish one day. "*Mă simt de parcă, dacă ar fi să mă întrebi, as fi de acord cu o relatie cu tine. Una de natură mai intimă,*" he said, and as he glanced at Zalith's curious face, he smirked in amusement.

"What did you say?"

The vampire sipped from his glass and shrugged. "Maybe you'll know vone day."

"Why can I not know now?"

"Because I said so," Alucard sneered.

"Please," Zalith pleaded, smirking.

"No."

Zalith laughed quietly and sipped from his glass. "Fine. Would you tell your best friend if he couldn't already understand you?" he teased.

Alucard frowned at him. "Best vriend?"

"Attila," he said, finishing his drink.

As Zalith placed his empty glass on the table, Alucard snarled and looked down into his glass. "Attila is *not* my best vriend."

"Do you intend to do anything about him?" the demon asked.

"Vor wrecking my castle?" he grumbled. "You zidn't tell me vhat vas 'e said about me zhat made you veel zhe need to vight vith 'im. Vhat vas zhat?"

Zalith sighed hesitantly and looked down at his lap. "He called me a filthy, disgusting fag, and said that I'm turning you into a soft, emotional fairy," he explained, glancing at the vampire. "With the lack of an accent, I might add," he said with a skeptical but slightly amused look on his face.

Alucard frowned in confusion. He didn't understand what that statement meant, but he almost felt like he shouldn't ask. Why had it angered Zalith enough to start a fight with Attila, though? A fight that may have ended in his old associate's death.... He wanted to know. He looked at Zalith and admitted, "I zon't...know vhat zhat means."

"They are both...derogatory terms for gay men."

The vampire scowled and looked down at his drink. Unprecedented anger began to simmer inside him. It was one thing for Attila to degrade Zalith in front of him, but to go to Zalith and do it to him even after Alucard warned him to drop it? That angered him beyond words. While Alucard wasn't an openly gay man, Zalith *was*, and for Attila to see that and insult him because of it...*and* it was Zalith he offended, someone Alucard felt a deep, strong need to defend. Such words upset the demon, and he couldn't and *wouldn't* ignore that.

Evidently noticing the anger on the vampire's face, Zalith frowned in concern. "Are you okay?"

But he didn't reply. The vampire glared ahead, trying to process what he felt now knowing what Attila said. Alucard wanted to ensure that he wouldn't even *think* of upsetting Zalith again.

With a slight smile on his face, Zalith slowly moved his hand over to Alucard's left shoulder, leaning closer to him. However, as he moved to place his other hand on the right side of Alucard's face, the vampire frowned uncomfortably—but Zalith used his fingers to tuck the vampire's hair behind his ear.

He then smirked as Alucard glanced at him. "You never told me why you wear this," he said, lightly tapping the gold earring in Alucard's right ear.

Alucard took his eyes off the demon and glared at the window. "I made zhe ving," he uttered with such hostility that he felt like he might unsettle Zalith. But he was *furious*. Attila had upset his friend and he wasn't going to let that go unpunished.

He hastily stood up, escaping the demon's grip, and then stormed over to his front door.

"Where are you going?" Zalith asked as he stood up.

Pulling his front door open, Alucard made his way out. "Outside," he growled.

The demon followed and stopped in the doorway as Alucard headed over to the fountain.

Alucard lifted his hand and jerked it, and a black aura surrounded his palm. He summoned Attila…and as he glared up into the sky, he watched, waiting…and when a screeching little bat appeared in the distance, he clenched his fists and scowled in anger, preparing for what he was about to unleash.

Chapter Sixty-Four

— ⸕ ✝ ⸖ —

The Evening's End

| Zalith |

Zalith watched Attila land beside the fountain.

The dog-faced man smiled and held out his arms as he approached Alucard. "Alucard," he greeted contently, but whatever followed was in Dor-Sanguian, which Zalith couldn't understand.

Before Attila could finish whatever he was saying, though, Alucard smashed his fist into his face. Attila's skull cracked loudly, and blood exploded from his mouth and nose as he stumbled back. He only just managed to remain on his feet and held his hands over his bloody nose as he stared at Alucard in shock.

Attila had no time to question Alucard's attack or try to dodge—Alucard struck him again, his fist colliding with the left side of his face. The man was flung off his feet, and as he hit the ground, Alucard grabbed the back of his collar and pulled him back up, turning him to face him.

Alucard then mercilessly smashed his fist into Attila's bloody face once again. Attila stumbled back, trying to speak before each hit met his face, but he didn't have the chance to do so. As Alucard came at him again, he moved in what might be an attempt to counter, but Alucard was faster. Alucard gripped Attila's right wrist with his left hand, snapped it, and crashed his right fist into his face.

When he hit the ground, Attila coughed painfully. Alucard kicked him onto his back and slammed his foot down on his throat, glaring down at him. He seemed to ponder for a moment—Zalith hoped he was considering killing him—but then, with an irritated snarl, Alucard moved his foot from Attila's throat and instantly snatched hold of it with his hand. He pulled Attila to his feet, let go of him again, and smashed his fist into his face once more, but this time, with such force that Attila was sent flying back, and as he crashed through the wall surrounding Alucard's manor, Alucard snarled evilly.

Attila groaned in torment as he tried to pull himself from the rubble, but Alucard appeared over him before he had a chance to try and get up himself. Alucard began to repeatedly smash his fists into Attila's face one after the other, his blood spraying over the rubble and grass beneath him.

"Zon't you *ever* insult Zaliv again!" Alucard yelled, an almost distorted, *estranged* echo to his voice as he stopped hitting Attila's face and glared down at him. "Get your miserable, revolting vace out of my sight bevore I kill you!"

Without a word, Attila struggled to his feet and scurried off into the night with several uncomfortable-looking limps, leaving a trail of blood splattered along the grass as he fled.

Zalith stared over at Alucard as he stood up and wiped the blood from his face. He had no control over whatever expression might be on his face—all he could think about was how much he wanted Alucard in every way possible. Right now, he was severely aroused, so intensely that he couldn't stop his mind from wandering. If Alucard wasn't so volatile and nervous, Zalith would have already taken himself over there, grabbed the vampire, and kissed him so aggressively that his desire to fuck him until he whined in sheer delight would be made clear. Just imagining the sound of Alucard's blissful moans made him tense up.

But…he couldn't. As immutable as his own desires might currently be, he respected Alucard's boundaries and feelings far too much. So, he took his eyes off the vampire for a moment and glanced down at his hand, which was resting on the porch's fence. He hadn't even realized he'd dug his claws into the wood. He exhaled quietly, calming his thumping heart and racing thoughts; he took his hand off the porch and set his eyes back on Alucard, who was making his way over with an irritated look on his face—the face Zalith just wanted to kiss and touch. He couldn't—but…he wanted to…how *sorely* he wanted to.

However, as Alucard passed him, he raised his hand in an attempt to touch the vampire's neck, but Alucard hissed irritably as a warning and walked straight past him into his house.

Zalith laughed quietly and followed the vampire, closing the door behind them. He trailed Alucard back into the lounge, and as the vampire slumped down on the couch, he sat beside him. He made sure to leave a reasonable amount of space between them because he felt he might unintentionally get carried away. The demon sat there, calming down as he watched Alucard clean the blood from his knuckles with an aggravated scowl on his pale face.

The demon smiled as he watched the vampire pour himself a half glass of wine. "I thoroughly enjoyed that."

Alucard rolled his eyes and sipped from his glass. Once he finished the wine, he placed it down, made himself comfortable, and glanced at Zalith. "Zhat's been dealt vith;

ve von't talk about zhat anymore. Do you vant anozzer drvink?" he offered, picking up the almost empty wine bottle.

Zalith admired the vampire while he replied, "Actually if we're going to sleep soon, I'd prefer something warm." But as Alucard looked over at him, he smirked. "Or perhaps…something cold—and pale."

Alucard frowned strangely. "I'd…call my butler, but I vink 'e died."

"Of blood loss, I assume."

"Probably. Sergiu must 'ave disposed of 'im vhilst ve vere out earlier."

"Well, if your butler is absent, I could make us both tea if you'd like to show me to the kitchen."

Alucard nodded and stood up. "Zhis vay," he said. He led the way back into the entrance hall and through to the kitchen.

As he followed the vampire, Zalith took a moment to observe. Judging by the relatively pristine state of the kitchen, it looked as though it had never been used. That wasn't much of a surprise, though. Alucard was a vampire—well…more or less; he was a type of demon that could live solely off blood, and clearly, Alucard did just that. The kitchen appeared to have everything a typical one would possess, though, which made Zalith suspect that the vampire used to eat once upon a time, but one day simply chose to stop. Either that or he had a whole kitchen full of appliances for his butler to use.

"I zon't know vhat you need, so just do vhatever you need to do," Alucard mumbled, leaning back against the island in the centre of the large kitchen.

"I assume you never come out here?" Zalith asked, looking around to see if he could locate a container of tealeaves before he started physically searching. But there wasn't a single thing in the kitchen that looked as if it contained such a thing.

"I 'ave no need to. Emil did everyving. I gazzer 'e vould keep vings 'ere vor 'imselv—'e spent a lot of time out 'ere, come to vink."

Nodding, Zalith wandered over to one of the countertops lined with opaque, black containers and peeked into each one, hoping to find something he could use. "Do you ever eat, Alucard?" he asked curiously, glancing back at the vampire.

"No," he answered, watching Zalith as he lifted the lid of one of many containers.

As he checked the contents of the next jar, Zalith felt slightly relieved. He had successfully located some lemongrass—and doing so made him smile amusedly. He hadn't long come to realize that the vampire's unique, intoxicating scent often carried a hint of such a thing, and seeing it now made him linger on the fact for a few moments. Undeniably, that was yet another thing he found so very appealing about the vampire.

But he was allowing himself to drift into his thoughts, so he smiled and turned to face Alucard, trying to quickly come up with something else for them to discuss while he completed the unnecessarily perilous task of making tea.

He thought back to earlier—when they had captured Detlaff—and frowned. "You never did tell me what you got from Detlaff," he said, making his way over to the stove, and placing the already water-filled kettle on it.

"Vhy are you concerned?"

"Curious," he said, "and to make conversation."

Alucard shrugged. "Not much more zhan vhat you alveady 'eard vhen you vere in zhe room. I vound out vhat 'e did to Ben, so I know 'ow to veturn 'is voice to 'im if I get zhe time. I vound zhat zhe Diabolus *'ave* retreated because of Zamien. Luciver is still just as desperate to vind me—'e veels as zhough zhe creature avter 'im and zhe ozzer Numen vill arrive soon, so 'is desperation to veach zhe safety of zhis vorld is increasing as each day passes. Zetlaff is also vather odd. 'E is loyal to Luciver, but I veel as zhough 'e vould betray 'im if zhe vight opportunity presented itself. 'E likes…people, creatures. 'E desires a vreedom to vork, vone Luciver von't give 'im because 'e vinks Zetlaff is too young."

Zalith smiled, leaning back against the countertop beside the stove. "Do you plan to give him what he wants?"

"No."

"Then…what *do* you plan to do with him?"

"Keep 'im 'ere. I can't let 'im go, 'e vill tell Luciver vhere I am. Maybe I'll decide to do someving vone day vith 'im, so I von't kill 'im. 'E could be useful."

"Indeed," Zalith agreed. "What of Lucifer? Are you confident he won't find you?"

"Yes," Alucard confirmed. "Zamien dealt vith zhe Diabolus as 'e said 'e vould, so I 'ave no veason to doubt 'is oath to protect me vrom my vather."

Glancing down at the slowly boiling kettle, Zalith frowned in concern. He still didn't like Damien at all, and he couldn't help but feel as though there was something more to his attachment to Alucard. It wasn't his business, though. He looked back over at the vampire and smiled. "As for Ben, you *are* going to restore him, aren't you?"

The vampire rolled his eyes. "Maybe," he muttered. "Only because I need 'im."

"Speaking of voices," he then said. "Attila: I know you wanted to leave that subject behind, but I can't help but wonder why he spoke to me without his accent, without a single sign of his broken Deiganish."

"Vhat?"

It seemed as though Alucard didn't know what he was talking about. He stood up straight and took two cups from the cupboard beside him. As he placed them down and added a small amount of lemongrass to each of them, he glanced at the vampire. "He spoke as clearly as you and I—without your accent, of course. If I didn't know better, I'd say he was a born Deiganish speaker."

Alucard took his eyes off the demon and looked down at the floor for a few moments. "Attila is…my best subordinate. 'E ovten appears as many people and pretends to be ozzer people. 'E dresses like Dor-Sanguian vampire and speaks like vone vhen 'e is in Dor-Sanguis. Vhen 'e goes to DeiganLupus, 'e dresses like Deiganish man, speaks like vone. I guess 'e spoke to you like Deiganish man because you are Deiganish. Zhat's all zhere is to zhat."

"If that is the case, why did he choose to speak to me as if he was Dor-Sanguian when we first met?" he asked, pouring the hot water into the cups.

"Takes much effort to put on an accent. I assume zhat because 'e zoesn't like you, 'e zidn't vant to make zhe effort to continue to be fake vith you."

"So, what is his truth? Is he Deiganish, or Dor-Sanguian?"

"You tell me."

Picking up both cups of tea, Zalith made his way over to the vampire and frowned. "I can't, can I? Otherwise, I wouldn't be asking."

Alucard smirked. "Exactly."

Zalith smiled in amusement and followed the vampire as he made his way back into the hall and returned to the couch in the lounge. As he sat beside the vampire, he exhaled contently and smiled over at him. "So, tomorrow...."

"Tomorrow," Alucard agreed, placing his tea on the table. "Ve can meet at zhe usual time, but I vant to take 'alf of zhe vemaining vampires."

The demon took a small sip from his tea to try and hide his worried expression. "Is there a reason for this decision?"

"Zamien vants me to make more progress," he answered, looking down at his tea.

Alucard was obviously slipping into sadness once again—Zalith didn't want that. However, he didn't want to disregard the subject. If Alucard took half of the remaining vampires tomorrow, that would shorten the number of meetings they would have, ultimately shortening the amount of time they would get to spend together. He didn't want to lose a single moment with Alucard. And so, he couldn't help but ask, "Once we've completed these vampire relocations, what will become of us?"

The vampire looked over at him, waiting.

"What happens to the time we spend together?"

With a conflicted frown, Alucard looked back down at his lap. "Ve can still meet," he said without hesitation. "And...do vhatever."

Zalith smiled contently in both agreement and relief. "Of course we can."

"I need you to even zhe groups out. I vill take 'alf tomorrow, and avter zhat...vell...I'll vork zhat out. Can you do zhat?"

"Of course," Zalith agreed, but sadness clung to his face. Despite the reassurance, he still feared that he and Alucard might not get to see each other as often. But he knew that he'd do whatever he could to make sure they did.

As he picked up his tea, Alucard glanced at Zalith. He then sipped from his cup and looked down at his lap. "Ve can talk about zhis more tomorrow if need be. Is late, so…ve should probably get some rest. I can show you to zhe guest room," he offered.

Once he finished his tea, Zalith nodded and said, "Okay."

He then stood up and walked with Alucard as he led the way upstairs and along the landing. When they got to the door to the guestroom Zalith saw the night they spent getting drunk, Alucard pushed the door open. However, the room was empty and bland; there weren't even any blankets on the bed.

Alucard frowned awkwardly and looked at Zalith. "Zhere's um…I guess Emil vas in zhe middle of cleaning zhis room bevore 'e died." He then turned around and made his way to his own room. "I 'ave some spare covers," he said, glancing back at Zalith, who followed him.

The vampire pushed open his bedroom door and hastily hurried over to the dresser against the back wall.

Zalith waited in the doorway, watching him with a curious smile as he opened the dresser in search of blankets. His eyes, however, caught sight of something quite out of place in the gothic-styled gloomy bedroom. Lying on the floorboards, just visible under the vampire's bed, was a piece of folded parchment. The floor around it was dotted with silvery glitter, and Zalith just couldn't ignore it.

While Alucard was distracted, Zalith swooped over and snatched the paper from the floor. With a smirk on his face, he unfolded it—but what he set his eyes on was *not* what he'd been expecting *at all*. Hand-drawn on the parchment was a rather gruesomely detailed drawing of Ada; she was without a single piece of clothing, sitting with a forced shy look on her face with her right index finger in her mouth and her legs as widely spread as she could get them.

When Alucard turned to face Zalith, he frowned as soon as he noticed the paper in his hands. "Vhat is zhat?"

"You tell me," Zalith said amusedly as he held it out so that Alucard could see the drawing.

As soon as he saw it, the vampire snatched it from Zalith and aggressively tore it up. He then threw the shreds of paper out his window.

"Why was that under your bed, Alucard?" Zalith asked with a suggestive smirk.

Red-faced, Alucard snarled and returned to looking for a blanket. "Must 'ave slipped out zhe invitation she sent me," he grumbled.

"Are you sure?" Zalith teased.

Finally locating a blanket, Alucard pulled it from the drawer and handed it to the demon. "Yes," he hissed. "Vhat vould I be doing vith a naked picture of a voman I despise?"

Zalith then laughed slightly. "Why so defensive?"

Alucard rolled his eyes, pouted, and glared down at the floor. "I zidn't know vas zhere—is embarrassing."

"And the glitter?" Zalith asked as Alucard glared at him. "Was that in her invitation too?"

"Yes."

With a grin on his face, Zalith backed out of the room, dropping the subject as he could see he'd made Alucard uncomfortable. "Well, I'll see you in the morning," he said. As much as he might want to kiss or even *hug* the vampire goodnight, he felt as though Alucard wasn't at all in the mood for it.

Nodding, Alucard sighed quietly. "If you need anyving, you can just… do vhatever."

"Goodnight," he said, smiling.

"*Noapte bună,*" Alucard said.

Zalith then headed to the guest room, and before he stepped inside, he looked down the hall at Alucard and smirked. The vampire pouted shyly and swiftly disappeared into his room, closing the door behind him.

Every time he saw Alucard, Zalith's heart grew fonder, and tonight, he'd only become surer of his feelings. But the night was over, and it was time to rest. Knowing he'd get to see Alucard in the morning made him smile, though. So, he'd head to bed and focus on the fact he'd be seeing that adorable, volatile vampire again tomorrow.

ARCFOUR

✝

DESPAIR

Chapter Sixty-Five

Izuret

| Alucard |

Alucard woke to the sound of singing birds and rain. The heavy, *pouring* rain. The vampire stared out of his window as he lay in bed; the sky was a miserable grey as the sun slowly crept over the horizon. Skyfish swam around above, their scales shimmering like flashes of lightning. The sight reminded him of Aditus-Insula, the Island of Doorways—the same island he had to travel to every two weeks to transfer vampires from Eltaria to Aegisguard. It was an island he hated at first, but now it was part of his much-adored ritual of seeing Zalith. Soon, he'd probably never see that island again—or Zalith.

He wasn't sure what would happen once the mission was complete; Damien would give him a new task, and he was certain that if he was seen with Zalith while they weren't working together, Damien would be far less lenient in his punishments. Alucard scowled and rolled over onto his back, glaring up at the ceiling. He didn't want to think about Damien, or about never seeing Zalith again. All he wanted was to see that demon, be with that demon…. He didn't want to waste what little time they had left thinking about the what-ifs.

With a quiet sigh, he shuffled onto his right side and stared over at the wall. He felt strange and suddenly restless. His sullen thoughts were the cause, and he knew he wasn't going to be able to fall back asleep. It was already getting lighter outside; he was sure Zalith would wake up soon, and when he did, they'd probably have things to discuss before they parted ways. So, he thought he might as well get up and start his day now.

The vampire climbed out of bed and dragged himself into his bathroom—but as he stood in front of his mirror and went to pull off his shirt, he set his eyes on what appeared to be a bruise on the left side of his neck. How had that got there? He frowned in confusion, pulled off his shirt, and leaned closer, glaring at the bruise. How could he forget that Zalith had been, for the lack of a better explanation, sucking on his neck? The bruise-like mark must have been what the demon intended to leave on his skin—and there it was.

Alucard scowled and pouted, unsure of how he felt. Zalith had taken the opportunity to leave his mark on him, and he felt strangely okay with it. In fact, it made him feel some sort of happiness. He wasn't sure why, but he wasn't going to give it too much thought. It would soon fade, he was sure.

As he sighed irritably, he proceeded to brush his teeth and tidy his hair. He then took one last glance at the mark on his neck before leaving the bathroom. He changed into a new black shirt and trousers, left his room, and headed up to his study, which sat in the highest reaches of his house. Once he got inside, he sat behind his desk, took a book from the bottom drawer, and flicked through to the page he last read.

Today, he said he would restore Ben's voice, so he had to make sure he knew what he was doing—the last thing he wanted to do was hurt Ben. The things he needed would already be waiting at the castle; all he needed now was Ben, who he could send Sergiu to collect later. However, as he stared at the pages, he couldn't engross it very well. He still felt uncomfortably restless. So, he returned the book to the drawer, closed it, and impatiently tapped his claws on his desk as he looked around his study for something else to do.

His eyes immediately shifted to his violin on one of the top shelves. While he would usually practice, he knew he shouldn't. Zalith was still sleeping downstairs, and the last thing Alucard wanted to do was wake him.

He looked at the papers stacked on his desk, three of which were the letters Dirk sent him a week ago. As much as he disliked that human, he couldn't continue to ignore his reports—especially now that they'd been translated for him. He rolled his eyes, picked them up, and read through them. It didn't take very long, though, and they weren't exciting or the least bit important.

The vampire sighed, dropped the letters back on the pile, and rested his arms on the desk with a lazy, irritated sigh. While he sat there in silence, his earlier despondent thoughts tried to consume him once more—but he didn't allow it. He couldn't. He stood up and made his way over to the left wall shelf. He snatched the first item his eyes set themselves on—a gold ticking fog watch—and took it back to his desk. He slumped down, took a moment to eye the fog watch from all its angles, and then began slowly and carefully taking it apart. The last thing he wanted was to sit there without something to preoccupy himself; that was when his thoughts became most overbearing. So, he'd distract himself the way he knew best.

He'd not be on his own for long, though. He'd become too focused on his work that he hadn't heard Zalith wake up, open his door, and make his way through the house. It wasn't long until the demon was knocking on the door to his study, and as it opened, Alucard glanced at it, watching as Zalith stepped inside. As the demon smiled at him and closed the door behind him, Alucard looked back down at the fog watch he'd taken apart and begun transforming into something else completely.

"Good morning," Zalith said as he sat in the seat in front of Alucard's desk.

"*Dimineată*," Alucard mumbled, focusing on what he was doing.

Watching as Alucard fiddled with the small, intricate parts of what had once been a fog watch, Zalith asked, "Have you been up long?"

Alucard fixed the last tiny cog into place, creating an owl-like construction. Then, he looked over at Zalith. "No. About… an hour or so."

Zalith smirked in amusement. "That looks as though it's taken you more than an hour," he said, nodding at the owl. "It's impressive."

Glancing back at his window, Alucard saw that it had not only stopped raining, but it was a lot later in the morning than he thought. He frowned and tucked the owl into one of his drawers. "I zidn't vealize vas zhis late," he said, slowly looking back at Zalith.

"Do you play?" Zalith abruptly asked.

"Vhat?"

Zalith looked over at the violin on Alucard's shelf and then back at the vampire. "It was one of the first things I noticed upon entering."

The vampire shrugged. "Maybe."

Zalith smirked, but before he could speak, a light tapping at the window caught both his and Alucard's attention. They looked up at the single rounded window, setting their eyes on a small, bat-like creature. It patted on the glass with its tiny hands, asking to be let in as it floated silently outside.

Alucard had no idea what he was looking at. The creature's huge, deep-purple-coloured eyes stared in at them both, and its imp-like body was covered in short, fuzzy, steely-blue fur, ceasing at its ankles and neckline to reveal scaley pink skin. Its head was strangely large and looked much like a hairless cat with larger bat-like ears on either side. The creature appeared to be around a foot and a half in height with a pair of leathery wings on its back—but it wasn't flapping them to stay suspended in the sky. It seemed to just… float.

The creature tapped at the window again with its right hand, an almost desperate look appearing on its face while it waited to be let in.

Zalith took his eyes off the creature and looked at Alucard. "How long have you been playing?"

"Since… I vas a boy," he answered, shifting his gaze back to Zalith.

"Will you play for me?" he asked with a smirk, resting his arms on the table.

A nervous look found its way to Alucard's face as he looked at the shelves to his right. "Vell…."

The creature tapped at the window again, but this time, it was tapping on the one directly behind Alucard, who frowned and looked back at it. It waved and then pointed down at the window's lock, chittering quietly. Alucard then watched as the creature's large eyes shifted to Zalith, who he also turned to look at.

Zalith didn't look at all happy to see it, but with an irritated sigh, he leaned back in his seat. "Can you let it in, please?"

Alucard reached back behind his seat, unlocked the window, and pushed it open so the cat-like creature could float in. It landed on his desk in front of Zalith, who stared at it with total disinterest, but Alucard wasn't sure what to make of it. Could it be Zalith's pet? Probably not.

"Vhat…is it?" Alucard asked.

"An izuret. They're little messenger demons."

"Oh…."

Looking down at the izuret as it pouted, Zalith rolled his eyes and sighed. "Speak."

The creature wiggled around, planting its feet firmly onto the desk so it was comfortable, and then opened its mouth. In a voice not of its own, the izuret spoke, "I know that you're out doing God only knows what with God knows who—probably some irrelevant peasant—but at least do me the courtesy of sharing whether you'll be coming home for the night or not. I'm tired of waking up to mystery every morning. How am I supposed to know whether you've been killed?! Show me some respect!" It was a *woman's* voice.

Rolling his eyes once more, Zalith glared at the creature as it held out its hands and chattered quietly, asking for payment in exchange for its services. He, however, had nothing to offer it at the moment. "I will pay you later. Tell her: I am alive, and I will be home later," he grumbled, waving his hand in dismissal.

The izuret pouted and chirped quietly to itself as it waddled around to face the window. But before it could leave, Alucard frowned upon noticing something in the creature's left arm.

"Vhat 'appened?" he asked quietly, pointing to the creature's arm, spotting a small cut beneath its fur.

It stopped in its tracks, glanced down at its arm, and pouted sadly. It then answered him with a short series of chattering chirps, holding out its left arm.

With a sympathetic frown, Alucard allowed the imp-like creature to lay its arm in his hand so that he could look at it closely. The small cut in its shoulder looked to be fairly recent; another few smaller cuts were lined down the majority of its fuzzy arm, and in the palm of its scaley-skinned hand was a small, black thorn. As the creature mumbled sadly to him, the vampire carefully removed the thorn.

It squeaked quietly in response and pulled its hand away from Alucard. But when it noticed its pain was gone, it looked back down at its hand and started to chirp happily in thanks.

Watching, Zalith sighed and shook his head, clearly trying to hide his smile. "It is fine," he insisted. "Let it go."

"No," Alucard sneered, glancing at Zalith. He then set his eyes back on the cat-like creature. "Are you okay now?"

Looking down at its hand, the creature thought to itself for a few moments and then shook its head. It waddled closer to him, pouting with a pained look on its face. It chattered quietly as it got closer to the vampire, who looked down at it with a sympathetic frown.

Alucard couldn't ignore a creature in need of help; he scooped it into his arms as if it were an infant. "Zon't vorry," he mumbled quietly, looking down at it as it stared up at him. "I'll 'elp you," he assured it as he began to remove another thorn from its arm. "Vhy vould you fall into a rose bush?"

The creature replied once more with a series of sad chirps and chatters as it stared up at Alucard, an awed look in its huge, purple eyes.

"Next time, vatch vhere you are going," he said as he pulled the last thorn out. The izuret nodded and chittered. He then glanced over at Zalith and frowned down at it. "Vhat does 'e pay you?"

The creature's eyes widened as a look of admiration appeared on its face. It chattered, moving its hands to imitate a large object. It then rested its arms on its body and gawped up at him.

Something shiny? Alucard smiled slightly and reached into the drawer he'd stored his recently-made trinket in. As he handed the small hand-crafted owl to the creature, it squealed excitedly and clutched the trinket close to its chest.

Alucard then helped the izuret to stand on his desk once more. "You can go now, and vemember vhat I said."

With a frantic nod, the izuret chittered in thanks. It then glanced back over its shoulder at Zalith before spreading its wings. It flapped them once and ascended, floating out of the same window it entered through, leaving Zalith and Alucard alone

When the creature left, Zalith smiled as he set his eyes back on the vampire.

"Who sent zhat?" Alucard asked with a skeptical frown. "Zhe message."

"Varana," he answered. "She's a good friend of mine."

Alucard's suspicion grew. He hadn't forgotten what the creature's message said, and he felt the need to question it. He was, after all, undeniably allowing himself to fall for Zalith, and he didn't want to keep letting that to happen if this demon had something he didn't wish for Alucard to know. "Vhy does she speak as if she is your keeper?" he questioned. "'Ome for zhe night? You live togezzer?"

Zalith laughed slightly. "She is very loud and rather demanding, but she means well. And yes, we *do* live together, and probably will be for the foreseeable future."

As much as he wanted to ask why they lived together, Alucard kept himself from doing so. He wasn't sure what the answer might be, and he was admittedly afraid to hear it. While he was already relatively certain that Zalith wasn't romantically interested in women, he still felt slightly afraid that such a living arrangement might disregard that fact. He didn't want to ask about it; he didn't want to *think* about it.

Alucard took his eyes off the demon and looked down at his desk. "Tonight, vill I be meeting you in zhe same place—zhe catacomb?" he asked, changing the subject.

"Seventy-three vampires remain, and you wish to take half. Thirty-six vampires will be at least twenty-too-many to fit in that small room," Zalith replied, smirking. "Unless you're one for tight spaces, Alucard, I'd advise we meet somewhere more…spacious."

"Vhat do you suggest?" he asked tonelessly. He didnt want to show any reaction to Zalith's flirtatious tone.

For a few moments, Zalith thought to himself but then smiled again. "There is a barn, I believe, not too far from the ruins of the castle. I can meet you in there with them," he suggested.

"Vine."

"Are you…okay?" Zalith asked in concern.

The vampire stood up. "Vhy vould I not be? I 'ave stuff to do bevore ve meet tonight, so I should get veady to go and do zhat."

With a worried frown on his face, Zalith followed Alucard as he left his study and started to make his way down the stairs. "You seem upset," he said, walking behind him.

"I'm not upset," he muttered.

Following Alucard down towards the entrance hall, Zalith sighed quietly. "Are you upset about Varana?"

The vampire stopped in his tracks, rolled his eyes, and looked back at him. "Vhy do you live vith a voman who asks vhy you zidn't come 'ome last night and seems overly mad about zhat?"

"I live with her because she's my best friend; she's not my wife, and she never will be. It's purely platonic, and you have nothing to worry about. She's just obnoxiously dependent on me because that's the kind of person she is. And I've said before that I'm gay," he explained. He then glanced at Alucard's neck and smirked. "I'm sure I've also made that clear. Do you like it?" he asked with an unseemly smile.

Seeing Zalith's eyes glance at the mark on his neck, Alucard pouted, moved his hand over the mark the demon left on his skin, and looked away from him, trying to hide his embarrassed expression. "Vhatever," he mumbled before continuing towards his front door.

Zalith smiled in amusement and followed the vampire. He watched silently as Alucard put on his blazer and cape, and then pulled the door open.

As much as Alucard enjoyed spending time with Zalith, he knew they had to part ways for now. Zalith needed to gather the vampires for tonight's move, and *he* needed to see Ben. He also felt that he needed time to reflect on everything that happened—Ada's death, his feelings for Zalith, Zalith's feelings for him—he couldn't sink into his thoughts if someone was going to be watching him.

He led the way out into the manor grounds and sighed as he turned to face Zalith. "I'll see you tonight, hmm?"

The demon smiled. "That you will," he confirmed.

"I'm…sorry vor my 'aste in saying goodbye, I just 'ave a vew vings to do today and vant to get zhem done bevore I come to Eltaria."

"You don't need to be sorry because you're busy," Zalith said, smiling. He then stepped closer and hesitated for half a moment. "Can I…hug you, vampire?"

A nervous expression smothered Alucard's face before he had the chance to turn away. Why had Zalith made a point of asking *this* time? Alucard felt as if he would have much preferred him to just do it—he did, however, appreciate him considering the fact that he might not welcome such contact.

He *did* want the demon to hug him. So, he looked away and frowned. "Yes."

With a content smile, Zalith moved closer and wrapped his arms around the vampire.

Alucard frowned in confliction—but not because he didn't like being in Zalith's embrace. He found that he profoundly enjoyed it. Being so close to him, being in his arms; it made him feel safer than he already did with this demon. He fought off his anxiety and gradually moved his arms around Zalith, too…and held him, but not so tight as to make him uncomfortable. He wasn't even sure how tightly he should hug him.

However, the longer he remained in Zalith's tight embrace, the more he felt himself wishing they didn't have to leave each other. He couldn't risk allowing himself to ask the demon to stay, so he pulled free of their hug and stepped back. "I 'ave to go now."

Zalith nodded and contently said, "Until tonight." Then, he headed off towards the wall to create a rift.

Alucard made his way over to the stables. It felt like it was going to be a long afternoon, but he had tonight to look forward to; knowing he'd get to see Zalith again so soon made him feel content, a feeling he'd been experiencing a whole lot more lately. And it was all because of a demon he'd once thought he'd hate forever.

Chapter Sixty-Six

— ⸜ ✝ ⸝ —

Voices

| Alucard |

When Alucard reached the stables, he set his eyes on Sergiu, who was tending to Sebastian's mane.

"*Aici*," the vampire called.

Sergiu ceased his task and made his way over to Alucard. "Yes, sir?"

"Did you dispose of Emil?"

The groundskeeper nodded. "Yes, sir. He collapsed whilst changing the bird feeder. I tried to save his life, but I was too late."

Alucard rolled his eyes. "Vind me a new butler."

"Of course, sir."

"And bring me Sebastian."

With a humble bow, Sergiu turned around and disappeared back into the stables to prepare the black stallion.

While he stood there, Alucard glanced back to see if Zalith was still hanging around, but he was gone. That made him feel despondent. He'd become so fond of being in Zalith's company that any time without him felt dull and empty. Zalith was the only person he wished to talk to, spend time with, and have fun with. The thought of anyone else repelled him.

"Here, sir," the groundskeeper said.

Alucard took Sebastian's reins from him. "Get a message to Ben, too. I need 'im at zhe castle in virty minutes."

"Of course."

Then, the vampire mounted and tapped the stallion's side, instructing it to trot forward. He left his manor and made his way along the path that would take him to his castle. As he journeyed onwards, he allowed himself to drift into his thoughts, and of course, his first thought was Zalith. He'd become so fond of that demon; he'd come to enjoy everything about him, even the things that irritated him or made him feel nervous. Zalith's smile was one such thing: he could never work out whether the demon was smiling because he was amused or because he was happy. Either way, Alucard no less than adored it.

While Zalith might be becoming more forward with his flirtatious comments, Alucard didn't feel at all uncomfortable. As nervous as they made him, he also *enjoyed* them. It was simply a part of who Zalith was, and Alucard felt there might not be a thing he didn't like about him—other than the fact that he appeared to live with some woman who insisted upon knowing where he was. Alucard didn't like that, but that wasn't his business. He was sure that Zalith was pursuing *him* and would continue to do so until they ended up somewhere other than where they were now, whether it be good or bad. Of course, he hoped for the former.

As his castle came into view, Alucard thought about what he was going to do with Detlaff. He didn't want to kill him, but he couldn't risk leaving him in a dungeon. That Satan spawn was undeniably smart, and Alucard expected him to find a way out sooner or later. He had to make sure that didn't happen, and he had a few ideas in mind. There were many ways to ground a demon—he knew that all too well. However, he was sure that Detlaff was *not* going to be as enthusiastic to see him since he tore away his horns, which were—aside from a demon's wings—a demon's most prized possession. There was a high chance that Detlaff would give him a hard time, but he wasn't unprepared.

Just then, his thought trail was broken when he caught a glimpse of mahogany in the corner of his eye. He frowned irritably, and as none other than Elvin yelled his name, he looked to his left, setting his blue eyes on the bard. Elvin approached on horseback, adorned in his usual get-up, and with a wide, bright smile on his face as he waved and sang, "Aleksei, Aleksei!" so many times that Alucard felt he might just change his middle name.

"Aleksei!" Elvin called, instructing his coffee-brown horse to walk alongside Alucard's.

"Vhat, Elvin?" Alucard grumbled, glaring ahead.

The bard scoffed. "It's been a week since I last saw you and all I get is a 'vhat Elvin'. Rude."

Alucard rolled his eyes and glanced at him. "'Ow vas your veek?" he asked, trying to sound interested.

"Well, now that you ask," the bard said, clapping. "You know that barmaid from that place I was in the night you killed that werewolf all over me?"

"No."

"We went on a date!"

With a confused, surprised frown, Alucard glanced at him again. "You?"

"Right!? Me!" he exclaimed happily.

"Is she deaf?"

The bard pouted. "You're so awful."

Alucard rolled his eyes and glared ahead.

"Anyway, we went for a drink, talked about stuff—"

"I can probably guess vhere zhis is going," he mumbled to himself.

"One thing led to another, and before I know it—"

"I zon't vant to know," Alucard snarled.

The bard chuckled to himself. "She's such a nice lady, Aleksei; you'd like her."

"Doubtvul."

"Why're you being so sour?" Elvin frowned irritably. "She really *is* nice. Anyway, I invited her to whatever you have planned for my birthday this year," he said, smiling.

Birthday? How could he forget? He always made a point of doing something for Elvin when his birthday came around to keep the bard from aggravating him with it. It was this coming Friday…in six days. He didn't have anything planned, and he didn't exactly have the mind space to try and *make* a plan.

"You…didn't forget, did you?" Elvin asked sadly.

"No," Alucard said. "You can come to my 'ouse…vith Ben, Tobias…and anyvone else you vant to invite."

Elvin nodded slowly…but then frowned skeptically. "Um…what's that?"

"Vhat?" Alucard grumbled.

Elvin tapped the side of his own neck. "Did…why do you have that?"

Alucard rolled his eyes and glared ahead again, not at all in the mood to entertain Elvin's jealousy.

But the bard was relentless. "Did that stupid demon do that?"

He ignored him.

"So, you're still seeing him?"

Still, he remained silent, setting his eyes on his castle as they came closer to it.

"Are you like…dating or something…together? Is that where you've been all this week? With *him*?"

Alucard sighed quietly, closing his eyes, trying to keep himself calm.

"You shouldn't see him, you know. He still looks shady, and I don't like him. I know you told me to stop, but…I don't want you to get hurt, and…he's—"

"Zon't make me tell you again," Alucard warned him. "Zhis time, I von't be so nice as to let you continue living."

Utterly shocked, Elvin scoffed and looked away. "All right, sheesh…I just…is he going to be there for my birthday?"

The vampire sighed as they passed the castle gates and made their way up to its entrance. "No," he answered. "Is *your* event, so only zhe people you vant zhere vill be zhere."

"Thank God," Elvin muttered as they stopped outside the castle door.

"Go," Alucard said before the bard could try to dismount his horse. "I 'ave shit to do—alone."

Elvin pouted. "What time should I be at your house on Friday?"

"Noon," the vampire answered, dismounting his horse. "I zon't vant to see you until zhen."

"Fine, god," he muttered.

As the bard left him alone, Alucard made his way inside. He walked across the empty entrance hall, through the busted wall which once held the door to his half of the castle, and down to the dungeon he stored Detlaff in. Upon opening the door, the estranged demon set his crimson eyes on the vampire, watching his every move with an evil, murderous scowl on his bloodied face.

"You came back for me, hmm?" he asked with a smile as the vampire closed the door behind him and lit the single lantern which hung from the wall to Detlaff's right. "Have you come to wriggle around in my head again? Or perhaps…to steal something else from me? Detlaff, your poor baby brother who just wants to be loved." He pouted sadly, his hair hanging over his tilted head, his wings drooping behind his back, and his pale skin painted an almost black purple with the dried blood from his broken horns.

Alucard approached the weakened demon and stood a few feet away from where he sat.

"What did you do with the information you stole from me, Vlady-poo? Did you find a way to help your precious Ben? You're not smart enough to reverse my handiwork," he said, grinning. "I was always smarter than my sisters and obviously smarter than you, or you would have killed me by now."

"I can do vorse zhan kill you."

"Ugh, please!" Detlaff begged with a longing tone. "It's so *boring* down here!" he screamed, wriggling around in his seat. "Have you come to gloat?!" he then yelled, realizing he couldn't escape from the black chains binding his wrist. "What is this?!" he asked, looking down at the chains.

"Mortem-metallum," Alucard said with a shrug. "Anti-zemon metal; grim reapers' scythes are crafted vrom zhat."

Detlaff then smirked. "And you came across this…how, big brother?"

"By killing zhe previous owner," he answered, stepping closer.

"Did *you*…kill a grim reaper? If that were the case, you'd have a *death mark* on you…but I don't detect it…so I assume the previous owner wasn't a grim reaper, but someone who had, in fact, killed one!" Detlaff sang.

Alucard snatched the demon's throat, glared into his eyes, and snarled irritably. He was done playing his little games. "I 'ave no veason to keep you alive, but I veel like I may 'ave use vor you vone day. Until zhen, I vill keep you 'ere. As vor now, you 'ave two choices: give me Ben's voice villingly, or I vill tear vrom you."

Looking up at him, Detlaff smiled and laughed amusedly. "Take it from me, if you wish," he invited, his tone becoming something more serious. "But before you do, ask yourself one question: *what* do you want to do right now? Do you want to kill me? Do you want to let me live? Do you *really* want Ben's voice back?" he asked. His eyes then glanced at the mark on Alucard's neck. "Nice love bite, by the way—who's the lucky lady? Or perhaps it's Mr Stare At Your Ass All Day? Where is he right now? Did you kill him? Eat him? Do tell me, big brother."

Confused by Detlaff's sudden change of tone and character, Alucard frowned and let go of him, backing off slightly.

Smiling deviously, Detlaff asked, "You get it, right?"

"Get vhat?" he asked, scowling at him.

"This," Detlaff said with a shrug, looking around. "The confusion, the sudden change—you get it, surely you must, big brother." He smiled with a pout. "The voices—the one that's telling you to kill me, the one that's telling you to keep me here, the one telling you to take back that vampire's voice, and perhaps…the one that's telling you to let me go. There might even be one telling you to make out with me," he giggled, licking his lips.

Disgusted, Alucard snarled and snatched Detlaff's throat again—

Detlaff laughed crazily through his struggled chokes. "Haven't you ever wondered what they are?" he asked desperately. "I can help, you know…if you want. You don't have to lock me away! Why lock me away when you can learn so much from me?"

"I zon't need to talk to you to get answers," Alucard snarled, tightening his grip on the demon's throat.

"Okay, but if you weren't interested in what I have to say, why would you come in here and talk to me? Why not just rip out my throat and go help that Ben vampire?" he asked, smiling. "Admit it, big brother, you wanna listen to little brother Detlaff, don't you? You won't kill me because you know I know so much more about Daddy than you do."

The vampire dug his claws into Detlaff's neck—

Before Alucard could tear his throat out, Detlaff squealed in panic. "W-wait!" he pleaded with a laugh. "You listen to them, right? They tell you so many things. They confuse you, anger you; they're not just voices, it's like they're totally different versions of yourself, right—I'm talking sense now, right?"

Alucard couldn't deny that Detlaff *was* making sense. By voices, he gathered the demon must be referring to thoughts, the conflicting thoughts Alucard experienced far too often to disregard.

Seeing that he had Alucard's attention, Detlaff continued, "There's so many of them, and sometimes you can't help but wonder if these thoughts are actually yours or someone else's. But you ignore them, right? When they become too loud, too intense—oh, the anger is intense, big brother, but so fun!" he giggled but then gagged as Alucard tightened his grip impatiently. "You should listen to them more, let them talk to you—*Father* talks to them. All of them. It's fun to watch, you know. He sits there, talking like there are five other people in the room. I tried it…but the anger…the desire…so hard to control. If you're not careful, they might gain control, consciousness."

He waited.

"Your loud thoughts, big brother, they're more than you think. Father has a problem, sick," he said, rolling his eyes. "Anyone who doesn't know will just think he's insane, talking to himself, seeing things. But not me, no, not little old Detlaff. I know…*we* know. Different versions of Father all live in his one body. They all get to talk with his mouth, move with his body, and sometimes more than one tries to take control—it's rather entertaining. Sometimes, he's angry—so angry. Then, sometimes—" he giggled, "—he's screwing every female in sight. Then, then…then…he's Mr Philosophical, sitting in his reading room trying to foresee prophecies. We never know what version of Father he'll be when we see him."

Glaring at him, Alucard frowned strangely. Detlaff was telling him that their father had multiple personalities but could somehow talk to them like they were their own people. Was Detlaff trying to say that he, too, possessed such a sickness? Was that why his own conflicting, overbearing thoughts were as loud and confounding as they were? Was that why he tried to keep his anger under control with the understanding that it could become devastating if he let it consume him? What *would* happen if he let go? If he let his anger boil past the limit he'd set himself so long ago? He wasn't sure, but after hearing Detlaff's rant, he was sure that he shouldn't find out.

Watching Alucard think to himself, Detlaff grinned. "I'm right, aren't I, big brother? You've felt it. You probably even feel it right now. I know how to control it, so…if you agree to spend some time with little brother, I'll teach you," he said, smiling.

Alucard wasn't in the mood to entertain *anyone* today. Detlaff was just looking for an excuse to escape his inevitable fate of being locked away like an animal. The vampire had come to take Ben's voice back, and that was what he was going to do.

With a vacant stare, Alucard mercilessly tore Detlaff's throat from his neck. The demon gagged and tried to scream, but his blood sprayed everywhere, and Alucard stepped back to keep it from dirtying his clothes. He watched as Detlaff healed, but the skin which slowly replaced that which had been torn away wasn't like that of his human body; it was scaled and a dark, ocean-like blue. Then, as Detlaff hissed at him, Alucard smirked and turned around, leaving the room with the majority of Detlaff's throat in his hand.

He didn't waste time returning to the castle's main hall, where Ben was sitting at the table. Sergiu had told him to arrive, as asked. All Alucard needed now were the things he'd sent one of his castle's butlers to retrieve. He made his way over to the table, pulled out the chair in front of Ben, and dropped Detlaff's throat on the surface.

As he glanced down at it, Ben frowned in confusion.

"Zon't vorry, you zon't 'ave to eat zhis," Alucard said amusedly.

With a nervous smirk, Ben nodded.

Alucard then looked back over his shoulder. "*Veni!*" he yelled.

They waited a few moments. One of the castle butlers emerged from the kitchens with a small box in his hands and hurried over. He placed it in front of Alucard, bowed respectfully, and then disappeared.

"I assume zhis looks vamiliar?" Alucard asked, opening the box to reveal a sealed jar of purple-red goop.

Looking at it, Ben shook his head.

"Hmm… did you not see vhat Zetlaff did to steal your voice?"

He shook his head.

"Vell, zhis—as vell as your vroat—'ad to be consumed. Zhis is Zetlaff's throat," he said, pointing to the bloody mess he'd put on the table, "and zhis is zhe concoction zhat must be consumed vith zhat," he said, pulling the lid from the jar he'd taken from the box. "You vill drink all of zhis," he instructed, picking up what was left of Detlaff's throat, and once he dropped it into the jar of strange goop, he held it out to Ben.

Taking it, Ben frowned unsurely.

"Vill probably taste vorse zhan anozzer vampire's blood, but at least vill vestore your voice, hmm?"

Ben didn't hesitate. With a deep sigh, he moved the jar to his mouth and started gulping it down.

"Vill probably take an hour or two to set, to 'eal. Until zhen, vest. I'm travelling to Eltaria tonight, and I vant you zhere. You can meet me at zhe docks, zhe same time as usual. Do not try to speak until at least an hour 'as passed."

With a revolted grimace, Ben finished the concoction, set the empty jar down, and shook his head. But then, as he looked at Alucard's expectant face, he nodded in confirmation.

"Bring a 'uman, too. Zhis transveral is going to drain me. I vill need zhe blood. I vill be veturning to my 'ome now to vest bevore zhe transveral."

He nodded again.

Alucard then stood up, and without another word, left the castle. All he wanted to do now was sleep until it was time to see Zalith again.

Chapter Sixty-Seven

— ⌣ ⟨ † ⟩ ⌣ —

Infirmity

| **Alucard** |

Alucard reached the docks as midnight crept closer. He dismounted Sebastian and made his way over to Ben, who stood with a rather content look on his face and a tied, panicking human at his side.

The vampire didn't care to ask why Ben looked so happy, so once he reached him, he walked past and up onto the ship, ignoring his smile of greeting. "Let's go," he called irritably, waving his hand back at Sergiu, who followed Alucard and Ben up onto the ship.

Sergiu went up to the quarterdeck and began preparing to disembark as Ben followed Alucard into the cabin.

"I wanted to say thank you," Ben said, stopping a few feet from Alucard's desk as he watched the vampire sit behind it. "You restored my voice, and you didn't have to. But you did, so, thank you."

Slumping down in his seat, Alucard glanced at Ben. "Vhat good are you vithout a voice, hmm?"

Ben laughed unsurely.

"Sit," Alucard then said, resting his arms on his desk.

As he was told, Ben sat across from Alucard.

"I'll be bringing 'alf zhe vampires tonight, so you vill 'ave a lot of vork to do 'ousing zhem."

Ben nodded and confidently said, "I'll get it done." But then he frowned in concern. "Are you…sure you should bring that many at once? The last time you brought a fair few, you didn't look so good, and—"

"I'll be vine," Alucard mumbled. "Do your job, and I'll do mine."

"Of course," Ben agreed.

"I 'ope your vife is less murdery," Alucard then said.

"Murdery?"

"She vreatened to kill me if I zidn't save you," he said, smirking.

Ben laughed nervously as he dragged his hand over the back of his neck. "Y-yeah…she's uh…a handful sometimes—sorry."

Alucard shrugged. "She cares, so…*de inteles*."

Ben then gained a curious smirk. "Speaking of caring, am I right in assuming I know the man who gave that to you?" he asked, glancing at the mark Zalith had left on Alucard's neck.

With an embarrassed scowl, Alucard snarled and turned his head to face the wall so Ben couldn't see his neck.

"Sorry, I don't mean to pry."

The vampire glanced back over at him. "Vhat do you know about 'im?"

"Zalith?"

"Yes."

He laughed unsurely and shrugged. "I know…a fair amount about him."

Alucard scowled impatiently as he tapped his claws on his desk, waiting for Ben to elaborate.

Ben looked anxious and conflicted. He jolted his leg up and down, and his eyes frantically shot around the room to avoid Alucard's gaze. "Is there uh…anything specific you want to know?"

"Zhe voman 'e lives vith," Alucard instantly answered. "Who is she? To 'im."

"Well…" Ben started, "they've been friends for a very long time; Zalith and his father worked for her, too. That's just public knowledge back home, and it's all I know."

Alucard rolled his eyes and glared at the window as the ship started moving along the ocean. "Vight," he mumbled, trying to dismiss his impatience, sure that it was soon going to become something quite like anger. Despite Detlaff appearing to be estranged and not entirely within typical mental capacities, Alucard couldn't help but consider what he told him, and it made him feel almost reluctant to allow himself to become angry.

Detlaff had fundamentally said that Lucifer, Alucard's father—by blood—possessed some sort of sickness, a sickness which caused him to own several different personalities, all of which he spoke to, and all of which might very well have their own consciousnesses. Detlaff also hinted at it being hereditary, which would mean Alucard might also possess the sickness. As much as he didn't want to consider the fact, he couldn't sit there and deny that Detlaff was right about his overbearing thoughts, some of which would often feel more like voices.

If it were true—if he did possess this sickness—and if it would eventually awaken into something worse, the best he could do would be to try and keep it from happening. In the four hundred years he'd lived, he hadn't once spoken to himself; he hadn't once let his thoughts control him in a way Detlaff had explained. He felt that all he could do was keep it that way, to not let his emotions become so overbearing that they turned him into whatever his father was.

With a quiet sigh, he looked back over at Ben. "Go."

Without question, Ben stood up and left the cabin, pulling the door shut behind him.

As Ben left, Alucard stared at the ocean outside. Now that he'd given it some thought, he couldn't stop thinking about it. Was he going to lose his mind? Despite how hard he tried *not* to become his father, was he cursed to become him regardless? He tapped his claws on his desk, frowning in both worry and anger. Did Detlaff have such a sickness? Was that why *he* acted so strangely? Was that why he instantly leapt from emotion to emotion as if he was someone else each time? Alucard looked down at his hands—did *he* already possess the sickness? He was aware of how volatile he could be, and he couldn't help but wonder if that was a symptom.

Then, he focused on more than one negative perspective. He hoped that if he did have the sickness, it was and had already been awake inside him. That way, he'd know that he could control whatever it was and whatever it did. Whenever he found himself erratically switching from emotion to emotion, he was still in control; he was still himself—he was still Alucard. He could still say what he wanted to say, do what he wanted to do. Perhaps because he was Lucifer's son, this problem wouldn't be so potent, and maybe all it would do to him was cause his emotions to be so very overwhelming at times.

The vampire snarled irritably and glared back out at the ocean. He didn't want to keep thinking about it. He was confident that there was nothing *wrong* with him and never would be.

As the sound of the island's rain and crashing thunder became louder, he stood up and made his way over to the cabin door. All he wanted to think about now was Zalith. He'd see him in just a few minutes, and he'd been looking forward to it since the moment the demon left this morning.

When he stepped out onto the ship's deck, he set his eyes on the island. He glanced up at the quarterdeck, eyeing Sergiu. He then glanced over at Ben, who was leaning back against the foremast, staring out at the water.

Alucard made his way over to him. "Vill you need my 'elp 'ousing zhe vampires? I could 'ave given you more notice."

Ben looked at him and smiled slightly. "No, I'll be all right. There's enough inns in the city to house a hundred people. I just hope there's enough room aboard this ship for them."

Glancing back at the door to his cabin, Alucard sighed. "If zhere isn't enough voom, zhere's a door in my cabin zhat leads beneath zhe deck. If you need to take anyvone down zhere, be careful, zhere are…vragile vings down zhere."

A curious frown found its way to Ben's face, but he knew better than to pry. He nodded. "Understood."

Then, without falter, Alucard morphed into vermillion smoke and swiftly made his way over to the rainy island. Once he landed on the rocky black ground, he sighed and hurried into the portal without stopping for a moment to think as he usually would. He felt strangely keen to see Zalith, and he didn't want to waste a moment.

Chapter Sixty-Eight

Reverberation

| Alucard |

When he emerged from the portal into the Eltarian castle ruins, Alucard brushed the rainwater from his shoulders and hair.

The vampire morphed into his owl form, flew up to the top of the tallest, slanted tower, and perched himself on the scorched bricks. He scoured the moonlit land with his eyes, searching for the barn Zalith mentioned. It stood behind a collection of tall, rotting trees, and the grass surrounding it was overgrown and twisting into the wood. It looked as though it had been standing there for at least a hundred or so years and might have homed many an animal in its time. It was large enough to home at least twelve horses, so Alucard was sure it wouldn't be too cramped inside with thirty or so vampires.

Obviously, he wasn't going to enter through the large front doors—they looked welded shut by the grass and dirt, so if Zalith and the vampires were inside, there must be another entrance. He silently flapped his feathered wings and glided around the barn from above, searching for another door, and when he set his eyes on one left ajar at its rear, he descended and morphed back to his usual self as he silently landed.

While he made his way towards the door, Alucard sensed a single heartbeat inside, and he knew exactly who it belonged to. However, when he entered the barn, Zalith was nowhere to be seen—again. Alucard was sure that the demon was planning another stunt, probably to sneak up on him again, and he felt as though he wasn't in the mood for it.

He stood in the doorway, eyeing each of the thirty-six vampires Zalith had gathered. As he looked at them, hesitation began to grip hold of him. Most of the vampires were at least a hundred years old, so he'd be taking a *whole* lot more than double his own age in vampires back with him. He couldn't change his mind now, however. How stupid would that make him look?

Just then, Zalith appeared out of nowhere and rested his arm around the vampire's shoulders, smiling at him, and his face was just a few inches from Alucard's. "I said: hello, Alucard," he greeted, smirking.

"Vhat?" Alucard frowned, glancing at him. He mustn't have heard Zalith speaking to him or sensed his approach—he was too busy calculating the ages of the vampires. He sighed and glared at them. "I zidn't 'ear you coming," he admitted.

Zalith took his eyes off the vampire and glared at the crowd standing in the centre of the barn. "I evened out the total age of this group and the remaining group. You were very specific about such a thing the first time we did this," he said, looking at him again.

"*Multemesc*," Alucard thanked.

"So, how was your day?"

Alucard shrugged as best he could with the demon's arm around him. "Normal," he answered. "I spoke to Zetlaff."

"Did he give you anything of interest?"

"No, just zhe usual nonsense."

"And Ben?"

"I vecovered 'is voice vor 'im. 'E's vaiting back in Aegisguard vor me and zhese vampires."

"I still think it's rather admirable of you to go out of your way to help him," Zalith said, still staring at him.

"I just need 'im to be able to speak. Vonce Attila gets back vrom DeiganLupus, I vink I'll 'ave Ben veplace 'im. 'E's pissed me off vor zhe last time," Alucard grumbled.

The demon smirked and asked, "I trust the werewolves have been quiet since Ada's removal?"

"Noving 'as come to my attention, and if Tobias saw anyving suspicious, 'e'd come to me. I'm still certain a war vill break out soon enough, zhough."

"I'm still more than happy to help you if you need it."

Alucard glanced at him but then looked back at the vampires. "Vell, I shouldn't vait avound 'ere too long."

Zalith then frowned in concern as he moved his arm from around Alucard and turned to face him. "Are you sure you're going to be okay moving this many at once? I've noticed these transferals tire you."

"I'll be vine," he mumbled. "I vound a vay to prevent zhe exhaustion vrom overvhelming me."

"And what way would that be?" he asked, smiling.

The vampire shrugged. "Blood. A lot, but vorks."

Zalith didn't look very convinced. He took his eyes off the vampire and stared over at the crowd. "Okay."

Alucard frowned at him. "Vhat?" he asked, sure that Zalith was irritated.

"I just care about you, and I don't want to see you hurt because of this—because of anything."

Taking his eyes off the demon, Alucard looked down at the straw-covered ground. He hadn't necessarily lied to Zalith, but he hadn't been entirely truthful, either. While that might not bother him with anyone else, it bothered him when it came to Zalith. He felt guilty for lying to him knowing that he cared. It was true that the blood helped him feel somewhat less dead after moving the vampires, but it didn't completely cure his fatigue. He was sure that, despite draining a human of their blood, this transferal was going to leave him utterly exhausted for days—weeks even. Should he warn Zalith about that possibility?

He glanced at Zalith again. He was sure that if he told him he might not feel so great after this, then Zalith would try to make it easier or even stop him altogether. He couldn't risk that. He didn't want to have to fight Zalith, nor did he want to reveal that Damien would punish him if he didn't do this. "Just makes me tired," he said. "I 'ave Ben vith me in case I need any sort of assistance, but I'll be vine."

"Okay."

Alucard then scowled at him. "Okay," he mocked with a sneer. "Do you vink I zon't know vhat I'm doing?" he snarled.

"I'm sure you know what you're doing, Alucard. But personally, it doesn't sound like the best idea to move so many at once. This group totals over three thousand years old; when you took Ben, his two friends, and me, our group was just over a single thousand in age, and that caused you to no less than pass out at your desk. I don't want that to happen again, and if you take three times as much, I'm sure it'll do worse than put you to sleep for thirty minutes," he stated with a stern but worried tone.

The vampire now felt as though Zalith was being condescending. Clearly, the demon didn't think he could manage; he obviously felt that Alucard hadn't come prepared, and that angered him. But as much as Zalith may have irritated him, and as much as he felt the urge to fight and argue, he kept himself from doing so. Not only was he still conflicted because of his earlier thoughts regarding Lucifer's sickness, but he was also hesitant to argue with Zalith. He...*cared* too much to fight and potentially damage their relationship. He also couldn't deny that Zalith had a point—and he was right, too. Alucard was sure this move would make him so tired that he'd need to sleep through the journey home, but he'd come prepared. He was confident he'd be fine.

However, he wasn't going to act so meekly and back down in front of Zalith. He scowled over at the vampires. "I'm not going to stand 'ere and argue," he said. As Zalith glanced at him, he sighed and glared over at the wall. "Is not like I 'ave a choice in zhe matter, anyvay," he added. "I 'ave to leave now."

Zalith turned to face Alucard again and frowned in concern. "Why do you not have a choice?"

"You know vhy," he grumbled, trying to hide how despondent it made him feel. Then, he stepped forward and set his eyes on the vampires. "Ve are leaving," he called. As all the vampires fell silent and looked over at him, he turned around and led the way outside, leaving Zalith alone. He didn't want to talk about it anymore.

| **Zalith** |

Once all the vampires left the barn, Zalith followed behind them. He didn't want to argue…but he wasn't going to apologize for caring. As much as he wanted to know why Alucard was risking himself by taking back these vampires, he felt as though he should stay silent to keep the already tense atmosphere between them from escalating. He suspected Damien had something to do with it, and Alucard's recent answer told him that he *did*. Alucard was always so closed off and standoffish when it came to talking about Damien, so he wasn't going to ask about him and make the situation worse.

However, he couldn't remain completely silent. The last thing he wanted was to say goodbye to Alucard on negative terms. He cared too much to leave a wound on the vampire's conscience or his own.

When they reached the castle ruins, Zalith sighed and caught up with Alucard. He walked beside the vampire as he led the way towards the portal. "Alucard," he said, placing his hand on his shoulder.

Alucard stopped a few feet from the portal and glared into it. "Vhat?"

"I don't want to leave things tense between us," Zalith said quietly. "I'm sorry that we argued and if I made you feel as though I was questioning your capability to do things. I just care. I don't want you to suffer unnecessarily."

Glancing back at the vampires as they filed into the ruins, Alucard huffed quietly. He then looked at Zalith. "Ve are vine—*zhis* is vine—and I vill be vine. I'll see you next veek."

A sullen frown appeared on Zalith's face as he stared at the vampire. It upset him to think that he'd hurt Alucard. He was aware of his own undeniable habit of arguing with literally anyone where an opportunity presented itself, and Alucard was the last person he wanted to subject to such a thing. He hadn't wanted to argue with Alucard, and he felt as though if he could have avoided it in any way, he would have. But it happened, and there wasn't anything he could do but hope that Alucard wasn't upset because of him.

He sighed sadly and moved his hand from Alucard's shoulder and to his back. He then guided his other arm around the vampire and embraced him tightly. And when

Alucard reciprocated his hug, he smiled in relief. Then, as he let Alucard go, he stepped back so that the vampire could take the others into the portal. "If you need me sooner than next week, you know how to contact me. Until then."

Alucard nodded and snatched the wrist of the vampire closest to him. "All of you need to 'old 'ands or arms or vhatever; just vemain connected physically and zon't let go until ve're all on zhe ozzer side," he instructed. "Make sure everyvone knows zhat."

The vampire he grabbed nodded and looked down the hallway, muttering Alucard's instructions to the others, who then passed it on to those who were further away until everyone was either holding hands or linked arm-in-arm.

Alucard looked at Zalith. "*La revedere.*"

"Farewell," Zalith said with a smile.

And then, Alucard disappeared into the portal.

Zalith watched as each vampire followed him though. Part of him wanted to meet Alucard on the other side—he'd been enjoying their time so much lately that all he wanted to do was continue to be with him. But he also felt conflicted. What if he was spending *too* much time with Alucard? He knew how often he got tired of people; he knew that there was only so much time he could and would spend with someone before things started to become boring—before the connection began to dry up. He was afraid that might happen with Alucard if he continued to spend so much time with him…and he didn't want that. He'd become so attached to that vampire in such little time that he was concerned their relationship might burn out just as quickly as it ignited.

It was rare for him to become this close to someone. He found himself feeling and doing things for this vampire that he'd never do for anyone else. Alucard already meant so much to him—so much that he'd gone out of his way to make everything easier on him, so much that all he wanted to do was help, even if it inconvenienced himself. He didn't want to run down the clock, and he didn't want to hurt Alucard because of his own unavoidable habits.

No…he'd not head over there and join him. He'd give him some space—it was probably for the best right now. So, as the last of the vampires disappeared into the portal, he turned around…and started heading home.

| Alucard |

As Alucard emerged on the rainy island, he scowled irritably and walked along the shore, but he was beginning to feel the tiring effects of the portal as each vampire stepped through.

He glanced at the ship, setting his eyes on Ben, who watched from the forecastle deck. Then, he looked back over his shoulder, observing as each vampire stepped through one after the other. Alucard frowned when pain shot throughout his entire body, increasing into something quite like agony as each vampire came through. He gritted his teeth, continuing forward, but when the sudden dizziness kept him from being able to walk straight, *that* was when he stopped.

The overbearing disorientation consumed him as the pain in his head became an intense migraine. His eyes ached, his ears rang, and his body felt as though it was in the process of healing multiple missing limbs at once. He rested his arm on the side of a large standing rock, closing his eyes and gripping the side of his face with his free hand. If the vampire standing beside him hadn't muttered something worriedly, Alucard wouldn't have known that the rain wasn't the only thing pouring down his face. When the man asked if he was okay, Alucard took his hand from the side of his face and stared at it; his own blood smothered his palm, and the rain slowly washed it away.

With an aggravated snarl, he waved his bloody hand, telling the vampires to keep coming, and as they continued to make their way through, he felt his strength wane into nothing. His ethos decreased so suddenly until even his reserves were gone. He had nothing left, and now, the vampires were using up his very life force. But he couldn't stop. He had to wait. He had to bear through it. And he did, even when his blood poured from not only his eyes but his ears and nose, too. What choice did he have, though? He'd receive far worse than bleeding orifices if Damien were to find out he'd failed again.

As the last vampire walked through the portal, Alucard dropped to his knees and let go of the wrist of the vampire he had been holding as he snarled in hostility. The man backed off in confusion, leaving Alucard to struggle alone. He'd never felt so weak, so vulnerable. Every ounce of his ethos was gone; his body was numb, his head was spinning, and he was starving so agonizingly, but he had not the strength to do anything about it. The world around him slowed, the mumbles of the vampire crowd faded to silence, and as his consciousness slowly left him, the last thing he saw was a glimpse of Ben's mortified face before black consumed everything.

| **Ben** |

Ben forced his way through the vampire crowd and hurried to where Alucard had fallen. He skidded along the ground as he crouched beside him, placing his hands on his shoulders and lightly shaking him. "Aleksei?" he asked—despite it being obvious that he wouldn't answer.

Alucard's bloody face mortified him to the point he knew he wouldn't be able to do much for him. So, with a panicked look on his face, Ben pulled off his coat and folded it; he placed it on the ground and rested Alucard's head on it before standing up.

He held out his arm. "*Veni foras!*" he demanded hastily.

In just moments, an izuret appeared in a small blast of dark mist and landed on Ben's extended arm. It stared at him with its huge, emerald-green eyes and waited.

"Tell him Aleksei's hurt," he instructed.

The izuret nodded and chirped; it swiftly took off and disappeared.

Ben then returned to the vampire's side, ignoring the concerned mumbles from the group behind him. He had no idea what to do, but he felt that what he'd just done was the best he could do. And it took no time at all for actual help to come.

"Move," Zalith demanded, shoving Ben aside as he appeared out of nowhere.

As he was shoved, Ben stumbled back and stood up straight, watching.

"What happened?" Zalith asked as he checked Alucard's pulse.

"He just…dropped," Ben said, confused. "This happened before, though—not as bad, but—he said blood helps, so we brought a guy, and—"

Before Ben could finish, Zalith picked Alucard up in his arms. He created a rift in the side of the huge boulder beside them and disappeared inside, leaving the island.

Ben stared wide-eyed as the rift sizzled into the rock and disappeared. "Okay then."

He hoped Alucard would be okay. If anyone could help him, it was Zalith, and there evidently wasn't anything else *he* could do. So, he turned around and headed for the ship. He still had a job to do.

| Zalith |

Zalith emerged through a rift in the stone wall of Alucard's kitchen. He silently carried the vampire through the pitch-black halls; he wasn't entirely sure what to do, but he was confident that he had a good idea of what might help. However, he couldn't help but dwell on the fact that he was right—he knew something would happen, and he felt he should have tried harder to get Alucard to take fewer vampires. But he let him go, and now, Alucard was unconscious, and Zalith wasn't sure what might be happening to him.

He glanced down at Alucard's bloody face as he carried him upstairs. He could barely sense the vampire's life force, and it was becoming weaker as each moment passed. There wasn't an ounce of detectable ethos in his body, either; demons *always* had reserves, but even those were gone. He couldn't silence his dread, his worry, or his angst. Alucard could—and possibly was—dying. He didn't want to lose Alucard—he couldn't. He already felt so attached to him; he cared for him so sorely that the thought of losing him because of this horrified him.

When he reached the door to Alucard's room, he turned around, pushed it open with his back, and made his way in. He placed the still, silent vampire onto his bed and stared down at him for a moment. His thoughts were racing so fast through his head that he couldn't figure out what to do first.

Seeing him in such a state, knowing he had suffered—it hurt him, it *angered* him. Alucard was only in this state because of Damien and his ridiculous mission to move the vampires from Eltaria to Aegisguard—the task he'd quite clearly forced on Alucard. Now, because of whatever Damien had over Alucard, the vampire was suffering…*his* vampire was suffering. Zalith felt nothing could make him angrier. But he couldn't focus on his anger, not now. Alucard needed his help, and he would do whatever it took to make sure he was comfortable and that he woke up.

Both Alucard and Ben said that blood helped the vampire the last time the portal made him feel exhausted, so Zalith assumed that was what he needed. He felt no hesitation and used his claws to cut his palm. He then lightly gripped either side of Alucard's jaw and allowed his blood to trickle into the vampire's mouth. It was to no instant avail, however. The blood didn't wake Alucard, nor did it cause any physical improvement. But Zalith *could* feel the vampire's life force halt. It didn't dramatically improve, but it did settle—that was something, at least.

Over the next few minutes, he gave Alucard more of his blood in hopes that it would revive him. But all it was doing was ever so slowly revitalizing his life force. The demon was already sure it would take more than a few days to wake Alucard up, but that didn't matter. He didn't care if it would take weeks or months; he'd take care of Alucard for however long it took. He could only spare so much blood at a time, though, and once he reached what he felt to be a limit, he sighed quietly and stared down at the silent vampire. The sight of Alucard's bloody face still forced a strange fear upon him—it wasn't odd because he never felt it before; it was strange because he *had* thought about it before. To lose someone he cared about…he couldn't bear that.

With a despondent frown, he carefully moved Alucard's fringe out of his face. He was covered in blood, and Zalith felt that he should at least clean it away. So, he went into the bathroom connected to the vampire's bedroom, found a rag, and dampened it under the tap. Once he returned to Alucard's side, he carefully cleaned the blood from the vampire's face, trying to keep his worry from overwhelming him. There wasn't much else he could do other than tidy him up, give him blood, and keep an eye on him until he woke up.

If he would wake up.

Chapter Sixty-Nine

Keeper

| Zalith |

The days were long and daunting. Despite Zalith's efforts to feed him blood and keep him comfortable, Alucard only seemed to worsen. His life force still dwindled, his ethos remained utterly undetectable, and it looked like he was becoming become paler as each moon passed.

Zalith spent the majority of the night in Alucard's room, reluctant to leave him for more than ten minutes. But when his need for sleep became overbearing, he retreated to the guest room; although he worried fiercely for the vampire, he still respected his boundaries and slept in a different bed. He'd most likely be giving his blood to Alucard for a while, and if he was to keep it up, he needed rest.

⊷◆⊶

As the first morning of his newfound duty of care came, Zalith chose to check on Alucard before anything else of importance. But the vampire was just as still, silent and no better than last night. The demon carefully took Alucard's bloody, damp cape, coat, and blazer off, and then pulled the bed covers over him in hopes that he would be comfortable during his sleep—however long it may last.

The demon sat on the vampire's bedside and fed him his blood again. Alucard was still alive, and his blood was clearly helping, and that seemed to be all he could do right now—check on him, and give him blood three times a day. Maybe he'd wake up soon, or maybe not…either way, Zalith had no intention to abandon him. Although he may have his own business to tend to, he cared too much to leave the vampire for longer than an hour at a time. Despite the fact that Alucard might not even be aware Zalith was with him, the demon didn't want Alucard to be or feel alone. And he himself didn't want to be too far away from him for too long. His attachment to Alucard was already fierce, and he wouldn't let any more harm come to him.

Monday wasn't much different. The morning came, Zalith spared his blood once again and made sure Alucard was as comfortable as he could be, and then went about his own business until noon came, checking in on Alucard every so often. He had both seen and sensed Ben coming towards Alucard's manor, but the guy hesitated and turned around, changing his mind. Zalith was relieved he chose to leave of his own accord; the demon didn't want *anyone* near Alucard. Not only had he gained his own protective instincts, but he was also sure that Alucard didn't want any of his subordinates to see him in such a state.

Dusk, however, exhibited strange developments. Zalith returned to check on and feed the vampire, but when he sat and stared down at him, his eyes caught sight of something peculiar. At first glance, he might have thought it was the love bite he left on the vampire's neck, but a second look proved it to be something different entirely. His skin around the bruise-like mark had started to darken, almost as if the mark was spreading. It stretched beneath the collar of the vampire's shirt, so he pulled it away from Alucard's neck and shoulder, setting his eyes on what lay beneath.

The vampire's skin was no longer ice-pale—it didn't even look human. What could only be described as scales had begun to appear on Alucard's shoulder; they were almost black in colour and shimmered in the light that found its way into the darkened room through the slightly parted curtains.

Zalith also didn't fail to notice that Alucard's life force had somewhat spiked. It was stronger, that was for sure, but only his… demon ethos? No… that wasn't demon ethos. It was *Numen* ethos—of course it was; he was the son of a Numen—and it was reviving itself, but his demon ethos was silent, dormant. Zalith wasn't sure what that meant, but he was certain that Alucard was recuperating.

He let go of the vampire's neck, fed him as usual, and left. What more could he do?

Tuesday soon came. The morning was cold, even more so within the walls of the vampire's empty, silent house. Zalith made his way to the vampire's room to discover that the night had left Alucard's physical condition deteriorating even more. The black scale-like markings on his skin had spread up his neck, stopping just below his ear. They had also begun to appear on the right side of Alucard's neck, too. The vampire's life force was livelier than it was yesterday, and when Zalith check his pulse, he noticed that it was close to normal.

With a perturbed frown, the demon dragged his fingers over the darkened skin on Alucard's neck. It felt quite like the skin of a snake, but Zalith knew that it was of demon origin. Alucard's Numen ethos was quickly recovering, but his demon energies weren't any better. If Zalith didn't know better, he'd assume Alucard's Numen form was breaking free of his body—and not the type of form which consisted of wings and horns on his human likeness, but his *true* form. Obviously, being trapped in a coma kept Alucard from being able to maintain his human likeness, and Zalith was sure that if he couldn't do something to stop or at least slow this transformation, Alucard might be faced with a whole lot more trouble when he woke.

But what more could Zalith do? He was struggling with his worry, but he didn't know how to stop Alucard's Numen form from consuming his body. All he could do was keep him alive and fed.

Wednesday, however, was when Zalith decided he had no choice but to ask for assistance in Alucard's recovery. Varana, being a child of Lucifer herself, must have had to go through the same process of gaining her human likeness as Alucard. There was no one better to ask. Did he want to ask her? Not particularly—he'd have to be careful with what he said. The last thing he wanted to do was give away Alucard's location to someone who might possibly give him up to Lucifer.

As morning came, he returned to the vampire's room. What was visible of Alucard's left arm was dotted with patches of darkened skin and demon scales. His once pale claws were now blackening and increasing in length, and the scales on his neck were beginning to creep along the left side of his face and over his forehead.

Zalith's first priority was to feed him, but when he opened the vampire's mouth, he instantly noticed that four fangs were no longer all he possessed. His teeth to the left and right of his top fangs had sharpened into smaller fangs. He had to try and do something before it got any worse.

He cut his hand, he fed the vampire—if that was even an appropriate name anymore. All Zalith could detect within Alucard was Numen ethos. Whatever was happening to him, Zalith was sure that if he left it much longer, Alucard might not even be Alucard when and if he woke up.

The demon hastily made his way back to the guest room. He closed the door and walked over to the wall with a large black mirror hanging between two cabinets. With a specific tap and quiet mumble of a spell, the mirror flickered and faded to black. He waited, and not too long after, the mirror faded to reveal a completely different room inside it. The walls were a boring, plain white, the sunlight shining in through the windows on the left wall. Sitting in front of the mirror in a black, silky halter dress, however, was the black-haired, crimson-eyed demon, Varana.

An irritated smile clung to her face while she eyed him through the mirror. "Oh, look who decided to check in."

Zalith sighed quietly. "I'm sorry," he said, hoping to avoid an argument. "I've been busy."

"With who?" she asked, frowning.

"No one in particular," he answered, his tone as vacant as it could be. "I've just been working on things."

Varana scowled skeptically, her eyes shifting from Zalith to the room he was standing in. "Whose home are you in?"

"A colleague's."

Irritancy smothered her face once more. "Which colleague?" she questioned.

He shrugged lightly. "No one that you know."

She scoffed. "Well, of course I don't know them; it's like pulling teeth to get you to introduce me to any of your apparent colleagues these days," she said, pouting. "Am I just not all that important to you anymore? I introduce you to everybody *I'm* sleeping with. I mean, that's *obviously* what you're doing—you just can't help yourself. Being an incubus—"

With his impatience growing, Zalith rolled his eyes. "Are you done?" he interjected. "The difference here is that I don't care about your business, Varana. Meanwhile, you care far too much about mine—"

"Is it such a crime for me to want to know where you are?!" she exclaimed, losing her temper. "Is it so awful of me to want to know if you're alive?! Surely, you remember that just last month you were almost *killed* by a mob of humans—"

He sighed tiredly. "I wasn't almost killed—"

"—And you expect me to sit here and pretend like everything's okay?! What if you die, Z? What am I supposed to do then?!"

"I'm *not* going to die, Varana," he mumbled, antagonized.

Varana scoffed loudly. "Famous last words."

Zalith exhaled quietly and closed his eyes, trying to keep his aggravation under control. He then set his sights back on her. "Are we about done with this conversation? I have something I need to ask you."

She crossed her arms, but in doing so, made sure that it complimented her chest, placing her arms beneath her breasts. She pouted stubbornly and rolled her eyes. "What?"

For a moment, Zalith hesitated. He wasn't yet ready to have a conversation with Varana involving Alucard. Not only did he not want to tell her of his feelings for this vampire, but Alucard so happened to be her brother, and that was a whole different thing.

She'd make a huge deal out of both factors, and he just couldn't find the strength to deal with it. While he might not like to lie to her, he simply had no choice. Coping with her when she was upset took a lot of energy—she was such a handful—and he was already overly stressed with Alucard's condition.

He huffed and started, "So, I didn't get much sleep last night—"

Varana groaned in revolt.

Zalith rolled his eyes in response to her unpleasant grunt. "—And my colleague has this fantastic library, so I decided I might as well read something. There was this wonderful little fiction book about the Numen and a handful of their offspring that the author had made up."

She tutted, and Zalith was sure she was thinking about humans and their fiction—like they knew anything about *her* life. "Okay, and?" she grumbled.

His chosen approach seemed to be working so far. "In the story—" he continued, "—the main character…who is one of the aforementioned offspring and is also a demon, overworked themselves beyond belief. They drained all of their ethos, even their reserves to the point they were pulled into a coma. Their…lover started feeding them their blood in an attempt to revive them, but the main character's body began to change. They began to look less and less human as each day passed as if their Numen likeness was beginning to reappear. Is that possible?" he asked. Of course, he knew that it *was* possible, for it was currently happening to Alucard. But he had to bring it up to Varana *somehow*.

Looking at him, she thought to herself for a few moments. "Yes…but only if the lover is a demon, too. The demon blood would increase the deterioration of the main character's human form," she explained. But she then frowned suspiciously. "How does the author know that? What book are you reading?"

He dismissed her with a slight wave of his hand. "I can't remember its name. That's very interesting though, thank you," he digressed.

She smiled contently. "You're welcome."

"Actually, I fell asleep before I could get any further into the story. I'm curious to know if this were to happen to a Numen's offspring in the real world, would it be better to give them human blood?"

Varana shrugged. "Well, if the lover wants results, then the demon blood would wake them up faster, but the drawback is that they'll keep reverting back to their true form, and then they'll have to consume humans to regain their human appearance. It just depends on how impatient the lover is."

"Humans? How many?"

Enjoying their conversation, she leaned forward—so much that her breasts almost broke free of her dress. "Well, how bad is it?"

Still with a vacant look on his face, Zalith shrugged. "I believe the character had minor scales on their arms and neck. His claws were darkening, increasing in length; some more of his teeth also started becoming fangs."

"Hmm…." She frowned, thinking to herself. "How old is this character?"

"Let me remember, I believe it was mentioned," he said, pretending to think to himself. "I think the author said he was around four hundred, maybe five hundred years old."

She nodded. "Okay, so based on what I know, I'd say that—if the reversion is minor—they'd only have to drain four or maybe five humans of their life force."

"Interesting," he said, nodding.

"If this was real life, though," she continued, "devouring them all at once would likely result in the character getting carried away—there would be a massacre," she giggled.

He smirked in amusement. "Noted."

Varana then smiled and rested her arms on the table she was sitting at. "This was nice," she said. "Look at us; we aren't even arguing anymore."

"How uncharacteristic of us," he concurred.

She then pouted sadly. "I really wish we could keep talking, but you caught me at a bad time. I just had a bath drawn for me. If you can sneak that book out of your 'colleague's' house, though, I'd love to take a look at it. I'd like to know more about what this author knows—or what they *think* they know."

"I'll see what I can do," he agreed.

"Well, I'll talk to you later, honey," she said, smiling.

"Goodbye," he said with a nod before disabling the ethos he'd infused into the mirror, tapping its side with his fingers once more.

Alucard would need humans once he woke, and Zalith had to make sure that there were some for him to feed on. So, he made his way over to the window, pulled it open, and muttered under his breath. Moments later, an emerald-green-eyed izuret appeared before him, hovering outside the window.

"Tell Ben I need five humans in the next few hours. Bring them to Aleksei's manor."

The izuret chirped and nodded before it disappeared.

Zalith then closed the window and sat on the edge of the bed. What more could he do now other than wait for Ben to deliver the humans? He could always get some of his own work done. There weren't many other options. But no matter how hard he tried to keep himself occupied, he knew that he wouldn't be able to stop worrying about Alucard. At least he knew how to help thanks to Varana, but there was still no way for him to know *when* he'd wake up.

All he could do was wait.

Chapter Seventy

— ⸴ ✝ ⸲ —

Amelioration

| Zalith |

There was finally a little improvement on Thursday. Varana's advice was informative, so at least Zalith knew what was happening to Alucard. However, there wasn't much else he could do until the vampire woke up.

As per Varana's information, continuing to feed Alucard demon blood was the fastest way to get him back on his feet. But once he woke, he'd need humans to take life force from to quickly regain his human likeness. Ben had delivered them, and Zalith told Alucard's groundskeeper to stow them somewhere the vampire wouldn't find them. The last thing he wanted was a massacre.

But Zalith felt hesitant about Alucard feeding on anyone else's blood. He already knew he didn't want anyone to touch *his* vampire, but in this case, it was necessary. Alucard needed human blood *and* life force, and the only way he'd get it would be to feed on humans.

As he fed the vampire his blood, he stared at his lifeless face. He sorely wished there was more he could do; he wished he could somehow speak to Alucard. There weren't words to describe how much he missed their conversations…his company, his voice, and his accent. Although Alucard was slowly recuperating, Zalith still felt the dread of losing him. Seeing him like this, seeing him so vulnerable, so weak—it made Zalith hurt so profoundly. Alucard didn't deserve this—any of it. He was suffering; he probably thought he was alone, and he might not even know where he was or if he'd ever wake up. He was just…trapped in his subconscious.

While his hand healed, Zalith sighed quietly and tucked the vampire's hair behind his ear. He gazed at him with a despondent look on his face. "Alucard," he said quietly, hoping that by some miracle, he might respond. But nothing came of it.

He sighed and placed his hand on the vampire's shoulder, trying to silence his dread, trying to ignore the heart-retching hurt he felt knowing that Alucard was in pain. He was only in this state because of Damien, the same creature who spoke to him as if he was some incompetent child. Alucard *wasn't* incompetent at all. Zalith knew and saw how hard the vampire worked. He saw what he did for other people, and while Alucard might like to claim that what he was doing was for his own benefit, Zalith knew he was doing it for the vampires—for *his* people.

A slight smile found its way to Zalith's face. He *adored* Alucard. Everything about him from the things he did and said to his reactions and responses. There wasn't a single thing Zalith didn't like about him. He might appear as a cold, awful creature that most people feared, but Zalith knew who he really was beneath that. He was kind. He was gentle. He didn't deserve the awful things Damien threw his way; he didn't deserve to suffer for that man—he didn't deserve to suffer for anyone. Alucard deserved to be happy, but he was so sad—so sad that it hurt Zalith to think about it.

Why was he sad? Zalith wasn't sure, but what he *was* sure about was the fact that he would make Alucard happy…if the vampire would let him.

He then sighed sullenly, taking his hand off the vampire's shoulder. He felt he should get himself something to drink, but the moment he stood up, he sensed the life force of a very annoying, very ugly man approaching Alucard's front door. As the door knocked, Zalith left the room—pulling the door shut behind him—and made his way downstairs. He unlocked the front door and set his eyes on Dirk, Alucard's human informant.

"Ah, is Aleksei home?" he asked, taking his eyes off the paper in his hands to look at Zalith.

"No," he said with a disinterested expression.

Dirk frowned. "Where might I find him?"

"You won't. Why do you need to see him?"

With an irritated tut, Dirk held his arms behind his back and eyed the demon. "I'm not at liberty to expose that information."

Zalith kept his disinterested look because he had no interest in talking to this man. But if he had important information for Alucard, then he'd have to be…nice. "He is indisposed. I'm taking care of him. Whatever you might have for him, you can give to me."

"Indisposed?"

The demon scowled in hostility.

Dirk evidently understood Zalith's glare as a warning. He cleared his throat and stood up straight. "I have returned from Boszorkány; I spoke to their leaders, most of which are some nasty witches. They're open to negotiations regarding Aleksei's offer of alignment, but they will only speak to him. I set up meetings for Decem thirty-first, which is when Aleksei holds his yearly party. The Boszorkány leaders will attend as guests. They are also willing to come at an earlier date if Aleksei prefers."

"Is that all?" Zalith uttered.

"Tomorrow is Elvin's birthday. He says Aleksei is hosting a small celebration here at his house. Is that still going ahead? If he is ill, I can inform everyone—"

"Someone will tell you tomorrow," he dismissed. He wasn't sure whether Alucard would wake up in time, but he didn't want to cancel the vampire's plans if he *did* wake up and still wanted to participate.

Looking at him, Dirk nodded slowly. "Is Aleksei... all right?"

Without answering, Zalith closed the door, ending their conversation. He then made his way back upstairs, returned to the vampire's room, and sat on the other side of his bed. He glanced over at him, noticing not a single change—but at least he wasn't getting worse.

With a quiet sigh, he took the book he'd been reading from the cabinet beside him, leaned back against the bed's headboard, and immersed himself in his reading, waiting for whatever might present itself to him next.

| **Alucard** |

Alucard didn't know where he was. But it was comfortable. He couldn't possibly still be on the rainy island; there was no rain falling on his face, but the pain remained. His body felt weak, his head was aching, and the hunger—the unrelenting hunger. He felt no motivation to do anything about it, though. He was too weak, too tired. The darkness still had hold of him. He couldn't open his eyes, nor could he move his body. All he could do was lay there.

However, some relief came to him when the familiar scent of bergamot caught his attention. Zalith was with him.

Where was he? Where were *they*? Was this even real? It took him quite some time to fight through the confusing, conflicting thoughts, but he soon remembered. He took the vampires through the portal, and it weakened him so much that he passed out. How long had he been unconscious? Why had Zalith come? How long had Zalith been there? He wanted to know, so he tried to open his eyes, but he didn't have the strength.

But as he lay there, his energy began to slowly return to him. Although his body still ached, he felt that he might be able to move. He waited for what felt like a few minutes and tried once again to open his eyes. They opened to reveal more darkness, though... more pain. His head felt as though it was on fire, but he needed to see—he needed to know where he was and what happened.

"Alucard?" Zalith's voice asked quietly.

The vampire couldn't speak, but he frowned in acknowledgement.

It took a long moment, but Alucard managed to open his eyes enough to set them on Zalith's familiar face. The demon stared down at him with a smile not of amusement but relief. If Alucard didn't know better, he'd assume Zalith thought he was dead. *Had* he died? He wasn't sure. He sure felt like he had, though. All he could do was lay there and stare.

The sunlight was shining in through the curtains, so he must have slept the entire night. That wasn't much of a surprise. He glanced around the room, and seeing that it was just him and Zalith, he felt slightly more relieved.

He set his eyes back on the demon. "Zaliv…" he breathed, but he couldn't finish his sentence. A single word was all he had the strength for, and he felt as though the word he said was the one he would always say if he had but a single word left. Despite his confusion, despite his pain, seeing Zalith gave him relief.

Zalith smiled. "There you are." But as the vampire frowned in confusion, he lost his smile. "You're home," he said. "I brought you here after you fell unconscious. Ben contacted me when it happened. I've been taking care of you."

Alucard kept his frown, unable to ask what he wanted to. All he could do was gaze up at Zalith and hope that he would continue telling him what happened.

And Zalith seemed to know exactly what he was wondering. "That was four days ago," he said quietly.

Dread filled Alucard's eyes—four whole days?

Zalith lightly placed his hand on the side of the vampire's face. "Nothing has happened," he assured him. "Dirk came by with some information, but that's all. No werewolves, no Damien, no vampires."

Although he was relieved to hear it, he was more concerned about the threat *he* posed. His hunger—he could feel it increasing as each moment passed. He needed blood—human blood. Zalith was safe with him, so that was a relief, but he knew the moment he regained the strength to do so, he'd leave his bed—he'd head straight for the city and kill whatever he set his eyes on first. As inviting as such an activity sounded, he couldn't do it. The treaty was in place; rules had been set. Even *he* wouldn't break them. So what could he do?

"I know that you need humans," Zalith said; once again, he somehow knew what Alucard was thinking. "I've contacted Ben, and he's brought the necessary amount through your organized sources."

Was Zalith reading his mind? Was that how he knew what he was thinking? At this point, he didn't care. He was *too weak* to care.

With a slow, tired blink, Alucard turned his head and glared over at the curtains. He felt too tired to try and hide the horrific state that he knew his face must be in—that his entire *body* must be in. He could feel what happened. His ethos had waned, and his strength was close to nought. Being this weak and unconscious for more than a day would cause him to lose the ability to maintain his human likeness—his body would use what energy it could to keep him alive, even that which kept his human body in place, and he was certain it had already deteriorated too much. Why else would Zalith be telling him he had humans ready? The demon knew he needed to drain their life force, didn't he?

He didn't want to think about what Zalith thought seeing him like this. He just wanted to recover; the last thing he wanted was to look so weak and fragile in front of someone like Zalith... in front of someone he cared about, someone *he* wanted to protect. How could he do such a thing if the person he wanted to take care of was taking care of *him*?

"Alucard?" Zalith asked quietly. "I..." he paused, hesitating. "I'll go and get a human for you. You need blood."

However, as Zalith stood up, Alucard's eyes darted from the curtains and to the demon. Despite his need for human blood, the scent of *Zalith's* almost captivated Alucard in a strange but dangerous way. Right now, he was so starved that even the blood of a creature he didn't need would suffice. His thoughts were racing; his strength was forcibly returning so that he could feed and recover. He knew what would happen the moment his body provided him with the miraculous strength to attack whatever was close by... and that was Zalith. He knew he wouldn't be able to stop himself; all he could do was hope that Zalith could stop him.

In the blink of an eye and with a quiet *thud*, Alucard burst out of bed and pinned Zalith against the wall before he could reach the bedroom door. The vampire moved so quickly that the bed covers were only just settling back down onto the bed as he gripped Zalith's throat in his right hand. But the vampire didn't sink his fangs into his neck. He just stared at him. And Zalith stared back with an almost expectant look on his face. He didn't look the least bit afraid. If anything, he looked concerned for Alucard, not himself.

Breathing frantically with a look of hunger in his eyes, Alucard stared eagerly into Zalith's almost black eyes. He wanted *something* from Zalith, but he didn't understand what. It wasn't blood, that was for sure, and that was all that mattered to him right now. Blood. He needed it, he wanted it, and he would get it. His miraculous, predatory strength wouldn't last much longer, and he didn't plan to waste it.

Alucard let go of Zalith's throat and threw him aside—but not with enough force to throw the demon off his feet. He didn't care, though. He had but one focus, and it was the heartbeat coming from his manor's grounds.

Focusing on the sound, he left his room and prowled through his house and down the stairs. Zalith, who was following him, reached out and grabbed his arm to try and help him walk, but he snarled back at the demon. He wasn't about to let him stop him.

He reached the front door, pulled it open, and stepped out into the sun. The scent of the human he was hunting was now stronger than ever. He sharply turned his head, setting his ice-blue eyes on the cedar-brown-haired man tending to a black stallion. He cared not to remember who this man was; he was human and exactly what Alucard needed.

Without a moment's hesitation, Alucard sprung forward, using every ounce of what remained of his accumulated energy. The man screamed in horror as the vampire appeared in the blink of an eye and grabbed the side of his face, digging his claws into his skin. Alucard pulled the man's head aside to expose his neck and mercilessly sank his fangs into his throat, silencing his panicked pleas. Alucard dropped to his knees, holding the man as tightly as he could as he drained him of his blood and life force, and in a few short moments, his victim was dead. He stopped struggling, took his final breath, and as his blood was devoured, his body began to wither until it was nothing but a husk.

Alucard exhaled in satisfaction as the scales on his face started receding and fading, and he watched his claws return to their usual, pale colour. But his first kill didn't completely recover his human likeness. He was going to need more.

With a tired sigh, he leaned his back against the legs of the unfazed black stallion, who was still standing where Sergiu left him. Alucard didn't feel so exhausted anymore, but he was still weary. His senses were returning to normal, the world around him became relevant again, and as the gravel crunched beneath someone's boots, he slowly turned his head towards the sound and set his eyes on Zalith.

He knew he attacked the demon, and it made him feel so disappointed in himself; he couldn't look at him a moment longer. He took his eyes off Zalith, looking down at the ground, waiting for his body to heal a little more before he spoke. He calmed down, finding it less of a challenge to focus on what he was doing and feeling. But the hunger still lingered. He needed more—he *wanted* more. But where would he get it?

Zalith crouched beside him and slowly placed his hand on his shoulder. "Alucard?" he asked quietly. "Do you feel any better now?"

The vampire frowned, keeping his eyes on the ground. He didn't need nor want demon blood, but for some reason, Zalith being so close to him enticed him. This time, however, he felt as though he could keep himself from attacking him. "Yes," he answered wearily.

"Let me help you," he said, placing his other hand on Alucard's right shoulder. The vampire didn't refuse, so he helped him to his feet. "You still need to rest."

Alucard did his best not to fight. Zalith was right. He *did* need to rest. So, as Zalith held his arm and escorted him back towards and into his house, he followed silently. He kept his eyes focused on the floor, trying to ignore the urge to sink his fangs into the demon. He still didn't understand why he felt so eager for his blood—he was a demon, Alucard didn't need that. He needed human blood, so why did he feel as though he needed Zalith's? He frowned in confusion while they made their way up the stairs, down the hall, and back into his bedroom.

As Zalith helped him back into his bed, he glanced up at him. "Vhy are you 'ere? Vhy…did you take care of me?" he asked, unsure why anyone would stick around for *four* days and look after him.

Looking down at him, Zalith smiled. "Because I care about you, Alucard," he said with sincerity. "Now, stay in bed and rest, or I'll spank you," he warned with a smirk.

Alucard didn't know how to take Zalith's threat. It made him feel strangely nervous, and he was sure that his statement was meant to be flirtatious. Even when he was weak and tired, Zalith didn't miss an opportunity to embarrass him, and it made him pout and look away.

Zalith smiled as he stood up and straightened his blazer. "I have a few things to do, so I'll leave you to rest. I'll be back in a short while, and I'll bring someone else for you to devour," he said, smirking.

The vampire glanced up at him. "I'm…sorry vor attacking you. Vhen zhis 'appens, I—"

"You don't need to apologize, Alucard. Now, rest," he repeated.

With a slight nod, Alucard made himself comfortable, and as the demon left his room, he sighed quietly. He still felt weary and hungry. His desire for blood was close to overbearing, but after draining Sergiu, he felt as if he could control himself. The life force he took would slowly restore his physical appearance, and the blood would help his ethos slowly recuperate. He just hoped it wouldn't take too long.

The last time the portal affected him this way, he felt exhausted for more than a week. He was sure that this time, he'd feel even more so for much longer. But…at least Zalith was there. He'd never imagined allowing someone to care for him while he was so vulnerable—no one but Zalith. He felt he'd let that demon do just about anything, but that unnerved him. To be so helpless as to allow someone into his life like that—could he let it happen?

Alucard frowned and slowly rolled onto his side. He couldn't allow himself to overthink. He had to rest; he had to recover. He could think about Zalith later. But despite that decision, he still found the demon on his mind as he slowly drifted off to sleep. It seemed as though Zalith had earned a permanent home inside Alucard's mind, and it might very well remain that way for a long, long time.

The vampire had no quarrels with that, though. Zalith meant a great deal to him already, so much that he was comfortable allowing him to not only take care of him but to remain in his house and keep him out of harm's way while he healed. He felt safe with Zalith. *No one* made Alucard feel safe…but *he* did. And that fact made his wish to be around Zalith more of a need.

Chapter Seventy-One

Need

| Alucard |

Alucard woke when someone knocked on his front door. Of course, he didn't have the strength or motivation to get up and answer it, but he didn't need to. He lay in the darkness of his room, listening as Zalith opened the door and greet Ben, who hadn't come alone.

The scent of human blood immediately snatched the vampire's attention, forcing him to become something of a starved, manic animal. He needed it, he wanted it, and he was going to get it. But by the time he was on his feet, Zalith had already opened his bedroom door and stepped into the darkness with a rather confused-looking woman at his side. Alucard didn't care who she was or why she looked as if she had no idea where she was—she was human; that was all that mattered.

He sprung out of his bed, grabbed the woman from Zalith's grip, and pinned her against the wall in the hall. He sunk his four fangs into her neck, biting so hard she couldn't even scream. He didn't care. She was nothing but food to him. And the moment he tasted blood, he felt as though an awful burden had been lifted.

The vampire drained every drop from her, and every ounce of her life force, revitalizing his own. Now, he felt a whole lot better than earlier, but his hunger wasn't yet sated. It calmed, but it didn't cease. He snarled quietly, threw the woman's corpse to the floor, and turned around, resting his back against the wall as he waited for the high that human blood gave him to fade.

"Are you feeling better?" Zalith asked, walking over to him.

As the demon stopped in front of him, Alucard thoughtlessly moved his hand towards Zalith's face, but as he snapped out of his blood-induced trance, he quickly diverted his hand to the demon's shoulder.

He gripped Zalith's shoulder, staring at his own hand, waiting for his voice to return to him. It took a moment, but once his high faded, he pulled his hand away, frowned, and glanced at Zalith's intrigued but concerned face.

"Maybe," the vampire uttered. He then sighed deeply as he rested his head back against the wall and glared up at the ceiling. "Vhat…day is zhis?" he asked, unsure whether he'd slept longer than he felt he had.

Zalith slowly placed his hand on the vampire's arm and pulled him away from the wall. He led the vampire back into his room, directed him over to his bed, and sat him down. As he sat beside him, he answered, "Thursday."

An irritated, tired huff escaped Alucard's breath as he dragged his hand over his face. Tomorrow was Elvin's birthday, and as much as he might like to cancel, he felt as though he couldn't. He was on his feet, he was recovering, and he knew Elvin would make a huge deal of it if he failed to come through with his promise. He didn't want to let him down either, despite his weakened state. At least his face and hands were no longer scaled. If he still looked like a man-turning-lizard, there'd be no way he could be seen by anyone, least of all someone who would write about it.

He glanced at Zalith, who was staring at him—of course. "I 'ave…a ving tomorrow."

"Yes, Dirk informed me. Elvin's birthday," he said with a disapproving tone. "You don't look the least bit ready to be walking around, let alone host a party."

Alucard shook his head and looked down at his lap. "I can't cancel. I said I vould do zhis."

"What's more important, Alucard? A birthday—something that could be celebrated at a later date—or your own physical *and* mental health?"

He rolled his eyes and sighed quietly. "I'm not cancelling. I just…need to ask you someving."

Zalith seemed to frown expectantly—almost as if he was hoping for something.

The vampire sighed again and glanced at him. "I zon't know 'ow long zhe effects of vhatever zhis is vill last; vhen zhis 'appens, leaves me veeling…unrelentingly 'ungry. I von't lose control of myselv, but…just in case I do, I vant you to keep an eye on me, especially since at least two of zhe guest vill be 'uman," he explained. The last thing he wanted was to attack and maybe even kill Elvin or his new barmaid girlfriend. He didn't want to cancel the occasion, either. He and Elvin may not have been on the best of terms lately, but he didn't want to let the bard down. So, asking Zalith to keep an eye on him was the best thing he could do. He trusted him to keep him from doing anything he might regret.

Zalith sighed but smiled slightly. "Of course. But*why*must this occasion go ahead?"

"I just…." He huffed and shrugged. "I zon't like to let people down. Zhat's all. I'll be vine tomorrow. I just need you to make sure I zon't try to eat Elvin or 'is girlvriend."

Amused, Zalith scoffed. "That*dwarf*has a girlfriend?"

Alucard grunted irritably and looked at him. "I vhought you'd be glad to 'ear zhat 'e's not pining vor me anymore."

"Why? He was never a threat in the first place," Zalith said confidently.

"You seemed vreatened enough to ask who 'e vas," Alucard sneered.

"General curiosity, vampire," the demon said with a smile.

With an exasperated sigh, Alucard took his eyes off the demon and looked back down at his lap. "Vight," he muttered. "Vank you."

Zalith smiled curiously. "For what?"

"Vor taking care of me," he said quietly, but the bravery it had taken for him to say it quickly waned, just as his composure always did in Zalith's presence. However, he wasn't going to cut his appreciative speech short. He wanted to tell Zalith how much it meant to him—for him to care for him and give up his time to make sure he was okay. "You zidn't 'ave to, but you did, and…I'd never expect anyvone to care vor me, and especially not vor zhis long, eizer."

He smiled and placed his hand on the vampire's shoulder. "There is nothing I wouldn't do for you," he said firmly.

Alucard glanced at him again. They stared at one another for a moment, neither of them speaking a word. But Alucard looked away when he saw Zalith move a little closer. "Vhat vill you do?" he asked, changing the subject, still far too nervous to talk about his thoughts and feelings.

"Tonight?"

"Yes."

"Sleep," he answered. "It would seem we have things to do tomorrow."

Alucard nodded at the corpse in the hall. "I'd say Sergiu can deal vith zhat, but I vemember I relieved 'im of 'is vork earlier," he said with a smirk.

Amused, Zalith laughed slightly. "Don't worry. I'll have someone deal with it. What time do your guests arrive tomorrow?"

"Noon," Alucard answered.

"All right. Get some more rest, and I'll see you in the morning…and remember what I said about staying in bed," he said, smirking.

AsZalith stood up, keeping his hand on Alucard's shoulder, the vampire looked up at him. He didn't want to say goodnight yet, but he didn't have the words or courage to ask him to stay longer.

"Oh, Alucard," Zalith said with a frown.

"Vhat?"

"I thought I should say something since Sergiu's now dead. I saw him a few weeks back talking to himself. I focused on him, and I think he was communicating with someone telepathically."

Alucard frowned strangely. "Sergiu vas 'uman…as var as I vas avare."

"He was definitely talking to *someone*."

The vampire's frown thickened; he couldn't believe he hadn't pieced it together until now. Damien seemed to *always* know what he was doing and where he was… almost as if someone was feeding him information. What if it was Sergiu? His groundskeeper knew a lot of the details of his private life, things which somehow got back to Damien. And if he was right… then Damien was going to come looking for his messenger's killer.

"Are you okay?" Zalith asked worriedly.

Alucard nodded. "I'm vine. *Noapte bună*," he said.

Zalith smiled and let go of his shoulder. "Goodnight."

Then, as the demon left his room, Alucard climbed back into bed and stared over at the curtains. While he might usually lay there and overthink, he didn't have the strength to do so tonight. He closed his eyes, focused on resting, and soon drifted off to sleep once more.

He could think about Sergiu tomorrow.

When he woke up the following morning, Alucard's thoughts overbore him. Zalith—of course—was the first thing on his mind. That seemed to be the case a lot recently, so much that it felt strange *not* to be thinking about the demon. All he wanted was to see him, to hear him—to even *feel* him despite his hate for physical contact. Zalith was the only person he'd come to appreciate contact with, and he thought that he might just crave more than what he currently received.

He sighed quietly, rolling onto his back, and as he stared up at the ceiling, he frowned sullenly. What should he do? Was now the time to tell Zalith how he felt? The fact that he felt so very safe with this demon encouraged him to believe that now was a better time than any to talk to him… to tell him. But *what* should he tell him? That he craved his presence? That he adored his touch? That he didn't want to spend a moment without him? Or should he just tell him that he wanted to be with him in every way? To date him—that was how Zalith put it. Alucard wanted that. *That* was what he should tell him. But when? Should he get up, go to his room, and tell him right this moment? He should, right?

But… hesitation gripped him before he could get out of bed. Perhaps he ought to wait until he felt better. What if his current state of weakness was affecting his judgment? Where had this confidence come from? Why did he feel so eager to tell him now when he could have told him on countless other occasions? Was he*really*prepared to expose his feelings? He sat up and stared down at his lap, trying to decide whether he was ready. He wanted to, he needed to, but how could he be sure that Zalith wouldn't eventually tire of him? He was convinced that he wasn't an interesting enough person for someone like Zalith to want to be around for a long while.

Alucard sighed in hopelessness. But he wouldn't be alone with his thoughts much longer. He could hear the demon making his way down the hall towards his room. Then, when he knocked quietly, Alucard lifted his head and looked over at the door. He watched as Zalith opened it and walked in with a smile on his face.

"Good morning," the demon said, leaving the door ajar as he made his way over to Alucard's bed.

As the demon sat on the side of his bed not too far from where he was sitting, Alucard frowned slightly and glanced at him. "*Buna dimineata*," he said, trying to ignore the fact that, despite having just woken up, his hunger was already beginning to overwhelm him.

He didn't understand why, but something about Zalith seemed to confuse not only his thoughts but also his senses—his instincts. He didn't need nor want demon blood, so why did he feel what could only be described as a need for Zalith's? Perhaps his weakened state was just affecting him in more ways than he knew. Maybe his fatigue convinced him that any blood could help. He knew that not to be true, though. He needed humans, not demons.

"Do you feel better this morning?" Zalith asked.

"Somevhat," Alucard said. Although his hunger might still be screaming at him, his body didn't feel so weak. He thought it would be less of a struggle to walk around, and considering Elvin would soon arrive for his celebration, that relieved him.

"Good. I imagine your guests will be here soon; do you want me to bring another human now or later?"

Alucard wasn't sure what he wanted. He was hungry; he needed the blood and life force to heal himself, but all he could think about was Zalith. He couldn't stop thinking about what he wanted to say and what he felt he might do. Seeing him now, and with him being so close… it made him more nervous than he'd ever felt before.

He took his eyes off Zalith, looked down at the floor, and shrugged. "Now… please," he muttered, sure that it would be best to try and sate his hunger before Elvin arrived.

"I'll be right back," Zalith said with a smile before standing up.

Then, as Zalith left the vampire's bedroom, Alucard slowly pulled himself out of bed, making sure that he could actually walk without feeling as though he was going to pass out again. He slowly made his way over to the curtains, pulled them open, and stared down at his manor gardens. The sun was high in the sky, his eyes shimmering ice blue as he glanced up at it. He frowned and looked down at his hands, watching as they trembled in response to his hunger. It irritated him—it *angered* him. But there was no avoiding it.

The moment he heard Zalith returning, Alucard snapped back into his thirst-driven trance. But he didn't fling himself at the human this time. Zalith stood in the doorway, gripping the wrist of a confused, horrified woman. Alucard looked back over his shoulder, setting his eyes on not his food…but Zalith. The demon smiled as his eyes met Alucard's—Alucard didn't know why he was staring at him. Just as he had yesterday, he felt there was something he wanted from Zalith, something he *needed*. Something to say, something to do—he didn't know. But there *was*…something. However, just as he also had yesterday, he ignored the confusing, strange desire to snatch Zalith's throat instead of the human's.

With a tired look on his face, he made his way over to where Zalith stood, harshly snatched the woman's throat, and pinned her against the door. He felt hesitant to kill her, though. Before sinking his fangs into her, he glanced at Zalith and frowned in response to the demon's smirk.

"Vhere are you getting zhem vrom?" the vampire asked.

"Ben sent them. I assume he gets them from a safe source."

With a frown, Alucard looked back at the choking woman. "And is zhere a veason zhey 'ave all been vomen?" he asked skeptically.

"Have they?" Zalith smirked. "I hadn't noticed."

Alucard rolled his eyes and sank his fangs into the woman's neck, slowly draining her of her blood and silencing his thirst.

Zalith started to move closer to Alucard. "How do you feel now?" he asked quietly, leaning into Alucard's ear.

He didn't reply; he was too busy feeding.

The demon grinned as he carefully placed his right hand on Alucard's lower back.

Alucard frowned but didn't stop him from dragging his hand down until he lightly gripped his ass.

"And *now*?" the demon murmured, still leaning into the vampire's ear.

With a confused expression, Alucard pulled his fangs from the woman's throat, trying to decide whether he wanted to tell Zalith to back off. But he felt no need to. Before, he thought he wanted something from this demon, and he didn't know what. Now, however, he felt as though *this* might be what he desired. He felt strangely content— strangely *inviting* of Zalith's flirting and touching. Whether it be because of the high he felt or not, he didn't care. It cleared his conflicted thoughts, and he was certain that what was happening right now was what he wanted.

The vampire exhaled quietly in anticipation, refusing to pay attention to his thoughts any longer. He threw the silent woman away and turned around and grabbed Zalith's collar, pulling him closer as he leaned his back against the door. Zalith smiled excitedly, but as he leaned in to kiss the vampire's lips, Alucard placed his hand on the back of the demon's head and diverted his face to his neck. He slightly tilted his head aside, giving Zalith space to kiss, and when the demon did as he wished, Alucard closed his eyes and sighed in relief.

Zalith guided his right hand down to the vampire's ass and gripped it tightly while he playfully bit Alucard's neck between his kisses. He then grabbed Alucard's right wrist with his free hand and pinned his arm against the door, and as he kissed his way over to the other side of the vampire's neck, he began to move his hand up and under his shirt. He waited, making sure Alucard was comfortable—Alucard was sure that his lack of reluctant fidgets told Zalith that he *was*—so the demon continued.

As Zalith placed his hand on Alucard's bare waist, the vampire flinched a little, but he didn't ask him to stop—he didn't *want* him to. Zalith then stopped kissing his neck and started sucking on it again. Was he giving him another love bite?

Alucard exhaled quietly as Zalith dragged his hand over his abs, caressing each one with his fingers. He felt no need to flee or tell Zalith to stop; he enjoyed the demon's attention. His touch made him feel a new kind of excitement, something he hadn't felt before, and he profoundly enjoyed it.

While Zalith continued to suck on the right side of his neck, Alucard gripped a fistful of the demon's hair, trying to contain a strange new eagerness that seemed to increase as each moment passed. His entire body shivered in desperation as Zalith lightly dragged his fingers over it; whatever Zalith was doing, whatever it was he was causing Alucard to feel, the vampire longed for more.

But that was when the front door knocked. The sound startled Alucard so much that he snapped out of whatever excitement he was drowning in. He sharply turned his head, staring over at the window as Zalith moved his face from his neck. He could sense an entire group of people outside—humans, werewolves, vampires—which had to mean that his guests had arrived, and his overly nervous thoughts returned the moment he realized that Zalith had his hand beneath his shirt and on his left pec.

With an anxious look on his reddening face, he pulled free from Zalith's grip, lightly pushed him away, and silently left his bedroom, heading for the front door. He wasn't sure what had come over him…but all he felt now was overwhelmingly embarrassed. He'd never experienced anything like that before…and he didn't know how to feel.

Chapter Seventy-Two

— ⸱ ✝ ⸱ —

Elvin's Birthday

| **Alucard** |

When he answered the door, Alucard set his eyes on Elvin, who smiled and clapped his hands. At his side was a brunette woman a few inches taller than him, and behind him were Tobias and Ben, who were arguing with each other. Ben's wife was shaking her head, and the four women Tobias brought with him were comparing the jewellery on their hands. Dirk lingered in the background along with a very stubborn-looking, platinum-blonde-haired woman.

"Aleksei!" Elvin cheered, but he frowned when his eyes wandered to the right side of Alucard's neck—of course, he was staring at the new love bite Zalith had given him. He pouted, rolled his eyes, and took the hand of the woman beside him. "This is Maia," he introduced as the woman smiled pleasantly.

"Hi," she said, holding out her hand towards the vampire.

"Yo, you got somewhere I can put this?" Tobias then called from behind Elvin, holding up a crate of alcohol.

Alucard stepped aside. "Zhe kitchen."

"All right," Tobias said with a grin as he led the way into the house, and the four women followed him.

Elvin then hurried into the house, dragging his female companion with him.

"You look better," Ben said with a smirk, stopping beside Alucard. "Zalith here?"

"Maybe. Go and make sure Tobias' vives zon't steal my shit," he grumbled. Then, he looked at Lillian. "You can come in."

Nodding, Ben made his way inside with his wife.

"I trust your stubborn friend shared my news with you?" Dirk asked, stopping in front of Alucard as the woman he brought with him went with Ben and his wife.

Zalith hadn't yet told him what Dirk informed him of, but it could wait. So, he nodded.

"Do you wish for me to change the date?"

Alucard rolled his eyes and closed his door. "Ve can talk about zhis later."

Dirk replied, "All right," and trailed the rest of the guests through to the kitchen.

With a quiet sigh, Alucard closed the door and followed them. When he entered his kitchen, he eyed each guest closely. Tobias was already pouring everyone a drink—Elvin downed his straight away, and that made Alucard roll his eyes harder than he might ever have. That man shouldn't drink, but it was his birthday, so who was he to stop him?

Once Tobias caught sight of Alucard, he made his way through the crowd and handed him a glass of whiskey. "Hey, I heard you were kinda sick. You all right?"

Taking the glass from him, Alucard shrugged. "I'm vine."

Tobias smirked. "You gonna tell me where your boyfriend is?"

"Vhat?" Alucard asked, frowning.

"Don't play dumb with me, man. Ben told me about that hickey—didn't tell me about that one, though," he said with a grin, gesturing to Alucard's new love bite with his hand.

Alucard sighed and sipped from his glass. "Who are zhe vomen you brought vith you?" he asked, taking his eyes off Tobias to glare over at the four black-haired women.

"Oh, them?" Tobias mumbled, leaning back against the wall beside Alucard. "Those are the Wynen-Blood sisters."

Alucard waited for him to elaborate.

"They uh…come from another, smaller pack. Met them in the city. They're lookin' to unite with a pack of similar size, and I was like, hey, I got a small pack, let's talk. And here we are," he said, shrugging.

"Can you trust zhem?" Alucard asked with a scowl.

"Yeah, don't worry, man. I checked them out—"

"I'm sure you did."

Tobias chuckled, but when Alucard didn't laugh with him, he calmed down. "They come from Drydenheim. Apparently, some shit's happening there with the elves and humans; wolves got caught up in it. Came here 'cause they heard wolves were native to this land. They didn't come looking for Ada, that's for sure."

"She's dead," Alucard said.

"Yeah?" he asked, surprised.

"Keep an eye on your vomen," Alucard then warned. "If a single piece of my jewellery—or anyving vor zhat matter—goes missing, I'll be coming to you."

Holding up his free hand, Tobias smiled. "Hey, don't worry, man. I'll keep an eye on them."

With a slight nod, Alucard made his way over to Elvin, and Tobias returned to pouring drinks for everyone as they all gathered and conversed in the kitchen.

"It's a nice house," Elvin's female companion, Maia, said as she set her eyes on Alucard.

"What happened?" Elvin asked as Alucard stopped in front of them. "You look kinda…tired."

"Noving," he mumbled.

Elvin pouted, and as he finished his drink, he gagged and looked disgusted.

"You shouldn't drink that," Maia said, taking the empty glass from him.

Elvin tutted stubbornly. "Why not?"

"Because you get drvunk var too easily; you vrow up and start singing. Ve zon't vant any of zhose vings to 'appen," Alucard said and then finished his own drink.

The bard scoffed as he watched Alucard place his glass on the countertop they were standing beside. "I ain't ever seen *you* drunk, but you only get drunk with annoying, rude, ugly demons," he sneered.

"Oh?" Maia asked.

"Is he here?" Elvin questioned. "Of course he is."

Alucard rolled his eyes and glanced at Tobias, who handed him another glass. The vampire set his eyes back on Elvin and said, "If I let you drvink, vill you keep your nose out of my business?"

Taking the glass, Elvin muttered, "Whatever."

The vampire smirked. "'Appy birvday."

Surprised, Elvin stared in silence, watching as the vampire turned around and headed over to Ben and Lillian.

"I never said vank you," Alucard said, stopping behind Ben, who turned to face him, pausing the conversation he was having with Lillian. "Vor contacting Zaliv."

Ben smiled. "You don't have to say thanks. I'm just doing my job."

"Hmm. I gazzer Zetlaff is still in zhe dungeon?"

"Yeah, he's still down there. Sings a lot, asks to see you."

"I'll deal vith 'im tomorrow."

"Okay, so," Tobias said, joining Ben, Alucard, and Lillian with his four women. "These are Betisa—" he said, pointing to the woman with the longest hair— "Kistie—" he held his hand towards the woman with the ponytail— "Nicola—" he tapped the shoulder of the woman with the ear-length hair— "and Sonja Wynen-Blood," he said, placing his hand on the shoulder of the last sister, whose hair was plaited and tied into a bun. "Girls, this is Aleksei, Ben, and Lillian."

All four sisters smiled, waved, and said their words of greeting.

Nicola smiled and lightly stroked Alucard's arm. "Hey," she said, smiling.

Tobias then chuckled and pulled her away from the vampire, who glared in hostility. "Yeah, no," he warned. "Not your type, lady."

"I gather your companion is here, too?" Dirk asked, joining the huddle of people as he looked at Alucard.

The vampire glanced around the room, but he couldn't see Zalith. He was still upstairs. Why?

"You haven't paid up yet," Ben muttered, glancing at Tobias.

"Hey, I ain't paying shit til I see it for myself," Tobias argued.

"Vhat are you talking about?" Alucard questioned.

Lillian rolled her eyes. "These two morons made a bet that you and Ben's old boss were a thing. Tobias bet against it."

Alucard frowned, looking around at each of their curious faces.

"Well…are you?" Tobias asked.

"I don't think they are," Elvin announced, joining them.

Noticing the uncomfortable look on Alucard's face, Ben sighed and placed his hand on Tobias' shoulder. "All right, let's not all huddle out here in the kitchen. Should we move to one of the sitting rooms?"

"Vhrough zhere," Alucard said, waving his towards the doorway which would take them through to the conference room. "And zhen into zhe next voom."

Everyone did as instructed and followed Ben through the conference lounge and into the large dining room. The four black-haired sisters pulled out chairs and sat at the table, chattering quietly with one another. Elvin stuck close to Maia by one of the windows with Dirk and his female friend. Ben, Tobias, and Lillian also remained together and talked about werewolf heirachy.

Alucard didn't know what to do with himself; he stood by the arched doorway and kept a watchful eye on Tobias' women. He'd already caught them eyeing many of his smaller possessions lined around the room's shelves. He didn't want to have to argue with anyone today, but if one of those women so much as *thought* about taking something, he'd not hesitate to confront them.

"I see everyone has a companion at their side…other than you, vampire," Zalith said with a smirk, appearing beside him.

Not at all startled by his appearance, Alucard glanced at him. "I 'ave no idea who Dirk's voman is, and Tobias never vails to 'ave a voman at 'is side."

As he leaned against the wall beside Alucard, Zalith smiled at him. "You don't look like you want to be here."

"I told Elvin I'd do someving vor 'im. 'E seems content, zhat's all zhat matters," Alucard mumbled, looking across the room at Elvin, who was laughing with Maia.

"I'll get Ben to dispose of the body in your room," Zalith said quietly.

He glanced at the demon again. "I vorgot about zhat."

"I'm not surprised," he said with a flirty tone. "We *were* a little preoccupied."

As an embarrassed frown stole his vacant expression, Alucard pouted and looked back over at Elvin.

"I'll get us something to drink," Zalith then said before leaving the vampire's side.

Watching him head towards the kitchen, Alucard frowned and went back to keeping an eye on Tobias' friends. His attention, however, didn't remain on *them*. His thoughts quickly reverted to Zalith and what was going on before Elvin arrived. He wasn't sure what happened to him, but for a moment, he felt as eager as he'd ever felt for Zalith's attention, so keen that he'd been able to ignore his nervousness. He felt as though his blood high had helped with that, but he couldn't deny that he enjoyed each moment of it. He also couldn't help but wonder what might have happened if Elvin hadn't shown up.

"Here," Zalith said with a smile, handing Alucard a glass of wine. Then, while he sipped from *his* glass of wine, he eyed each person in the room. "I assume all of these people aren't only your subordinates, then?"

"Vhat does zhat matter?" Alucard uttered.

"It doesn't. I'm just creating conversation in an attempt to keep myself from dragging you back upstairs—unless, of course, you want that."

Pouting, Alucard glared down at his glass, trying to hide his nervousness. "No."

"Shame. You seemed to be rather enjoying it."

"Stop," Alucard muttered.

"Why?" he asked, turning to face him. He rested his arm against the wall beside him and smiled in his face. "Would you prefer to continue here?"

Right now, Alucard was beginning to feel rather agitated. Elvin's arrival had irritated him, and now, so was Zalith. Despite it not being the demon's fault that he was annoyed, he couldn't control his aggravated mood. He took his eyes off his glass and scowled into Zalith's eyes, ignoring his seductive look. But Zalith didn't seem to take him seriously.

The demon smiled and moved his hand to Alucard's shoulder, but the vampire snatched his wrist. Zalith stared at him, evidently only just understanding that Alucard really *did* want him to stop. So, he stepped back, and as Alucard let go of his wrist, he made sure to stay away.

"Sorry," Zalith said quietly. "I don't mean to make you uncomfortable."

"I'm *not* uncomfortable," he snarled and sipped from his glass.

"Then what's upset you?"

"Noving," he lied.

"I thought you said he wasn't coming," Elvin interjected, appearing beside them, eyeing Zalith evilly.

"Hey now," Tobias said, pulling Elvin away as both Zalith and Alucard scowled at him.

Alucard sighed quietly. He was becoming *very* irritable already, and the last thing he wanted to do was snap at somebody. So, he wordlessly moved away from Zalith and observed as Elvin was dragged away by Tobias.

The bard pouted. "I didn't invite him."

"You didn't invite my girls or Ben's wife, but they're here," Tobias said, putting his arm around Elvin's shoulders as he escorted him towards the crowd.

"So?" Elvin argued. "I don't mind *them* because they're not stuck up or rude or shady!"

"What's shady about Aleksei's... well, whatever he is to him?"

"I don't like him." Elvin pouted and leaned against the table as he and Tobias stopped in front of Ben and his wife.

"What's not to like?" Tobias mumbled.

"Where's your girlfriend?" Ben then asked, looking for Maia, who wasn't at Elvin's side.

Elvin shrugged. "She went to use the bathroom."

"Where'd you meet her?" Lillian asked.

Dirk and his female friend then joined them. He refilled all of their glasses with the whiskey bottle he'd just come back from the kitchen with.

Alucard took his eyes off them for a moment to look for Maia, but the woman wasn't in the room. He wasn't concerned, though. The only women he needed to keep a close eye on were Tobias' companions.

The bard replied, "Well, it was a while ago—a couple of months, actually. Just before Aleksei started going to meet that guy over there," he grumbled, glancing at Zalith, who was standing alone in the arched doorway. "I was in a tavern in Wrodiff telling Aleksei's story. The patrons didn't exactly like what I had to say about the vampire who was leading the human-vampire treaty up in the city, so they kinda just chased me off stage."

Tobias laughed and gripped the bard's shoulder. "Did you scream?"

"No!" Elvin insisted, crossing his arms. "Anyway!" he growled, "I went to the bar while I waited for Aleksei to come meet me, and this nice lady just starts talking to me."

"That's a barmaid's job, you know," Ben said, smirking.

"Whatever!" Elvin snapped. "All we did was talk a bit about Aleksei. But I went back there after you guys just abandoned me in the city a few weeks back, and she was there. I was sitting on my own, and she came over, asked if I was okay 'cause I was sad you guys left me. She sat with me, we talked a lot, and then I went back home with her. Now we see each other every day," he explained with a proud smile on his face.

Ben and Tobias nodded and smiled suggestively as Lillian rolled her eyes.

"You're dating this barmaid?" Dirk asked.

"I mean... I guess," Elvin said with a shrug.

"What happened to your little crush on Aleksei?" Lillian asked. "Ben told me about it," she said as everyone gawped at her.

"I didn't have a crush on him!" Elvin squealed before gulping down his drink, which he choked on.

Tobias patted the bard's back and shook his head. "There, there. It's not for everyone."

With an angry huff, Elvin held out his glass for a refill. "Who's *your* lady friend?" he questioned, looking at Dirk while he refilled his drink.

The platinum-blonde-haired woman held out her hand. "Lady White," she said, setting her almost-white eyes on Elvin.

"Girlfriend, huh?" Tobias winked, nudging Dirk.

"No," she said with an offended frown as Elvin shook her hand. "I am manó."

"A-what-o?" Tobias blurted.

"Manó," Dirk said, looking around at their curious faces. "An all-female species of elf."

Tobias smirked. "Cool. But… if you're all girls, how do you like… you know… make more?"

"We selectively breed with males of other species," she answered.

"You taking applications?" Tobias asked, grinning.

"No."

He pouted with embarrassment and sipped from his drink.

"Your luck doesn't seem to exceed the women of your own species, does it?" Ben asked Tobias, amused.

Tobias wordlessly glared over at the windows.

"What are you doing in Dor-Sanguis?" Lillian asked curiously.

Lady White replied, "I met Dirk on a trade ship back from Boszorkäny. He looked rather interesting, so I told him of my mission. Now, I am here."

"Mission?" Elvin questioned.

"She told us, man," Tobias mumbled.

"Seen anyone of interest?" Lillian asked with a smirk.

"Perhaps," she said, smiling.

Tobias then sighed loudly. "All right, who wants shots?"

No one disagreed.

"All right, I'll be back."

Alucard took his eyes off the group as Tobias left for the kitchen and looked at Zalith, who was heading over to where he was.

When Zalith reached Alucard, he frowned hesitantly. "I wanted to suggest something, considering as our mutual mission will soon be complete."

He didn't want to think about the end of their mission, and Zalith's mention of it saddened him. But there was no point in avoiding it. He was right. Soon, the last of the vampires would be moved to Aegisguard, and their mission would be over.

"Vhat?" he asked, trying to keep himself from sinking into dismay. He hoped that the demon's suggestion would involve them continuing to see one another after the mission was complete.

Zalith smiled and said, "Another means of contact. I know of an ethos that will allow us to speak and see one another through any mirror. If you would like to use such a way of speaking, I can show you how to use it."

With an intrigued frown, Alucard turned to face him. "Vhat sort of ethos?"

"An enchanting ethos. As long as you are aware of the link you wish to make, any mirror can be used. Or, if it's easier for you, I can simply make it so a mirror of yours is always connected to one of mine."

"And…vhat? I can see you vhrough zhat, and you can see me? Ve can…talk to each ozzer?"

"Yes," he said, smiling.

He took his eyes off the demon and looked down at his glass for a moment. While he liked the sound of that, he couldn't help but wonder if this was Zalith's way of suggesting that they might not see one another again for a while once their mission was complete. He couldn't help but ask, "And…I *vill* still see you avter zhis, vight?"

"Of course. I was going to ask you the same question."

Alucard shrugged. "Ve can still meet vor…coffee."

"We can," Zalith agreed with a smirk. He then glanced at Ben, who left the crowd and stood over by the table on his own, pouring another drink. "Don't go anywhere," he said, looking back at Alucard, "I need to have a word with Ben."

The vampire nodded.

Zalith smiled and then turned around, making his way over to Ben.

Alucard watched him for a moment…but the mention of their mission ending hurt him a lot more than he'd thought it would. He knew that Damien was likely to ensure that they wouldn't get to spend time together once it was over, and that brought a deep, *drowning* sadness to his heart. But he wasn't going to stand around and let people see just how despondent he felt. So, while Zalith was distracted, he turned around and left the room. He needed some air.

| Zalith |

"I trust you are well," Zalith said, standing beside Ben.

Ben stopped pouring his drink, picked up his half-filled glass, and smiled slightly. "Very. I'm glad to have my voice back, too."

"Good. Thank you for contacting me when Alucard collapsed."

"No problem. You were the only person I could think to contact. *You* are the one he's working with, after all. I thought it might hinder progress if I didn't contact you."

"On the subject of working and business, I believe our time together has reached a natural conclusion."

Fear filled Ben's eyes. "Why?"

"You work for Alucard now, and I don't want him to think I'm trying to undermine him or pry into his private affairs. The last thing I want is him thinking we can't trust each other," Zalith explained.

The dread on Ben's face was unmissable.

Zalith smiled in amusement. "I'm not going to kill you. I'm sure I can trust you enough to know that you're not going to share any information about myself or my work with anyone... are you?"

Astonished, Ben frowned and shook his head. "Uh...yeah...." He laughed nervously. "No, never. You can trust me; I'd die before I exposed either of you."

Zalith nodded and said, "If there ever happens to be another emergency, you can contact me using the izurets."

"Of course—thank you," Ben said with relief in his voice.

Then, Zalith turned around and went to return to where he left Alucard, but the vampire was gone. He stopped in his tracks and looked around, searching the room for him. Not only was Alucard missing, but so were Tobias and Elvin's girlfriend. Either one of them could become Alucard's next snack, and he agreed to keep Alucard from unintentionally attacking someone because of his current state. But where was he? He ought to find him before he decided it was time to devour someone else.

As his worry grew and his heart raced a little harder, Zalith left the room and began his search for the vampire.

Chapter Seventy-Three

— ⟨ † ⟩ —

Almost Goodbye

| Alucard |

In the manor's back garden, Alucard was sitting on a bench on the porch. The clouds above denied the sunlight from hitting the ground, thus hiding his ice-blue eyes. He stared ahead, watching a fox as it crept out of the tree line, stalking a lonely hare in the grass. He held his wine glass in his left hand and had his right rested in his lap.

A sullen look clung to his pale face. Despite being surrounded by the people he might one day allow himself to call his friends, he felt no less alone. All he could think about was how he'd soon be utterly alone again. Zalith was the only person who could make him feel wanted, who could make him feel needed, safe, and as if he wasn't alone. But Zalith would be a piece of his past soon. Once the vampire relocation mission was complete, Damien would never let him see that demon again. And although Zalith said that they'd stay in contact, he wouldn't get his hopes up.

He hated it. He hated *himself.* He couldn't understand why he allowed himself to grow so close to someone, to become so attached to someone he knew would only be in his life temporarily. The pain it caused him to even*think*about never seeing Zalith again made him struggle to keep tears from his eyes, and the agony that would come once he was actually gone… Alucard was sure it would torment him worse than any punishment Damien had ever given him.

He looked down into his glass, staring at the dull, crimson wine. Depravity was his life; he had always known that. So why did he think it would be any different this time? What happened earlier with Zalith—that moment along with Zalith saying they'd be seeing one another after the mission was complete—dragged him into the darkest parts of his heart. While Zalith seemed so convinced, Alucard knew the truth. Once it was over, *they'd* be over.

With a hopeless look in his eyes, he glared at the forest which sat at the end of the garden. He'd probably not see his home again after, either. Damien would most likely be sending him elsewhere to work. He didn't want to leave his home; he didn't want to leave the people who had found their way into his life. He didn't want to leave Zalith.

"I hope you're thinking about me," Zalith called, making his way over to where Alucard was sitting.

Snapping out of his thoughts, Alucard sharply turned his head and looked over at him, watching as he made his way over and sat beside him. "Vhat?" he asked, staring at him.

"You make the same faces when you're thinking," Zalith said with a smirk.

Alucard frowned and looked down at his lap. Did he?

Zalith adorned a concerned expression and shuffled closer to him. "Why did you leave the room?"

"I just needed some air," he said quietly.

"And here I was thinking you ran away from *me*," Zalith said with a quiet laugh as he rested his right leg over his left. He sipped from the glass of wine he'd brought with him.

"No," Alucard muttered in response.

Zalith placed his glass on the bench's arm, moved closer, and put his hand on Alucard's right wrist. "What's bothering you?"

Alucard glanced at Zalith's hand and then frowned at him. "Vhy are you so convinced zhat someving is vrong vith me?"

"You make a face, Alucard. I've known you long enough to know when you're overthinking something. I may not understand *all* of your expressions, but I understand when you're sad. Why are you sad?"

Alucard looked away from Zalith's worried face and stared down at his lap again. "I'm not sad," he lied.

"If anything I've said or done has upset you, please tell me."

He shook his head. "Noving you 'ave said or done 'as upset me."

"Then tell me," Zalith implored. "Why are you sad?"

But Alucard didn't answer.

The demon lightly gripped Alucard's jaw with his hand and turned the vampire's head so that he was facing him. "Tell me," he pleaded softly.

Staring into the demon's eyes, Alucard frowned in distress. He pulled his jaw from Zalith's grip and glared down at his wine. "I von't see you avter ve are done vith zhe vampires," he uttered, his heart aching.

"What?" Zalith asked as a look of disbelief struck his face. "Will you be busy?"

Alucard hesitated. He could tell that Zalith was upset, and that was the last thing he wanted, but there was no avoiding it. He deserved to know the truth—to know that Damien wouldn't let them see each other again and that he would *kill* Zalith if he were caught with him once the mission was done. Alucard couldn't keep lying to himself, he couldn't keep lying to Zalith, and he couldn't continue to let Zalith believe that they'd stay in contact once the mission was complete. As much as he'd like to believe it, as much as he wished it could happen, he knew that it just wouldn't.

He took his eyes off his lap and glanced at Zalith's confused face. "Zamien varned you," he said, "…and *me*. Ve vork togezzer vor *'im*, and vonce zhat is over, ve von't need to see each ozzer anymore. Zamien vill kill you if 'e sees you vith me avter ve are done."

Zalith frowned and sternly said, "I've told you before, Alucard. I'm not afraid of Damien. If I want to see you, I will see you. And I *do* want to see you—every day if it were possible. Whatever he may have made you think, we *will* see each other after the mission is over."

"I'd like to believe zhat," Alucard mumbled sullenly.

With a quiet sigh, Zalith placed his hand over Alucard's. "When you move the last of the vampires, I'll come and see you here the day after. Then, we can make plans. It's still not safe for you to visit my world, but I'm sure there are plenty of things we can do here. Do you—"

"You zon't get zhis," Alucard interrupted, pulling his hand from under Zalith's. "Ve *can't* see each ozzer avter ve're done. Zhis vas fun—zhese last months—but zhat's all zhis ever can be. Zhere are vings you zon't know, vings you *von't* know. Vings I von't tell you. But vhat I *can* tell you is zhat you need…I need…to stop. I zon't even know vhy I let myselv get so close—zhis is vhy I zon't 'ave vriends, vhy I zon't talk to people or socialize. I *can't*. All I do is vork—is all I'll ever do. I can't…be vith you. If zhat's even vhat you vant. I zon't know vhy you vould vant zhat; I'm not intervesting or attractive, I'm just…." He took his eyes off the demon, whose expression faded from a smile to an almost heart-breaking frown. He sighed in regret and glared at his glass. "Stop vasting your time on me."

Before Zalith could say anything, Alucard stood up—he couldn't sit near him anymore. He had said what needed to be said, and now, he had to walk away. If he stayed, he'd lose his composure and yearn for Zalith's embrace. He couldn't give in. What he was doing—although it broke his heart—was saving Zalith's life. Zalith mattered to him so much, so much that he'd give up his own happiness so that he could be safe. If losing him meant he remained alive, then lose him he would.

As Zalith also stood up, Alucard frowned at him. "You should go, and I'll contact you vhen I'm veady to move more vampires," he said.

But Zalith didn't say anything. He just stood there, looking at him with an unreadable look on his face. Alucard felt he might say something else; he thought he should insist that he left, but he couldn't bring himself to do it. He couldn't speak another word. He could feel his sadness growing, and his throat was sore from holding back his tears. He hesitated, but he had to walk away. And so, he exhaled quietly, taking his eyes off the demon.

However, before Alucard could walk off, Zalith snatched his wrist, pulled him back towards him, and tightly wrapped his arms around him. He buried his face in the vampire's shoulder and shook his head, tightening his grip as each moment passed by.

"Don't leave me," he pleaded quietly. "I can't…lose you."

Alucard didn't fight. He stood there, staring at the wall behind them, feeling Zalith tighten his grip around him. Zalith's plea, Zalith's response—it conflicted him so profoundly. He didn't want to leave him; of course he didn't. How could he? What he felt for Zalith was something he'd never felt before, something he wanted to hold onto. He wanted to be with him whenever he could. He*needed*Zalith. But that need could get either one of them killed—maybe even both of them. He'd never felt so pressured, so stressed. What could he do? Allow them both to suffer so that they could live? Or allow them both to enjoy their time together as much as they could before Damien inevitably ended their lives?

The pain of it all was unbearable—so unbearable that he couldn't keep himself from moving his arms around Zalith. He held him firmly, trying to contain his sadness. He didn't want to let go; he didn't want to let*him*go. Was it worth it? Spending whatever time they may have together? To have just a little while of happiness? Would it be worth their lives?

Yes.

Alucard had never felt so content, so positive—so…alive, even. Zalith made him feel so many things in such a short time, and he already knew he wanted to spend whatever time he had left with this demon. They could die tomorrow and he'd go happily knowing that he had the chance to share something like this with someone, knowing that he had been given a chance to care for someone so much that he'd give his life for them. He was quite sure what that was—this feeling. And he would hold onto it for as long as he could.

With a sullen pout on his face, Alucard rested the side of his head against Zalith's.

They stood there for a few moments…but then Zalith moved his head from the vampire's shoulder and stared into his eyes, their faces just inches from one another. Alucard didn't frown, he didn't cower—he waited as Zalith slowly moved his hand from the vampire's back and held it up to his face. Then, he gradually moved it closer until he placed it on Alucard's cheek.

Alucard didn't hesitate. Zalith's hand on his face no longer panicked him. He didn't feel uncomfortable, he didn't feel nervous—he felt…curious. He waited, allowing Zalith to move his face closer to his own and his hand to the back of his head. When he saw Zalith close his eyes, slightly slanting his head to his right, Alucard closed his eyes, too. Whatever was about to happen…he felt it was long overdue.

Zalith edged his face nearer…and gently pressed his lips against Alucard's. The vampire*was* instantly overwhelmed with nervousness when he felt their warm, wet touch—how could he not? But he didn't let it ruin their moment. He just wished he had let Zalith kiss him like this when he'd tried many times before. It felt gratifying in a way he couldn't explain; all he understood was that he enjoyed it, needed it, and wanted it. After what might be considered such a long time, after so many confusing, immutable thoughts, he felt he finally understood what he and Zalith *both* wanted from one another.

As a few seconds passed, though, he couldn't hold back his nervous thoughts. He moved his hands from around Zalith, carefully gripped the front of his blazer, and lightly pressed his hands into his chest, hoping Zalith would understand that he was telling him it was time to move away.

Zalith slowly pulled back and smiled, and then he rested his forehead against Alucard's. He stared into Alucard's eyes, but the vampire's face reddened as he looked away from him. That just made Zalith's smile grow into a smirk, though.

"Any time with you is never wasted," the demon told him quietly, caressing the vampire's hair as he kept his hand on the back of his head. "I'm not going anywhere, and neither are you," he said with a possessive yet seductive tone in his voice. "You are *mine* now, vampire. Nothing and no one will keep you from me, not even Damien."

Alucard slowly took his sights off the ground and set them on Zalith, staring into his dark eyes, a shimmer of red flickering through them for half a second. He felt no need to disapprove or digress. To be Zalith's—that was what he wanted, and it seemed as though that was now what he was. He couldn't feel any more content with that fact.

A smile nervously found its way to Alucard's face as he lifted his hand and placed it over Zalith's left cheek. He took a moment to admire the demon's face, but before he could say or do anything more, the sound of the door to his left creaking snatched his confidence away. The vampire sharply turned his head and set his eyes on Tobias, who was standing in the doorway with an apologetic look on his face.

"Oh…" Tobias dragged out his reaction. "Uh…sorry," he said, shrugging as he watched them both glare at him. "I can come back…I'll just…come back," he said with a nod, disappearing back into the house.

Zalith sighed and looked at Alucard. "Every time," he mumbled…but then he smiled as Alucard gazed at him.

The vampire took his hands off Zalith, stepped back, and tried his best to hide his look of embarrassment. "Ve can…talk later," he said, glancing at Zalith before he started making his way towards the door.

"Wait," Zalith called. As Alucard stopped and looked back at him, he frowned unsurely. "Do you still want me to leave?" he asked with a smirk.

Alucard looked down at the ground. "No. I vant you to stay…indelibly."

And then, as Zalith smiled, the vampire headed into the house, leaving Zalith alone. He was content with what happened and just as happy with his decision to spend and enjoy what time he had left with Zalith. That demon was worth any punishment Damien could inflict.

| Zalith |

A smile of great relief clung to Zalith's face as he stood on the porch. For an awful moment, he thought he might lose Alucard. If he lost him, it would drown him in a deep, dark, *lonely* sea forever. He'd be lost without him. In such a short time, Alucard had come to mean so much to him; he wanted to spend every moment with him. He longed for their future, for the day they would be together—a day he wished would come soon.

Alucard was *his*. He'd do whatever it took to ensure it remained that way. Almost losing him just now made him realize that he wanted to give *all* his time to Alucard—decades, centuries, millennia. He could feel his own fears slapping him in the face, but he ignored them. This wasn't going to be like every other time before. Alucard was different…he knew it.

He was also now sure that Alucard suffered a similar if not the same fear that he suffered from—the fear of losing each other. As vexed as he may feel about yet another of their moments being intruded on, he was so very relieved to know that Alucard felt the same about spending as much time as they could together.

With a smirk on his face, he lightly dragged his thumb over his bottom lip, revelling in the fact that he had finally kissed Alucard. The first of many kisses, he hoped. Despite finally getting what he so sorely wanted, he felt undeniably greedy. He wanted more, and he knew he'd get more. He'd just have to be patient. While he might not be so patient with anyone else, Alucard was different. He waited months for that first kiss, and he'd wait however long was necessary for another…maybe.

He sighed quietly, picked up his wine glass, and began to make his way back into the house.

Chapter Seventy-Four

— ⸱ ✝ ⸱ —

Never Have I Ever

| Alucard |

Alucard stopped in the entrance hall on his way back to the dining room. The human presence upstairs snatched his attention. The only time he would expect any of his guests to be upstairs would be to use the bathroom, but this human wasn't on the second floor, the third, or the fourth. No, they were on the *fifth* floor, the floor where his study was. What were they doing up *there*?

Silently and swiftly, he made his way upstairs. He continued down the hall towards the doors of his study, which had been left ajar, and the sound of hasty shuffling came from within. He didn't waste any time entering the room, and when he stepped inside, he set his eyes on the brunette woman, Maia, who was shuffling through the papers on his desk. She nosed through the drawers, and lifted open the boxes on his shelves, continuing to rummage through his things.

Of course, if people weren't aware of his presence, they couldn't see him unless he wanted them to. So, he closed the doors behind him, making Maia flinch in shock.

"O-oh!" she gasped, leaning back against the desk, trying to hide the pile of papers she'd messed up while looking through them. "I didn't see you there. Sorry, I was looking for, uh...."

"Vor?" Alucard asked with a skeptical scowl.

She laughed nervously and looked around. "The um... bathroom."

"Does zhis look like a bavroom to you?"

Maia frowned nervously as she set her dull green eyes on him. "N-no, I...."

"Vhat are you doing in 'ere?" he questioned, moving closer to her, and when he glanced behind her, he saw that she'd been looking through his registry—the registry which displayed each name of the people he already had under his thumb as well as those he planned to control in time.

She grinned anxiously as he stopped a few feet in front of her. "Just…curious, I guess."

Alucard smiled condescendingly. "Vight."

But before she could say anything else, he snatched her throat, pulled her away from his desk, and pinned her back against the wall. She struggled and tried to scream, but he slammed his hand over her mouth and glared into her horrified, panicked eyes. She gripped his wrists and tried to kick him in an attempt to get away, but he lifted her off her feet and snarled aggressively in her face.

While he felt that he might just kill her, he needed to know exactly what it was she was doing. Obviously, she had a motive; what she'd been looking at on his desk was very specific, and she'd only know what it was if it was what she'd been looking for in the first place. He tightened his grip on her throat so she couldn't make a sound, took his other hand from over her mouth, and placed his fingers on her face so that he could invade her thoughts and memories, and everything was made clear to him.

Maia Vidali, Diabolus operative, infiltration specialist. She hadn't done a great job of that, had she? She'd been sent to Dor-Sanguis years ago, waiting around until word of Lucifer's son came her way. Posing as a barmaid in the most popular tavern in the city, she was sure to hear something one day or another. And she did. Elvin had come along preaching about a vampire named Aleksei, a vampire the world had branded as a monster, but Elvin insisted that he was a good guy—how Elvin of Elvin to do such a thing. The bard said he was Aleksei's friend—best friend, even. She'd relayed that information back to headquarters, and they instructed her to get closer to the bard to get to the vampire. She was using Elvin.

Alucard scowled evilly, tightening his grip so much that her neck could snap any moment. Elvin was so happy to know this woman, to think that they had something. But she was just using him—playing with him. As much as Elvin might annoy Alucard, the fact that someone was toying with him made him furious.

Before he could end her life, though, Zalith—who Alucard hadn't even noticed come into the room—abruptly snatched his arms and pulled him away from the panicking woman. She dropped to the floor, gasping frantically for air as Alucard snarled and struggled, trying to escape Zalith's tight grip.

"*What* is going on up here?" the demon asked.

Maia choked, "He just attacked—"

"I wasn't asking you," Zalith snapped at her. Then, he looked at the vampire. "Alucard?"

Glaring at Maia, Alucard gritted his teeth and stopped struggling. "She's Diabolus," he hissed. "I caught 'er looking vhrough—"

"I wasn't!" she yelled.

Alucard growled angrily and tried to pull free from Zalith again—this time, Zalith let him go.

Immediately, Alucard snatched Maia's throat, pinned her up against the wall, and moved to end her life, but he hesitated. She squirmed around in his grip, struggling to breathe, trying to escape. He wished he hadn't just chosen to examine her life force—but he had to. He couldn't just consume her blood without making sure it didn't contain something that might poison him. And what he found...he couldn't bring himself to kill her. Instead, he scowled irritably and chucked her to the floor.

Alucard then turned around and dragged his hand over his face in frustration.

Zalith frowned in concern. "Alucard?"

The vampire turned around and glared back down at the woman. He wanted to kill her—it was the logical thing to do. But how could he? He glanced at Zalith, looked back down at Maia, and looked at the demon once more. What should he do?

Zalith frowned and glanced down at the woman, who was sitting where she had fallen, too afraid to attempt to run. It clearly took Zalith no time at all to work out what Alucard had discovered: Maia was pregnant, just two weeks gone, and as much as he wanted to kill this woman...he didn't want to kill an unborn child, no matter how old it was.

"Are you going to kill her?" Zalith asked, looking back over at Alucard.

Dragging his hand over his face again, Alucard glared at the woman. If she had been anyone else's girlfriend, he would have killed her. But she was Elvin's—fake or not— and she was most likely carrying *his* child. Alucard couldn't bring himself to take two people from Elvin. Despite Elvin probably not even knowing Maia was pregnant, he couldn't deny him the truth. But Maia was Diabolus. She'd seen his records, his information. She knew where he lived; she knew the names of his subordinates *and* associates. She'd seen Zalith, she'd seen Ben, Tobias, Dirk...she was far too great a risk to let go...to let live.

He turned his back on them both, glaring out of the window, trying to decide what to do. What *could* he do? He sighed deeply, shrugging, shaking his head. "I zon't fucking know," he mumbled.

"Can I make a suggestion?" Zalith asked, moving closer to Alucard. He then stopped beside him and placed his hand on his shoulder. "You have guests downstairs. As much as I enjoy watching you kill, now might not be the best time. However, your reaction tells me you care that she's possibly carrying your bard friend's child. If that's the case, I can manipulate her memories. I can make her forget what she's seen, and I can even make her forget that she's Diabolus. It would be up to you whether you want to grant her that mercy or not."

With a conflicted frown, Alucard glanced back at Maia—who was still on the floor— and then looked at Zalith.

"Once Elvin's party has concluded, we can decide what to do with her. I feel as though the best option right now would be to have her forget. But, as I said, it's your choice," Zalith said.

Alucard snarled quietly and made his way over to Maia. He snatched her throat and pinned her against the wall. "Who else 'ave you been vith?" he demanded, glaring into her eyes.

"W-what?" she stuttered.

He tightened his grip.

Maia choked and shook her head. "N-no one!"

"*Prost*," he snarled irritably, dropping her to the floor again. He then looked back at Zalith. "Do vhatever."

Zalith didn't waste time. Ignoring Maia's pleas, he grabbed the woman's throat, placed his fingers on her face, and did as he said he would.

Alucard waited, watching....

Once he was done, Zalith let go of her and stepped back. "No one will notice," he said, looking at Alucard.

The vampire looked down at her; she seemed to have no idea where she was, looking around as though she had just woken up from a coma. "Vhat did you veplace 'er memories vith?"

"She became lost on her way to the bathroom *and* on the way back. You have such a large house, after all, Alucard," Zalith said, smirking. "She'll be somewhat confused for the next minute or so. I believe we should place her somewhere less likely to confuse her once she comes around. I also took the liberty of erasing her past—I replaced her memories of working for the Diabolus with her attending bard school, failing, and becoming a barmaid instead."

"Vank you," he grumbled. Then, with an irritated snarl, he snatched Maia's arm, pulled her to her feet, and started to drag her out of the room as she looked around in utter confusion.

Zalith followed, pulling the doors to Alucard's study shut behind him.

When Alucard and Zalith returned to the dining room with Maia, everyone stopped chattering about Tobias' girlfriends and looked over at them.

Tobias grinned at them. "Hey, there's your girlfriend," he said, glancing at Elvin.

Maia smiled and rushed over to the bard, who stumbled into her arms, barely able to stand on his own.

"Where was she?" Ben asked as Alucard and Zalith stopped beside him. "She was gone a good while; I was about to look for her myself."

"She got lost," Alucard mumbled.

"Understandable," Lillian said.

Tobias then turned to face them both. "We're doing shots."

"Vhat?" Alucard asked with a frown, and as Tobias handed him a minuscule glass of whiskey, he looked down at it.

As he was also handed a shot glass, Zalith nodded in thanks.

"None for you," Tobias denied when Elvin tried to snatch a shot glass from him. "Ladies," he said with a smile, handing the four sisters a glass each. Once everyone had a drink, he stood in the centre of the crowd and held his up. "To…Elvin."

Everyone concurred and downed their drinks.

Ben smirked as Tobias began filling everyone's glasses. "We should play never have I ever."

"Hell yeah, man," Tobias agreed. He then glanced around at everyone else. "Ya'll down for that?"

"Vhat is zhat?" Alucard asked Ben.

"Well, we each take turns, and we'll say something like…never have I ever…hmm…stolen something, for example. If you *have* stolen something, you drink your shot. If you haven't, you don't. Pretty simple," Ben explained.

"Let's…do it!" Elvin yelled.

Alucard frowned in confliction, and as he glanced at Zalith, he saw that he, too, had a reluctant look on his face. But then a devious thought came to him. If he were to play, he was sure Zalith would agree, too. Alucard didn't know much about him, and this childish game seemed like a rather interesting way to learn some small facts about the demon he'd come to adore.

So, he looked back over at Tobias, who was waiting for him to answer. "Vine," he agreed.

"And you?" Tobias asked, holding out the whiskey bottle to Zalith.

The demon glanced at Alucard's expectant face and sighed quietly. "Sure," he answered, holding out his glass, and Tobias filled it.

"All right, I'll start," Tobias said once everyone's glasses were full. "Never have *I* ever…slept in a house."

Everyone looked around at each other and collectively drank their shots.

"That's pretty obvious," Dirk said as Tobias refilled his glass. "I mean…the state of you half the time."

"Whatever, man. I'd rather be covered in dirt than dress in a fancy suit every day—no offence," Tobias said to Zalith.

Zalith evidently didn't care; he was deadpan.

"My turn!" Elvin yelled, insisting that Tobias filled his glass—so he did. The bard then stared into his drink for a moment and shrugged. "Never…ever…have I ever…won a fight."

Ben and Tobias snickered as they, along with everyone else, drank—all except Dirk.

"You've never won a fight?" Lady White asked Dirk.

Dirk shrugged. "I haven't ever been involved in any."

"Hmm." She frowned, watching Tobias as he refilled everyone's glasses.

"Your turn, bro," Tobias said, nodding at Ben.

Ben thought to himself for a few moments. "Never have *I* ever…uh…made out with another guy," he said, smirking.

Alucard glanced at Zalith, who rolled his eyes. The vampire was sure that Zalith knew just as well as he did that Ben's question was aimed towards them—Ben and Tobias seemed to have made it their personal mission to find out whether they were seeing one another. He should have known they'd use this game to find out more.

All of the women downed their drinks. Dirk drank, as did Elvin and Alucard. Zalith stood still, and so did Tobias.

"What?" Ben laughed, frowning at Tobias. "When?"

Tobias shrugged. "Ages ago, man. Like…too long. We was drunk, and I'm straight as all hell; it was just a bit of fun."

"Uh-huh," Ben uttered with a skeptical smirk.

"Why'd you drink, man?" Tobias then asked Alucard. "I swear you two—"

"No," Alucard warned.

"All right," Tobias said with a smile, holding up his hands.

Elvin pouted as if he was about to speak, but Maia gripped his arm and shook her head in disapproval.

Refilling everyone's glasses with the last of the whiskey, Tobias looked at Alucard again. "All right, your turn."

Alucard looked down into his glass, unsure of what to say. What had he never done that wouldn't have everyone question him? There were so many things. But he had to be careful; was there something that he was comfortable with not only his subordinates knowing but Zalith, too?

The vampire's silence lasted at least two minutes, but everyone waited patiently.

He soon frowned and shrugged slightly. "I 'ave never…seen my parents," he revealed.

"Damn, man," Tobias mumbled and downed his drink along with everyone but Elvin.

"Is a vact," Alucard said with very little care in his voice.

Zalith gazed sadly at him for a moment…but drank his shot and smiled at him.

Tobias then took a bottle of vodka from the table, opened it, and all but Alucard's and Elvin's glasses. As he filled Zalith's, he pointed at him. "Your go."

"No," Zalith said with a smile.

"You can't skip," Tobias said, frowning.

"Y-yeah!" Elvin yelled. "Tell…tell us…ssss…something!"

Zalith deadpanned again. "I have never met someone as annoying as *you*."

Everyone laughed in response. The only people who downed their drinks were Maia and the four sisters sitting at the table.

"Okay girls, your turns," Tobias said, looking at the sisters.

Nicola, the sister with the ear-length hair, smirked at Alucard and said, "Never have I ever slept with a vampire."

Ben and Lillian drank, as did the other three sisters, and so did Zalith.

A conflicted frown made its way onto Alucard's face as he glanced at Zalith, seeing that he was drinking. Obviously, he wasn't the first vampire Zalith had shown interest in, and that undeniably bothered him.

Betisa, the sister with the longest hair, giggled as Tobias refilled glasses. "Never have *I* ever made out with another woman."

None of the sisters drank. The only people who did were Ben, Tobias, Elvin, and Lady White.

"I thought you only went with men?" Dirk asked, looking over at Lady White.

"It was for fun," she said with a smile.

At that point, they were beginning to follow the same path as Elvin. While the bard was moments from passing out, everyone else was well on their way to being unable to stand on their own two feet. Tobias leaned back against the table, filling everyone's glasses. Lillian and Ben leaned on one another, Elvin sunk down to Maia's feet as she leaned against the table, and Zalith moved his arm around Alucard's shoulders despite either of them actually needing support to stand—yet. Lady White and Dirk also leaned back against the table, waiting for the next sister to speak.

Kistie, the sister with the ponytail, tapped her chin. "Hmm…never…have I ever…fallen in love!" she laughed, watching as none of her sisters drank.

"So, that's how it is, huh?" Tobias said with a huff and then downed his drink.

Lillian and Ben both smiled at one another as they drank.

Maia stared down at Elvin awkwardly as he snored at her ankles.

Dirk ignored his drink, glaring at the floor.

Lady White quickly sipped her drink.

Neither Alucard nor Zalith drank. They both donned the same conflicted look as if they were both too afraid to answer. Alucard glanced at Zalith, who also glanced at him, both waiting to see if the other would drink. But they didn't.

Sonja, the last sister, held up her glass. "Never have I ever seen a god."

Tobias shrugged and looked around at everyone. No one but Dirk, Alucard, and Zalith drank. But no one dared to ask where, how, or why.

"Okay, I guess it's my turn?" Maia asked.

"Go for it, lady," Tobias said, smirking.

She thought to herself for a few moments. "Never have I ever…met a more interesting group of people," she said, smiling

Alucard stopped himself from rolling his eyes at her stupid answer.

Tobias shrugged. "Yeah, you guys are all right," he said with a grin, looking around at everyone. "All right, last person is you—go," he said, looking at Lillian.

"Hmm…I suppose…never have I ever…seen a werewolf pup?" she said unsurely.

"Lord," Tobias groaned ad downed his drink. "Annoying, feisty little shits. You remember those brats I had to take care of, don't you?" he asked, nodding over at Alucard, who slowly sipped his drink alongside Zalith. The only people that didn't drink were Maia, Dirk, and Lady White.

Alucard sighed and nodded. "'Ow could I vorget?"

"Do tell me," Zalith said with a curious smile, looking at Alucard.

The vampire shrugged. "Vas…many years ago. Avound zhe time Tobias 'adn't been a verevolf vor long. Zhere vere six children—pups, I guess. Zhe parents died, and Tobias 'ad to take care of zhem until 'e vound adoptive parents. I 'elped 'ere and zhere."

"You played dad to a bunch of werewolf kids?" Ben asked Alucard, surprised.

"Not veally," Alucard mumbled. "I just checked up on zhem and Tobias vrom time to time."

Zalith smiled and rested his head on the side of Alucard's, succumbing to the alcohol. "Sounds fun."

"Eh," Alucard said, shrugging.

"Never again," Tobias said, shaking his head.

Ben then cleared his throat quietly and waved. "I uh…think we ought to sit down," he said, stumbling over to the table with Lillian. They both sat down, also succumbing to the excessive amount of drink they'd both had.

Tobias looked back over his shoulder, seeing that the four sisters were pretty much passing out in each other's arms. He looked at Alucard and Zalith—two of the only still-standing people. Lady White and Dirk were stumbling, but they remained where they were, waiting. Maia had sunk to the floor, sleeping with Elvin.

"Huh…guess we know who the lightweights are then," Tobias said with a grin.

"I'm surprised your liver still exists," Alucard said with an amused smirk.

"Me too, man, me too."

Dirk then held up his hand. "I think uh…Lady White and I are going to head out," he uttered, pointing at the dining room doorway.

"What? And you?" Tobias asked, looking at Alucard and Zalith as Dirk left with Lady White.

The vampire and the demon glanced at one another, both waiting for the other to answer.

"You're still up for a few more, right?" Tobias asked.

Alucard shrugged. "I guess. Ve can move to zhe lounge, zhough. If I'm going to pass out, I'd vather not do so in 'ere."

"Understandable," Tobias said, pointing at them both. "Lead the way, boss man."

Slowly, Alucard and Zalith turned around, walking with their arms around one other. But walking only made Alucard feel a whole lot more overwhelmed. They reached the lounge, and that was when he stumbled over the white, fluffy rug and decided it was time to rest.

He hit the rug, groaned irritably, and closed his eyes. He didn't want to move, so he allowed himself to sink into his fatigue, ignoring Zalith's muffled, concerned voice.

The evening was over, and when he felt the warmth of the demon's body beside him, he drifted off feeling content.

Chapter Seventy-Five

— ⸱ ✝ ⸱ —

Thunder

| Alucard |

As a crash of thunder echoed loudly through the silence, Alucard jolted awake. He tensed up; the cold of the night scraped at his skin. The rain poured loudly outside, and his almost pitch-black house was lit by the occasional flash of white lightning. It was just a storm.

He frowned as he stared at the ceiling; his head was cloudy due to the amount he'd had to drink, and it took him a moment to come to his senses. The weight on his stomach was strange, so he looked down and set his eyes on Zalith, who had his head rested on him, sleeping silently. His head started spinning from that simple movement. He couldn't have had so much to drink that his hangover could be as bad as it was; he felt like the state the portal left him in was contributing to his current discomfort. But he didn't want to move. He felt content despite his aching head. It seemed as though Zalith not only helped him to feel both relaxed and safe in his consciousness but also while he slept.

But as he lay there, his headache became worse. The pain turned into hunger, and he was already sure that he knew what he needed. He could hear Ben and Lillian mumbling quietly in the dining room, but he didn't care to listen to their conversation. As carefully as he could, he moved Zalith's head from his stomach and shuffled away from him—but Zalith mumbled quietly in disapproval, trying to snatch whatever he could of the vampire. Alucard caught his hand and placed it on the rug, waiting for him to fall back asleep before departing.

The vampire quietly made his way through his house and to the kitchen. He opened the cabinet in which he would usually keep blood—he wasn't sure *why* he opened it; he knew it had been empty since Emil's death. However, when he opened it, he set his eyes on several bottles that he recognized from the castle. Ben must have delivered some when he helped Zalith find the humans the demon had been feeding him. He took one of the bottles over to the countertop closest to him, grabbed a wine glass, and filled it.

He then leaned back against the countertop, staring at the other side of his kitchen as he sipped the blood. His headache didn't relent entirely, but it calmed enough for him to think at least. And, of course, his thoughts immediately focused on Zalith. But it didn't vex Alucard. He smiled ever so slightly, thinking back to the moment they kissed. Not only had it been his and Zalith's first kiss, but it had been Alucard's first-*ever* kiss. And he felt he'd not rather it have been with anyone else. Although Damien would inevitably end their relationship, he felt content knowing he'd continue to grow closer to Zalith, and perhaps one day, they might become something more than what they currently were.

As the storm outside worsened, he placed the bottle back into the cupboard and returned to the lounge.

"I kinda wondered where you went," Tobias said with a smirk from the armchair he was sitting on.

Alucard glared at him for a moment but made his way over and sat on his couch.

"Storm wake you up?" Tobias asked.

The vampire shrugged, flicking his hand towards the fireplace. As it lit with crimson flames, he looked back over at Tobias. "Vere you zhe only vone who zidn't pass out?"

He shrugged. "Looks like it. Ya'll died around seven. I'd say it's close to midnight now."

Alucard then frowned, noticing that Tobias' usual perky attitude was absent from both his voice and face. They were alone, they weren't working; what harm would there be in asking him if he was okay? "Are you…okay?" Alucard asked. It felt strange to ask such a thing for what might be the first time ever.

Tobias shrugged again. "Yeah, you?"

"I can tell vhen you lie, you know."

The man sighed and stared at the fire. "Well, not to be a dippy-downer or anything man, but…I dunno. Seeing everyone with their girlfriends or…whatever you and he are," he said, nodding at Zalith. "It kinda makes me realize I should stop fucking around and look for a wifey, right?"

Alucard smirked. "You and I both know zhat's not your style."

"Hey," Tobias said with a smirk, shrugging, "everyone's gotta settle down one day or another, right?"

"Maybe," Alucard muttered, looking down into his glass.

Tobias then shuffled to the end of his seat, rested his arms on his knees, and stared at Alucard. "You and that Zalith guy—"

"No," Alucard denied.

"Come on, man. It's just us."

"So?"

"So? We're pals, right?"

"Are ve?"

"Yeah, I mean…we've had our fair share of good times. Been a while since we hung out—too long, to be honest. One day, we were buddies, then you disappear for a while, and when you come back, you're cold as ice—no offence. But you kinda dropped me. What happened?"

"Business," Alucard answered.

"Right," Tobias said with a sigh, leaning back in his seat. "But seriously, I ain't ever seen you with anyone until now. Oh, sorry if I was intruding earlier, too. I just came to find you. I didn't expect to—"

"Is vine," he interjected.

Tobias shuffled closer again. "Pleeeease," he drawled. "Tell me *something*."

"Like vhat?"

"Well…are you two dating?"

"No."

"Seeing each other?"

Alucard frowned and glanced at Tobias. "Vell…ve see each ozzer outside of vork if zhat's vhat you mean."

"Well, you seem happier," Tobias said with a smirk. "You're not so cold anymore."

The vampire rolled his eyes. "You vant a vife?" he asked, changing the subject.

"I mean…one day, yeah, maybe."

"Vhy not marry vone of your packmates?"

He shrugged. "I dunno. I don't really see any of them as like…a wife, you know? I kinda wanna meet someone new, someone that like…doesn't work for me. I imagine you can relate to that, huh?"

Looking back into his glass, Alucard shrugged. "I guess."

"I'm thinking like…someone that's *not* a werewolf. Someone outside that part of my life."

"Go to zhe city; zhere are many people zhere."

"Nah," Tobias said with a sigh. "Rich people are snobby. I just wanna meet a cool, chilled-back gal, you know? Someone that ain't gonna flake or whatever. Someone that don't mind the outside."

"Zhere are many options," Alucard said with a shrug and a smirk. "Dirk vound Lady Vhite, so maybe you can vind an elf, too."

"Maybe…or a hot vampire chick," he snickered.

"Good luck vith zhat. Vampires and verevolves vill alvays be enemies."

"Yeah, well, the same's said about demons and vampires, but here *you* are, Lord of all vampires, making out with a demon," he said, winking.

Alucard scowled. "Ve did not."

Tobias scoffed amusedly. "Come on, man. I ain't blind. Tell me!" he encouraged, shuffling around in his seat with an excited grin on his face. "You know I ain't gonna blab. I just miss the times you and I would hang out and talk about whatever. It was always me talking about my girls; let me hear something from *you*."

He hesitated, staring into the fireplace. As much as he might like to keep his life private, he felt like he actually *wanted* to talk about Zalith. To talk about how he made him feel, about how *he* felt. Attila shut him down the first time he tried, but Tobias wasn't likely to do that. He knew this werewolf well enough to know his interest was purely curiosity. He was right, after all. There was a time he and Tobias were closer, a time they'd hang out just as they were now. Perhaps…it would be good to rekindle such a friendship. Zalith had quietened the despondency that once caused Alucard to distance himself from everyone, so much that he felt he might just be able to slowly repair the friendships he had to sever.

The vampire slowly looked at Tobias and shrugged. "Ve just…kissed."

A look of surprise smothered Tobias' face. "Yo," he drawled, smirking. "Lemme guess—first-*ever* kiss?"

Alucard frowned strangely. How did he know?

Tobias shrugged. "Just a guess, man. You never told me about being with anyone else, so. I just assumed."

The vampire sighed. "Vell, you're not vrong."

"Damn, man. Four hundred years old, and you just had your first kiss? What you been doing all those years?"

"Vork."

"A lot of work, clearly."

Alucard looked back into the blood-red flames burning in the fireplace.

"Well…is it serious? Whatever you guys are?"

"I zon't know," Alucard said quietly.

Tobias frowned. "You two not talk about it?"

"Not yet," he said, glancing at him. "You interrupted us."

"Yeah…sorry about that again," he said nervously, dragging his hand over the back of his head.

"Zoesn't matter," Alucard uttered and sipped from his glass. "Zhere vill be more time later."

"Well, whatever happens, best of luck to you, man."

Alucard frowned over at him again. "Vhen vill you begin your search vor a vife?"

"Tomorrow…next week…next year—who knows?"

"Stay avay vrom zhe vampires, hmm?"

"Gotcha, boss man," he said with a grin.

The pair then fell silent for a few moments.

But Tobias was never without something to say. He smirked at Alucard. "Hey, speaking of vampires, you wanna teach me some more of those slick moves? Like old times, right? Since we're buddies again."

"Is zhat vhat ve are?"

"Yeah. Come on," he said as he stood up, inviting Alucard to join him. "Kick my ass, and then show me how you do it. Never know, could save my life one day."

Alucard sighed hesitantly. "Is now veally zhe best time? I'm pretty sure I'm still drunk."

"Nah, you been out for like…six hours, man. Come on."

The vampire sighed and hesitated, but then rolled his eyes and got up. He placed his glass on the mantlepiece and stood ready as Tobias moved the coffee table from the centre of the room. Alucard then stared vacantly. "Vhen you're veady."

"All right," Tobias said, smirking. He held up his fists, preparing—he almost instantly struck his right fist forward, but Alucard dodged, leaning his head to the side.

Grinning, Tobias struck his right fist forward. Alucard dodged again. He then swiftly struck his left forward, but Alucard dodged once more and then grabbed hold of Tobias so quickly that the guy didn't realize until it might have been too late.

"You're dead," Alucard snarled, his face just inches from Tobias' neck as he stood behind him, holding both his arms behind his back.

Laughing nervously, Tobias struggled, trying to pull free. "All right, man. Now show me how to counter it."

Alucard let go of Tobias and lightly shoved him forward.

He stumbled forward and turned to face Alucard, his back now to the couch.

"Move your arm as if you're trying to 'it me," the vampire instructed.

As he was told, Tobias extended his right arm.

Alucard then snatched his wrist. "Zon't let me get be'ind because zhat's vhen you vill die. Vhen I grab your wrist, 'it me 'ere," he said, tapping his own chest. "Vill startle me. Vhen a vampire uses zheir speed, zhe vest of zheir body is somevhat more vulnerable. If you can 'it me, zhis vill stop me."

Tobias nodded as the vampire let go of his wrist. "All right…show me how you get behind me first, so I know what to look out for."

The vampire nodded. "Try to 'it me again."

He struck his right fist forward; Alucard snatched it, but instead of subduing him in the blink of an eye, he did it at the speed of a normal man. He swiftly moved behind Tobias and snatched his other wrist from his side, pinning both of his arms against his back as he grunted and struggled.

"All right, I think I got it," he laughed, gritting his teeth in pain. Then, as the vampire let go of him, he turned to face him so that his back was to the window once again. "Can I try *that*?"

"Vhy vould you need to get be'ind someone?"

"I dunno. Could come in handy," he said, shrugging.

"Vine."

"All right," Tobias said with a grin, preparing to try. Then, as Alucard lazily struck his fist forward, Tobias snatched his wrist, but when he went to move just as Alucard had, he couldn't shift the vampire's arm. He scowled and pouted. "Come on, man. Don't be a prick."

Alucard smirked and pulled his wrist from Tobias' grip. He then struck his fist forward again—this time, as Tobias snatched his wrist, he allowed the werewolf to perform the same attack he'd shown him. But he almost instantly pulled free from Tobias' grasp, not at all comfortable in his grip.

"It's kinda simple, really," Tobias said with a frown, scratching his head as he walked around and stood in front of Alucard again. "Except I guess it's far more effective when you can move faster than light, huh?"

"*Da*," Alucard confirmed.

"All right, now I gotta learn the counter," he said, readying himself. "Okay…you ready?"

Alucard went to answer, but before he could, Zalith gripped either side of his waist and pulled him into his lap when he slumped on the couch. The vampire squirmed in confusion and embarrassment to try and escape, but Zalith nuzzled his neck and smiled. Alucard held out both his arms, unsure of where to place them, and uncertain whether he should move from Zalith's lap. But he gave in when the demon wrapped his arms around him. He pouted as he rested his right arm around Zalith's shoulders and his left beside him. He didn't understand why Zalith insisted on doing this in front of Tobias, but he undeniably enjoyed the attention.

"Guess we'll pick it up another time," Tobias said, smiling. "You want anything from the kitchen? I need a drink."

"A coffee," Zalith muttered.

"Sure."

As Tobias left the room, Alucard looked at Zalith and pouted. "Vhat are you doing?"

"Holding you," he replied, resting his head on Alucard's pec as he looked up at him. "Is that okay?"

Alucard shrugged and looked over at the window, watching as the rain poured outside. "Yes."

"Good," Zalith said with a smile, hugging him tighter.

"Is late, so…I should probably vake everyvone up soon and send zhem 'ome."

"And *me*?" Zalith asked.

A nervous look found its way to Alucard's face as he glanced at the front door. "You can…stay—if you vant…in zhe guest voom."

Zalith smiled. "Thank you."

"Vhat vill you do tomorrow?" Alucard asked, glancing down at him. "Do you 'ave to veturn 'ome?"

"I'm still taking care of you," he replied quietly. "You still haven't recovered entirely. I'm not going to leave until I'm sure you're completely better. I might also add that we still haven't spoken about what happened outside earlier. Maybe we talk about it after your guests have left?"

"Here, man," Tobias then said, appearing beside them with a white coffee cup in his right hand, which he held out towards Zalith.

As Zalith took the cup from Tobias, Alucard shuffled out of his lap and sat beside him.

"I'm gonna go gather my shit, get ready to leave," Tobias said. "I left the pack long enough."

Alucard nodded.

"Oh and uh…Elvin's waking up, so, heads up on that. The four sisters left earlier, too—they didn't take any of your shit, though. I checked them before they left," Tobias said, and as Alucard nodded at him again, he walked off and disappeared back into the kitchen.

Sipping from his coffee, Zalith set his eyes on Alucard. "How do you feel? Well enough to drink from a bottle, I see," he said, glancing up at the glass of blood Alucard left on the mantlepiece.

Alucard shrugged and looked down at his lap. "Better, I guess."

"And now? The last time we had so many drinks together, I'm sure we both spent the next day feeling utterly awful."

"I'll be vine," he mumbled, watching as Zalith sipped his coffee again. He then sighed and looked down at his lap. "You said zhat ve'll see each ozzer avter zhe mission is done. I cut you off bevore you could vinish vhat you vere going to ask me."

Zalith smiled at him. "I was going to ask if there was anywhere you wanted to make a point of visiting here, and then I was going to suggest we go together."

Alucard thought to himself for a few moments. "Vell…I've alvays vanted to visit Samjang; is vone of zhe only places I 'aven't yet been to."

"Then Samjang it is," Zalith said and sipped from his coffee again. Then, he offered his cup to him. "It's not brimmed with sugar, but you *can* have some."

Once he took the cup, Alucard stared into the coffee for a few moments, remembering just how awful it tasted without his preferred amount of sugar. But that didn't stop him from wanting some.

As Alucard took a small sip, Zalith smiled. "Did you have a nice time today?" he asked curiously.

Alucard shrugged, handing the cup back to Zalith. "Vas more eventvul zhan I vhought vould be. But aside vrom vhat 'appened in my study, vas a nice time, yes. Did *you* 'ave a good time?"

"I did. Of course, the highlights of my day were just before the guests arrived and when you and I were alone in the garden. Now is also rather nice," he said with a smirk.

The vampire looked down at his lap and frowned sullenly. "I'm sorry if I 'urt you…vith vhat I said about seeing each ozzer. I just…vorry. Zamien zoesn't like—" he stopped speaking when he heard someone approaching. He looked back over his shoulder and saw Elvin, who sleepily stumbled out of the dining room, dragged himself over to the armchair, and slumped down on it. Alucard pouted irritably, took the coffee from Zalith again, and scowled at Elvin as he sipped from it.

"What…time is it?" Elvin asked, staring at them both.

"Vay past your bedtime," Alucard mumbled, handing Zalith the cup back.

The bard pouted. "I don't remember falling asleep. Where's Dirk? And Tobias?"

"Dirk levt earlier vith Lady Vhite, and Tobias is preparing to leave now. You should probably do zhe same; is late, and I need to go to sleep," Alucard answered.

Elvin watched as Alucard and Zalith shared their cup of coffee. He eyed the demon with irritancy and revolt, and then rolled his eyes as he said to Alucard, "Thanks for doing this for me—you do so much for me."

Alucard looked over at him with a confused frown. Did he? "Is vor your birvday."

"Yeah, but…you didn't have to do it. I don't imagine you'd do it for anyone else."

"Zhere are a select vew," Alucard denied.

Elvin pouted. "Well…thanks again, anyway."

The vampire then stared vacantly. "Vhat do you plan to do vith your girlvriend?"

"Maia?"

Alucard nodded.

"Well, she's not really my girlfriend, I just…well, I dunno. Maybe she will be, though. What do you think? Do you like her?"

"Vhat I vink zoesn't matter," Alucard said, also muttering his thanks as Zalith handed him his coffee again.

The bard frowned. "If what you think didn't matter, I wouldn't ask. Do you *not* like her?"

"I zon't like anyvone," he grumbled, glaring at him.

"That's a lie," Elvin said with a pout. "You like *him*."

As Elvin nodded in Zalith's direction, Alucard rolled his eyes and sipped from the cup. He then handed it back to Zalith, made himself comfortable, and sighed. "Maybe you should go and vake 'er up and 'ead 'ome bevore gets too late. Sergiu isn't 'ere anymore, so I'll get Ben to escort you back to zhe city."

"What happened to Sergiu?"

"Occupational 'azard," Alucard said with a slight smile, and as Zalith laughed quietly beside him, he shook his head. "Anyvay, go and get veady to go."

Elvin sighed and stood up. "Can't *you* walk me back? It's been a while since you told me anything new for my novel."

A reluctant frown found its way onto Alucard's face as he thought to himself for a few moments. It *was* Elvin's birthday, so it was the least he could do to bring the day to a close. He sighed, waved his hand in dismissal, and glanced at the bard. "Vine, vine. Go get veady."

Excited, Elvin clapped his hands and went to leave the room—but a horrific, deafening crash lit up the dark with a bright, blinding red. The ground shook, the air went still, and the rain ceased. Alucard shot to his feet, staring out of the window across the room. Elvin frowned strangely, and Zalith stared up at the vampire in conflicted confusion.

Alucard ignored both Elvin and Zalith's concerned questions. His body trembled and tensed up at the same time, and dread filled his eyes and thoughts. Of all times, now couldn't be any worse for Damien to show up—and what a coincidence it had to be. His house was full of guests, all of whom he didn't want to bear witness to what was about to happen. He knew Damien was there to scold him—to *punish* him. And he was sure that it was because of Sergiu.

He could only dread what the next few minutes might hold for him… and for his guests. But he couldn't avoid it. Whatever was about to happen, Damien would make sure he knew he deserved it.

The Daegelus stood beside the fountain outside, his wings folded against his back, and a glimmer of hatred in his eyes as he glared at Alucard's manor.

"Aleksei?" Elvin asked worriedly. "What… what's wrong?"

The vampire took his eyes off Damien and looked at the bard. He then glanced at Zalith, who placed his hand on his shoulder. What should he do? He couldn't hang around inside for much longer; patience was not something Damien had much of. No. He'd have to go outside; he'd have to face him and accept whatever was about to happen. So, he turned his back on them, preparing to head for the door—

Zalith asked, "Do you want me to—"

"No," Alucard instantly denied, cutting him off. He *didn't* want Zalith to follow him; that would only make this worse.

So, as Alucard made his way over to the front door and left, Zalith remained where he was.

And Alucard could only hope he'd stay there.

Chapter Seventy-Six

— ₹ † ₴ —

Means to an End

| Zalith |

Zalith stared out of the window, watching as Alucard approached Damien. He felt dread pooling in his heart. The last time Damien descended, he'd *very* harshly punished Alucard for socializing instead of working himself tirelessly to please the Daegelus, and he was sure that something similar was about to happen again.

He wanted nothing more than to help Alucard—he wanted to head out there and tell Damien this was his idea, not Alucard's…but the vampire had told him to stay, and he didn't want to do something that would upset or maybe even worsen the situation for Alucard.

So he waited…staring…. He could hope that Damien wasn't about to hurt Alucard and cause a scene, but he knew such a thing would only thicken his impending despair.

| Alucard |

Alucard approached Damien, who scowled in revolt, and when he reached him, the vampire stared up at him as his heart raced in his chest. He tried his best to keep as much of his fear hidden as possible, but as each moment passed, he struggled to contain it. He knew what was coming.

Damien held out his arms. "Aleksei," he greeted pleasantly. "Aren't you going to ask me how I've been?"

He shakily asked, "'Ow…'ave you been?"

"Great, now that you ask. Going out of my way to keep the Diabolus off your ass has been straining—or did you fail to remember that is what I have been doing?"

"No," Alucard answered.

"Why don't you tell me why *I'm* out here spending my time protecting *you* whilst you're sitting around here being a lazy fuck sleeping for an *entire* week? And then when you finally get the fuck up off your indolent, incompetent ass, you decide it's time to throw a party?!" He snatched Alucard's collar and pulled him closer and up off his feet. He inhaled deeply and snarled in revolt. "You stink of alcohol…demons…werewolves—what the fuck have you been doing?"

As Damien dropped him back to his feet, Alucard stared up at him in fear. "Someving 'appened vith zhe portal. I took too many at vonce, and…zhat caused me to comatose."

The Daegelus burst out into cruel, hysterical laughter. He then slammed his hand onto Alucard's shoulder. "I knew you were weak and pathetic, Aleksei, but never would I have expected you to be *this* weak! Is it really so much work to move some measly vampires across the worlds? Are you so fucking worthless that you can't even do *that* without hindrance?!"

Alucard stared at him, waiting, too dread-stricken to try and explain himself further. What would be the point? Damien wouldn't listen.

Damien soon lost his smile and glared into his eyes. "I've been told a very special *someone* has been taking care of you—is that right, Aleksei?"

"J-just…I—"

"Why don't you come on out here?" Damien called. "I know you're listening." He then shook his head and dug his claws into Alucard's shoulder. "No, why don't you *all* come out? Before I lose my patience."

Alucard stood there, grimacing as Damien's claws tore his skin. He listened as everyone inside his house shuffled around and began to make their way out into the grounds. Elvin, Tobias, Maia, Ben, Lillian, and Zalith. They walked outside and stood by the door. They all possessed a confused frown, but Zalith's scowl was one of concern.

Eyeing each of the people who filed outside, Damien snarled in disgust. He set his sights on Zalith and smirked. "This is the second time I've caught you where you shouldn't be, Eladarin."

Zalith didn't say anything. He remained as silent as everyone else.

Damien then looked back at Alucard, ever so slowly moving his claws around inside the wounds they had already created in his shoulder. "Are these your little friends, Aleksei?" he asked with a challenging frown.

"No," Alucard answered.

"That wouldn't be a filthy little lie, would it?" He scowled, moving his hand from Alucard's shoulder to grip his throat.

Choking, Alucard frowned in angst. "N-no," he repeated.

Damien scoffed with a smile and once again glanced at the group. "Your ugly little pet human and its pregnant girlfriend—" he sneered, glaring at Elvin, who frowned in confusion and looked at Maia, who seemed just as perplexed. "Two of the very vampires I sent you to Eltaria to bring back here—" he said, eying Ben and Lillian— "a werewolf, Aleksei?" He smiled, taking his eyes off Tobias to look at Alucard. "Do I even *want* to know why you have his revolting stench all over you? And of course, Eladarin's here, too. Have you moved on to better things, Eladarin? Two at once, now?" he asked Zalith, who kept the same vacant look on his face. The Daegelus then scowled at Alucard and tightened his grip on his throat. "Are these creatures the reason for your laziness, Aleksei?"

Alucard struggled but shook his head.

The Daegelus smiled the way he always did before taking something from Alucard.

"P-please zon't…kill anyvone," Alucard stuttered quietly, finding it hard to breathe in Damien's grasp. "Zhey're just subordinates."

"Subordinates?" Damien laughed. He let go of Alucard's throat and turned him to face everyone. He then placed his hands on his shoulders and leaned into his ear. "*I'm* not going to kill anyone, Aleksei—*you* are."

Alucard's eyes darted from person to person as he frowned in confusion. "V-vhat?"

"You heard me. Pick one," Damien snarled.

Pick one? Kill…one? Alucard's thoughts were so erratic that he couldn't think. He couldn't understand; he couldn't decide what to do. Damien wanted him to kill someone…someone he cared about. As much as he wanted to refuse and fight Damien, he couldn't. He didn't have the strength or the will. When Damien said something was going to happen, it happened—one way or another. Damien wanted him to kill one of the people in front of him, and he knew he had no choice. If he didn't, Damien would kill them all. But he couldn't kill any of these people…Zalith, Elvin, Ben, Tobias…he couldn't even kill Lillian or Maia. But…he had to.

"Are you fucking deaf?" Damien snapped impatiently, shaking Alucard's shoulders.

The vampire slowly looked back at him—but he had no words. The look of dread in his eyes was something contagious; it spread to the eyes of every person in front of him. Even Zalith looked wary.

Damien had zero patience. He snarled, shoved Alucard aside, and held his left hand down towards the ground. In an instant, everyone but Zalith was pulled to the concrete; they all grunted and groaned in confusion and pain, unable to move, unable to speak.

Alucard watched in horror. He had to do it—but who?

"Pick one, Aleksei, or I will kill them all," Damien growled.

The vampire's eyes shifted to Zalith, the only one of them left standing.

Damien noticed—of course he did. He pointed at Zalith. "You. Here. Now," he instructed.

Zalith couldn't refuse. *No* demon could refuse when Damien barked an order, not even someone as resilient as Zalith, and that worsened Alucard's fear.

When Zalith reached them, Damien snatched the demon's throat and grinned over at Alucard. "Or should I kill him? Surely, *this* must motivate you, Aleksei?"

It *didn't* motivate him. It horrified him. Before, he hadn't felt any incitement to approach and kill one of these people, but now…he felt a painful duty to do so. He didn't want Zalith to die. Nothing could get him to kill one of these people unless Zalith's life was at stake. And it was. So, he had no choice. He'd not hesitate—how could he? It took him no time at all to consider whether he'd rather let Zalith die to save everyone else or kill one of them. It was cruel, it was cold, merciless—but he'd not lose the man he'd come to care for so intensely.

A harsh, amused grin stretched across Damien's face as Alucard made his way towards the subdued group. The sound of Zalith's stifled breaths caused an ache in the vampire's racing heart, and knowing that Damien could snap the demon's neck in half a moment had him stricken with such terror. He didn't want to lose Zalith.

He reached the grounded group, staring at them one by one with a dismayed glare. He didn't take long to decide who he had to kill. The only person who meant nothing to him was Maia. She would inevitably die one day, anyway—she was Diabolus. If he didn't kill her himself, then the Diabolus would eventually track her down and end her life. It would break Elvin, especially now that he knew she was pregnant, but what other choice did he have? He wouldn't take Lillian from Ben…he wouldn't kill Ben, either. He wouldn't kill Tobias or Elvin. Maia was the only option.

He approached the woman, who was crying next to Elvin; the pair tried to reach one another with their hands. But Alucard had to dismiss his guilt. If Elvin hated him after this…then he wouldn't blame him. He snatched the woman's throat and pulled her to her feet; she cried and begged, but her words were useless. Without remorse, the vampire forced his hand into her chest and tore her heart from her body, ending her life before Elvin could finish his plea of mercy. Maia was dead.

But it wasn't over.

The vampire turned to face Damien, who had an entertained grin on his face, still holding Zalith's throat in his hand.

"That wasn't so hard, was it?" the Daegelus called. But before Alucard could walk back over, Damien pointed at him. "You're not done yet," he said with a scowl, tightening his grip on Zalith's throat, and slowly lifting him off his feet. "Do you think I'm so stupid that I wouldn't know which of these people mean the most to you? I've been watching you far longer than you might think. Try again."

Someone else? Despair smothered Alucard's face as the world around him came back into contact with his senses. He could hear Elvin's sorrowful cries; Tobias was trying to tell the bard to shut up, and Ben told Lillian that they'd be okay. Would they? Would any of them be okay? Damien obviously knew that he cared about these people—why else would Maia not be enough?

Alucard stood there, staring at the Daegelus and Zalith. His thoughts were silent, his body was still. He wasn't sure whether he was overwhelmed with shock or horror…or if he just didn't know what to do.

He *didn't* know what to do. It was either Zalith…or one of the people who found their way into his life. And whoever it was, it had to be someone Damien knew meant something to him. How could he do that? Elvin, Tobias, or Ben? He couldn't kill them. He *wouldn't*. Elvin had been with him for seven years—that might not be long for him, but for Elvin, that was almost a third of his life. How could he kill someone who'd spent that much time looking up to him?

And Tobias…he'd been around just as long as Elvin. Alucard couldn't disregard that he was his friend. And Ben? He may not have been around as long, but Alucard cared about him—of course he did. Why would he go out of his way to help him after what happened with Detlaff if he didn't care about him? Not only that, but he *needed* Ben. However, one of them had to go…someone had to die, or he'd lose Zalith forever.

How could he have let this happen? He looked down at Elvin, watching as the bard grieved for Maia. How could he have let himself love someone? To be put in a position where he had to kill someone he cared about to save another. How could he have let that happen? How could he have allowed himself to think that it was okay to stray from Damien's rules? He shouldn't have. He knew this would happen—he *knew*. And there he was. Killing his friends. Killing…Elvin.

He didn't realize he had the bard's throat in his hand until Elvin was screaming and kicking in an attempt to escape. But what more could he do? He had to be cold; he had to be heartless—he had to think about his *own* future. His thoughts shifted from reluctance to something logical. Something…cruel. He didn't want to lose Zalith, that was something he knew for sure, so he would kill one of these people.

And what did *Elvin* do for him? Nothing. The bard had served his purpose. He didn't become a wolf once he matured, he was just a human…a *useless* human. Elvin would live the rest of his life hating him if he lived beyond this point anyway, and the people who hated him would always end up becoming his enemy. He didn't want that for Elvin. He'd like to think of his choice as a mercy, but that wasn't what it was. He was doing this to save himself even greater pain, wasn't he?

Elvin…or Zalith?

There was no debate.

No hesitation.

But there *was* sorrow.

He frowned sullenly as his eyes met those of the terrified bard. "I'm sorry," he uttered.

Elvin stared in horror. He knew his life was at its end. And just as Alucard suspected he would, the bard burst into tears and started to plead.

"W-wait!" he wailed. "I-I'm your friend! Aleksei!" he screamed as Alucard grabbed his throat and picked him up. "You don't have to do this! You're not like this! Aleksei!"

Alucard couldn't bear to listen to his cries anymore. He knew what Elvin must be thinking, and it would haunt him forever. But he had no choice.

In the blink of an eye, he mercilessly broke the bard's neck, silencing him before he could beg further. Alucard held back his own pain, fighting the agonizing torture which gripped him. He allowed Elvin's lifeless body to slowly slip from his grip and drop to the ground beside Maia.

Lillian screamed in horror, Ben stared in mortification, and Tobias—he looked as though he had lost every ounce of faith he'd ever had in Alucard. The vampire didn't expect any less of his remaining subordinates. They'd all hate him for this, but what other option did he have?

Elvin was dead, and with him, seven years of Alucard's life withered as though they were meaningless. To save a boy just to kill him years later. He'd not save anyone ever again, lest they suffer the same fate. Because they would. They *all* would.

Damien grinned in satisfaction, watching Alucard as he slowly turned to face him again. "You finally got there. Well done."

Alucard's eyes shifted to Zalith, who stared at him with a sorrowful frown. He wasn't sure what the demon must be thinking, but he was sure that he now thought much less of him for killing someone as innocent as Elvin—for not trying to resist Damien's orders. But Zalith didn't understand—he didn't know what Damien would do to him if he didn't listen.

"Here," Damien instructed, pointing to the ground in front of him.

And as he was told, Alucard slowly made his way over, ignoring Tobias' confused plea for an explanation.

The Daegelus wasn't yet done, though. He snarled and sharply turned his head to glare at Zalith. "I don't know who you think you are, demon scumbag, but you *are* expendable," he said, lifting Zalith up. He then slammed him down into the ground, making Zalith grunt painfully as Damien crouched over him and held both his hands around his throat. "You've been living on borrowed time since I caught you with my boy. You might think you can wriggle your way out of anything, but not this time. You've pissed me off for the last time. Finish the mission…and say your goodbyes to whoever it might be you care about—if you're even capable of such a thing."

Alucard stared at Zalith in despair as he glared up at Damien. He knew the demon didn't feel threatened so easily, but right now, there was a glimmer of fear in his dark eyes. Damien had sentenced him to death…and Alucard…what could he do?

Damien snarled and stood up, harshly pressing his foot against Zalith's throat. "Do I make myself clear?" he growled.

The demon scowled. "You do," he agreed tonelessly.

With a smile on his face, Damien then swung around and snatched Alucard's throat.

But the vampire didn't react. How could he? Killing Elvin had all but destroyed him. He didn't have the strength to respond, to fight, to argue. He just stood there, staring at Damien, waiting for whatever might come next.

"I hope you've learned a lesson here, Aleksei. Remove these people from your life, or I will do it for you. And say goodbye to your demon. I'm sure you won't see him again once you finish your mission—tomorrow. No later than midnight. I want the rest of the vampires in Aegisguard. If you die whilst doing so, then so be it," he sneered, dragging the claw of his thumb over Alucard's cheek, cutting into his skin. "And if you live, I will make sure it is with pain and suffering. No more will you continue to defy me, to try and cheat me. Never, *ever* will you even *think* about crossing me again."

Alucard stared at him with a hopeless, despondent look in his eyes.

"Get the fuck out of my face!" he yelled, picking Alucard up off his feet. He then mercilessly threw the vampire to his left with such force that most of the trees in his path snapped and fell for miles.

And Alucard didn't even try to fight it or slow himself. He felt utterly defeated.

| Zalith |

Watching as Alucard disappeared into the darkness, Zalith felt suffocating dismay grip him. Alucard didn't deserve any of this, and Zalith wanted nothing more than to kick the living shit out of Damien right now…but he couldn't. He had no choice but to stand there and wait like a schoolboy.

Damien looked back down at him. "Make the most of the time you have left. Get to work."

Zalith stared up at the sky behind Damien; he didn't want to see his ugly face. He didn't care about his threats, all he cared about was Alucard and all the pain he must be in. Not just from being thrown for miles through a forest, but the pain he must feel for executing his friend.

He couldn't help but feel guilty…awfully guilty. It might not be entirely his fault that this happened, but he shared the blame. It wasn't long ago that Alucard tried to warn him about Damien and how they couldn't be together because of him. But Zalith dismissed his worries like they were nothing, and now, he'd come to see that the vampire's worries were very real and very true. That didn't inspire him to want to leave Alucard, though; it only made his desire to protect him so much stronger.

The demon remained on the ground as Damien backed off and disappeared in his usual fashion—a blinding flash of crimson light and a deafening boom. Zalith then climbed to his feet, trying to silence his conflicting thoughts. His life was at stake, and he had to do something about it, but he cared about Alucard far much more than he cared about himself. He ignored Ben's call and disappeared, following the scent of Alucard's blood.

He swiftly raced through the forest, following the destruction left by the force of Damien's throw, and when he found Alucard, he frowned in *panic*.

The vampire lay still on his right side, miles away from his home. His blood oozed from the many cuts on his body, smothering the soil beneath him. Pain lingered in his hell-fiery eyes, which seemed to dim in his sadness.

"Alucard?" Zalith asked quietly, trying to help him up, but Alucard's agonized murmurs of disapproval forced him to take his hands off him, unsure of where he was hurt. But he wasn't just going to leave him lying in the dirt. Kneeling on the ground, he gently pulled the vampire's head into his lap, staring down at his vacant face—but the pain in his teary eyes was heartbreaking.

From what he could tell, Alucard's left arm was broken, but it was slowly repairing itself, as were his broken ribs. The only injury that wouldn't heal was the cut on his face. Damien had inflicted that himself and Zalith knew too well that injuries inflicted by Numen and other demons healed a whole lot more slowly than any other wound. It didn't take him long to summarize that Damien was the one responsible for the three slashes that had been healing on Alucard's face the second time he met him for their mission, and he couldn't help but suspect that Damien was the reason Alucard was so fearful of his face being touched. It made sense. And it made Zalith's heart ache.

Staring at the silent vampire, Zalith's hurt morphed into anger. He took his eyes off Alucard for a short moment and glared into the trees in the direction his house was. Damien had done this, and he was very likely responsible for so many things Zalith knew Alucard suffered from. He treated Alucard like a slave, like a plaything, like an insolent child—so many things Alucard *wasn't*. He was so enraged that he felt he could kill Damien…that he *should* kill him. Zalith already felt an undying need to protect *his* vampire from harm, and Damien seemed to be the biggest harm that could ever come to Alucard.

The only thing Damien had just achieved was gaining *him* as an enemy. But Zalith couldn't focus on that right now. Alucard was hurt. *That* was what mattered. He looked down at him again. "Alucard?" he asked, moving his crimson hair out of his face.

Alucard didn't look at him. "Ve 'ave to move zhe vampires—tomorrow," he mumbled, his voice quiet and toneless.

Zalith frowned but didn't question him. Damien was their superior, and they couldn't defy him. But the last time Alucard had taken as many vampires as were left, he almost died. Zalith spent the last week nursing him back to health. This could very well kill him, and Zalith wasn't at all willing to let Alucard suffer—least of all *die* because of Damien. He had to figure out a way to make it easier on Alucard… and he wasn't short on options. He wasn't, however, going to silence his concern.

He shook his head slightly. "That's going to kill you, Alucard. I can't just stand around and let you—"

"So?" Alucard interjected, still avoiding eye contact. "I zon't 'ave a choice."

"No, but I'm sure we can find a solution. I care about you too much to let you suffer."

Alucard scowled and struggled to sit up. He allowed Zalith to help him to his feet, and once he was up, he turned to face him. "Zhere is no solution," he said, gripping his slowly healing left arm with his right hand. "Ve move zhe vampires, zhat's all zhere is to zhis. I zon't vant to argue about zhis or talk about zhis; I just need you to bring zhem and meet me tomorrow."

As Alucard turned around and slowly walked back towards his house, Zalith frowned in denial and followed. Alucard had already decided what he was going to do, that was for sure. Zalith couldn't deter him from that; he couldn't even discuss possible solutions with him—Alucard wouldn't listen. Right now, he felt like he didn't know what to do. He knew Alucard wouldn't want to talk about Damien or what just happened, either, so he didn't ask. He just walked beside him, glancing at him every few seconds. What more could he say?

Chapter Seventy-Seven

— ᛉ ✝ ᛣ —

No More

| Alucard |

Alucard didn't realize he reached his manor until he saw Tobias walking backwards in front of him, and his voice echoed through his head. The vampire stared past the nattering man, ignoring both him and Zalith. He didn't care to answer. He couldn't. He hoped he could wait to reflect once everyone left, but his thoughts had always been so overbearing.

Just as Alucard knew he would, Damien showed up and caught him with everyone—*everyone*. Now, Elvin was dead, and *he* had been the one to kill him. Damien humiliated him in front of Zalith and his subordinates. But he couldn't be angry at Damien—he wasn't capable. He could only feel fearfully motivated to do as he was told. Because that's what it was, right? Fear. He was afraid of Damien—who wouldn't be? Anyone who wasn't fearful of Damien was a fool. *Zalith* was a fool to think not fearing Damien was something to share aloud. The Daegelus sentenced Zalith to death for his lack of fear and respect. As much as Alucard felt he appreciated Zalith's lack of fear, he now knew that was a foolish thing to do. *He* was foolish. They both were.

With a sullen look in his eyes, he glanced over at Zalith. Despite having just been sentenced to death, the demon didn't look at all shaken. The same vacant stare clung to his face, but there was a hint of worry in his eyes when he glanced at Alucard.

Zalith seemed to be more worried for the vampire than for himself. As much as Alucard might like to enjoy that, he couldn't. No longer could he indulge in the things Zalith made him feel. The only thing he would think about was saving Zalith's life. If he spoke to Damien, if he reasoned with him…and if Zalith were to never see him again, then Alucard was sure that he could save him from his sentence. Damien *did* need Zalith. If Alucard could present a case and make the Daegelus reconsider, then Zalith might live. That was all he cared about right now. But that would mean he'd never get to see him again.

Confliction warped his thoughts once again. Earlier, he considered these truths; he considered the fact that Damien would kill them. But he accepted it, and he decided he'd continue to risk their lives just to spend whatever time he had left with Zalith. That was selfish. Now that he'd seen Zalith's life at risk with his own eyes, it wasn't hard for him to realize that he made a mistake. He cared far too much to let him die—to risk his life—so much that he killed Elvin to save him. And that in itself was a whole different matter. Damien used Zalith to control him, to get him to kill someone he cared about. That type of vulnerability was something he didn't want to possess.

There was much to think about, much to consider—but not now.

"Dude?!" Tobias then yelled, stopping in his path, glaring at Alucard.

The vampire stopped walking, and as Zalith stopped beside him, he set his vacant eyes on Tobias. "Vhat?"

Tobias scoffed and held out his arms. "What the fuck, man? The hell just happened?"

"Elvin died," Alucard responded tonelessly, walking around Tobias and continuing towards where Elvin lay with Maia.

Ben and Lillian were standing nearby in one another's arms, waiting for him to join them.

Following him, Zalith remained silent but kept his eyes on Alucard. The vampire was glad, though, that he'd chosen to not try and console him in front of everyone.

Ben watched Alucard approach, holding his mortified wife's hand. But the look of animosity Alucard shot him evidently told Ben that it was time to leave. And without hesitation, he and Lillian hurried towards the manor's exit.

Tobias wasn't as easily frightened off. He slowly shadowed Alucard and Zalith over to Elvin and Maia's bodies. "Man…I don't even know what to say. Just…tell me what I can do, yeah?"

Alucard took his vacant eyes off Elvin and glared at Tobias. "Go 'ome," he instructed and then looked back down at Elvin, trying to decide what to do with him and Maia.

Tobias scoffed. "I ain't going nowhere, man. You just…are you all right?"

"Go 'ome," Alucard repeated sternly with an impatient scowl.

He crossed his arms and frowned. "Dude, come on. The fuck just happened? I…you just…" he paused and looked down at Elvin. "You…Elvin…and…."

The vampire clenched his fists impatiently and glowered at him.

Backing off, Tobias held up his hands. "All right, man," he said with a nod. "I'll piss off. But…what are you gonna do? I can't—"

"He told you to leave," Zalith then warned, glaring at him from the corner of his eye.

With a deep sigh, Tobias dragged his hand over his head and nodded. "Yeah," he said, turning around. Then, without another word, he left the manor.

"Alucard?" Zalith asked quietly, raising his hand towards Alucard's shoulder, but he hesitated and let it fall back at his side.

"I zon't know vhat to do," Alucard mumbled, staring down at Elvin and Maia.

Zalith turned to face him. "Do you want to bury your friend?"

"No," Alucard answered. "Ve zon't bury people 'ere. Ghouls."

"Oh, I see" Zalith responded sympathetically. "Is there anything else you want to do…perhaps to honour them, somehow? You're just staring at them."

Alucard didn't respond. He stood there, staring at Elvin and trying his best not to sink into dismay. But how could he not? Elvin didn't deserve to die, and although it may have been easy to end his life, now that it was over, he regretted it so sorely. He didn't regret saving Zalith's life, no, but he did regret allowing himself to see Elvin as an expired resource. If he hadn't thought such a thing, though, he might not have been able to do what he had to. What he did was to save Zalith. Zalith mattered more to him than Elvin did—it was a cold, harsh truth, and as awful as he felt to admit it to himself, he had to. He had to face the facts. He'd have killed everyone if it was what had been necessary to save Zalith.

But that wasn't something to admire. He couldn't allow himself to possess such a weakness. Damien would use Zalith against him again now that he knew it sufficed as a way to control him. He didn't want that. As much as he cared for Zalith, as much as he wanted to continue to see him and keep him in his life, he couldn't. And as much as it would pain him, he'd have no choice but to tell Zalith—and this time, he'd have to make sure the demon understood, and Alucard would have to make sure he didn't let Zalith charm him away from his decision.

Right now, though, he had to decide what he was doing with Elvin, Maia, and the depravity he'd been left with. He couldn't bury them; he didn't want to drag them away like they were some lowlifes he'd had to kill. He also had to consider the fact that, even though he didn't become a werewolf in his life, in death, Elvin might still become possessed. The only way to make sure that didn't happen was to completely eradicate his body.

That was what he'd do. He kept his right arm at his side but ever so slightly twisted his hand—and instantly, both bodies were consumed by blood-red flames. He and Zalith watched in silence as the flames erased any trace of the bodies' existence in just minutes. But while Elvin's body had been removed from existence, he would always remain a memory in Alucard's mind. He'd never forget what happened, and he felt as though it was a lesson Damien wished for him to learn from.

And he had. No more friends. No more socializing. No more Zalith.

"You should go," Alucard said, glancing at Zalith.

The demon frowned and stared at him. "I'm not leaving until I know that you're okay," he said sternly.

"I'm vi—"

"You're not fine, Alucard," he interjected.

Alucard turned to face him and scowled in hostility.

"He just made you kill your friend," Zalith said sadly. "He then threw you halfway across the island. Tell me, honestly: are you okay?"

The vampire pouted and looked down at the ground, watching as his crimson flames slowly diminished. He wasn't okay. He was nowhere *near* okay. All he wanted to do was feel Zalith's comforting embrace, but if he allowed that to happen, his decision to put an end to their friendship would waver. He looked back at Zalith. "Yes," he answered.

Zalith didn't look convinced. He sighed and slowly placed his hand on the vampire's shoulder. But Alucard shrugged his hand off.

"I 'ave to prepare vor tomorrow. You should, too," the vampire said, glaring down at the ground where Elvin and Maia had once been.

"Alucard—"

"Go," he insisted, shifting his gaze back to Zalith. "I'll meet you tomorrow just bevore midnight in zhe same place as last time."

A frown of worry claimed Zalith's face, but he sighed and nodded. "I will see you tomorrow night."

"Yes."

"And if you need me, you know how to contact me."

Glancing at him, Alucard replied, "*La revedere.*"

"Goodbye," Zalith said with a sad smile.

As the demon left the grounds, Alucard looked back down at the ground. There was no point in dwelling on it anymore. What was done was done, and he couldn't do anything about it.

He walked away, heading towards his front door. When he stepped into his silent, empty house, he took a moment to stop...to look around...to frown despondently. Tonight may be the last night he spent in this house. If the portal didn't kill him this time, then Damien would send him off to work elsewhere the moment he got back—there was no doubt about it. He closed the front door behind him and dragged himself up to the fifth floor.

The vampire made his way into his study—his disorganised mess of a study. What better way to spend the night than clearing it up? He didn't have much else to do, and if he didn't do *something*, then his thoughts would consume him. So, he closed the doors behind him, walked over to his desk, and began tidying the paper on it. He didn't want to think ill of Damien, but if he really was keeping the Diabolus off his back, then how had Maia found him? Why had she been allowed into his home? Perhaps she managed— somehow—to avoid the Daegelus' watchful eye, an eye which always seemed to be on Alucard.

He finished tidying the papers and moved onto the shelves. But his thoughts focused on Zalith once again. Tomorrow would be the last time Alucard would see him.

Tomorrow would be when he told Zalith that whatever they were…it had to end—it *would* end. They couldn't see each other anymore. Damien would kill Zalith, and that was something Alucard would do anything to keep from happening. If he had to sacrifice his own happiness, then he would. He knew he'd be a whole lot less sad if Zalith were to remain in his life, but he just couldn't have him. They just couldn't be together. They could never see each other again, and Alucard had to make sure of it.

There was no way for Alucard to win—there never was. He'd never get to see Zalith again either way; he'd stop seeing him to save his life, and if he continued to see him, Damien would kill him. As much as it would hurt, and as miserable as it would make him, Alucard had to do whatever it took to keep Zalith alive. If he had to live knowing that Zalith was dead because of him…then it would cause him pain he'd never be able to relieve.

The thought of losing Zalith felt like a nightmare. To wake up knowing that the day was another day where Zalith was living in some other world—alive, breathing, probably with someone else, someone better. It hurt. But Alucard would have to suffer that if he wanted Zalith to live. He'd suffer. He'd always suffer. For Zalith, he'd do anything.

Once he finished tidying his shelves, he slumped down in his seat and stared vacantly at the doors ahead of him. What would come next? When the vampires were all in Aegisguard, what would his next task be? Would he be able to remain in Dor-Sanguis? Probably not. Where would he go? Would he at least stay in Aegisguard? It was possible that he wouldn't. But wherever he may end up, he sorely wished that Zalith would be with him.

But he wouldn't be there.

He'd not be there ever again.

Chapter Seventy-Eight

— ⸝ ✝ ⸝ —

The Orphanage

| **Alucard, *Iunius 5th*, *950(TG)*—*7 Years ago*** |

Attila asked Alucard, "Why do you care?"

Alucard stared out the window of the locomotive cabin, watching the countryside as it passed by outside. Why *did* he care? Why was he in DeiganLupus? Why was he heading to the same orphanage he dropped that little boy off at seventeen years ago?

He took his eyes off the vast farmland and set them on the vampire opposite him. "I told you vhy," he answered.

Attila sat with his legs widely spread, leaning back in his seat with a perturbed look on his pale face. He nodded, glancing at the cabin door as a small group of people walked past. "I remember," he said. Then, he looked back over at Alucard and frowned. "Tomorrow is his eighteenth birthday, correct? He hasn't yet turned; the guys you had me watching him haven't reported anything. What if you're wrong? What if he's just human?"

"Zhen I vill get vid of 'im. I 'ave no use vor 'umans."

"And if he's *not*?"

"I use 'im vor vhat I intend to use 'im vor."

"Become his friend, get him to convince the wolves that war isn't the only option?"

"Precisely," Alucard confirmed, looking back out the window.

"How can you be sure he's of the royal bloodline?" Attila then asked, scratching the side of his stubble-covered face.

Alucard frowned irritably. "'Is mother vas Ada's descendant; I'd recognize zhat ugly bitch's offspring anyvhere."

Amused, Attila scoffed and crossed his arms. "I still don't get why you don't try to become Ada's friend. Yeah, she's a little psycho, but aren't we all?"

"No," Alucard snarled.

"All right," he said with a sigh, holding up his hands. He then rested his arms behind his head and looked out the window, watching as the locomotive began to approach its final destination. The countryside faded into brick and steel buildings, the once clear air now thick with steam and smoke. "Of all places, why here?" he then asked, looking back at Alucard. "If we were alive, I'm sure we'd both catch something life-threatening from our visit."

"Is zhe only place currently vree of war," Alucard answered.

Eventually, the large, black-steel train halted in DeiganLupus' main city station. Passengers flooded off and onto the platform, bustling towards the exit as quickly as they could. Alucard and Attila were two of the last people to disembark—of course, the last thing they wanted to do was arouse suspicion, so the best thing to do would be to avoid larger crowds. Despite the people of the city being busy with their own lives, it wasn't hard to spot a vampire, and if either of them were noticed, their journey would become an unnecessary challenge. However, their unique ability to walk in the sunlight *should* keep them safe.

"Do you know where we're going?" Attila asked.

"Speak Deiganish," Alucard muttered.

Attila slipped his hands into his pockets and followed Alucard as he led the way forward, trailing the crowd of people ahead of them. "Is it far from station?" he asked in Deiganish, as told.

Alucard glared ahead, watching as the ticket inspectors verified each passing person's ticket. "A small valk," he confirmed, reaching into his left blazer pocket. He pulled out two small pieces of card, and as they approached the inspectors, he held them out to the man who halted them. As the inspector nodded and let them pass, Alucard glanced over at Attila. "Keep your mouth shut zhis time, hmm?"

Attila smirked as they left the building and stepped out onto the busy street. "No worries," he said. But when he walked beside Alucard, he frowned in revolt, examining the smoke-filled sky, the dirty roads, and the mass amount of people bustling through the streets. "Could you… live in place like this?"

"Per'aps… not *in*, but close by," Alucard answered.

"Ugly city… ugly people," Attila mumbled.

Soon, they left the busy city behind and made their way down an abandoned road. A few tall, browned trees were lined along the sidewalks in front of two-story houses, which were all either white or black. Horse-drawn carriages were stowed outside most of the homes, some with horses still attached.

They walked until a large iron-gated building came into view at the end of the road. A huge estate rested within the walls, and a small hut sat just outside with a rather irritated-looking man sitting inside. He eyed both vampires as they approached and stood up when he realized they were looking to enter.

"What's yer business 'ere?" he called.

"Is this a prison or an orphanage?" Attila asked in Dor-Sanguian.

The man then scoffed as they both stopped in front of him. "Aye, I don't speak whatever you do. Get outta here."

"I'm 'ere to pick somevone up," Alucard said.

"Is that right?"

Alucard reached into his blazer pocket and took out a rolled piece of parchment. He handed it to the man, who eyed him for a few moments before unwrapping it to read what was written on it.

"I told zhem I'd be back vor 'im vonce 'e turned eighteen," Alucard said.

Nodding slowly, the man rolled the parchment back up and handed it back to Alucard. "Yeah, right. Go on in; the sisters will be inside."

As the gates unlocked, Alucard led the way inside.

"Not that I make a habit of pointing out the obvious, but…how do you suppose we get inside? Nuns, Alucard? They're gonna know what we are the second they see us waiting outside the threshold like a couple of indecisive cats," Attila said in Dor-Sanguian.

"You can vait outside," Alucard grumbled. "I've already been inside. And I told you to speak Deiganish."

"Right, apologies. Why I wait outside? Make me look stupid."

Alucard glanced at him, and as he smiled amusedly, watching Attila frown in offence, he replied, "You might get lucky; somevone might invite you in."

When they reached the front door, Attila pouted and shook his head. "Why this even a thing?" he asked as Alucard knocked on the door. "Whose idea was it to make us not able to enter homes? Places? Stupid rule."

"Ask my father—if you can contact 'im."

"Tch," Attila uttered, leaning back against the wall beside the door.

The front door then unlocked from inside, and as a small, old woman no more than four feet tall answered it, she stared at Alucard with her dull greyed eyes.

"I've come vor—"

"Yes, I remember you," she said, smiling brightly. "You've not aged a day, Aleksei," she said, taking his wrist and guiding him inside.

He smiled just as pleasantly. "I take care of myselv."

"You *must* share your secrets with me; I'd die to look twenty again," she said, leading him over to the front desk.

"You vere tventy sixteen years ago," he said, frowning—now, she looked to be in her hundreds.

She sighed as she let go of his wrist and hobbled behind the desk. She shuffled into her seat and looked up at him as he rested his arms on the desk. "This place—it's not so kind to us people. The smoke: if it doesn't make you sick, it makes you look like an old woman after a decade or so of exposure. I live next to one of the factories, so…it was bound to happen. I'd love to move somewhere the smoke isn't so thick, but it's too expensive."

"Vight," Alucard mumbled.

"So, you're here for the same child you brought in here all those years ago?"

He nodded.

"You got the paperwork?"

The vampire handed her the same roll of parchment he'd handed to the man outside. "Is zhere a cure?" he asked curiously. "Vor zhis…effect of zhe smoke."

Taking the parchment from him, she sighed. "There is, but…once again, too expensive. Anyway, enough about me. Yeah, you kept it intact all these years, huh?" she asked, smiling down at the parchment, the same parchment *she* had given him when he dropped off the kid sixteen years ago. "Well, he's called himself Elvin—didn't like any of the names we tried to give him. I was his main supervisor, but he preferred to just sit in the corner and write silly stories most of the time."

"Vhy Elvin?" Alucard asked with a frown.

She shrugged. "I don't know. He tells us it means noble friend—spent weeks looking through the books we have here to find it. He doesn't even have any friends," she explained, stamping the parchment before handing it back to Alucard. "Wait here. I'll go and fetch him for you."

As she left the room, Alucard leaned back against the desk and stared over at the door, tucking the parchment back into his pocket. It didn't take long for her to return with a small teenager; his short hair was a dull brown, as were his eyes, and he clung fondly onto a lute with both his hands. He followed the woman out of the door, and as she guided him over to Alucard, the vampire eyed him closely.

"This is him. Elvin, this is Aleksei. He's come to take you home," she said with a smile, looking at the boy's confused face.

"Home?" Elvin asked nervously. "Isn't *this* my home?"

"Vas," Alucard said.

Elvin then frowned strangely. "You have an accent; you're not from here. Where do you come from? How can you be taking me home if you're not even from the same place as me?" he asked skeptically. He then looked at the woman. "I don't wanna go! I wanna stay here!"

"Now, Elvin, you know you can't do that. Everyone leaves the home once they turn eighteen. For you, that's tomorrow. Most of the kids here don't even have anywhere to go, so you should count yourself lucky. Aleksei will take care of you."

The boy pouted, eyeing Alucard up and down again. "Your suit looks expensive—are you rich? Are you taking me and planning to sell me to the slave trade?"

"Vhat?" the vampire questioned.

"Elvin!" the woman exclaimed, smacking the boy's wrist. She then sighed and shook her head. "He's a little funny, this one," she mumbled, looking up at Alucard.

"Me, or *him*," Elvin muttered.

"*Multemesc*," Alucard said. "I vill take 'im now."

"Behave, Elvin," the woman said as she nudged him towards Alucard.

Mumbling to himself, the boy made his way over to Alucard and stood beside him.

"Is zhat all 'e 'as?" Alucard asked, nodding at the boy's lute.

"He's had it since he turned twelve; saved up all the money he made from cleaning windows and bought it."

"You're not taking it from me!" Elvin insisted, gripping his lute as tightly as he could.

"No," Alucard said with an amused smile, glancing at him. He then looked back at the small woman. "I appreciate you taking care of 'im all zhese years," he said, reaching into his right pocket. He pulled out a small black envelope and handed it to her. "Take zhis to zhe bank—a vank you vor all you've done. I also expect you vill not mention zhis to anyvone?"

Taking the envelope with an excited look on her face, the old woman shook her head and smiled. "Not a word."

"Zhen zhis is goodbye."

"You don't need anything else from me?" she asked in disappointment.

"If I 'appen across anozzer kid who needs an 'ome, I vill be sure to come to you."

As Alucard then left with the boy slowly following, the woman waved goodbye.

"Who even are you?" Elvin asked, looking up at Alucard as he followed him out of the building.

"He is new guardian, kid," Attila said as he joined them both, placing his hand on Elvin's shoulder.

Startled, the boy flinched but continued to follow Alucard. "Guardian? You adopted me for one day? I'll be eighteen tomorrow, and then I can go wherever I want."

"Zhat may be zhe case, but until zhen, you vollow me and do vhat I say," Alucard said.

The boy pouted and glared ahead as they left the orphanage gates.

"Ve're going to veturn to my 'omeland—Dor-Sanguis. Vonce ve're zhere, ve'll vind you a place to live."

"Why?" Elvin asked. "You're just strangers. Why do you care about me?"

"We don't, kid," Attila said.

"I wasn't asking you, creepy guy," Elvin grumbled.

Attila scoffed in offence as Alucard smirked amusedly.

"You vant to become a bard, I imagine?" Alucard asked, looking down at Elvin. "I 'eard you vere pretty good. Per'aps I vish to sponsor your career."

"Really?!" Elvin asked excitedly.

"Sure."

"What's it like in this Sanguis place?" he asked with a look of admiration in his eyes. "Is it smokey like the big city?"

"No," Alucard answered. "Is mostly… country and sea. Zhere is a city, zhough, many places vor you to sing or tell your stories."

Elvin clapped his hands together. "I'm so excited! I won't let you down!"

"Let's 'ope not, hmm?"

Chapter Seventy-Nine

Endings

| **Alucard, *Iunius 6th, 957(TG)—Present* |**

Alucard woke when he heard his door knock. He lifted his head from his desk, and the paper which stuck to the side of his face floated back down to its surface. He focused on who was outside, and when he realized that it was Tobias, he huffed irritably.

He knocked again, and after a few minutes passed, he knocked once more. What could he possibly want?

The vampire looked back over his shoulder, setting his eyes on the moons outside as they slowly crept higher into the sky. Soon, he'd head to Eltaria, where he'd see Zalith for the last time…the last time *ever*. But how was he supposed to tell him? He hadn't even thought it through. He couldn't tell him that they couldn't see each other anymore; he already tried that, and Zalith convinced him otherwise. One thing he'd come to learn about Zalith was that he might just be as stubborn as he was. He wouldn't take no for an answer, so Alucard was going to have to be as stern as possible.

Then, the door knocked once again. With an irritated scowl, Alucard stood up, left his study, made his way down through his house to the entrance hall, and yanked the door open. "Vhat?!" he snapped.

Shocked by his appearance, Tobias flinched and frowned. "Uh…sorry. Look, I just came to see if you were all right, man. Ain't seen you since yesterday. You uh…not get that looked at?" he asked, pointing to the slowly healing cut on the side of Alucard's face.

"Go 'ome, Tobias. I 'ave places to be."

Alucard went to shut the door, but Tobias slammed his hand against it and frowned in worry. "Come on, dude. What happened was fucked up, and I get it if you don't wanna talk about it. But at least like…don't lock yourself away, yeah? Maybe…come for a drink or something?" he suggested.

"No," he refused. "Take your 'and off my door bevore I make you."

Tobias scoffed and let go of the door. "Come on, man. At least let me try and help."

"I zon't need anyvone's 'elp," he denied, shutting the door in Tobias' face.

The vampire sighed heavily as he leaned his back against the door. He'd slept so long that he was now moments away from having to leave for the portal, and Zalith would be waiting for him on the other side. He could think about what to tell him on the way; it would keep him from dwelling on his regret for what happened to Elvin. Dreaming about the day he'd picked the bard up hadn't exactly helped; it just made him feel even worse for killing him as if he was nothing.

Alucard grabbed his blazer and pulled it on, leaving his cape on the coat rack as he turned around and opened his door again. He stepped outside, setting his eyes on Tobias, who was making his way towards the gates but turned to face him when he heard the door shut.

"You change your mind?" the man called from across the grounds.

Ignoring him, Alucard prepared to shift into his mist form and head for the docks.

"Hey!" Tobias called, hurrying over.

Alucard hesitated. Tobias was only trying to be kind; he was the only person who tried to do so without becoming overbearing and annoying. And he was also the only person Alucard felt he could stand to listen to for more than a few minutes—other than Zalith. He sighed, turned to face Tobias as he reached him, and waited.

Tobias smiled. "You coming?"

"No," Alucard repeated. "I 'ave to meet Zaliv."

"Oh…well…tomorrow, then?"

The vampire thought to himself for a few moments. He wasn't the type to talk about his problems or feelings, and that had to be what Tobias was suggesting. He couldn't hang out with him anyway; he had to head to the portal, and he wasn't even sure he'd be coming back from it. However, he was sure Tobias wouldn't leave him alone unless he agreed, so he thought he might as well do so. He looked at him and frowned irritably. "I'll see 'ow I veel vhen I get back later."

"All right, sweet."

"Now go 'ome."

Tobias winked. "You got it." He turned around and made his way towards the exit.

Then, Alucard morphed into vermillion smoke and hurried towards the docks.

❧ ❖ ❧

As Alucard landed on the ship's deck, Ben watched with a fearful look on his face.

"Let's go," Alucard immediately instructed. He made his way to the edge of the ship, tapped its side, letting Drac know it was time to leave, and then disappeared into his cabin. He sat behind his desk, staring aimlessly out of the window.

Ben stepped into the room.

"Vhat do you vant?" Alucard grumbled.

Ben moved closer and rested his arms on the back of the chair in front of Alucard's desk. "You all right?"

"You're zhe second person to ask me zhat tonight."

"Sorry. I'm just concerned. The guy that came last night…who was he?"

"Get out," Alucard uttered, not at all interested in talking to him.

As he was told, Ben nodded and respectively left the cabin, closing the door behind him.

Alucard glared down at his hands, trying to shroud his despondent thoughts with irritancy, with *anger*…but he couldn't. Soon, he'd see Zalith for the last time. He'd have to tell him that they couldn't see each other anymore. It was painful enough to try and tell him before, but then they kissed, they spent much more time together, and now, he had to do it again. He had to ignore his need for that demon; he had to forget what he felt and wanted. It was to save Zalith's life, and that was something he'd do anything for. It was going to hurt; it would cause him such pain—but he had to do it. And he would.

He'd just tell him straight. Damien would kill Zalith if they saw each other again once the mission was complete. The only way to ensure he'd stay alive was to forget him, move on, and find someone else. Alucard was sure Zalith wouldn't struggle in such a feat. After all, Alucard wasn't special, was he? The demon he'd come to appreciate so much would soon forget who he was. But that was okay. He'd be alive, he'd be happy with someone else, and as much as that may hurt, Alucard just wanted Zalith to be safe, content, and alive, even if it meant he couldn't be there with him.

With a sullen frown, he turned to face the window and stared out at the sea. He should have known this would happen. Why did he let himself grow so close to someone? To *fall* for someone. He could never have such a thing—he could never have a relationship; he couldn't have love. Was that what this was? Was that what he felt? No, it couldn't be. If it were love, surely he wouldn't be sitting there trying to work out how to say goodbye, would he?

He scowled and looked down at the floor. All he knew was that he needed to accept that he'd never see Zalith again after this. He needed to stop thinking about him, his feelings, and whatever Zalith might do once they said farewell. It didn't matter. All that mattered was goodbye.

When the ship halted beside the island, dread filled his heart as it began to beat just a little faster. He didn't want to go. He didn't want to say goodbye. He didn't want the mission to end. But what choice did he have? He couldn't keep Zalith in his life if he wanted him to live. He *had* to say goodbye, or he'd condemn Zalith to death.

He silenced his hesitation, his regret, his *pain*. He stood up, left the cabin, and stepped down onto the island. The vampire slowly made his way towards the portal, staring into the shimmering blackness within. Zalith was waiting on the other side; this would be the last time Alucard stepped through to Eltaria, the last time he would set foot in Zalith's homeworld. It was the last time for many things he wished he could change. But he had no control over any of it. And he had no one to blame but himself. He shouldn't have let it happen.

With a vacant glare, he stepped through the portal and emerged into the ruins. He stopped for a moment, staring ahead at the night sky. The same thought lingered inside his head no matter how many times he tried to accept it. Tonight was the last night he'd see Zalith. Ever. He already accepted it, so why did he continue to dwell on it? There was nothing he could do to change it. He just needed to work out how to tell Zalith, how to get him to understand that he was serious. There was no escaping Damien—he needed to make Zalith understand that.

Banishing his sullen frown, Alucard walked forward, making his way out of the ruins and down towards the barn. He didn't care to focus and work out how many vampires were inside; the only aura he could seem to focus on was Zalith's. He'd never feel it again, would he? He scowled and made his way down to the barn, heading towards the same back entrance he used last time.

As soon as he entered, he set his eyes on the demon, who was dressed just as attractively as usual. Black shirt, black waistcoat, both fitted rather elegantly. Even when Zalith set his almost-black eyes on him, Alucard didn't look away. He'd not see him after tonight, after all. He wanted to make the most of whatever time they had left.

The demon smiled and made his way over. "Hey," he said, slowly moving in for a hug—and Alucard let it happen.

Alucard knew he probably shouldn't let Zalith hug him and that he shouldn't be hugging him back, but how could he not? Tonight was goodbye, and he'd rather it be on a comforting note, not something bitter or confounding. He wanted to make sure Zalith knew what he meant to him, that saying goodbye was hard, and that it also had to be done. He didn't want to hurt or upset Zalith by lying, by making up some bullshit story about not wanting to see him again. Zalith deserved the whole truth, and that was what Alucard would give him.

"How are you feeling?" Zalith asked, stepping back but keeping his hands on Alucard's shoulders.

Looking at him, Alucard shrugged slightly. "Vine," he mumbled.

The vampire took his eyes off Zalith for a moment, realizing that the barn wasn't as densely populated as he had thought. There were only nine vampires; there should be almost forty. Where were the others?

He frowned at Zalith, "Vhere are zhe rest?"

"They changed their minds about wanting to relocate," Zalith answered.

Alucard scowled skeptically. "Did *you* change zheir minds?"

The demon smiled. "I can be very persuasive."

"Vhy vould you do zhat?" Alucard exclaimed in disbelief.

"Why do you think, Alucard?"

"Enlighten me," he snarled. "If I zon't take zhem all back tonight, Zamien vill vink I vailed, and 'e'll do vorse zhan vrow me into some vorest!"

Zalith sighed quietly. "I did it because I don't want you to die. You shouldn't have to suffer just because that creature swings his fists around like an ape and whines about things not progressing at an impossible rate," he said.

As Alucard scowled irritably, Zalith moved his left hand from his shoulder and to the side of his neck.

"I care about you so much, Alucard—more than anything. If what I've done makes things between you and Damien any tenser, then I'm sincerely sorry; that was never my intention. But I won't play a part in your death. What I've done is to protect you— to *help* you. If Damien asks for an explanation, then you can tell him that the humans discovered where the last of the vampires were hiding and attacked. He isn't at all likely to check, and if he so happens to, then I've made sure to cover all of my tracks. I did everything I could to save us both from suspicion."

Staring at him, Alucard frowned sullenly and looked away. "I zidn't ask you to do zhat."

Zalith shook his head. "You don't have to ask me to do anything. If your life is at risk, there is nothing I wouldn't do."

It would seem that Zalith might understand what Alucard had to tell him. But how to tell him? When? He needed to move the vampires first…then he could focus on saying what needed to be said.

"Are you sure you're okay, Alucard?" Zalith asked quietly.

Alucard dismissed his sullen frown and looked back at the demon. "Yes."

Zalith sighed and smiled slightly. "I'm always here if you need me—whether it be to talk or…just my company."

The vampire acknowledged his answer with a slight nod. Alucard didn't have the heart to tell him that he wouldn't always be there. After tonight, they'd never see each other again. Perhaps now was the time to tell him.

"Hey, are we going?" one of the vampires called, waving his hand over at Alucard and Zalith.

The Vampire Lord glanced over at him, scowled, and looked back at Zalith.

"I'll walk with you," the demon said with a smile.

Alucard nodded and called to the vampires, "Ve're leaving." Then, as the vampires followed, he led the way out of the barn with Zalith at his side.

"I'll allow you to rest tonight, but tomorrow I'll come and see you," Zalith said.

Alucard didn't know what to say. He knew it wouldn't happen, but he wasn't yet ready to explain that to Zalith—especially not with a bunch of strangers behind them, either. It would be a huge, painful struggle, and he didn't want them to witness it. He'd not expose himself like that to anyone other than Zalith. But he had to respond; otherwise, Zalith was going to assume something was wrong and question him.

The vampire nodded and sighed quietly. "Vill tire me. I ovten sleep a day or two avter I vinish zhese moves."

"Then I will come the day after," Zalith said contently.

The fact that Zalith seemed so content right now broke Alucard's heart. Was he smiling in an attempt to lie to himself? Did he know what was coming?

"Vhat vill you do?" Alucard asked, glancing at him. "Vonce zhis mission is complete, vill you do someving else vor Zamien?"

"Damien still needs me for his grand plan," he uttered irritably. "I'm not sure whether he'll give me a new job, though. All I plan to do after this is spend more time with you."

Alucard couldn't concur as much as he wanted to. He kept his eyes forward, trying to hide his sullen, despondent frown. "Vhen do you vink 'e vill initiate zhat plan?"

Zalith frowned slightly, realizing that Alucard was avoiding the subject of meeting after the mission was complete. "I…don't know. Alucard, is—"

"I zon't know if 'e needs me vor zhat still," he interjected. "'E might look vor somevone else now zhat I've pissed 'im off as much as I 'ave."

Once they reached the portal, Zalith grabbed Alucard's shoulder and turned him to face him. "Tell me what's wrong," he insisted, a horribly worried look on his face. "Has Damien said something else? Did he come back after I left?"

"No," Alucard mumbled, shrugging his hand off his shoulder. He glanced at the vampires. "Link arms or join 'ands; zon't let go until ve are all on zhe ozzer side," he instructed. Then, he looked at Zalith. "I…ve…" he hesitated, Zalith's look of worry making it a whole lot harder to tell him. He couldn't stand around, though—not with the vampires. He needed to get them through the portal first; what he had to say would take too long to risk keeping them waiting. So, he snatched the wrist of the vampire closest to him and sullenly asked Zalith, "Can you…meet me on zhe other side?"

Zalith kept his concerned frown but nodded and smiled slightly. "Of course."

Without a moment of hesitation, Alucard scowled in struggle and stepped through the portal, pulling the vampires with him.

When he emerged back onto the rainy island, Alucard continued forward, leading the nine vampires through. Once they were all free, he let go and sent them on their way to the ship. He then waited in the rain, watching as Ben greeted each of the vampires with a smile on his face.

In just moments, he'd have to say his final goodbye. And he wasn't ready for it. He'd never be ready for it. But he had to do it. To save Zalith…he had to remove himself from his life.

"Alucard," Zalith said, appearing beside him. "Listen to me. I know you're worried about Damien's threat, and your reason for avoiding the subject of us seeing each other is most likely because of that. But I can assure you, he is *not* going to kill either of us. Not only did I convince most of the vampires to change their minds, but I also spent the majority of last night removing every candidate Damien had lined up to replace me. Now he has no choice but to keep me alive if he wants his plan to succeed. And I don't even need to tell you why he will keep you alive, but I will anyway. You're Lucifer's son; there is no way he will give up someone as valuable as you."

As the rain poured around them, Alucard stared sullenly, trying to work out where to begin. What Zalith said didn't matter. Damien would kill him anyway. Zalith may have killed every other Lilith-descended male currently alive, but Damien could just ask her to create another. Zalith had tried—and that pained Alucard so sorely. He knew Zalith wanted to keep him in his life just as much as he wanted to keep *him*, but it couldn't happen. Alucard could never see Zalith again. That was the way it had to be.

The vampire slowly shifted his eyes to Zalith. He had to say something now before it became harder to speak. But he couldn't find the words. He didn't have the will. All he could do was stare at him and wish he didn't have to do it.

Gazing at his despondent face, Zalith frowned in worry. "It might not solve all of our problems, but it *will* solve a large one. We can work out what to do *together*. I'm not going to let anything come between us, let alone someone as cruel and insufferable as Damien."

Alucard couldn't listen anymore. Zalith was so convinced that they could fight Damien, that they could defy him. Alucard knew the truth, the facts, the reality, and he had to make Zalith understand. There was no way…no version of this where they could be together. As much as Alucard might like to believe there was, there just wasn't. Zalith's attempts to change his mind were futile.

As the rain poured over his face, he turned to look at the demon. "You can't make zhat choice. You can't stop Zamien—*ve* can't stop 'im. You're not avraid of 'im because you zon't know 'im like I do. You killed all zhe people zhat 'e vould veplace you vith? Zhat's not going to stop 'im vrom killing you. 'E is cruel and spitevul. 'E vill just kill you anyvay and adjust 'is plan. Zhere's no vay ve can come out of zhis alive and still able to see vone anozzer."

Zalith frowned in both sadness and concern. "There *has* to be a way."

"Zhere isn't," the vampire stated sternly. "I tried to tell you bevore. I tried to explain zhat I just…can't be vith you. I can't pretend zhat zhere's a vay avound zhis, zhat zhere's a vay ve can continue to see each ozzer. I'm not going to allow you to visk your life just to see me—is not vorth zhis. As much as I vish ve could share more, as much as I vish I could see you avter tonight, zhis 'as to be zhe last time ve see each ozzer."

The demon shook his head and placed his hand on Alucard's shoulder. "No, it doesn't," he denied strongly. "Damien isn't the be-all and end-all of everything, least of all *us*. We *will* figure this out, you and I—together. Trust me, please?" he pleaded.

"Stop trying to change my mind," Alucard exclaimed painfully. Why did Zalith have to fight him? Why did he have to continue to try and convince him that there was a way they could be together, a way to escape Damien? There was no way out. Why couldn't he see that? Why couldn't he just listen? Understand? Why did he have to make this so much harder than it already was? "I care too much to allow you to visk your life just to see me," he uttered, shoving Zalith's arm away, but the demon snatched his wrist and stared at him with a look of such intense refusal that Alucard wasn't sure what to expect next.

Zalith stared at him for a few moments; he moved his hand up the vampire's arm and placed it on the side of his face. "Let me help you," he begged quietly. Let me free you from Damien's vile grip. I told you before, and I'll tell you again: I know someone. I know of a way to hide you even from Damien. *We* can hide from him," he said, moving closer to him. "You don't have to leave—we don't have to end this."

Alucard shook his head, trying to hide his dismayed expression by looking down at the ground. "Ve *do*," he mumbled, his voice breaking. "'E'll vind us, and 'e'll kill you. 'E'll make me kill you, 'e'll make me vatch…and I can't…do zhat," he said, slowly looking back at Zalith's face, watching as a despondent frown appeared on it. "I can't…be vith you. I can't ever see you again. I can't ever *talk* to you again. I vish I could, but…zhis 'as to be goodbye."

"It doesn't," Zalith insisted, moving as close as he could get to him.

The vampire stared at him, trying to hold back his tears. But he couldn't. They slid down his face, masked by the rain which seemed to fall heavier. He placed his hand on Zalith's face, staring into his despondent eyes. "If I could spend my life vith you, zhen I vould. But our time togezzer is over. I—"

Zalith didn't let him finish. The demon moved his distraught face into Alucard's and placed a kiss so passionate on his lips that every word Alucard planned to speak withered. For a small moment, his agony lifted. It was a feeling he wished could last forever, but it couldn't. That didn't mean he couldn't enjoy it while it lasted, though.

The demon sighed and rested his forehead against Alucard's. "I'll wait for you," he said, opening his eyes to stare into his. "You might not see it now because of what happened, but there *are* ways we can be together. When I want something, there's very little that can stop me—and I want *you*. I *need* you. This may be goodbye, vampire, but only for now. I *will* be back for you."

Then, before Alucard could say anything else, Zalith let go of him, backed off, and with one last look at the vampire, he disappeared into the rift that formed behind him.

He was gone. So suddenly, so easily. Gone.

Alucard stared at the scorched rock Zalith disappeared into, every type of sadness building up inside him. Zalith was still so convinced that they'd see each other again, and Alucard failed to make him understand that never again would they lay eyes on one another. Never again would they hear one another's voice. And never again would they share one another's company. Whatever they were, whatever they had—it was over.

| Zalith |

Zalith leaned back against the wall he emerged in front of as his rift faded. He could feel his heart aching in his chest—it had *broken*, and he'd done his best to hide it. But he tried his best to focus on his determination. Alucard was *his* and nobody and nothing would take him from him. Not Damien, not anyone. He would do *anything* for Alucard; he would do whatever it took to be with him.

He wasn't sure if his words had convinced Alucard that he wasn't going to let this be the end—that he wasn't afraid of Damien and his empty threats. Damien wasn't going to kill *either* of them. He needed them for his pathetic plan, especially now that Zalith killed anyone who could replace himself.

But Alucard was so scared; Zalith saw that heart-breaking fear in his eyes. He knew Alucard didn't want to say any of the things he did, and he was confident that Alucard wanted to be together as much as he wanted it. But Damien scared him—*tormented* him into thinking that he would kill them both if they ever saw each other again. How was he going to get Alucard to see that that wouldn't happen?

He sighed and dragged his hand over his face. There wasn't much he could do right now. He wasn't going to force Alucard, he wasn't going to pressure him. He'd just... wait. Alucard was worth waiting for, and no matter how long it took, he'd give the vampire as much time as he needed to decide what he *really* wanted. Next week, next month, next *year*. However long Alucard needed...he'd give it to him.

With a sullen frown, he moved away from the wall and started heading home. While he waited for Alucard, he'd bury himself in work.

Chapter Eighty

— ⟨ † ⟩ —

Tobias and Alucard

| Alucard |

Alucard didn't remember getting back on his ship. He had tried to shut everything out—his feelings, his thoughts, even the world around him, but the crashing waves woke him from his trance. And it all came flooding back to him. That goodbye. The end of his happiness. No one could make him feel the things Zalith did, and now, he was gone. *It* was gone. All he felt was a bitter, endless emptiness, something quite familiar.

But at least Zalith would live. Alucard sacrificed his once-in-a-lifetime chance to be happy to save Zalith—and he'd do it again if he had to. The days, the months, and the years ahead without Zalith would be painful; they'd be lonely, empty, and boring, but Alucard would endure it knowing Zalith was safe. That was all that mattered to him.

He had to work out what he would do next, but all he could think about was Zalith. What was *he* doing right now? What would he be doing tomorrow? The day after? Next week? Next month? It didn't matter. He'd move on—and that was okay. That was what Alucard wanted; he wanted him to be happy, safe, and alive. Even if it was without him.

When he felt the ship slowing, Alucard irritably wiped his face, unsure whether the wet on it was rain or tears. He didn't want to figure out which. He stood up, made his way out onto the deck, and watched as his castle edged closer.

The muttering vampires were drowned out by the crashing water, and as Alucard glanced down at the waters, he caught a glimpse of Drac's shimmering blue scales. Who would look after his dragon now that Rodney was gone? Who would look after Elvin's kitten? And who would look after his homeland once he was gone, too? He wouldn't be in Dor-Sanguis much longer, he was sure. Damien was more than likely to send him elsewhere to work alone, and he was certain that Damien would never make him work alongside someone else ever again.

He took his eyes off the water and stared at his castle as the docks edged closer.

"You're Aleksei, right?" someone then asked.

Alucard took his eyes off the castle and glanced at the tall, blonde-haired vampire standing beside him. He frowned in disinterest and looked back out at his castle. "Obviously," he mumbled. Why did these people always want to talk to him like he was their friend?

"I'm Vespin, somewhat good friends with Ben. He says you might have work for us. I'd rather do something than sit around in some city—no offence."

He didn't care. "Talk to Ben about zhat," he grumbled, walking off.

The Vampire Lord made his way up onto the forecastle deck, rested his arms on the fence, and glared ahead. He waited while the ship halted, listening as Ben and two other vampires docked the boat. Usually, Alucard found himself with many things to think about and consider. But right now, his mind was blank. Zalith was gone—he'd never see him again, and the way Zalith said he'd be back hurt Alucard deeply. He *wouldn't* be back. Their farewell was the last they would ever share.

As Ben led the vampires off the ship, Alucard turned around and walked down to the docks. He followed silently behind them, heading towards the city. What would he do with the rest of his night? Continue to follow Ben, help him house the vampires? No, that was Ben's job, not his. Tobias wanted to meet for a drink—he could always do that. As annoying as that werewolf could be, the sound of company was a rather inviting one. If he were to dwell alone for the rest of the night, he was sure he'd sink deeper into his depression. All he'd be able to think about was Zalith, how he sorely wished they didn't have to say goodbye, and how empty and pointless his life would be now that the demon was gone. He didn't want to do that to himself.

So, he broke off from the group and headed towards the forest, hoping to find Tobias in the same place his pack always was. But his ethos was weakened; the portal was still affecting him despite the fact that he'd only transported nine vampires. However, he had enough to morph into a melanistic fox and scurried through the forest.

When he came close to the tree line, he scanned the opening ahead with his eyes. The same quiet folk music carried on the light breeze; each of the caravans had lights lit within, and some had small campfires burning outside with either two or three people sitting around them with drinks.

Morphing out of his fox form, Alucard stepped out into the glade and made his way towards the only caravan with its door open. Once he reached it, he knocked and stepped back, waiting. It didn't take long for the shuffling inside to result in Tobias' appearance. He stepped outside and greeted Alucard with a bright smile, clapping his hands together, standing in nothing but torn, black ripped-at-the-knee jeans.

"Sup, man? Come for that drink?" he asked.

Alucard looked around for a moment with a hesitant look on his face. But he soon shrugged and looked back at Tobias. "I guess so," he muttered.

"Sweet. I know this pretty little bar in—"

"No," Alucard interjected. "No bars, I'd vather just…stay 'ere," he said, not at all interested in sitting in some ram-packed tavern surrounded by bumbling, screaming idiots.

Tobias nodded and dragged his hand over the back of his neck. "Yeah, sure thing, man. You want in here or out there?" he asked, pointing his thumb back at his caravan.

"Outside," he grumbled, not having failed to have noticed the two black-haired women sleeping side by side in Tobias' bed—two of the four sisters he brought to Elvin's party.

He held up his thumbs. "Gotcha, man. I'll be right out," he said, disappearing back into the caravan.

The vampire turned around and walked a short distance from the caravan, staring into the darkness of the forest. He felt himself almost cringe listening to Tobias mutter sweet nothings to the girls in his bed, telling them he'd be back for them—he wouldn't. Everyone knew that Tobias never slept with the same woman twice. But it wasn't Alucard's business, nor did he care to tell the girls Tobias had pretty much used them. He didn't care.

"How'd it go with the not-boyfriend, huh?" Tobias called, heading over to Alucard with two beers in his right hand.

Alucard turned to face him. "Vhy do you sleep vith so many vomen, Tobias?" he asked with an unintentional condescending look on his face.

But Tobias didn't take offence. "I mean…I dunno. Looking for the one, I guess," he said with a shrug, handing the vampire one of the bottles. He then led the way over to the quietly flowing river. "Something to pass the time sometimes, too, not gonna lie. Like…nah, I don't think you'd get it—no offence."

"Enlighten me," Alucard said, stopping in front of the river as Tobias did.

Slumping down, resting his arms on his knees, Tobias said, "At first, y'know, I kinda thought it was just outta boredom. I was some young stud, getting all the girls." He grinned, watching Alucard as he slowly sat on the grass beside him. "But then I kinda figured I was just looking for the right babe. Either that or I kinda got addicted to the game. Either way, I feel like it's all some path to me finally settling down."

With a frown on his face, Alucard took his eyes off Tobias and looked at the river.

"Why you ask?" Tobias questioned, using his hands to open both beers.

"Is zhat vhat 'appens?" he asked, taking the bottle from Tobias. "Do you just…vind somevone, spend a little time vith zhem, and move on to somevone else—vorever until you vind zhe vight vone?"

"I mean…nah—me, personally, yeah. But like…some other people are lucky and find the right gal right away—or…dude," he said with a smile, tapping the neck of his bottle onto Alucard's. He took a sip, sighed, and looked back at the vampire. "Something happen with you and the demon?" he asked with a concerned expression.

Staring down at his drink, Alucard shrugged. "I zon't know."

"You guys… fight? Break up or… what?"

"Ve vere never veally togezzer," he said sadly. "Ve vere just… 'eading tovards someving, I guess. But I ended vhatever zhat vas."

Tobias frowned, sipping from his drink again. "You like… cut it off?"

"I 'ad to," he uttered, setting his eyes back on the river.

"Why? If you got scared, that's a natural thing, man, especially if it's your first-*ever* relationship. He probably gets it, so if you're worried about him forgetting about you, don't. From what I seen, he's into you like crazy," he said enthusiastically. "Sleep on it or something; talk to him tomorrow. That's kinda what happens with these things— but couples should always talk to each other. Like me and Mary—god was she—"

"I zon't vant to 'ear about your conquests," Alucard dismissed. He then looked at the forest beside them and frowned sullenly. "Is not like zhat. I can never see 'im again, and I zon't know vhere to go now. Do you just… vorget about zhe vings you veel vor somevone over time?" he asked, glancing at Tobias. "Do zhe vings you veel just… go avay?"

Tobias sighed heavily and took several gulps from his bottle. "I mean… personally, not really. I've only ever really loved one chick for real—that shit don't leave you, period. If you really love someone, those kinda feelings just don't fuck off. You think about them constantly, even when you try not to. Even when you're having the goddamn time of your life with someone else, you still sit there and think, 'damn, I really fucking wish she was here instead.' It sucks, man. You can tell yourself you're over her, you can bed as many hot as all hell chicks as you want, but you ain't ever forgetting *her*. That shit sticks like fucking blood on white, man. Ain't going anywhere anytime soon," he lamented.

Alucard frowned despondently and looked down at the grass. He asked himself before if what he felt for Zalith was love. Was it? Everything Tobias said made some sort of sense. But Alucard still wasn't sure. It didn't even matter now, did it? Zalith was gone. Alucard would have to move on.

He didn't want to share that with Tobias, but he didn't want their conversation to end, either. So, he asked him, "Who did you love?"

Tobias looked hesitant; a tormented look sat on his scruffy face. "Ana Reiss," he said as he smiled sadly. "Amazing, talented girl. Knew her before I became a wolf; she worked in the relief clinic with me. We'd go to the same ugly little café every Thursday 'cause it was the place we first met. We'd get the same tea—shit tasted like dirt water, but that didn't matter. The memory was what mattered. And we liked the little old lady who ran the place; always gave us an extra cookie. You ever had a cookie, man?"

"No," Alucard admitted.

He guided his hand over the grass and said, "Ana used to love 'em."

"Vhat 'appened?"

"Well, war happened, man. Everyone lost someone. *I* lost Ana. After I became a wolf, I got all these weird instincts, especially when I became an Alpha. I didn't spare her a thought until I found myself leading this pack. I thought this was what I wanted, you know? To be at the top, to be in charge, to rule a little bit of the world. But it ain't. Not that I don't appreciate what you've done for me, not that at all. Sometimes, I just sit here, and I realize…you think you want the world when really you just wanna be a part of someone else's world."

He paused and looked up at the stars, clearly trying to keep a straight face.

Tobias continued, "I'd do anything to see Ana again. I'd give this all up in a heartbeat. But she's gone, and I'll never see her again. I'll never…hear her, feel her—she's just…nowhere," he said sullenly. "Can't feel her, can't talk to her; it's like she just…went. Is there even anything after this, man?" he asked, looking back over at Alucard. "After living?"

Alucard thought to himself for a few moments, trying to remain on the subject Tobias threw his way to keep himself from sinking into his own despairing thoughts.

The vampire shrugged and looked down at his untouched drink. "Zhere are so many stories—each Numen-vocused veligion 'as zheir own. Of course, zhis land's main veligion vocuses on zhe Demiurge. Zhey believe in 'eaven and 'ell. If you praise Levoldus all your life, if you're a good little 'uman, you get to go to 'eaven, and 'ell if you're bad," he mocked.

"Sounds like you don't believe that horseshit."

"Do you?"

"Nah. Also sounds like you know—I mean, you're the son of Satan, right? Surely, *you* must know what happens to us after we die."

The vampire glanced at him. "Can you 'andle zhe truth?"

"Try me," Tobias said, smirking. "Unless…you just…well, only tell me if there's something and not just an end."

"Zhere's someving. Zhere's a place called Nirvana. Vithin Nirvana is purgatory. Grim veapers guide zhe souls of zhe dead zhere vhere Arbiters judge zhem and decide vhether zhey are sent to zhe Undervorld to suffer vor eternity or sent back to zhe vorld to live again—veincarnation, zhey call it," he explained.

"Shit…" Tobias drawled and sipped from his drink. "How are people judged? Like…what do you have to have done to be sent to the Underworld?"

"If I ever go zhere, I'll be sure to ask," Alucard mumbled.

Tobias then laughed and downed the rest of his drink.

Amused, Alucard smiled slightly. But then he looked back down at his drink. "I zon't vink I'll ever go zhere."

"Course not," Tobias agreed, placing his empty bottle on the grass. "You'll live forever, right? Hey, maybe you can come find me when I reincarnate, have me work for you again, huh?"

"You von't vemember me," Alucard said. "Veincarnation is a new life—you become a new person entirely. You could 'ave lived vive or six lives bevore zhis vone and not even know."

He scoffed. "Yeah, but you could make me remember, right?"

"Zoesn't vork like zhat. Vonce you're gone, you're gone. Is your soul zhat comes back, but not as you—as somevone new."

Tobias sighed deeply and stared into the river. "Don't people say it's your soul that makes you who you are, though? I mean…what about you and your past life, huh? I bet you were still some awesome leader before you became this," he said with a smirk, looking Alucard up and down.

Alucard smirked slightly. "I 'ave alvays been me."

"Huh?"

"I zon't 'ave a soul," he revealed. "None of zhe Numen do. Vonce I am gone, I am gone. Vell…maybe."

"You don't…got a soul? How's that work? Why? What happens if you get dead, man?"

The vampire shrugged. "I zon't know," he admitted. "Maybe I'll vind out vone day. All I know is zhe only ving zhat can kill a Numen permanently is anozzer Numen. Zhey sort of…eat each ozzer," he said with a slight laugh. "Ve are…vorever, but only vonce. If ve die, zhat's zhe end of our vorever."

Tobias frowned, nodding. "Dark."

Alucard shrugged. "A necessary sacrivice to make zhe Numen as untouchable as zhey are."

"So…untouchable as in like…immortal?"

"Not me. But zhe Numen, to an extent."

Nodding, Tobias looked back over at the river. "I mean, it's not surprising. They *are* gods, after all. But, if *you're* a god's kid, don't that make *you* a god too? Or a like…lesser…god?"

"No," Alucard said. "Vell…I zon't know. I zon't veally care."

"Makes sense," Tobias said, smirking. "What would you do if *you* were one of those big-shot Numen guys?"

What *would* he do if he were a Numen? He stared into the slowly flowing water, thinking to himself. What would he do if he had all the power in the world? What would he do if he wasn't bound by Damien's rules? By the laws of the world he lived in? The body he was trapped in?

"I know what I'd do," Tobias said. "I'd bring Ana back for starters, and then…well…I guess that's all I really want. A world without war would be nice, too."

"If I vere a Numen," Alucard said slowly. "I vink…I'd kill zhe ozzers."

Tobias scoffed and looked around unsurely. "Uh…why?"

"Zhey're tyrants. Zhey aren't gods, zhey aren't vulers. Zhey zon't care vhat 'appens to zhe people who live in zhe vorlds zhey created. All zhey do is vight amongst vone anozzer; zoesn't matter who suffers or dies in zheir vake. A god should be protecting zhe land zhey own, zhe people zhey made; zheir people shouldn't be slaves to zhem. Zhey vill continue to vight vone anozzer, people vill continue to die, and zhey von't care. If I vere a Numen, I'd vemove zhose who see zhese vorlds as playgrounds. Is vine vor a god to be governing, to be disciplinary—zhere are vules vor a veason. But zhe Numen zon't vork like zhat. I'd change zhat, just as I'm trying to vebuild my empire, and turn zhis vorld back into a warless place," he explained.

Tobias had a bewildered look on his face. "Fuck, man…that's some real shit. You really got goals, huh? I mean, I've known that, yeah, but like…damn. If I were a god, I'd really only be doing shit for myself, looking at it now. You're all about the people, yeah?"

"Sometimes."

"I mean…can you?"

"Can I vhat?"

"Kill those Numen guys?"

"I alveady said," Alucard muttered, glaring into the river. "Only anozzer Numen can kill a Numen."

Tobias shrugged and looked down at the grass. "Yeah, I guess that's why you didn't fight back against that guy yesterday, huh?"

A despondent frown clung to Alucard's face.

"What was that, man? What…happened? I ain't ever seen you—"

"Ve're not talking about zhat," Alucard denied, glaring at him.

Tobias held up his hands. "Yeah, sorry. Sure thing, man."

Alucard then sighed, handed Tobias his untouched drink, and stood up. "I should 'ead 'ome. I'll probably 'ave someving to do tomorrow."

"You sure, man?" Tobias asked, also standing up.

The vampire nodded and turned around, heading for the forest.

"All right, well, I'll catch you later then," he called, waving.

Then, Alucard walked silently through the forest. He didn't want to let his sullen thoughts consume him, but he could feel them creeping, and the harder he tried to fight, the more his heart hurt. If he were a Numen, he could be with Zalith.

But there was no use thinking about it. He wasn't a Numen, and he couldn't be with Zalith.

Chapter Eighty-One

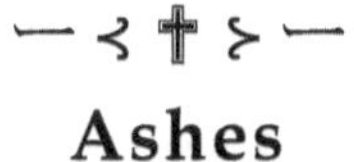

Ashes

| **Alucard** |

Alucard made his way through the dark forest in his fox form. Although it wasn't his fault, Tobias didn't help him feel any better. He just couldn't stop thinking about Zalith.

He tried to focus on what Damien might have planned for him instead. However, the further away he got from Tobias' camp, the stronger the smell of smoke became. At first, he thought it was the fires the pack were sitting around, but the camp was far behind him, too far for the smell to be as strong as it was.

It was coming from the direction he was heading in. Was the city in flames? He morphed into his owl form and raced up until he broke free of the trees; he set his eyes on the huge blur of smoke ahead. It wasn't coming from the city but the direction of his manor, the orange flames building higher and higher into the sky as each moment passed.

He might not have much ethos left, but if his home was on fire, he had to put it out as fast as he could manage. So he morphed into vermillion smoke and raced through the night sky, arriving at his burning home in moments. He returned to his usual form, stumbled to a halt in front of the fountain, and stared in horror. His *entire* house was engulfed in bright orange flames; every window was smashed, and the fire spewed out from within. Parts of the building had already caved in, Sebastian was dead, and Alucard had no idea what to do.

Why? Who? He thought about silencing the flames, but trying to save it would be futile. The smoke was so thick that he could barely see a few feet ahead of him, and the smell of ash was overbearing. But it wasn't as overbearing as the thought of losing everything inside. Not just his possessions, but the memories the place held, too. It was like a part of his heart had been torn away.

It was all gone, and there wasn't a thing he could do. And that was the least of his problems.

The entire area around him suddenly filled with quiet, low growls. Alucard took his eyes off his house and looked around slowly. He watched the shimmering golden eyes of werewolves appear through the smoke; there were over four dozen of them, their black silhouettes dancing through the murk as they snickered like hyenas, taunting him while he turned again and again, unsure of where they might strike from.

He scowled and gritted his teeth in anger. *Werewolves* did this? He clenched his fists, and he turned around, counting every wolf as they revealed themselves. There were now at least a hundred—but that didn't unsettle him. All of his anger, hurt, and pain—it morphed into something dreadful. He had no more patience, no more room for chances. The werewolves had pushed him way beyond his limits, and now? They'd taken one of the last things he cared about. His ability to grant mercy withered. His wish for peace disappeared. It was time to kill without hindrance. To kill until every single wolf in this place and beyond was dead.

But he had no weapons. He didn't need weapons; he had his hands, and they were all he needed. They were all he ever needed. He turned around and set his eyes on his first target—but the wolves were still lingering inside the smoke, circling him almost as if they were waiting for an order. But who was leading them?

Something came at him, whistling through the tense air—he swung around and snatched a steel arrow in his right hand, glaring in the direction it had come from. For a moment, the smoke thinned, revealing the outline of a long-haired, pear-shaped woman with a marksman at her side, who lowered his bow.

A distraction? Is that what the wolves were? And an *arrow*? He frowned and glanced at the arrow in his hand, but its head wasn't steel like its body. It shimmered silver. With an irritated snarl, he threw the arrow into the smoke, and as the yelp of a wolf echoed from within, he almost laughed in amusement.

"Aleksei!" came a hauntingly familiar voice.

The vampire shuddered and froze where he stood, slowly looking back over his shoulder. He set his eyes on the woman as she made her way out of the smoke; her eyes lemon-yellow, her hair shimmering blonde and a twisted smile clung to her face— her *teary* face. Her cheeks were red, her skin was wet—had she been crying? She sniffled, dragged her hand over her eyes, and scowled at him.

And that was when the wolves attacked. Simultaneously, every wolf in his smoky grounds charged at him—he had to think fast and move just as quickly. The first wolf pounced at him, but he swung around and smashed his fist into its face, the creature's head tearing clean off its body before it dropped to the ground. He then turned around and grabbed the next by its throat, but two more jumped at him as he grabbed it. He tore out the wolf's throat, threw its corpse at one of the jumping wolves, and caught the other before it could sink its teeth into his arm. He gripped its muzzle in one hand and bottom jaw in his other, tearing the beast horizontally in half.

They kept coming—and he kept fighting while Ada watched. It wasn't until he'd killed close to a third of her wolves that she held up her hand, calling off the attack. Before Alucard could recover from his last kill, the woman flung herself forward and wrapped her arms around the blood-smothered vampire. He snarled in revolt and shoved her back, reaching to grab and kill her, but she was a lot faster than any other wolf.

"Why do you continue to break my heart, Aleksei?" she sniffled, slouching forward, tears streaming down her face as the wolves backed off into the smoke.

He had no intention to entertain her estranged antics. His house was in flames, his friends were dead, and he was alone. He'd already experienced too much pain for one night, so much that he couldn't maintain his composure. He was angry—furious. All he wanted to do was kill. It was the only thing that took the pain of losing Zalith away. It was the only thing he could focus on.

Ada caused him so much annoyance, so much inconvenience, and he was finished with her. He wasted no time. He reached forward to snatch her throat, but his weariness made him slower than usual. Ada grabbed his wrist and stared sullenly into his irritated eyes.

"You would leave me?" she asked, tilting her head to the left. "You would…let someone harm me?"

The vampire had no idea what she was talking about, and he didn't give a shit. He pulled his wrist free and prepared to attack again—but Ada sprung forward, and before Alucard even knew what her intentions were, she impaled a silver stake through his chest, through his heart, and as it pieced out through his back, he grunted and gagged in both confusion and agony. His blood sprayed to the ground and oozed through his teeth as he gritted them in struggle. How could he have been so careless?

"You made me do this, Aleksei!" Ada cried, moving her face just an inch away from his. "You made this happen!"

He stared into her tormented eyes, gripping her wrists, trying to pull the stake from his body, but his strength was withering at an alarming rate.

Sniffling with tears streaming down her face, Ada started twisting the stake, a crazed laugh escaping her stifled breaths as Alucard yelled in anger and torment. He fell back, so she fell with him, and as his back hit the scorched ground, she laid on top of him. "We could have been together forever, Aleksei," she cried, using her right hand to stroke the side of his bloody face, still holding the stake with her left. "We could have ruled the world!"

Staring up at her, Alucard snarled and gritted his teeth. But then he laughed a strained, mocking laugh.

Distraught, Ada scowled and twisted the stake harshly. "Did you really think you could get away from me? Did you think some demon would save you? You're mine, Aleksei, you always have been! If I can't have you in life, then we shall die together!"

she sang, sitting up, straddling his lap as he lay there, helpless. She inhaled excitedly and looked back down at his agonized face. "We'll be lovers in our next lives, Aleksei!"

He had nothing to say. He stared up at what he could see of the sky, feeling the life fading from his body. But he didn't care. Any point he thought he had for living was gone. His empire? What was the point? That wouldn't fill the hole in his life—in his heart. He knew what he wanted, what he *needed*, and he couldn't have it. So what point was there in life? How could he have thought he could go on knowing that Zalith would be with someone else? How could he continue living and pretending that his life wasn't some fucked up, miserable, useless, pointless waste? He couldn't. Zalith made him feel so many things he didn't want to lose, but Zalith was gone, and the things he made him feel went with him.

As Ada stroked the side of his face again, he took his eyes off the sky and looked at her revolting face. It would be *her* who killed him, wouldn't it? He wasn't surprised. She tore down his life's work, and now she'd torn away what was left of his life. And that was okay. He felt content. He'd die, and he'd no longer have to suffer. It was a strange feeling—to be so welcoming of death. But to die sounded much more inviting than continuing to live his life under Damien's thumb—to live in misery. Dying was an escape, one he so sorely needed his entire life.

But he'd not break free tonight.

The sound of battling beasts echoed around him. He kept his eyes on Ada, watching as a confused, almost terrified look appeared on her face. He couldn't hear her voice, his weakness numbing his senses, but her lips uttered the word 'demon' several times.

Zalith?

She screamed her orders, the look of horror on her face increasing as the smell of blood became a miasma in moments. She soon let go of the stake, stood up, and backed off. She yelled angrily and transformed into her wolf form. But before she could ready herself, a dark blur raced over Alucard and smashed into her.

Ada tumbled across the scorched grass, her golden coat smothered in blood and ash as she dug her claws into the ground and slowed her momentum. She then snarled, stood up on her hind legs, and set her eyes on her attacker. Not too far from where Alucard lay stood another werewolf, his dark coat smothered in the blood of the wolves he'd slaughtered.

While his vision blurred and his head spun, Alucard watched Ada sprint at the wolf, and they engaged in a bloody battle. They sunk their teeth into one another, slashing their claws, tearing huge wounds into each other's flesh. Neither of them yielded, even when the ground around them was drenched in blood.

But when the dark wolf smashed his right foot into her stomach, she tumbled back and hit the manor's surrounding wall. With all her wolves dead, she was best to run, and that was exactly what she did. She snarled and sprinted on all fours, disappearing into the smoke before the other wolf had a chance to attack again.

It was then that the wolf transformed into a man. He hurried to where Alucard lay, dropping to the ground beside him. But Alucard couldn't make out his face. The vampire groaned painfully when he pulled the weapon from his chest, and as agony burned through his body, Alucard snatched the man's arm.

"Aleksei?" the man's distorted voice asked.

Alucard felt *anger*. He wanted to die. Why couldn't he just die? All of this would be over if he could slip away.

But his fury quickly withered. He'd lost so much blood, and as his instincts began taking over, all he could concentrate on was the sound of a single beating heart. His hunger was taking control the same way it always did when he was inches from death. Did he want to let his hunger save him?

No.

What was the point? Why would he want to return to a life of misery and suffering? He had *no one* to return to. The struggle to rebuild his empire had been for nothing. Damien would send him away for so many years, and what he'd come to rebuild would crumble again. Elvin was dead; the boy he hoped to give a better life after he'd all but caused the death of his parents. He could lay there and tell himself he only saved that boy because he might have been useful, but he did it because he wanted to. Because he wanted to do some good. But that was over. His home was in flames. He had nothing left. No one left. Zalith was gone—the only person who made him feel *alive*. He'd never see him again, so why live?

He didn't have a choice. His body was acting on its own—it was almost as if he wasn't *allowed* to die. Alucard couldn't stop himself. He couldn't stop his hands from gripping hold of the man who pulled the stake from his heart; he couldn't stop himself from savagely sinking his fangs into his throat. It wasn't until the disgusting taste of wolf blood hit his tongue that he knew he'd lost yet another person he cared about.

But he didn't stop. He *couldn't* stop. Tobias' confused, struggled voice echoed through his head—he tried to push Alucard away, but the vampire pinned him to the ground so mercilessly that he heard the man's bones break in his grip.

And he still didn't stop; he drained every ounce of blood from Tobias' body. He scowled in agony, aware of what he was doing, but he had no control. He took the life of the last person he could rely on. The life of a man who'd done nothing but pledge loyalty to him. Tobias was his friend—his *best* friend. And now, he was dead, and this time, there was no one to blame but himself.

It took too long for control to return to him. He pulled his fangs from Tobias' cold neck and exhaled in dismay, letting go of his friend's broken, bruised wrists. And he stared at him. He stared in dread, in horror, in *pain* at the lifeless face of the only person he had left. His entire body ached, not because he'd almost died, but because he killed someone else he cared for. Tobias had come and saved his life, and all Alucard could offer in return was a meaningless death.

Meaningless. That's all any of this was. His life, his goals, his dreams—everything he had ever done and would ever do. Meaningless. *He* was meaningless. What was he even doing? Why did he do any of the things he did? No one cared. No one appreciated it. What was he but a meaningless creature among billions of other meaningless creatures?

He was Lucifer's son. Like his father, he was a killer—a heartless murderer who didn't deserve something as precious as a friend—as *love*. Why did he ever think he could have anything so *human*? He couldn't. He wasn't deserving of it. He'd been sent to kill this world, and now that he realized it, he felt something break inside himself.

It broke his will; it withered like ash in the wind. His morals burned like the house behind him. He stared at Tobias, his pain and sorrow shrinking into something quite like pity. Whatever compassion he might have possessed was banished like a demon on holy ground. Anything human about him—it died, leaving him with nothing but anger; screaming, scratching, burning rage so potent that it was like a storm of hellish fire smouldering within him, begging desperately to be set free.

He didn't deny it. He sat there, staring at the lifeless face of his friend. His hell-fiery eyes burned devilishly, his wounds healing as an ominous shroud of darkness spread across the ground like the shadows of creatures unseen. The world around him tensed up in fear of his presence, the look on his face so vacant that it was as though emotion was a myth.

And then...the voices.

The whispers.

The screaming.

The cries of pain and agony.

And that face. Alucard might have sworn it was Damien...staring into his soul, encouraging him to let go, and he continued to do just that.

Staring, listening, waiting. His rage was already so overbearing that he couldn't do anything but sit there. The darkness poured into his shadow, the voices becoming louder, edging him into something quite like madness. But the madness was like a home. It felt inviting—it felt...right. Whatever this was, whatever was awakening inside him, he didn't have the strength nor the desire to deny it.

Silence.

The vampire stared.

The smoke around him began to settle.

The raging fire which consumed his home calmed.

But the fire within him had only just begun to burn.

"Aleksei?"

Alucard slowly turned his head and set his eyes on Ben. He had a mortified look on his face, waiting while his troupe of vampires searched the mounds of dead wolves for anything that might still be alive. But everything was dead.

Everything but the one thing that should be.

Wherever she had gone, wherever she might think she was going, Alucard would find her. He would find her, he would kill her—no, that was too simple. She'd taken enough from him—*too* much. He'd find her, he'd find the people *she* loved, and he'd make her watch as he killed each and every one of them. Then—only *then* would he kill her.

Wordlessly, he stood up. For a moment, he stared down at Tobias' body, but there was nothing to wait for. He stepped forward, ignoring the concerned voices of the vampires around him, even when they followed. Alucard had made his choice, and nothing would keep him from doing what he decided.

He scowled, he gritted his teeth, and with a look of murder in his fiery eyes, he burst into vermillion smoke, racing into the night sky and through it faster than he ever had before. Nothing but murder was on his mind—nothing but rage, anger, revenge. Ada should have died so long ago, and it was long overdue. He caught the bitch's scent, and he followed it to a small cottage in the hills. He didn't know if she was inside, but this was where the trail ended, and so, he morphed out of the smoke, and with an enraged, agonized yell, he launched a devastating storm of blood-red fire down onto the cottage.

He landed on the ground, watching as *she* and her brood fled from the burning building, screaming in fear. The vampire wasted not a moment. He reached her in the blink of an eye, appearing before her so suddenly that her glare of shock and horror was unlike anything anyone might have seen. He snatched her throat and slammed her down into the ground—he broke her left leg, her right leg, her arms, and her back, making it impossible for her to heal normally. And without hesitation, he began his rampage of merciless murder.

First, he grabbed Ada's youngest son; he tore the kid's head from his body, making sure Ada was watching. As she screamed in horror—as she *begged* for mercy—he appeared before the next child, who tried to flee into the woods. He grabbed her by her hair, and as she screamed in terror, he tore her head from her body with his teeth and threw her corpse towards her paralyzed mother.

Ada wailed in mortification, shaking her head, tears streaming down her face, continuing to beg as she watched Alucard set his eyes on her eldest son. The boy transformed, but before he had a chance to attack, the vampire reached him, tore out his eyes, and grabbed him by his right wrist. He lifted him and flung him towards his mother, and when he hit the floor, he tried to drag himself away. Alucard left him, seeing to the last of Ada's daughters. The girl stood there, having watched the whole thing, the torment in her eyes near to that of her mother. Alucard didn't care that she had no idea what to do. He grabbed her neck, pulled her closer, and once she was finally able to scream, he gripped her jaw and tore it from her face.

In mere minutes, Ada's entire family was dead. Her entire bloodline had ended, and Alucard wasn't yet done.

He dropped the girl's corpse, turned around, and set his eyes on Ada. She lay there, wailing and bawling—unable to move, unable to heal. She didn't deserve relief, and Alucard would make sure she'd never get it.

Still with his vacant stare, Alucard transformed into his wingless, dragon-like true form. He prowled on all fours to where Ada lay, dragging his spiked, scaled tail along the grass. Ada stared up at him, surrounded by the corpses of her family; her son was still alive, crawling away—but not anymore. Alucard kept his eyes on her, and with a flick of his right talon, several shards of black crystal arose from the ground and impaled the wolf's body, severing his head in an explosion of blood and fur. Now, she was the only one left.

Ada screamed in desperation, crying over at her dead son. She had no one. She had nothing. And that was the type of pain Alucard wished her to feel—*forever*. He'd never forget, so why should she be granted release? He snatched her throat, and as he stood on his hind legs, he lifted and held her up so that she was at eye level with him. She choked, she whimpered, and she cried like the pathetic, weak creature Alucard had always known she was. And now, she'd know what it felt like to suffer a life immortal.

He widened his monstrous jaws, and before she could scream a final time, he snapped them shut over her head. But it wasn't her blood he was taking; he took her soul, her life force—her *everything*. Forever she would live in a realm quite like hell, a place Alucard had only just been made aware of. It was *his* place. It was *his* hell. His father had such a place, so why shouldn't he? Whether it had always been there or whether he created it in his moment of awakening, he didn't know, but it didn't matter. It existed, and that was where he would send Ada to suffer for as long as he might live.

He dropped her corpse to the ground, and with no sound at all, he morphed back to his usual self.

It was over.

Wasn't it?

The silent sky was scathed by the crashing crimson light of lightning and a rumble of thunder so loud that the ground shook beneath him. But he didn't fret. He stood there in the light of the burning cottage, staring at the massacre he'd so profoundly enjoyed—but the vacant stare on his face didn't reflect the joy he felt in murder. As he heard the creature approach behind him, he slowly turned and faced him.

Damien, for the first time, possessed a look of worry. "Aleksei…" he said slowly, approaching the blood-smothered vampire.

Alucard waited, staring at him, not a single word escaping his silent breath.

"Are you going to tell me what happened here?" Damien asked calmly, slowly placing his hand on Alucard's shoulder.

The vampire looked up at him like a child without a voice.

"What did you see?" he asked with a concerned frown on his face.

"You," he answered.

"Me?" he asked in slight surprise. "That *is* peculiar."

Alucard stared at him, unsure of what to say.

"Aleksei," he said with what looked like a threatened look on his face. "Listen to me."

He waited.

"Something has happened to you—something… dangerous. If you don't let me help you, Lucifer will find you—and he will kill you. What you are experiencing is the same disease he suffers from—you don't want to suffer, do you?"

Alucard *didn't* want to suffer. He wanted it all to be over.

"I'm going to take it away, but you have to let me."

The vampire didn't hesitate.

Damien placed his other hand on Alucard's shoulder, staring down at him. "Repeat the words I tell you, and then you'll be just fine," Damien instructed.

Staring up at him, Alucard began to feel confused. But he willfully did as Damien told him. The Daegelus uttered a few True Speech words, and Alucard repeated them. As he did, the rage burning inside him began to simmer down. His ache to murder and destroy started weakening. Everything that just happened… the sense it made began to disappear. It made no sense… none of it. What happened? Why did he murder Ada's entire family so viciously?

"Aleksei?" Damien asked, taking his hands off his shoulders.

The vampire flinched in horror, his fear of Damien returning in his rage's absence.

"This is what happens," Damien said with a condescending scowl. "You get too close to people… and they die. I taught you that the only thing you need in this world or any other is *me*. *I* came to save you from your father's fate. *I* will always be here to save you, Aleksei. Do you see that now? After all this death, do you finally understand?"

Did he?

He stared up at Damien, but the only person he could think about was Zalith. Where was *Zalith*? Why wasn't *he* here? Alucard couldn't be angry. He told Zalith to stay away, and he was doing just that. And Damien was right. *He* was here. *He* had come and pulled him out of whatever murderous trance he sank into. Damien had been and always would be protecting him from Lucifer. Damien was the only permanent person in his life—his meaningless, pointless life. What else did he have left now?

Damien. He had Damien. He would always have Damien, and Damien would always have him. But that was okay. That was the way things had been and would be. Why deviate? Trying to escape that fate only caused him a whole world of agony. It was high time he accepted the fact that he belonged where he was—in Damien's grip, under his rule. Where would he be without him, after all?

"Come, Aleksei," Damien said with a smile, placing his arm around the vampire's shoulders and escorting him forward. "Come home."

Home. Where was home now? Where it had always been. With Damien in the Underworld. Alucard didn't refuse. Where else would he go? He followed Damien without hesitation. He was tired. He wanted to rest. He wanted to sleep. And he wanted to forget the pain. The sorrow. The *agony*. Where better to do that than in the company of someone who taught him how irrelevant emotion was?

As the fire died down behind them, both the vampire and the Daegelus disappeared back up into the night sky, leaving the world that had caused Alucard such pain behind one last time. Perhaps this time, he'd not have to return. Perhaps now…his place was somewhere else.

NOSFERATU
Numen Chronicles | Volume One

Arc Five

— † —

Farewell

Chapter Eighty-Two

— ⸜ † ⸝ —

Absent

| Ben, 1 week later |

Ben lay on his back, comfortable but unable to settle in his bed beside Lillian in their dark, lightless bedroom. A week passed since Alucard vanished, and he was worried about him.

He'd gone to Alucard's burning manor to find The Vampire Lord with Tobias' dead body beneath him; Alucard had killed him, obviously, and it unnerved Ben. He saw his new boss kill *two* of the people closest to him, and he couldn't help but wonder: who was next? He didn't even know where Alucard was. The Vampire Lord had taken off in what seemed to be a fit of rage, disappearing into the night sky, never to be seen again. He'd be back, though. Ben was sure of it.

Or at least he *hoped* so.

Lillian rolled over to face him, and when she noticed that he was awake, she frowned and shuffled closer. "This is the third night this week I've woken to you just staring up at the ceiling," she said with concern in her voice. "What's wrong?"

Staring at the white ceiling above, he sighed quietly. Why *did* Alucard's disappearance worry him so much? Was it because no one was around to keep things running? Or was it because he was afraid he might be next to die? Or…because he considered Alucard his friend? Tobias was dead, and Ben was sure he was Alucard's *best* friend. That must have hurt him—so much that Ben found himself worrying for Alucard's wellbeing…wherever he was.

"Ben?" Lillian insisted, sitting up to look down at him.

He took his eyes off the ceiling and looked at her worried face. "I'm fine," he said with a smile. "I'm just worried about Aleksei. Things are going to go to shit if he doesn't show up soon."

She sighed and laid back down. "I don't know why you sit up all night worrying about someone who would kill you without a second thought. He's probably with Zalith somewhere."

"Maybe," he said, looking back up at the ceiling.

"Go back to sleep."

With a quiet sigh, he rolled onto his side, closed his eyes, and did as his wife told him, dismissing his worried thoughts.

He woke later to the sound of birds outside. Usually, he'd be getting out of bed the moment he was awake, but he didn't know what he was supposed to do. His job was complete; all of the vampires had homes. Alucard wasn't around to give him a new job, so all he could do was linger around the house and try his best not to irritate Lillian. But she wasn't beside him; a disappointed frown clung to his face when he looked over his shoulder to see if she was still in the room. She must be downstairs.

Ben climbed out of bed, pulled on the shirt closest to him, and made his way down to the living room, where he found his wife silently reading a novel. "Morning," he called from the doorway, smiling over at her.

She glanced at him and said, "Someone's been trying to get through to you for the last thirty minutes. Three guesses who."

He instantly frowned as he watched her gesture at the lounge, the same lounge he kept his mirror link in. Ben swiftly hurried to the wall-mounted mirror—which was fogged black—and prepared for the irritable remarks he would receive for taking as long as he had to answer.

Without a moment longer of hindrance, he tapped the side of the blackened mirror and watched as it faded to reveal an entirely new room on the other side.

"I'm sorry I didn't come sooner," he insisted, dragging his hand over the back of his neck. "I slept in."

Zalith, who was sitting on the other side of the mirror behind a desk, ignored the vampire and continued writing. So, Ben waited. It wasn't until a few tense moments had passed that the demon put his quill down and glanced at him.

"How is Alucard?" Zalith asked tonelessly.

"Well…he's…missing," he answered worriedly.

A look of both concern and confusion spread across the demon's once emotionless face. "Missing?"

Ben nodded. "About a week's passed. I assume it happened just after we came back from collecting the vampires. I was up in the city, so it took me a while to get there—to his house—and by the time I *did* get there, he'd already killed Tobias and took off into the night. If I didn't know better, I'd say he was off to kill whoever burned his house to the ground."

Zalith frowned, slowly looking back down at the papers spread across his desk. "Do you know who burned his house?"

"No," Ben replied. "But there were werewolf corpses everywhere, so I assume it had something to do with *them*. Revenge for Ada, perhaps?"

"Perhaps," he said, nodding. "I want you to tell me as soon as Alucard gets back," he instructed sternly. "Or if you hear anything of his whereabouts."

Ben nodded. "Yeah, don't worry. I'll let you know."

As his mirror faded back to reflective glass, Ben dragged his hand over his face and sighed heavily. Not even *Zalith* knew where Alucard was. He was still sure that The Vampire Lord would show up eventually, though. He had to…right?

It wasn't until just over a week later that Ben finally received a message from Alucard. He was sitting out on his balcony watching over the bustling city when a half-dead crow descended from the sky and dropped a rolled piece of parchment into his lap.

With a curious frown, he watched the bird disappear and then looked down at the parchment it had more or less thrown at him. His eyes immediately jumped to the name that had signed it, and seeing that it was from Alucard gave him some sort of relief.

Ben,

You need not know where I am, only that I am currently preoccupied with business elsewhere. In my absence, I'd like you to take over and keep things running for me until I return. When that will be, I'm not sure, but it will be someday.

There is an office in the tallest tower of my castle Attila used to use. It is now yours. I have sent a similar message to Dirk, Attila, and my other contacts in the city. They have all been made aware of your new temporary position. If I need anything specific done, I'll contact you again.

Aleksei.

Reading it over a few times, Ben frowned, sighed, and lifted his head to stare back out at the city. He hoped for a little more information, but the letter in his hand seemed to be all he would get. At least he had a new job, something he'd been waiting for. But to take over for Alucard? Could he manage such a thing? He'd have to.

He folded up the paper and tucked it into his back pocket, pondering to himself. He now had his own office; that was rather exciting. But again…to do Alucard's job? He felt anxious, but Alucard wouldn't ask him to do it if he didn't think he was capable. How long would he be in charge, though? He didn't know, but he was strangely nervous but eager to begin.

Without any further hindrance, he stood up and made his way back into his house, preparing to tell Lillian of his new position. He knew she wouldn't be so happy to know he was now running things for Alucard while he dealt with business elsewhere, but how hard could it be? It would probably only be for a few weeks, too. He was ready to start and make the most of being the big boss for once.

But it might not be as excitingly thrilling as he used to think.

Chapter Eighty-Three

— ‹ † › —

Waiting

| **Zalith,** *Eltaria, Decem 6th—4 months later* |

Zalith sat behind a light, tawny wooden desk. He was busy working, holed up in a cramped little bedroom with a small blue couch and a bed, and the white, panelled walls were adorned with needlepoint artwork of flowers and kind-looking animals. This wasn't his décor of choice, but in times such as these, he had to make do with what he was given.

The farmhouse that Zalith found himself in was surrounded by endless golden fields, planted exclusively with something that Zalith didn't have the knowledge to name. A faint wind caused the plants to sway, the surface rippling as though it were an ocean of gold water.

There was a certain serenity to be found in this secluded little farmhouse. Perhaps it was the way the warm sun filtered into the windows, causing the white curtains to become almost sheer in the light—or perhaps it was due to the lack of noise. Aside from the quiet farmer who came by every so often to care for the few animals that still lived in the barn, Zalith and his companion were entirely alone on the property. Either way— even despite the kitschy décor—he felt content.

In his happiness, Zalith's mind drifted to Alucard. He wondered what the vampire was doing right now, pondering about whether or not Alucard ever thought of him in return. It had been four long months since their farewell, a farewell that pained him more than he might have liked to admit at the time. He'd only known the vampire for half a year, and the thought of losing him already caused him a deep heartache. He told Alucard he'd be back for him, that he wouldn't let Damien keep them apart, and he wished to keep to that promise—but he had to be careful.

Alucard said his goodbyes; the vampire tried to send him away to protect him from the Daegelus. Of course, Zalith made sure that Damien *couldn't* kill him. But he still had to be cautious. As much as he wanted to go and find Alucard, as much as he wanted to go to him and save him from Damien's tyranny, he had to make sure that he wasn't as expendable as Damien once said he was. All of Damien's Lilith-descended candidates were dead; all Zalith had to do now was wait until Damien came to tell him he was the last. Only then could he be sure that he wouldn't be killed for being in Alucard's company.

That wasn't the only thing keeping him from finding the vampire, though. In all truth, the demon had no idea *where* he was. A week after their farewell, Zalith contacted Ben and asked him how Alucard was doing, and Ben corresponded with some rather strange news: Alucard disappeared, his house had been burned to the ground, and not one of his friends remained alive. Zalith was sure Damien was involved, and as desperate as he felt to hunt them down—to find Alucard—he couldn't. All he could do was sit around and wait for Ben to tell him that Alucard had returned—if that would ever happen.

Where could he have gone? Why had his manor been destroyed? Something happened, and not knowing cursed Zalith with god-awful angst. The thought of never seeing Alucard again caused him such pain, but the thought of him being dead? The thought of him suffering because of Zalith's choice to reduce the vampires' numbers.... He'd never be able to forgive himself if he was the cause of Alucard's disappearance. As horrifying as such a thought was, however, Zalith felt strangely confident that the vampire *was* alive—he was *somewhere*. Alucard told him before their farewell that Damien would most likely send him off to work elsewhere as soon as the vampire relocation mission was over, and Zalith *hoped* that was the case.

Sighing, Zalith shook his head; he couldn't let himself get carried away by his worried, confounding thoughts. As much as he missed Alucard, as much as he wished he knew where he was and what he was doing...he had work to do.

With a small frown, the demon looked away from the window and to his right, where his little messenger stood on top of the desk, waiting for his instructions. The bipedal, imp-like izuret jiggled its wings, gawping at him with its huge, green eyes. While the creature wasn't necessarily threatening to behold, it was still a demon, and their species had been serving Zalith's family for centuries. Some might say they could be considered something of a pet, but to do so would be an insult. Izurets were much smarter than they looked.

"Let me know when you're ready," Zalith said to the creature as he leaned back in his chair.

The izuret's large ears twitched, and a soft chattering noise left its mouth in confirmation.

Zalith slowly said, "A contact of mine is working on establishing an underground settlement in Siall. I assume that if we play our cards right, he may let us use a portion of that space for your operations. I can send more details if you find yourself interested...." He then looked out of the nearby window, gathering his thoughts before he continued, "Also, tell Baron that I'm tired of waiting; if I don't hear from him by this time next week, then I will send someone to take what is mine. We both know he can be difficult, so if you need to draw blood to get the message across, then I suggest you do so."

With a chirp, the creature nodded.

Finished, Zalith looked down at the creature, and its massive eyes happily returned the glance. "Let me hear it back."

The izuret, which otherwise communicated in a series of light chirps and chatters, opened its mouth and began to speak. With complete ease, the creature repeated the words that Zalith said, and the voice which came from its small mouth sounded identical to his. Zalith nodded as he listened, his eyes drifting out towards the window once more. Once the izuret had finished, it grinned pridefully, revealing a row of sharp, jagged fangs.

"Good. I need this message to go to the usual contact. When do you expect to be there?"

The creature chirped and held up one of its four slender fingers.

"One day?"

It nodded.

"That's fine," Zalith said as he reached down to the bottom drawer of his desk and pulled out a small wooden box.

The creature chattered in anticipation as Zalith lifted off the lid and revealed a small collection of shiny trinkets.

"Here's payment for your last task—you may have one," he said firmly, holding the box out to the tiny demon.

The izuret's fur bristled on its back in excitement. Immediately, the creature's hands ravenously rifled through the box for a few moments, pushing items aside as it searched for something that piqued its interest. It didn't take long for the izuret to narrow down what it wanted; it held a small, smooth, brass knight in one hand and a shiny silver horse in the other. The creature flattened its ears, its eyes darting back and forth between the two items in its hand. With a sad little chirp, its large, shiny eyes sparkling sadly in the sunlight, it looked up at Zalith and clutched the two items to its chest.

With a sigh, Zalith shook his head. "I said one."

The tiny demon chattered sadly to itself as it looked down at the two items. With a gloomy little whine, it placed the knight back in the box and took a step back.

Satisfied that the creature had chosen its prize, Zalith covered up the box and put it back in his drawer. "Do you want me to hold on to it for you? Until you return, of course."

With a sweet little smile, the creature handed the horse off to him. But as its shiny silver legs touched Zalith's palm, the izuret hesitated. It pulled the horse away from the demon's hand, rubbing it lovingly on the side of its face.

Sure that it had changed its mind, Zalith withdrew his hand with a roll of his eyes. "Just don't lose it. I'm not replacing it next time."

The creature nodded in understanding, its large eyes blinking intelligently.

With a silent wave, Zalith dismissed his messenger. Horse in hand, it spread its wings and quickly soared across the room towards the open window. Just as its small body slowly began to disappear into thin air, the door to Zalith's room swung open on its hinges.

Varana stood in the doorway with a tight although casual deep-green linen dress clinging to her body. With a look of disgust on her face, she threw her long, shiny hair behind her shoulders as she watched the izuret disappear. "Honestly, Z, I'm not sure why you keep those things around," she uttered as she approached Zalith's desk.

Zalith was accustomed to having friends in high places, and Varana was no exception. Although the war hadn't ended in their favour, Varana was still the queen of demons and all manner of creatures who bowed to their species. She and Zalith had been close friends for centuries, so it was only natural that Varana had chosen Zalith to latch onto both during and after the war. The woman was absolutely more than capable of taking care of herself, but she always seemed to turn to Zalith for help—even when she didn't necessarily need it.

Varana took a seat on the desk's surface, not particularly mindful of any of the papers she was sitting on. "Why not use something more intimidating than an izuret to send your messages?"

Zalith sighed and pulled a thin book out from underneath her. "They're discrete, they're dangerous, they're fiercely loyal, and they accept anything shiny as payment. What's not to love?"

Varana crossed her legs, the high slit in her dress revealing the pale skin of her leg. "I just think, aesthetically speaking, that they're not sending the right message."

"Well, what do you suggest we use?" Zalith asked her. "A dragon?"

The woman shrugged. "If we have one available, yes."

An amused smile spread across Zalith's face. "We don't," he told her, his dark eyes looking down at the disorganised desk. "Now, if you don't mind...." He tilted his head, indicating that it was best if Varana moved.

The woman huff dramatically and headed to the small couch under the window. With her hand on her forehead, she laid down, the slit in her dress once again revealing her pale, naked leg almost in its entirety.

Zalith rolled his eyes and looked down at his desk, returning to his work.

"How much longer must we stay in this dreadful little farmhouse?" the woman lamented.

The demon sighed; it seemed that all Varana did was complain, no matter what he did to try and accommodate her. When he agreed to stay there, Zalith knew that she wasn't going to like the farmhouse, but they were quickly running out of dignified options when it came to their living arrangement. Zalith was too tired to fight her on these sorts of things; his days of trying to get their lives back in order were far too long to waste time arguing with someone as relentless as Varana.

"If I knew, I'd tell you," he answered.

"This morning, I saw a cow outside of my window, Zalith," the woman said with a scowl. "A cow."

If the demon was meant to feel sorry for her, he couldn't find the energy to do so. There were things after the two demons that were far worse than cows. "Terrible," he uttered.

"And it looked at me, too," Varana whined, her hand still on her forehead. "As though I was just some farm girl who's expected to…brush it, or something—or feed it a potato."

"We won't be staying here permanently," he reminded her. "Instead of pouting, perhaps you should be appreciative that Danford found this house for us in the first place."

She sighed and then fell silent. Zalith watched her close her crimson eyes while she sadly shook her head in complete displeasure. The two demons were used to the finer things in life, Varana especially. The war exposed the woman to parts of society that she was ignorant of and not used to, and even now, she struggled to accept that she wasn't going back to her castle any time soon. That life was over for both of them. They lost. Still, Varana was who she was, and Zalith had made his peace with that long ago. She was difficult, haughty, and obsessed with appearances, but she was his oldest and dearest friend.

"I'll speak to Danford about the cow," Zalith muttered, picking up his quill. "Perhaps he can get the farmer to move it elsewhere."

Varana nodded, her eyes still closed tight. "And the pig."

"There's a pig?"

"Yes," the woman's voice cracked as though she were on the verge of tears. "In the yard."

Zalith did his best to hold back his entertained smile. "I'll see what I can do."

"Thank you, sweetheart," the woman mumbled with her hand still on her forehead.

The duo sat in silence for quite some time while Zalith worked. His eyes peered down at maps, treaties, and all sorts of messages that were sent to him regarding the war. There was so much that needed to be done, and so many people counting on him—but his mind began to wander.

Alucard. Zalith felt as though he was fighting a war with himself at almost every minute of the day. That vampire always seemed to find a way to creep into his thoughts. Something like this hadn't happened to him in a very long time; Zalith found himself missing the vampire to a somewhat alarming extent. Why was this happening? He had so much more that he needed to focus on right now; he couldn't afford to sit around and daydream about something so frivolous—

"How did all that business go with the vampires?" Varana abruptly asked, still lying on the couch.

"Good," Zalith said with a nod, unable to hide his frown.

"You're done with them now, aren't you?"

"I'm done with them now. They're safe, and I can move on."

Move on. The thought pained him. Why? The work was done. The vampires were no longer on his long list of things to worry about… but with them gone, it meant that Alucard was gone, too. Zalith grimaced; he thought that perhaps kissing the vampire would have gotten all of this out of his system, but obviously, it hadn't worked—neither time. All it did was increase his want for Alucard—his *need*. Frivolous? How could he have just thought of his and Alucard's relationship as such a thing? The vampire already meant so much to him, and despite his attempts to silence his thoughts, they so very easily found their way back to the front of his mind.

Varana scoffed. "Move on to what, another farmhouse? Perhaps Danford can find us a hut made of mud and hay when we inevitably get chased out of here."

The demon rolled his eyes, not too keen on engaging with her. Still, despite his silence, his friend continued.

"You know what I think?" Varana grumbled.

"What, Varana?"

"You should have had someone in Aegisguard find us somewhere to stay while you were at it."

Zalith knew that Varana was right; moving to Aegisguard was one of the more logical things to do, even if it was just for a few years. He was reluctant to abandon his colleagues, but he couldn't deny the fact that, even in this farmhouse, he was already miles and miles away from all of them. Zalith was working through messengers already; what was the harm in doing it in Aegisguard instead?

But then Alucard burst to the very forefront of the demon's mind again. The thought of seeing his beautiful face, his red-as-blood hair, and his eyes—those eyes which looked as though fire itself raged within them… those beautifully *sad* eyes. His alluring, natural scent of cedarwood, warm amber, roses, and cinnamon. The feel of his warm, soft skin— something he'd not expect a vampire to possess. Everything about Alucard was perfectly confounding, strangely alluring, and so beautifully unique that Zalith couldn't keep himself from thinking about him all the time. He was confident he knew what he felt for Alucard, but it had been such a long time; he wasn't sure if Alucard felt the same anymore, and that thought cut him so deeply. He missed him so sorely—his presence, his voice, his endearing reactions.

The demon could only imagine how frequently Alucard would fill his mind if they were practically next door to each other. Zalith knew himself well enough; if he went to Aegisguard, he wouldn't be able to stop himself from seeing Alucard as often as he could. He couldn't afford that—he couldn't risk his work in Eltaria by allowing the vampire to take up all his time, and he couldn't risk the relationship he and Alucard had built. Zalith had a history of playing with hearts, and he didn't want to ruin what he and Alucard shared. He figured that if he kept his distance, then perhaps he'd find a way to do things the right way.

He shook his head, returning to his conversation with Varana. "This may surprise you to hear, but I don't have as many friends in other worlds as I do here."

"I'm sure you can figure something out," Varana insisted, dismissing him with a wave of her hand. "You usually do."

Zalith shook his head again as a small grimace appeared on his face. He knew that it was hard to get Varana to let go of something she'd already set her mind on. He also knew that Varana wasn't going to take any mentions of his being romantically involved with anyone very well. But he wasn't romantically involved with Alucard, was he? They spent an unusually long amount of time together...they shared some delicate moments—they even kissed twice. But that was all it was, right? A few intimate moments between friends; there was nothing serious about it. However, what he felt...it might be more—he *wanted* it to be more. But when would be the right time to tell Alucard?

He then sighed. He didn't want to bring up the vampire, but it *was* better than dealing with the consequences of leaving Varana in the dark. "I'm concerned," he said.

Varana looked over at him with her red eyes. "About what?"

"Do you recall when I told you about the individual who was working with me on the vampire relocation project?"

She nodded. "The rude one?"

"Yes," he said, his finger drumming on the desk. He hadn't told her anything about Alucard outside of their initial meeting with Damien, and it was strange to hear that he once thought of Alucard as rude. Now, everything Alucard did was endearing.

"What about him?" Varana questioned, although the dark look that passed over her face suggested that she had already somewhat pieced things together.

"It would seem..." he carefully began, "that he and I kissed."

The woman's eyes widened in shock, but her surprised face quickly twisted into bitterness. "Of course you did."

"However, I value the relationship that he and I have built—"

Varana scoffed.

"And I'm worried that if we go to Aegisguard, I'm going to pursue something more with him, and—"

"And then get tired of him and leave," Varana continued. "Like you always do."

"Yes," Zalith muttered. "Like I always do."

The woman shrugged as a happy little smile grew on her face. "I, for one, see no problem with that."

Varana was always a jealous woman; Zalith wasn't at all surprised by her words.

"I don't want to hurt this one," he told her. "I think I've found myself…caring about him…severely."

Zalith watched a sour look take hold of Varana's face as she cringed in disgust.

"Ugh," she groaned.

The demon nodded, heaving a great sigh. "I know."

"Leave it to you to find yourself a little boyfriend, even in times like these. Do you have no self-control?"

Zalith shook his head. "I'm starting to think not—"

"Well, you need to find some!" Varana snapped, sitting up from where she lay. "I'm not staying in this dirty little hovel just because you can't find strength enough to control your urges! Be a man!"

Sighing quietly, Zalith began to gather up some of the papers on his desk, giving himself a moment of silence to think. He hated to admit it, but he was being foolish— Varana was right. Why risk their safety over something so silly? They were in danger every day of their lives, and Aegisguard was the best place to hide from their hunters. Zalith had underestimated them before, but he knew with absolute certainty that they wouldn't be able to find them in another world.

"Fine," he uttered, tucking the papers into his drawer.

Varana exclaimed, "What?"

"We'll go to Aegisguard."

The woman gasped in shock as a wide smile spread on her face. "Really?"

Zalith nodded. He wasn't entirely happy with it, but he knew he was just being stubborn. This was the right thing to do. Alucard wasn't even in Aegisguard anymore, so looking for him would still be out of the question, even if he was in the same world the vampire lived in.

"Yes," he said.

Varana stood up immediately, and in her excitement, she hurried over to Zalith and kissed him hard on the cheek. The woman grinned from ear to ear, straightened out her dress, and headed out the door.

"Where are you going?" Zalith asked with a small laugh.

"To pack!"

The demon sighed for what felt like the thousandth time that day. "We need to work out specifics first, Varana," he called after her.

Zalith heard an eager *"I don't care!"* from down the hallway before the sound of her bedroom door closing shut.

Shaking his head, the demon quietly resumed the task of reorganizing his desk. Alucard entered his mind yet again, and this time, Zalith wasn't so quick to brush his thoughts away. He'd have to try to get used to it because whether he was ready to face his feelings or not, he and Varana were going to Aegisguard.

Chapter Eighty-Four

— ⸖ † ⸖ —

Return

| **Ben,** *Dor-Sanguis, Decem 12th* |

Ben was sitting behind the desk in his office. He still had no idea where Alucard was, but he had been given his orders, and they were to take care of things whilst his boss was away.

Since Alucard's vanishing, things had been tense. Ben wasn't fully aware of how Alucard handled things, so when something dire came to his attention, he wasn't entirely certain which approach to take. However, he felt he was doing an exceptional job so far—if it weren't for the constant riots and protests in the city, he might say things were running smoothly.

The city council called upon Alucard for answers regarding the sudden arrival of so many more vampires, and Ben had done his best to explain that Alucard was currently off elsewhere taking care of business, but the humans didn't take kindly to an answer that didn't give them what they wanted.

Most of the vampires had left the city; some moved back into the castle, and others were simply missing. Ben was searching for them but without avail. Most of his time was consumed by the city's outrage—the humans didn't want the vampires around, and despite his efforts, Ben hadn't done too well in keeping the peace. He wasn't sure when Alucard would return, but when he eventually did, Ben had no idea how he would explain what happened.

He hadn't long woken from his sleep; the shadows under his eyes were clear indicators of his lack of such a thing. But that didn't keep him from working. How people like Alucard and Zalith managed this amount of work bewildered him; he found himself glad that this was only temporary. He shuffled the papers on his desk, unsure of what to start the day with, but he was sure something would present itself to him sooner or later.

Sooner appeared to be the case. He sharply lifted his head and glared up at the ceiling as a rather loud thump came from above. He frowned, listening as footsteps made their way along the floor above—that space was an attic, he was sure. His office sat in one of the tallest towers closest to the guard of savage, demonic birds surrounding the sky above. Who or what could have passed them to enter the attic? He wasted no time in heading off to find out.

Swiftly as any vampire, he left his office and made his way down the hall and towards the stairs that would take him to the attic. But before he reached the stairs, he halted his inhuman rush at the sight of the crimson-haired vampire, who stepped down from them. For a moment, Ben didn't believe what he was seeing, but it was as clear as day—*Alucard* was as clear as day. Standing there with the same frown he always possessed no matter his emotion, and his face was unusually scruffy with red stubble. An expectant look lingered in Alucard's eyes, but Ben had no idea what he was waiting for. A greeting? An update? Or perhaps…The Vampire Lord hadn't wanted to be seen.

Ben smiled ever so slightly, trying to hide his confoundment. "Aleksei?"

"Obviously," he replied, glaring at Ben, standing in the same clothes he had worn the night of his disappearance—but they were scorched, bloody, and torn.

Unsure of how to respond, Ben frowned slightly. "I didn't know when you'd be back," he said as calmly as he could. "I did as you asked, kept things running."

Alucard didn't look at all interested.

"Where…what happened?" he asked; the guy looked like he'd been through more than one type of hell, and Ben couldn't help but ask why.

But Alucard wasn't going to tell him. "Vind me in my study in vive minutes," he grumbled, walking off down the hall before Ben could say anything else.

After four months, Alucard so suddenly showed up as if he'd been away for a day or so, and that confused Ben more than anything else. It almost seemed as though his abrupt vanishing hadn't even happened. What was he supposed to think or say? Clearly, he was meant to meet Alucard in his study in five minutes; perhaps he should do that first. Or should he inform Zalith that Alucard had returned? He turned around and started to make his way back to his office. He told Zalith he'd tell him as soon as Alucard returned, but wouldn't it be best to find out where he'd been? He wasn't even sure Alucard would tell him such a thing, but he felt it would be better to come to Zalith with as many answers to the questions he would undoubtedly have as possible.

He turned back around and instead headed down the hall and towards the stairs that would take him down to the castle's main corridors.

Ben walked from the vampires' side of the castle, through the main entrance hall, and towards the recently repaired door to Alucard's side of the castle. He unlocked the door, closed it behind him, and walked through the silent, empty corridor, following it until he reached the wide-open door to the huge, hollowed-out tower in which Alucard's impressive study existed. He stepped inside, slowly making his way towards one of the desks, eyeing everything that caught his attention.

There were hundreds—maybe even *thousands* of books lined around the towering walls. He couldn't name all the trinkets and apparatuses, and there were so many things he might like to ask about, but it wasn't his business. Instead of investigating, he made his way over to the desk he'd set his eyes on, pulled out a chair, and sat down, waiting for Alucard to arrive.

He tapped his fingers on the desk, staring at the bookshelves ahead of him. Was Alucard back permanently? He could only hope. Recently, he realized that The Vampire Lord's job was one he couldn't manage for too long. Once again, he also found himself wondering where Alucard had been to have come back looking as though he'd gone through hell. He'd never seen him like that before, and he was quite certain that Alucard hadn't appreciated him seeing him that way. But it couldn't have been helped. Ben was just doing his job. For all he knew, an enemy could have landed in the attic.

With a quiet sigh, he continued to look around the room, waiting for Alucard to join him.

| Alucard |

Alucard made his way towards his study. He'd changed out of his scorched blazer, tidied his hair, and did his best to make himself look presentable. He thought about shaving his face, but he didn't have the energy. He wanted to get this over and done with.

He headed into the room unseen, setting his eyes on Ben, who was oblivious to his arrival. "I noticed zhe vampires 'ave moved back into zhe castle," he said, stopping beside Ben, who flinched in startle.

Ben sat up straight, watching as Alucard made his way around to the other side of the desk and sat down. "Uh…yeah. The humans haven't been accepting of them lately, especially since you brought just over thirty new vampires at one point. It almost seemed as though they were waiting for something to kick off about."

Alucard rested his arms on the desk in front of him. "Zhere are no vampires in zhe city anymore?"

"Protestors, riots—they wanted to get away from it. I'm sorry, I tried to—"

"Zoesn't matter," Alucard mumbled, waving his hand in dismissal. "I'll vix zhis."

A look of relief appeared on Ben's face. "Are you back permanently?"

"Vor now," he said, leaning back in his seat. "I 'ope zhere's noving else vor me to deal vith," he uttered irritably.

"No." Ben shook his head. "Other than that, everything else has been rather quiet. No werewolves, either."

"I took care of zhat bevore I levt."

"You did?"

"Ada vas still alive. I killed 'er and ended 'er bloodline. Zhe volves shouldn't be a problem anymore."

With an almost shocked look on his face, Ben looked down at his hands, which he rested on the desk. Then, he frowned and looked back at Alucard. "I thought…Zalith killed her ages ago?"

"So did I."

"So…what happened? If you don't mind my asking, that is."

Alucard frowned slightly and glanced over at the small window to his right. It might have been four months ago, but it still felt like it was only yesterday that Ada had shown her ugly face one last time and essentially caused the death of his only friend. But he couldn't blame her. He had been the one to kill Tobias. His friend was dead because he couldn't control himself—he couldn't control what he was. But it didn't matter now. Everyone was gone, he was alone, and he'd have to get used to it again.

He set his eyes back on Ben. "I came back to my 'ouse burning; Ada vas zhere, ve vought, she stabbed me, Tobias came to my rescue, and I killed 'im to save myselv. I voke up, I chased Ada down, killed 'er and 'er vamily, and zhen I levt."

With a dumbfounded stare on his face, Ben seemed to ponder his answer. "I did as you asked in your absence," he started. "I wasn't sure where you were, so I couldn't send updates."

"I vas in zhe Undervorld," he revealed.

"The…Underworld?" Ben asked. "As in…*the* Underworld?"

Alucard frowned irritably. "Zhere is only vone Undervorld."

"Right, sorry," Ben said sincerely.

The vampire then rolled his eyes and looked back over at the window. "Zhat zoesn't matter. I need to get back on track vith vhat I vas doing 'ere, starting vith my annual party. Dirk vill be inviting possible allies, and I need you to arrange zhe event vith 'im. You vill vind 'im in zhe city."

"Of course."

"I vill also need you to send invitations vor me to zhe people who are not of Dor-Sanguian origin. I vill call vor you vhen I need you. Go."

Nodding, Ben stood up, and without another word, he left the room, leaving Alucard alone.

Alucard leaned back in his seat, staring at the window. His time in the Underworld hadn't been great, but at least it helped him get over his overbearing sadness—or so he had thought. The moment Ben left the room, he found himself reminiscing. He and Zalith spent time in this room; it was the same room where the demon told him that he cared about him, the same room Alucard felt he realized that he cared differently for Zalith—differently than he'd ever cared for anyone.

But he dismissed those thoughts. It had been four long months, and he was sure that Zalith had moved on. That demon didn't need him, and he was sure he didn't need Zalith, either. At least that was what he told himself.

He took his eyes off the window and looked down at his desk. At least he had work to do, work that would distract him. The humans were acting with hostility towards the vampires, so he'd have to put them back in their places. He then had relations and treaties to work out with Dirk and possible new associates once his birthday came around. All he had to do was work out who he'd personally invite. But he had no one. Tobias was gone. Elvin was gone. Who did he have left?

Zalith. He scowled angrily but then frowned miserably. Even after all this time, he found himself thinking about him; how much he missed his company, his annoying, smirky face, his voice—even his strange remarks. But he sent Zalith away, and despite him—and more recently Damien—telling him that Zalith was the last of the Lilidian bloodline and that he needed to be protected, Alucard didn't feel as though contacting him was a good idea. He was sure the demon would have moved on, and he was sure Zalith didn't spare a moment of his time to think about Alucard. So why was *he* sitting there dwelling on what couldn't be undone?

The vampire leaned forward, resting his arms on the desk, staring down at them. He should have listened to him because he was right. Damien wasn't going to kill Zalith. Zalith made sure of that. Alucard, however, had been too convinced that the Daegelus would find a way to remove Zalith from existence. But…during his time in the Underworld, he overheard Damien talking to his associates, telling them that Zalith was the last of the Lilidian bloodline, and Alucard couldn't help but consider what he learned….

| *Two months ago, the Underworld* |

Alucard wandered the empty corridors of his uncle's dark, gloomy castle with regret heavy on his mind. Ever since leaving Aegisguard, all he could think about was Zalith, how he'd never see him again, how he sent him away, hurt him, and destroyed what could have been something serene for them both. It didn't matter now.

Damien brought him home. Two months ago, something happened to him. He killed his best friend because he couldn't control who or what he was, and that had woken something inside him—something…dark. Damien saved him from whatever it was.

Damien told him it was similar to Lucifer's disease, something he'd learned of through Detlaff, and it was something he knew he didn't want to carry the burden of. Damien had potentially saved his sanity, and he should focus on *that*, not some demon he allowed himself to carelessly fall for.

But the moment he heard that demon's name echo from the room ahead, his desire to forget him withered. Damien's voice had spoken Zalith's name—*Eladarin*—a name he'd not forget any time soon. So, he made his way towards the slightly parted door and leaned back against the wall, listening to the conversation within. He wasn't sure who Damien was talking to, but it didn't matter. He wanted to know why Zalith had been mentioned.

"I don't know what happened," came Damien's frustrated voice.

"So, somebody kills all the males of a particularly important bloodline, and you don't have the slightest idea who did it?" his associate asked, concern in his strangely similar but accented voice. Alucard didn't recognize this person, but he was sure it was another of Damien's errand boys, one he shared a closer relationship with. Anyone who spoke so casually to Damien was always close to him in one way or another.

Damien scoffed. "I don't have eyes everywhere, do I?" he argued, slamming his fist into what Alucard could only assume to be a wall.

"Clearly not. No wonder it takes you so long to catch up with what's been going on out there. You were lucky you caught Caedis when you did. That was probably the only time you've arrived on time somewhere."

Irritated, Damien snarled and shuffled around inside the room. "I'm busy."

"No, you're not. You sit around here all day, all night, fucking around with magic you don't understand. Half the shit you do you only do because I tell you how to do it."

"Tch," Damien scoffed. "What you tell me doesn't matter."

"No. What *does* matter is what you're going to do about this situation. Eladarin is the last of Lilith's bloodline, but you want to kill him for messing around with Caedis. What will you do, Damien?"

The Daegelus snarled a few times and tapped his fingers on what sounded like a desk. "I can't kill him, can I? I need him. I need *him*. I need Aleksei."

"So let them live."

"So they can fuck around behind my back? Make fun of me? No. I swore I would kill him if he even thought of approaching that boy again."

"Why do you insist upon keeping them apart?"

"Aleksei doesn't need anyone else. I should be the only beacon in his life."

"Why?"

"Because!" Damien yelled.

"Because…you hate his father. You can't take your anger out on Lucifer, so you decide to beat the shit out of his son instead. Why? Does it fuel your ego? Does it satisfy you to hurt someone who looks so much like the creature you hate most?"

Damien scoffed again, but this time in amusement. "Do I need a reason? Lucifer abandoned that boy, and I took him under *my* wing. He is mine, he will stay mine, and no one, least of all some fucking *demon,* will take him from me."

His associate laughed slightly. "I thought you liked to see him suffer."

"Only when necessary."

"We know what Eladarin is like. He'll hurt Caedis in a way you can't; won't that teach him a lesson? Won't *that* teach him to listen to you when you tell him you're the only person he can and will rely on?"

Damien went silent.

Alucard frowned, staring down at the floor. He wasn't sure what to think at first. Of course, he knew Damien's reason for being so possessive of him—he raised him, and he cared for him. But who was he talking to? Who would be allowed to talk to him so unprofessionally? So…strangely? Not even Zalith dared to speak in such a condescending way to Damien. So who in the worlds was in that room with him?

"You're right," Damien said. "I can't kill him, so I may as well use him to strengthen Aleksei's faith in me. I don't know how much longer I'll be keeping him here, but I know for a fact he'll scurry back to that demon the moment I let him go."

"Good."

"Looks like Eladarin slithers away from death once again," Damien muttered.

"He has a habit of doing that. Keep an eye on them both; we need them, remember."

"When is this happening?" Damien then asked. "You shared this plan to create another Daegelus with me near to a year ago. When will it happen?"

"When I am ready. It might not be for a while, but it will happen. There are other factors of the prophecy to focus on. Have you found a matriarch yet?"

"There are a few I have contacted, yes. Do you have a preference?" Damien asked.

"The eldest. The older a demon is, the greater their power."

Damien went silent once again…but then sighed. "I'll contact her."

"Don't manifest me again unless you have a *real* problem," his associate then warned. "Finish with Caedis, and then send him back to Aegisguard."

"Right," Damien mumbled irritably.

Sure that the conversation was over, Alucard silently hurried away from the door, down the corridors, and a reasonable distance from where Damien was. Now he had time to think. He heard so much, yet the only thing he could focus on was the fact that Damien wasn't going to kill Zalith. Did that mean they could see each other again? Did that mean they could…no. Alucard leaned back against the wall and frowned sullenly. It had been two months; Zalith would have most likely moved on by now. And that was okay.

Alucard expected that to happen. All that mattered was that Zalith was safe. That gave him enough relief for now.

| *Present, Alucard's castle* |

The vampire stared down at his arms. Zalith was safe, and he wasn't going to die, but that didn't change the fact that he and Zalith couldn't be together. It had now been *four* months. Zalith had to have moved on, and as much as Alucard missed him, as much as he felt he might still feel the same way he did before, he still felt afraid. Despite what he heard, he still feared that Damien might intervene. Damien changed his mind so erratically that he could kill Zalith at any given time, with or without reason. Alucard didn't want to risk that happening.

That didn't stop Alucard's mind from wandering, though. What if Zalith *wasn't* seeing someone else? What if the demon waited as he said he would? Would he wait this long just to be with someone like him? Probably not. But…Alucard pondered. If he somehow saw Zalith again, if the demon wished to be with him, he felt…maybe…no.

Sighing, Alucard stood up and silenced his thoughts. He had work to do. Perhaps he could give the demon more thought later. Right now, he had to fix whatever happened in the city in his absence.

Chapter Eighty-Five

Updates

| Ben |

Ben waited, standing in front of the small mirror on the wall in his room, its glass fading to an ominous, empty black. A few hours ago, Alucard returned from his hiatus. Ben had sworn to tell Zalith of his return the moment it occurred, but The Vampire Lord put him to work the moment he got home.

But he had no resentment. He was glad to be back to his usual tasks. He'd much rather be running around for Alucard than doing *his* job. Now, he had the chance to contact Zalith and inform him of Alucard's return, but he'd been waiting in front of the enchanted mirror for at least ten minutes, and there still hadn't been a reply. He thought he might try again later, but it might irritate Zalith if he failed to wait at least a little longer. He was a busy man, after all. Ben knew that too well.

He crossed his arms and tapped his fingers, looking around as he huffed and puffed. Lillian was waiting for him, too, and Alucard could call upon him at any moment. He was sure The Vampire Lord wouldn't take too well to him contacting his old boss with the intention of telling him his business. But Zalith clearly cared about Alucard, and Ben wasn't sure whether he was doing this because he admired that or because he was scared that Zalith might not be so happy if he failed to live up to his word.

As patiently as he could, he stared into the mirror, waiting for Zalith to appear within it.

| Zalith |

Zalith sat behind his desk, sighing quietly as he placed his mug of coffee down. As busy as his day had been already, he was eager to hear the updates Ben had regarding Alucard.

He reached over and tapped the side of his standing mirror, and as it faded from black to reveal Ben, he waited for him to speak.

"Aleksei came back," Ben started.

Staring vacantly, Zalith nodded slightly. "From where?" he asked tonelessly.

"He said he was in the Underworld. He didn't specify why, though."

Zalith rolled his eyes. *Of course* Damien would be involved—just as he suspected. But Alucard was now home, which relieved him of many of his overbearing worries. But he still wanted to know how he was. "How is he?"

"Different," Ben answered. "Well, he's…back to business as usual. He put me straight to work and went straight to work himself. He came back looking rather…battered, though. Dirty, awfully tired look on his face—I didn't think he had facial hair, and I've been made aware otherwise."

"Battered?" Zalith asked, concern in his voice. Was he hurt? Zalith already knew how badly Damien treated Alucard, and knowing that the vampire had spent a whole four months with him…horrified him. There was no way Alucard came out of that without wounds, and he wanted to know just how many there were.

Ben pondered. "I didn't see or detect any physical wounds. He was just covered in ash like he walked through a few wars to get here. After I learned he'd come from the Underworld, the scorches on his clothes made sense. That's about it—apart from like I said, he looked tired as all hell."

Of course he looked tired. Damien worked that vampire until he was but a moment from death. The first thought that came to his mind was just how much he wanted to phase to Dor-Sanguis, find Alucard, hug him, and tell him he was there for him. But he couldn't. He couldn't just intrude on Alucard's life without invitation. As much as he cared, as much as he desperately wanted to hurry to him now that he was back, he had to remain where he was. Alucard might not yet be ready to see him so soon after returning, and he respected that. There was also the chance that god forbid, Alucard didn't feel the same anymore. It was him, after all, who said things between them needed to end.

Why was he thinking about that right now? He should be happy to know Alucard was home and safe. But all he felt was sadness. He yearned to be with him now that he knew it was possible, but he had to wait. However, he didn't see any harm in sending Alucard something that might tell the vampire he was still waiting for him. But what?

He took his eyes off his desk and looked back at Ben. "What is he doing?"

"I'm not entirely sure. The humans here have been causing trouble for the vampires. I think he's been dealing with that. He has me working with Dirk to plan some party— an annual thing, he said."

Alucard's annual party—his *birthday* party. There was a time Zalith jokingly asked for an invitation. Now, he felt he might just try to get one. He undeniably wanted to see Alucard again—how could he not want to? But he wouldn't just show up unless the vampire wanted him there, as he already decided not too long ago. No, he wouldn't invite himself; he'd see if the vampire would invite him. Of course, he'd have to remind him somehow that he was still there…waiting for him, and what better way to do that than through Ben?

"He once mentioned that party to me. Has he written up a guest list yet?"

"Not that I'm aware of," Ben answered. "But he *did* tell me he'd need me to assist him with invitations for people who aren't from Dor-Sanguis. I assume that's because he's not Deiganish. I said I'd help, and he told me he'd contact me when—"

"Perhaps he may have forgotten in his months of absence. Would you be so kind as to discretely remind him that I would very much like to attend?" Zalith requested.

A smile appeared on Ben's face. "Of course," he agreed.

Zalith nodded. "Thank you for informing me."

"Sure thing."

Then, Zalith reached over and tapped the side of his mirror. As it faded to black, he sighed and took a sip of his coffee. There was no time for him to sit around and ponder, though. He had to get back to work.

Chapter Eighty-Six

— ⸲ † ⸱ —

Solving

| **Alucard,** *Decem 19th* |

A week passed.

Alucard sat in front of the desk on the highest floor of his huge study. In front of him lay the treaty he formed over half a year ago, the same treaty he had to revise in response to the humans' latest disturbance. He'd only been home a week and he was already overwhelmed with things to do. But that was how he preferred things to be. As long as he had something to do, his mind wouldn't wander.

He spent the last week catching up on what he missed, and more recently, he'd chosen to focus on the problems currently happening in the city, the problems that might result in the treaty he worked so hard to build shattering. He didn't want that, and he'd do what he could to make sure it stayed in place.

The vampire stared at the treaty, which had been translated from Deiganish to Dor-Sanguian. A conflicted look sat on his pale face. He wasn't entirely sure what happened to cause the humans to protest, but he'd invited Dirk over to explain everything to him. It wasn't going to be an enjoyable conversation, but Dirk must have seen everything since he lived in the city's main district, the place that saw most of Dargamoore's drama.

Listening as the door to his half of the castle crept open, Alucard took his eyes off the treaty and glanced over at the huge, shimmering telescope-like contraption to his left. Everything he looked at now reminded him of Zalith for reasons he felt to be illogical. Simply because Zalith asked about that telescope, it made Alucard think of him. How he missed him, how he wished he could be talking to him right now instead of the incoming boring human with an equally boring name. It wasn't like he had a choice, though. Zalith was gone, and Alucard had to make do with the people who were left around him.

Taking his eyes off the telescope, he looked back down at the treaty, and as Dirk entered the study, he sighed quietly.

"Aleksei?" Dirk called from the bottom of the tower.

The vampire stood up, made his way over to the edge of the floor he was working on, and glared down at him. As Dirk waved, Alucard disappeared into vermillion smoke and reappeared moments later in front of him.

Dirk stared at him. "I assume you've read the treaty over. I had my best translators work on it for you."

Inviting Dirk to sit in front of his desk, Alucard nodded and slumped down in his seat. "Vould be a lot easier to veigh options if I knew vhat exactly 'ad caused zhis tension."

"Of course," Dirk said with a nod, making himself comfortable in his seat. "In your absence—your sudden absence—some of your vampires began to… well… deviate. The newer ones, mostly. Ben was tied up with it; I think that Ben was overwhelmed and didn't deal with things as well as he could have."

"Get to zhe point. Vhy is zhis 'appening, and vhat must I do to vix zhis?"

"Luckily, nothing too widescale has broken out. Just a few human groups causing trouble with the vampires. Ben moved those of the vampires who hadn't already left out of the city to keep anything else from occurring. I've looked into it, and the people starting these riots and protests all lead back to one man. His name is Marcus, and he leads a small rebellion within the left district of the city. Anti-vampire protestors; never wanted them in the city in the first place. I advise you to try to reason with him. If you kill him, you'd make a martyr of him, and that would only inspire the rest of the city to support his movement."

"Vone man started all of zhis?"

Dirk nodded. "I don't have the entire story, but a vampire did something to piss him off. He took it to heart, started blaming *all* vampires, and he eventually gained a following. They'd harass the vampires, hence why they began to leave the city. Some have even left the country altogether. As I said, you simply need to talk to this one man."

"Vhere can I vind 'im?"

Looking at his vacant face, Dirk frowned unsurely. "I must… implore that you don't kill anyone, Aleksei. It might make things worse."

"Zhe treaty ve vormed applies to my vampires, not me personally. If I vant to kill zhe men causing problems vor my people, I vill kill zhem. If you try to tell me vhat to do vone more time, I vill top zhe pile of bodies vith yours," he warned.

Dirk nodded and looked down at the desk. "Of course."

"Vhere can I find zhis Marcus?" he repeated.

"Here is his address," Dirk said, taking a piece of paper from his pocket, and as he slid it across the table, he frowned slightly. "Might I know where you were these past months?"

"No."

"Forgive my intrusion. This is also the place he and his little gathering meet every night," he said, sliding another piece of paper across the table. "Should I prepare for an uproar?"

"Prepare to varn zhe city zhat I am back, and if zhey try shit like zhis again, I von't be so kind as to let zhem stay in my city."

Nodding, Dirk sat up straight. "And...Marcus?"

"I'll try to veason vith 'im virst. But in my absence, my patience 'as proved to vither even more. I'll give 'im a single chance to back down, and if 'e zoesn't, zhen I vill put an end to 'is miserable life. Anyving else to bring to my attention?"

Dirk thought to himself for a few moments and then said, "Your party. I've sent invitations to possible allies, and most have corresponded with acceptance. Ben tells me you're writing a guest list yourself, and that he'll be helping you write the invitations for those who are not Dor-Sanguian. Would you like my assistance with any of that?"

"No," Alucard denied, taking the two pieces of paper from the table. He slipped them into his blazer pocket. "Alzhough I'll need a new verevolf subordinate, a new scribe, 'orses, and a groundskeeper for zhe castle. Vind me such people—make sure zhey all speak Dor-Sanguian."

Dirk nodded. "What about your manor? Would you like me to have people search it for anything that might have survived the fire?"

"You can do zhat yourselv."

"Right..." Dirk agreed.

"Send Ben to me on your vay out."

Standing up, Dirk nodded. "Of course. Good luck with Marcus; he's a stubborn one."

As Dirk then left the room, Alucard stood up and disappeared, reappearing back on the highest floor where he'd been working. He sat down, folded up the treaty, and tucked it into a small box containing several rolled pieces of parchment. Then, he pulled open the top right drawer of his desk, took a piece of paper from within, and placed it down in front of it. Written on it were the names of the people he needed Ben to send invites to. The list was short, consisting only of five names. He felt he might like to add a specific sixth, but his reluctance kept him from doing so.

Would Zalith even come? Probably not. Did Alucard even want to invite him? He wasn't sure. He wanted to see him again—of course he did. Yes, he was still afraid that Damien might intervene in their friendship—if it could even be called that anymore. They hadn't seen each other or spoken in months. Whatever they had been building towards before, Alucard was sure it had withered. But that didn't stop him from considering sending Zalith an invitation.

Whether Zalith was seeing someone else or not, the vampire still wanted to see him. He still wanted to be in his company; he still wanted to talk to him, to hear his voice, to see his irritating smile. But what would be the point? He wasn't going to allow himself to care for a man who might no longer care about him. Zalith said he'd be back for him, but where was he? Nowhere. That made Alucard much surer that he'd moved on.

He sighed and rested his arms on the desk, glancing at the telescope. Despite everything that happened and everything that might happen, he couldn't banish Zalith from his thoughts. The temptation to invite him was high, but so was his reluctance. He didn't want to invite him only to learn that he was seeing someone new. He didn't want to send an invite and receive no correspondence—he didn't want to make a fool of himself by expecting Zalith to come at his call only for him to fail to turn up.

No, he'd not invite him. He was sure that whatever they shared before ended the moment Alucard sent him away.

"Aleksei?" Ben called, his voice echoing through the tower.

Snapping out of his thoughts, Alucard sighed, snatched the list from his desk, and stood up. He made his way to the edge of the floor and looked down at Ben, who was staring up at him, standing not too far from the door.

Alucard disappeared and reappeared behind his desk, where Ben headed. The vampire sat down, kicked out a chair, and invited Ben to sit.

Ben sat down and crossed his arms in front of him. "Dirk said you needed me."

Alucard slid a piece of paper across the desk towards him. "Zhese are zhe people I need you to vrite invitations to."

Taking the piece of paper, Ben frowned curiously. "Are you not inviting Zalith?"

"Vhy vould I invite 'im?" Alucard snapped.

"You're friends…or…something, right?"

"Maybe vonce upon a time," he mumbled.

"Oh…well I don't want to pry or anything, but…whatever happened between you two, I know Zalith, and…I'm sure he's…well if you invited him, I'm sure he'd come."

Alucard frowned in aggravation. "Vhat gives you zhe impression *I* vant 'im 'ere?"

Ben hesitated but sighed and tucked the paper into his pocket. "I'm sure he's worried. You were gone for four months; none of us knew where you were. I thought you might be with Zalith, which is why I was confused as to why his name isn't on this list. My mistake, my apologies."

Alucard took his eyes off Ben and looked down at his desk. He would have much rather spent the last four months with Zalith than Damien. But he didn't want to think about his time with the Daegelus. He'd shut it out of his mind as if it never happened, and he wanted to keep it that way. The only thing he wanted to remember from the last four months was finding out that Damien wouldn't kill either him or Zalith.

He opened the bottom left drawer of his desk, pulled out five silvery envelopes, and handed them to Ben. "Send zhe invitations in zhese," he instructed. He then opened the second to last drawer and pulled out a small card with a beautifully drawn N on it. He held it out to Ben. "Sign each envelope's back vith zhis sigil."

As he took the piece of card, Ben eyed it for a moment before looking at Alucard. "N?" he asked.

Alucard then laughed slightly. "You 'ave been vorking vor me vor over six months, and I 'ave vailed to tell you vhat my organization calls i'self."

Ben smiled nervously and nodded.

"Nosveratu," Alucard said.

"I've never heard that term before," Ben admitted, holding everything in his left hand.

"You vouldn't 'ave—not 'ere. Outside of my country, zhough, is vell known."

Nodding with an intrigued look on his face, Ben rested his arms on the desk. "Is there specific information I should write in these invitations?"

"Decem virty-virst, dusk. 'Ere in my castle. Zhat's all you veally need to put ozzer zhan zheir names," Alucard answered.

"And your name?"

"No," he denied. "Zhey'll know who is vrom because of zhat sigil."

"Got it," Ben said.

Closing his desk drawer, Alucard leaned back in his seat. "I'll be dealing vith zhe 'uman problem soon. Zon't be alarmed if dead bodies start to appear in zhe streets. Vill only be my doing."

With a concerned look on his face, Ben replied, "Understood."

"Go," Alucard then dismissed.

Nodding, Ben stood up and left the room.

As Ben left, Alucard remained at his desk with a conflicted, sullen look on his face. Ben was right…wasn't he? Zalith was probably worried…was he? No…well…Alucard wasn't sure. He liked to think that the demon was still waiting to see him again, but Alucard's anxiety told him that Zalith moved on in the four months they hadn't seen or even spoken to one another. Should he try to contact him? Should he invite him to his party and see if he'd come? His confliction was so overbearing that he was certain it would cause him to sit there for hours pondering. He couldn't afford to do that right now. He had humans to deal with.

Without further delay, he stood up, morphed into vermillion smoke, and disappeared out through one of the open windows.

In the city, lingering in a festering alley, was Marcus, the tall, coltish man who led the rebellion against the vampires. He stood at the end of the alley, his eyes dull and green, his hair scruffy and black. Surrounded by his followers, he evidently felt as though he meant something—as though he was important. A smug smile clung to his face while he relished in the success of his operations carried out by those willing to listen to him preach.

"The undead pests have been removed from our city," Marcus called, grabbing the attention of every man, woman, and child in attendance. "We will continue to do God's work; we will continue to cleanse this land of their filthy disease. Dor-Sanguis is only the beginning!"

The crowd nodded and murmured in agreement.

"Once this place is free of them, we'll move onto lands beyond!" he announced with a smug smile as his followers agreed. "With their creator gone, there's nothing to stop us—just as our ancestors did, we'll drive them into extinction!"

Observing from above, crouching on the edge of a nearby roof, Alucard fiddled with his small flask. His irritancy grew as the man continued to speak to his followers; he wasn't Diabolus, that was for sure. Alucard had heard enough Diabolus speeches, and this man was acting purely on his own, likely inspired by the stories about how the humans once cast vampires out. Of course, the stories left out the parts involving Alucard and his constant victories against the humans, but he didn't care. It was rather entertaining to watch little men like Marcus think they stood a chance.

Alucard drank from his flask, downing every ounce of blood within it in moments. Since Ada's ambush, he hadn't felt the same. His hunger was something devastating, and no matter how adamantly he kept up with his need to feed, his hunger and temptation to drain the life out of someone didn't fade. He could manage it, though, and he was sure this new struggle would wither soon enough.

The vampire went to screw the small cap back onto his flask, but it slipped through his fingers and pounced down to the alley below. It looked like his time of observing was over.

As the cap chimed in response to hitting the concrete, the human crowd gawped at it and then looked up, eventually setting their eyes on him. Most of them screamed and ran for their lives, ignoring Marcus' futile attempts to inspire them to fight. They all knew who Alucard was, and they knew it was best to run and forget that Marcus had ever existed.

Ignoring Marcus' and his remaining followers' religious chants of banishing, Alucard stood up and dropped to the ground. The moment The Vampire Lord's boots hit the ground, the rest of Marcus' men fled, leaving him alone.

Unafraid, Marcus pointed a wooden stake at Alucard, gripping the crucifix around his neck.

Alucard wasn't at all patient enough to deal with this. Before Marcus could comprehend it, Alucard smacked the stake out of his hand and pinned him back against the wall, glaring into his horrified eyes. "Dirk tells me you've been causing me unnecessary problems."

Grunting as he gripped Alucard's wrists, Marcus scowled evilly. "You undead filth," he growled. "This city doesn't belong to you—it never did!"

Glaring at him, Alucard felt he might argue with the man. But did he have the strength to do so? Not particularly. He felt no motivation to threaten him; he just wanted to kill him and be done with it. But he had to make sure this murder wouldn't make things worse. He sighed lazily and glared at Marcus. "I'll get straight to zhe point, hmm?"

Marcus frowned. "W-what?"

"You and your little band of fucking idiots aren't going to get very var vith zhis movement of yours. All you vill succeed in doing is causing me anozzer inconvenience. As much as I like to kill people like you, I 'ave much more pressing vings to attend to vight now. So, shut zhe fuck up, go 'ome, and live your life as vas bevore vone of my vampires 'urt your precious veelings. Or I vill 'ave to kill you and every single person to 'ave ever seen you. Do you vant zhat? Do you vant to vorce me to take zhe time out of my vather busy schedule to clean up your mess?" he asked with a condescending tone.

Staring at him, Marcus looked confused. He obviously had no idea what to say, and Alucard's patience was wearing thin.

"Vell? Live or die; is not veally zhat 'ard to understand, is zhat?"

Glaring at him, Marcus then scowled. "You don't scare me, I—"

"Die, zhen," Alucard mumbled and tore the man's throat out before he could finish what he was saying.

As Marcus' corpse dropped to the ground, Alucard stepped back and frowned irritably. Would he have to hunt down everyone who listened to this man's foolish preaching? No. He just wanted to go home. But…as he stared at Marcus' corpse, a familiar horror began to grip him. The blood…and his own lack of mercy—it reminded him of the night he killed Elvin, the night he killed Tobias. It made him think for a moment; it made him remember just how much he resented what he was and what he'd done because he couldn't control himself.

He wouldn't stand there and let his hatred of himself consume him. He picked up his flask cap, screwed it back on, and slowly made his way out of the alley. He'd have to make sure people saw him; he'd have to make the city aware he'd returned. And so, he silently made his way down the busy streets, ignoring the people's confused, horrified mutters and mumbles. Then, when a petrified screech echoed from the alley he just left, a smug smile clung to his face. He'd undeniably missed how easily humans were scared.

All that was left to do now was wait for Dirk to handle the rest. He'd make sure the city fell back in line, and then, Alucard could get Ben to move the vampires back into their homes. It had been solved fairly simply, but it didn't give Alucard the relief he'd been hoping for.

Once he reached the city exit, he sighed quietly, morphed into vermillion smoke, and disappeared. There wouldn't be much left to do until his party, but he was sure something would come up.

Chapter Eighty-Seven

— ⊰ ✝ ⊱ —

Invitation

| Alucard, *Decem 24th—One week until Alucard's birthday* |

Alucard stood on the balcony of the tower in which his bedroom was. His house was gone, and he'd done his best to make his old room in the castle feel like home.

He watched closely as the people below filed in and out of the castle's door, preparing the main hall for the event taking place in seven days. He didn't care to head down there and intervene; he hired people to boss the other people around for him. He wasn't feeling at all sociable; all he wanted to do was stand there, wait, watch, and try not to think about Zalith. But of course, trying *not* to think about him was a constant struggle.

His party was in a week, and he still hadn't decided whether he wanted to send Zalith an invitation. Ben tried to convince him to do so, but he didn't want to send one if it was going to result in no response or him turning up with news that he was seeing someone else. It didn't matter. He just wanted to see the demon. To remember what it felt like to be in the company of someone who made him feel something other than tired or miserable. He wanted to talk to him, to hear his voice. His company was something the vampire longed for each and every day, and he wasn't going to ignore that. But he wasn't ready to learn if Zalith had forgotten him or not.

He was finally able to silence his overbearing thoughts of worry and despondency once he spotted Dirk making his way up to the castle with four people following. Alucard could tell that one of them was a werewolf, and the others were human. It seemed as though Dirk had finally completed his tasks.

The vampire turned around; he made his way through his bedroom, down the corridors, and towards his study. Once he sat behind his desk, he waited for Dirk in silence.

When Dirk arrived, Alucard eyed the people he brought with him. The first person he was not only a werewolf but also a woman. She followed Dirk closely, dressed just as rugged as he'd expect a wolf to be—torn black jeans, a surprisingly clean white blouse, and a torn black leather jacket missing its zip. Her hair was long, curly, and blonde, and her eyes were a deep, dark orange. Everything about this woman reminded him of Ada, and he couldn't stand to look at her, let alone work with her.

He took his eyes off the woman and eyed the next person. Obviously, the smartly dressed, fedora-wearing man was a scribe. He carried his book and quill as proudly as a soldier carried his sword. He was also blonde, but one of his eyes was covered with a patch, the other brown in colour. A one-eyed scribe—how ridiculous.

The next man was dressed in a tailcoat and shirt. He was clearly the castle's new groundskeeper, which meant the last man following behind had to be a horse breeder. His stench spelt that out clearer than day.

"Aleksei," Dirk said pleasantly, approaching the desk. When he reached it, he invited himself to sit down, rested his arms on the table, and waited.

Not at all in a positive mood—which seemed to be the norm lately—Alucard scowled at him. "Did I say you could sit?"

Threatened and embarrassed, Dirk slowly stood up, cleared his throat, and glanced back at the others. "Ahem…uh…these are the people you asked me to bring to you. I've also been back to the remains of your manor, and the only thing that survived the flames was your cape. I handed it to one of the butlers to wash for you."

"Good," Alucard grumbled. Fire couldn't burn the materials his precious cape was made from. He then set his eyes on the woman. "Talk."

"Uh, this is—"

"Not you," Alucard snarled, pointing at Dirk, silencing him. "You," he said, pointing at the woman, and then to the seat she was standing beside.

With a sweet smile, she sat down. "My name is Freja," she said, holding out her hand. "Freja Ardelean."

Slowly, Alucard moved his hand from the arm of his seat and shook hers. Ardelean was Ada's bloodline, and while not all Ardeleans were Ada's blood relatives, knowing that this woman was of her wolf line made him feel cautious.

"I'm the East Pack's leader—or Queen, they like to call me. We stayed out of the business with the North Pack and West Pack. Dirk approached me with an offer of peace with the overlord of this land, and I felt inclined to accept. Ada's dead, so there's not really much reason for war. Hopefully, we can live in peace," she explained. "I'm a descendant of Ada, but I do not and have never shared her vision. I just want to live in peace."

Listening to her, Alucard concentrated, searching for any signs that would tell him she was lying. But her pulse was normal, any and all tells were absent. He hadn't heard much of the East Pack since returning home from DeiganLupus with Elvin many years ago; as far as he had been aware, the East Pack, along with the South Pack, kept themselves out of the recent trouble caused by the werewolves. Perhaps the spreading news of Ada's death was inspiring the cowering, silent packs to come out of hiding.

"Unless…you brought me here for some other reason." She frowned nervously, looking back at Dirk, the vampire's silence clearly frightening her.

"Vhere is zhe South pack?" Alucard asked.

She looked back at him. "I don't know. They've been silent for years."

"And you speak Dor-Sanguian?"

"I do," she confirmed. "My mother was born here, as was her mother."

"Vhere do you reside, and 'ow large is your pack?"

"We're currently holed up in a cave system not too far from the Dargamoore border. Currently, there are thirty-seven of us, two of my sisters are pregnant, and so are three of the other women."

"You vill velocate to a place closer to 'ere. Zhere is alveady a small pack zhere; you vill join vith zhem. I used to vork vith zheir Alpha, but 'e…passed," Alucard mumbled.

Freja nodded slowly. "You want me…to move my entire pack?"

"Zhat's vhat I said."

"Okay…I can do that, but…do you need me there right now? It's going to take some time to move that many people."

"Speak to Dirk about specivics."

Nodding, she stood up and returned to standing beside the seat.

"You," Alucard then said, pointing to the horse breeder. He went to sit, but the vampire scowled in warning.

The man stood there, looking at him.

"Sebastian died," Alucard said. "I need anozzer stallion like 'im."

"Of course, sir, but I currently have no shire mares."

"Vork zhat out," Alucard grumbled. He then looked at the scribe. "Vhy do you only 'ave vone eye?"

With a smile, the scribe shrugged. "Accidents happen, even in my field."

"Vight…you can speak, read, and write Deiganish?"

"Yes, I can."

"Good. You vill meet me 'ere every morning at dawn. No later."

He nodded. "Of course."

"And you," Alucard said, nodding at the new groundskeeper. "I'm sure you know vhat your job 'ere vill be."

The groundskeeper nodded. "Indeed, My Lord."

Alucard then waved his hand in dismissal. "You can all go."

"Before I leave," Dirk said as everyone else made their way towards the door. "All of your invited guests have responded to their invitations; no one has denied, so everyone will be attending."

With a slight nod, Alucard stood up. "Vight," he mumbled.

Then, without bidding farewell to Dirk, he disappeared into vermillion smoke and reappeared on the tallest floor of his study. He slumped down in his seat beside the large golden telescope. He waited, listening as everyone left his study, and once they were gone, he sighed quietly and rested his arms on the desk.

There wasn't much left to do until his party. He had no one else to look for, no one else to talk to. All he had to do was sit around and wait. Now, he had nothing to do with his free time. Everything he did hobby-wise burned with his home, and the only person he wanted to spend time with was gone. What was he supposed to do now? Sleep for a week? He could…but he didn't want to. Sleep wasn't an escape anymore; it only forced him to relive memories he didn't want to remember.

So, he sat there, staring aimlessly as the day ticked away. The sun was once high in the sky, and while he sat there, it slowly began to set. If it wasn't for the quiet tapping on something metal, he might have sat there a whole lot longer.

He took his eyes off the desk and frowned as he looked at the telescope. Usually, the arched gap in the roof would be open in case he wished to use the contraption, but the metal shutter had been pulled over it, trapping whatever was tapping on it outside. He stared closely, setting his eyes on what appeared to be a tiny pair of imp-like feet shuffling around on the part of the telescope which was outside. Then, as desperate chirping echoed from above, he saw an izuret trying to get in.

An izuret? Here? Why? He watched as the creature's small hands found their way under the shutter and tried to lift it. The creature's struggled grunts motivated him to get out of his seat and let it in; he stood up, made his way over to a lever on the wall to the right of the telescope, and pulled it down. The shutter began to slowly open, allowing the hairless cat-like creature to waddle in. It shuffled down the telescope carrying a differently coloured carnation flower in each of its hands. Once it was halfway down the telescope, it pounced forward and floated over to the vampire's desk.

Alucard sat back down and watched the izuret chirp while it held the flowers out to him. The vampire eyed them strangely. Flowers? An izuret? There was only one person this little demon could have been sent by, and Alucard felt too nervous to ask the izuret *why* it had been sent. He sat there, staring at the two carnations—one was blood-red, and the other was white with scattered splotches of red. Why had *he* sent them?

As Alucard took the crimson flower, the izuret chirped quietly and shuffled closer, holding the other flower closer to him. He took the second flower, holding them both in his right hand, gazing at them. Why would Zalith send carnations? How did he know he was back from his hiatus? What did this even mean? It could mean so many things. Was this Zalith's way of telling him that he was still waiting? Or was this just Zalith checking in because, despite everything, they were still friends? Alucard didn't know what to make of it. There was no note, no explanation, and the izuret looked rather clueless as to why it had been asked to deliver flowers, too.

He took his eyes off the flowers and looked down at the small demon. "Vhy did 'e send zhese?"

The creature shrugged, shook its head, and chirped quietly in confusion.

Glancing back down at the flowers, Alucard sighed. He still didn't know what he should do. He wanted to see Zalith again, and receiving the flowers gave him a little confidence that perhaps the demon was still waiting. But if that were true, why hadn't he just said so? Why hadn't he sent a message with the carnations? Alucard felt confused, conflicted, and despondent. His worry that Zalith had found someone else kept him from hoping; it kept him from thinking that these flowers had been sent as some sort of hint.

With a quiet sigh, he placed the flowers down to the right of his desk and looked back at the izuret, which was still waiting on his desk. "Vhat?" he asked irritably. "Go now."

The creature pouted and shuffled closer, muttering quietly.

"I 'ave noving to give you," the vampire mumbled.

But the izuret didn't leave. It gawped up at him with an expectant look lingering in its huge, purple eyes. It was then that Alucard realized the creature was the *same* izuret that had come to deliver Zalith a message a few months ago, the same izuret he'd taken several thorns out of. It chirped quietly, holding out its arm, thanking him again for his help.

Alucard couldn't keep himself from smiling. "You veel better?"

The izuret nodded and chattered quietly. But it then turned around and waddled over to the flowers. It pointed down at them, chirped, and frowned at him, waiting.

It told him to invite Zalith.

Should he? Ben had suggested he should do it…and despite his worry, despite his anxiety, *he* wanted to do it. So what if Zalith didn't show up? At least then Alucard would know where they stood. He wanted to know if their time apart had changed anything; he wanted to know if Zalith had moved on or forgotten whatever it was they had shared in their short time together. If Zalith didn't show up, then he'd know that whatever they were was now over, and if he *did* show up, then at least Alucard would have the chance to ask Zalith if they might still feel the same way.

He wanted to see him. He wanted to take the risk of getting hurt. He had to. If he didn't do this, he might never know—he might be left sitting around without answers for as long as he would live. So, with a stubborn pout, he took out a black piece of card, a dark envelope, and a quill. He placed them on his desk before reaching into the second drawer to pull out a vial of white ink, a small wax burner with a small stick of gold wax, and a seal-carved envelope stamp.

The izuret chirped in approval as it watched the vampire prepare everything he needed to send a personal invitation. It sat down, crossing its little legs, watching in fascination.

Alucard didn't even know what to write. He laid out the card, dabbed his quill into the ink, and then sat there, staring, thinking…what should he say? It had to be in Deiganish too, or Zalith wasn't going to be able to understand. He didn't want to ask someone to write it for him; he wanted to do it himself—which felt rather strange since he knew he wasn't any good at all writing Deiganish. But he wanted to at least try. It was a personal invitation, after all; it wouldn't be so private if he asked someone to write for him, would it?

He sighed and placed the quill down, trying to work out what to write as he set the wax to burn. "Vhat do I even say?" he asked, looking at the izuret.

The creature shrugged and chattered quietly. They both looked at one another, thinking, and the small demon's eyes soon lit up. It clapped its hands excitedly, chirping in suggestion.

Alucard pondered as he picked the quill back up. "Hmm…Zaliv," he said, writing as he spoke. "I…'ost a celebration each year vor All-'allows Eve at my castle. I make sure to invite all of my vriends and associates…." He then went silent, continuing to write as the izuret leaned closer, trying to see what he was writing.

Once he was done, Alucard didn't bother reading it over. If he did, he knew he'd tear it up and start again. He couldn't afford to do that; if he did, he'd become frustrated and give up.

With a hesitant frown, he allowed the white ink to dry and then slipped the black card into the envelope. He placed it down on the desk, carefully poured a small amount of wax onto the letter's flap, and placed the seal stamp over it. He waited for it to dry.

Watching, the izuret wriggled around excitedly.

"If 'e zoesn't show up, I'll blame you," Alucard grumbled, glancing at the little demon, which chirped confidently in response. He sighed and handed the izuret the sealed black envelope. "Delay a little. I zon't vant to seem desperate."

Holding the letter in its hands, the izuret nodded and chirped quietly.

"Zaliv vill 'ave to pay you zhis time. I 'ave noving."

The izuret frowned in worry.

"Eh, no." Alucard shrugged. "My 'ouse just burned down. Everyving I 'ad inside vent vith. I'll be vine, zhough," he said as the izuret pouted sadly in concern. "Go now. I 'ave vings to do."

The izuret waved its free hand in farewell as it flapped its wings once, allowing itself to levitate. It then floated up to the roof and disappeared out through the open shutter.

As the small demon disappeared, Alucard sighed quietly and looked down at the two carnations Zalith sent him. He was back to waiting. So many people were coming to his party in order to discuss business with him, but now that he'd actually sent Zalith an invitation, he found himself focused on whether he'd get to see the demon. *That* was all that he looked forward to. He didn't care about making alliances with new people; he didn't care about spreading his influence across Aegisguard. Right now, all he cared about was seeing Zalith again. It would relieve him of so much worry, pain, and regret.

But there was no way to know if the demon would come or not. All he could do was hope.

Chapter Eighty-Eight

⌐ ⸰ † ⸰ ⌐

Xaliv

| **Zalith** |

The minuscule light which came down from the overcast sky filtered in through the orange-tinted windows of Zalith's new, empty office. He and Varana had found themselves a charming manor in Nefastus, Aegisguard, and the work he'd had done on it was finally complete. It was starting to look like home, and although the place wasn't without its quirks, Zalith felt much more safe and content than he had in Eltaria.

With a quiet sigh, his mind began to rifle through the long list of things that needed to get done, his dark eyes transfixed on the sad, blank wall across the room. He left all the decorating to Varana, something that he knew would keep her occupied for a while. The remainder of the walls were lined with barren shelves which he knew would one day be full of books and other things, but for now, the room was empty aside from his chair, his large desk, and the three empty chairs that sat across from it.

Zalith heard a light knock on the door frame, and his eyes fell upon one of his new butlers.

"Your guests have arrived, sir," the man said.

Wordlessly, Zalith nodded, and the butler ushered three people into the room, closing the door behind them. The demon recognized his guests immediately; after all, he'd known them for quite some time. Two of the individuals—a man with long, icy blonde hair named Orin and a woman with brunette hair named Idina—sat down in the chairs across from Zalith's desk. The remaining guest, Tyrus, began to slowly and curiously wander around the room, his amber eyes glowing in the slight absence of light.

The three of these demons were not only Zalith's subordinates but also Alphas of their own packs—packs which answered to Zalith, too. This made Zalith what was known in demon society as an Apex, a demon that ruled over multiple Alphas and their packs. He was *very* highly respected and well-known.

"Is it just me or does shit feel different here?" Tyrus asked enthusiastically before inhaling loudly. "Maybe it's the air? I don't know. I feel like I've been called home to the motherland."

Zalith said nothing in response, but the two demons murmured in agreement.

"And this house isn't too shabby either," Tyrus continued, his glowing eyes soon settling on the tinted windows. "I mean, it's no castle, but it's better than some werewolf den or that fucking farmhouse. Kinda looks like your old house in Andora."

Idina nodded in agreement. "How is Her Highness adjusting to the move?"

"Good," Zalith said simply, watching Tyrus as he gazed out of the window.

Orin nodded pleasantly to hear so. "We'd very much like to see her and extend our gratitude…if possible."

Zalith looked at the man across from him, and a small smile spread across his previously stern face. "No."

The man frowned, but he didn't object. He knew better than to do so.

Zalith waited for Tyrus to sit down before he began his meeting, but it was clear that the man was preoccupied. His sights darted between the trees in the distance, like a cat watching birds feeding in the yard.

Rolling his eyes slightly, Zalith began to speak. "How are things in Eltaria?"

Idina sighed. "I've heard news that the werewolf Primes are considering making a move against the human and healer populations. They seem to think that with you and Her Highness gone, they can do whatever they'd like. I've tried to talk them out of it, but they think they stand a chance."

There were three Primes in Chronia, the Eltarian country that Zalith had come from. Each Prime reigned over what very little remained of the several sub-packs that spread throughout the country.

Zalith shook his head. "They don't have the numbers to take on the humans; they should know this well enough. Orin, I suggest that you pay each of the Primes a visit, let them know that I meant what I said when I told them to stand down."

"And if they don't comply?" the man asked, a sinister grin spreading on his face.

Zalith smiled. "Convince them."

The man cracked his knuckles. "It would be my pleasure."

"Anything else?" Zalith asked, his sights drifting back to Tyrus, who was still enthusiastically eyeing the scenery beyond the manor.

Idina answered, "Three of the four known remaining vampires in Eltaria approached me yesterday practically begging to be let into Aegisguard. They were the ones who turned down the offer initially. I told them that I'd speak with you first, but–"

"They had their chance," Zalith said firmly. "I'm not troubling my contact just to accommodate them. If they can find peace amongst themselves, the werewolves, or what little remains with the demon population, then I suggest they do so."

Idina nodded, taking his words as resolute. "Of course, sir."

"Anything else?" Zalith questioned, and when the two demons shook their heads, his eyes drifted over to Tyrus. "Tyrus?" he asked, a blank look on his face.

The orange-eyed demon sighed happily and looked away from the window. "What do we know of the demons here? Rankings? Social structures?"

Orin shrugged. "As far as I'm aware, there's very little difference between the demons of Aegisguard and Eltaria in terms of behaviour."

Zalith leaned back in his chair, trying to dismiss the sadness that came with thinking about Alucard and how they parted ways. All this talk of vampires and demons…how could he *not* think about Alucard?

He frowned, focusing on his subordinates. "On average, I suspect that they're a little more…instinctual in this world, but that's no cause for concern. You'll find the beginnings of a lot of old and powerful bloodlines here, too."

Idina looked at Tyrus with a skeptical frown. "What are you thinking?"

Tyrus grinned, revealing a set of sharp fangs as he sat down casually in his chair. "I just want to get to know the locals," he said with a fiendish smile. "What do the humans say? Hobnob? I'm just going to do some regular, wholesome hobnobbing."

Idina glowered. "Is that really important right now? What about Eltaria?"

"What *about* Eltaria?" he laughed. "This is *it*, Idina—Aegisguard. Didn't you hear me? We're in the motherland. I'm talking Damien, Lucifer, Lilith—"

"But we weren't born here, this isn't—"

"I just want to make some acquaintances," Tyrus grumbled, cutting her off, although his fiendish eyes met Zalith's with a look of amusement. "Friends, maybe."

Idina shook her head in aversion. "When has anybody ever expressed interest in being a friend of yours? You kill anything that moves—"

Tyrus smiled. "And more often than not, that ends in all of our favours."

"Well, if there's a mysterious string of deaths in the area with no obvious cause, we'll know who to blame," the woman said, turning up her nose at him.

"I guess we will," Tyrus said with a shrug.

Zalith smiled as he watched the two bicker back and forth, but when he finally began to speak, they immediately fell silent. "I don't intend on staying here forever, but I think it would be wise to make use of this place while your queen and I are still here. Nefastus is a lawless although colourful little sty, and I think that, as residents, it's our civic duty to do a little bit of cleaning up."

The three listened intently, although Idina didn't seem too enthusiastic about Zalith's proposal.

"Tyrus," Zalith began, "I want you and what remains of your men to settle in the nearby city and its outskirts. Find what demons you can. Gather them, exert your dominance, and then bring them to me once they've aligned themselves with you. We'll work on this location first, but we'll speak about branching outwards once we're a little more comfortable."

The orange-eyed demon grinned devilishly. "It would be my absolute pleasure, sir."

Zalith looked at Orin. "As for you, focus on Eltaria for the time being. If we lose the werewolves, we'll lose the other races, so deal with the Primes as soon as you can. When that's over and done with, I want you to come back to Aegisguard and do some scouting for me."

Orin nodded in agreement. "What are you looking for?"

"We need to make some friends in high places. Varana has a few connections through her sister, but I'm not entirely satisfied with what she brings to the table. Names, details, and locations will work for the time being."

"I'll see what I can find," the man said with a noble smile.

"Good," Zalith said, turning to Idina. "I want you stationed in Eltaria; you'll do best there. Keep things in order, and be sure to keep me updated. Make it clear that we haven't abandoned those who we've worked so tirelessly to protect. It may take a while, but once everybody loosens up and the next few generations of humans die out, we'll take back what's ours."

Idina nodded, exhaling happily to hear so. "Of course, sir."

Zalith leaned back in his chair, looking at the wall beyond his guests. "In the meantime, Varana and I are going to establish ourselves here in a very cosy, human way. Invest in a few businesses, make donations, clean up the city, win trust through good deeds."

Orin nodded. "Noble."

"Of course, if that doesn't work, then we have other methods of getting what we want," the demon continued, smirking. "I'm going to have to do some investigating, but I'm confident that we can move our way up socially fairly quickly. Soon enough, what we lost in Eltaria we just might gain in Aegisguard, and when it's time for us to make a comeback, we'll have everything we need."

The three demons nodded, each of them pleased with their individual tasks, but Zalith wasn't done speaking.

"And, of course, nobody in Eltaria needs to know where Varana and I can be found. I can count on your discretion, I'm sure." There was a pleasant smile on Zalith's face, but his tone was firm and near threatening.

Each of the demons offered a quick, verbal agreement in response. Satisfied, Zalith dismissed his guests with a wave of his hand. They disappeared into thin air, and Zalith was finally alone once again.

It wasn't long after their departure when the demon could hear Varana's cheerful voice from across the house. He didn't know why she was speaking so loudly, but he also truthfully didn't care.

Rolling his eyes, he opened his desk drawer and removed a small stack of letters that he had accumulated from his subordinates over the past few days. Sometimes Zalith felt as though his work would never end, but he couldn't deny that he was happy to have something to do. Something to keep his mind from wandering—but it didn't always prove effective.

As Zalith read a long, rambling, useless letter of apology from somebody who wronged him, his mind began to stray. Of course, the topic of choice was Alucard. They still hadn't spoken since their goodbye on Aditus-Insula, and Zalith's concern had done everything but lessen. Alucard hadn't contacted him—but to be fair, Zalith hadn't contacted him, either.

He felt horrible for not reaching out to his friend, but he had a compulsion to keep quiet. A part of him wanted to be naïve; it wanted to convince him that he trusted himself not to destroy whatever this relationship with Alucard was—but Zalith wasn't stupid. He knew what he was like, and he didn't want to subject the vampire to what he considered to be almost inevitable heartbreak. He didn't want Alucard to be a short little fling; the vampire deserved so much more than that. Alucard made him feel so much warmth—so many emotions that he rarely felt for others…but it didn't matter. The other shoe was bound to drop.

How many times had he found himself growing bored of somebody who once thrilled him? Far too many, and Zalith desperately didn't want to grow bored of Alucard. He wasn't just a silly game to Zalith; the demon was almost certain that he might want him for real. And so, Zalith desired nothing more than to protect the vampire from himself. Even in Aegisguard, the demon forced himself to keep a distance until he felt like he was ready, no matter how badly it made him feel.

Distance, however, wasn't enough to keep Alucard away from Zalith's thoughts. He still longed to be by Alucard's side. The demon knew that if Alucard were here, he'd be entirely unable to listen to his own rules. There was something captivating about that vampire, something that Zalith was powerless to let go of. He'd never been so fond of anyone before—he'd never been so consistently surprised, impressed, or utterly charmed by anyone else. He wasn't quite sure how this was possible, but it happened, and he was falling *hard*.

Smiling, Zalith silently daydreamed about Alucard for a long moment, but his ears couldn't help but overhear Varana's loud voice coming closer and closer. It wasn't long before she entered Zalith's office without a knock. The woman, who wore a long, black day dress, held a golden hand mirror up to her face as she walked. She had an effortless grace, an undeniable beauty that seemed to lure people inward. Even though she had a slew of obvious flaws, and even though he had no interest whatsoever in becoming an item with her, Zalith couldn't deny that there was nothing like walking into a room with that woman on his arm.

"And this is Z's office," Varana said, spinning slowly where she stood so that the mirror could see each barren corner. What someone might assume to be the woman's reflection gazed around the room and back down at her, but Zalith knew well enough to know that it wasn't Varana who was looking back at them.

"Are you *poor*?" a voice from within the mirror asked rudely. "Where's the furniture?"

"Of course we're not poor!" Varana snapped as she approached where Zalith sat. "We just moved in. It's much better than that louse-infested farmhouse, so I'm content for the time being."

Paying Zalith absolutely no mind, Varana sat down on the arm of his chair, angling the mirror so that the individual on the other side could see both of them clearly.

"There," Varana said with a content smile, her eyes looking at Zalith as she leaned into him. "We're settling in well, aren't we, sweetheart?"

Zalith nodded. "Well enough."

His dark eyes looked into the hand mirror to see Ysmay, Varana's twin sister. Upon first glance, the two women were identical in almost every way, but if Ysmay were to open her mouth, she would reveal several horrendously sharp, piranha-like teeth. On that basis alone, it was easy to tell the two apart. This wasn't always the case, however. Varana had her teeth painfully adjusted and filed down long ago in an attempt to better assimilate with the humans of Eltaria—a process that the two women bickered back and forth about for weeks.

Ysmay's loud, shrill laugh cut through the air. "*Sweetheart*? You've really committed yourself to pretending that he isn't gay, haven't you? You don't have a dick, Varana. It's not going to happen."

Varana huffed angrily, her face crumpling up in a bitter scowl. "Shut up. Bitch."

Zalith couldn't fight the amused smile that spread across his face. Ysmay was right; Varana was very committed to the idyllic, romantic fantasy between the two of them that she built up in her head long ago. He made it clear to her hundreds of times that they were never going to be together, but Varana often preferred delusion over the facts.

Ysmay laughed once more. "Z, my sister's insane, right?"

"I said *shut up*!" Varana hissed before Zalith could answer. "Why don't you focus your energy on being pregnant for the millionth time, you *hag*."

"Hag?!" Ysmay yelled.

Instead of replying to her sister, Varana irately slammed the mirror down on Zalith's desk, ending their conversation in an instant. The woman pouted and slid to her side, pressing more and more of her body against Zalith's until she was practically sitting on his lap.

"I hate her," Varana said with a soft pout, resting her head on his shoulder.

Zalith sighed. "No, you don't," he told her. "Now, get off of me. I'm trying to work."

"You're right. I don't," the woman murmured, ignoring Zalith's command as she wrapped her arms around his shoulders. "But she's so mean. All she does when we talk is tease me—I'm only ever nice to her, you know."

Zalith rolled his dark eyes. "Varana, you just called her a hag."

The woman scowled, her irritation returning. "She started it!"

Zalith sighed and looked up at her. As long as she wasn't attempting to seduce him in one way or another, the demon wasn't bothered by the woman's tendency for closeness—but he couldn't deny that something about it at that moment felt wrong. It felt inauthentic; she wasn't the one who he wanted to be close to right now.

"What's wrong?" Varana asked with a frown.

Zalith shook his head, a convincing smile spreading across his face. "Nothing."

"But why did—"

Relief spread through Zalith once he heard a knock on his office door.

Their butler stood in the doorway with a small stack of papers in his hand. "Your mail from the izuret, sir…madam."

Zalith nodded. "Thank you."

But the man remained in the doorway, his eyes looking between his hands and Varana. It was clear that he wasn't quite sure if he was allowed to entirely enter Zalith's office.

Varana scowled. "Well? Are we to wait all day?! Give it here!"

The man quickly crossed the room, placed the papers in her palm, and retreated back through the door.

Varana huffed loudly as she flipped through the small stack of paper, absently tossing what didn't intrigue her onto Zalith's desk. "I think that butler's afraid of you," she said.

"Do you?" Zalith laughed. "I've barely had the chance to interact with any of them. I think he's afraid of you and your horrible attitude."

Tutting quietly, Varana sorted through the letters. "Work….work…work…."

Zalith reached over, quickly scanning each of them with his eyes as Varana continued to dole them out.

"Work…work…more work," she muttered, quickly losing interest in what she was doing. "Oh, what's this?"

"Hmm?" Zalith asked absently, reading a quick update from one of their Eltarian colleagues.

"This," Varana said as she held a black envelope over the paper that Zalith was looking at.

The envelope was blank; the only thing on it was a golden wax seal. There was no addressee on the front, nothing to indicate who it was for or where it had come from, but Zalith had his suspicions. If not because of the black-on-gold aesthetic, then because of the imagery that had been pressed carefully into the wax surface. The letters A and R had been combined at the centre, the bottom of the A creating the line that ran through the middle of the letter R. Together, they created a shape that somewhat resembled an hourglass.

The demon immediately snatched the envelope from Varana's hands.

"Hey!" she yelped. "You gave me a paper cut."

"I'm sure I didn't," Zalith murmured, carefully lifting the golden seal from the paper.

Frowning, Varana raised her hand to her mouth. "Yes, you did," she whined, weakly sucking on the fictional wound on the webbing between her thumb and index finger. "What are you smiling about?"

Zalith hesitated. He *was* smiling, wasn't he? He couldn't deny it even if he wanted to. The blank envelope filled him with nothing but relief, happiness, and curiosity. As he carefully removed the parchment from inside, Zalith knew that this could very well be an angry letter. This could be Alucard telling him off, berating him for kissing him again and then disappearing—but Zalith found himself happy to hear from him all the same.

The demon did his best to keep the letter out of Varana's view, but with the way they were sitting, his efforts were futile. The two of them began to read, and Zalith's smile only grew. This was most certainly from Alucard.

Xaliv,

I host a selebrashun each yeer for All-Hallows' eve at my cassul. I make shure to invite all my friends and asosheits and fought this yeer you may want to come. All-Hallow's eve is seven days from now - this is not much notice so I can understand if you can't come. I wood like it for you to come, though. It has been some time since I have herd from you.

Alucard.

"Who in the world is *Xaliv*?" Varana asked confused frown.

"Me," Zalith said delightfully. He loved every little spelling error that Alucard had written, and it only made his heart grow fonder. And as he re-read the words, he swore he could hear that vampire's beautiful accent echoing through his head.

Varana scowled. "Who sent this to you?"

"My vampire," Zalith said, his dark eyes reading the letter once more.

"*Your* vampire?" Varana questioned, her face crumpled up in disfavour. "The one you kissed? I thought he worked for Damien?"

"He does."

The look of distaste on the woman's face only deepened. "So…why can't he spell?"

Zalith's smile fell, his joy quickly replaced by annoyance. He turned to look at her, his face void of any positive emotion. "This isn't his first language, Varana."

"So?" Varana said, a judgmental tone in her voice. "He spelt your name with an *X*…and it's not hard to spell castle."

"And yet we could both understand what he was saying, could we not?" Zalith grumbled.

"Yes, but I just feel like he could put a little more effort into—"

"Remind me, V, how many languages can you speak, exactly?" Zalith coldly asked. "Am I correct in assuming that it is still just the one?"

The woman clenched her jaw tightly, her eyes staring venomously back at Zalith. It was clear to the demon that she wanted to say more, but something kept her from lashing out. He almost wished that she would.

Varana closed her eyes and exhaled, only reopening them once she seemed calm. "I'm sorry," she said, crossing her arms against her chest.

Zalith put the letter carefully back into its envelope and then placed it safely in one of his desk drawers. The two demons sat in complete silence as Zalith began to quietly read the remainder of his mail, but he could feel Varana's energy practically bristling from within her. She wanted to do something, to say something, and he knew her well enough to know that she wouldn't be able to stay quiet for much longer.

Rolling his eyes, Zalith quietly waited for Varana to break the silence.

"The party's in a week," Varana murmured. "Do you know what you're going to wear?"

"Yes," Zalith said simply.

"Already?" Varana asked in bitter surprise.

Zalith nodded, and another silence fell between them, although Varana wasn't finished.

"Well, you'll have to let me know what you're thinking," Varana mused. "I don't want our outfits to clash—"

"You're not coming with me," Zalith said firmly, a small look of amusement on his face.

The woman pouted. "Why not?"

"Because I don't want you there," Zalith told her plainly.

The demon watched as Varana's jaw dropped in offence. "Why?!"

"Because you're unpleasant."

Varana squinted her crimson eyes in suspicion. "It's because you don't want me near that vampire, isn't it?"

"Yes," Zalith said, nodding. "Because to reiterate, you're *unpleasant*."

"I'm *not* unpleasant," Varana snapped.

Zalith wasn't convinced. He loved her, of course; she was practically family, but he wasn't wrong about her. Varana was always like this, especially when somebody that Zalith was seeing was involved. She'd resent them, plot against them, and childishly attempt to steal Zalith's attention away. He could only imagine what she might say or do in Alucard's company; he didn't want to risk it, not now.

"So you're just going to ignore me?" she questioned.

He shrugged. "It depends; are you going to continue to irritate me?"

Varana pouted. "We never used to be like this, you know. The war changed us, I suppose. We never used to bicker like this."

Zalith shook his head. "We absolutely did."

"Well…." Varana frowned. "I, *personally*, feel like everything's changing."

"Is that so?" Zalith asked with complete disinterest.

Varana nodded. "Yes. From rooms filled with beautiful art and pretty things, to…*this*. From the castle to dirty little farmhouses. From dukes to illiterate vampires—"

"Get out," Zalith growled. He'd had enough. Varana could say a million things about anybody else, but not Alucard.

Varana scowled. "Seriously?"

"Yes," Zalith snapped. "Don't bother speaking to me until you've learned some respect."

"Zalith—"

"*Leave*."

The demon put his hands on her shoulders and firmly pushed her off his lap and onto her feet. A violent, angry shriek came from Varana's mouth as she stood upright. The woman snatched her hand mirror off of his desk and stomped off into the hallway, slamming the door shut behind her. Along with the sound of her heavy, stomping footsteps in the hall, Zalith heard a shrill, high-pitched scream of anger from beyond the confines of his office. He didn't care. She could scream all she wanted; he wasn't going to react to her childish tantrum.

As the woman's angry sounds cleared, Zalith was left alone in the quiet with his thoughts. It was much more pleasant to think about Alucard's polite little invitation without Varana there. Another happy smile spread across Zalith's face. He was certainly going to attend, despite his previous preaching about keeping his distance for now. A party was perfect. They'd be in a room full of people, and Zalith would have to be on his best behaviour. Even if he and Alucard only had the chance to exchange brief greetings before the vampire was whisked away by his guests, at least Zalith would get the chance to see him again.

Chapter Eighty-Nine

— ⸨ † ⸩ —

Alucard's Party

| **Alucard,** *Decem 31st—Alucard's Birthday* |

The sun hadn't long set over the horizon; the sky was darkening, the moons were rising, and Alucard was sitting alone in the hall of his castle. The large, long oak table which usually spread through the middle of the hall was absent, and instead, several small tables were lined around the outside of the room. He sat at the table closest to the entrance hallway, staring aimlessly ahead.

Several butlers silently completed what little chores remained before Alucard's guests turned up for his annual All-Hallows' Eve party. He wasn't sure who might come, and he didn't care much, as long as he wouldn't have to spend the night alone. His loneliness weighed so intensely since the night he lost Tobias, the same night he'd also seen Zalith for what might just be the last time.

His thoughts were focused on his guests, namely those who *wouldn't* be attending this year, the people he'd taken so long to learn to openly care for and then lost in a heartbeat. It was only four months ago that he lost Elvin, the enthusiastic, talented bard he tried to give a better life to. But ultimately, he failed him, just as he failed everyone else who relied on him. Rodney, Tobias, Vanessa, Michael and Peter, Ben—he even felt as though he failed Zalith, who probably wasn't even going to turn up tonight. Why would he? Alucard hadn't made any effort to try and make contact after they finished the vampire relocation mission. Why would his stupid little invitation make any difference? Zalith had most likely moved on with someone else—someone better.

Alucard hadn't had much time to think about what happened before he returned to his burning manor, to Ada's last attempt to destroy what he'd built. But now that there was a possibility that he might be seeing Zalith tonight, there was no way to avoid thinking about it. Before they parted ways, Zalith kissed him again, and he accepted it so openly, so comfortably, despite his attempt to tell the demon that they could no longer see each other. Why? It was obvious—he felt something for Zalith he'd never felt for anyone else before, yet he had no idea what to do with it. He missed him so sorely; he craved his presence, and the thought of never seeing him again made him feel such an overwhelming ache deep within his heart.

Inviting Zalith tonight was all he could think of in his moment of agonizing yearning for his company, and if the demon didn't show, then he'd know that what he felt was absurdly nonsensical. He'd know that what they might have once shared was over. After all, if Zalith didn't feel the same way that Alucard still undeniably did, then what point was there in him feeling such a need for the embrace of a man who didn't want him? He told Zalith they could no longer see each other; he ended whatever they were becoming. Why would Zalith *not* move on after that? Why would he wait around after the things Alucard said?

He glanced over at the butlers, watching as they finished setting up the refreshment table. As far as Alucard was aware, his guests would all be human; he asked Dirk to invite whoever he wanted because Dirk was the only one of his subordinates left, and he was the only person Alucard knew who had such a vast majority of friends and contacts. He didn't even care who showed up; he just didn't want to spend this typically eventful night alone.

All Hallows' Eve was always a night of loud, ecstatic celebration in Dor-Sanguis, and despite his own depravity, he wasn't going to differ this year. All he hoped was that the one person he wanted to see would show, and if he didn't, well…he was quite sure he'd allow himself to sink into the despondency that had begun gripping him so tightly like the clawed hand of a painfully familiar creature, pulling him deeper into the dark that was his life.

Taking his eyes off the butlers, he looked down at his hands. Before he could retreat into his thoughts, the door knocked quietly. He stared over at the hallway which led to the castle's front door. No one was due to arrive for at least another fifteen minutes, and Dirk was never early, so why would any of his subordinates be? He wasn't at all interested in letting anyone in until it was time—why would he want to let these strangers in prematurely? However, if he remained sitting in silence, he was sure he'd allow his loneliness to grip him for the rest of the night. So, he stood up and started to make his way towards the front door.

Whoever was waiting on the other side of the door, he hoped it wasn't anyone too annoying—namely Dirk's fellow council members or Dirk himself. What did it matter? It wasn't like they would spend the evening talking to him; it wasn't like *anyone* would spend much time with him at all. They didn't care. He didn't care.

He lost his sullen frown, donned a vacant stare, and reached for the door handle. Then, he pulled the door open expecting to set his eyes on the ugly, uninteresting faces of humans; but instead, he set his fiery eyes on something much more appealing—and heart-wrenchingly unexpected.

Standing in front of him with a content smile on his almost pale face…was Zalith. The demon's dark eyes shimmered red in the light of the castle, his expression becoming something relieved as if to say the very thing Alucard was thinking: *at last*. Seeing him after so long…Alucard could feel his heart trembling. It felt as though the past four months had been *centuries*.

The demon had come dressed in a fitted, dark blue velvet suit adorned with a textured floral pattern of the same colour, and beneath his blazer, he wore a light grey waistcoat, a white shirt, and a light grey bowtie, along with black shoes. He looked as impressive as always.

"Hello, vampire," Zalith said, his voice like a breath of fresh air, like a cure for Alucard's immutable, despairing thoughts.

Alucard stared at him. He had no idea what to say. Seeing him caused a relieving yet nervous confusion to grip him; Zalith had come, even after he felt so convinced that he wouldn't. But there he was…with that same annoying smile on his face, the smile Alucard had come to enjoy seeing so often and missed so sorely whenever he was gone. Zalith appeared as calm and collected as always, something Alucard knew *he* currently wasn't. How could he be? He'd never felt like this before; he'd never felt such a need for a singular person's simple presence. He wasn't sure what it was, all he knew was that seeing Zalith right now was exactly what he needed.

The vampire found his voice and frowned. "You…came?" he asked, still surprised.

"Of course I did," Zalith said. He stepped forward, moving closer—

Alucard wasn't sure if he was moving in for a hug…or to come inside. His restless mind told him it was the latter. After all, it had been months since they'd seen each other. Surely, Zalith had moved on. But as the demon frowned slightly, Alucard drowned in angst—he'd wanted to hug him, hadn't he? It was too late now—too *embarrassing*.

Zalith glanced down the hallway. "Am I early?"

Setting his eyes back on Zalith, Alucard nodded. "You are," he said. Then, he led the way into the hall, trying to hide the fact that he was so overwhelmingly nervous. His thoughts, his feelings, his emotions: they were all over the place, and as much as he wanted to immediately tell Zalith how he hoped for his company, he knew he needed time to collect himself, otherwise what came out of his mouth would be a complete and utter disaster. He had no idea how to explain how he was feeling; he didn't know what to call these feelings—so he had to wait.

When they reached one of the small tables, Zalith lightly grabbed Alucard's arm and turned him to face him. "Is everything all right?" he asked with concern in his voice.

"Vhy vould not be?" Alucard answered, staring at him in confusion.

Zalith let go of his arm. "I won't impede," he said quietly…but then hesitated. He stared at him for a moment, almost as if he was unsure of what to say.

Alucard wasn't sure if he was waiting for him to speak, but he felt so overwhelmed with angst right now…he wasn't sure what he *could* say.

But the demon reached into his pocket. "Alucard," he said, and as the vampire took his eyes off the floor and looked at him, he held out a small black box. "I got something for you so that you'd know you never left my thoughts." He smiled, glancing down at the box. "And…because it's your birthday. I didn't forget."

Alucard's eyes slowly wandered from Zalith's face to the small black box he was holding in his left hand. He got something…for *him*? Why? Why would anyone feel the need to go out of their way and get something for him? He glanced at Zalith's face, unsure whether this was the beginning of some estranged gag. Was Zalith looking for amusement as he always seemed to be? He looked back down at the box in his hand. Should he take it?

With a smile of endearment, Zalith slowly and carefully grabbed Alucard's wrist with his right hand, pulled the vampire's hand forward, and placed the box in his palm.

Alucard stared at it. What could it be? What could Zalith have possibly thought to get him? He felt his anxiety growing; he wanted to open it, he wanted to see, but he also wanted to try and use this moment of mutual uncertainty to tell Zalith how he felt, to attempt to tell him what happened—so much had happened. Zalith was the only person he wanted to talk to, the only person he wanted to share his time with despite his sadness…because he knew that Zalith would help pull him from his despondency. If he didn't try to tell him now, he might not get another chance, and faltering was something he didn't much like to do.

He gazed at Zalith's expectant face. The demon was clearly waiting for a reaction or an answer. If Alucard told him why he invited him…if he asked Zalith if he still felt the same…would it ruin whatever it was they had? Did he want to risk ruining the only relationship he had left because he needed to understand where they stood? If he had to bury his immutable, yearning feelings for whatever might lay beyond friendship in order to keep Zalith in his life, then he would. After all, *Alucard* said goodbye; he ended whatever they shared and had most likely hurt Zalith doing it. If it had been Zalith telling him the things he told the demon, he knew he'd be so upset that he'd sink into his sadness for months—years, even. He'd probably caused Zalith a similar hurt, and he felt overwhelmingly guilty.

So, why would he expect Zalith to still feel the same after that goodbye and after so many months? He didn't know what to think. Zalith had come—he'd come *early*. He presented him with a gift, and a week ago, he sent flowers. What did all of this mean, if anything at all? *Did* Zalith still feel something? Or had he just come for some other unbeknown reason? Alucard wanted to ask, but he still didn't know how or if doing so was the best thing to do right now.

Taking his eyes off Zalith, he looked back down at the box—

"Alucard, please tell me what's wrong," Zalith pleaded quietly, still holding Alucard's left wrist with his right hand, moving his other hand to the vampire's right arm.

As his desperate need for understanding found its way to his face in the form of a sullen frown, Alucard stared at the demon. But he didn't have the words. His depravity lingered over him like a cold, dark cloud—there was so much to tell, so much to ask, but how to do it? He just didn't understand. But he could feel Zalith ever so slowly starting to pull him closer in his own unsureness. He waited, sure that Zalith was about to embrace him—and he felt as though maybe *that* was what he needed. This demon was the only person he felt no desire to push away, the only person whose physical contact didn't alarm nor distress him. He wanted to feel closer; he wanted to be reminded of what it felt like to have the arms of someone he yearned to be close to around him.

But he wouldn't get to feel such comfort tonight.

Before Zalith could pull him any closer, the door to his castle knocked loudly. The sound startled Alucard out of his moment of calm—the fact that he was so close to Zalith now caused him to feel both angst and embarrassment. And so, he moved away, pulling himself from Zalith's affectionate grip. He slipped the box into his pocket and silently made his way towards the door, trying to replace his nervous expression with a vacant one.

It was going to be a long, disheartening night.

Chapter Ninety

Opportunities

| Zalith |

Zalith watched Alucard in both regret and dismal as he walked towards the front door. All he wanted to do was embrace the vampire, and just now might have been his chance, but he took too long. The only thing he could do now was watch as Alucard walked away once more and try to keep his own despondency from ruining the evening for him. He wanted to know what Alucard was thinking, what he might be feeling in regard to their relationship, but he wasn't sure if he'd get an answer, let alone the one he wanted.

He felt so relieved to see him; it may have only been four months, but it felt as though it had been a short eternity. He missed the sound of his voice—his beautiful accent, the way he spoke a little too fast sometimes, and how he stuttered with some words he hadn't fully grasped the pronunciation of. And his *eyes*—Zalith could stare into them forever. He hadn't failed to notice that same sadness lingering within them, though.

Did Alucard still feel the same way? He tried to end their growing relationship that night on Aditus-Insula…and how he was acting now…his attitude, his body language, and his avoidance of Zalith's hug—of course, it could have been Alucard mistaking his intentions, but he couldn't help but feel as though it was Alucard trying to tell him…it was over. However, if that were the case, then why would the vampire have invited him to his party? Why would he have gone out of his way to *hand-write* an invitation?

Tonight wasn't another goodbye, was it? Zalith didn't want to think so, nor did he want to ruin what looked like an evening Alucard had put so much effort into. For now, he'd do his best to silence his anxious, dismaying thoughts…and let Alucard come to him.

| Alucard |

When he reached the front door, Alucard pulled it open and set his eyes on Dirk. The council member had his blonde hair combed back over his head, and his blue eyes gleamed brightly. Behind him was a large crowd of formally dressed men and women, and they were all chatting excitedly.

"Aleksei," Dirk said with a smile. "As you asked, I invited a fair amount of people—most of them are potential associates, of course."

Alucard didn't care to know who any of them were. He stepped aside, holding out his arm, inviting everyone inside. He did, however, catch sight of a familiar, scruffy-faced vampire among the crowd, standing arm-in-arm with his auburn-haired wife.

"Aleksei," Ben greeted, grabbing his hand and shaking it. "How are you doing?" he asked quietly. "I haven't heard from you since last week."

"I'm vine," Alucard mumbled, leaving the door open as he led the way back towards the hall, where everyone had gathered.

Ben smiled pleasantly as he and his wife walked beside Alucard. "I noticed that some of the vampires moved back into the city."

"Yes," he grumbled. He didn't want to remember any of the awful, heart-breaking things that unfolded in the past six months, the things that caused his absence, an absence that resulted in difficulties for everyone around him. He just wanted to live this night and forget his sadness for a while—if that were even possible.

Once they reached the hall, Ben and his wife followed Alucard over to his table and sat with him. The couple took a quick glance around the room, eyeing the unimportant humans as they helped themselves to the food that the butlers had laid out prior to their arrival. A small orchestra was also preparing to start playing on the stage. Then, they looked back at Alucard.

Ben asked, "So, did Zalith respond to your invite?"

The vampire took his eyes off the table and scoured the room with his eyes, searching for the demon, and when his eyes met with Zalith's from across the room, he felt his sadness yield ever so slightly. He would always catch Zalith staring at him, whether it be from afar or from a few small feet away, and it was yet another thing he had come to miss. For a moment, it made him ponder…if Zalith was still acting the same way he was before their goodbye, could that mean he hadn't moved on? Could it mean he still felt something? Or was he just admiring him because he found amusement in doing so? Alucard wasn't sure.

Looking in the direction Alucard was staring, Ben spotted Zalith—he raised his hand to wave, and Zalith responded with a slight smirk.

Ben then said to Alucard, "I told you he'd come."

Then, the music started to play.

Lillian tapped Ben's hand excitedly. "Let's dance."

Ben nodded and sighed quietly as he glanced at Alucard. "If you need me, I'll be around," he offered. Then, he stood up and escorted his wife to the centre of the room, where several couples had already started to slow-dance.

Once Ben left, Alucard slowly scoured the room once more, searching for Zalith—

"Aleksei, this is Dean," Dirk said, appearing in front of him.

Alucard glared up at him, uninterested in whoever he just introduced.

Dirk held his arm out towards the chubby, ecstatic-faced man beside him. "He's interested in sharing his business with ours—well, yours, but… you know what I mean."

Dean held out his hand and grinned. "I hear you have effective ways of dealing with one's enemies."

Slowly, Alucard's eyes shifted from Dirk to Dean; he shook the man's hand and then returned to staring vacantly at whatever his eyes so happened to set themselves on.

"He's not really… much of a talker," Dirk said nervously, looking back over at Dean. "Aleksei, Dean's from Solitudinem; he's a member of the country's parliament. They wish to discuss opportunities."

Dean adorned an enthusiastic smile. "We're currently on the verge of war with both vampires and lycans, much like most other continents in the world. We were hoping for your assistance in response to our willingness to cooperate with you and whatever you might want to—"

"Dirk vill sort zhis out. Stop bothering me," Alucard mumbled, waving his hand in dismissal.

"Uh… great, we'll get right on that," Dirk said as he turned his back on Alucard and walked away, muttering quietly to Dean.

After a few moments of loneliness, Freja then sat opposite Alucard, handing him a glass of red wine. He frowned, watching as the woman made herself comfortable and smiled at him.

The amber-eyed, blonde-haired werewolf rested her arms on the table. "There are far fewer vampires here than I suspected there would be," she mumbled in Dor-Sanguian.

Alucard took the glass and stared down into it, pondering to himself for a few moments. "Zhey are busy," he replied, unsure of what else to say to his new subordinate. He didn't like the fact that she reminded him of Ada appearance-wise, but he couldn't let that keep him from forming a professional relationship with her. If he chose to resent her, working with her wouldn't be as easy as he'd like.

"Who are all these people?" she asked, looking around at the packed room.

He shrugged and grumbled, "I zon't know ninety-nine percent of zhe people 'ere. Dirk invited possible allies and some of 'is vriends."

"Well, I've spent the last week moving my pack, as ordered. Most of them have set up camp in the little area Dirk showed me; we're just moving the last of our supplies over—I have my Betas doing it as we speak. We'll unite with the pack that is already there. One of my sisters has offered to marry one of their Betas."

"Good," he said, staring into his drink.

"Is there anything else you need me to do right now?"

"No," he answered. "Go and enjoy zhe party, or do vhatever. Leave me alone."

With a nod, Freja stood up and wandered off into the crowd.

Then, Alucard sighed and went to take a sip of his wine—

"So, *this* is Lin-Hong from Lâohû-Zhī-Dì," Dirk introduced, standing in front of Alucard once again with his arm around a Lâohunese man, who was around five foot five in height, and with not a single hair on his head.

Lin-Hong stared down at Alucard, a mutual vacant stare on his face.

"Who?" Alucard asked with a frown, utter disinterest in his voice. How many more people would Dirk introduce him to tonight?

"Lin-Hong. He's an emperor of Lâohû-Zhī-Dì. He wishes to offer a chance to work collaboratively with you in regard to his country's war. The nations have been at each other's throats for years, competing to win the favour of their gods. For your assistance, he offers you allegiance," Dirk explained.

Alucard sighed irritably and stood up. He pulled Dirk aside. "Vhat are you doing?"

Dirk frowned and answered, "You asked me to find allies and possible opportunities to expand. That's what I've been doing, and I invited the current candidates tonight so that you could meet them. That... *is* what you told me to do."

He was right. Alucard *had* asked him to search for possible allies, people he could convince to work with or for him so that he could spread his empire across Aegisguard once again—an empire he started creating in what he thought was a quest to gain what he wanted most: recognition, purpose—value. But he'd already come to see that he wouldn't get the kind of appreciation or affection he wanted from an empire. He would only get it from a single person, and that man was standing somewhere in the same room as him.

With a quiet sigh, Alucard looked down at his drink. "Vork zhat out vith Lin-'Ong."

"Of course," Dirk said, leaving him again.

There was a time and place for this sort of business, and this just wasn't it. Right now, Alucard didn't have the motivation to work on his business affairs; he didn't even have the motivation to drink what he had in his hand. All he could do was stare at it. The commotion of the party around him seemed all but still and silent—he paid no mind to any of it. He thought that filling his castle with people would spare him from his tired, lonely life for a moment at least, but it just made him feel a whole lot more empty.

If Elvin were there, he would be making a complete and utter fool of himself while Alucard tried to keep him from stumbling. Tobias would be in the far corner with several women hanging off his arms, inviting the vampire to join him, and Rodney would be having a political conversation with a woman who very clearly wasn't interested. But not one of those three people was present. And they never would be again.

| **Zalith** |

From across the room, Zalith kept his watchful yet concerned gaze on Alucard. He'd never seen him look so sad before—it was disheartening. He still didn't know why Alucard was so despondent, so quiet, so distant, and he still didn't know whether his actions played a part in what he must be feeling. What *was* he feeling? The demon longed to know. Despite his own worries, he wanted to know how Alucard felt about *him*. Was Alucard questioning their relationship, or could Alucard possibly still feel what Zalith believed to be the same way he did?

Zalith knew what *he* wanted; what he felt was so much more than anything that had come before. The need he felt for Alucard's company, for his affection—it was *real*. It wasn't of lust or entertainment—it was of something pure-hearted. To him, Alucard was so important, so…precious, even. Whenever he thought about this vampire, he felt nothing but content, nothing but a longing to experience more with him. Seeing him after what felt like so long only intensified his desire. But the worry that Alucard might no longer feel the same way still lingered in the back of Zalith's mind. For quite some time, he'd been confident that he wanted more than a friendship with Alucard, and he still found himself hoping Alucard might just feel that way, too.

As Alucard sipped from his glass, Zalith's sullen frown withered. Why was the vampire just standing there? He was alone, and he looked so upset that it hurt Zalith's heart. This was *his* party; he should surely be having a good time, but he didn't even bother to mingle with any of the guests. He stood alone, staring into his glass, a look of vacancy on his pale face. Zalith didn't want to leave him standing by himself, and he wanted to take whatever chance he could to spend more time with the vampire.

However, when Dirk placed another random, boring group of humans in front of Alucard, Zalith scowled. He watched as they all nattered on to one another, glancing at Alucard so that he might feel involved in a conversation that had nothing to do with him, his life, or his party—these people simply wanted to be seen in Alucard's presence, to feel important, and that made Zalith so dangerously furious that he thought he might just head over there and put them in their lowly, pathetic places.

But he might get carried away. His own feelings might cause him to do something that would upset Alucard, and he didn't want that. So, he kept his distance, admiring the vampire from afar, keeping his eyes on him as he made his way over to a butler and took a glass of wine from him. Zalith was sure the evening would be a long one, but he wasn't certain of when he might get to speak to Alucard again. Whenever it may be, though, he'd be sure to use the time wisely.

Chapter Ninety-One

At Last

| **Alucard** |

Hours passed and Alucard was still standing in the same place since the party started. Dirk placed person after person in front of him, and not a single thing any of them said made an impact. It all went in one ear and out the other. Alucard had no interest in anything anyone else might have to say. The only person he wanted to hear from was Zalith.

"…He's from Samjang," Dirk concluded, patting the shoulder of the black-haired, slender man standing beside him.

Alucard blinked slowly in disinterest. He didn't remember the names of anyone Dirk introduced to him through the evening. He nodded in response, sending Dirk away for what he hoped to be the last time.

He stared down into his wine glass; he hoped that Zalith would have come over by now, but he hadn't. Alucard tried to convince himself that maybe the demon was taking time to collect his thoughts—if he even had anything else to say. He then glanced down at his pocket; perhaps *now* he'd get a chance to look at the gift Zalith gave him. But as he lowered his hand towards his pocket, Dirk stopped in front of him once again.

"This is the Divinos clan," he introduced, holding his arm out to present the three midnight-purple-robed men. "They're interested in your knowledge of Janus."

The vampire looked at each of the Divinos wizards and frowned in disinterest. "Vhatever," he mumbled, having already decided that he was now going to look at what might be inside the box Zalith had given him. He'd held onto it for long enough, and Dirk's annoyance helped him banish his despondency just enough so that he could spare a moment to allow his curiosity to seep in.

Dirk frowned. "You…don't have anything to—"

"No," Alucard snarled quietly. "I'm busy. Go and deal vith zhat."

Nodding, Dirk led the wizards away.

However, Alucard felt his confidence wane. Did he want to open the box in front of everyone? Not exactly. He knew Zalith was still watching him, too, and that made him nervous enough on its own—but to look at his gift under his watchful eye? He couldn't do that... could he? He looked down at his pocket again, but when he heard Dirk making his way over, he snarled, scowled irritably, and moved away from the wall he'd spent the entire night standing against.

He headed towards the door to his half of the castle; he glanced through the crowd, and that was when he spotted Zalith. The demon was glancing at Ben, who chatted contentedly with him. It seemed as though Zalith *wasn't* still watching him after all. Why did that hurt him so much?

Alucard scowled down at the floor and reached the door. Without so much as a sound, he left the party and walked through the deserted hallways. But his brief moment of anger withered into sadness. Anyone he'd ever felt close to was taken from him in one way or another; why would Zalith be any different? He wasn't sure why he allowed himself to hope that perhaps Zalith still felt the way he did before Alucard ended what they once shared.

With a despondent scowl, he made his way upstairs, the party echoing behind him. Where he'd started to feel as if he might be ready to tell Zalith he still felt the same, he now knew that he wasn't—he couldn't. What was the point? He was convinced that Zalith no longer felt that way, so now he'd have to bury these feelings—feelings he'd never felt before... and that fact kept him from doing so so easily. How could he ignore them? How could he ignore this painful need for someone's attention? This weighted feeling of sorrow he felt every time he thought about losing Zalith, about never seeing him again. He had no idea what to do with any of it; he had no idea what to call any of it—how to explain it. All he was sure of was that he never needed anyone in the way he needed that demon, a demon who didn't need him.

No one needed him.

He went into his study and disappeared into vermillion smoke, reappearing on one of the top floors. The vampire pulled the balcony doors open and walked to the edge. He rested his arms on the railings as he glared down at the ground, watching as the humans in the castle courtyard laughed, conversed, and made use of the wine he spent so long making in his spare time.

His thoughts wandered back to Zalith and the gift that sat in his pocket. He denied himself falling into sadness once more and reached into his pocket. He pulled the small black box out and stared down at it as it sat in his palm. Confliction gripped him as a sullen frown replaced his vacant stare. No one had *ever* given Alucard a gift—no one. Zalith was the first—the first to do so many things for him—and despite his worry that Zalith might not feel the same anymore, he still felt happiness knowing that the demon thought fondly enough of him to go out of his way to get him a gift. But what could it be?

Angst consumed him. He was afraid to open it. He had no idea what to expect—he *never* knew what to expect when it came to Zalith…but he liked that. He then scowled; he didn't want to think about what he liked about Zalith, not when he was too busy talking to Ben, paying *him* no mind. He wasn't sure why that made him feel so strangely angry…almost *jealous*, but it soon faded.

He glanced down at the main building where the party was continuing. Should he go back and find Zalith? Should he just stop being so stupidly shy and tell him how he felt? He wanted to make his feelings known—he *had* to; it was the only way he'd understand what it meant. But what if it pushed Zalith away? What if Zalith found it funny? What if Zalith didn't feel the same way he did? He couldn't bear to lose him, not now. So perhaps his silence was better.

The vampire looked at the box again, despondency smothering his face. He slowly pulled the lid off to reveal the inside of it, which was dark grey and adorned with black floral-like patterns similar to those on Zalith's suit. Alucard placed the lid on the top of the balcony railings and proceeded to look at what was inside. Something sat within, wrapped in black silk, which shimmered in the coloured moonlight. He carefully took whatever it was out and placed the rest of the box aside. Then, he started to gently unwrap what was inside the silk while his angst increased.

Alucard had no idea what it might be, and as each moment of slow, suspenseful unwrapping passed, he felt his heart beat just a little faster. Why was he so nervous to see what Zalith got him? Was it because no one had ever given him anything before, or was it because it was Zalith who gave it to him? He wasn't sure, but as he pulled the last of the silk away, he stared at what sat in his palm.

A silver crucifix; each of the cross' ends were shaped in an almost cloud-like form, each point with a small silver circle inlaid into it. The outline of a slightly smaller cross sat within it, its ends pointed, and embedded in the centre of the crucifix was a rounded shape almost reminiscent of a flower with a deep black gemstone encrusted in it. A silvery chain was attached to it, but the item shimmered with an almost pale grey hue that couldn't be silver—if it was, he couldn't wear it. Of course, Zalith somehow knew that, and he wouldn't be so foolish as to get him something made with silver.

The vampire smiled. He loved it. He loved the crucifix, and he loved that Zalith seemed to know that he would appreciate it as much as he did. He placed the silk alongside the box, unclipped the chain's clip, and then tried to put it around his neck. However, he couldn't manage on his own.

And that was when he felt a familiar touch against his cold hands—but he wasn't startled.

"Let me do that for you," Zalith said with a smile, taking each end of the chain from Alucard's grip.

Lowering his hands to his sides, Alucard waited as Zalith clipped the chain back together around his neck.

The demon then moved in front of him and straightened it before smiling contentedly. "It looks perfect on you."

Trying to hide his nervous smile, Alucard looked down at the crucifix. "You zidn't 'ave to get me anyving."

"I wanted to," Zalith replied, resting his left arm on the railings.

"Vhy?" Alucard asked, and as his eyes met with the demon's, he hesitated and looked down at the courtyard.

Zalith smiled amusedly in response to Alucard's nervousness. "Because I want you to know that you're important to me."

Alucard glanced at him; he wanted to ask Zalith to elaborate, he wanted to know just what he meant by that; why was he important to him? Did he still feel the same way he had before? Did he still mean the things he said when Alucard asked him why he cared? Did Zalith…perhaps still want to be with him? He had to ask, but all he could do was stand there, look down at his hands, and pout in silence.

However, Zalith wasn't so reluctant to speak up. "You *are* important to me, Alucard," he said quietly, gazing at him. "So much that it pains me to see you in such distress. What's happened?" he asked, placing his hand on the vampire's arm.

There had never been a time Alucard could hide his expression from Zalith; he always seemed to know what he was experiencing. He *was* distressed—but about so many different things. He didn't understand his feelings, his friends had all been taken from him, and he was afraid he might lose the only person he felt a disheartening, confusing attachment to because he allowed his fear to force him to push him away. Did Zalith see *that*? Did he suspect that he might be feeling this way? He wasn't sure. Even if Zalith *could* tell, what would he be able to do about it? Alucard didn't know. There were so many things he just didn't know.

He shifted his sights to Zalith's gaze, gripping the demon's wrist with his hand. Hesitation kept him from even attempting to try and tell Zalith he needed him. Even after what happened—after Damien's threats, his own worries…now that he knew Damien *couldn't* kill Zalith, Alucard's fear withered. He wanted to be with Zalith, he wanted to tell him that, but now that he was here standing in front of him, he didn't know where to go or what to say. All he could do was stare at his face and hold onto his wrist so tightly as to show how desperately he wanted to keep him in his life.

With the music from the party playing quietly in the distance, Zalith gazed at him for a moment. But then he moved his hand from Alucard's arm, gripped the vampire's hand, and smiled sweetly. "Dance with me," he requested.

"Vhat?" Alucard asked, frowning unsurely.

Zalith laughed quietly. "I said dance with me, Alucard," he repeated, slowly placing his left hand on Alucard's waist, still holding the vampire's left hand in his right.

Alucard didn't hesitate. He slowly placed his right hand on Zalith's left shoulder, staring sullenly into his eyes as they stood inches apart. And as they began a calming, slow dance, the vampire started to feel his sorrow fading. Whenever he was in Zalith's presence, his sadness would always yield, his loneliness and depravity would stop drowning him, and he'd feel such an intense need to hold on that he knew he couldn't let him go. But he couldn't make him stay, either. He couldn't make *anyone* stay. He could only sorely hope that Zalith *would*—and right now, he felt as though maybe…he might just want to.

Was now the right moment to tell Zalith how he felt? Why would the demon want to dance with him if he didn't feel the same? Why would he want to be as close as they now were? Alucard didn't fully understand his feelings, but he *did* understand that right now, what they were doing couldn't possibly be only because they were friends. Even if it was, he liked it, and he didn't want it to end. This closeness was unlike anything he'd been given before; he felt so deprived of contact since Zalith showed him what it was like to crave it from someone. He'd never needed to feel someone's hand in his own, never longed to have his face just a mere inch from someone else's. And not once had he so desperately needed to feel the warmth of someone's embrace.

His eyes wandered from Zalith's face, and as his heartbreaking need for more weighed down on him, he moved his hand to Zalith's back. He then slowly rested the side of his head on the demon's right shoulder; he pulled him so close that the majority of Zalith's body was against his own. Relief banished his conflicted, uncertain thoughts as he closed his eyes, holding onto Zalith as tightly as he could manage. He needed this so much that he was sure he would never let go—how could he? This demon was the only person he had ever craved to be so close to, and now that he was *this* close, he didn't want there to ever be a distance between them again.

Zalith moved both his arms around Alucard, holding him just as tightly. Then he smiled, resting his head on Alucard's. "Whatever's upsetting you, I want you to know that you don't have to be sad anymore, Alucard," he said quietly. "I want to make you happy in whatever way you need."

Alucard slowly lifted his head from Zalith's shoulder and stared at him as he gazed back. "I'm not…sad," he said with an unsure tone. "I'm…avraid."

"Afraid?" he questioned, frowning. "Of what?"

Alucard looked down to hide his despondency. "Zhat you might leave," he mumbled.

Zalith smiled and rested his forehead against Alucard's. "I'm not going anywhere," he said softly, still holding him tightly.

The vampire then stared into Zalith's convincing eyes. Whether that was true or not, Zalith's words gave him the relief he had so long been searching for. He'd been sure quite some time ago that he wanted this demon to remain in his life indefinitely and that he wanted them to move on to whatever came after friendship. But…to do that, he needed to tell Zalith—to assure him that what he said that night in front of the portal was no longer relevant. Yes, he was still afraid that something might happen one day with Damien, but it wouldn't happen any time soon. That was what Alucard wanted to focus on.

Alucard frowned sadly at him. "I…zhe vings I said vour months ago—avter ve moved zhe vampires," he started, looking down so he could hide his nervous expression. "I zidn't mean to 'urt you or make you vink zhat I zidn't vant to be vith you anymore. I just…'ad to do zhat. I vas convinced Zamien vas going to kill you, and zhe only vay to stop zhat vrom 'appening vould be to stop seeing you. Zhat pained me—to vink I vould never see you again."

He stopped for a moment, trying to fight against the pain his aching heart burdened him with. He glanced at Zalith, unsure whether he would say anything in response or not. But the demon just stood there, smiling at him. Was he waiting for more?

Alucard looked back down and continued, "I zon't know vhat else to say. I 'eard Zamien talking to somevone not too long bevore I came 'ome. 'E said 'e vasn't going to kill you. I'm still avraid of vhat 'e might vink or do if 'e sees us togezzer, but I veel like I zon't care. I…zon't know if you still vant to be vith me—if zhat's even vhat you vanted in zhe virst place—but *I* vant zhat," he admitted quietly. "I vant to be vith you."

Zalith stared at Alucard as a content, relieved smile appeared on his face. "You don't have to apologize," he said quietly, moving his hand to the side of Alucard's face and making him look at him. "I understand."

They gazed at one another for a moment…and when Zalith moved his hand and lightly gripped the vampire's jaw, Alucard didn't hesitate. Zalith pulled his face into his and gently pressed his lips against his, and Alucard felt both their tense bodies relax.

Alucard wasn't going to shy away this time. He moved his hand to the side of Zalith's face, allowing their single kiss to turn into a few caresses of one another's lips…and when he felt the demon's tongue ease into his mouth, Alucard tensed up nervously. His heart beat a little faster, and his need for closeness became desperation. He widened his jaw a little more, exhaling through his nose as their tongues embraced one another. And *at last*, he felt the serenity returning—the serenity this demon had blessed him with.

But then the sky flashed red. The clouds parted, thunder rumbling. Alucard knew too well what that meant, and before Zalith could stop him, he pulled himself from the demon's grip so hastily that Zalith seemed staggered and confused.

Before either of them could speak, a blur of black and white landed between them.

Alucard stared in sheer terror, watching as Damien stood up straight, folding his wings against his back with a condescending, cruel frown on his face. But he then looked over his shoulder, setting his red eye on Zalith. "Leave us," he ordered.

Zalith glanced at Alucard in regret and worry but did as he was asked and left the balcony, disappearing into Alucard's study.

Damien set his begrudging gaze on the vampire. "Am I interrupting something, Aleksei?" he questioned skeptically.

Of course Damien would come. Why would he not? He hadn't yet informed him of his new task, and what better night to ruin than his birthday? Alucard hung his head, staring miserably down at the floor. "No," he answered.

The Daegelus prowled towards him. "That wouldn't be a little lie, would it?" he growled with a challenging tone in his cold voice. "Have you forgotten what I've taught you about lying?"

Alucard lifted his head to stare at Damien's face. "No," he repeated.

Damien smiled—but then he gripped Alucard's shoulders and forced him back against the railings with such force that it almost felt like he tried to push him over, but he held the vampire tightly, digging his claws into his skin. "You wouldn't be making it so that I may have to kill my favourite errand boy, would you?" he snarled, his face just inches from Alucard's.

Staring in horror, Alucard frowned. "No," he answered.

Glaring at him, Damien's hostile scowl slowly faded into something of concern. "He's using you," he stated matter-of-factly, almost as if he was attempting a new approach to keep them away from each other. "I've known him near enough his whole life, Aleksei, and this is what he does. He finds a…hmm…I'd say pretty, but you're not exactly that, are you?" he asked, grinning.

Alucard stared, waiting.

"He finds someone like you—someone weak, someone he can manipulate, and he makes them believe he loves them. He'll confuse you, he'll fuck you, and then he'll forget that you exist. Do you really think someone like him would *actually* care for someone like *you*?" he laughed cruelly. "Demons prey on the weak, Aleksei, and you're as weak as they come…aren't you?"

Confused, Alucard stared in silence. Was that what was going on? Was Zalith using him? Lying to him? Was this all just some game? No, it couldn't be. While Alucard might not understand something so strange as love, he did understand the seriousness in Zalith's words. Zalith said he wanted to make him happy, so why would he do any of the things Damien just insisted on? But then again, Zalith was hard to read; he was smart and sly, and Alucard knew how he loved to be amused. Did he find amusement in playing him like some game? Was his goal to break him? Was that the highest form of entertainment for someone like Zalith?

Damien grinned cruelly. "I've told you so many times; don't get attached to people, they will all throw you away once they've taken what they want from you. You are worthless, pathetic, and dirty," he snarled, looking him up and down. "No one could ever care for you, least of all *love* you. Get out of your head whatever you think it might be Zalith feels for you because I can assure you it will only be something you don't want to hear. As much as I despise you, I won't let you be subjected to his games. I'm the only one you can trust to never leave and hurt you in such a way. Did I not prove my undying care when I pulled you from your insanity?"

Alucard stared sullenly, unsure of what might be true or not anymore. He didn't have the strength to consider anything. All he knew was that despite Damien's threats, he still wanted to be back in Zalith's arms, even if it wasn't going to end the way he wanted.

"Your next task is ready," Damien told him.

The vampire waited.

"You will travel to Tengetso; you will eradicate several of Letholdus' discarded experiments and bring them to me. Then, you will return here and locate the men I need for my dominion. I assume with your ever-growing empire that locating people won't be much of a bother anymore."

He nodded.

"Good. Last but never least, you will meet with Lucious, a grounded angel once sent by Ephriel to gather allies. You will convince him to join my cause."

"Vhere is 'e?" Alucard asked.

"Avalmoor," he said with a cruel smirk. "Be careful, Aleksei. I hear Letholdus' children reside there, along with one of Lucifer's other…spawns. If I were you, I'd do my best not to be seen by any of them."

He had no motivation to fight, nor did he really care. He knew how to handle himself. He answered, "Yes."

Damien gripped his throat. "Don't fail me," he growled. Then, with a revolted snarl, he harshly let go of Alucard, and as the vampire dropped to his knees, the Daegelus scowled. "Leave now," he ordered and spread his wings. He swiftly ascended back into the night sky, leaving Alucard alone.

The vampire sat there, staring vacantly as a sense of worthlessness drowned him. He didn't even care that his next task was as risky as it was. All he could think about was Zalith and what Damien just said about him. Was it true? He wasn't sure, and he didn't want to think about it. His need for Zalith blinded his judgement, it kept him from considering Damien's statement, and as Zalith walked back out onto the balcony, relief pulled him from his sadness once again.

"Are you okay?" the demon asked quietly as he helped him back to his feet.

Alucard nodded once in response.

Keeping his hand on the vampire's shoulder, Zalith frowned. "What did he want?" he asked as if he hadn't been listening—Alucard knew he'd heard every word.

"I…'ave to go," Alucard uttered sadly.

"Go?"

"To Avalmoor. 'E 'as me searching vor somevone. I 'ave to travel to vone of zhe ozzer vorlds."

Denial smothered Zalith's face. "Right now?"

"Soon," Alucard said, slowly turning to face him.

Zalith placed his hand on the side of Alucard's face. "Then I'll wait for you."

But Alucard shook his head. "Zhis vone vill take me a vhile—longer zhan vour months. 'E vants me to vind all zhe people 'e needs vor 'is cause. I zon't…know vhen I'll be back," he mumbled, looking away from him. He didn't want to go, but what choice did he have? He couldn't deny Damien, and he couldn't falter, either. And their moment had been ruined. His confidence withered, his nervousness returned, and so did his conflicting thoughts.

He walked away from Zalith, moving back into his study. The demon followed him in as he picked up his blazer and pulled it on over his shirt.

"Will you stay in contact with me?" Zalith asked almost desperately.

Tucking his colt-like pistols into his blazer, Alucard frowned at him. "Vhy?" he asked despondently.

"Because…I'll miss you," Zalith said, moving closer to him. "If I can't see you like this, at least let me see you through the mirror. We can set up the links I mentioned."

The vampire glanced over at the mirror and then set his eyes back on Zalith, who stopped in front of him. "I vill probably be gone a long time."

"Then talk to me whenever you can," he said, smiling. "Please."

With a conflicted frown, Alucard looked back over at the mirror. The fact that Zalith was asking him to keep in contact with him made him feel…strange but in an almost relieving way. Even though he'd be preoccupied, Zalith was telling him he'd wait for him—*again*. That withered any ounce of worry he once had. But there was no telling how long this mission might take. It could take *six* months, a year, ten, thirty—maybe even longer. Would Zalith wait *that* long to see him?

The vampire looked at him. "Vhat vill you do?"

Zalith smirked and said, "I've come to find myself faced with many new, intriguing tasks—but I'll always have time for you."

Alucard smiled slightly, looking down at the floor. "Zhen…I'll see you vhen I'm done?"

"You certainly will," Zalith assured him. "You can speak to me through any mirror; just imbue it with your demon ethos and think of me. It's fairly simple."

Alucard glanced at the mirror in the corner of the room and then looked back at Zalith. "Okay."

"I'm going to write to you, too," he said, smirking.

With an almost embarrassed look on his face, Alucard looked away. "Zhat's vine."

Still smiling, Zalith placed his hand on the side of Alucard's face, made him look at him, and kissed him one last time. "Goodbye, vampire—for now."

Staring at him, Alucard smiled ever so slightly and nodded. "Goodbye."

The vampire then moved away from Zalith and made his way out onto the balcony. He glanced back over his shoulder at him, taking one final look for what might be a long, long time. But he was confident that whatever they had wouldn't end here. Zalith asked him to keep in contact, and he'd do his best to do so.

As Zalith smiled at him, he turned away, trying to hide his own smile. And then, without another word, he dematerialized into vermillion smoke, determined to complete Damien's next tasks as quickly as possible so that he could see Zalith again.

And he *would* get to see him again.

At least…he hoped.

That demon turned his entire life upside down, but he wouldn't change a single thing about it. Zalith had shown him *everything* he was missing…and *nothing* would make him let go now that he had it.

Not even Damien.

THE NUMEN CHRONICLES
SERIES ONE

Nosferatu
The Numen Chronicles | Volume 1

Demon's Fate
The Numen Chronicles | Volume 2

Light
The Numen Chronicles | Volume 3

Demon's Bane
The Numen Chronicles | Volume 4

Ascendant
The Numen Chronicles | Volume 5

Icarus
The Numen Chronicles | Volume 6

Demon's Curse
The Numen Chronicles | Volume 7

Renascence
The Numen Chronicles | Volume 8

Demon's Reclamation
The Numen Chronicles | Volume 9

[And more...]

THE NUMENVERSE
OTHER SERIES/STORIES

Aldergrove Chronicles

Set in the year 1176 after Aegisguard's second world war. After being told he has only six months left to live, Clementine decides to track down his sister's murderers, leading him to Aldergrove Academy, a place where a hundred students must fight to the death to earn their right to travel to the New World. But he soon learns that the students aren't the only ones prowling the corridors at night in search of blood.

Where The Wild Wolves Have Gone

Set in the year 1330. Following Luan, a young transman werewolf who belongs to a pack owned by Lyca Corp., a military-focused organization. The pack have served them for generations, but after a mission goes sideways, Luan begins to learn the horrifying truth about the people they serve.

Greykin Chronicles

Set in the year 1332, following Jackson, a journalist who heads to the snowy mountains of Ascela in search of his missing best friend, Wilson. But he discovers that not only is there a whole different world hidden out there, but death isn't necessarily the end for some creatures.

The Numen Chronicles Series Two

Set in the year 1335. While hunting for his missing friend, Elijah stumbles upon a fiery journalist, who so happens to be looking for the same people as him: the doctors who experimented on him when he was a child. But when the two are forced to go on the run together, Elijah's healing wounds are opened, and he realises that Lyca Corp. took more than his childhood.

To stay up to date with future releases, follow the author through their website!

www.numenverse.com/